THE WORLD GUIDE TO
GNOMES, FAIRIES, ELVES
AND
OTHER LITTLE PEOPLE

THE WORLD GUIDE TO
GNOMES, FAIRIES, ELVES
AND
OTHER LITTLE PEOPLE

BY

THOMAS KEIGHTLEY

Another sort there be, that will
Be talking of the Fairies still ;
Nor never can they have their fill,
 As they were wedded to them
                    DRAYTON.

AVENEL BOOKS
NEW YORK

Originally published in 1880 as
The Fairy Mythology.
Culver Pictures, Inc. have
provided the illustrations that
fall opposite pages 54, 55, 74, 75, 78,
152, 153, 207, 258, 281, 316, 317, 420, 464.
All other illustrations have been
provided by the courtesy of
the New York Public Library
Picture Collection.

Picture research was done
by Anita Duncan.

This edition is published by Avenel Books,
distributed by Crown Publishers, Inc.
a b c d e f g h

AVENEL 1978 PRINTING

Library of Congress Cataloging in Publication Data

Keightley, Thomas, 1789-1872.
    The world guide to gnomes, fairies,
elves, and other little people.

    Reprint of the 1878 ed. published
by G. Bell; London under title:
The fairy mythology, with added ill.
    1. Fairy tales.   2. Folk-lore. 3. Folk
literature.   4. Fairies.   I. Title.
GR550.K4   1978   398.2′1   78-12628
ISBN 0-517-26313-0

PREFACE.

A PREFACE is to a book what a prologue is to a play—a usual, often agreeable, but by no means necessary precursor. It may therefore be altered or omitted at pleasure. I have at times exercised this right, and this is the third I have written for the present work.

In the first, after briefly stating what had given occasion to it, I gave the germs of the theory which I afterwards developed in the Tales and Popular Fictions.* The second contained the following paragraph:—

"I never heard of any one who read it that was not pleased with it. It was translated into German as soon as it appeared, and was very favourably received. Goethe thought well of it. Dr. Jacob Grimm—perhaps the first authority on these matters in Europe—wrote me a letter commending it, and assuring me that even to *him* it offered something new; and I was one Christmas most agreeably surprised by the receipt of a letter from Vienna, from the celebrated orientalist, Jos Von Hammer, informing me that it had been the companion of a journey he had lately made to his native province of Styria, and had afforded much pleasure and information to himself and to some ladies of high rank and cultivated minds in that country. The initials at the end of the preface, he said, led him to suppose it was a work of mine. So far for the Continent. In this

*A sequel to this volume.

country, when I mention the name of Robert Southey as that of one who has more than once expressed his decided approbation of this performance, I am sure I shall have said quite enough to satisfy any one that the work is not devoid of merit."

I could now add many names of distinguished persons who have been pleased with this work and its pendent, the Tales and Popular Fictions. I shall only mention that of the late Mr. Douce, who, very shortly before his death, on the occasion of the publication of this last work, called on me to assure me that "it was many, many years indeed, since he had read a book which had yielded him so much delight."

The contents of the work which gave such pleasure to this learned antiquary are as follows:—

I. Introduction—Similarity of Arts and Customs—Similarity of Names—Origin of the Work—Imitation—Casual Coincidence—Milton—Dante. II. The Thousand and One Nights—Bedoween Audience around a Story-teller—Cleomades and Claremond—Enchanted Horses—Peter of Provence and the fair Maguelone. III. The Pleasant Nights—The Dancing Water, the Singing Apple, and the Beautiful Green Bird—The Three Little Birds—Lactantius—Ulysses and Sindbad. IV. The Shâh-Nâmeh—Roostem and Soohrâb—Conloch and Cuchullin—Macpherson's Ossian—Irish Antiquities. V. The Pentamerone—Tale of the Serpent—Hindoo Legend. VI. Jack the Giant-killer—The Brave Tailoring—Thor's Journey to Utgard—Ameen of Isfahân and the Ghool—The Lion and the Goat—The Lion and the Ass. VII. Whittington and his Cat—Danish Legends—Italian Stories—Persian Legend. VIII. The Edda—Sigurd and Brynhilda—Völund—Helgi—Holger Danske—Ogier le Danois—Toko—William Tell. IX. Peruonto—Peter the Fool—Emelyan the Fool—Conclusion. Appendix.

Never, I am convinced, did any one enter on a literary career with more reluctance than I did when I found it to be my only resource—fortune being gone, ill health and delicacy of constitution excluding me from the learned professions, want of interest from every thing else. As I journeyed to the metropolis, I might have sung with the page whom Don Quixote met going a-soldiering:

A la guerra me lleva—mi necesidad,
Si tuviera dineros—no fuera en verdad :

for of all arts and professions in this country, that of literature is the least respected and the worst remunerated. There is something actually degrading in the expression " an author by trade," which I have seen used even of Southey, and that by one who did not mean to disparage him in the slightest degree. My advice to those who may read these pages is to shun literature, if not already blest with competence.

One of my earliest literary friends in London was T. Crofton Croker, who was then engaged in collecting materials for the Fairy Legends of the South of Ireland. He of course applied to his friends for aid and information; and I, having most leisure, and, I may add, most knowledge, was able to give him the greatest amount of assistance. My inquiries on the subject led to the writing of the present work, which was succeeded by the Mythology of Ancient Greece and Italy, and the Tales and Popular Fictions; so that, in effect, if Mr. Croker had not planned the Fairy Legends, these works, be their value what it may, would in all probability never have been written.

Writing and reading about Fairies some may deem to be the mark of a trifling turn of mind. On this subject I have given my ideas in the Conclusion; here I will only remind such critics, that as soon as this work was completed, I commenced, and wrote in the space of a few weeks, my Outlines of History; and whatever the faults of that work may be, no one has ever reckoned among them want of vigour in either thought or expression. It was also necessary, in order to write this work and its pendent, to be able to read, perhaps, as many as eighteen or twenty different languages, dialects, and modes of orthography, and to employ different styles both in prose and verse. At all events, even if it were trifling, *dulce est desipere in loco;* and I shall never forget the happy hours it caused me, especially those spent over the black-letter pages of the French romances of chivalry, in the old reading-room of the British Museum.

Many years have elapsed since this work was first published. In that period much new matter has appeared in various works, especially in the valuable Deutsche Mythologie of Dr. Grimm. Hence it will be found to be greatly enlarged, particularly in the sections of England and France. I have also inserted much which want of space obliged me to omit in the former edition. In its present form, I am presumptuous enough to expect that it may live for many years, and be an authority on the subject of popular lore. The active industry of the Grimms, of Thiele, and others, had collected the popular traditions of various countries. I came then and gathered in the harvest, leaving little, I apprehend, but gleanings for future writers on this subject. The legends will probably fade fast away from the popular memory; it is not likely that any one will relate those which I have given over again; and it therefore seems more probable that this volume may in future be reprinted, with notes and additions. For human nature will ever remain un_ changed; the love of gain and of material enjoyments, omnipotent as it appears to be at present, will never totally extinguish the higher and purer aspirations of mind; and there will always be those, however limited in number, who will desire to know how the former dwellers of earth thought, felt, and acted. For these mythology, as connected with religion and history, will always have attractions.

T. K.

England

CONTENTS.

LIST OF ILLUSTRATIONS

THE FAIRY MYTHOLOGY.

INTRODUCTION.

—◆—

In oldè dayès of the King Artoúr,
Of which that Bretons spoken gret honoúr,
All was this lond fulfilled of faërie;
The elf-qrene with hir jolie companie
Danced full oft in many a grenè mede.
CHAUCER.

ORIGIN OF THE BELIEF IN FAIRIES.

ACCORDING to a well-known law of our nature, effects suggest causes; and another law, perhaps equally general, impels us to ascribe to the actual and efficient cause the attribute of intelligence. The mind of the deepest philosopher is thus acted upon equally with that of the peasant or the savage; the only difference lies in the nature of the intelligent cause at which they respectively stop. The one pursues the chain of cause and effect, and traces out its various links till he arrives at the great intelligent cause of all, however he may designate him; the other, when unusual phenomena excite his attention, ascribes their production to the immediate agency of some of the inferior beings recognised by his legendary creed.

The action of this latter principle must forcibly strike the minds of those who disdain not to bestow a portion of their attention on the popular legends and traditions of different

countries. Every extraordinary appearance is found to have
its extraordinary cause assigned; a cause always connected
with the history or religion, ancient or modern, of the
country, and not unfrequently varying with a change of
faith.*

The noises and eruptions of Ætna and Stromboli were, in
ancient times, ascribed to Typhon or Vulcan, and at this day
the popular belief connects them with the infernal regions.
The sounds resembling the clanking of chains, hammering of
iron, and blowing of bellows, once to be heard in the island
of Barrie, were made by the fiends whom Merlin had set to
work to frame the wall of brass to surround Caermarthen.†
The marks which natural causes have impressed on the solid
and unyielding granite rock were produced, according to the
popular creed, by the contact of the hero, the saint, or the
god: masses of stone, resembling domestic implements in
form, were the toys, or the corresponding implements of the
heroes and giants of old. Grecian imagination ascribed to
the galaxy or milky way an origin in the teeming breast of
the queen of heaven: marks appeared in the petals of
flowers on the occasion of a youth's or a hero's untimely
death: the rose derived its present hue from the blood of
Venus, as she hurried barefoot through the woods and lawns;
while the professors of Islâm, less fancifully, refer the origin
of this flower to the moisture that exuded from the sacred
person of their prophet. Under a purer form of religion,
the cruciform stripes which mark the back and shoulders of

---

* The mark on Adam's Peak in Ceylon is, by the Buddhists, ascribed to
Buddha; by the Mohammedans, to Adam. It reminds one of the story of
the lady and the vicar, viewing the moon through a telescope; they saw in it,
as they thought, two figures inclined toward each other: "Methinks," says
the lady, "they are two fond lovers, meeting to pour forth their vows by earth-
light." "Not at all," says the vicar, taking his turn at the glass; "they are
the steeples of two neighbouring churches."

† Faerie Queene, III. c. iii. st. 8, 9, 10, 11. Drayton, Poly-Olbion, Song
VI. We fear, however, that there is only poetic authority for this belief.
Mr. Todd merely quotes Warton, who says that Spenser borrowed it from
Giraldus Cambrensis, who picked it up among the romantic traditions propa-
gated by the Welsh bards. The reader will be, perhaps, surprised to hear
that Giraldus says nothing of the demons. He mentions the sounds, and endeavours to explain them by natural causes. Hollingshed indeed (l. i. c. 24.)
says, " whereof the superstitious sort do gather many toys."

the patient ass first appeared, according to the popular tradition, when the Son of God condescended to enter the Holy City, mounted on that animal; and a fish only to be found in the sea * stills bears the impress of the finger and thumb of the apostle, who drew him out of the waters of Lake Tiberias to take the tribute-money that lay in his mouth. The repetition of the voice among the hills is, in Norway and Sweden, ascribed to the Dwarfs mocking the human speaker, while the more elegant fancy of Greece gave birth to Echo, a nymph who pined for love, and who still fondly repeats the accents that she hears. The magic scenery occasionally presented on the waters of the Straits of Messina is produced by the power of the Fata Morgana; the gossamers that float through the haze of an autumnal morning, are woven by the ingenious dwarfs; the verdant circlets in the mead are traced beneath the light steps of the dancing elves; and St. Cuthbert forges and fashions the beads that bear his name, and lie scattered along the shore of Lindisfarne.†

In accordance with these laws, we find in most countries a popular belief in different classes of beings distinct from men, and from the higher orders of divinities. These beings are usually believed to inhabit, in the caverns of earth, or the depths of the waters, a region of their own. They generally excel mankind in power and in knowledge, and like them are subject to the inevitable laws of death, though after a more prolonged period of existence.

How these classes were first called into existence it is not easy to say; but if, as some assert, all the ancient systems of heathen religion were devised by philosophers for the instruction of rude tribes by appeals to their senses, we might suppose that the minds which peopled the skies with their thousands and tens of thousands of divinities gave birth also to the inhabitants of the field and flood, and that the numerous tales of their exploits and adventures are the production of poetic fiction or rude invention. It may

---

* The Haddock.

† For a well-chosen collection of examples, see the very learned and philosophical preface of the late Mr. Price to his edition of Warton's History of English Poetry, p. 28 *et seq.*

further be observed, that not unfrequently a change of religious faith has invested with dark and malignant attributes beings once the objects of love, confidence, and veneration.*

It is not our intention in the following pages to treat of the awful or lovely deities of Olympus, Valhalla, or Merû. Our subject is less aspiring; and we confine ourselves to those beings who are our fellow-inhabitants of earth, whose manners we aim to describe, and whose deeds we propose to record. We write of FAIRIES, FAYS, ELVES, *aut alio quo nomine gaudent.*

ORIGIN OF THE WORD FAIRY.

Like every other word in extensive use, whose derivation is not historically certain, the word Fairy has obtained various and opposite etymons. Meyric Casaubon, and those who like him deduce everything from a classic source, however unlikely, derive Fairy from Φήρ, a Homeric name of the Centaurs;† or think that *fée*, whence Fairy, is the last syllable of *nympha*. Sir W. Ouseley derives it from the Hebrew פאר (*peër*), *to adorn;* Skinner, from the Anglo-Saxon ꝼaꞃan, *to fare, to go;* others from Feres, companions, or think that Fairy-folk is *quasi* Fair-folk. Finally, it has been queried if it be not Celtic.‡

But no theory is so plausible, or is supported by such names, as that which deduces the English Fairy from the Persian Peri. It is said that the Paynim foe, whom the warriors of the Cross encountered in Palestine, spoke only Arabic; the alphabet of which language, it is well known, possesses no *p*, and therefore organically substitutes an *f* in such foreign words as contain the former letter; consequently Peri became, in the mouth of an Arab, Feri, whence the crusaders and pilgrims, who carried back to Europe the marvellous

---

* In the Middle Ages the gods of the heathens were all held to be devils.

† Φήρ is the Ionic form of θήρ, and is nearly related to the German *thier*, beast, animal. The Scandinavian *dyr*, and the Anglo-Saxon ꝺeoꞃ, have the same signification; and it is curious to observe the restricted sense which this last has gotten in the English *deer*.

‡ Preface to Warton, p. 44; and Breton philologists furnish us with an etymon; not, indeed, of Fairy, but of Fada. "Fada, fata, etc.," says M. de Cambry (Monumens Celtiques), "come from the Breton *mat* or *mad*, in construction *fat*, good; whence the English, *maid*."

tales of Asia, introduced into the West the Arabo-Persian word *Fairy*. It is further added, that the Morgain or Morgana, so celebrated in old romance, is Merjan Peri, equally celebrated all over the East.

All that is wanting to this so very plausible theory is something like proof, and some slight agreement with the ordinary rules of etymology. Had Feërie, or Fairy, originally signified the individual in the French and English, the only languages in which the word occurs, we might feel disposed to acquiesce in it. But they do not: and even if they did, how should we deduce from them the Italian Fata, and the Spanish Fada or Hada, (words which unquestionably stand for the same imaginary being,) unless on the principle by which Menage must have deduced Lutin from Lemur—the first letter being the same in both? As to the fair Merjan Peri (D'Herbelot calls her Merjan Banou*), we fancy a little too much importance has been attached to her. Her name, as far as we can learn, only occurs in the Cahermân Nâmeh, a Turkish romance, though perhaps translated from the Persian.

The foregoing etymologies, it is to be observed, are all the conjectures of English scholars; for the English is the only language in which the name of the individual, Fairy, has the canine letter to afford any foundation for them.

Leaving, then, these sports of fancy, we will discuss the true origin of the words used in the Romanic languages to express the being which we name Fairy of Romance. These are *Faée*, *Fée*, French; *Fada*, Provençal (whence *Hada*, Spanish); and *Fata*, Italian.

The root is evidently, we think, the Latin *fatum*. In the fourth century of our æra we find this word made plural, and even feminine, and used as the equivalent of Parcæ. On the reverse of a gold medal of the Emperor Diocletian are three female figures, with the legend *Fatis victricibus;* a *cippus*, found at Valencia in Spain, has on one of its sides

---

* D'Herbelot *titre* Mergian says, " C'est du nom de cette Fée que nos anciens romans ont formé celui de *Morgante la Déconnue.*" He here confounds Morgana with Urganda, and he has been followed in his mistake. D'Herbelot also thinks it possible that *Féerie* may come from *Peri ;* but he regards the common derivation from *Fata* as much more probable. Cambrian etymologists, by the way, say that Morgain is Mor Gwynn, the *White Maid.*

Fatis Q. Fabius ex voto, and on the other, three female
figures, with the attributes of the Mœræ or Parcæ.* In
this last place the gender is uncertain, but the figures
would lead us to suppose it feminine. On the other hand,
Ausonius† has *tres Charites, tria Fata;* and Procopius‡
names a building at the Roman Forum τὰ τρία φάτα, adding
οὕτω γὰρ 'Ρωμαῖοι τὰς μοίρας νενομίκασι καλεῖν. The Fatæ
or Fata, then, being persons, and their name coinciding so
exactly with the modern terms, and it being observed that
the Mœræ were, at the birth of Meleager, just as the Fées
were at that of Ogier le Danois, and other heroes of
romance and tale, their identity has been at once asserted,
and this is now, we believe, the most prevalent theory. To
this it may be added, that in Gervase of Tilbury, and other
writers of the thirteenth century, the Fada or Fée seems to
be regarded as a being different from human kind.§

On the other hand, in a passage presently to be quoted
from a celebrated old romance, we shall meet a definition of
the word *Fée*, which expressly asserts that such a being was
nothing more than a woman skilled in magic; and such, on
examination, we shall find to have been all the Fées of the
romances of chivalry and of the popular tales; in effect, that
fée is a participle, and the words *dame* or *femme* is to be
understood.

In the middle ages there was in use a Latin verb, *fatare*,‖
derived from *fatum* or *fata*, and signifying to enchant. This

---

* These two instances are given by Mdlle. Amélie Bosquet (La Normandie
Romanesque, etc. p. 91.) from Dom Martin, *Rel. des Gaulois*, ii. ch. 23
and 24.

† Gryphus ternarii numeri.   ‡ De Bell. Got. i. 25.

§ See below, *France*. It is also remarked that in some of the tales of
the Pentamerone, the number of the *Fate* is three; but to this it may be
replied, that in Italy every thing took a classic tinge, and that the Fate of those
tales are only Maghe; so in the Amadigi of Bernardo Tasso we meet with
La *Fata* Uganda. In Spain and France the number would rather seem to
have been seven. Cervantes speaks of "los siete castillos de las *siete* fadas;"
in the Rom. de la Infantina it is said, "*siete* fadas me *fadaron*, en brazos de
una ama mia," and the *Fées* are *seven* in La Belle au Bois dormant. In the
romance, however, of Guillaume au Court-nez, the *Fées* who carry the sleeping
Renoart out of the boat are *three* in number.—See Grimm Deutsche Mythologie,
p. 383.

‖ A MS. of the 13th century, quoted by Grimm (*ut sup.* p. 405), thus
relates the origin of Aquisgrani (Aix la Chapelle): Aquisgrani dicitur Ays, et

verb was adopted by the Italian, Provençal* and Spanish languages; in French it became, according to the analogy of that tongue, *faer, féer.* Of this verb the past participle is *faé, fé;* hence in the romances we continually meet with *les chevaliers faés, les dames faées, Oberon la faé, le cheval étoit faé, la clef était fée,* and such like. We have further, we think, demonstrated † that it was the practice of the Latin language to elide accented syllables, especially in the past participle of verbs of the first conjugation, and that this practice had been transmitted to the Italian, whence *fatato-a* would form *fato-a,* and *una donna fatata* might thus become *una fata.* Whether the same was the case in the Provençal we cannot affirm, as our knowledge of that dialect is very slight; but, judging from analogy, we would say it was, for in Spanish *Hadada* and *Hada* are synonymous. In the Neapolitan Pentamerone *Fata* and *Maga* are the same, and a Fata sends the heroine of it to a sister of hers, *pure fatata.* Ariosto says of Medea—

> E perchè per virtù d' erbe e d'incanti
> Delle Fate una ed immortal fatta era.
> *I Cinque Canti,* ii. 106.

The same poet, however, elsewhere says—

> Queste che or Fate e dagli antichi foro
> Già dette Ninfe e Dee con più bel nome.—*Ibid.* i. 9.

and,

> Nascemmo ad un punto che d'ogni altro male
> Siamo capaci fuorchè della morte.—*Orl. Fur.* xliii. 48.

---

dicitur eo, quod Karolus tenebat ibi quandam *mulierem fatatam,* sive quandam *fatam,* quæ alio nomine *nimpha* vel *dea* vel *adriades* (l. *dryas*) appellatur, et ad hanc consuetudinem habebat, et eam cognoscebat; et ita erat, quod ipso accedente ad eam vivebat ipsa, ipso Karolo recedente moriebatur. Contigit dum quadam vice ad ipsam accessisset ut cum ea delectaretur, radius solis intravit os ejus, et tunc Karolus vidit *granum auri* lingue ejus affixum, quod fecit abscindi et contingenti (l. in continenti) mortua est, nec postea revixit.

    * " Aissim *fadaro* tres serors
       En aquella ora qu' ieu sui natz
       Que totz temps fos enamoratz."—*Folquet de Romans.*
(Thus three sisters *fated,* in the hour that I was born, that I should be at all times in love.)

    " Aissi fuy de nueitz *fadatz* sobr' un puegau."—*Guilh. de Poitou.*
    (Thus was I *fated* by night on a hill.)—Grimm, *ut sup.* p. 383.
       † See our Virgil, Excurs. ix.

which last, however, is not decisive. Bojardo also calls the water-nymphs Fate; and our old translators of the Classics named them *fairies*. From all this can only, we apprehend, be collected, that the ideas of the Italian poets, and others, were somewhat vague on the subject.

From the verb *faer, féer*, to enchant, illude, the French made a substantive *faerie, féerie*,* illusion, enchantment, the meaning of which was afterwards extended, particularly after it had been adopted into the English language.

We find the word Faerie, in fact, to be employed in four different senses, which we will now arrange and exemplify.

1. Illusion, enchantment.

> Plusieurs parlent de Guenart,
> Du Loup, de l'Asne, de Renart,
> De *faeries* et de songes,
> De phantosmes et de mensonges.
> *Gul. Giar. ap. Ducange.*

Where we must observe, as Sir Walter Scott seems not to have been aware of it, that the four last substantives bear the same relation to each other as those in the two first verses do.

> Me bifel a ferly
> Of *faërie*, me thought.
> *Vision of Piers Plowman*, v. 11.

> Maius that sit with so benigne a chere,
> Hire to behold it seemed *faërie*.
> *Chaucer, Marchante's Tale.*

It (*the horse of brass*) was of *faërie*, as the peple semed,
Diversè folk diversëly han demèd.— *Squier's Tale.*

> The Emperor said on high,
> Certes it is a *faërie*,
> Or elles a vanité.—*Emare.*

> With phantasme and *faërie*,
> Thus she bleredè his eye.—*Libeaus Disconus.*

The God of her has made an end,
And fro this worldès *faërie*
Hath taken her into companie.—*Gower, Constance.*

---

* Following the analogy of the Gotho-German tongues, *zauberei*, Germ. *trylleri*, Dan. *trolleri*, Swed. illusion, enchantment. The Italian word is *fattucchieria*.

Mr. Ritson professes not to understand the meaning of
faerie in this last passage. Mr. Ritson should, as Sir Hugh
Evans says, have ' prayed his pible petter;' where, among
other things that might have been of service to him, he
would have learned that ' man walketh in a *vain* shew,' that
' all is *vanity*,' and that ' the fashion of this world passeth
away;' and then he would have found no difficulty in com-
prehending the pious language of ' moral Gower,' in his
allusion to the transitory and deceptive vanities of the
world.

2. From the sense of illusion simply, the transition was
easy to that of the land of illusions, the abode of the Faés,
who produced them; and Faerie next came to signify the
country of the Fays. Analogy also was here aiding; for
as a Nonnerie was a place inhabited by Nonnes, a Jewerie a
place inhabited by Jews, so a Faerie was naturally a place
inhabited by Fays. Its termination, too, corresponded with
a usual one in the names of countries: Tartarie, for instance,
and ' the regne of Feminie.'

> Here beside an elfish knight
> Hath taken my lord in fight,
> And hath him led with him away
> Into the *Faërie*, sir, parmafay.—*Sir Guy.*

La puissance qu'il avoit sur toutes *faeries* du monde.
Huon de Bordeaux.

En effect, s'il me falloit retourner en *faerie*, je ne sçauroye ou prendre
mon chemin.—*Ogier le Dannoys.*

> That Gawain with his oldè curtesie,
> Though he were come agen out of *faërie*.
> *Squier's Tale.*

> He (Arthur) is a king y-crowned in *Faërie*,
> With sceptre and pall, and with his regalty
> Shallè resort, as lord and sovereigne,
> Out of *Faerie*, and reignè in Bretaine,
> And repair again the ouldè Roundè Table.
> *Lydgate, Fall of Princes*, bk. viii. c. 24.

3. From the country the appellation passed to the inhabitants in their collective capacity, and the Faerie now signified
the people of Fairy-land.*

---

* Here too there is *perhaps* an analogy with *cavalry, infantry, squierie,*
and similar collective terms.

Of the fourth kind of Spritis called the Phairie.
K. James, Demonologie, 1. 3.

Full often time he, Pluto, and his quene
Proserpina, and alle hir *faërie*,
Disporten hem, and maken melodie
About that well.—*Marchante's Tale.*

The feasts that underground the *Faërie* did him make,
And there how he enjoyed the Lady of the Lake.
Drayton, Poly-Olb., Song IV.

4. Lastly, the word came to signify the individual denizen of Fairy-land, and was equally applied to the full-sized fairy knights and ladies of romance, and to the pygmy elves that haunt the woods and dells. At what precise period it got this its last, and subsequently most usual sense, we are unable to say positively; but it was probably posterior to Chaucer, in whom it never occurs, and certainly anterior to Spenser, to whom, however, it seems chiefly indebted for its future general currency.* It was employed during the sixteenth century † for the Fays of romance, and also, especially by translators, for the Elves, as corresponding to the Latin Nympha.

They believed that king Arthur was not dead, but carried awaie by the *Fairies* into some pleasant place, where he should remaine for a time, and then returne again and reign in as great authority as ever.
Hollingshed, bk. v. c. 14. Printed 1577.

Semicaper Pan
Nunc tenet, at quodam tenuerunt tempore nymphæ.
Ovid, Met. xiv. 520.

The halfe-goate Pan that howre
Possessed it, but heretofore it was the *Faries'* bower. *Golding,* 1567.

---

* The Faerie Queene was published some years before the Midsummer Night's Dream. Warton (Obs. on the Faerie Queene) observes : "It appears from Marston's Satires, printed 1598, that the Faerie Queene occasioned many publications in which Fairies were the principal actors.

Go buy some ballad of the FAERY KING.—*Ad Lectorem.*

Out steps some Faery with quick motion,
And tells him wonders of some flowerie vale—
Awakes, straight rubs his eyes, and prints his tale.
B. III. Sat. 6.''

† It is in this century that we first meet with *Fairy* as a dissyllable, and with a plural. It is then used in its fourth and last sense.

Hæc nemora indigenæ fauni nymphæque tenebant,
Gensque virum truncis et duro robore nata.
Virgil, Æneis, viii. 314.

With nymphis and faunis apoun every side,
Qwhilk *Farefolkis* or than *Elfis* clepen we.
Gawin Dowglas.

The woods (quoth he) sometime both fauns and nymphs, and gods of
ground,
And *Fairy-queens* did keep, and under them a nation rough.
Phaer, 1562.

Inter Hamadryadas celeberrima Nonacrinas
Naïas una fuit.—*Ovid, Met.* l. i. 690.

Of all the nymphes of Nonacris and *Fairie* ferre and neere,
In beautie and in personage this ladie had no peere.
Golding.

Pan ibi dum teneris jactat sua carmina nymphis.
Ov. Ib. xi. 153.

There Pan among the *Fairie-elves,* that daunced round togither.
Golding.

Solaque Naïadum celeri non nota Dianæ.—*Ov. Ib.* iv. 304.

Of all the *water-fayries,* she alonely was unknowne
To swift Diana.—*Golding.*

Nymphis latura coronas.—*Ov. Ib.* ix. 337.

Was to the *fairies* of the lake fresh garlands for to bear.
Golding.

Thus we have endeavoured to trace out the origin, and
mark the progress of the word Fairy, through its varying
significations, and trust that the subject will now appear
placed in a clear and intelligible light.

After the appearance of the Faerie Queene, all distinctions
were confounded, the name and attributes of the real Fays
or Fairies of romance were completely transferred to the
little beings who, according to the popular belief, made ' the
green sour ringlets whereof the ewe not bites.' The change
thus operated by the poets established itself firmly among
the people; a strong proof, if this idea be correct, of the
power of the poetry of a nation in altering the phraseology
of even the lowest classes* of its society.

---

* The Fata Morgana of the Straits of Messina is an example ; for the name
of Morgana, whencesoever derived, was probably brought into Italy by the
poets.

Shakspeare must be regarded as a principal agent in this revolution; yet even he uses Fairy once in the proper sense of Fay; a sense it seems to have nearly lost, till it was again brought into use by the translators of the French Contes des Fées in the last century.

> To this great Fairy I 'll commend thy acts.
> *Antony and Cleopatra*, act iv. sc. 8.

And Milton speaks

> Of Faery damsels met in forests wide
> By knights of Logres or of Lyones,
> Lancelot, or Pelleas, or Pellinore.

Yet he elsewhere mentions the

> Faery elves,
> Whose midnight revels by a forest side
> Or fountain some belated peasant sees.

Finally, Randolph, in his Amyntas, employs it, for perhaps the last time, in its second sense, Fairy-land:

> I do think
> There will be of Jocastus' brood in Fairy.
> Act i. sc. 3.

We must not here omit to mention that the Germans, along with the French romances, early adopted the name of the Fées. They called them Feen and Feinen.* In the Tristram of Gottfried von Strazburg we are told that Duke Gylan had a syren-like little dog,

Dez wart dem Herzoge gesandt	'Twas sent unto the duke, pardé,
Uz Avalun, der *Feinen* land,	From Avalun, the Fays' countrie,
Von einer Gottinne.—V. 1673.	By a gentle goddess.

In the old German romance of Isotte and Blanscheflur, the hunter who sees Isotte asleep says, I doubt

Dez sie menschlich sei,	If she human be,
Sie ist schöner denn eine *Feine.*	She is fairer than a Fay.
Von Fleische noch von Beine	Of flesh or bone, I say,
Kunte nit gewerden	Never could have birth
So schönes auf der erden.	A thing so fair on earth.

---

* Dobenek, des deutschen Mittelalters und Volksglauben. Berlin, 1816.

Our subject naturally divides itself into two principal branches, corresponding to the different classes of beings to which the name Fairy has been applied. The first, beings of the human race, but endowed with powers beyond those usually allotted to men, whom we shall term FAYS, or FAIRIES OF ROMANCE. The second, those little beings of the popular creeds, whose descent we propose to trace from the cunning and ingenious Duergar or dwarfs of northern mythology, and whom we shall denominate ELVES or POPULAR FAIRIES.

It cannot be expected that our classifications should vie in accuracy and determinateness with those of natural science. The human imagination, of which these beings are the off-spring, works not, at least that we can discover, like nature, by fixed and invariable laws; and it would be hard indeed to exact from the Fairy historian the rigid distinction of classes and orders which we expect from the botanist or chemist. The various species so run into and are confounded with one another; the actions and attributes of one kind are so frequently ascribed to another, that scarcely have we begun to erect our system, when we find the foundation crumbling under our feet. Indeed it could not well be otherwise, when we recollect that all these beings once formed parts of ancient and exploded systems of religion, and that it is chiefly in the traditions of the peasantry that their memorial has been preserved.

We will now proceed to consider the Fairies of romance; and as they are indebted, though not for their name, yet perhaps for some of their attributes, to the Peries of Persia, we will commence with that country. We will thence pursue our course through Arabia, till we arrive at the middle-age romance of Europe, and the gorgeous realms of Fairy-land; and thence, casting a glance at the Faerie Queene, advance to the mountains and forests of the North, there to trace the origin of the light-hearted, night-tripping elves.

ORIENTAL ROMANCE.*

صانند تو ادصي در افاق
صمكن نبود پري نديدم

All human beings must in beauty yield
To you; a PERI I have ne'er beheld.

PERSIAN ROMANCE.

THE pure and simple religion of ancient Persia, originating, it is said, with a pastoral and hunting race among the lofty hills of Aderbijân, or, as others think, in the elevated plains of Bactria, in a region where light appears in all its splendour, took as its fundamental principle the opposition between light and darkness, and viewed that opposition as a conflict. Light was happiness; and the people of Irân, the land of light, were the favourites of Heaven; while those of Turân, the gloomy region beyond the mountains to the north, were its enemies. In the realms of supernal light sits enthroned Ormuzd, the first-born of beings; around him are the six Amshaspands, the twenty-eight Izeds, and the countless myriads of Ferohers.† In the opposite kingdom of darkness

---

* See D'Herbelot, Richardson's Dissertation, Ouseley's Persian Miscellanies, Wahl in the Mines de l'Orient, Lane, Thousand and One Nights, Forbes, Hatim Taï, etc., etc.

† Ormuzd employed himself for three thousand years in making the heavens and their celestial inhabitants, the Ferohers, which are the angels and the unembodied souls of all intelligent beings. All nature is filled with Ferohers, or guardian angels, who watch over its various departments, and are occupied in performing their various tasks for the benefit of mankind.—*Erskine on the Sacred Books and Religion of the Parsis, in the Transactions of the Literary Society of Bombay*, vol. ii. p. 318. The Feroher bears in fact a very strong resemblance to the Genius of the ancient Roman religion : see our Mythology of Greece and Italy

Aherman is supreme, and his throne is encompassed by the six Arch-Deevs, and the numerous hosts of inferior Deevs. Between these rival powers ceaseless warfare prevails; but at the end the prince of darkness will be subdued, and peace and happiness prevail beneath the righteous sway of Ormuzd.

From this sublime system of religion probably arose the Peri-* or Fairy-system of modern Persia; and thus what was once taught by sages, and believed by monarchs, has shared the fate of everything human, and has sunk from its pristine rank to become the material and the machinery of poets and romancers. The wars waged by the fanatical successors of the Prophet, in which literature was confounded with idolatry, have deprived us of the means of judging of this system in its perfect form; and in what has been written respecting the Peries and their country since Persia has received the law of Mohammed, the admixture of the tenets and ideas of Islam is evidently perceptible. If, however, Orientalists be right in their interpretation of the name of Artaxerxes' queen, Parisatis, as Pari-zadeh † (*Peri-born*), the Peri must be coeval with the religion of Zoroaster.

The Peries and Deevs of the modern Persians answer to the good and evil Jinn of the Arabs, of whose origin and nature we shall presently give an account. The same Suleymans ruled over them as over the Jinn, and both alike were punished for disobedience. It is difficult to say which is the original; but when we recollect in how much higher a state of culture the Persians were than the Arabs, and how well this view accords with their ancient system of religion, we shall feel inclined to believe that the Arabs were the borrowers, and that by mingling with the Persian system ideas derived from the Jews, that one was formed by them which is now the common property of all Moslems.

In like manner we regard the mountains of Kâf, the abode alike of Jinn and of Peries and Deevs, as having belonged originally to Persian geography. The fullest account of it

---

* This word is pronounced *Perry* or rather *Parry*.

† پَرِي زَادَه Hence it follows that the very plausible idea of the Peri having been the same with the Feroher cannot be correct.

appears in the Persian romance of Hatim Taï,* the hero of which often visited its regions. From this it would seem that this mountain-range was regarded as, like that of the ancient Greek cosmology, surrounding the flat circular earth like a ring, or rather like the bulwarks of a ship, outside of which flowed the ocean ; while some Arab authorities make it to lie beyond, and to enclose the ocean as well as the earth.† It is said to be composed of green chrysolite, the reflection of which gives its greenish tint to the sky. According to some, its height is two thousand English miles.

Jinnestân is the common appellation of the whole of this ideal region. Its respective empires were divided into many kingdoms, containing numerous provinces and cities. Thus in the Peri-realms we meet with the luxuriant province of Shad-u-kâm (*Pleasure and Delight*), with its magnificent capital Juherabâd (*Jewel-city*), whose two kings solicited the aid of Cahermân against the Deevs,‡ and also the stately Amberabâd (*Amber-city*), and others equally splendid. The metropolis of the Deev-empire is named Ahermanabâd (*Aherman's city*); and imagination has lavished its stores in the description of the enchanted castle, palace, and gallery of the Deev monarch, Arzshenk.

The Deevs and Peries wage incessant war with each other. Like mankind, they are subject to death, but after a much longer period of existence ; and, though far superior to man in power, they partake of his sentiments and passions.

We are told that when the Deevs in their wars make prisoners of the Peries, they shut them up in iron cages, and hang them from the tops of the highest trees, exposed to every gaze and to every chilling blast. Here their companions visit them, and bring them the choicest odours to feed on ; for the ethereal Peri lives on perfume, which has moreover the property of repelling the cruel Deevs, whose malignant nature is impatient of fragrance.§

When the Peries are unable to withstand their foes, they

---

* Translated by Mr. Duncan Forbes. It is to be regretted that he has employed the terms Fairies and Demons instead of Peries and Deevs.

† See Lane, Thousand and One Nights, i. p. 21, *seq.*

‡ The Cahermân Nâmeh is a romance in Turkish. Cahermân was the father of Sâm, the grandfather of the celebrated Roostem.

§ It is in the Cahermân Nâmeh that this circumstance occurs.

solicit the aid of some mortal hero. Enchanted arms and
talismans enable him to cope with the gigantic Deevs, and
he is conveyed to Jinnestân on the back of some strange
and wonderful animal. His adventures in that country
usually furnish a wide field for poetry and romance to
expatiate in.

The most celebrated adventurer in Jinnestân was Tahmuras, surnamed Deev-bend (*Deev-binder*),* one of the
ancient kings of Persia. The Peries sent him a splendid
embassy, and the Deevs, who dreaded him, despatched another. Tahmuras, in doubt how to act, consults the wonderful bird Seemurgh,† who speaks all languages, and whose
knowledge embraces futurity. She advises him to aid the
Peries, warns him of the dangers he has to encounter, and
discloses his proper line of action. She further offers to

---

* دیو بند   The Tahmuras Nâmeh is also in Turkish. It and the
Cahermân Nâmeh are probably translations from the Persian. As far as
we are aware, Richardson is the only orientalist who mentions these two
romances.

† سیمرغ   It signifies 'thirty birds,' and is thought to be the roc of
the Arabs. The poet Sâdee, to express the bounty of the Almighty says

چنان پهن خوان کرم کسترد
که سیمرغ در قاف قسمت خورد

His liberal board he spreadeth out so wide,
On Kâf the Seemurgh is with food supplied.

The Seemurgh probably belongs to the original mythology of Persia. for she
appears in the early part of the Shâh Nâmeh. When Zâl was born to Sâm
Nerimân, his hair proved to be white. The father regarding this as a proof o
Deev origin, resolved to expose him, and sent him for that purpose to Mount
Elburz. Here the poor babe lay crying and sucking his fingers till he was
found by the Seemurgh, who abode on the summit of Elburz, as she was
looking for food for her young ones. But God put pity into her heart, and she
took him to her nest and reared him with her young. As he grew up, the
caravans that passed by, spread the fame of his beauty and his strength, and a
vision having informed Sâm that he was his son, he set out for Elburz to claim
him from the Seemurgh. It was with grief that Zâl quitted the materna.
nest. The Seemurgh, when parting with her foster-son, gave him one of her
feathers, and bade him, whenever he should be in trouble or danger, to cast it
into the fire, and he would have proof of her power; and she charged him at
the same time strictly never to forget his nurse,

convey him to Jinnestân, and plucks some feathers from her breast, with which the Persian monarch adorns his helmet.

Mounted on the Seemurgh, and bracing on his arm the potent buckler of Jân-ibn-Jân,* Tahmuras crosses the abyss impassable to unaided mortality. The vizier Imlân, who had headed the Deev embassy, deserting his original friends, had gone over to Tahmuras, and through the magic arts of the Deev, and his own daring valour, the Persian hero defeats the Deev-king Arzshenk. He next vanquishes a Deev still more fierce, named Demrush, who dwelt in a gloomy cavern, surrounded by piles of wealth plundered from the neighbouring realms of Persia and India. Here Tahmuras finds a fair captive, the Peri Merjân,† whom Demrush had carried off, and whom her brothers, Dâl Peri and Milân Shâh Peri, had long sought in vain. He chains the Deev in the centre of the mountain, and at the suit of Merjân hastens to attack another powerful Deev named Houndkonz; but here, alas! fortune deserts him, and, maugre his talismans and enchanted arms, the gallant Tahmuras falls beneath his foe.

The great Deev-bend, or conqueror of Deevs, of the Shâh-Nâmeh‡ is the illustrious Roostem. In the third of his Seven Tables or adventures, on his way to relieve the Shâh Ky-Caoos, whom the artifice of a Deev had led to Mazenderân, where he was in danger of perishing, he encounters in the dark of the night a Deev named Asdeev, who stole on him in a dragon's form as he slept. Twice the hero's steed, Reksh, awoke him, but each time the Deev vanished, and Roostem was near slaying his good steed for giving him a false alarm. The third time he saw the Deev and slew him after a fearful combat. He then pursued his way to the cleft in the mountain in which abode the great Deev Sefeed, or White Deev. The seventh Table brought him to where lay an army of the Deev Sefeed's Deevs, commanded by Arzshenk, whose head he struck off, and put his troops to flight. At length he reached the gloomy cavern of the Deev

---

* See *Arabian Romance.*

† مرجان a pearl. Life, soul also, according to Wilkins.

‡ Ferdousee's great heroic poem. It is remarkable that the Peries are very rarely spoken of in this poem. They merely appear in it with the birds and beasts among the subjects of the first Iranian monarchs.

Sefeed himself, whom he found asleep, and scorning the advantage he awoke him, and after a terrific combat deprived him also of life.

Many years after, when Ky-Khosroo sat on the throne, a wild ass of huge size, his skin like the sun, and a black stripe along his back, appeared among the royal herds and destroyed the horses. It was supposed to be the Deev Akvân, who was known to haunt an adjacent spring. Roostem went in quest of him; on the fourth day he found him and cast his noose at him, but the Deev vanished. He re-appeared; the hero shot at him, but he became again invisible. Roostem then let Reksh graze, and laid him to sleep by the fount. As he slept, Akvân came and flew up into the air with him; and when he awoke, he gave him his choice of being let fall on the mountains or the sea. Roostem secretly chose the latter, and to obtain it he pretended to have heard that he who was drowned never entered paradise. Akvân thereupon let him fall into the sea, from which he escaped, and returning to the fount, he there met and slew the Deev. Roostem's last encounter with Deevs was with Akvân's son, Berkhyas, and his army, when he went to deliver Peshen from the dry well in which he was confined by Afrasiâb. He slew him and two-thirds of his troops. Berkhyas is described as being a mountain in size, his face black, his body covered with hair, his neck like that of a dragon, two boar's tusks from his mouth, his eyes wells of blood, his hair bristling like needles, his height 140 ells, his breadth 17, pigeons nestling in his snaky locks. Akvân had had a head like an elephant.

In the Hindoo-Persian Bahar Danush (*Garden of Knowledge*) of Ynâyet-ûllah, written in India A.D. 1650,* we find the following tale of the Peries, which has a surprising resemblance to European legends hereafter to be noticed.†

---

* Chap. xx. translation of Jonathan Scott, 1799.
† See below, *Shetland.*

The Peri-Wife.

THE son of a merchant in a city of Hindostan, having been driven from his father's house on account of his undutiful conduct, assumed the garb of a Kalenderee or wandering Derweesh, and left his native town. On the first day of his travels, being overcome with fatigue before he reached any place of rest, he went off the high road and sat down at the foot of a tree by a piece of water : while he sat there, he saw at sunset four doves alight from a tree on the edge of the pond, and resuming their natural form (for they were Peries) take off their clothes and amuse them-selves by bathing in the water. He immediately advanced softly, took up their garments, without being seen, and con-cealed them in the hollow of a tree, behind which he placed himself. The Peries when they came out of the water and missed their clothes were distressed beyond measure. They ran about on all sides looking for them, but in vain. At length, finding the young man and judging that he had possessed himself of them, they implored him to restore them. He would only consent on one condition, which was that one of them should become his wife. The Peries asserted that such a union was impossible between them whose bodies were formed of fire and a mortal who was composed of clay and water; but he persisted, and selected the one which was the youngest and handsomest. They were at last obliged to consent, and having endeavoured to console their sister, who shed copious floods of tears at the idea of parting with them and spending her days with one of the sons of Adam; and having received their garments, they took leave of her and flew away.

The young merchant then led home his fair bride and clad her magnificently; but he took care to bury her Peri-raiment in a secret place, that she might not be able to leave him. He made every effort to gain her affections, and at length succeeded in his object · "she placed her foot in

the path of regard, and her head on the carpet of affection."
She bore him children, and gradually began to take pleasure
in the society of his female relatives and neighbours. All
doubts of her affection now vanished from his mind, and he
became assured of her love and attachment.

At the end of ten years the merchant became embarrassed
in his circumstances, and he found it necessary to undertake a long voyage. He committed the Peri to the care
of an aged matron in whom he had the greatest confidence,
and to whom he revealed the secret of her real nature, and
showed the spot where he had concealed her raiment. He
then " placed the foot of departure in the stirrup of travel,"
and set out on his journey. The Peri was now overwhelmed
with sorrow for his absence, or for some more secret cause,
and continually uttered expressions of regret. The old
woman sought to console her, assuring her that "the dark
night of absence would soon come to an end, and the
bright dawn of interview gleam from the horizon of divine
bounty." One day when the Peri had bathed, and was dry-
ing her amber-scented tresses with a corner of her veil, the
old woman burst out into expressions of admiration at her
dazzling beauty. "Ah, nurse," replied she, "though you
think my present charms great, yet had you seen me in my
native raiment, you would have witnessed what beauty and
grace the Divine Creator has bestowed upon Peries; for
know that we are among the most finished portraits on the
tablets of existence. If then thou desirest to behold the
skill of the divine artist, and admire the wonders of creation, bring the robes which my husband has kept concealed,
that I may wear them for an instant, and show thee my
native beauty, the like of which no human eye, but my lord's,
hath gazed upon."

The simple woman assented, and fetched the robes and
presented them to the Peri. She put them on, and then,
like a bird escaped from the cage, spread her wings, and,
crying Farewell, soared to the sky and was seen no more.
When the merchant returned from his voyage " and found
no signs of the rose of enjoyment on the tree of hope, but
the lamp of bliss extinguished in the chamber of felicity, he
became as one Peri-stricken,* a recluse in the cell of mad-

---

* *i. e.* possessed, insane. It is like the νυμφόληπτος of the Greeks.

ness. Banished from the path of understanding, he remained lost to all the bounties of fortune and the useful purposes of life."

The Peri has been styled "the fairest creation of poetical imagination." No description can equal the beauty of the female Peri,* and the highest compliment a Persian poet can pay a lady is to liken her to one of these lovely aerial beings.† Thus Sâdee, in the lines prefixed to this section, declares that only the beauty of a Peri can be compared with that of the fair one he addresses; and more lately, Aboo Taleeb Khân says to Lady Elgin, as he is translated by M. von Hammer,‡

> The sun, the moon, the Peries, and mankind,
> Compared with you, do far remain behind;
> For sun and moon have never form so mild,
> The Peries have, but roam in deserts wild.

Sir W. Ouseley is at a loss what to compare them to. They do not, he thinks, resemble the Angels, the Cherubim and Seraphim of the Hebrews, the Dæmons of the Platonists, or the Genii of the Romans; neither do they accord with the Houri of the Arabs. Still less do they agree with the Fairies of Shakspeare; for though fond of fragrance, and

---

* It must be recollected that the Peries are of both sexes: we have just spoken of Peri *kings*, and of the *brothers* of Merjân.

† In the Shâh Nâmeh it is said of Prince Siyawush, that when he was born he was *bright as a Peri*. We find the poets everywhere comparing female beauty to that of superior beings. The Greeks and Romans compared a lovely woman to Venus, Diana, or the nymphs; the Persians to a Peri: the ancient Scandinavians would say she was Frith sem Alfkone, "fair as an Alf-woman;" and an Anglo-Saxon poet says of Judith that she was *Elf-sheen*, or fair as an Elf. In the Lay of Gugemer it is said,

> Dedenz la Dame unt trovée
> Ki de biauté resanbloit *Fée*.

The same expression occurs in Méon (3, 412); and in the Romant de la Rose we meet, *jure que plus belle est que fée* (10, 425). In the Pentamerone it is said of a king's son, *lo quale essenno bello comme a no fato*.

‡ Mines de l'Orient, vol. iii. p. 40. To make his version completely English, M. von Hammer uses the word Fairies; we have ventured to change it.

living on that sweet essential food, we never find them
employed in

> Killing cankers in the musk-rose buds,

or obliged

> To serve the fairy queen
> To dew her orbs upon the green.

Neither is their stature ever represented so diminutive as to
make key-holes pervious to their flight, or the bells of
flowers their habitations. But Milton's sublime idea of a
'faery vision,' he thinks, corresponds more nearly with
what the Persian poets have conceived of the Peries.

> Their port was more than human, as they stood;
> I took it for a faery vision
> Of some gay creatures of the element
> That in the colours of the rainbow live
> And play i' the plighted clouds. I was awestruck,
> And as I pass'd I worshipp'd.—*Comus.*

"I can venture to affirm," concludes Sir William gallantly,
"that he will entertain a pretty just idea of a Persian Peri,
who shall fix his eyes on the charms of a beloved and beautiful mistress."

If poetic imagination exhausted itself in pourtraying the
beauty of the Peries, it was no less strenuous in heaping.
attributes of deformity on the Deevs. They may well vie in
ugliness with the devils of our forefathers. "At Lahore, in
the Mogul's palace," says William Finch, "are pictures of
Dews, or Dives, intermixed in most ugly shapes, with long
horns, staring eyes, shaggy hair, great fangs, ugly paws, long
tails, with such horrible difformity and deformity, that I
wonder the poor women are not frightened therewith."*

Such then is the Peri-system of the Mohammedan
Persians, in which the influence of Islâm is clearly perceptible, the very names of their fabled country and its kings
being Arabic. Had we it as it was before the Arabs forced
their law on Persia, we should doubtless find it more con-
sistent in all its parts, more light, fanciful, and etherial.

---

* In Purchas' Pilgrims, vol. i., quoted by Sir W. Ouseley.

ARABIAN ROMANCE.

THE Prophet is the centre round which every thing connected with Arabia revolves. The period preceding his birth is regarded and designated as the times of ignorance, and our knowledge of the ancient Arabian mythology comprises little more than he has been pleased to transmit to us. The Arabs, however, appear at no period of their history to have been a people addicted to fanciful invention. Their minds are acute and logical, and their poetry is that of the heart rather than of the fancy. They dwell with fondness on the joys and pains of love, and with enthusiasm describe the courage and daring deeds of warriors, or in moving strains pour forth the plaintive elegy; but for the description of gorgeous palaces and fragrant gardens, or for the wonders of magic, they are indebted chiefly to their Persian neighbours.*

What classes of beings the popular creed may have recognised before the establishment of Islâm we have no means of ascertaining.† The Suspended Poems, and Antar, give us little or no information; we only know that the tales of Persia were current among them, and were listened to with such avidity as to rouse the indignation of the Prophet. We must, therefore, quit the tents of the Bedoween, and the valleys of 'Araby the Blest,' and accompany the khaleefehs to their magnificent capital on the Tigris, whence emanated all that has thrown such a halo of splendour around the genius and language of Arabia. It is in this seat of empire that we must look to meet with the origin of the marvels of Arabian literature.

Transplanted to a rich and fertile soil, the sons of the

---

* Compare Antar and the Suspended Poems (translated by Sir W. Jones) with the later Arabic works. Antar, though written by Asmai the court-poet of Haroon-er-Rasheed, gives the manners and ideas of the Arabs of the Desert.

† The Jinn are mentioned in the Kurân and also in Antar.

desert speedily abandoned their former simple mode of life; and the court of Bagdad equalled or surpassed in magnificence any thing that the East has ever witnessed. Genius, whatever its direction, was encouraged and rewarded, and the musician and the story-teller shared with the astronomer and historian the favour of the munificent khaleefehs. The tales which had amused the leisure of the Shahpoors and Yezdejirds were not disdained by the Haroons and Almansoors. The expert narrators altered them so as to accord with the new faith. And it was thus, probably, that the delightful Thousand and One Nights * were gradually produced and modified.

As the Genii or Jinn † are prominent actors in these tales, where they take the place of the Persian Peries and Deevs, we will here give some account of them.

According to Arabian writers, there is a species of beings named Jinn or Jân (Jinnee *m.*, Jinniyeh *f. sing.*), which were created and occupied the earth several thousand years before Adam. A tradition from the Prophet says that they were formed of " smokeless fire," *i.e.* the fire of the wind Simoom. They were governed by a succession of forty, or, as others say, seventy-two monarchs, named Suleyman, the last of whom, called Jân-ibn-Jân, built the Pyramids of Egypt. Prophets were sent from time to time to instruct and admonish them; but on their continued disobedience, an army of angels appeared, who drove them from the earth to the regions of the islands, making many prisoners, and slaughtering many more. Among the prisoners, was a young Jinnee, named 'Azâzeel, or El-Hârith (afterwards called Iblees, from his *despair*), who grew up among the angels, and became at last their chief. When Adam was created, God commanded the angels to worship him; and they all obeyed except Iblees, who, for his disobedience, was turned into a Sheytân or Devil, and he became the father of the Sheytâns.‡

* See Tales and Popular Fictions, p. 37, *seq.* Lane, Thousand and One Nights, *passim.*

† Genius and Jinn, like Fairy and Peri, is a curious coincidence. The Arabian Jinnee bears no resemblance whatever to the Roman Genius.

‡ " When we said unto the Angels, Worship ye Adam, and they worshiped except Iblees (who) was of the Jinn."—Kurân. chap. xviii. v. 48. Worship

The Jinn are not immortal; they are to survive mankind, but to die before the general resurrection. Even at present many of them are slain by other Jinn, or by men; but chiefly by shooting-stars hurled at them from Heaven. The fire of which they were created, circulates in their veins instead of blood, and when they receive a mortal wound, it bursts forth and consumes them to ashes. They eat and drink, and propagate their species. Sometimes they unite with human beings, and the offspring partakes of the nature of both parents. Some of the Jinn are obedient to the will of God, and believers in the Prophet, answering to the Peries of the Persians; others are like the Deevs, disobedient and malignant. Both kinds are divided into communities, and ruled over by princes. They have the power to make themselves visible and invisible at pleasure. They can assume the form of various animals, especially those of serpents, cats, and dogs. When they appear in the human form, that of the good Jinnee is usually of great beauty; that of the evil one, of hideous deformity, and sometimes of gigantic size.

When the Zôba'ah, a whirlwind that raises the sand in the form of a pillar of tremendous height, is seen sweeping over the desert, the Arabs, who believe it to be caused by the flight of an evil Jinnee, cry, Iron! Iron! (*Hadeed! Hadeed!*) or Iron! thou unlucky one! (*Hadeed! yâ meshoom!*) of which metal the Jinn are believed to have a great dread. Or else they cry, God is most great! (*Allâhu akbar!*) They do the same when they see a water-spout at sea; for they assign the same cause to its origin.*

The chief abode of the Jinn of both kinds is the Mountains of Kâf, already described. But they also are dispersed through the earth, and they occasionally take up their residence in baths, wells, latrinæ, ovens, and ruined houses.†

is here prostration. The reply of Iblees was, " Thou hast created *me* of fire, and hast created *him* of earth."—*Ib.* vii. 11; xxxviii. 77.

* It was the belief of the Irish peasantry, that whirlwinds of dust on the roads were raised by the Fairies, who were then on a journey. On such occasions, unlike the Arabs, they used to raise their hats and say, " God speed you, gentlemen!" For the power of iron, see *Scandinavia.*

† The Arabs when they pour water on the ground, let down a bucket into a well, enter a bath, etc., say, " Permission!" (*Destoor!*) or, Permission, ye blessed! (*Destoor, yâ mubârakeen!*)

They also frequent the sea and rivers, cross-roads, and market-places. They ascend at times to the confines of the lowest heaven, and by listening there to the conversation of the angels, they obtain some knowledge of futurity, which they impart to those men who, by means of talismans or magic arts, have been able to reduce them to obedience.*

The following are anecdotes of the Jinn, given by historians of eminence.†

It is related, says El-Kasweenee, by a certain narrator of traditions, that he descended into a valley with his sheep, and a wolf carried off a ewe from among them; and he arose and raised his voice, and cried, " O inhabitant of the valley ! " whereupon he heard a voice saying, " O wolf, restore him his sheep ! " and the wolf came with the ewe and left her, and departed.

Ben Shohnah relates, that in the year 456 of the Hejra, in the reign of Kaiem, the twenty-sixth khaleefeh of the house of Abbas, a report was raised in Bagdad, which immediately spread throughout the whole province of Irak, that some Turks being out hunting saw in the desert a black tent, beneath which there was a number of people of both sexes, who were beating their cheeks, and uttering loud cries, as is the custom in the East when any one is dead. Amidst their cries they heard these words—*The great king of the Jinn is dead, woe to this country !* and then there came out a great troop of women, followed by a number of other rabble, who proceeded to a neighbouring cemetery, still beating themselves in token of grief and mourning.

The celebrated historian Ebn Athir relates, that when he was at Mosul on the Tigris, in the year 600 of the Hejra, there was in that country an epidemic disease of the throat ; and it was said that a woman, of the race of the Jinn, having lost her son, all those who did not condole with her on account of his death were attacked with that disease ; so that to be cured of it men and women assembled, and with all their strength cried out, *O mother of Ankood, excuse us ! Ankood is dead, and we did not mind it !*

---

* For the preceding account of the Jinn, we are wholly indebted to Lane's valuable translation of the Thousand and One Nights, i. 30, *seq.*

† The first is given by Lane, the other two by D'Herbelot.

MIDDLE-AGE ROMANCE.

Ecco quei che le carte empion di sogni,
Lancilotto, Tristano e gli altri erranti,
Onde conven che il volgo errante agogni.
PETRARCA.

FEW will now endeavour to trace romantic and marvellous fiction to any individual source. An extensive survey of the regions of fancy and their productions will incline us rather to consider the mental powers of man as having an uniform operation under every sky, and under every form of political existence, and to acknowledge that identity of invention is not more to be wondered at than identity of action. It is strange how limited the powers of the imagination are. Without due consideration of the subject, it might be imagined that her stores of materials and powers of combination are boundless; yet reflection, however slight, will convince us that here also 'there is nothing new,' and charges of plagiarism will in the majority of cases be justly suspected to be devoid of foundation. The finest poetical expressions and similes of occidental literature meet us when we turn our attention to the East, and a striking analogy pervades the tales and fictions of every region. The reason is, the materials presented to the inventive faculties are scanty. The power of combination is therefore limited to a narrow compass, and similar combinations must hence frequently occur.

Yet still there is a high degree of probability in the supposition of the luxuriant fictions of the East having through Spain and Syria operated on European fancy. The poetry and romance of the middle ages are notoriously richer in detail, and more gorgeous in invention, than the more correct and chaste strains of Greece and Latium; the island of Calypso, for example, is in beauty and variety left far behind by the retreats of the fairies of romance. Whence arises this difference? No doubt

> When ancient chivalry display'd
> The pomp of her heroic games,
> And crested knights and tissued dames
> Assembled at the clarion's call,
> In some proud castle's high-arch'd hall,

that a degree of pomp and splendour met the eye of the minstrel and romancer on which the bards of the simple republics of ancient times had never gazed, and this might account for the difference between the poetry of ancient and of middle-age Europe. Yet, notwithstanding, we discover such an Orientalism in the latter as would induce us to acquiesce in the hypothesis of the fictions and the manner of the East having been early transmitted to the West; and it is highly probable that along with more splendid habits of life entered a more lavish use of the gorgeous stores laid open to the plastic powers of fiction. The tales of Arabia were undoubtedly known in Europe from a very early period. The romance of Cleomades and Claremonde, which was written in the thirteenth century,* not merely resembles, but actually is the story of the Enchanted Horse in the Thousand and One Nights. Another tale in the same collection, The two Sisters who envied their younger Sister, may be found in Straparola, and is also a popular story in Germany; and in the Pentamerone and other collections of tales published lo g before the appearance of M. Galland's translation of the Eastern ones, numerous traces of an oriental origin may be discerned. The principal routes they came by may also be easily shown. The necessities of commerce and the pilgrimage to Mecca occasioned a constant intercourse between the Moors of Spain and their fellow-sectaries of the East; and the Venetians, who were the owners of Candia, carried on an extensive trade with Syria and Egypt. It is worthy of notice, that the Notti Piacevoli of Straparola were first

---

* On the subjects mentioned in this paragraph, see Tales and Popular Fictions, chap. ii. and iii.

published in Venice, and that Basile, the author of the Pentamerone, spent his youth in Candia, and was afterwards a long time at Venice. Lastly, pilgrims were notorious narrators of marvels, and each, as he visited the Holy Land, was anxious to store his memory with those riches, the diffusal of which procured him attention and hospitality at home.

We think, therefore, that European romance may be indebted, though not for the name, yet for some of the attributes and exploits of its fairies to Asia. This is more especially the case with the romances composed or turned into prose in the fourteenth, fifteenth, and sixteenth centuries; for in the earlier ones the Fairy Mythology is much more sparingly introduced.

But beside the classic and oriental prototypes of its fairies, romance may have had an additional one in the original mythology of the Celtic tribes, of which a being very nearly allied to the fay of romance appears to have formed a part. Such were the damoiselles who bestowed their favours upon Lanval and Graelent. This subject shall, however, be more fully considered under the head of Brittany.

Romances of chivalry, it is well known, may be divided into three principal classes; those of Arthur and his Round Table, of Charlemagne and his Paladins, and those of Amadis and Palmerin, and their descendants and kindred. In the first, with the exception of Isaie le Triste, which appears to be a work of the fifteenth century, the fairies appear but seldom; the second exhibits them in all their brilliancy and power; in the third, which all belong to the literature of Spain, the name at least does not occur, but the enchantress Urganda la Desconecida seems equal in power to La Dame du Lac, in the romance of Lancelot du Lac.[*]

Among the incidents of the fine old romance just alluded to,[†] is narrated the death of King Ban, occasioned by grief at the sight of his castle taken and in flames through the treachery of his seneschal. His afflicted queen had left her

---

[*] In the Amadigi of B. Tasso, she is La Fata Urganda.

[†] Lancelot is regarded as probably the earliest prose romance of chivalry. It was first printed in 1494. The metrical romance called La Charrette, of which Lancelot is the hero, was begun by Chrestien de Troyes, who died in 1191, and finished by Geoffrey de Ligny. We may here observe that almost

new-born infant on the margin of a lake, while she went to soothe the last moments of the expiring monarch. On her return, she finds her babe in the arms of a beautiful lady. She entreats her pathetically to restore the orphan babe; but, without heeding her entreaties, or even uttering a single word, she moves to the edge of the lake, into which she plunges and disappears with the child. The lady was the celebrated Dame du Lac: the child was Lancelot, afterwards styled Du Lac. The name of the lady was Vivienne, and she had dwelt "en la marche de la petite Bretaigne." Merlin the demon-born, the renowned enchanter, became enamoured of her, and taught her a portion of his art; and the ill-return she made is well known in the annals of female treachery.* In consequence of the knowledge thus acquired she became a fairy; for the author informs us that "the damsel who carried Lancelot to the lake was a fay, and in those times all those women were called fays who had to do with enchantments and charms—and there were many of them then, principally in Great Britain—and knew the power and virtues of words, of stones, and of herbs, by which they were kept in youth and in beauty, and in great riches, as they devised." †

The lake was a *feerie*, an illusion raised by the art which the devil had taught Merlin, and Merlin the lady. The

---

all the French romances of chivalry were written originally in verse in the twelfth and thirteenth centuries, principally by Chrestien de Troyes and Huon de Villeneuve. The prose romances in general were made from them in the fifteenth century.

* For while it was in hand, by loving of an elf,
  For all his wondrous skill was cozened of himself:
  For walking with his Fay, her to the rock he brought,
  In which he oft before his nigromancies wrought.
  And going in thereat, his magics to have shown,
  She stopt the cavern's mouth with an enchanted stone,
  Whose cunning strongly crossed, amazed while he did stand,
  She captive him conveyed unto the Fairy-land.
  Drayton, *Poly-Olb*. Song IV.—See above, p. 2.

† La damoiselle qui Lancelot porta au lac estoit une *fée*, et en cellui temps estoient appellées *fees* toutes celles qui sentremeloient denchantements et de charmes, et moult en estoit pour lors principallement en la Grand Bretaigne, et savoient la force et la vertu des parolles, des pierres, et des herbes, parquoi elles estoient en jeunesse, et en beaulte, et en grandes richesses, comment elles divisoient.

romance says : " The lady who reared him conversed only in the forest, and dwelt on the summit of a hill, which was much lower than that on which King Ban had died. In this place, where it seemed that the wood was large and deep, the lady had many fair houses, and very rich ; and in the plain beneath there was a gentle little river well-stored with fish ; and this place was so secret and so concealed, that right difficult was it for any one to find, for the semblance of the said lake covered it so that it could not be perceived." *

When her young *protégé* had gone through his course of knightly education, she took him to King Arthur's court, and presented him there ; and his subsequent history is well known.

In the romance of Maugis d'Aygremont et de Vivian son Frère, when Tapinel and the female slave had stolen the two children of Duke Bevis of Aygremont, the former sold to the wife of Sorgalant the child which he had taken, whose name was Esclarmonde, and who was about fifteen years of age, and was " plus belle et plus blanche qu'une fée." The slave having laid herself to rest under a white-thorn (*aube-spine*), was devoured by a lion and a leopard, who killed one another in their dispute for the infant. " And the babe lay under the thorn, and cried loudly, during which it came to pass that Oriande la Fée, who abode at Rosefleur with four other fays, came straight to this thorn ; for every time she passed by there she used to repose under that white-thorn. She got down, and hearing the child cry, she came that way and looked at him, and said, ' By the god in whom we believe, this child here is lying badly (*mal gist*), and this shall be his name ;' and from that time he was always called Maugis."

Oriande la Fée brought the child home with her and her

---

* La dame qui le nourissoit ne conversoit que en forest, et estoít au plain de ung tertre plus bas assez que celui ou le roy Ban estoit mort : en ce lieu ou il sembloit que le bois fust grant et parfont (*profond*) avoit la dame moult de belles maisons et moult riches ; et au plain dessoubs y avoit une gente petite riviere moult plantureuse de poissons ; et estoit ce lieu si cele et secret que bien difficille estoit a homme de le trouver, car la semblance du dit lac le couvroit si que il ne pouvoit estre apperceu. And farther, La damoiselle nestoit mie seulle, mais y avoit grande compaignie de chevaliers et de dames et damoiselles.

damsels; and having examined him, and found, by a precious ring that was in his ear, that he was of noble lineage, "she prayed our Lord that he would be pleased of his grace to make known his origin (*nation*)." When she had finished her prayer, she sent for her nephew Espiet, "who was a dwarf, and was not more than three feet high, and had his hair yellow as fine gold, and looked like a child of seven years, but he was more than a hundred; and he was one of the falsest knaves in the world, and knew every kind of enchantment." Espiet informed her whose child he was; and Oriande, having prayed to our Lord to preserve the child, took him with her to her castle of Rosefleur, where she had him baptised and named Maugis. She and her damsels reared him with great tenderness; and when he was old enough she put him under the care of her brother Baudris, "who knew all the arts of magic and necromancy, and was of the age of a hundred years;" and he taught what he knew to Maugis.

When Maugis was grown a man, the Fay Oriande clad him in arms, and he became her *ami;* and she loved him "de si grand amour qu'elle doute fort qu'il ne se departe d'avecques elle."

Maugis shortly afterwards achieved the adventure of gaining the enchanted horse Bayard, in the isle of Boucaut. Of Bayard it is said, when Maugis spoke to him, "Bayard estoit *feyé,* si entendoit aussi bien Maugis comme s'il (*Bayard*) eust parlé." On his return from the island, Maugis conquers and slays the Saracen admiral Anthenor, who had come to win the lands and castle of Oriande, and gains the sword Flamberge (Floberge), which, together with Bayard, he afterwards gave to his cousin Renaud.

In Perceforest, Sebille la Dame du Lac, whose castle was surrounded by a river on which lay so dense a fog that no one could see across the water, though not called so, was evidently a fay. The fortnight that Alexander the Great and Floridas abode with her, to be cured of their wounds, seemed to them but as one night. During that night, "la dame demoura enceinte du roy dung filz, dont de ce lignage yssit le roi Artus." *

* Vol. i. ch. 42.

In the same romance * we are told that " en lysle de Zellande jadis fut demourante une *faee* qui estoit appellee Morgane." This Morgane was very intimate with " ung esperit (named Zephir) qui repairoit es lieux acquatiques, mais jamais nestoit veu que de nuyt." Zephir had been in the habit of repairing to Morgane la Faee from her youth up, " car elle estoit malicieuse et subtille et tousjours avoit moult desire a aucunement sçavoir des enchantemens et des conjurations." He had committed to her charge the young Passelyon and his cousin Bennucq, to be brought up, and Passelyon was detected in an intrigue with the young Morgane, daughter of the fay. The various adventures of this amorous youth form one of the most interesting portions of the romance.

In Tristan de Leonois,† king Meliadus, the father of Tristan, is drawn to a chase *par mal engin et negromance* of a fairy who was in love with him, and carries him off, and from whose thraldom he was only released by the power of the great enchanter Merlin.

In Parthenopex of Blois,‡ the beautiful fairy Melior, whose magic bark carries the knight to her secret island, is daughter to the emperor of Greece.

In no romance whatever is the fairy machinery more pleasingly displayed than in Sir Launfal, a metrical romance, composed § by Thomas Chestre, in the reign of Henry VI.

Before, however, we give the analysis of this poem, which will be followed by that of another, and by our own imitations of this kind of verse, we will take leave to offer some observations on a subject that seems to us to be in general

---

* Vol. iii. ch. 31.

† Tristan was written in verse by Chrestien de Troyes. The prose romance was first printed in 1489.

‡ Parthenopex was written in French in the twelfth century, according to Le Grand; in the thirteenth, according to Roquefort.

§ *Composed*—for to call it, with Ellis, Ritson, and others, a translation, would be absurd. How Ellis, who had at least read Le Grand's and Way's Fabliaux, could say of Chestre, that he " seems to have given a *faithful* as well as spirited version of this old Breton story," is surprising. It is in fact no translation, but a poem on the adventures of Sir Launfal, founded chiefly on the Lais de Lanval and de Graelent, in Marie de France, with considerable additions of Chestre's own invention, or derived from other sources. These Lais will be considered under Brittany.

but little understood, namely, the structure of our old English verse, and the proper mode of reading it.

Our forefathers, like their Gotho-German kindred, regulated their verse by the number of accents, not of syllables. The foot, therefore, as we term it, might consist of one, two, three, or even four syllables, provided it had only one strongly marked accent. Further, the accent of a word might be varied, chiefly by throwing it on the last syllable, as *natúre* for *náture, honoúr* for *hónour*, etc. (the Italians, by the way, throw it back when two accents come into collision, as, *Il Pástor Fido**) ; they also sounded what the French call the feminine e of their words, as, *In oldè dayès of the King Artoúr ;* and so well known seems this practice to have been, that the copyists did not always write this *e*, relying on the skill of the reader to supply it.† There was only one restriction, namely, that it was never to come before a vowel, unless where there was a pause. In this way the poetry of the middle ages was just as regular as that of the present day ; and Chaucer, when properly read, is fully as harmonious as Pope. But the editors of our ancient poems, with the exception of Tyrwhitt, seem to have been ignorant or regardless of this principle ; and in the Canterbury Tales alone is the verse properly arranged.

We will now proceed to the analysis of the romance of Sir Launfal.

Sir Launfal was one of the knights of Arthur, who loved him well, and made him his steward. But when Arthur married the beautiful but frail Gwennere, daughter of Ryon, king of Ireland, Launfal and other virtuous knights manifested their dissatisfaction when she came to court. The queen was aware of this, and, at the first entertainment given by the king,

> The queen yaf (*gave*) giftès for the nones,
> Gold and silver, precious stones,
> Her courtesy to kythe (*show*) :
> Everiche knight she yaf broche other (*or*) ring,
> But Sir Launfal she yaf no thing,
> That grieved him many a sythe (*time*).

---

* Thus we ourselves say *the Príncess Royal, éxtreme need,* etc. This, by the way, is the cause why the Greeks put a grave and not an acute accent on words accented on the last syllable, to show that it is easily moveable.

† As this seems to be one of the lost arts, we will here and elsewhere mark the feminine e and the change of accent.

Launfal, under the feigned pretext of the illness of his
father, takes leave of the king, and retires to Karlyoun,
where he lives in great poverty. Having obtained the loan
of a horse, one holyday, he rode into a fair forest, where,
overcome by the heat, he lay down under the shade of a
tree, and meditated on his wretched state.   In this situation
he is attracted by the approach of two fair damsels splendidly
arrayed.

> Their faces were white as snow on down,
> Their rode * was red, their eyne were brown;
>   I saw never none swiche.
> That one bare of gold a basín,
> That other a towel white and fine,
>   Of silk that was good and riche;
> Their kerchevès were welè skire (*clear*)
> Araid (*striped*) with richè goldè wire—
>   Launfal began to siche—
> They comè to him over the hoth (*heath*),
> He was curteís, and against them goeth,
>   And greet them mildeliche.

They greet him courteously in return, and invite him to
visit their mistress, whose pavilion is at hand.   Sir Launfal
complies with the invitation, and they proceed to where the
pavilion lies.   Nothing could exceed this pavilion in magnificence.   It was surmounted by an *erne* or eagle, adorned
with precious stones so rich, that the poet declares, and we
believe, that neither Alexander nor Arthur possessed "none
swiche jewel."

> He foundè in the paviloun
> The kingès daughter of Oliroun,
>   Dame Tryamour that hight;
> Her father was king of Faërie,
> Of occientè† fer and nigh,
>   A man of mickle might.

'he beauty of dame Tryamour was beyond conception.

> For heat her cloathès down she dede
> Almostè to her girdle stede (*place*),
>   Than lay she uncover't;
> She was as white as lily in May,
> Or snow that snoweth in winter's day:
>   He seigh (*saw*) never none so pert (*lively*).

---

* Rode—complexion ; from *red*.

† Occient—*occident* or *océan?* The Gascon peasantry call the Bay of
Biscay *La Mer d'Occient*. The Spaniards say *Mar Oceano*.

The redè rose, when she is new,
Against her rode was naught of hew
    I dare well say in cert;
Her hairè shone as goldè wire:
May no man redè her attire,
    Ne naught well think in hert *(heart)*.

This lovely dame bestows her heart on Sir Launfal, on condition of his fidelity. As marks of her affection, she gives him a never-failing purse and many other valuable presents, and dismisses him next morning with the assurance, that whenever he wished to see her, his wish would be gratified on withdrawing into a private room, where she would instantly be with him. This information is accompanied with a charge of profound secrecy on the subject of their loves.

The knight returns to court, and astonishes every one by his riches and his munificence. He continues happy in the love of the fair Tryamour, until an untoward adventure interrupts his bliss. One day the queen beholds him dancing, with other knights, before her tower, and, inspired with a sudden affection, makes amorous advances to the knight. These passages of love are received on his part with an indignant repulse, accompanied by a declaration more enthusiastic than politic or courteous, that his heart was given to a dame, the foulest of whose maidens surpassed the queen in beauty. The offence thus given naturally effected an entire conversion in the queen's sentiments; and, when Arthur returned from hunting, like Potiphar's wife, she charges Launfal with attempting her honour. The charge is credited, and the unhappy knight condemned to be burned alive, unless he shall, against a certain day, produce that peerless beauty. The fatal day arrives; the queen is urgent for the execution of the sentence, when ten fair damsels, splendidly arrayed, and mounted on white palfreys, are descried advancing toward the palace. They announce the approach of their mistress, who soon appears, and by her beauty justifies the assertion of her knight. Sir Launfal is instantly set at liberty, and, vaulting on the courser his mistress had bestowed on him, and which was held at hand by his squire, he follows her out of the town.

The lady rode down Cardevile,
Fer into a jolif ile,

Oliroun that hight; *
Every year upon a certain day,
Men may heare Launfales steedè neighe,
    And him see with sight.
He that will there axsy (*ask*) justes
To keep his armès fro the rustes,
    In turnement other (*or*) fight,
Dar (*need*) he never further gon;
There he may find justès anon,
    With Sir Launfal the knight.
Thus Launfal, withouten fable,
That noble knight of the roundè table,
    Was taken into the faërie;
Since saw him in this land no man,
Ne no more of him tell I ne can,
    For soothè, without lie.†

No romance is of more importance to the present subject than the charming Huon de Bordeaux.‡   Generally
known, as the story should be, through Wieland's poem and
Mr. Sotheby's translation, we trust that we shall be excused
for giving some passages from the original French romance,
as Le petit roy Oberon appears to form a kind of connecting
link between the fairies of romance and the Elves or Dwarfs
of the Teutonic nations.   When we come to Germany it
will be our endeavour to show how the older part of Huon
de Bordeaux has been taken from the story of Otnit in the
Heldenbuch, where the dwarf king Elberich performs

---

* It is strange to find the English poet changing the Avalon of the Lai de
Lanval into the well-known island of Oléron.   It is rather strange too, that
Mr. Ritson, who has a note on "Oliroun," did not notice this.

† The Lai ends thus:

Od (*avec*) li sen vait en Avalun,
Ceo nus recuntent le Bretun;
En une isle que mut est beaus,
La fut ravi li dameiseaus,
Nul humme nen ot plus parler,
Ne jeo nen sai avant cunter.

In Graelent it is said that the horse of the knight used to return annually to
the river where he lost his master.   The rest is Thomas Chestre's own, taken
probably from the well-known story in Gervase of Tilbury.

‡ Huon, Hue, or Hullin (for he is called by these three names in the
poetic romance) is, there can be little doubt, the same person with Yon king
of Bordeaux in the Quatre Filz Aymon, another composition of Huon de
Villeneuve, and with Lo Re Ivone, prince or duke of Guienne in Bojardo
and Ariosto.   See the Orl. Inn. l. i. c. iv. st. 46.   I Cinque Canti, c. v. st. 42

nearly the same services to Otnit that Oberon does to Huon, and that, in fact, the name Oberon is only Elberich slightly altered.*

Huon, our readers must know, encounters in Syria an old follower of his family named.Gerasmes; and when consulting with him on the way to Babylon he is informed by him that there are two roads to that city, the one long and safe, the other short and dangerous, leading through a wood, "which is sixteen leagues long, but is so full of Fairie and strange things that few people pass there without being lost or stopt, because therewithin dwelleth a king, Oberon the Fay. He is but three feet in height; he is all humpy; but he hath an angelic face; there is no mortal man who should see him who would not take pleasure in looking at him, he hath so fair a face. Now you will hardly have entered the wood, if you are minded to pass that way, when he will find how to speak to you, but of a surety if you speak to him, you are lost for evermore, without ever returning; nor will it lie in you, for if you pass through the wood, whether straightforwards or across it, you will always find him before you, and it will be impossible for you to escape at all without speaking to him, for his words are so pleasant to hear, that there is no living man who can escape him. And if so be that he should see that you are nowise inclined to speak to him, he will be passing wroth with you. For before you have left the wood he will cause it so to rain on you, to blow, to hail, and to make such right marvellous storms, thunder and lightning, that you will think the world is going to end. Then you will think that you see a great flowing river before you, wondrously black and deep; but know, sire, that right easily will you be able to go through it without wetting the feet of your horse, for it is nothing but a phantom and enchantments that the dwarf will make for you, because he wishes to have you with him, and if it so be that you keep

* Otnit was supposed to have been written by Wolfram von Eschembach, in the early part of the thirteenth century. It is possibly much older. Huon de Bordeaux was, it is said, written in French verse by Huon de Villeneuve, some time in the same century. It does not appear in the list of Huon de Villeneuve's works given by Mons. de Roquefort. At the end of the prose romance we are told that it was written at the desire of Charles seigneur de Rochefort, and completed on the 29th of January, 1454.

firm to your resolve, not to speak to him, you will be surely able to escape," etc.*

Huon for some time followed the sage advice of Gerasmes, and avoided Oberon le fayé. The storms of rain and thunder came on as predicted, the magic horn set them all dancing, and at last the knight determined to await and accost the dwarf.

"The Dwarf Fay came riding through the wood, and was clad in a robe so exceeding fine and rich, that it would be a marvel to relate it for the great and marvellous riches that were upon it; for so much was there of precious stones, that the great lustre that they cast was like unto the sun when he shineth full clear. And therewithal he bare a right fair bow in his fist, so rich that no one could value it, so fine it was; and the arrow that he bare was of such sort and manner, that there was no beast in the world that he wished to have, that it did not stop at that arrow. He had at his neck a rich horn, which was hung by two rich strings of fine gold."†

---

* Qui a de long seizes lieues, mais tant est plain de faerie et chose estrange que peu de gens y passent qui n'y soient perdus ou arrestez, pour ce que la dedans demeure un roi, Oberon le fayé. Il n'a que trois pieds de hauteur; il est tout bossu ; mais il a un visage angelique ; il n'est homme mortel que le voye que plaisir ne prengne a le regarder tant a beau visage. Ja si tost ne serez entrez au bois se par la voulez passer qu'il ne trouve maniere de parler a vous, si ainsi que a luy parliez perdu estus a tousjours sans jamais plus revenir ; ne il ne sera en vous, car se par le bois passez, soit de long ou de travers, vous le trouverez tousjours au devant de vous, et vous sera impossible que eschappiez nullement que ne parliez a luy, car ses parolles sont tant plaisantes a ouyr qu'il n'est homme mortel qui de luy se puisse eschapper. Et se chose est qu'il voye que nullement ne vueillez parler a luy, il sera moult troublé envers vous. Car avant que du bois soyez parti vous fera pleuvoir, venter, gresiller, et faire si tres-mervueilleux orages, tonnerres, et esclairs, que advis vous sera que le monde doive finir. Puis vous sera advis que par devant vous verrez une grande riviere courante, noire et parfonde a grand merveilles ; mais sachez, sire, que bien y pourrez aller sans mouiller les pieds de vostre cheval, car ce n'est que fantosme et enchantemens que le nain vous fera pour vous cuider avoir avec lui, et se chose est que bien tenez propos en vous de non parler a luy, bien pourrez eschapper, etc.

† Le Nain Fee s'en vint chevauchant par le bois, et estoit vestu d'une robbe si tres-belle et riche, que merveilles sera ce racompter pour la grand et merveilleuse richesse que dessus estoit, car tant y avoit de pierres precieuses, que la grand clarté qu'elles jettoient estoit pareille au soleil quant il luit bien clair. Et avec ce portoit un moult bel arc en son poing, tant riche que on ne le sauroit estimer tant estoit beau. Et la fleche qu'il portoit estoit de telle

This horn was wrought by four Fairies, who had endowed it with its marvellous properties.

Oberon, on bringing Huon to speech, informed him that he was the son of Julius Cæsar, and the lady of the Hidden Island, afterwards called Cephalonia. This lady's first love had been Florimont of Albania, a charming young prince, but being obliged to part from him, she married, and had a son named Neptanebus, afterwards King of Egypt, who begot Alexander the Great, who afterwards put him to death. Seven hundred years later, Cæsar, on his way to Thessaly, was entertained in Cephalonia by the lady of the isle, and he loved her, for she told him he would defeat Pompey, and he became the father of Oberon. Many a noble prince and noble fairy were at the birth, but one Fairy was unhappily not invited, and the gift she gave was that he should not grow after his third year, but repenting, she gave him to be the most beautiful of nature's works. Other Fairies gave him the gift of penetrating the thoughts of men, and of transporting himself and others from place to place by a wish; and the faculty, by like easy means, of raising and removing castles, palaces, gardens, banquets, and such like. He further informed the knight, that he was king and lord of Mommur; and that when he should leave this world his seat was prepared in Paradise—for Oberon, like his prototype Elberich, was a veritable Christian.

When after a variety of adventures Oberon comes to Bordeaux to the aid of Huon, and effects a reconciliation between him and Charlemagne, he tells Huon that the time is at hand that he should leave this world and take the seat prepared for him in Paradise, " en faerie ne veux plus demeurer." He directs him to appear before him within four years in his city of Mommur, where he will crown him as his successor.

Here the story properly ends, but an addition of considerable magnitude has been made by a later hand, in which the story is carried on.

Many are the perils which Huon encounters before the period appointed by Oberon arrives. At length, however, he

---

sorte et maniere, qu'il n'estoit beste au monde qu'il vousist souhaiter qu'a icelle fleche elle ne s'arrestast. Il avoit a son cou un riche cor, lequel estoit pendu a deux riches attaches de fin or.

and the fair Esclairmonde (the Rezia of Wieland) come to Mommur. Here, in despite of Arthur (who, with his sister Morgue la faée and a large train, arrives at court, and sets himself in opposition to the will of the monarch, but is reduced to order by Oberon's threat of turning him into a *Luyton de Mer**), Huon is crowned king of all Faerie "tant du pais des Luytons comme des autres choses secretes reservées dire aux hommes." Arthur gets the kingdom of Bouquant, and that which Sybilla held of Oberon, and all the Faeries that were in the plains of Tartary. The good king Oberon then gave Huon his last instructions, recommending his officers and servants to him, and charging him to build an abbey before the city, in the mead which the dwarf had loved, and there to bury him. Then, falling asleep in death, a glorious troop of angels, scattering odours as they flew, conveyed his soul to Paradise.

Isaie le Triste is probably one of the latest romances, certainly posterior to Huon de Bordeaux, for the witty but deformed dwarf Tronc, who is so important a personage in it, is, we are told, Oberon, whom Destiny compelled to spend a certain period in that form. And we shall, as we have promised, prove Oberon to be the handsome dwarf-king Elberich. In Isaie the Faery ladies approach to the Fées of Perrault, and Madame D'Aulnoy. Here, as at the birth of Oberon and of Ogier le Danois, they interest themselves for the new-born child, and bestow their gifts upon it. The description in this romance of the manner in which the old hermit sees them occupied about the infant Isaie is very pleasing. It was most probably Fairies of this kind, and not the diminutive Elves, that Milton had in view when writing these lines :

> Good luck betide thee, son, for, at thy birth,
> The Faery ladies danced upon the hearth.
> Thy drowsy nurse hath sworn she did them spy
> Come tripping to the room where thou didst lie,
> And, sweetly singing round about thy bed,
> Strew all their blessings on thy sleeping head.

---

* This sort of transformation appears to have been a usual mode of punishing in a Fairy land. It may have come from Circe, but the Thousand and One Nights is full of such transformations. For *luyton* or *lutin*, see below, *France.*

The description of the Vergier des Fées in Isaie le Triste, and of the beautiful valley in which it was situated, may rival in richness and luxuriancy similar descriptions in Spenser and the Italian poets.*

We have now, we trust, abundantly proved our position of the Fairies of romance being, at least at the commencement, only 'human mortals,' endowed with superhuman powers, though we may perceive that, as the knowledge of Oriental fiction increased, the Fairies began more and more to assume the character of a distinct species. Our position will acquire additional strength when in the course of our inquiry we arrive at France and Italy.

Closely connected with the Fairies is the place of their abode, the region to which they convey the mortals whom they love, 'the happy lond of Faery.'

---

* We are only acquainted with this romance through Mr. Dunlop's analysis.

FAIRY LAND.

There, renewed the vital spring,
Again he reigns a mighty king
And many a fair and fragrant clime,
Blooming in immortal prime,
By gales of Eden ever fanned,
Owns the monarch's high command.

T. WARTON.

AMONG all nations the mixture of joy and pain, of exquisite delight and intense misery in the present state, has led
the imagination to the conception of regions of unmixed bliss
destined for the repose of the good after the toils of this life,
and of climes where happiness prevails, the abode of beings
superior to man. The imagination of the Hindoo paints his
Swergas as 'profuse of bliss,' and all the joys of sense are
collected into the Paradise of the Mussulman. The Persian
lavished the riches of his fancy in raising the Cities of
Jewels and of Amber that adorn the realms of Jinnestân;
the romancer erected castles and palaces filled with knights
and ladies in Avalon and in the land of Faerie; while the
Hellenic bards, unused to pomp and glare, filled the Elysian
Fields and the Island of the Blest with tepid gales and
brilliant flowers. We shall quote without apology two
beautiful passages from Homer and Pindar, that our readers
may at one view satisfy themselves of the essential difference
between classic and romantic imagination.

In Homer, Proteus tells Menelaus that, because he had
had the honour of being the son-in-law of Zeus, he should
not die in "horse-feeding Argos."

But thee the ever-living gods will send
Unto the Elysian plain and distant bounds
Of Earth, where dwelleth fair-hair'd Rhadamanthus.
There life is easiest unto men; no snow,

Or wintry storm, or rain, at any time,
Is there; but evermore the Ocean sends
Soft-breathing airs of Zephyr to refresh
The habitants.—*Od.* iv. 563.

This passage is finely imitated by Pindar, and connected
with that noble tone of pensive morality, so akin to the
Oriental spirit, and by which the 'Dircæan Swan' is distinguished from all his fellows.

They speed their way
To Kronos' palace, where around
The Island of the Blest, the airs
Of Ocean breathe, and golden flowers
Blaze; some on land
From shining trees, and other kinds
The water feeds.   Of these
Garlands and bracelets round their arms they bind,

Beneath the righteous sway
Of Rhadamanthus.—*Ol.* ii. 126.

Lucretius has transferred these fortunate fields to the
superior regions, to form the abode of his *fainéans,* gods;
and Virgil has placed them, with additional poetic splendour,
in the bosom of the earth.

Widely different from these calm and peaceful abodes of
parted warriors are the Faeries of the minstrels and romancers.   In their eyes, and in those of their auditors, nothing
was beautiful or good divested of the pomp and pride of
chivalry; and chivalry has, accordingly, entered deeply into
the composition of their pictures of these ideal realms.

The Feeries of romance may be divided into three kinds
Avalon, placed in the ocean, like the Island of the Blest;
those that, like the palace of Pari Banou, are within the
earth; and, lastly, those that, like Oberon's domains, are
situate 'in wilderness among the holtis hairy.'

Of the castle and isle of Avalon,* the abode of Arthur and
Oberon, and Morgue la faye, the fullest description is to be

* Avalon was perhaps the Island of the Blest, of Celtic mythology, and
then the abode of the Fees, through the Breton Korrigan.   Writers, however,
seem to be unanimous in regarding it and Glastonbury as the same place,
called an isle, it is stated, as being made nearly such by the "river's embrace-

seen in the romance of Ogier le Danois, from which, as we
know no sure quarter but the work itself to refer to for the
part connected with the present subject, we will make some
extracts.*

At the birth of Ogier several Fairies attended, who
bestowed on him various gifts. Among them was Morgue
la Faye, who gave him that he should be her lover and friend.
Accordingly, when Ogier had long distinguished himself in
love and war, and had attained his hundredth year, the
affectionate Morgue thought it was time to withdraw him
from the toils and dangers of mortal life, and transport him
to the joys and the repose of the castle of Avalon. In pur-
suance of this design, Ogier and king Caraheu are attacked
by a storm on their return from Jerusalem, and their vessels
separated. The bark on which Ogier was "floated along the
sea till it came near the castle of loadstone, which is called
the castle of Avalon, which is not far on this side of the
terrestrial paradise, whither were rapt in a flame of fire
Enock and Helias; and where was Morgue la Faye, who at
his birth had endowed him with great gifts, noble and
virtuous."†

The vessel is wrecked against the rock; the provisions
are divided among the crew, and it is agreed that every man,
as his stock failed, should be thrown into the sea. Ogier's
stock holds out longest, and he remains alone. He is nearly
reduced to despair, when a voice from heaven cries to him:
"God commandeth thee that, as soon as it is night, thou go
unto a castle that thou wilt see shining, and pass from bark to
bark till thou be in an isle which thou wilt find. And
when thou wilt be in that isle thou wilt find a little path,
and of what thou mayest see within be not dismayed at anything. And then Ogier looked, but he saw nothing."‡

When night came, Ogier recommended himself to God,

---

ment." It was named Avalon, we are told, from the British word *Aval*, an
apple, as it abounded with orchards; and *Ynys gwydrin ;* Saxon Glaytn-ey,
glassy isle; Latin, Glastonia, from the green hue of the water surrounding it.

    * See Tales and Popular Fictions, ch. ix., for a further account of Ogier.

    † Tant nagea en mer qu'il arriva pres du chastel daymant quon nomme le
chasteau davallon, qui nest gueres deca paradis terrestre la ou furent ravis en
une raye de feu Enoc et Helye, et la ou estoit Morgue la faye, qui a sa nais-
sance lui avoit donne de grands dons, nobles et vertueux.

    ‡ Dieu te mande que si tost que sera nuit que tu ailles en ung chasteau que

and seeing the castle of loadstone all resplendent with light, he went from one to the other of the vessels that were wrecked there, and so got into the island where it was. On arriving at the gate he found it guarded by two fierce lions. He slew them and entered; and making his way into a hall, found a horse sitting at a table richly supplied. The courteous animal treats him with the utmost respect, and the starving hero makes a hearty supper. The horse then prevails on him to get on his back, and carries him into a splendid chamber, where Ogier sleeps that night. The name of this horse is Papillon, "who was a Luiton, and had been a great prince, but king Arthur conquered him, so he was condemned to be three hundred years a horse without speaking one single word, but after the three hundred years he was to have the crown of joy which they wore in Faerie." *

Next morning he cannot find Papillon, but on opening a door he meets a huge serpent, whom he also slays, and follows a little path which leads him into an orchard "tant bel et tant plaisant, que cestoit ung petit paradis a veoir." He plucks an apple from one of the trees and eats it, but is immediately affected by such violent sickness as to be put in fear of speedy death. He prepares himself for his fate, regretting "le bon pays de France, le roi Charlemaigne ... et principallement la bonne royne dangleterre, sa bonne espouse et vraie amie, ma dame Clarice, qui tant estoit belle et noble." While in this dolorous state, happening to turn to the east, he perceived "une moult belle dame, toute vestue de blanc, si bien et si richement aornee que cestoit ung grant triumphe que de la veoir."

Ogier, thinking it is the Virgin Mary, commences an Ave; but the lady tells him she is Morgue la Faye, who at his birth had kissed him, and retained him for her loyal amoureux, though forgotten by him. She places then on his finger a

tu verras luire, et passe de bateau en bateau tant que tu soies en une isle que tu trouveras. Et quand tu seras en lisle tu trouveras une petite sente, et de chose que tu voies leans ne tesbahis de rien. Et adonc Ogier regarda mais il ne vit rien.

* Lequel estoit luiton, et avoit este ung grant prince ; mais le roi Artus le conquist, si fust condampne a estre trois cens ans cheval sans parler ung tout seul mot ; mais apres les trois cens ans, il devoit avoir la couronne de joye de laquelle ils usoient en faerie.

ring, which removes all infirmity, and Ogier, a hundred
years old, returns to the vigour and beauty of thirty. She
now leads him to the castle of Avalon, where were her
brother king Arthur, and Auberon, and Mallonbron, " ung
luiton de mer."

"And when Morgue drew near to the said castle of
Avalon, the Fays came to meet Ogier, singing the most
melodiously that ever could be heard, so he entered into the
hall to solace himself completely. There he saw several
Fay ladies adorned and all crowned with crowns most
sumptuously made, and very rich, and evermore they sung,
danced, and led a right joyous life, without thinking of
any evil thing whatever, but of taking their mundane
pleasures."*   Morgue here introduces the knight to Arthur,
and she places on his head a crown rich and splendid beyond
estimation, but which has the Lethean quality, that whoso
wears it,

> Forthwith his former state and being forgets,
> Forgets both joy and grief, pleasure and pain ;

for Ogier instantly forgot country and friends.   He had no
thought whatever " ni de la dame Clarice, qui tant estoit belle
et noble," nor of Guyon his brother, nor of his nephew
Gauthier, " ne de creature vivante."   His days now rolled
on in never-ceasing pleasure.   " Such joyous pastime did
the Fay ladies make for him, that there is no creature in
this world who could imagine or think it, for to hear them
sing so sweetly it seemed to him actually that he was in
Paradise ; so the time passed from day to day, from week
to week, in such sort that a year did not last a month
to him."†

---

* Et quand Morgue approcha du dit chasteau, les Faes vindrent au devant
dogier, chantant le plus melodieusement quon scauroit jamais ouir, si entra
dedans la salle pour se deduire totallement.   Adonc vist plusieurs dames Faes
aournees et toutes courronnees de couronnes tressomptueusement faictes, et
moult riches, et tout jour chantoient, dansoient, et menoient vie tresjoyeuse,
sans penser a nulle quelconque meschante chose, fors prandre leurs mondains
plaisirs.

† Tant de joyeulx passetemps lui faisoient les dames Faees, quil nest
creature en ce monde quil le sceust imaginer ne penser, car les ouir si doulce-
ment chanter il lui sembloit proprement quil fut en Paradis, si passoit temps
de jour en jour, de sepmaine en sepmaine, tellement que ung an ne lui duroit
pas ung mois.

But Avalon was still on earth, and therefore its bliss was not unmixed. One day Arthur took Ogier aside, and informed him that Capalus, king of the Luitons, incessantly attacked the castle of Faerie with design to eject king Arthur from its dominion, and was accustomed to penetrate to the basse court, calling on Arthur to come out and engage him. Ogier asked permission to encounter this formidable personage, which Arthur willingly granted. No sooner, however, did Capalus see Ogier than he surrendered to him; and the knight had the satisfaction of leading him into the castle, and reconciling him to its inhabitants.

Two hundred years passed away in these delights, and seemed to Ogier but twenty: Charlemagne and all his lineage had failed, and even the race of Ogier was extinct, when the Paynims invaded France and Italy in vast numbers; and Morgue no longer thought herself justified in withholding Ogier from the defence of the faith. Accordingly, she one day took the Lethean crown from off his head: immediately all his old ideas rushed on his mind, and inflamed him with an ardent desire to revisit his country. The Fairy gave him a brand which was to be preserved from burning, for so long as it was unconsumed, so long should his life extend. She adds to her gift the horse Papillon and his comrade Benoist. " And when they were both mounted, all the ladies of the castle came to take leave of Ogier, by the command of king Arthur and of Morgue la Faye, and they sounded an aubade of instruments, the most melodious thing to hear that ever was listened to; then, when the aubade was finished, they sung with the voice so melodiously, that it was a thing so melodious that it seemed actually to Ogier that he was in Paradise. Again, when that was over, they sung with the instruments in such sweet concordance that it seemed rather to be a thing divine than mortal."*   The

---

* Et quand ils furent tous deux montes, toutes les dames du chasteau vindrent a la departie dogier, par le commandement du roi Artus et de Morgue la fae, et sonnerent une aubade dinstrumeus, la plus melodieuse chose a ouir que on entendit jamais; puis, l'aubade achevee, chanterent de gorge si melodieusement que cestoit une chose si melodieuse que il sembloit proprement a Ogier quil estoit en Paradis.   De rechief, cela fini, ils chanterent avecques les instrumens par si doulce concordance quil sembloit mieulx chose divine que humaine.

knight then took leave of all, and a cloud, enveloping him
and his companion, raised them, and set them down by a fair
fountain near Montpellier.   Ogier displays his ancient
prowess, routs the infidels, and on the death of the king is
on the point of espousing the queen, when Morgue appears
and takes him back to Avalon.   Since then Ogier has never
reappeared in this world.

Nowhere is a Faerie of the second kind so fully and
circumstantially described as in the beautiful romance of
Orfeo and Heurodis.   There are, indeed, copious extracts
from this poem in Sir Walter Scott's Essay on the Fairies
of Popular Superstition; and we have no excuse to offer
for repeating what is to be found in a work so universally
diffused as the Minstrelsy of the Scottish Border, but that
it is of absolute necessity for our purpose, and that romantic
poetry is rarely unwelcome.

Orfeo and Heurodis were king and queen of Winchester.
The queen happening one day to sleep under an ymp* tree
in the palace orchard, surrounded by her attendants, had a
dream, which she thus relates to the king:

> As I lay this undertide (*afternoon*)
> To sleep under the orchard-side,
> There came to me two faire knightes
> Well arrayed allè rightes,
> And bade me come without letting
> To speakè with their lord the king;
> And I answér'd with wordès bolde
> That I ne durstè ne I nolde:
> Fast again they can (*did*) drive,
> Then came their kingè all so blive (*quick*)
> With a thousand knights and mo,
> And with ladies fifty also,
> And riden all on snow-white steedes,
> And also whitè were their weedes.
> I sey (*saw*) never sith I was borne
> So fairè knightès me by forne.
> The kingè had a crown on his head,
> It was not silver ne gold red;

---

* Imp tree is a grafted tree.   Sir W. Scott queries if it be not a tree consecrated to the imps or fiends.   Had imp that sense so early?   A grafted tree
had perhaps the same relation to the Fairies that the linden in Germany and
the North had to the dwarfs.

All it was of precious stone,
As bright as sun forsooth it shone.
All so soon he to me came,
Wold I, nold I he me name (*took*),
And madè me with him ride
On a white palfrey by his side,
And brought me in to his palís,
Right well ydight over all ywis.
He shewed me castels and toures,
Meadows, rivers, fields and flowres,
And his forests everiche one,
And sith he brought me again home.

The fairy-king orders her, under a dreadful penalty, to await him next morning under the ymp tree. Her husband and ten hundred knights stand in arms round the tree to protect her,

And yet amiddès them full right
The queenè was away y-twight (*snatched*);
With Faëry forth y-nome (*taken*);
Men wist never where she was become.

Orfeo in despair abandons his throne, and retires to the wilderness, where he solaces himself with his harp, charming with his melody the wild beasts, the inhabitants of the spot. Often while here,

He mightè see him besides
Oft in hot undertides
The king of Faëry with his rout
Come to hunt him all about,
With dim cry and blowíng,
And houndes also with him barkíng.
Ac (*yet*) no beastè they no nome,
Ne never he nist whither they be come;
And other while he might them see
As a great hostè by him te.*
Well atourned ten hundred knightes
Each well y-armed to his rightes,
Of countenancè stout and fierce,
With many displayéd bannérs,
And each his sword y-drawè hold;
Ac never he nistè whither they wold.
And otherwhile he seigh (*saw*) other thing,
Knightès and levedis (*ladies*) come dauncíng

---

* *Te* or *tew* (Drayton, Poly-Olb. xxv.) is to draw, to march; from **A. S.** τeóᵹan, τuᵹan, τeón (Germ. *ziehen*), whence *tug, team.*

In quaint attirè guisëly,
Quiet pace and softëly.
Tabours and trumpès gede (*went*) him by,
And allè manere minstracy.
And on a day he seigh him beside
Sixty levedis on horse ride,
Gentil and jolif as brid on ris (*bird on branch*),
Nought o (*one*) man amonges hem ther nis,
And each a faucoun on hond bare,
And riden on hauken by o rivér.
Of game they found well good haunt,
Mallardes, heron, and cormeraunt.
The fowlès of the water ariseth,
Each faucoun them well deviseth,
Each faucoun his preyè slough * (*slew*).

Among the ladies he recognises his lost queen, and he determines to follow them, and attempt her rescue.

In at a roche (*rock*) the levedis rideth,
And he after and nought abideth.
When he was in the roche y-go
Well three milès other (*or*) mo,
He came into a fair countráy
As bright soonne summers day,
Smooth and plain and allè grene,
Hill ne dale nas none y-seen.
Amiddle the lond a castel he seigh,
Rich and real and wonder high.
Allè the utmostè wall
Was clear and shinè of cristal.
An hundred towers there were about,
Deguiselich and batailed stout.
The buttras come out of the ditch,
Of redè gold y-arched rich.
The bousour was anowed all
Of each manere diverse animal.
Within there werè widè wones
All of precious stones.
The worstè pillar to behold
Was all of burnished gold.
All that lond was ever light,
For when it should be therk (*dark*) and night,

---

* Beattie probably knew nothing of Orfeo and Heurodis, and the Fairy Vision in the Minstrel (a dream that would never have occurred to any minstrel) was derived from the Flower and the Leaf, Dryden's, not Chaucer's, for the personages in the latter are not called Fairies. In neither are they Elves.

> The richè stonès lightè gonne (*yield**)
> Bright as doth at nonne the sonne,
> No man may tell ne think in thought
> The richè work that there was wrought.

Orfeo makes his way into this palace, and so charms the king with his minstrelsy, that he gives him back his wife. They return to Winchester, and there reign, in peace and happiness.

Another instance of this kind of Feerie may be seen in Thomas the Rymer, but, restricted by our limits, we must omit it, and pass to the last kind.

Sir Thopas was written to ridicule the romancers; its incidents must therefore accord with theirs, and the Feerie in it in fact resembles those in Huon de Bordeaux. It has the farther merit of having suggested incidents to Spenser, and perhaps of having given the idea of a queen regnante of Fairy Land. Sir Thopas is chaste as Graelent.

> Full many a maidè bright in bour
> They mourned for him *par amour;*
>   When hem were bete to slepe;
> But he was chaste and no lechour,
> And sweet as is the bramble flour
>   That bereth the red hepe.

He was therefore a suitable object for the love of a gentle elf-queen. So Sir Thopas one day "pricketh through a faire forest" till he is weary, and he then lies down to sleep on the grass, where he dreams of an elf-queen, and awakes, declaring

> An elf-queen wol I love, ywis.
>
> All other women I forsake,
> And to an elf-queen I me take
>   By dale and eke by down.

He determines to set out in quest of her.

> Into his sadel he clombe anon,
> And pricked over style and stone,
>   An elf-quene for to espie;
> Till he so long had ridden and gone,
> That he found in a privee wone
>   The countree of Faerie,†

> Wherein he soughtè north and south,
> And oft he spied with his mouth
>   In many a forest wilde;
> For in that countree n'as there none
> That to him dorst ride or gon,
>   Neither wif ne childe.

The " gret giaunt " Sire Oliphaunt, however, informs him
that

> Here is the quene of Faërie,
> With harpe and pipe and simphonie,
>   Dwelling in this place.

Owing to the fastidiousness of " mine hoste," we are
unable to learn how Sir Thopas fared with the elf-queen,
and we have probably lost a copious description of Fairy
Land.

From the glimmering of the morning star of English
poetry, the transition is natural to its meridian splendour,
the reign of Elizabeth, and we will now make a few remarks
on the poem of Spenser.

rather with the Feeries of Huon de Bordeaux than with Avalon, or the region
into which Dame Heurodis was taken.

The Fays

Spenser's Faerie Queene

SPENSER'S FAERIE QUEENE.

A braver lady never tript on land,
Except the ever-living Faerie Queene,
Whose virtues by her swain so written been
That time shall call her high enhanced story,
In his rare song, the Muse's chiefest glory.
                                          BROWN.

DURING the sixteenth century the study of classical literature, which opened a new field to imagination, and gave it a
new impulse, was eagerly and vigorously pursued. A classic
ardour was widely and extensively diffused. The composi-
tions of that age incessantly imitate and allude to the
beauties and incidents of the writings of ancient Greece
and Rome.

Yet amid this diffusion of classic taste and knowledge,
romance had by no means lost its influence. The black-
letter pages of Lancelot du Lac, Perceforest, Mort d'Arthur,
and the other romances of chivalry, were still listened to
with solemn attention, when on winter-evenings the family
of the good old knight or baron ' crowded round the ample
fire,' to hear them made vocal, and probably no small degree
of credence was given to the wonders they recorded. The
passion for allegory, too, remained unabated. Fine moral
webs were woven from the fragile threads of the Innamorato
and the Furioso; and even Tasso was obliged, in compliance
with the reigning taste, to extract an allegory from his
divine poem; which Fairfax, when translating the Jerusalem,
was careful to preserve. Spenser, therefore, when desirous
of consecrating his genius to the celebration of the glories
of the maiden reign, and the valiant warriors and grave
statesmen who adorned it, had his materials ready prepared. Fairy-land, as described by the romancers, gave him

a scene; the knights and dames with whom it was peopled, actors; and its court, its manners, and usages, a facility of transferring thither whatever real events might suit his design.

It is not easy to say positively to what romance the poet was chiefly indebted for his Faery-land. We might, perhaps, venture to conjecture that his principal authority was Huon de Bordeaux, which had been translated some time before by Lord Berners, and from which it is most likely that Shakespeare took his Oberon, who was thus removed from the realms of romance, and brought back among his real kindred, the dwarfs or elves. Spenser, it is evident, was acquainted with this romance, for he says of Sir Guyon,

> He was an elfin born of noble state
> And mickle worship in his native land;
> Well could he tourney and in lists debate,
> And knighthood took of good *Sir Huon's* hand,
> When with King Oberon he came to Fairy-land.
> B. ii. c. 1. st. vi.

And here, if such a thing were to be heeded, the poet commits an anachronism in making Sir Huon, who slew the son of Charlemagne, a contemporary of Arthur.

Where "this delightful land of Faery" lies, it were as idle to seek as for Oberon's realm of Mommur, the island of Calypso, or the kingdom of Lilliput. Though it shadow forth England, it is distinct from it; for Cleopolis excels Troynovant in greatness and splendour, and Elfin, the first Fairy king, ruled over India and America. To the curious the poet says,

> Of Faery-lond yet if he more inquire,
> By certain signes here sett in sondrie place,
> He may it fynd, ne let him then admyre,
> But yield his sence to be too blunt and bace,
> That no'te without an hound fine footing trace.

The idea of making a queen sole regnante of Fairy-land was the necessary result of the plan of making "the fayrest princesse under sky" view her "owne realmes in lond of faery." Yet there may have been sage authority for this settlement of the fairy throne. Some old romancers may have spoken only of a queen; and the gallant Sir Thopas

does not seem to apprehend that he is in pursuit of the
wedded wife of another. This doughty champion's dream
was evidently the original of Arthur's.

> Forwearied with my sportes, I did alight
> From loftie steede, and downe to sleepe me layd;
> The verdant grass my couch did goodly dight,
> And pillow was my helmett fayre displayd;
> Whiles every sence the humour sweet embayd,
> Me seemed by my side a royall mayd
> Her dainty limbes full softly down did lay,
> So faire a creature yet saw never sunny day.
>
> Most goodly glee and lovely blandishment
> She to me made, and badd me love her deare,
> For dearly, sure, her love was to me bent,
> As, when iust time expired, should appeare:
> But whether dreames delude, or true it were,
> Was never hart so ravisht with delight,
> Ne living man such wordes did never heare
> As she to me delivered all that night,
> And at her parting said, she queen of Faries hight.
>
>   *   *   *   *   *
>
> From that day forth I cast in carefull mynd
> To seek her out with labor and long tyne,
> And never vow to rest till her I fynd—
> Nyne months I seek in vain, yet n'ill that vow unbynd.
> > B. i. c. 9. st. xiii., xiv., xv.

The names given by Spenser to these beings are Fays
(*Feés*), Farys or Fairies, Elfes and Elfins, of which last
words the former had been already employed by Chaucer,
and in one passage it is difficult to say what class of beings
is intended. Spenser's account of the origin of his Fairies
is evidently mere invention, as nothing in the least resembling it is to be found in any preceding writer. It bears,
indeed, some slight and distant analogy to that of the origin
of the inhabitants of Jinnestân, as narrated by the Orientals.
According to the usual practice of Spenser, it is mixed up
with the fables of antiquity.

> Prometheus did create
> A man of many parts from beasts deryved;
>
> That man so made he called Elfe, to weet,
> Quick,* the first author of all Elfin kynd,
> Who, wandring through the world with wearie feet,

---

* That is, *elfe* is *alive*.

> Did in the gardins of Adonis fynd
> A goodly creature, whom he deemed in mynd
> To be no earthly wight, but either spright
> Or angell, the authour of all woman-kynd;
> Therefore a Fay he her according hight,
> Of whom all Faryes spring, and fetch their lignage right.
>
> Of these a mighty people shortly grew,
> And puissant kings, which all the world warrayd,
> And to themselves all nations did subdue.
>
> B. ii. c. 9. st. lxx., lxxi., lxxii.

Sir Walter Scott remarks with justice (though his memory played him somewhat false on the occasion), that " the stealing of the Red Cross Knight while a child, is the only incident in the poem which approaches to the popular character of the Fairy." It is not exactly the *only* incident; but the only other, that of Arthegal, is a precisely parallel one :—

> He wonneth in the land of Fayëree,
> Yet is no Fary born, ne sib at all
> To Elfes, but sprung of seed terrestriall,
> And whyleome by false Faries stolne away,
> Whyles yet in infant cradle he did crall :
> Ne other to himself is knowne this day,
> But that he by an Elfe was gotten of a Fay.
>
> B. iii. c. 3. st. xxvi.

Sir Walter has been duly animadverted on for this dangerous error by the erudite Mr. Todd. It would be as little becoming as politic in us, treading, as we do, on ground where error ever hovers around us, to make any remark. Freedom from misconception and mistake, unfortunately, forms no privilege of our nature.

We must here observe, that Spenser was extremely injudicious in his selection of the circumstances by which he endeavoured to confound the two classes of Fairies. It was quite incongruous to style the progeny of the subjects of Gloriane a " base elfin brood," or themselves " false Fairies," especially when we recollect that such a being as Belphœbe, whose

> whole creation did her shew
> Pure and unspotted from all loathly crime,
> That is ingenerate in fleshly slime,

was born of a Fairie.

Our poet seems to have forgotten himself also in the Legend of Sir Calidore; for though the knight is a Faerie himself, and though such we are to suppose were all the native inhabitants of Faerie-land, yet to the "gentle flood" that tumbled down from Mount Acidale,

> ne mote the ruder clown
> Thereto approach ne filth mote therein drown;
> But Nymphs and Faeries on the banks did sit
> In the woods shade which did the waters crown.
> B. vi. c. 10. st. vii.

And a little farther, when Calidore gazes on the "hundred naked maidens lily white," that danced around the Graces, he wist not

> Whether it were the train of beauty's queen,
> Or Nymphs or Faeries, or enchanted show,
> With which his eyes mote have deluded been.—St. xvii.

The popular Elves, who dance their circlets on the green, were evidently here in Spenser's mind.*

It is now, we think, if not certain, at least highly probable, that the Fairy-land and the Fairies of Spenser are those of romance, to which the term Fairy properly belongs, and that it is without just reason that the title of his poem has been styled a *misnomer*.† After the appearance of his Faerie Queene, all distinction between the different species was rapidly lost, and Fairies became the established name of the popular Elves.

Here, then, we will take our leave of the potent ladies of romance, and join the Elves of the popular creed, tracing their descent from the Duergar of northern mythology, till we meet them enlivening the cottage fireside with the tales of their pranks and gambols.

---

* These Fairies thus coupled with Nymphs remind us of the Fairies of the old translators. Spenser, in the Shepherd's Calendar, however, had united them before, as

> Nor elvish ghosts nor ghastly owls do flee,
> But friendly *Faeries* met with many Graces,
> And light-foot *Nymphs*.—Æg. 6.

† "Spenser's *Fairy Queen*, which is one of the grossest misnomers in romance or history, bears no features of the Fairy nation."—Gifford, note on B. Jonson, vol. ii. p. 202.

EDDAS AND SAGAS.

En sång om strålende Valhalla,
Om Gudar och Gudinnar alla.
TEGNER.

A song of Vallhall's bright abodes,
Of all the goddesses and gods.

THE ancient religion of Scandinavia, and probably of the whole Gotho-German race, consisted, like all other systems devised by man, in personifications of the various powers of nature and faculties of mind. Of this system in its fulness and perfection we possess no record. It is only from the poems of the elder or poetic Edda,* from the narratives of the later or prose Edda and the various Sagas or histories written in the Icelandic language,† that we can obtain any knowledge of it.

The poetic or Sæmund's Edda was, as is generally believed, collected about the end of the eleventh or beginning of the twelfth century by an Icelander named Sæmund, and styled Hinns Fròda, or The Wise. It consists of a number of mythological and historical songs, the production of the ancient Scalds or poets, all, or the greater part, composed before the introduction of Christianity into the north. The measure of these venerable songs is alliterative rime, and they present not unfrequently poetic beauties of a high and striking character.‡

* *Edda* signifies grandmother. Some regard it as the feminine of *othr*, or *odr*, wisdom.
† This language is so called because still spoken in Iceland. Its proper name is the Norræna Tunga (*northern tongue*). It was the common language of the whole North.
‡ See Tales and Popular Fictions, chap. ix.

The prose Edda is supposed to have been compiled in the thirteenth century by Snorro Sturleson, the celebrated historian of Norway. It is a history of the gods and their actions formed from the songs of the poetic Edda, and from other ancient poems, several stanzas of which are incorporated in it. Beside the preface and conclusion, it consists of two principal parts, the first consisting of the Gylfa-ginning (*Gylfa's Deception*), or Hárs Lygi (*Hár's* i. e. *Odin's Fiction*), and the Braga-rædur (*Braga's Narrative*), each of which is divided into several Dæmi-sagas or Illustrative Stories; and the second named the Kenningar or list of poetic names and periphrases.*

The Gylfa-ginning narrates that Gylfa king of Sweden, struck with the wisdom and power of the Æser,† as Odin and his followers were called, journeyed in the likeness of an old man, and under the assumed name of Ganglar, to Asgard their chief residence, to inquire into and fathom their wisdom. Aware of his design, the Æser by their magic art caused to arise before him a lofty and splendid palace, roofed with golden shields. At the gate he found a man who was throwing up and catching swords, seven of which were in the air at one time. This man inquires the name of the stranger, whom he leads into the palace, where Ganglar sees a number of persons drinking and playing, and three thrones, each set higher than the other. On the thrones sat Har (*High*), Jafnhar (*Equal-high*), and Thridi (*Third*). Ganglar asks if there is any one there wise and learned. Har replies that he will not depart in safety if he knows more than they.‡ Ganglar then commences his interrogations, which embrace a variety of recondite subjects, and extend from the creation to the end of all things. To each he receives a satisfactory reply. At the last reply Ganglar hears a loud

---

* It was first published by Resenius in 1665.

† By the Æser are understood the Asiatics, who with Odin brought their arts and religion into Scandinavia. This derivation of the word, however, is rather dubious. Though possibly the population and religion of Scandinavia came originally from Asia there seems to be no reason whatever for putting any faith in the legend of Odin. It is not unlikely that the name of their gods, Æser, gave birth to the whole theory. It is remarkable that the ancient Etrurians also should have called the gods Æsar.

‡ So the Iötunn or Giant Vafthrudnir to Odin in the Vafthrudnismal.—Strophe vii.

rush and noise : the magic illusion suddenly vanishes, and he
finds himself alone on an extensive plain.

The Braga-rædur is the discourse of Braga to Ægir, the
god of the sea, at the banquet of the Immortals.   This part
contains many tales of gods and heroes old, whose adventures
had been sung by Skalds, of high renown and lofty genius.

Though both the Eddas were compiled by Christians, there
appears to be very little reason for suspecting the compilers
of having falsified or interpolated the mythology of their
forefathers.   Sæmund's Edda may be regarded as an Antho-
logy of ancient Scandinavian poetry ; and the author of the
prose Edda (who it is plain did not always understand the
true meaning of the tales he related) wrote it as a northern
Pantheon and Gradus ad Parnassum, to supply poets with
incidents, ornaments, and epithets.   Fortunately they did so,
or impenetrable darkness had involved the ancient religion
of the Gothic stock !

Beside the Eddas, much information is to be derived from
the various Sagas or northern histories.   These Sagas, at
times transmitting true historical events, at other times containing the wildest fictions of romance, preserve much valuable mythic lore, and the Ynglinga, Volsunga, Hervarar, and
other Sagas, will furnish many important traits of northern
mythology.

It is not intended here to attempt sounding the depths
of Eddaic mythology, a subject so obscure, and concerning
which so many and various opinions occur in the works of
those who have occupied themselves with it.   Suffice it to
observe that it goes back to the most remote ages, and that
two essential parts of it are the Alfar (*Alfs* or *Elves*) and
the Duergar (*Dwarfs*), two classes of beings whose names continue to the present day in all the languages of the nations
descended from the Gotho-German race.

" Our heathen forefathers," says Thorlacius,* " believed,
like the Pythagoreans, and the farther back in antiquity the
more firmly, that the whole world was filled with spirits of
various kinds, to whom they ascribed in general the same
nature and properties as the Greeks did to their Dæmons.
These were divided into the Celestial and the Terrestrial,

---

* Thorlacius, Noget om Thor og hans Hammer, in the Skandinavisk
Museum for 1803.

from their places of abode. The former were, according to the ideas of those times, of a good and elevated nature, and of a friendly disposition toward men, whence they also received the name of White or Light Alfs or Spirits. The latter, on the contrary, who were classified after their abodes in air, sea, and earth, were not regarded in so favourable a light. It was believed that they, particularly the *land ones*, the δαίμονες ἐπιχθόνιοι of the Greeks, constantly and on all occasions sought to torment or injure mankind, and that they had their dwelling partly on the earth in great thick woods, whence came the name Skovtrolde* (*Wood Trolls*), or in other desert and lonely places, partly in and under the ground, or in rocks and hills; these last were called Bjerg-Trolde (*Hill Trolls*) : to the first, on account of their different nature, was given the name of Dverge (*Dwarfs*), and Alve, whence the word Ellefolk, which is still in the Danish language. These Dæmons, particularly the underground ones, were called Svartálfar, that is Black Spirits, and inasmuch as they did mischief, Trolls."

This very nearly coincides with what is to be found in the Edda, except that there would appear to be some foundation for a distinction between the Dwarfs and the Dark Alfs.†

---

* Thorlacius, *ut supra*, says the thundering Thor was regarded as particularly inimical to the Skovtrolds, against whom he continually employed his mighty weapon. He thinks that the *Bidental* of the Romans, and the rites connected with it, seem to suppose a similar superstition, and that in the well-known passage of Horace,

> Tu parum castis inimica mittes
> Fulmina lucis,

the words *parum castis lucis* may mean groves or parts of woods, the haunt of unclean spirits or Skovtrolds, *satyri lascivi et salaces*. The word *Trold* will be explained below.

† The Dark Alfs were probably different from the Duergar, yet the language of the prose Edda is in some places such as to lead to a confusion of them. The following passage, however, seems to be decisive :

> Náir, Dvergar
> *Ok* Döck-Álfar.
> Hrafna-Galdr Othins, xxiv. 7.

> Ghosts, Dwarfs
> *And* Dark Alfs.

Yet the Scandinavian literati appear unanimous in regarding them as the same. Grimm, however, agrees with us in viewing the Döck-Alfar as distinct from the Duergar. As the abode of these last is named Svartálfaheimr, he thinks that the Svartálfar and the Duergar were the same.—Deutsche Mythologie, p. 413, *seq.* See below, *Isle of Rügen.*

THE ALFAR.

Ther ro meth Alfum.
BRYNHILDAR QUIDA,

Those are with the Alfs.

IN the prose Edda, Ganglar inquires what other cities beside that in which the Nornir dwelt were by the Urdar
fount, under the Ash Yggdrasil.* Hár replies,

"There are many fair cities there. There is the city which
is called Alf-heim, where dwelleth the people that is called
Liosálfar (*Light Alfs*). But the Döckálfar (*Dark Alfs*)
dwell below under ground, and are unlike them in appearance,
and still more unlike in actions. The Liosálfar are whiter
than the sun in appearance, but the Döckálfar are blacker
than pitch."†

The Nornir, the Parcæ, or Destinies of Scandinavian
mythology, are closely connected with the Alfar.

"Many fair cities are there in Heaven," says Hár, "and
the divine protection is over all. There standeth a city
under the ash near the spring, and out of its halls came three
maids, who are thus named, Udr, Verthandi, Skulld (*Past,
Present, Future*). These maids shape the life of man. We
call them Nornir. But there are many Nornir; those who
come to each child that is born, to shape its life, are of the
race of the gods; but others are of the race of the Alfs; and
the third of the race of dwarfs. As is here expressed,

> Sundry children deem I
> The Nornir to be—the same
> Race they have not.
> Some are of Æser-kin,
> Some are of Alf-kin,
> Some are the daughters of Dualin." (*i.e.* of the Dwarfs.)

* The ash-tree, Yggdrasil, is the symbol of the universe, the Urdar-fount
is the fount of light and heat, which invigorates and sustains it. A good
representation of this myth is given in Mr. Bohn's edition of Mallet's " Northern
Antiquities," which the reader is recommended to consult.

† This Grimm (*ut sup.*) regards as an error of the writer, who confounded
the *Döck* and the *Svartálfar.*

" Then," said Ganglar, " if the Nornir direct the future destiny of men, they shape it very unequally.   Some have a good
life and rich, but some have little wealth and praise, some
long life, some short."   " The good Nornir, and well descended," says Hár, " shape a good life; but as to those
who meet with misfortune, it is caused by the malignant
Nornir."

These Nornir bear a remarkable resemblance to the classical Parcæ and to the fairies of romance.   They are all alike
represented as assisting at the birth of eminent personages,
as bestowing gifts either good or evil, and as foretelling the
future fortune of the being that has just entered on existence.*   This attribute of the fairies may have been derived
from either the north or the south, but certainly these did
not borrow from each other.

Of the origin of the word Alf nothing satisfactory is to be
found.   Some think it is akin to the Latin *albus*, white;
others, to *alpes*, Alps, mountains.   There is also supposed to
be some mysterious connexion between it and the word Elf,
or Elv, signifying water in the northern languages; an analogy which has been thought to correspond with that between
the Latin Nympha and Lympha.   Both relations, however,
are perhaps rather fanciful than just.   Of the derivation of
Alf, as just observed, we know nothing certain,† and the
original meaning of Nympha would appear to be a new-
married woman,‡ and thence a marriageable young woman;
and it was applied to the supposed inhabitants of the mountains, seas, and streams, on the same principle that the
northern nations gave them the appellation of men and
women, that is, from their imagined resemblance to the
human form.

Whatever its origin, the word Alf has continued till the
present day in all the Teutonic languages.   The Danes have
Elv, pl. *Elve;* the Swedes, *Elf* pl. *Elfvar* m. *Elfvor* f.; and
the words *Elf-dans* and *Elf-blæst*, together with *Olof* and
other proper names, are derived from them.   The Germans
call the nightmare *Alp;* and in their old poems we meet

---

* See Tales and Popular Fictions, p. 274.

† The analogy of Deev, and other words of like import, might lead to the
supposition of Spirit being the primary meaning of Alf.

‡ See Mythology of Greece and Italy, p. 248, second edition.

with *Elbe* and *Elbinne*, and *Elbisch* occurs in them in the bad sense of *elvish* of Chaucer and our old romancers; and a number of proper names, such as Alprecht, Alphart, Alpinc, Alpwin,* were formed from it, undoubtedly before it got its present ill sense.† In the Anglo-Saxon, Ælf or Ælfen, with its feminine and plural, frequently occurs. The Oreas, Naias, and Hamodryas of the Greeks and Romans are rendered in an Anglo-Saxon glossary by ꝣunꞇ-ælfen, ꝼǽ-ælfen, and ꝼelꝺ-ælfen.‡ Ælf is a component part of the proper names Ælfred and Ælfric; and the author of the poem of Judith says that his heroine was Ælf-ꞃcıne (*Elf-sheen*), bright or fair as an elf. But of the character and acts of the elfs no traditions have been preserved in Anglo-Saxon literature. In the English language, Elf, Elves, and their derivatives are to be found in every period, from its first formation down to this present time.

THE DUERGAR.

By ek fur jörth nethan,
A ek, undir stein, stath.
ALVIS-MAL.

I dwell the earth beneath,
I possess, under the stone, my seat.

THESE diminutive beings, dwelling in rocks and hills, and distinguished for their skill in metallurgy, seem to be peculiar to the Gotho-German mythology.§ Perhaps the most probable account of them is, that they are personifications of

* After the introduction of Christianity, *Engel*, angel, was employed for *Alp* in most proper names, as Engelrich, Engelhart, etc.
† See MM. Grimm's learned Introduction to their translation of the Irish Fairy Legends, and the Deutsche Mythologie of J. Grimm.
‡ MM. Grimm suppose with a good deal of probability, that these are compounds formed to render the Greek ones, and are not expressive of a belief in analogous classes of spirits.
§ Some think, but with little reason, they were originally a part of the Finnish mythology, and were adopted into the Gothic system

the subterraneous powers of nature ; for it may be again
observed, that all the parts of every ancient mythology are
but personified powers, attributes, and moral qualities. The
Edda thus describes their origin :—

" Then the gods sat on their seats, and held a council, and
called to mind how the Duergar had become animated in the
clay below in the earth, like maggots in flesh. The Duergar
had been first created, and had taken life in Ymir's * flesh,
and were maggots in it, and by the will of the gods they
became partakers of human knowledge, and had the likeness
of men, and yet they abode in the ground and in stones.
Modsogner was the first of them, and then Dyrin."

The Duergar are described as being of low stature, with
short legs and long arms, reaching almost down to the ground
when they stand erect.† They are skilful and expert workmen in gold, silver, iron, and the other metals. They form
many wonderful and extraordinary things for the Æser, and
for mortal heroes, and the arms and armour that come from
their forges are not to be paralleled. Yet the gift must be
spontaneously bestowed, for misfortune attends those ex-
torted from them by violence.‡

In illustration of their character we bring forward the
following narratives from the Edda and Sagas. The homely
garb in which they are habited, will not, it is hoped, be displeasing to readers of taste. We give as exact a copy as we
are able of the originals in all their rudeness. The tales are
old, their date unknown, and they therefore demand respect.
Yet it is difficult to suppress a smile at finding such familiar,
nay almost vulgar terms § applied to the great supernal
powers of nature, as occur in the following tale from the
Edda.

---

* The giant Ymir is a personification of Chaos, the undigested primal matter.
The sons of Börr (other personifications) slew him. Out of him they formed
the world ; his blood made the sea, his flesh the land; his bones the mountains ;
rocks and cliffs were his teeth, jaws, and broken pieces of bones ; his skull
formed the heavens.

† Gudmund Andreas in notis ad Völuspá.

‡ That they are not insensible to kindness one of the succeeding tales
will show.

§ The habitual reader of the northern and German writers, or even our old
English ones, will observe with surprise his gradually diminished contempt for
many expressions now become vulgar. He will find himself imperceptibly
falling into the habit of regarding them in the light of their pristine dignity.

Loki and the Dwarf.

—•—

LOKI, the son of Laufeiar, had out of mischief cut off all the hair of Sif. When Thor found this out he seized Loki, and would have broken every bone in his body, only that he swore to get the Suartalfar to make for Sif hair of gold, which would grow like any other hair.

Loki then went to the Dwarfs that are called the sons of Ivallda. They first made the hair, which as soon as it was put on the head grew like natural hair; then the ship Skidbladni,* which always had the wind with it, wherever it would sail; and, thirdly, the spear Gugner, which always hit in battle.

Then Loki laid his head against the dwarf Brock, that his brother Eitri could not forge three such valuable things as these were. They went to the forge; Eitri set the swine-skin (bellows) to the fire, and bid his brother Brock to blow, and not to quit the fire till he should have taken out the things he had put into it.

And when he was gone out of the forge, and that Brock was blowing, there came a fly and settled upon his hand, and bit him; but he blew without stopping till the smith took the work out of the fire; and it was a boar, and its bristles were of gold.

He then put gold into the fire, and bid him not to stop blowing till he came back. He went away, and then the fly came and settled on his neck, and bit him more severely than before; but he blew on till the smith came back and took out of the fire the gold-ring which is called Drupner.†

Then he put iron into the fire, and bid him blow, and said ·

---

* Skidbladni, like Pari Banou's tent, could expand and contract as required. It would carry all the Æser and their arms, and when not in use it could be taken asunder and put in a purse. "A good ship," says Ganglar, "is Skid-bladni, but great art must have been employed in making it." Mythologists say it is the clouds.   † i. e. The *Dripper.*

that if he stopped blowing all the work would be lost. The fly now settled between his eyes, and bit so hard that the blood ran into his eyes, so that he could not see; so when the bellows were down he caught at the fly in all haste, and tore off its wings; but then came the smith, and said that all that was in the fire had nearly been spoiled. He then took out of the fire the hammer Miölner,* gave all the things to his brother Brock, and bade him go with them to Asgard and settle the wager.

Loki also produced his jewels, and they took Odin, Thor, and Frey, for judges. Then Loki gave to Odin the spear Gugner, and to Thor the hair that Sif was to have, and to Frey Skidbladni, and told their virtues as they have been already related. Brock took out his jewels, and gave to Odin the ring, and said that every ninth night there would drop from it eight other rings as valuable as itself. To Frey he gave the boar, and said that he would run through air and water, by night and by day, better than any horse, and that never was there night so dark that the way by which he went would not be light from his hide. He gave the hammer to Thor, and said that it would never fail to hit a Troll, and that at whatever he threw it it would never miss it; and that he could never fling it so far that it would not of itself return to his hand; and when he chose, it would become so small that he might put it into his pocket. But the fault of the hammer was that its handle was too short.

Their judgment was, that the hammer was the best, and that the Dwarf had won the wager. Then Loki prayed hard not to lose his head, but the Dwarf said that could not be. "Catch me then," said Loki; and when he went to catch him he was far away, for Loki had shoes with which he could run through air and water. Then the Dwarf prayed Thor to catch him, and Thor did so. The Dwarf now went to cut off his head, but Loki said he was to have the head only, and not the neck. Then the Dwarf took a knife and a thong, and went to sew up his mouth; but the knife was bad, so the Dwarf wished that his brother's awl were there; and as soon as he wished it it was there, and he sewed his lips together.†

---

* *i. e.* The *Bruiser* or *Crusher*, from *Myla*, to bruise or crush. Little the Fancy know of the high connexions of their phrase *Mill.*

† Edda Resenii, Dæmisaga 59.

Northern mythologists thus explain this very ancient fable. Sif is the earth, and the wife of Thor, the heaven or atmosphere; her hair is the trees, bushes, and plants, that adorn the surface of the earth. Loki is the Fire-God, that delights in mischief, *bene servit, male imperat*. When by immoderate heat he has burned off the hair of Sif, her husband compels him so by temperate heat to warm the moisture of the earth, that its former products may spring up more beautiful than ever. The boar is given to Freyr, to whom and his sister Freya, as the gods of animal and vegetable fecundity, the northern people offered that animal, as the Italian people did, to the earth. Loki's bringing the gifts from the under-ground people seems to indicate a belief that metals were prepared by subterranean fire, and perhaps the forging of Thor's hammer, the mythic emblem of thunder, by a terrestrial demon, on a subterranean anvil, may suggest that the natural cause of thunder is to be sought in the earth.

Thorston and the Dwarf.

WHEN spring came, Thorston made ready his ship, and put twenty-four men on board of her. When they came to Vinland, they ran her into a harbour, and every day he went on shore to amuse himself.

He came one day to an open part of the wood, where he saw a great rock, and out a little way from it a Dwarf, who was horridly ugly, and was looking up over his head with his mouth wide open; and it appeared to Thorston that it ran from ear to ear, and that the lower jaw came down to his knees. Thorston asked him, why he was acting so foolishly. "Do not be surprised, my good lad," replied the Dwarf; "do you not see that great dragon that is flying up there? He has taken off my son, and I believe that it is Odin himself that has sent the monster to do it. But I shall burst and die if I lose my son." Then Thorston shot at the dragon, and hit him under one of the wings, so that he fell dead to the earth; but Thorston caught the Dwarf's child in the air, and brought him to his father.

The Dwarf was exceeding glad, and was more rejoiced than any one could tell; and he said, "A great benefit have I to reward you for, who are the deliverer of my son; and now choose your recompense in gold and silver." "Cure your son," said Thorston, "but I am not used to take rewards for my services." "It were not becoming," said the Dwarf, "if I did not reward you; and let not my shirt of sheeps'-wool, which I will give you, appear a contemptible gift, for you will never be tired when swimming, or get a wound, if you wear it next your skin."

Thorston took the shirt and put it on, and it fitted him well, though it had appeared too short for the Dwarf. The Dwarf now took a gold ring out of his purse and gave it to Thorston, and bid him to take good care of it, telling him that he never should want for money while he kept that ring. He next took a black stone and gave it to Thorston, and said, "If you hide this stone in the palm of your hand no one will see you. I have not many more things to offer you, or that would be of any value to you; I will, however, give you a fire-stone for your amusement."

He then took the stone out of his purse, and with a steel point. The stone was triangular, white on one side and red on the other, and a yellow border ran round it. The Dwarf then said, "If you prick the stone with the point in the white side, there will come on such a hail-storm that no one will be able to look at it; but if you want to stop this shower, you have only to prick on the yellow part, and there will come so much sunshine that the whole will melt away. But if you should like to prick the red side, then there will come out of it such fire, with sparks and crackling, that no one will be able to look at it. You may also get whatever you will by means of this point and stone, and they will come of themselves back to your hand when you call them. I can now give you no more such gifts."

Thorston then thanked the Dwarf for his presents, and returned to his men, and it was better for him to have made this voyage than to have stayed at home.*

---

* Thorston's Saga, c. 3, in the Kämpa Dater.

The Dwarf-Sword Tirfing.

SUAFORLAMI, the second in descent from Odin, was king over Gardarike (Russia). One day he rode a-hunting, and sought long after a hart, but could not find one the whole day. When the sun was setting he found himself immersed so deep in the forest that he knew not where he was. There lay a hill on his right hand, and before it he saw two Dwarfs; he drew his sword against them, and cut off their retreat by getting between them and the rock. They proffered him ransom for their lives, and he asked them then their names, and one of them was called Dyren, and the other Dualin. He knew then that they were the most ingenious and expert of all the Dwarfs, and he therefore imposed on them that they should forge him a sword, the best that they could form; its hilt should be of gold, and its belt of the same metal. He moreover enjoined, that the sword should never miss a blow, and should never rust; and should cut through iron and stone, as through a garment; and should be always victorious in war and in single combat for him who bare it. These were the conditions on which he gave them their lives.

On the appointed day he returned, and the Dwarfs came forth and delivered him the sword; and when Dualin stood in the door he said, "This sword shall be the bane of a man every time it is drawn; and with it shall be done three of the greatest atrocities. It shall also be thy bane." Then Suaforlami struck at the Dwarf so, that the blade of the sword penetrated into the solid rock. Thus Suaforlami became possessed of this sword, and he called it Tirfing, and he bare it in war and in single combat, and he slew with it the Giant Thiasse, and took his daughter Fridur.

Suaforlami was shortly after slain by the Berserker*

---

* The Berserkers were warriors who used to be inflamed with such rage and fury at the thoughts of combats as to bite their shields, run through fire,

Andgrim, who then became master of the sword. When the twelve sons of Andgrim were to fight with Hialmar and Oddur for Ingaborg, the beautiful daughter of King Inges, Angantyr bore the dangerous Tirfing; but all the brethren were slain in the combat, and were buried with their arms.

Angantyr left an only daughter, Hervor, who, when she grew up, dressed herself in man's attire, and took the name of Hervardar, and joined a party of Vikinger, or Pirates. Knowing that Tirfing lay buried with her father, she determined to awaken the dead, and obtain the charmed blade; and perhaps nothing in northern poetry equals in interest and sublimity the description of her landing alone in the evening on the island of Sams, where her father and uncles lay in their sepulchral mounds, and at night ascending to the tombs, that were enveloped in flame,* and by force of entreaty obtaining from the reluctant Angantyr the formidable Tirfing.

Hervor proceeded to the court of King Gudmund, and there one day, as she was playing at tables with the king, one of the servants chanced to take up and draw Tirfing, which shone like a sunbeam. But Tirfing was never to see the light but for the bane of man, and Hervor, by a sudden impulse, sprang from her seat, snatched the sword and struck off the head of the unfortunate man. Hervor, after this, returned to the house of her grandfather, Jarl Biartmar, where she resumed her female attire, and was married to Haufud, the son of King Gudmund. She bare him two sons, Angantyr and Heidreker; the former of a mild and gentle disposition, the latter violent and fierce. Haufud would not permit Heidreker to remain at his court; and as he was departing, his mother, with other gifts, presented him Tirfing. His brother accompanied him out of the castle. Before they

---

swallow burning coals, and perform such like mad feats. " Whether the avidity for fighting or the ferocity of their nature," says Saxo, " brought this madness on them, is uncertain."

* The northern nations believed that the tombs of their heroes emitted a kind of lambent flame, which was always visible in the night, and served to guard the ashes of the dead; they called it *Hauga Elldr*, or The Sepulchral Fire. It was supposed more particularly to surround such tombs as contained hidden treasures.—*Bartholin, de Contempt. a Dan. Morte*, p. 275.

parted, Heidreker drew out his sword to look at and admire it; but scarcely did the rays of light fall on the magic blade, when the Berserker rage came on its owner, and he slew his gentle brother.

After this he joined a body of Vikinger, and became so distinguished, that King Harold, for the aid he lent him, gave him his daughter Helga in marriage. But it was the destiny of Tirfing to commit crime, and Harold fell by the hand of his son-in-law. Heidreker was afterwards in Russia, and the son of the king was his foster-son. One day, as they were out hunting, Heidreker and his foster-son happened to be separated from the rest of the party, when a wild boar appeared before them; Heidreker ran at him with his spear, but the beast caught it in his mouth and broke it across. He then alighted and drew Tirfing, and killed the boar; but on looking around, he could see no one but his foster-son, and Tirfing could only be appeased with warm human blood, and he slew the unfortunate youth. Finally, King Heidreker was murdered in his bed by his Scottish slaves, who carried off Tirfing; but his son Angantyr, who succeeded him, discovered and put them to death, and recovered the magic blade. In battle against the Huns he afterwards made great slaughter; but among the slain was found his own brother Laudur. And so ends the history of the Dwarf-sword Tirfing.*

Like Alf, the word Duergr has retained its place in the Teutonic languages. Dverg† is the term still used in the north; the Germans have Zwerg, and we Dwarf,‡ which, however, is never synonymous with Fairy, as Elf is. Ihre

---

* Hervarar Saga *passim*. The Tirfing Saga would be its more proper appellation. In poetic and romantic interest it exceeds all the northern Sagas.

† In Swedish Dverg also signifies a spider.

‡ In the old Swedish metrical history of Alexander, the word *Duerf* occurs. The progress in the English word is as follows : Anglo-Saxon ðþeonȝ; thence *dwerke ;*

> A maid that is a messingere
> And a *dwerkè* me brought here,
>   Her to do socoúr.
> *Lybeaus Disconus.*

lastly, *dwarf*, as in old Swedish.

Thor with his magic hammer and the giant

Giant and Dwarfs

rejects all the etymons proposed for it, such, for example, as that of Gudmund Andreæ, θέοι ἔργον ; and with abundant reason.

Some have thought that by the Dwarfs were to be understood the Finns, the original inhabitants of the country, who were driven to the mountains by the Scandinavians, and who probably excelled the new-comers in the art of working their mines and manufacturing their produce. Thorlacius, on the contrary, thinks that it was Odin and his followers, who came from the country of the Chalybes, that brought the metallurgic arts into Scandinavia.

Perhaps the simplest account of the origin of the Dwarfs is, that when, in the spirit of all ancient religions, the subterranean powers of nature were to be personified, the authors of the system, from observing that people of small stature usually excel in craft and ingenuity, took occasion to represent the beings who formed crystals and purified metals within the bowels of the earth as of diminutive size, which also corresponded better with the power assigned them of slipping through the fissures and interstices of rocks and stones. Similar observations led to the representation of the wild and awful powers of brute nature under the form of huge giants.

SCANDINAVIA.

De vare syv og hundrede Trolde,
De vare baade grumme og lede,
De vilde gjöre Bonden et Gjæsterie,
Med hannem baade drikke og æde.
ELINE AF VILLENSKOV.

There were seven and a hundred Trolls,
They were both ugly and grim,
A visit they would the farmer make,
Both eat and drink with him.

UNDER the name of Scandinavia are included the kingdoms of Sweden, Denmark, and Norway, which once had a common religion and a common language. Their religion is still one, and their languages differ but little; we therefore feel that we may safely treat of their Fairy Mythology together.

Our principal authorities are the collection of Danish popular traditions, published by Mr. Thiele,* the select Danish ballads of Nyerup and Rahbek,† and the Swedish ballads of Geijer and Afzelius.‡ As most of the principal Danish ballads treating of Elves, etc., have been already translated by Dr. Jamieson, we will not insert them here; but translate, instead, the corresponding Swedish ones, which are in general of greater simplicity, and often contain additional traits of popular belief. As we prefer fidelity to polish, the reader must not be offended at antique modes of expression and imperfect rimes. Our rimes we can, however, safely say shall be at least as perfect as those of our originals.

These ballads, none of which are later than the fifteenth

---

* Danske Folkesagn, 4 vols. 12mo. Copenh. 1818—22.
† Udvalgde Danske Viser fra Middelaldaren, 5 vols. 12mo. Copenh. 1812.
‡ Svenska Folk-Visor från Forntiden, 3 vols. 8vo. Stockholm, 1814—16. We have not seen the late collection of Arvidsson named Svenska Fornsånger, in 3 vols. 8vo.

century, are written in a strain of the most artless simplicity;
not the slightest attempt at ornament is to be discerned in
them; the same ideas and expressions continually recur;
and the rimes are the most careless imaginable, often a mere
assonnance in vowels or consonants; sometimes not possessing even that slight similarity of sound. Every Visa or
ballad has its single or double Omquæd * or burden, which,
like a running accompaniment in music, frequently falls in
with the most happy effect; sometimes recalling former joys
or sorrows; sometimes, by the continual mention of some
attribute of one of the seasons, especially the summer, keeping up in the mind of the reader or hearers the forms of
external nature.

It is singular to observe the strong resemblance between
the Scandinavian ballads and those of England and Scotland,
not merely in manner but in subject. The Scottish ballad
first mentioned below is an instance; it is to be met with in
England, in the Feroes, in Denmark, and in Sweden, with
very slight differences. Geijer observes, that the two last
stanzas of 'William and Margaret,' in Percy's Reliques,
are nearly word for word the same as the two last in the
Swedish ballad of 'Rosa Lilla,' † and in the corresponding

---

* The reader will find a beautiful instance of a double Omquæd in the
Scottish ballad of the Cruel Sister.

> There were two sisters sat in a bower,
> *Binnōrie o Binnōrie*
> There came a knight to be their wooer
> *By the bonny mill-dams of Binnōrie.*

And in the Cruel Brother,

> There were three ladies played at the ba',
> *With a heigh ho and a lily gay;*
> There came a knight and played o'er them a',
> *As the primrose spreads so sweetly.*

The second and fourth lines are repeated in every stanza.

† These are the Swedish verses:

> Det växte upp *Liljor* på begge deres graf,
> *Med äran och med dygd—*
> De växte tilsamman med alla sina blad.
> *J vinnen väl, J vinnen väl både rosor och liljor.*
> Det växte upp *Rosor* ur båda deras mun,
> *Med äran och med dygd—*
> De växte tilsammans i fagreste lund.
> *J vinnen väl, J vinnen väl både rosor och liljor.*

Danish one. This might perhaps lead to the supposition of many of these ballads having come down from the time when the connexion was so intimate between this country and Scandinavia.

We will divide the Scandinavian objects of popular belief into four classes :—1. The Elves ; 2. The Dwarfs, or Trolls, as they are usually called ; 3. The Nisses ; and 4. The Necks, Mermen, and Mermaids.*

ELVES.

Säg, kännar du Elfvornas glada slägt?
De bygga ved flodernas rand;
De spinna af månsken sin högtidsdrägt,
Med liljehvit spelande hand.
STAGNELIUS.

Say, knowest thou the Elves' gay and joyous race?
The banks of streams are their home;
They spin of the moonshine their holiday-dress,
With their lily-white hands frolicsome.

THE Alfar still live in the memory and traditions of the peasantry of Scandinavia. They also, to a certain extent, retain their distinction into White and Black. The former, or the Good Elves, dwell in the air, dance on the grass, or sit in the leaves of trees; the latter, or Evil Elves, are regarded as an underground people, who frequently inflict sickness or injury on mankind; for which there is a particular kind of doctors called *Kloka män*,† to be met with in all parts of the country.

* Some readers may wish to know the proper mode of pronouncing such Danish and Swedish words as occur in the following legends. For their satisfaction we give the following information. J is pronounced as our *y ;* when it comes between a consonant and a vowel, it is very short, like the y that is expressed, but not written, in many English words after *c* and *g* : thus *kjær* is pronounced very nearly as *care :* ö sounds like the German ö, or French *eu :* *d* after another consonant is rarely sounded, Trold is pronounced Troll : *aa,* which the Swedes write *å,* as o in *more, tore.* Aarhuus is pronounced *Ore-hoos.*

† That is, Wise People or Conjurors. They answer to the Fairy-women of Ireland.

Gnomes terrifying a miner

Dark Elves of old Scandinavia

The Elves are believed to have their kings, and to celebrate their weddings and banquets, just the same as the dwellers above ground. There is an interesting intermediate class of them in popular tradition called the Hill-people (*Högfolk*), who are believed to dwell in caves and small hills : when they show themselves they have a handsome human form. The common people seem to connect with them a deep feeling of melancholy, as if bewailing a half-quenched hope of redemption.*

There are only a few old persons now who can tell any thing more about them than of the sweet singing that may occasionally on summer nights be heard out of their hills, when one stands still and listens, or, as it is expressed in the ballads, "lays his ear to the Elve-hill" (*lägger sitt öra till Elfvehögg*): but no one must be so cruel as, by the slightest word, to destroy their hopes of salvation, for then the spritely music will be turned into weeping and lamentation.†

The Norwegians call the Elves Huldrafolk, and their music Huldraslaat: it is in the minor key, and of a dull and mournful sound. The mountaineers sometimes play it, and pretend they have learned it by listening to the underground people among the hills and rocks. There is also a tune called the Elf-king's tune, which several of the good fiddlers know right well, but never venture to play, for as soon as it begins both old and young, and even inanimate objects, are impelled to dance, and the player cannot stop unless he can play the air backwards, or that some one comes behind him and cuts the strings of his fiddle.‡

The little underground Elves, who are believed to dwell

---

* Afzelius is of opinion that this notion respecting the Hill-people is derived from the time of the introduction of Christianity into the north, and expresses the sympathy of the first converts with their forefathers, who had died without a knowledge of the Redeemer, and lay buried in heathen earth, and whose unhappy spirits were doomed to wander about these lower regions, or sigh within their mounds till the great day of redemption.

† "About fifteen years ago," says Ödman (Bahuslän, p. 80), "people used to hear, out of the hill under Gärun, in the parish of Tanum, the playing, as it were, of the very best musicians. Any one there who had a fiddle, and wished to play, was taught in an instant, provided they promised them salvation ; but whoever did not do so, might hear them within, in the hill, breaking their violins to pieces, and weeping bitterly." See Grimm. Deut. Myth. 461.

‡ Arndt, Reise nach Schweden, iv. 241.

under the houses of mankind, are described as sportive and
mischievous, and as imitating all the actions of men. They
are said to love cleanliness about the house and place, and to
reward such servants as are neat and cleanly.

There was one time, it is said, a servant girl, who was for
her cleanly, tidy habits, greatly beloved by the Elves, particularly as she was careful to carry away all dirt and foul
water to a distance from the house, and they once invited
her to a wedding. Every thing was conducted in the greatest
order, and they made her a present of some chips, which she
took good-humouredly and put into her pocket. But when
the bride-pair was coming there was a straw unluckily lying
in the way, the bridegroom got cleverly over it, but the poor
bride fell on her face. At the sight of this the girl could
not restrain herself, but burst out a-laughing, and that
instant the whole vanished from her sight. Next day, to her
utter amazement, she found that what she had taken to be
nothing but chips, were so many pieces of pure gold.*

A dairy-maid at a place called Skibshuset (*the Ship-house*),
in Odense, was not so fortunate. A colony of Elves had taken
up their abode under the floor of the cowhouse, or it is more
likely, were there before it was made a cowhouse. However,
the dirt and filth that the cattle made annoyed them beyond
measure, and they gave the dairy-maid to understand that
if she did not remove the cows, she would have reason to
repent it. She gave little heed to their representations ;
and it was not very long till they set her up on top of the
hay-rick, and killed all the cows. It is said that they were
seen on the same night removing in a great hurry from the
cowhouse down to the meadow, and that they went in little
coaches ; and their king was in the first coach, which was
far more stately and magnificent than the rest. They have
ever since lived in the meadow.†

* Svenska Folk-Visor, vol. iii. p. 159. There is a similar legend in
Germany. A servant, one time, seeing one of the little ones very hard-set to
carry a single grain of wheat, burst out laughing at him. In a rage, he
threw it on the ground, and it proved to be the purest gold. But he and his
comrades quitted the house, and it speedily went to decay.—Strack. Beschr. v.
Eilsen, p. 124, *ap.* Grimm, Introd., etc., p. 90.

† Thiele, vol. iv. p. 22. They are called Trolls in the original. As they
had a king, we think they must have been Elves. The Dwarfs have long since
abolished monarchy.

The Elves are extremely fond of dancing in the meadows, where they form those circles of a livelier green which from them are called Elf-dance (*Elfdans*). When the country people see in the morning stripes along the dewy grass in the woods and meadows, they say the Elves have been dancing there. If any one should at midnight get within their circle, they become visible to him, and they may then illude him. It is not every one that can see the Elves; and one person may see them dancing while another perceives nothing. Sunday children, as they are called, *i. e.* those born on Sunday, are remarkable for possessing this property of seeing Elves and similar beings. The Elves, however, have the power to bestow this gift on whomsoever they please. People also used to speak of Elf-books which they gave to those whom they loved, and which enabled them to foretell future events.

The Elves often sit in little stones that are of a circular form, and are called Elf-mills (*Elf-quärnor*); the sound of their voice is said to be sweet and soft like the air.*

The Danish peasantry give the following account of their Ellefolk or Elve-people.

The Elle-people live in the Elle-moors. The appearance of the man is that of an old man with a low-crowned hat on his head; the Elle-woman is young and of a fair and attractive countenance, but behind she is hollow like a dough-trough. Young men should be especially on their guard against her, for it is very difficult to resist her; and she has, moreover, a stringed instrument, which, when she plays on it, quite ravishes their hearts. The man may be often seen near the Elle-moors, bathing himself in the sun-beams, but if any one comes too near him, he opens his mouth wide and breathes upon them, and his breath produces sickness and pestilence. But the women are most frequently to be seen by moonshine; then they dance their rounds in the high grass so lightly and so gracefully, that they seldom meet a denial when they offer their hand to a rash young man. It is also necessary to watch cattle, that they may not graze in any place where the Elle-people have been; for

---

* The greater part of what precedes has been taken from Afzelius in the Svenska Visor, vol. iii.

if any animal come to a place where the Elle-people have spit, or done what is worse, it is attacked by some grievous disease which can only be cured by giving it to eat a handful of St. John's wort, which had been pulled at twelve o'clock on St. John's night. It might also happen that they might sustain some injury by mixing with the Elle-people's cattle, which are very large, and of a blue colour, and which may sometimes be seen in the fields licking up the dew, on which they live. But the farmer has an easy remedy against this evil; for he has only to go to the Elle-hill when he is turning out his cattle and to say, "Thou little Troll! may I graze my cows on thy hill?" And if he is not prohibited, he may set his mind at rest.*

The following ballads and tales will fully justify what has been said respecting the tone of melancholy connected with the subject of the Elves.†

Sir Olof in the Elve-Dance.

SIR Olof he rode out at early day,
And so came he unto an Elve-dance gay.
    The dance it goes well,
    So well in the grove.

The Elve-father reached out his white hand free,
"Come, come, Sir Olof, tread the dance with me."
    The dance it goes well,
    So well in the grove.

"O nought I will, and nought I may,
To-morrow will be my wedding-day."
    The dance it goes well,
    So well in the grove.

---

* Thiele, iv. 26.

† In the distinction which we have made between the Elves and Dwarfs we find that we are justified by the popular creed of the Norwegians.—Faye, p. 49, ap. Grimm, Deutsche Mythologie, p. 412.

And the Elve-mother reached out her white hand free,
" Come, come, Sir Olof, tread the dance with me."
  The dance it goes well,
  So well in the grove.

" O nought I will, and nought I may,
To-morrow will be my wedding-day."
  The dance it goes well,
  So well in the grove.

And the Elve-sister reached out her white hand free,
" Come, come, Sir Olof, tread the dance with me."
  The dance it goes well,
  So well in the grove.

" O nought I will, and nought I may,
To-morrow will be my wedding-day."
  The dance it goes well,
  So well in the grove.

And the bride she spake with her bride-maids so,
" What may it mean that the bells thus go ?"
  The dance it goes well,
  So well in the grove.

" 'Tis the custom of this our isle," they replied ;
" Each young swain ringeth home his bride."
  The dance it goes well,
  So well in the grove.

" And the truth from you to conceal I fear,
Sir Olof is dead, and lies on his bier."
  The dance it goes well,
  So well in the grove.

And on the morrow, ere light was the day,
In Sir Olof's house three corpses lay.
  The dance it goes well,
  So well in the grove.

It was Sir Olof, his bonny bride,
And eke his mother, of sorrow she died.
  The dance it goes well,
  So well in the grove.*

 * Svenska Visor, iii. 158, as sung in Upland and East Gothland.

The Elf-Woman and Sir Olof.

Sir Olof rideth out ere dawn,
  Breaketh day, falleth rime ;
Bright day him came on.
    Sir Olof cometh home,
    When the wood it is leaf-green.

Sir Olof rides by Borgya,
  Breaketh day, falleth rime ;
Meets a dance of Elves so gay.
    Sir Olof cometh home,
    When the wood it is leaf-green.

There danceth Elf and Elve-maid,
  Breaketh day, falleth rime ;
Elve-king's daughter, with her flying hair.
    Sir Olof cometh home,
    When the wood it is leaf-green.

Elve-king's daughter reacheth her hand free,
  Breaketh day, falleth rime ;
" Come here, Sir Olof, tread the dance with me."
    Sir Olof cometh home,
    When the wood it is leaf-green.

" Nought I tread the dance with thee,"
  Breaketh day, falleth rime ;
" My bride hath that forbidden me."
    Sir Olof cometh home,
    When the wood it is leaf-green.

" Nought I will and nought I may,"
  Breaketh day, falleth rime ;
" To-morrow is my wedding-day."
    Sir Olof cometh home,
    When the wood it is leaf-green.

"Wilt thou not tread the dance with me?"
    Breaketh day, falleth rime;
"An evil shall I fix on thee."
      Sir Olof cometh home,
      When the wood it is leaf-green.

Sir Olof turned his horse therefrom,
    Breaketh day, falleth rime;
Sickness and plague follow him home.
      Sir Olof cometh home,
      When the wood it is leaf-green.

Sir Olof to his mother's rode,
    Breaketh day, falleth rime;
Out before him his mother stood.
      Sir Olof cometh home,
      When the wood it is leaf-green.

"Welcome, welcome, my dear son,"
    Breaketh day, falleth rime;
"Why is thy rosy cheek so wan?"
      Sir Olof cometh home,
      When the wood it is leaf-green.

"My colt was swift and I tardy,"
    Breaketh day, falleth rime;
"I knocked against a green oak-tree."
      Sir Olof cometh home,
      When the wood it is leaf-green.

"My dear sister, prepare my bed,"
    Breaketh day, falleth rime;
"My dear brother, take my horse to the mead."
      Sir Olof cometh home,
      When the wood it is leaf-green.

"My dear mother, brush my hair,"
    Breaketh day, falleth rime;
"My dear father, make me a bier."
      Sir Olof cometh home,
      When the wood it is leaf-green.

" My dear son, that do not say,"
    Breaketh day, falleth rime ;
To-morrow is thy wedding-day."
    Sir Olof cometh home,
    When the wood it is leaf-green.

" Be it when it will betide,"
    Breaketh day, falleth rime ;
" I ne'er shall come unto my bride."
    Sir Olof cometh home,
    When the wood it is leaf-green.*

The Young Swain and the Elbes.

I WAS a handsome young swain,
And to the court should ride.
I rode out in the evening-hour ;
In the rosy grove I to sleep me laid.
    Since I her first saw.

I laid me under a lind so green,
My eyes they sunk in sleep ;
There came two maidens going along,
They fain would with me speak.
    Since I her first saw.

The one she tapped me on my cheek,
The other whispered in my ear :
" Stand up, handsome young swain,
If thou list of love to hear."
    Since I her first saw.

* Svenska Visor, iii. 165, from a MS. in the Royal Library. This and
the preceding one are variations of the Danish Ballad of Elveskud, which has
been translated by Dr. Jamieson (Popular Ballads, i. 219), and by Lewis in
the Tales of Wonder. The Swedish editors give a third variation from East
Gothland. A comparison of the two ballads with each other, and with the
Danish one, will enable the reader to judge of the modifications a subject
undergoes in different parts of a country.

They led then forth a maiden,
Whose hair like gold did shine :
" Stand up, handsome young swain,
If thou to joy incline."
     Since I her first saw.

The third began a song to sing,
With good will she did so ;
Thereat stood the rapid stream,
Which before was wont to flow.
     Since I her first saw.

Thereat stood the rapid stream,
Which before was wont to flow ;
And the hind all with her hair so brown,
Forgot whither she should go.
     Since I her first saw.

I got me up from off the ground,
And leaned my sword upon ;
The Elve-women danced in and out,
All had they the Elve fashión.
     Since I her first saw.

Had not fortune been to me so good,
That the cock his wings clapped then,
I had slept within the hill that night,
All with the Elve-womén.
     Since I her first saw.*

---

* Svenska Visor, iii. p. 170.   This is the Elveshöj of the Danish ballads,
translated by Jamieson (i. 225), and by Lewis.   In the different Swedish variations, they are Hafsfruen, i. e. Mermaids, who attempt to seduce young men to
their love by the offer of costly presents.

A Danish legend (Thiele, i. 22) relates that a poor man, who was working
near Gillesbjerg, a haunted hill, lay down on it to rest himself in the middle
of the day.   Suddenly there appeared before him a beautiful maiden, with a
gold cup in her hand.   She made signs to him to come near, but when the
man in his fright made the sign of the cross, she was obliged to turn round
and then he saw her back that it was hollow.

Svend Fælling and the Elle-Maid.

SVEND FÆLLING was, while a little boy, at service in
Sjeller-wood-house in Framley ; and it one time happened
that he had to ride of a message to Ristrup. It was evening
before he got near home, and as he came by the hill of
Borum Es, he saw the Elle-maids, who were dancing without
ceasing round and round his horse. Then one of the Elle-
maids stept up to him, and reached him a drinking cup,
bidding him at the same time to drink. Svend took the
cup, but as he was dubious of the nature of the contents, he
flung it out over his shoulder, where it fell on the horse's back,
and singed off all the hair. While he had the horn fast in
his hand, he gave his horse the spurs and rode off full speed.
The Elle-maid pursued him till he came to Trigebrand's
mill, and rode through the running water, over which she
could not follow him. She then earnestly conjured Svend
to give her back the horn, promising him in exchange twelve
men's strength. On this condition he gave back the horn,
and got what she had promised him ; but it very frequently
put him to great inconvenience, for he found that along
with it he had gotten an appetite for twelve.*

* Thiele, ii. 67. Framley is in Jutland. Svend (i. e. *Swain*) Fælling is a
celebrated character in Danish tradition ; he is regarded as a second Holger
Danske, and he is the hero of two of the Kjempe Viser. In Sweden he is
named Sven Färling or Fotling. Grimm has shown that he and Sigurd are
the same person. Deutsche Mythologie, p. 345. In the Nibelungen Lied
(st. 345) Sifret (Sigurd) gets the strength of twelve men by wearing the
tarnkappe of the dwarf Albrich. Another tradition, presently to be mentioned, says it was from a Dwarf he got his strength, for aiding him in battle
against another Dwarf. It is added, that when Svend came home in the
evening, after his adventure with the Elle-maids, the people were drinking
their Yule-beer, and they sent him down for a fresh supply. Svend went
without saying anything, and returned with a barrel in each hand and one
under each arm.

The Elle-Maids.

THERE lived a man in Aasum, near Odense, who, as he was coming home one night from Seden, passed by a hill that was standing on red pillars, and underneath there was dancing and great festivity. He hurried on past the hill as fast as he could, never venturing to cast his eyes that way. But as he went along, two fair maidens came to meet him, with beautiful hair floating over their shoulders, and one of them held a cup in her hand, which she reached out to him that he might drink of it. The other then asked him if he would come again, at which he laughed, and answered, Yes. But when he got home he became strangely affected in his mind, was never at ease in himself, and was continually saying that he had promised to go back. And when they watched him closely to prevent his doing so, he at last lost his senses, and died shortly after.*

Maid Vae.

THERE was once a wedding and a great entertainment at Œsterhæsinge. The party did not break up till morning, and the guests took their departure with a great deal of noise and bustle. While they were putting their horses to their carriages, previous to setting out home, they stood talking about their respective bridal-presents. And while they were talking loudly, and with the utmost earnestness, there came from a neighbouring moor a maiden clad in green, with plaited rushes on her head; she went up to the man who was loudest, and bragging most of his present, and said to him: "What wilt thou give to maid Væ?" The

---

* Thiele, iii. 43. Odense is in Funen.

man, who was elevated with all the ale and brandy he had been drinking, snatched up a whip, and replied: "Ten cuts of my whip;" and that very moment he dropt down dead on the ground.[*]

The Elle-Maid near Ebeltoft.

A FARMER's boy was keeping cows not far from Ebeltoft. There came to him a very fair and pretty girl, and she asked him if he was hungry or thirsty. But when he perceived that she guarded with the greatest solicitude against his getting a sight of her back, he immediately suspected that she must be an Elle-maid, for the Elle-people are hollow behind. He accordingly would give no heed to her, and endeavoured to get away from her; but when she perceived this, she offered him her breast that he should suck her. And so great was the enchantment that accompanied this action, that he was unable to resist it. But when he had done as she desired him, he had no longer any command of himself, so that she had now no difficulty in enticing him with her.

He was three days away, during which time his father and mother went home, and were in great affliction, for they were well assured that he must have been enticed away. But on the fourth day his father saw him a long way off coming home, and he desired his wife to set a pan of meat on the fire as quick as possible. The son then came in at the door, and sat down at the table without saying a word. The father, too, remained quite silent, as if every thing was as it ought to be. His mother then set the meat before him, and his father bid him eat, but he let the food lie untouched, and said that he knew now where he could get much better food. The father then became highly enraged, took a good large switch, and once more ordered him to take

---

[*] Thiele, i. 109. (*communicated*). Such legends, as Mr. Thiele learned directly from the mouths of the peasantry, he terms *oral;* those he procured from his friends, *communicated.* Œsterhæsinge, the scene of this legend, is in the island of Funen.

his food. The boy was then obliged to eat, and as soon as he had tasted the flesh he ate it up greedily, and instantly fell into a deep sleep. He slept for as many days as the enchantment had lasted, but he never after recovered the use of his reason.*

Hans Puntleder.

THERE are three hills on the lands of Bubbelgaard in Funen, which are to this day called the Dance-hills, from the following occurrence. A lad named Hans was at service in Bubbelgaard, and as he was coming one evening past the hills, he saw one of them raised on red pillars, and great dancing and much merriment underneath. He was so enchanted with the beauty and magnificence of what he saw, that he could not restrain his curiosity, but was in a strange and wonderful manner attracted nearer and nearer, till at last the fairest of all the fair maidens that were there came up to him and gave him a kiss. From that moment he lost all command of himself, and became so violent, that he used to tear to pieces all the clothes that were put on him, so that at last they were obliged to make him a dress of sole-leather, which he could not pull off him; and ever after he went by the name of Hans Puntleder, i. e. Sole-leather.†

According to Danish tradition, the Elle-kings, under the denomination of Promontory-kings, (*Klintekonger*), keep watch and ward over the country. Whenever war, or any other misfortune, threatens to come on the land, there may be seen, on the promontory, complete armies, drawn up in array to defend the country.

One of these kings resides at Möen, on the spot which still bears the name of King's-hill (*Kongsbjerg*). His queen

---

* Thiele, i. 118. (*communicated*). Ebeltoft is a village in North Jutland.
† Thiele, iv. 32. From the circumstances, it would appear that these were Elves and not Dwarfs ; but one cannot be positive in these matters.

is the most beautiful of beings, and she dwells at the Queen's Chair (*Dronningstolen*). This king is a great friend of the king of Stevns, and they are both at enmity with Grap, the promontory-king of Rügen, who must keep at a distance, and look out over the sea to watch their approach.

Another tradition, however, says, that there is but one king, who rules over the headlands of Möen, Stevns, and Rügen. He has a magnificent chariot, which is drawn by four black horses. In this he drives over the sea, from one promontory to another. At such times the sea grows black, and is in great commotion, and the loud snorting and neighing of his horses may be distinctly heard.*

It was once believed that no mortal monarch dare come to Stevns; for the Elle-king would not permit him to cross the stream that bounds it. But Christian IV. passed it without opposition, and since his time several Danish monarchs have been there.

At Skjelskör, in Zealand, reigns another of these jealous promontorial sovereigns, named king Tolv (*Twelve*). He will not suffer a mortal prince to pass the bridge of Kjelskör. Wo, too, betide the watchman who should venture to cry twelve o'clock in the village, he might chance to find himself transported to the village of Borre or to the Windmills.

Old people that have eyes for such things, declare they frequently see Kong Tolv rolling himself on the grass in the sunshine. On New-year's night he takes from one smith's forge or another nine new shoes for his horses; they must be always left ready for him, and with them the necessary complement of nails.

The Elle-king of Bornholm† lets himself be occasionally heard with fife and drum, especially when war is at hand; he may then be seen in the fields with his soldiers. This king will not suffer an earthly monarch to pass more than three nights on his isle.

In the popular creed there is some strange connexion between the Elves and the trees. They not only frequent them, but they make an interchange of form with them. In

---

* Möen and Stevns are in Zealand. As Rügen does not belong to the Danish monarchy, the former tradition is probably the more correct one. Yet the latter may be the original one.

† Bornholm is a *holm*, or small island, adjacent to Zealand.

the church-yard of Store Heddinge,* in Zealand, there are
the remains of an oak wood. These, say the common people,
are the Elle-king's soldiers; by day they are trees, by night
valiant warriors. In the wood of Rugaard, in the same
island, is a tree which by night becomes a whole Elle-people,
and goes about all alive. It has no leaves upon it, yet it
would be very unsafe to go to break or fell it, for the underground-people frequently hold their meetings under its
branches. There is, in another place, an elder-tree growing
in a farm-yard, which frequently takes a walk in the twilight
about the yard, and peeps in through the window at the
children when they are alone.

It was, perhaps, these elder-trees that gave origin to the
notion. In Danish *Hyld* or *Hyl*—a word not far removed
from Elle—is Elder, and the peasantry believe that in or
under the elder-tree dwells a being called Hyldemoer (*Elder-
mother*), or Hyldequinde (*Elder-woman*), with her ministrant
spirits.† A Danish peasant, if he wanted to take any part
of an elder-tree, used previously to say, three times—" O,
Hyldemoer, Hyldemoer! let me take some of thy elder, and
I will let thee take something of mine in return." If this
was omitted he would be severely punished. They tell of a
man who cut down an elder-tree, but he soon after died suddenly. It is, moreover, not prudent to have any furniture
made of elder-wood. A child was once put to lie in a cradle
made of this wood, but Hyldemoer came and pulled it by
the legs, and gave it no rest till it was put to sleep elsewhere. Old David Monrad relates, that a shepherd, one
night, heard his three children crying, and when he inquired
the cause, they said some one had been sucking them. Their
breasts were found to be swelled, and they were removed to
another room, where they were quiet. The reason is said
to have been that that room was floored with elder.

The linden or lime tree is the favourite haunt of the
Elves and cognate beings; and it is not safe to be near it
after sunset.‡

---

* The Elle-king of Stevns has his bedchamber in the wall of this church.
† This is evidently the Frau Holle of the Germans.
‡ The preceding particulars are all derived from M. Thiele's work.

DWARFS OR TROLLS.

Ther bygde folk i the bärg,
Quinnor och män, för mycken duerf.
HIST. ALEX. MAG. *Suedice.*

Within the hills folk did won,
Women and men, dwarfs many a one.

THE more usual appellation of the Dwarfs is Troll or Trold,[*]
a word originally significant of any evil spirit,[†] giant monster, magician,[‡] or evil person; but now in a good measure
divested of its ill senses, for the Trolls are not in general
regarded as noxious or malignant beings.

The Trolls are represented as dwelling inside of hills,
mounds, and hillocks—whence they are also called Hill-
people (*Bjergfolk*)—sometimes in single families, sometimes
in societies. In the ballads they are described as having
kings over them, but never so in the popular legend.
Their character seems gradually to have sunk down to the
level of the peasantry, in proportion as the belief in them
was consigned to the same class. They are regarded as

---

[*] There is no etymon of this word. It is to be found in both the Icelandic
and the Finnish languages; whether the latter borrowed or communicated it is
uncertain. Ihre derives the name of the celebrated waterfall of Trollhæta,
near Göaenturg, from Troll, and Haute *Lapponice*, an abyss. It therefore
answers to the Irish *Poul-a-Phooka*. See *Ireland*.

[†] In the following lines quoted in the Heimskringla, it would seem to
signify the Dii Manes.

> Tha gaf hann Trescegg Tröllum,
> Torf-Einarr drap Scurfo.

> Then gave he Trescegg to the Trolls,
> Turf-Einarr slew Scurfo.

[‡] The ancient Gothic nation was called Troll by their Vandal neighbours
(Junii Batavia, c. 27); according to Sir J. Malcolm, the Tartars call the
Chinese Deevs. It was formerly believed, says Ihre, that the noble family of
Troll, in Sweden, derived their name from having killed a Troll, that is,
probably, a Dwarf.

extremely rich for when, on great occasions of festivity, they have their hills raised up on red pillars, people that have chanced to be passing by have seen them shoving large chests full of money to and fro, and opening and clapping down the lids of them. Their hill-dwellings are very magnificent inside. "They live," said one of Mr. Arndt's guides, "in fine houses of gold and crystal. My father saw them once in the night, when the hill was open on St. John's night. They were dancing and drinking, and it seemed to him as if they were making signs to him to go to them, but his horse snorted, and carried him away, whether he would or no. There is a great number of them in the Guldberg (*Goldhill*), and they have brought into it all the gold and silver that people buried in the great Russian war."*

They are obliging and neighbourly; freely lending and borrowing, and elsewise keeping up a friendly intercourse with mankind. But they have a sad propensity to thieving, not only stealing provisions, but even women and children.

They marry, have children, bake and brew, just as the peasant himself does. A farmer one day met a hill-man and his wife, and a whole squad of stumpy little children, in his fields;† and people used often to see the children of the man who lived in the hill of Kund, in Jutland, climbing up the hill, and rolling down after one another, with shouts of laughter.

The Trolls have a great dislike to noise, probably from a recollection of the time when Thor used to be flinging his hammer after them; so that the hanging of bells in the churches has driven them almost all out of the country. The people of Ebeltoft were once sadly plagued by them, as they plundered their pantries in a most unconscionable manner; so

* Arndt, Reise nach Schweden, vol. iii. p. 8.

† Like our Fairies the Trolls are sometimes of marvellously small dimensions: in the Danish ballad of Eline af Villenskov we read—

Det da meldte den mindste Trold,
Han var ikke stiirre end en myre,
Her er kommet en Christen mand,
Den maa jag visseligen styre.

Out then spake the tinyest Troll,
No bigger than an emmet was he,
Hither is come a Christian man,
And manage him will I surelie.

they consulted a very wise and pious man; and his advice was, that they should hang a bell in the steeple of the church. They did so, and they were soon eased of the Trolls.[*]

These beings have some very extraordinary and useful properties; they can, for instance, go about invisibly,[†] or turn themselves into any shape; they can foresee future events; they can confer prosperity, or the contrary, on a family; they can bestow bodily strength on any one; and, in short, perform numerous feats beyond the power of man.

Of personal beauty they have not much to boast: the Ebeltoft Dwarfs, mentioned above, were often seen, and they had immoderate humps on their backs, and long crooked noses. They were dressed in gray jackets,[‡] and they wore pointed red caps. Old people in Zealand say, that when the Trolls were in the country, they used to go from their hill to the village of Gudmandstrup through the Stone-meadow, and that people, when passing that way, used to meet great tall men in long black clothes. Some have foolishly spoken to them, and wished them good evening, but they never got any other answer than that the Trolls hurried past them, saying, Mi! mi! mi! mi!

Thanks to the industry of Mr. Thiele, who has been indefatigable in collecting the traditions of his native country, we are furnished with ample accounts of the Trolls; and the following legends will fully illustrate what we have written concerning them.[§]

We commence with the Swedish ballads of the Hillkings, as in dignity and antiquity they take precedence of the legends.

---

[*] Thiele, i. 36.

[†] For this they seem to be indebted to their hat or cap. Eske Brok being one day in the fields, knocked off, without knowing it, the hat of a Dwarf who instantly became visible, and had, in order to recover it, to grant him every thing he asked. Thiele iii. 49. This hat answers to the Tarnkappe or Hel-kaplein of the German Dwarfs; who also become visible when their caps are struck off.

[‡] In the Danish ballad of Eline af Villenskov the hero is called *Trolden graae*, the Gray Trold, probably from the colour of his habiliments.

[§] We deem it needless in future to refer to volume and page of Mr. Thiele's work. Those acquainted with the original will easily find the legends.

Sir Thynne.

AND it was the knight Sir Thynnè,
   He was a knight so grave;
Whether he were on foot or on horse,
   He was a knight so brave.*

And it was the knight Sir Thynnè
   Went the hart and the hind to shoot,
So he saw Ulva, the little Dwarf's daughter,
   At the green linden's foot.

And it was Ulva, the little Dwarf's daughter,
   Unto her handmaid she cried,
" Go fetch my gold harp hither to me,
   Sir Thynnè I 'll draw to my side."

The first stroke on her gold harp she struck,
   So sweetly she made it ring,
The wild beasts in the wood and field
   They forgot whither they would spring.

The next stroke on her gold harp she struck,
   So sweetly she made it ring,
The little gray hawk that sat on the bough,
   He spread out both his wings.

The third stroke on her gold harp she struck,
   So sweetly she made it ring,
The little fish that went in the stream,
   He forgot whither he would swim.

---

* We have ventured to omit the Omquæd. *I styren väll de Runor !*
(Manage well the runes !) The final *e* in Thynnè is marked merely to indicate that it is to be sounded.

Then flowered the mead, then leafed all,
   'Twas caused by the runic lay;*
Sir Thynnè he struck his spurs in his horse,
   He no longer could hold him away.

And it was the knight Sir Thynnè,
   From his horse he springs hastily,
So goeth he to Ulva, the little Dwarf's daughter,
   All under the green linden tree.

" Here you sit, my maiden fair,
   A rose all lilies above ;
See you can never a mortal man
   Who will not seek your love."

" Be silent, be silent, now Sir Thynnè,
   With your proffers of love, I pray ;
For I am betrothed unto a hill-king,
   A king all the Dwarfs obey.

" My true love he sitteth the hill within,
   And at gold tables plays merrily ;
My father he setteth his champions in ring,
   And in iron arrayeth them he.

" My mother she sitteth the hill within,
   And gold in the chest doth lay ;
And I stole out for a little while,
   Upon my gold harp to play."

And it was the knight Sir Thynnè,
   He patted her cheek rosie :
" Why wilt thou not give a kinder reply
   Thou dearest of maidens, to me ? "

---

   * *Runeslag,* literally Rune-stroke. Runes originally signified letters, and
then songs. They were of two kinds, Maalrunor (*Speech-runes*), and Troll-
runor (*Magic-runes*). These last were again divided into Skaderunor
(*Mischief-runes*) and Hjelprunor (*Help-runes*), of each of which there were
five kinds. See Verelius' notes to the Hervarar Saga, cap. 7.
   The power of music over all nature is a subject of frequent recurrence in
northern poetry. Here all the wild animals are entranced by the magic tones
of the harp ; the meads flower, the trees put forth leaves ; the knight, though
grave and silent, is attracted, and even if inclined to stay away, he cannot
restrain his horse.

" I can give you no kinder reply ;
  I may not myself that allow ;
I am betrothed to a hill-king,
  And to him I must keep my vow."

And it was Thora, the little Dwarf's wife,
  She at the hill-door looked out,
And there she saw how the knight Sir Thynnè,
  Lay at the green linden's foot.

And it was Thora, the little Dwarf's wife,
  She was vext and angry, God wot :
" What hast thou here in the grove to do ?
  Little business, I trow, thou hast got.

" 'Twere better for thee in the hill to be,
  And gold in the chest to lay,
Than here to sit in the rosy grove,*
  And on thy gold harp to play.

" And 'twere better for thee in the hill to be,
  And thy bride-dress finish sewing,
Than sit under the lind, and with runic lay
  A Christian man's heart to thee win."

And it was Ulva, the little Dwarf's daughter,
  She goeth in at the hill-door :
And after her goeth the knight Sir Thynnè,
  Clothed in scarlet and fur.

And it was Thora, the little Dwarf's wife,
  Forth a red-gold chair she drew :
Then she cast Sir Thynnè into a sleep,
  Until that the cock he crew.

And it was Thora, the little Dwarf's wife,
  The five rune-books she took out ;
So she loosed him fully out of the runes,
  Her daughter had bound him about.

---

* *Rosendelund.* The word *Lund* signifies any kind of grove, thicket, &c.

" And hear thou me, Sir Thynnè,
   From the runes thou now art free;
This to thee I will soothly say,
   My daughter shall never win thee.

" And I was born of Christian kind,
   And to the hill stolen in;
My sister dwelleth in Iseland,*
   And wears a gold crown so fine.

" And there she wears her crown of gold,
   And beareth of queen the name;
Her daughter was stolen away from her,
   Thereof there goeth great fame.

" Her daughter was stolen away from her,
   And to Berner-land brought in;
And there now dwelleth the maiden free,
   She is called Lady Hermolin.

" And never can she into the dance go,
   But seven women follow her;
And never can she on the gold-harp play,
   If the queen herself is not there.

" The king he hath a sister's son,
   He hopeth the crown to possess,
For him they intend the maiden free,
   For her little happiness.

" And this for my honour will I do,
   And out of good-will moreover,
To thee will I give the maiden free,
   And part her from that lover."

Then she gave unto him a dress so new,
   With gold and pearls bedight;
Every seam on the dress it was
   With precious stones all bright.

---

* Not the island of Iceland, but a district in Norway of that name. By Berner-land, Geijer thinks is meant the land of Bern (*Verona*), the country of Dietrich, so celebrated in German romance

Then she gave unto him a horse so good,
    And therewith a new sell;
" And never shalt thou the way inquire,
    Thy horse will find it well."

And it was Ulva, the little Dwarf's daughter,
    She would show her good-will to the knight;
So she gave unto him a spear so new,
    And therewith a good sword so bright.

" And never shalt thou fight a fight,
    Where thou shalt not the victory gain;
And never shalt thou sail on a sea
    Where thou shalt not the land attain."

And it was Thora, the little Dwarf's wife,
    She wine in a glass for him poured:
" Ride away, ride away, now Sir Thynnè,
    Before the return of my lord."

And it was the knight Sir Thynnè,
    He rideth under the green hill side,
There then met him the hill-kings two,
    As slow to the hill they ride.

" Well met! Good day, now Sir Thynnè!
    Thy horse can well with thee pace;
Whither directed is thy course?
    Since thou 'rt bound to a distant place."

" Travel shall I and woo;
    Plight me shall I a flower;
Try shall I my sword so good,
    To my weal or my woe in the stour."

" Ride in peace, ride in peace, away, Sir Thynnè,
    From us thou hast nought to fear;
They are coming, the champions from Iseland,
    Who with thee long to break a spear."

And it was the knight Sir Thynnè,
    He rideth under the green hill side;
There met him seven Bernisk champions,
    They bid him to halt and abide.

" And whether shall we fight to-day,
    For the red gold and the silvér ;
Or shall we fight together to-day,
    For both our true loves fair ? "

And it was the king's sister's son,
    He was of mood so hastý ;
" Of silver and gold I have enow,
    If thou wilt credit me."

" But hast thou not a fair true love,
    Who is called Lady Hermolin ?
For her it is we shall fight to-day,
    If she shall be mine or thine."

The first charge they together rode,
    They were two champions so tall ;
He cut at the king's sister's son,
    That his head to the ground did fall.

Back then rode the champions six,
    And dressed themselves in fur ;
Then went into the lofty hall,
    The aged king before.

And it was then the aged king,
    He tore his gray hairs in woe.
" Ye must avenge my sister's son's death :
    I will sables and martins bestow. ' *

Back then rode the champions six,
    They thought the reward to gain,
But they remained halt and limbless :
    By loss one doth wit obtain.

And he slew wolves and bears,
    All before the high chambér ;
Then taketh he out the maiden free
    Who so long had languished there.

---

* *Sabel och Mård.*   These furs are always mentioned in the northern
ballads, as the royal rewards of distinguished actions.

And now hath Lady Hermolin
    Escaped from all harm;
Now sleeps she sweet full many a sleep,
    On brave Sir Thynnè's arm.

And now has brave Sir Thynnè
    Escaped all sorrow and tine;
Now sleeps he sweet full many a sleep,
    Beside Lady Hermolin.

Most thanketh he Ulva, the little Dwarf's daughter,
    Who him with the runes had bound,
For were he not come inside of the hill,
    The lady he never had found.*

Proud Margaret.

PROUD Margaret's† father of wealth had store,
    Time with me goes slow.—
And he was a king seven kingdoms o'er,
    But that grief is heavy I know.‡

To her came wooing good earls two,
    Time with me goes slow.—
But neither of them would she hearken unto,
    But that grief is heavy I know.

* This fine ancient Visa was taken down from recitation in West Gothland. The corresponding Danish one of Herr Tönne is much later.

† Niebuhr, speaking of the Celsi Ramnes, says, " With us the salutation of blood relations was *Willkommen stolze Vetter* (Welcome, proud cousins)· and in the Danish ballads, proud (*stolt*) is a noble appellation of a maiden."— Römische Geschichte, 2d edit. vol. i. p. 316.

It may be added, that in English, *proud* and the synonymous term *stout* (*stolz, stolt*) had also the sense of noble, high-born.
      Do now your devoir, yonge knightes *proud*.
                    Knight's Tale.
      Up stood the queen and ladies *stout*.
                    Launfal.
    ‡ *Men jag vet at sorge är tung.*

To her came wooing princes five,
    Time with me goes slow.—
Yet not one of them would the maiden have,
    But that grief is heavy I know.

To her came wooing kings then seven,
    Time with me goes slow.—
But unto none her hand has she given,
    But that grief is heavy I know.

And the hill-king asked his mother to read,
    Time with me goes slow.—
How to win proud Margaret he might speed,
    But that grief is heavy I know.

" And say how much thou wilt give unto me,"
    Time with me goes slow.—
" That herself may into the hill come to thee ?"
    But that grief is heavy I know.

" Thee will I give the ruddiest gold,"
    Time with me goes slow.—
" And thy chests full of money as they can hold,"
    But that grief is heavy I know.

One Sunday morning it fell out so,
    Time with me goes slow.—
Proud Margaret unto the church should go,
    But that grief is heavy I know.

And all as she goes, and all as she stays,
    Time with me goes slow.—
All the nearer she comes where the high hill lay,
    But that grief is heavy I know.

So she goeth around the hill compassing,
    Time with me goes slow.—
So there openeth a door, and thereat goes she in,
    But that grief is heavy I know.

Proud Margaret stept in at the door of the hill,
    Time with me goes slow.—
And the hill-king salutes her with eyes joyful,
    But that grief is heavy I know.

So he took the maiden upon his knee,
   Time with me goes slow.—
And took the gold rings and therewith her wed he,
   But that grief is heavy I know.

So he took the maiden his arms between,
   Time with me goes slow.—
He gave her a gold crown and the name of queen,
   But that grief is heavy I know.

So she was in the hill for eight round years,
   Time with me goes slow.—
There bare she two sons and a daughter so fair,
   But that grief is heavy I know.

When she had been full eight years there,
   Time with me goes slow.—
She wished to go home to her mother so dear,
   But that grief is heavy I know.

And the hill-king spake to his footpages twain,
   Time with me goes slow.—
" Put ye the gray pacers now unto the wain,"*
   But that grief is heavy I know.

And Margaret out at the hill-door stept,
   Time with me goes slow.—
And her little children they thereat wept,
   But that grief is heavy I know.

And the hill-king her in his arms has ta'en,
   Time with me goes slow.—
So he lifteth her into the gilded wain,
   But that grief is heavy I know.

" And hear now thou footpage what I unto thee say,"
   Time with me goes slow.—
" Thou now shalt drive her to her mother's straightway,"
   But that grief is heavy I know.

---

* Wain, our readers hardly need be informed, originally signified any kind of carriage : see Faerie Queene, *passim*. It is the Ang. Sax. þǽn, and not a contraction of *waggon*.

Proud Margaret stept in o'er the door-sill,
  Time with me goes slow.—
And her mother saluteth her with eyes joyful,
  But that grief is heavy I know.

" And where hast thou so long stayed?"
  Time with me goes slow.—
" I have been in the flowery meads,"
  But that grief is heavy I know.

" What veil is that thou wearest on thy hair?"
  Time with me goes slow.—
" Such as women and mothers use to wear,"
  But that grief is heavy I know.

" Well may I wear a veil on my head,"
  Time with me goes slow.—
" Me hath the hill-king both wooed and wed,"
  But that grief is heavy I know.

" In the hill have I been these eight round years,"
  Time with me goes slow.—
" There have I two sons and a daughter so fair,"
  But that grief is heavy I know.

" There have I two sons and a daughter so fair,"
  Time with me goes slow.—
" The loveliest maiden the world doth bear,"
  But that grief is heavy I know.

" And hear thou, proud Margaret, what I say unto thee,"
  Time with me goes slow.—
" Can I go with thee home thy children to see?"
  But that grief is heavy I know.

And the hill-king stept now in at the door,
  Time with me goes slow.—
And Margaret thereat fell down on the floor,
  But that grief is heavy I know.

" And stayest thou now here complaining of me,"
  Time with me goes slow.—
" Camest thou not of thyself into the hill to me?"
  But that grief is heavy I know.

"And stayest thou now here and thy fate dost deplóre?"
 Time with me goes slow.—
"Camest thou not of thyself in at my door?"
 But that grief is heavy I know.

The hill-king struck her on the cheek rosie,
 Time with me goes slow.—
"And pack to the hill to thy children wee,"
 But that grief is heavy I know.

The hill-king struck her with a twisted root,
 Time with me goes slow.—
"And pack to the hill without any dispute,"
 But that grief is heavy I know.

And the hill-king her in his arms has ta'en,
 Time with me goes slow.—
And lifted her into the gilded wain,
 But that grief is heavy I know.

"And hear thou my footpage what I unto thee say,"
 Time with me goes slow.—
"Thou now shalt drive her to my dwelling straightway,"
 But that grief is heavy I know.

Proud Margaret stept in at the hill door,
 Time with me goes slow.—
And her little children rejoiced therefòre,
 But that grief is heavy I know.

"It is not worth while rejoicing for me,"
 Time with me goes slow.—
"Christ grant that I never a mother had been,"
 But that grief is heavy I know.

The one brought out a gilded chair,
 Time with me goes slow.—
"O rest you, my sorrow-bound mother, there,"
 But that grief is heavy I know.

The one brought out a filled up horn,
 Time with me goes slow.—
The other put therein a gilded corn,
 But that grief is heavy I know.

The first drink she drank out of the horn,
    Time with me goes slow.—
She forgot straightway both heaven and earth,
    But that grief is heavy I know.

The second drink she drank out of the horn,
    Time with me goes slow.—
She forgot straightway both God and his word,
    But that grief is heavy I know.

The third drink she drank out of the horn,
    Time with me goes slow.—
She forgot straightway both sister and brother,
    But that grief is heavy I knów.

She forgot straightway both sister and brother,
    Time with me goes slow.—
But she never forgot her sorrow-bound mother,
    But that grief is heavy I know.*

The Troll Wife.

THE grandfather of Reor, who dwelt at Fuglekärr (i.e. *Bird-marsh*), in the parish of Svartsborg (*Black-castle*), lived close to a hill, and one time, in the broad daylight, he saw sitting there on a stone a comely maiden. He wished to intercept her, and for this purpose *he threw steel* between her and the hill; whereupon her father laughed within the hill, and opening the hill-door asked him if he would have his daughter. He replied in the affirmative and as she was *stark naked* he took some of his own clothes and covered her with them, and he afterwards had her christened. As he was going away, her father said to him, " When you are going to have your wedding (*bröllup*) you must provide twelve barrels of beer and bake a heap of bread and the flesh of four oxen, and drive to the barrow or hill where I keep, and when the bridal gifts are to be bestowed, depend on it I will give mine." This also came to pass; for when

* From Vermland and Upland.

others were giving he raised the cover of the cart and cast into it so large a bag of money that the body of it nearly broke, saying at the same time:—"This is *my* gift!" He said, moreover, "When you want to have your wife's portion (*hemmagifta*),* you must drive to the hill with four horses, and get your share. When he came there afterwards at his desire he got copper-pots, the one larger than the other till the largest pot of all was filled with the smaller ones. He also gave him other things,† which were helmets, of that colour and fashion which are large and thick, and which are still remaining in the country, being preserved at the parsonage of Tanum. This man Reor's father surnamed I Foglekärsten, had a number of children by this wife of his, whom he fetched out of the hill, among whom was the aforesaid Reor. Olaf Stenson also in Stora Rijk, who died last year, was Reor's sister's son.‡

The Altar-Cup in Aagerup.

BETWEEN the villages of Marup and Aagerup in Zealand, there is said to have lain a great castle, the ruins of which are still to be seen near the strand. Tradition relates that a great treasure is concealed among them, and that a dragon there watches over three kings' ransoms.§ Here, too, people frequently happen to get a sight of the underground folk, especially about festival-times, for then they have dancing and great jollity going on down on the strand.

One Christmas-eve, a farmer's servant in the village of

---

* This we suppose to be the meaning of *hemmagifta*, as it is that of *hemgift*, the only word approaching to it that we have met in our dictionary.

† *Brandcreatur*, a word of which we cannot ascertain the exact meaning. We doubt greatly if the following *hielmeta* be helmets.

‡ Grimm (Deut. Mythol. p. 435) has extracted this legend from the Bahuslän of Ödman, who, as he observes, and as we may see, relates it quite seriously, and with the real names of persons. It is we believe the only legend of the union of a *man* with one of the hill-folk.

§ "Three kings' ransoms" is a common maximum with a Danish peasant when speaking of treasure.

Aagerup went to his master and asked him if he might take a horse and ride down to look at the Troll-meeting. The farmer not only gave him leave but desired him to take the best horse in the stable; so he mounted and rode away down to the strand. When he was come to the place he stopped his horse, and stood for some time looking at the company who were assembled in great numbers. And while he was wondering to see how well and how gaily the little dwarfs danced, up came a Troll to him, and invited him to dismount, and take a share in their dancing and merriment. Another Troll came jumping up, took his horse by the bridle, and held him while the man got off, and went down and danced away merrily with them the whole night long.

When it was drawing near day he returned them his very best thanks for his entertainment, and mounted his horse to return home to Aagerup. They now gave him an invitation to come again on New-year's night, as they were then to have great festivity; and a maiden who held a gold cup in her hand invited him to drink the stirrup-cup. He took the cup; but, as he had some suspicion of them, he, while he made as if he was raising the cup to his mouth, threw the drink out over his shoulder, so that it fell on the horse's back, and it immediately singed off all the hair. He then clapped spurs to his horse's sides, and rode away with the cup in his hand over a ploughed field.

The Trolls instantly gave chase all in a body; but being hard set to get over the deep furrows, they shouted out, without ceasing,

> " Ride on the lay,
> And not on the clay."*

He, however, never minded them, but kept to the ploughed field. However, when he drew near the village he was forced to ride out on the level road, and the Trolls now gained on him every minute. In his distress he prayed unto God, and he made a vow that if he should be delivered he would bestow the cup on the church.

He was now riding along just by the wall of the church-yard, and he hastily flung the cup over it, that it at least might be secure. He then pushed on at full speed, and at

---

* ' Rid paa det Bolde,
    Og ikke paa det Knolde. "

last got into the village; and just as they were on the point of catching hold of the horse, he sprung in through the farmer's gate, and the man clapt to the wicket after him. He was now safe; but the Trolls were so enraged, that, taking up a huge great stone, they flung it with such force against the gate, that it knocked four planks out of it.

There are no traces now remaining of that house, but the stone is still lying in the middle of the village of Aagerup. The cup was presented to the church, and the man got in return the best farm-house on the lands of Eriksholm.*

Origin of Tiis Lake.

A TROLL had once taken up his abode near the village of Kund, in the high bank on which the church now stands; but when the people about there had become pious, and went constantly to church, the Troll was dreadfully annoyed by their almost incessant ringing of bells in the steeple of the church. He was at last obliged, in consequence of it, to take his departure; for nothing has more contributed to the emigration of the Troll-folk out of the country than the increasing piety of the people, and their taking to bell-ringing. The Troll of Kund accordingly quitted the country, and went over to Funen, where he lived for some time in peace and quiet.

Now it chanced that a man who had lately settled in the town of Kund, coming to Funen on business, met on the road with this same Troll: " Where do you live ? " said the

---

* *Oral.* This is an adventure common to many countries. The church of Vigersted in Zealand has a cup obtained in the same way. The man, in this case, took refuge in the church, and was there besieged by the Trolls till morning. The bridge of Hagbro in Jutland got its name from a similar event. When the man rode off with the silver jug from the beautiful maiden who presented it to him, an old crone set off in pursuit of him with such velocity, that she would surely have caught him, but that providentially he came to a running water. The pursuer, however, like Nannie with Tam o' Shanter, caught the horse's hind leg, but was only able to keep one of the cocks of his shoe : hence the bridge was called Hagbro, *i. e.* Cock Bridge.

Troll to him. Now there was nothing whatever about the
Troll unlike a man, so he answered him, as was the truth.
" I am from the town of Kund." " So ?" said the Troll. " I
don't know you, then ! And yet I think I know every man
in Kund. Will you, however," continued he, "just be so
kind to take a letter from me back with you to Kund ? "
The man said, of course, he had no objection. The Troll
then thrust the letter into his pocket, and charged him
strictly not to take it out till he came to Kund church, and
then to throw it over the churchyard wall, and the person
for whom it was intended would get it.

The Troll then went away in great haste, and with him
the letter went entirely out of the man's mind. But when
he was come back to Zealand he sat down by the meadow
where Tiis Lake now is, and suddenly recollected the Troll's
letter. He felt a great desire to look at it at least. So he
took it out of his pocket, and sat a while with it in his hands,
when suddenly there began to dribble a little water out of
the seal. The letter now unfolded itself, and the water came
out faster and faster, and it was with the utmost difficulty
that the poor man was enabled to save his life ; for the malicious Troll had enclosed an entire lake in the letter. The
Troll, it is plain, had thought to avenge himself on Kund
church by destroying it in this manner ; but God ordered it
so that the lake chanced to run out in the great meadow
where it now flows.*

---

* *Oral.* Tiis Lake is in Zealand. It is the general belief of the peasantry
that there are now very few Trolls in the country, for the ringing of bells has
driven them all away, they, like the Stille-folk of the Germans, delighting in
quiet and silence. It is said that a farmer having found a Troll sitting very
disconsolate on a stone near Tiis Lake, and taking him at first for a decent
Christian man, accosted him with—" Well ! where are you going, friend ? "
" Ah !" said he, in a melancholy tone, " I am going off out of the country.
I cannot live here any longer, they keep such eternal ringing and dinging ! "

" There is a high hill," says Kalm (Resa, &c. p. 136), " near Botna in
Sweden, in which formerly dwelt a Troll. When they got up bells in Botna
church, and he heard the ringing of them, he is related to have said :

> " *Det är så godt i det Botnaberg at bo,*
> *Vore ikke den leda Bjällcko.*"

> " Pleasant it were in Botnahill to dwell,
> Were it not for the sound of that plaguey bell,"

A Farmer tricks a Troll.

A FARMER, on whose ground there was a little hill, resolved not to let it lie idle, so he began at one end to plough it up. The hill-man, who lived in it, came to him and asked him how he dared to plough on the roof of his house. The farmer assured him that he did not know that it was the roof of his house, but at the same time represented to him that it was at present equally unprofitable to them both to let such a piece of land lie idle. He therefore took the opportunity of proposing to him that he should plough, sow, and reap it every year on these terms: that they should take it year and year about, and the hill-man to have one year what grew over the ground, and the farmer what grew in the ground; and the next year the farmer to have what was over, and the hill-man what was under.

The agreement was made accordingly; but the crafty farmer took care to sow carrots and corn year and year about, and he gave the hill-man the tops of the carrots and the roots of the corn for his share, with which he was well content. They thus lived for a long time on extremely good terms with each other.*

Skotte in the Fire.

NEAR Gudmanstrup, in the district of Odd, is a hill called Hjulehöi (*Hollow-hill*). The hill-folk that dwell in this mount are well known in all the villages round, and no one ever omits making a cross on his beer-barrels, for the Trolls are in the habit of slipping down from Hjulehöi to steal beer.

One evening late a farmer was passing by the hill, and he

* This story is told by Rabelais with his characteristic humour and extravagance. As there are no Trolls in France, it is the devil who is deceived in the French version. A legend similar to this is told of the district of Lujhmân in Afghanistân (Masson, Narrative, etc., iii. 297); but there it was the Shâitan (*Satan*) that cheated the farmers. The legends are surely independent fictions.

saw that it was raised up on red pillars, and that underneath there was music and dancing and a splendid Troll banquet. The man stood a long time gazing on their festivity; but while he was standing there, deeply absorbed in admiration of what he saw, all of a sudden the dancing stopped, and the music ceased, and he heard a Troll cry out, in a tone of the utmost anguish, "Skotte is fallen into the fire! Come and help him up!" The hill then sank, and all the merriment was at an end.

Meanwhile the farmer's wife was at home all alone, and while she was sitting and spinning her tow, she never noticed a Troll who had crept through the window into the next room, and was at the beer-barrel drawing off the liquor into his copper kettle. The room-door was standing open, and the Troll kept a steady eye on the woman. The husband now came into the house full of wonder at what he had seen and heard. "Hark ye, dame," he began, "listen now till I tell you what has happened to me!" The Troll redoubled his attention. "As I came just now by Hjulehöi;" continued he, "I saw a great Troll-banquet there, but while they were in the very middle of their glee they shouted out within in the hill, 'Skotte is fallen into the fire; come and help him up!'"

At hearing this, the Troll, who was standing beside the beer-barrel, was so frightened, that he let the tap run and the kettle of beer fall on the ground, and tumbled himself out of the window as quickly as might be. The people of the house hearing all this noise instantly guessed what had been going on inside; and when they went in they saw the beer all running about, and found the copper kettle lying on the floor. This they seized, and kept in lieu of the beer that had been spilled; and the same kettle is said to have been a long time to be seen in the villages round about there.*

---

* *Oral.* Gudmanstrup is in Zealand. In Ouröe, a little island close to Zealand, there is a hill whence the Trolls used to come down and supply themselves with provisions out of the farmers' pantries. Niel Jensen, who lived close to the hill, finding that they were making, as he thought, over free with his provisions, took the liberty of putting a lock on the door through which they had access. But he had better have left it alone, for his daughter grew stone blind, and never recovered her sight till the lock was removed.— *Resenii Atlas,* i. 10. There is a similar story in Grimm's Deutsche Sagen, i. p. 55.

The Legend of Bodedys.

THERE is a hill called Bodedys close to the road in the neighbourhood of Lynge, that is near Soröe. Not far from it
lived an old farmer, whose only son was used to take long
journeys on business. His father had for a long time heard
no tidings of him, and the old man became convinced that
his son was dead. This caused him much affliction, as was
natural for an old man like him, and thus some time passed
over.

One evening as he was coming with a loaded cart by
Bodedys, the hill opened, and the Troll came out and desired
him to drive his cart into it. The poor man was, to be sure,
greatly amazed at this, but well knowing how little it would
avail him to refuse to comply with the Troll's request, he
turned about his horses, and drove his cart straight into the
hill. The Troll now began to deal with him for his goods,
and finally bought and paid him honestly for his entire cargo.
When he had finished the unloading of his vehicle, and was
about to drive again out of the hill, the Troll said to him,
" If you will now only keep a silent tongue in your head
about all that has happened to you, I shall from this time
out have an eye to your interest; and if you come here
again to-morrow morning, it may be you shall get your son."
The farmer did not well know at first what to say to all this;
but as he was, however, of opinion that the Troll was able to
perform what he had promised, he was greatly rejoiced, and
failed not to come at the appointed time to Bodedys.

He sat there waiting a long time, and at last he fell asleep,
and when he awoke from his slumber, behold! there was his
son lying by his side. Both father and son found it difficult to
explain how this had come to pass. The son related how he
had been thrown into prison, and had there suffered great
hardship and distress; but that one night, while he was
lying asleep in his cell, there came a man to him, who said,
" Do you still love your father?" And when he had answered

that he surely did, his chains fell off and the wall burst open. While he was telling this he chanced to put his hand up to his neck, and he found that he had brought a piece of the iron chain away with him. They both were for some time mute through excess of wonder; and they then arose and went straightway to Lynge, where they hung up the piece of the chain in the church, as a memorial of the wonderful event that had occurred.*

Kallundborg Church.

WHEN Esbern Snare was about building a church in Kallundborg, he saw clearly that his means were not fully adequate to the task. But a Troll came to him and offered his services; and Esbern Snare made an agreement with him on these conditions, that he should be able to tell the Troll's name when the church was finished; or in case he could not, that he should give him his heart and his eyes.

The work now went on rapidly, and the Troll set the church on stone pillars; but when all was nearly done, and there was only half a pillar wanting in the church, Esbern began to get frightened, for the name of the Troll was yet unknown to him.

One day he was going about the fields all alone, and in great anxiety on account of the perilous state he was in; when, tired, and depressed, by reason of his exceeding grief and affliction, he laid him down on Ulshöi bank to rest himself a while. While he was lying there, he heard a Troll-woman within the hill saying these words:—

" Lie still, baby mine !
To-morrow cometh Fin,
Father thine,
And giveth thee Esbern Snare's eyes and heart to play with."†

---

* This legend is oral.
† *Tie stille, barn min !*
Imorgen kommer Fin,
Fa'er din,
Og gi'er dig Esbern Snares öine og hjerte at lege med.

When Esbern heard this, he recovered his spirits, and went back to the church. The Troll was just then coming with the half-pillar that was wanting for the church; but when Esbern saw him, he hailed him by his name, and called him " Fin." The Troll was so enraged at this, that he went off with the half-pillar through the air, and this is the reason that the church has but three pillars and a half.*

The same is told of a far greater than Esbern Snare. As St. Olaf, the royal apostle of the North, was one day going over hill and dale, thinking how he could contrive to build a splendid church without distressing his people by taxation, he was met by a man of a strange appearance, who asking him what he was thinking about, Olaf told him, and the Troll, or rather Giant (*Jätte*), for such he was, undertook to do it within a certain time, stipulating, for his reward, the sun and moon, or else St. Olaf himself. Olaf agreed, but gave such a plan for the church as it seemed to be impossible ever could be executed. It was to be so large that seven priests could preach in it at the same time without disturbing each other; the columns and other ornaments both within and without should be of hard flintstone, and so forth. It soon, however, was finished, all but the roof and pinnacle. Olaf, now grown uneasy, rambled once more over hill and dale, when he chanced to hear a child crying within a hill, and a giantess, its mother, saying to it, " Hush, hush! Thy father, Wind-and-Weather, will come home in the morning, and bring with him the sun and moon, or else St. Olaf him-self." Olaf was overjoyed, for the power of evil beings ceases when their name is known. He returned home, where he saw every thing completed—pinnacle and all. He im-mediately cried out, " Wind-and-Weather, you 've set the

---

* *Oral.* Kallundborg is in Zealand. Mr. Thiele says he saw four pillars at the church. The same story is told of the cathedral of Lund in Funen, which was built by the Troll Finn at the desire of St. Laurentius.

Of Esbern Snare, Holberg says, " The common people tell wonderful stories of him, and how the devil carried him off; which, with other things, will serve to prove that he was an able man."

The German story of Rumpelstilzchen (Kinder and Haus-Märchen, No. 55) is similar to this legend. MM. Grimm, in their note on this story, notice the unexpected manner in which, in the Thousand and One Days, or Persian Tales, the princess Turandot learns the name of Calaf.

pinnacle crooked!"* Instantly the Giant fell witn a great crash from the ridge of the roof, and broke into a thousand pieces, which were all flintstone.†

The Hill-Man invited to the Christening.

THE hill-people are excessively frightened during thunder. When, therefore, they see bad weather coming on, they lose no time in getting to the shelter of their hills. This terror is also the cause of their not being able to endure the beating of a drum, as they take it to be the rolling of thunder. It is therefore a good receipt for banishing them to beat a drum every day in the neighbourhood of their hills; for they immediately pack up and depart to some more quiet residence.

A farmer lived once in great friendship and unanimity with a hill-man, whose hill was on his lands. One time when his wife was lying-in, it gave him some degree of perplexity to think that he could not well avoid inviting the hill-man to the christening, which might not improbably bring him into bad repute with the priest and the other people of the village. He was going about pondering deeply, but in vain, how he might get out of this dilemma, when it came into his head to ask the advice of the boy that kept his pigs, who was a great head-piece, and had often helped him before. The pig-boy instantly undertook to arrange the matter with the hill-man in such a manner that he should not only stay away without being offended, but moreover give a good christening-present.

      * *Wind och Veder !*
          Du har satt spiran spedar !
Others say it was
          Bläster ! sätt spiran väster !
          Blester ! set the pinnacle westwards !
Or,
          Slät ! sätt spiran rätt !
          Slätt ! set the pinnacle straight !

† Afzelius Sago-häfder, iii. 83.   Grimm, Deut. Mythol. p. 515.

Accordingly, when it was night he took a sack on his shoulder, went to the hill-man's hill, knocked, and was admitted. He delivered his message, giving his master's compliments, and requesting the honour of his company at the christening. The hill-man thanked him, and said, " I think it is but right that I should give you a christening-gift." With these words he opened his money-chests, bidding the boy to hold up his sack while he poured money into it. " Is there enough now ?" said he, when he had put a good quantity into it. " Many give more, few give less," replied the boy.

The hill-man then fell again to filling the sack, and again asked, " Is there enough now ?" The boy lifted up the sack a little off the ground to try if he was able to carry any more, and then answered, "It is about what most people give." Upon this the hill-man emptied the whole chest into the bag, and once more asked, " Is there enough now ?" The guardian of the pigs saw that there was as much in it now as ever he was able to carry, so he made answer, " No one gives more, most people give less."

" Come, now," said the hill-man, "let us hear who else is to be at the christening ?" " Ah," said the boy, " we are to have a great parcel of strangers and great people. First and foremost, we are to have three priests and a bishop ! " " Hem !" muttered the hill-man ; " however, these gentlemen usually look only after the eating and drinking : they will never take any notice of me. Well, who else ? " " Then we have asked St. Peter and St. Paul." " Hem ! hem ! however, there will be a by-place for me behind the stove. Well, and then ? " " Then our Lady herself is coming ! " " Hem ! hem ! hem ! however, guests of such high rank come late and go away early. But tell me, my lad, what sort of music is it you are to have ?" " Music ! " said the boy, " why, we are to have drums." " Drums ! " repeated he, quite terrified ; " no, no, thank you, I shall stay at home in that case. Give my best respects to your master, and I thank him for the invitation, but I cannot come. I did but once go out to take a little walk, and some people beginning to beat a drum, I hurried home, and was just got to my door when they flung the drum-stick after me and broke one of my shins. I have been lame of that leg ever since, and I shall take good care in future to avoid that sort of music." So saying, he helped the boy to put the sack on his back, once more charging him to give his best respects to the farmer.*

The Troll turned Cat.

ABOUT a quarter of a mile from Soröe lies Pedersborg, and a little farther on is the town of Lyng. Just between these towns is a hill called Bröndhöi (*Spring-hill*), said to be inhabited by the Troll-people.

There goes a story that there was once among these Troll-people of Bröndhöi an old crossgrained curmudgeon of a Troll, whom the rest nick-named Knurremurre (*Rumble-grumble*), because he was evermore the cause of noise and uproar within the hill. This Knurremurre having discovered what he thought to be too great a degree of intimacy between his young wife and a young Troll of the society, took this in such ill part, that he vowed vengeance, swearing he would have the life of the young one. The latter, accordingly, thought it would be his best course to be off out of the hill till better times; so, turning himself into a noble tortoise-shell tom-cat, he one fine morning quitted his old residence, and journeyed down to the neighbouring town of Lyng, where he established himself in the house of an honest poor man named Plat.

Here he lived for a long time comfortable and easy, with nothing to annoy him, and was as happy as any tom-cat or Troll crossed in love well could be. He got every day plenty of milk and good groute† to eat, and lay the whole day long at his ease in a warm arm-chair behind the stove.

Plat happened one evening to come home rather late, and as he entered the room the cat was sitting in his usual place,

---

* This event happened in Jutland. The Troll's dread of thunder seems to be founded in the mythologic narratives of Thor's enmity to the Trolls.

† Groute, Danish *Gröd*, is a species of food like furmety, made of shelled oats or barley. It is boiled and eaten with milk or butter.

scraping meal-groute out of a pot, and licking the pot itself carefully. "Harkye, dame," said Plat, as he came in at the door, " till I tell you what happened to me on the road. Just as I was coming past Bröndhöi, there came out a Troll, and he called out to me, and said,

"Harkye Plat,
Tell your cat,
That Knurremurre is dead."*

The moment the cat heard these words, he tumbled the pot down on the floor, sprang out of the chair, and stood up on his hind-legs. Then, as he hurried out of the door, he cried out with exultation, "What! is Knurremurre dead? Then I may go home as fast as I please." And so saying he scampered off to the hill, to the amazement of honest Plat; and it is likely lost no time in making his advances to the young widow.†

Kirsten's-Hill.

THERE is a hill on the lands of Skjelverod, near Ringsted, called Kirsten's-hill (*Kirstens Bjerg*). In it there lived a Hill-troll whose name was Skynd, who had from time to time stolen no less than three wives from a man in the village of Englerup.

It was late one evening when this man was riding home from Ringsted, and his way lay by the hill. When he came there he saw a great crowd of Hill-folk who were dancing round it, and had great merriment among them. But on looking a little closer, what should he recognise but all his three wives among them! Now as Kirsten, the

* *Hör du Plat,*
Siig til din Kat,
At Knurremurre er död.

† The scene of this story is in Zealand. The same is related of a hill called Ornehöi in the same island. The writer has heard it in Ireland, but they were cats who addressed the man as he passed by the churchyard where they were assembled.

second of them, had been his favourite, and dearer to him
than either of the others, he called out to her, and named
her name. Troll Skynd then came up to the man, and
asked him why he presumed to call Kirsten. The man told
him briefly how she had been his favourite and best beloved
wife, and entreated of him, with many tears and much
lamentation, to let him have her home with him again.
The Troll consented at last to grant the husband's request,
with, however, the condition, that he should never hurry
(*skynde*) her.

For a long time the husband strictly kept the condition;
but one day, when the woman was above in the loft, getting
something, and it happened that she delayed a long time, he
called out, Make haste, Kirsten, make haste, (*Skynde dig
Kirsten*); and scarcely had he spoken the words, when the
woman was gone, compelled to return to the hill, which has
ever since been called Kirsten's Bjerg.*

The Troll-Labour.

"In the year 1660, when I and my wife had gone to my
farm (*fäboderne*), which is three quarters of a mile from
Ragunda parsonage, and we were sitting there and talking a
while, late in the evening, there came a little man in at the
door, who begged of my wife to go and aid his wife, who was
just then in the pains of labour. The fellow was of small
size, of a dark complexion, and dressed in old grey clothes.
My wife and I sat a while, and wondered at the man; for
we were aware that he was a Troll, and we had heard tell
that such like, called by the peasantry Vettar (*spirits*),
always used to keep in the farmhouses, when people
left them in harvest-time. But when he had urged his
request four or five times, and we thought on what evil the
country folk say that they have at times suffered from the
Vettar, when they have chanced to swear at them, or with

---

* This legend was orally related to Mr. Thiele.

uncivil words bid them go to hell, I took the resolution to read some prayers over my wife, and to bless her, and bid her in God's name go with him. She took in haste some old linen with her, and went along with him, and I remained sitting there. When she returned, she told me, that when she went with the man out at the gate, it seemed to her as if she was carried for a time along in the wind, and so she came to a room, on one side of which was a little dark chamber, in which his wife lay in bed in great agony. My wife went up to her, and, after a little while, aided her till she brought forth the child after the same manner as other human beings. The man then offered her food, and when she refused it, he thanked her, and accompanied her out, and then she was carried along, in the same way in the wind, and after a while came again to the gate, just at ten o'clock. Meanwhile, a quantity of old pieces and clippings of silver were laid on a shelf, in the sitting-room, and my wife found them next day, when she was putting the room in order. It is to be supposed that they were laid there by the *Vettr*. That it in truth so happened, I witness, by inscribing my name. Ragunda, the 12th of April, 1671.

"PET. RAHM."*

The Hill-Smith.

BIORN MARTINSSON went out shooting, one day, with a gamekeeper, on the wooded hill of Ormkulla. They there found a hill-smith (*bergsmed*) lying fast asleep. Biörn directed the gamekeeper to secure him, but he refused, saying "Pray to God to protect you! The hill-smith will fling you down to the bottom of the hill." He was, however, bold and determined, and he went up and seized the sleeping hill-smith, who gave a cry, and implored him to let him go, as he had a wife and seven little children. He said he would also do any iron work that should be required; it

* Hülpher, Samlingen om Jämtland. Westeras, 1775. p. 210 *ap.* Grimm, Deut. Mythol., p. 425.

would only be necessary to leave iron and steel on the side
of the hill, and the work would be found lying finished in
the same place. Biörn asked him for whom he worked; he
replied, "For my companions." When Biörn would not
let him go, he said, "If I had my mist-cap (*uddehat*) you
should not carry me away. But if you do not let me go,
not one of your posterity will attain to the importance
which you possess, but continually decline;" which certainly
came to pass. Biörn would not, however, let him go, but
brought him captive to Bahus. On the third day, however,
he effected his escape out of the place in which he was
confined.*

The following legend is related in Denmark:—
On the lands of Nyegaard lie three large hills, one of
which is the abode of a Troll, who is by trade a blacksmith.
If any one is passing that hill by night, he will see the fire
issuing from the top, and going in again at the side. Should
you wish to have any piece of iron-work executed in a
masterly manner, you have only to go to the hill, and saying
aloud what you want to have made, leave there the iron and
a silver shilling. On revisiting the hill next morning, you
will find the shilling gone, and the required piece of work
lying there finished, and ready for use.†

The Girl at the Troll-Dance.

A GIRL, belonging to a village in the isle of Funen, went out,
one evening, into the fields, and as she was passing by a
small hill, she saw that it was raised upon red pillars, and a

* Ödmans Bahuslän, *ap.* Grimm. Deut. Mythol. p. 426. Ödman also
tells of a man who, as he was going along one day with his dog, came on a
hill-smith at his work, using a stone as an anvil. He had on him a light grey
coat and a black woollen hat. The dog began to bark at him, but he put on
so menacing an attitude that they both deemed it advisable to go away.

† Thiele, iv. 120. In both these legends we find the tradition of the
artistic skill of the Duergar and of Völundr still retained by the peasantry :
see Tales and Popular Fictions, p. 270.

Troll-banquet going on beneath it. She was invited in, and such was the gaiety and festivity that prevailed, that she never perceived the flight of time. At length, however, she took her departure, after having spent, as she thought, a few hours among the joyous hill-people. But when she came to the village she no longer found it the place she had left. All was changed; and when she entered the house in which she had lived with her family, she learned that her father and mother had long been dead, and the house had come into the hands of strangers. She now perceived that for every hour that she had been among the Trolls, a year had elapsed in the external world. The effect on her mind was such that she lost her reason, which she never after recovered.*

The Changeling.

THERE lived once, near Tiis lake, two lonely people, who were sadly plagued with a changeling, given them by the underground-people instead of their own child, which had not been baptised in time. This changeling behaved in a very strange and uncommon manner, for when there was no one in the place, he was in great spirits, ran up the walls like a cat, sat under the roof, and shouted and bawled away lustily; but sat dozing at the end of the table when any one was in the room with him. He was able to eat as much as any four, and never cared what it was that was set before him; but though he regarded not the quality of his food, in quantity he was never satisfied, and gave excessive annoyance to every one in the house.

---

* Thiele, iv. 21. In Otmar's Volksagen, there is a German legend of Peter Klaus, who slept a sleep of twenty years in the bowling-green of the Kyffhäuser, from which Washington Irving made his Ripp van Winkle. We shall also find it in the Highlands of Scotland. It is the Irish legend of Clough na Cuddy, so extremely well told by Mr. C. Croker (to which, by the way, we contributed a Latin song), in the notes to which further information will be found. The Seven Sleepers seems to be the original.

When they had tried for a long time in vain how they could best get rid of him, since there was no living in the house with him, a smart girl pledged herself that she would banish him from the house. She accordingly, while he was out in the fields, took a pig and killed it, and put it, hide, hair, and all, into a black pudding, and set it before him when he came home. He began, as was his custom, to gobble it up, but when he had eaten for some time, he began to relax a little in his efforts, and at last he sat quite still, with his knife in his hand, looking at the pudding.

At length, after sitting for some time in this manner, he began—"A pudding with hide!—and a pudding with hair! a pudding with eyes!—and a pudding with legs in it! Well, three times have I seen a young wood by Tiis lake, but never yet did I see such a pudding! The devil himself may stay here now for me!" So saying, he ran off with himself, and never more came back again.[*]

Another changeling was got rid of in the following manner. The mother, suspecting it to be such from its refusing food, and being so ill-thriven, heated the oven as hot as possible. The maid, as instructed, asked her why she did it. "To burn my child in it to death," was the reply. When the question had been put and answered three times, she placed the child on the peel, and was shoving it into the oven, when the Troll-woman came in a great fright with the real child, and took away her own, saying, "There's your child for you. I have treated it better than you treated mine," and in truth it was fat and hearty.

---

[*] *Oral.* See the Young Piper and the Brewery of Egg-shells in the Irish Fairy Legends, with the notes. The same story is also to be found in Germany where the object is to make the changeling laugh. The mother breaks an egg in two and sets water down to boil in each half shell. The imp then cries out: "Well! I'm as old as the Westerwald, but never before saw I any one cooking in egg-shells," and burst out laughing at it. Instantly the true child was returned.—Kinder and Haus-Märchen, iii. 39. Grose also tells the story in his Provincial Glossary. The mother there breaks a dozen of eggs and sets the shells before the child, who says, "I was seven years old when I came to nurse, and I have lived four since, and yet I never saw so many milkpans." See also Minstrelsy of the Scottish Border, and below, *Wales, Brittany, France.*

The Tile-Stove jumping over the Brook.

NEAR Hellested, in Zealand, lived a man, who from time to time remarked that he was continually plundered. All his suspicions fell on the Troll-folk, who lived in the neighbouring hill of Ildshöi (*Fire-hill*), and once hid himself to try and get a sight of the thief. He had waited there but a very short time when he saw, as he thought, his tile-stove jumping across the brook. The good farmer was all astonishment at this strange sight, and he shouted out " Hurra! there's a jump for a tile-stove!" At this exclamation the Troll, who was wading through the water with the stove on his head, was so frightened that he threw it down, and ran off as hard as he could to Ildshöi. But in the place where the stove fell, the ground got the shape of it, and the place is called Krogbek (*Hook-brook*), and it was this that gave rise to the common saying, " That was a jump for a tile-stove!" " *Det var et Spring af en Leerovn!* "*

Departure of the Trolls from Vendsyssel.

ONE evening, after sunset, there came a strange man to the ferry of Sund. He engaged all the ferry-boats there to go backwards and forwards the whole night long between that place and Vendsyssel, without the people's knowing what lading they had. He told them that they should take their freight on board half a mile to the east of Sund, near the alehouse at the bridge of Lange.

At the appointed time the man was at that place, and the ferrymen, though unable to see anything, perceived very clearly that the boats sunk deeper and deeper, so that they easily concluded that they had gotten a very heavy freight on board. The ferry-boats passed in this manner to and fro

---

* This legend is taken from Resenii Atlas, i. 36.

the whole night long; and though they got every trip a fresh cargo, the strange man never left them, but staid to have everything regulated by his directions.

When morning was breaking they received the payment they had agreed for, and they then ventured to inquire what it was they had been bringing over, but on that head their employer would give them no satisfaction.

But there happened to be among the ferrymen a smart fellow who knew more about these matters than the others. He jumped on shore, took the clay from under his right foot, and put it into his cap, and when he had set it on his head he perceived that all the sand-hills east of Aalborg were completely covered with little Troll-people, who had all pointed red caps on their heads. Ever since that time there have been no Dwarfs seen in Vendsyssel.*

Svend Fælling.

SVEND FÆLLING was a valiant champion. He was born in Fælling, and was a long time at service in Aakjær house, Aarhuus, and as the roads were at that time greatly infested by Trolls and underground-people, who bore great enmity to all Christians, Svend undertook the office of letter-carrier.

As he was one time going along the road, he saw approaching him the Troll of Jels-hill, on the lands of Holm. The Troll came up to him, begging him to stand his friend in a combat with the Troll of Borum-es-hill. When Svend Fælling had promised to do so, saying that he thought himself strong and active enough for the encounter, the Troll reached him a heavy iron bar, and bade him show his strength on that. But not all Svend's efforts availed to lift it: whereupon the Troll handed him a horn, telling him to drink out of it. No sooner had he drunk a little out of it than his strength increased. He was now able to lift the bar, which,

---

* Vendsyssel and Aalborg are both in North Jutland.—The story is told by the ferrymen to travellers : see Mythology of Greece and Italy, p. 68.

when he had drunk again, became still lighter; but when again renewing his draught he emptied the horn, he was able to swing the bar with ease, and he then learned from the Troll that he had now gotten the strength of twelve men. He then promised to prepare himself for combat with the Troll of Bergmond. As a token he was told that he should meet on the road a black ox and a red ox, and that he should fall with all his might on the black ox, and drive him from the red one.

This all came to pass just as he was told, and he found, after his work was done, that the black ox was the Troll from Borum-es-hill, and the red ox was the Troll himself of Jels-hill, who, as a reward for the assistance he had given him, allowed him to retain for his own use the twelve men's strength with which he had endowed him. This grant was, however, on this condition—that if ever he should reveal the secret of his strength, he should be punished by getting the appetite of twelve.

The fame of the prodigious strength of Svend soon spread through the country, as he distinguished himself by various exploits, such, for instance, as throwing a dairy-maid, who had offended him, up on the gable of the house, and similar feats. So when this report came to the ears of his master, he had Svend called before him, and inquired of him whence his great strength came. Svend recollected the words of his friend the Troll, so he told him if he would promise him as much food as would satisfy twelve men, he would tell him. The master promised, and Svend told his story; but the word of the Troll was accomplished, for from that day forth Svend ate and drank as much as any twelve.*

* See above p. 89. According to what Mr. Thiele was told in Zealand, Svend Fælling must have been of prodigious size, for there is a hill near Steenstrup on which he used to sit while he washed his feet and hands in the sea, about half a quarter of a mile distant. The people of Holmstrup dressed a dinner for him, and brought it to him in large brewing vessels, much as the good people of Lilliput did with Gulliver. This reminds us of Holger Danske, who once wanted a new suit of clothes. Twelve tailors were employed: they set ladders to his back and shoulders, as was done to Gulliver, and they measured away; but the man that was highest on the right side ladder chanced, as he was cutting a mark in the measure, to clip Holger's ear. Holger, forgetting what it was, hastily put up his hand to his head, caught the poor tailor, and crushed him to death between his fingers.

The Dwarfs' Banquet.

A NORWEGIAN TALE.*

THERE lived in Norway, not far from the city of Drontheim, a powerful man, who was blessed with all the goods of fortune. A part of the surrounding country was his property ; numerous herds fed on his pastures, and a great retinue and a crowd of servants adorned his mansion. He had an only daughter, called Aslog,† the fame of whose beauty spread far and wide. The greatest men of the country sought her, but all were alike unsuccessful in their suit, and he who had come full of confidence and joy, rode away home silent and melancholy. Her father, who thought his daughter delayed her choice only to select, forbore to interfere, and exulted in her prudence. But when, at length, the richest and noblest had tried their fortune with as little success as the rest, he grew angry, and called his daughter, and said to her, " Hitherto I have left you to your free choice, but since I see that you reject all without any distinction, and the very best of your suitors seem not good enough for you, I will keep measures no longer with you. What ! shall my family be extinct, and my inheritance pass away into the hands of strangers ? I will break your stubborn spirit. I give you now till the festival of the great Winter-night ; make your choice by that time, or prepare to accept him whom I shall fix on."

---

* This tale was taken from oral recitation by Dr. Grimm, and inserted in Hauff's Märchenalmanach for 1827. Dr. Grimm's fidelity to tradition is too well known to leave any doubt of its genuineness.

† Aslög (*Light of the Aser*) is the name of the lovely daughter of Sigurd and Brynhilda, who became the wife of Ragnar Lodbrok. How beautiful and romantic is the account in the Volsunga Saga of old Heimer taking her, when an infant, and carrying her about with him in his harp, to save her from those who sought her life as the last of Sigurd's race ; his retiring to remote streams and waterfalls to wash her, and his stilling her cries by the music of his harp !

Aslog loved a youth called Orm, handsome as he was brave and noble. She loved him with her whole soul, and she would sooner die than bestow her hand on another. But Orm was poor, and poverty compelled him to serve in the mansion of her father. Aslog's partiality for him was kept a secret; for her father's pride of power and wealth was such that he would never have given his consent to an union with so humble a man.

When Aslog saw the darkness of his countenance, and heard his angry words, she turned pale as death, for she knew his temper, and doubted not but that he would put his threats into execution. Without uttering a word in reply, she retired to her silent chamber, and thought deeply but in vain how to avert the dark storm that hung over her. The great festival approached nearer and nearer, and her anguish increased every day.

At last the lovers resolved on flight. "I know," says Orm, "a secure place where we may remain undiscovered until we find an opportunity of quitting the country." At night, when all were asleep, Orm led the trembling Aslog over the snow and ice-fields away to the mountains. The moon and the stars sparkling still brighter in the cold winter's night lighted them on their way. They had under their arms a few articles of dress and some skins of animals, which were all they could carry. They ascended the mountains the whole night long till they reached a lonely spot inclosed with lofty rocks. Here Orm conducted the weary Aslog into a cave, the low and narrow entrance to which was hardly perceptible, but it soon enlarged to a great hall, reaching deep into the mountain. He kindled a fire, and they now, reposing on their skins, sat in the deepest solitude far away from all the world.

Orm was the first who had discovered this cave, which is shown to this very day, and as no one knew any thing of it, they were safe from the pursuit of Aslog's father. They passed the whole winter in this retirement. Orm used to go a hunting, and Aslog stayed at home in the cave, minded the fire, and prepared the necessary food. Frequently did she mount the points of the rocks, but her eyes wandered as far as they could reach only over glittering snow-fields.

The spring now came on—the woods were green—the

meads put on their various colours, and Aslog could but
rarely and with circumspection venture to leave the cave.
One evening Orm came in with the intelligence that he
had recognised her father's servants in the distance, and
that he could hardly have been unobserved by them, whose
eyes were as good as his own. "They will surround this
place," continued he, "and never rest till they have found us;
we must quit our retreat, then, without a moment's delay."

They accordingly descended on the other side of the
mountain, and reached the strand, where they fortunately
found a boat. Orm shoved off, and the boat drove into the
open sea. They had escaped their pursuers, but they were
now exposed to dangers of another kind: whither should
they turn themselves? They could not venture to land, for
Aslog's father was lord of the whole coast, and they would
infallibly fall into his hands. Nothing then remained for
them but to commit their bark to the wind and waves. They
drove along the entire night. At break of day the coast had
disappeared, and they saw nothing but the sky above, the
sea beneath, and the waves that rose and fell. They had
not brought one morsel of food with them, and thirst and
hunger began now to torment them. Three days did they
toss about in this state of misery, and Aslog, faint and
exhausted, saw nothing but certain death before her.

At length, on the evening of the third day, they discovered an island of tolerable magnitude, and surrounded by
a number of smaller ones. Orm immediately steered for
it, but just as he came near it there suddenly rose a
violent wind, and the sea rolled every moment higher and
higher against him. He turned about with a view of
approaching it on another side, but with no better success;
his vessel, as oft as it approached the island, was driven
back as if by an invisible power. "Lord God!" cried he,
and blessed himself and looked on poor Aslog, who seemed
to be dying of weakness before his eyes. But scarcely had
the exclamation passed his lips when the storm ceased,
the waves subsided, and the vessel came to the shore,
without encountering any hindrance. Orm jumped out
on the beach; some mussels that he found on the strand
strengthened and revived the exhausted Aslog, so that she
was soon able to leave the boat.

The island was overgrown with low dwarf shrubs, and seemed to be uninhabited; but when they had gotten about to the middle of it, they discovered a house reaching but a little above the ground, and appearing to be half under the surface of the earth. In the hope of meeting human beings and assistance, the wanderers approached it. They listened if they could hear any noise, but the most perfect silence reigned there. Orm at length opened the door, and with his companion walked in; but what was their surprise, to find everything regulated and arranged as if for inhabitants, yet not a single living creature visible. The fire was burning on the hearth, in the middle of the room, and a pot with fish hung on it apparently only waiting for some one to take it up and eat it. The beds were made and ready to receive their wearied tenants. Orm and Aslog stood for some time dubious, and looked on with a certain degree of awe, but at last, overcome by hunger, they took up the food and ate. When they had satisfied their appetites, and still in the last beams of the setting sun, which now streamed over the island far and wide, discovered no human being, they gave way to weariness, and laid themselves in the beds to which they had been so long strangers.

They had expected to be awakened in the night by the owners of the house on their return home, but their expectation was not fulfilled; they slept undisturbed till the morning sun shone in upon them. No one appeared on any of the following days, and it seemed as if some invisible power had made ready the house for their reception. They spent the whole summer in perfect happiness—they were, to be sure, solitary, yet they did not miss mankind. The wild birds' eggs, and the fish they caught, yielded them provisions in abundance.

When autumn came, Aslog brought forth a son. In the midst of their joy at his appearance, they were surprised by a wonderful apparition. The door opened on a sudden, and an old woman stepped in. She had on her a handsome blue dress: there was something proud, but at the same time something strange and surprising in her appearance.

"Do not be afraid," said she, "at my unexpected appearance—I am the owner of this house, and I thank you for the clean and neat state in which you have kept it, and for

the good order in which I find everything with you.
I would willingly have come sooner, but I had no power to
do so till this little heathen (pointing to the new born-babe)
was come to the light. Now I have free access. Only
fetch no priest from the main-land to christen it, or I must
depart again. If you will in this matter comply with my
wishes, you may not only continue to live here, but all the
good that ever you can wish for I will do you. Whatever
you take in hand shall prosper; good luck shall follow you
wherever you go. But break this condition, and depend
upon it that misfortune after misfortune will come on you,
and even on this child will I avenge myself. If you want
anything, or are in danger, you have only to pronounce my
name three times and I will appear and lend you assistance.
I am of the race of the old Giants, and my name is Guru.
But beware of uttering in my presence the name of him
whom no Giant may hear of, and never venture to make the
sign of the cross, or to cut it on beam or board in the house.
You may dwell in this house the whole year long, only be
so good as to give it up to me on Yule evening, when the
sun is at the lowest, as then we celebrate our great festival,
and then only are we permitted to be merry. At least, if
you should not be willing to go out of the house, keep
yourselves up in the loft as quiet as possible the whole
day long, and as you value your lives do not look down into
the room until midnight is past. After that you may take
possession of everything again."

When the old woman had thus spoken she vanished, and
Aslog and Orm, now at ease respecting their situation, lived
without any disturbance contented and happy. Orm never
made a cast of his net without getting a plentiful draught;
he never shot an arrow from his bow that it was not sure to
hit; in short, whatever they took in hand, were it ever so
trifling, evidently prospered.

When Christmas came, they cleaned up the house in the
best manner, set everything in order, kindled a fire on the
hearth, and as the twilight approached, they went up to the
loft, where they remained quite still and quiet. At length
it grew dark; they thought they heard a sound of whizzing
and snorting in the air, such as the swans use to make in
the winter time. There was a hole in the roof over the fire-

place which might be opened and shut either to let in the
light from above, or to afford a free passage for the smoke.
Orm lifted up the lid, which was covered with a skin, and
put out his head. But what a wonderful sight then presented
itself to his eyes.! The little islands around were all lit up
with countless blue lights, which moved about without
ceasing, jumped up and down, then skipped down to the
shore, assembled together, and came nearer and nearer to
the large island where Orm and Aslog lived. At last they
reached it, and arranged themselves in a circle around a large
stone not far from the shore, and which Orm well knew.
But what was his surprise, when he saw that the stone had
now completely assumed the form of a man, though of a
monstrous and gigantic one! He could clearly perceive that
the little blue lights were borne by Dwarfs, whose pale clay-
coloured faces, with their huge noses and red eyes, disfigured
too by birds' bills and owls' eyes, were supported by misshapen bodies; and they tottered and wabbled about here
and there, so that they seemed to be at the same time merry
and in pain. Suddenly, the circle opened; the little ones
retired on each side, and Guru, who was now much enlarged
and of as immense a size as the stone, advanced with gigantic
steps. She threw both her arms round the stone image,
which immediately began to receive life and motion. As
soon as the first symptom of motion showed itself, the little
ones began, with wonderful capers and grimaces, a song, or
to speak more properly, a howl, with which the whole island
resounded and seemed to tremble at the noise. Orm, quite
terrified, drew in his head, and he and Aslog remained in
the dark, so still, that they hardly ventured to draw their
breath.

The procession moved on toward the house, as might be
clearly perceived by the nearer approach of the shouting and
crying. They were now all come in, and, light and active,
the Dwarfs jumped about on the benches; and heavy and
loud sounded at intervals the steps of the giants. Orm and
his wife heard them covering the table, and the clattering
of the plates, and the shouts of joy with which they celebrated their banquet. When it was over and it drew near
to midnight, they began to dance to that ravishing fairy-air
which charms the mind into such sweet confusion, and

which some have heard in the rocky glens, and learned by
listening to the underground musicians. As soon as Aslog
caught the sound of this air, she felt an irresistible longing
to see the dance. Nor was Orm able to keep her back.
" Let me look," said she, " or my heart will burst." She
took her child and placed herself at the extreme end of the
loft, whence, without being observed, she could see all that
passed. Long did she gaze, without taking off her eyes for
an instant, on the dance, on the bold and wonderful springs
of the little creatures who seemed to float in the air, and not
so much as to touch the ground, while the ravishing melody
of the elves filled her whole soul. The child meanwhile,
which lay in her arms, grew sleepy and drew its breath
heavily, and without ever thinking on the promise she had
given the old woman, she made, as is usual, the sign of the
cross over the mouth of the child, and said, " Christ bless
you, my babe ! "

The instant she had spoken the word there was raised a
horrible piercing cry. The spirits tumbled heads over heels
out at the door with terrible crushing and crowding, their
lights went out, and in a few minutes the whole house was
clear of them, and left desolate. Orm and Aslog frightened
to death, hid themselves in the most retired nook in the
house. They did not venture to stir till daybreak, and not
till the sun shone through the hole in the roof down on the
fire-place did they feel courage enough to descend from the
loft.

The table remained still covered as the underground-
people had left it; all their vessels, which were of silver, and
manufactured in the most beautiful manner, were upon it.
In the middle of the room, there stood upon the ground a
huge copper vessel half full of sweet mead, and by the side
of it, a drinking-horn of pure gold. In the corner lay against
the wall a stringed instrument, not unlike a dulcimer, which,
as people believe, the Giantesses used to play on. They
gazed on what was before them, full of admiration, but without venturing to lay their hands on anything : but great
and fearful was their amazement, when, on turning about,
they saw sitting at the table an immense figure, which Orm
instantly recognised as the Giant whom Guru had animated
by her embrace. He was now a cold and hard stone. While

they were standing gazing on it, Guru herself entered the room in her giant-form. She wept so bitterly, that her tears trickled down on the ground. It was long ere her sobbing permitted her to utter a single word: at last she spoke:—

"Great affliction have you brought on me, and henceforth I must weep while I live; yet as I know that you have not done this with evil intentions, I forgive you, though it were a trifle for me to crush the whole house like an egg-shell over your heads."

"Alas!" cried she, "my husband, whom I love more than myself, there he sits, petrified for ever; never again will he open his eyes! Three hundred years lived I with my father on the island of Kunnan, happy in the innocence of youth, as the fairest among the Giant-maidens. Mighty heroes sued for my hand; the sea around that island is still filled with the rocky fragments which they hurled against each other in their combats. Andfind won the victory, and I plighted myself to him. But ere I was married came the detestable Odin into the country, who overcame my father, and drove us all from the island. My father and sisters fled to the mountains, and since that time my eyes have beheld them no more. Andfind and I saved ourselves on this island, where we for a long time lived in peace and quiet, and thought it would never be interrupted. But destiny, which no one escapes, had determined it otherwise. Oluf * came from Britain. They called him the Holy, and Andfind instantly found that his voyage would be inauspicious to the giants. When he heard how Oluf's ship rushed through the waves, he went down to the strand and blew the sea against him with all his strength. The waves swelled up like mountains. But Oluf was still more mighty than he; his ship flew unchecked through the billows like an arrow from a bow. He steered direct for our island. When the ship was so near that Andfind thought he could reach it with his hands, he grasped at the forepart with his right hand, and was about to drag it down to the bottom, as he had often done with other ships. But Oluf, the terrible Oluf, stepped forward, and crossing his hands over each other, he cried with a loud voice, 'Stand there as a stone,

---

* This is Saint Oluf or Olave, the warlike apostle of the North.

till the last day,' and in the same instant my unhappy husband became a mass of rock. The ship sailed on unimpeded, and ran direct against the mountain, which it cut through, and separated from it the little island which lies out yonder.*

"Ever since my happiness has been annihilated, and lonely and melancholy have I passed my life. On Yule-eve alone can petrified Giants receive back their life for the space of seven hours, if one of their race embraces them, and is, at the same time, willing to sacrifice a hundred years of their own life. But seldom does a Giant do that. I loved my husband too well not to bring him back cheerfully to life every time that I could do it, even at the highest price, and never would I reckon how often I had done it, that I might not know when the time came when I myself should share his fate, and at the moment that I threw my arms around him become one with him. But alas! even this comfort is taken from me; I can never more by any embrace awake him, since he has heard the name which I dare not utter; and never again will he see the light until the dawn of the last day shall bring it.

"I now go hence! You will never again behold me! All that is here in the house I give you! My dulcimer alone will I keep! But let no one venture to fix his habitation on the little islands that lie around here! There dwell the little underground ones whom you saw at the festival, and I will protect them as long as I live!"

With these words Guru vanished. The next spring Orm took the golden horn and the silver ware to Drontheim,

---

* A legend similar to this is told of Saint Oluf in various parts of Scandinavia. The following is an example:—As he was sailing by the high strand-hills in Hornsherred, in which a giantess abode, she cried out to him,

> Saint Oluf with the red beard hear!
> My cellar-wall thou'rt sailing too near!

Oluf was incensed, and instead of guiding the ship through the rocks, he turned it toward the hill, replying:

> Hearken thou witch with thy spindle and rock!
> There shalt thou sit and be a stone-block!

and scarcely had he spoken when the hill burst and the giantess was turned into stone. She is still seen sitting on the east side with her rock and spindle; out of the opposite mass sprang a holy well. Grimm. Deutsche Mythologie, p. 516.

where no one knew him. The value of these precious metals was so great, that he was able to purchase everything requisite for a wealthy man. He laded his ship with his purchases, and returned back to the island, where he spent many years in unalloyed happiness, and Aslog's father was soon reconciled to his wealthy son-in-law.

The stone image remained sitting in the house; no human power was able to move it. So hard was the stone, that hammer and axe flew in pieces without making the slightest impression upon it. The Giant sat there till a holy man came to the island, who with one single word removed him back to his former station, where he stands to this hour. The copper vessel, which the underground people left behind them, was preserved as a memorial upon the island, which bears the name of House Island to the present day.

NISSES.*

——◆——

Og Trolde, Hexer, Nisser i hver Vraae.
FINN MAGNUSEN

And Witches, Trolls, and Nisses in each nook.

THE Nis is the same being that is called Kobold in Germany, Brownie in Scotland, and whom we shall meet in various other places under different appellations. He is in Denmark and Norway also called Nisse god-dreng (*Nissè good lad*), and in Sweden Tomtgubbe (*Old Man of the House*), or briefly Tomte.

He is evidently of the Dwarf family, as he resembles them in appearance, and, like them, has the command of money, and the same dislike to noise and tumult. He is of the size of a year-old child, but has the face of an old man. His

------

* Nisse, Grimm thinks (Deut. Mythol. p. 472) is Nicls, Niclsen, *i. e.* Nicolaus, Niclas, a common name in Germany and the North, which is also contracted to Klas, Claas.

usual dress is grey, with a pointed red cap ; but on Michael-mas-day he wears a round hat like those of the peasants.

No farm-house goes on well unless there is a Nis in it, and well is it for the maids and the men when they are in favour with him. They may go to their beds and give them-selves no trouble about their work, and yet in the morning the maids will find the kitchen swept up, and water brought in, and the men will find the horses in the stable well cleaned and curried, and perhaps a supply of corn cribbed for them from the neighbours' barns. But he punishes them for any irregularity that takes place.

The Nisses of Norway, we are told, are fond of the moon-light, and in the winter time they may be seen jumping over the yard, or driving in sledges. They are also skilled in music and dancing, and will, it is said, give instructions on the fiddle for a *grey sheep*, like the Swedish Strömkarl.*

Every church, too, has its Nis, who looks to order, and chastises those who misbehave themselves. He is called the Kirkegrim.

The Nis Removing.†

It is very difficult, they say, to get rid of a Nis when one wishes it. A man who lived in a house in which a Nis carried his pranks to great lengths resolved to quit the tenement, and leave him there alone. Several cart-loads of furniture and other articles were already gone, and the man was come to take away the last, which consisted chiefly of empty tubs, barrels, and things of that sort. The load was now all ready, and the man had just bidden farewell to his house and to the Nis, hoping for comfort in his new habita-tion, when happening, from some cause or other, to go to the back of the cart, there he saw the Nis sitting in one of

---

* Wilse *ap* Grimm, Deut. Mythol., p. 479, who thinks he may have con-founded the Nis with the Nöck.

† The places mentioned in the following stories are all in Jutland. It is remarkable that we seem to have scarcely any Nis stories from Sweden.

the tubs in the cart, plainly with the intention of going along with him wherever he went. The good man was surprised and disconcerted beyond measure at seeing that all his labour was to no purpose; but the Nis began to laugh heartily, popped his head up out of the tub, and cried to the bewildered farmer, " Ha! we 're moving to-day, you see."*

The Penitent Nis.

It is related of a Nis, who had established himself in a house in Jutland, that he used every evening, after the maid was gone to bed, to go into the kitchen to take his groute, which they used to leave for him in a wooden bowl.

One evening he sat down as usual to eat his supper with a good appetite, drew over the bowl to him, and was just beginning, as he thought, to make a comfortable meal, when he found that the maid had forgotten to put any butter into it for him. At this he fell into a furious rage, got up in the height of his passion, and went out into the cow-house, and twisted the neck of the best cow that was in it. But as he felt himself still very hungry, he stole back again to the kitchen to take some of the groute, such as it was, and when he had eaten a little of it he perceived that there was butter in it, but that it had sunk to the bottom under the groute. He was now so vexed at his injustice toward the maid, that, to make good the damage he had done, he went back to the cow-house and set a chest full of money by the side of the dead cow, where the family found it next morning, and by means of it got into flourishing circumstances.

---

* This story is current in Germany, England, and Ireland. In the German story the farmer set fire to his barn to burn the Kobold in it. As he was driving off, he turned round to look at the blaze, and, to his no small mortification, saw the Kobold behind him in the cart, crying " It was time for us to come out—it was time for us to come out !"

The Nis and the Boy

THERE was a Nis in a house in Jutland; he every evening got his groute at the regular time, and he, in return, used to help both the men and the maids, and looked to the interest of the master of the house in every respect.

There came one time an arch mischievous boy to live at service in this house, and his great delight was, whenever he got an opportunity, to give the Nis all the annoyance in his power. One evening, late, when everything was quiet in the place, the Nis took his little wooden dish, and was just going to eat his supper, when he perceived that the boy had put the butter at the bottom, and concealed it, in hopes that he might eat the groute first, and then find the butter when all the groute was gone. He accordingly set about thinking how he might repay the boy in kind; so, after pondering a little, he went up to the loft, where the man and the boy were lying asleep in the same bed. When he had taken the bed-clothes off them, and saw the little boy by the side of the tall man, he said, "Short and long don't match;" and with this word he took the boy by the legs and dragged him down to the man's legs. He then went up to the head of the bed, and "Short and long don't match," said he again, and then he dragged the boy up once more. When, do what he would, he could not succeed in making the boy as long as the man, he still persisted in dragging him up and down in the bed, and continued at this work the whole night long, till it was broad daylight.

By this time he was well tired, so he crept up on the window-stool, and sat with his legs hanging down into the yard. But the house-dog—for all dogs have a great enmity to the Nis—as soon as he saw him, began to bark at him, which afforded such amusement to Nis, as the dog could not get up to him, that he put down first one leg and then the other to him, and teazed him, and kept saying, "Look at my little leg! look at my little leg!" In the meantime the boy had wakened, and had stolen up close behind him, and while Nis was least thinking of it, and was going on with his "Look at my little leg!" the boy tumbled him down into the yard to the dog, crying out at the same time, "Look at the whole of him now!"

The Nis Stealing Corn.

THERE lived a man at Thyrsting, in Jutland, who had a Nis in his barn. This Nis used to attend to the cattle, and at night he would steal fodder for them from the neighbours, so that this farmer had the best fed and most thriving cattle in the country.

One time the boy went along with the Nis to Fugleriis to steal corn. The Nis took as much as he thought he could well carry, but the boy was more covetous, and said, "Oh, take more; sure we can rest now and then?" "Rest!" said the Nis; "rest! and what is rest?" "Do what I tell you," replied the boy; "take more, and we shall find rest when we get out of this."—The Nis then took more, and they went away with it. But when they were come to the lands of Thyrsting, the Nis grew tired, and then the boy said to him, "Here now is rest;" and they both sat down on the side of a little hill. "If I had known," said the Nis, as they were sitting there, "if I had known that rest was so good, I'd have carried off all that was in the barn."

It happened some time after that the boy and the Nis were no longer friends, and as the Nis was sitting one day in the granary-window, with his legs hanging out into the yard, the boy ran at him and tumbled him back into the granary. But the Nis took his satisfaction of him that very same night; for when the boy was gone to bed, he stole down to where he was lying, and carried him naked as he was out into the yard, and then laid two pieces of wood across the well, and put him lying on them, expecting that, when he awoke, he would fall from the fright down into the well and be drowned. But he was disappointed, for the boy came off without injury.

The Nis and the Mare.

———◆———

THERE was a man who lived in the town of Tirup, who had a very handsome white mare. This mare had for many years gone, like an heirloom, from father to son, because there was a Nis attached to her, which brought luck to the place.

This Nis was so fond of the mare, that he could hardly endure to let them put her to any kind of work, and he used to come himself every night and feed her of the best; and as for this purpose he usually brought a superfluity of corn, both threshed and in the straw, from the neighbours' barns, all the rest of the cattle enjoyed the advantage of it, and they were all kept in exceeding good case.

It happened at last that the farm-house passed into the hands of a new owner, who refused to put any faith in what they told him about the mare, so the luck speedily left the place, and went after the mare to his poor neighbour who had bought her; and within five days after his purchase, the poor farmer who had bought the mare began to find his circumstances gradually improving, while the income of the other, day after day, fell away and diminished at such a rate, that he was hard set to make both ends meet.

If now the man who had gotten the mare had only known how to be quiet, and enjoy the good times that were come upon him, he and his children, and his children's children after him, would have been in flourishing circumstances till this very day. But when he saw the quantity of corn that came every night to his barn, he could not resist his desire to get a sight of the Nis. So he concealed himself one evening, at nightfall, in the stable; and as soon as it was midnight, he saw how the Nis came from his neighbour's barn and brought a sackful of corn with him. It was now unavoidable that the Nis should get a sight of the man who was watching; so he, with evident marks of grief, gave the mare her food for the last time, cleaned, and dressed her to

the best of his abilities, and when he had done, turned round
to where the man was lying and bid him farewell.

From that day forward the circumstances of both the
neighbours were on an equality, for each now kept his own.

The Nis Riding.

THERE was a Nis in a farm-house, who was for ever torment-
ing the maids, and playing all manner of roguish tricks on
them, and they in return were continually planning how to
be even with him. There came one time to the farm-house a
Juttish drover and put up there for the night. Among his
cattle, there was one very large Juttish ox; and when Nis
saw him in the stable he took a prodigious fancy to get up
and ride on his back. He accordingly mounted the ox, and
immediately began to torment the beast in such a manner
that he broke loose from his halter and ran out into the
yard with the Nis on his back. Poor Nis was now terrified
in earnest, and began to shout and bawl most lustily. His
cries awakened the maids, but instead of coming to his
assistance they laughed at him till they were ready to break
their hearts. And when the ox ran against a piece of timber,
so that the unfortunate Nis had his hood all torn by it, the
maids shouted out and called him " Lame leg, Lame leg,"
and he made off with himself in most miserable plight. But
the Nis did not forget it to the maids; for the following
Sunday when they were going to the dance, he contrived,
unknown to them, to smut their faces all over, so that when
they got up to dance, every one that was there burst out a
laughing at them.

The Nisses in Vosborg.

THERE was once an exceeding great number of Nisses in Jutland. Those in Vosborg in particular were treated with so much liberality, that they were careful and solicitous beyond measure for their master's interest. They got every evening in their sweet-groute a large lump of butter, and in return for this, they once showed great zeal and gratitude.

One very severe winter, a lonely house in which there were six calves was so completely covered by the snow, that for the space of fourteen days no one could get into it. When the snow was gone, the people naturally thought that the calves were all dead of hunger; but far from it, they found them all in excellent condition; the place cleaned up, and the cribs full of beautiful corn, so that it was quite evident the Nisses had attended to them.

But the Nis, though thus grateful when well treated, is sure to avenge himself when any one does anything to annoy and vex him. As a Nis was one day amusing himself by running on the loft over the cow-house, one of the boards gave way and his leg went through. The boy happened to be in the cow-house when this happened, and when he saw the Nis's leg hanging down, he took up a dung fork, and gave him with it a smart rap on the leg. At noon, when the people were sitting round the table in the hall, the boy sat continually laughing to himself. The bailiff asked him what he was laughing at; and the boy replied, "Oh! a got such a blow at Nis to-day, and a gave him such a hell of a rap with my fork, when he put his leg down through the loft." "No," cried Nis, outside of the window, "it was not one, but three blows you gave me, for there were three prongs on the fork; but I shall pay you for it, my lad."

Next night, while the boy was lying fast asleep, Nis came and took him up and brought him out into the yard, then flung him over the house, and was so expeditious in getting to the other side of the house, that he caught him before he came to the ground, and instantly pitched him over again, and kept going on with this sport till the boy had been eight times backwards and forwards over the roof, and the ninth time he let him fall into a great pool of water, and then set up such a shout of laughter at him, that it wakened up all the people that were in the place.

In Sweden the Tomte is sometimes seen at noon, in summer, slowly and stealthily dragging a straw or an ear of corn. A farmer, seeing him thus engaged, laughed, and said, "What difference does it make if you bring away that or nothing?" The Tomte in displeasure left his farm, and went to that of his neighbour; and with him went all prosperity from him who had made light of him, and passed over to the other farmer. Any one who treated the industrious Tomte with respect, and set store by the smallest straw, became rich, and neatness and regularity prevailed in his household.*

NECKS, MERMEN, AND MERMAIDS.

Ei Necken mer i flodens vågor quäder,
Och ingen Hafsfru bleker sina kläder
Paa böljans rygg i milda solars glans.
STAGNELIUS.

The Neck no more upon the river sings,
And no Mermaid to bleach her linen flings
Upon the waves in the mild solar ray.

It is a prevalent opinion in the North that all the various beings of the popular creed were once worsted in a conflict with superior powers, and condemned to remain till doomsday in certain assigned abodes. The Dwarfs, or Hill (*Berg*) trolls, were appointed the hills; the Elves the groves and

---

* Afzelius, Sago Häfdar., ii. 169. On Christmas-morning, he says, the peasantry gives the Tomte, his wages, *i. e.* a piece of grey cloth, tobacco, and a *shovelful of clay.*

leafy trees; the Hill-people (*Högfolk**) the caves and caverns; the Mermen, Mermaids, and Necks, the sea, lakes, and rivers; the River-man (*Strömkarl*) the small waterfalls. Both the Catholic and Protestant clergy have endeavoured to excite an aversion to these beings, but in vain. They are regarded as possessing considerable power over man and nature, and it is believed that though now unhappy, they will be eventually saved, or *faa förlossning* (get salvation), as it is expressed.

The NECK (in Danish Nökke†) is the river-spirit. The ideas respecting him are various. Sometimes he is represented as sitting, of summer nights, on the surface of the water, like a pretty little boy, with golden hair hanging in ringlets, and a red cap on his head; sometimes as above the water, like a handsome young man, but beneath like a horse;‡ at other times, as an old man with a long beard, out of which he wrings the water as he sits on the cliffs. In this last form, Odin, according to the Icelandic sagas, has sometimes revealed himself.

The Neck is very severe against any haughty maiden who makes an ill return to the love of her wooer; but should he himself fall in love with a maid of human kind, he is the most polite and attentive suitor in the world.

Though he is thus severe only against those who deserve it, yet country people when they are upon the water use certain precautions against his power. Metals, particularly steel, are believed "*to bind the Neck*," (*binda Necken*) ; and when going on the open sea, they usually put a knife

* *Berg* signifies a larger eminence, mountain, hill; *Hög*, a height, hillock. The *Hög-folk* are Elves and musicians.

† The Danish peasantry in Wormius' time described the Nökke (Nikke) as a monster with a human head, that dwells both in fresh and salt water. When any one was drowned, they said, *Nökken tog ham bort* (the Nökke took him away) ; and when any drowned person was found with the nose red, they said the Nikke has sucked him : *Nikken har suet ham.*—Magnusen, Eddalære. Denmark being a country without any streams of magnitude, we meet in the Danske Folkesagn no legends of the Nökke ; and in ballads, such as " The Power of the Harp," what in Sweden is ascribed to the Neck, is in Denmark imputed to the Havmand or Merman.

‡ The Neck is also believed to appear in the form of a complete horse, and can be made to work at the plough, if a bridle of a particular description be employed.—*Kalm's Vestgötha Resa.*

in the bottom of the boat, or set a nail in a reed. In Norway the following charm is considered effectual against the Neck :—

> Nyk, nyk, naal i vatn !
> Jomfru Maria kastet staal i vatn !
> Du sök, äk flyt !

> Neck, neck, nail in water !
> The virgin Mary casteth steel in water !
> Do you sink, I flit !

The Neck is a great musician. He sits on the water and plays on his gold harp, the harmony of which operates on all nature. To learn music of him, a person must present him with a black lamb, and also promise him resurrection and redemption.

The following story is told in all parts of Sweden :—

"Two boys were one time playing near a river that ran by their father's house. The Neck rose and sat on the surface of the water, and played on his harp; but one of the children said to him, 'What is the use, Neck, of your sitting there and playing? you will never be saved.' The Neck then began to weep bitterly, flung away his harp, and sank down to the bottom. The children went home, and told the whole story to their father, who was the parish priest. He said they were wrong to say so to the Neck, and desired them to go immediately back to the river, and console him with the promise of salvation. They did so; and when they came down to the river the Neck was sitting on the water, weeping and lamenting. They then said to him, 'Neck, do not grieve so; our father says that your Redeemer liveth also.' The Neck then took his harp and played most sweetly, until long after the sun was gone down."

This legend is also found in Denmark, but in a less agreeable form. A clergyman, it is said, was journeying one night to Roeskilde in Zealand. His way led by a hill in which there was music and dancing and great merriment going forward. Some dwarfs jumped suddenly out of it, stopped the carriage, and asked him whither he was going. He replied to the synod of the church. They asked him if he thought they could be saved. To that, he replied, he could not give an immediate answer. They then begged

that he would give them a reply by next year. When he
next passed, and they made the same demand, he replied,
" No, you are all damned." Scarcely had he spoken the
word, when the whole hill appeared in flames.

In another form of this legend, a priest says to the Neck,
" Sooner will this cane which I hold in my hand grow
green flowers than thou shalt attain salvation." The Neck
in grief flung away his harp and wept, and the priest rode
on. But soon his cane began to put forth leaves and
blossoms, and he then went back to communicate the glad
tidings to the Neck who now joyously played on all the
entire night.*

The Power of the Harp.

LITTLE Kerstin she weeps in her bower all the day ;
Sir Peter in his courtyard is playing so gay.
    My heart's own dear !
    Tell me wherefore you grieve ?

" Grieve you for saddle, or grieve you for steed ?
Or grieve you for that I have you wed ? "
    My heart's, &c.

" And grieve do I not for saddle or for steed :
And grieve do I not for that I have you wed.
    My heart's, &c.

" Much more do I grieve for my fair gold hair,
Which in the blue waves shall be stained to-day.
    My heart's, &c.

" Much more do I grieve for Ringfalla flood,
In which have been drowned my two sisters proud.
    My heart's, &c.

" It was laid out for me in my infancy,
That my wedding-day should prove heavy to me."
    My heart's, &c.

* Afzelius, Sago-häfdar, ii. 156.

" And I shall make them the horse round shoe,
He shall not stumble on his four gold shoes.
    My heart's, &c.

" Twelve of my courtiers shall before thee ride,
Twelve of my courtiers upon each side."
    My heart's, &c.

But when they were come to Ringfalla wood,
There sported a hart with gilded horns proud.
    My heart's, &c.

And all the courtiers after the hart are gone ;
Little Kerstin, she must proceed alone.
    My heart's, &c.

And when on Ringfalla bridge she goes,
Her steed he stumbled on his four gold shoes.
    My heart's, &c.

Four gold shoes, and thirty gold nails,
And the maiden into the swift stream falls.
    My heart's, &c.

Sir Peter he spake to his footpage so—
" Thou must for my gold harp instantly go."
    My heart's, &c.

The first stroke on his gold harp he gave
The foul ugly Neck sat and laughed on the wave.
    My heart's, &c.

The second time the gold harp he swept,
The foul ugly Neck on the wave sat and wept.
    My heart's, &c.

The third stroke on the gold harp rang,
Little Kerstin reached up her snow-white arm.
    My heart's, &c.*

---

    * *Det tredje slag på gullharpan klang,*
      Liten Kerstin räckta upp sin snöhvita arm.
       Min hjerteliga kär !
       J sägen mig hvarfor J sörjen ?

He played the bark from off the high trees;
He played Little Kerstin back on his knees.
  My heart's, &c.

And the Neck he out of the waves came there,
And a proud maiden on each arm he bare.
  My heart's own dear!
  Tell me wherefore you grieve ?*

The Strömkarl, called in Norway Grim or Fosse-Grim†
(*Waterfall-Grim*) is a musical genius like the Neck.   Like
him too, when properly propitiated, he communicates his
art.   The sacrifice also is a black lamb,‡ which the offerer
must present with averted head, and on Thursday evening.
If it is poor the pupil gets no further than to the tuning of
the instruments ; if it is fat the Strömkarl seizes the votary
by the right hand, and swings it backwards and forwards
till the blood runs out at the finger-ends.   The aspirant is
then enabled to play in such a masterly manner that the
trees dance and waterfalls stop at his music. §
 The Havmand, or Merman, is described as of a handsome
form, with green or black hair and beard.   He dwells either
in the bottom of the sea, or in the cliffs and hills near the
sea shore, and is regarded as rather a good and beneficent
kind of being.‖
 The Havfrue, or Mermaid, is represented in the popular
tradition sometimes as a good, at other times as an evil and
treacherous being.   She is beautiful in her appearance.

---

   * As sung in West Gothland and Vermland.
    † *Fosse* is the North of England *force.*
  ‡ Or a white kid, Faye *ap.* Grimm, Deut. Mythol., p. 461.
 § The Strömkarl has eleven different measures, to ten of which alone
people may dance ; the eleventh belongs to the night spirit his host.   If any
one plays it, tables and benches, cans and cups, old men and women, blind
and lame, even the children in the cradle, begin to dance.—Arndt. *ut sup.*,
see above p. 80.
 ‖ In the Danske Viser and Folkesagn there are a few stories of Mermen,
such as Rosmer Havmand and Marstig's Daughter, both translated by Dr.
Jamieson, and Agnete and the Merman, which resembles Proud Margaret.   It
was natural, says Afzelius, that what in Sweden was related of a Hill King,
should, in Denmark, be ascribed to a Merman.

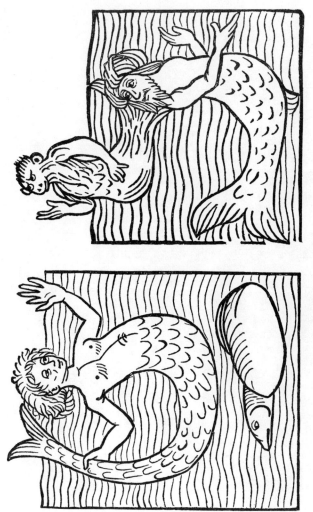

Mermaids and Mermen

The Knight and the Gnomes

Fishermen sometimes see her in the bright summer's sun, when a thin mist hangs over the sea, sitting on the surface of the water, and combing her long golden hair with a golden comb, or driving up her snow-white cattle to feed on the strands and small islands. At other times she comes as a beautiful maiden, chilled and shivering with the cold of the night, to the fires the fishers have kindled, hoping by this means to entice them to her love.* Her appearance prognosticates both storm and ill success in their fishing. People that are drowned, and whose bodies are not found, are believed to be taken into the dwellings of the Mermaids. These beings are also supposed to have the power of fore-telling future events. A Mermaid, we are told, prophesied the birth of Christian IV. of Denmark, and

> En Havfrue op af Vandet steg,
> Og spaade Herr Sinklar ilde.
> SINCLAR'S VISA.

> A mermaid from the water rose,
> And spaed Sir Sinclar ill.

Fortune-telling has been in all countries a gift of the sea-people. We need hardly mention the prophecies of Nereus and Proteus.

A girl one time fell into the power of a Havfrue and passed fifteen years in her submarine abode without ever seeing the sun. At length her brother went down in quest of her, and succeeded in bringing her back to the upper world. The Havfrue waited for seven years expecting her return, but when she did not come back, she struck the water with her staff and made it boil up and cried—

> Hade jag trott att du varit så falsk,
> Så skulle jag kreckt dig din tiufvehals !

> Had I but known thee so false to be,
> Thy thieving neck I'd have cracked for thee.†

---

* The appearance of the Wood-woman (*Skogsfru*) or Elve-woman, is equally unlucky for hunters. She also approaches the fires, and seeks to seduce young men.

† Arvidsson, ii. 320, *ap.* Grimm, p. 463.

Duke Magnus and the Mermaid.

DUKE MAGNUS looked out through the castle window,
How the stream ran so rapidly;
And there he saw how upon the stream sat
A woman most fair and lovelie,
    Duke Magnus, Duke Magnus, plight thee to me,
    I pray you still so freely;
    Say me not nay, but yes, yes!

" O, to you I will give a travelling ship,
The best that a knight would guide;
It goeth as well on water as on firm land,
And through the fields all so wide.
    Duke Magnus, &c.

" O, to you will I give a courser gray,
The best that a knight would ride;
He goeth as well on water as on firm land,
And through the groves all so wide."
    Duke Magnus, &c.

" O, how should I plight me to you?
I never any quiet get;
I serve the king and my native land,
But with woman I match me not yet."
    Duke Magnus, &c.

" To you will I give as much of gold
As for more than your life will endure;
And of pearls and precious stones handfuls;
And all shall be so pure."
    Duke Magnus, &c.

" O gladly would I plight me to thee,
If thou wert of Christian kind;
But now thou art a vile sea-troll,
My love thou canst never win."
    Duke Magnus, &c.

"Duke Magnus, Duke Magnus, bethink thee well,
And answer not so haughtily;
For if thou wilt not plight thee to me,
Thou shalt ever crazy be."
    Duke Magnus, &c.

"I am a king's son so good,
How can I let you gain me?
You dwell not on land, but in the flood,
Which would not with me agree."
    Duke Magnus, Duke Magnus, plight thee to me,
    I offer you still so freely;
    Say me not nay, but yes, yes! *

---

* This is a ballad from Småland. Magnus was the youngest son of Gustavus Vasa. He died out of his mind. It is well known that insanity pervaded the Vasa family for centuries.

NORTHERN ISLANDS.

Här Necken sin Harpa i Glasborgen slår,
Och Hafsfruar kamma sitt grönskande hår,
Och bleka den skinande drägten.
                                        STAGNELIUS.

The Neck here his harp in the glass-castle plays,
And Mermaidens comb out their green hair always,
And bleach here their shining white clothes.

UNDER the title of Northern Islands we include all those
lying in the ocean to the north of Scotland, to wit Iceland,
the Feroes, Shetland, and the Orkneys.

These islands were all peopled from Norway and Denmark
during the ninth century. Till that time many of them,
particularly Iceland and the Feroes, though, perhaps, occasionally visited by stray Vikings, or by ships driven out
of their course by tempests, had lain waste and desert from
the creation, the abode alone of wild beasts and birds.

But at that period the proud nobles of Norway and
Denmark, who scorned to be the vassals of Harold Fair-
hair and Gorm the Old, the founders of the Norwegian and
Danish monarchies, set forth in quest of new settlements,
where, at a distance from these haughty potentates, they
might live in the full enjoyment of their beloved indepen-
dence. Followed by numerous vassals, they embarked on
the wide Atlantic. A portion fixed themselves on the
distant shores of Iceland; others took possession of the
vacant Feroes; and more dispossessed the Peti and Papæ,
the ancient inhabitants of Shetland and the Orkneys, and
seized on their country.

As the Scandinavians were at that time still worshipers
of Thor and Odin, the belief in Alfs and Dwarfs accom-

panied them to their new abodes, and there, as elsewhere, survived the introduction of Christianity. We now
proceed to examine the vestiges of the old religion still to
be traced.

ICELAND.

Hvad mon da ei
Og her lyksalig leves kan? Jeg troer
Det mueligt, som för i Heden-Old
For raske Skander mueligt det var,
Paa denne kolde Öe.

ISLANDSKE LANDLEVNET.

What! cannot one
Here, too, live happy? I believe it now
As possible, as in the heathen age,
For the bold Scandinavians it was,
On this cold isle.

IT is in vain that we look into the works of travellers for
information on the subject of popular belief in Iceland.
Their attention was too much occupied by Geysers, volca-
noes, agriculture, and religion, to allow them to devote any
part of it to this, in their eyes, unimportant subject. So
that, were it not for some short but curious notices given by
natives of the island, we should be quite ignorant of the
fate of the subordinate classes of the old religion in Iceland.

Torfæus, who wrote in the latter end of the seventeenth
century, gives, in his preface to his edition of Hrolf Krakas
Saga, the opinion of a venerable Icelandic pastor, named
Einar Gudmund, respecting the Dwarfs. This opinion
Torfæus heard when a boy from the lips of the old man.

" I believe, and am fully persuaded," said he, " that this
people are the creatures of God, consisting of a body and
a rational spirit; that they are of both sexes; marry, and
have children; and that all human acts take place among
them as with us: that they are possessed of cattle, and of
many other kinds of property; have poverty and riches,
weeping and laughter, sleep and wake, and have all other

affections belonging to human nature; and that they enjoy a longer or a shorter term of life according to the will and pleasure of God. Their power of having children," he adds, "appears from this, that some of their women have had children by men, and were very anxious to have their offspring dipped in the sacred font, and initiated into Christianity; but they, in general, sought in vain. Thorkatla Mari, the wife of Kari, was pregnant by a Hill-man, but she did not bring the child Aresus into the world, as appears from the poems made on this fatal occasion.

"There was formerly on the lands of Haga a nobleman named Sigvard Fostre, who had to do with a Hill-woman. He promised her faithfully that he would take care to have the child received into the bosom of the church. In due time the woman came with her child and laid it on the churchyard wall, and along with it a gilded cup and a holy robe (presents she intended making to the church for the baptism of her child), and then retired a little way. The pastor inquired who acknowledged himself the father of the child. Sigvard, perhaps, out of shame, did not venture to acknowledge himself. The clerk now asked him if it should be baptised or not. Sigvard said ' No,' lest by assenting he should be proved to be the father. The infant then was left where it was, untouched and unbaptised. The mother, filled with rage, snatched up her babe and the cup, but left the vestment, the remains of which may still be seen in Haga. That woman foretold and inflicted a singular disease on Sigvard and his posterity till the ninth generation, and several of his descendants are to this day afflicted with it. Andrew Gudmund (from which I am the seventh in descent) had an affair of the same kind. He also refused to have the child baptised, and he and his posterity have suffered a remarkable disease, of which very many of them have died; but some, by the interposition of good men, have escaped the deserved punishment."

The fullest account we have of the Icelandic Elves or Dwarfs is contained in the following passage of the Ecclesiastical History of Iceland of the learned Finnus Johannæus.

"As we have not as yet," says he, "spoken a single word about the very ancient, and I know not whether more r:diculous or perverse, persuasion of our forefathers about semigods, this seems the proper place for saying a few words about this so celebrated figment, as it was chiefly in this period it attained its acmè, and it was believed as a true and necessary article of faith, that there are genii or semigods, called in our language Alfa and Alfa-folk.

" Authors vary respecting their essence and origin. Some hold that they have been created by God immediately and without the intervention of parents, like some kinds of spirits : others maintain that they are sprung from Adam, but before the creation of Eve :* lastly, some refer them to another race of men, or to a stock of præ-Adamites. Some bestow on them not merely a human body, but an immortal soul: others assign them merely mortal breath (*spiritum*) instead of a soul, whence a certain blockhead,† in an essay written by him respecting them, calls them our half-kin (*half-kyn*).

"According to the old wives' tales that are related about this race of genii who inhabit Iceland and its vicinity, they have a political form of government modelled after the same pattern as that which the inhabitants themselves are under. Two viceroys rule over them, who in turn every second year, attended by some of the subjects, sail to Norway, to present themselves before the monarch of the whole

---

* This was plainly a theory of the monks. It greatly resembles the Rabbinical account of the origin of the Mazckeen, which the reader will meet in the sequel.

Some Icelanders of the present day say, that one day, when Eve was washing her children at the running water, God suddenly called her. She was frightened, and thrust aside such of them as were not clean. God asked her if all her children were there, and she said, Yes ; but got for answer, that what she tried to hide from God should be hidden from man. These children became instantly invisible and distinct from the rest. Before the flood came on, God put them into a cave and closed up the entrance. From them are descended all the underground-people.—Magnussen, *Eddalære.*

† This was one Janus Gudmund, who wrote several treatises on this and similar subjects, particularly one " De Alfis et Alfheimum," which the learned bishop characterises as a work " nullius pretii, et meras nugas continens." We might, if we were to see it, be of a different opinion. Of Janus Gudmund Brynj Svenonius thus expresses himself to Wormius : *Janus Gudmundius, ære dirutus verius quam rude donatus, sibi et aliis inutilis in angulo* ronscnuit. Worm., Epist., 970.

race, who resides there, and to give him a true report concerning the fidelity, good conduct, and obedience of the
subjects ; and those who accompany them are to accuse the
government or viceroys if they have transgressed the bounds
of justice or of good morals. If these are convicted of
crime or injustice, they are forthwith stript of their office,
and others are appointed in their place.

"This nation is reported to cultivate justice and equity
above all other virtues, and hence, though they are very
potent, especially with words and imprecations, they very
rarely, unless provoked or injured, do any mischief to man ;
but when irritated they avenge themselves on their enemies
with dreadful curses and punishments.

" The new-born infants of Christians are, before baptism,
believed to be exposed to great peril of being stolen by
them, and their own, which they foresee likely to be feeble in
mind, in body, in beauty, or other gifts, being substituted
for them. These supposititious children of the semigods are
called Umskiptingar ; whence nurses and midwives were
strictly enjoined to watch constantly, and to hold the infant
firmly in their arms, till it had had the benefit of baptism,
lest they should furnish any opportunity for such a change.
Hence it comes, that the vulgar use to call fools, deformed
people, and those who act rudely and uncivilly, *Umskiptinga
eins og hann sie ko minnaf Alfum*, *i.e.* changelings, and come
of the Alfs.

" They use rocks, hills, and even the seas, for their habitations, which withinside are neat, and all their domestic
utensils extremely clean and orderly. They sometimes
invite men home, and take especial delight in the converse
of Christians, some of whom have had intercourse with their
daughters or sisters, who are no less wanton than beautiful,
and have had children by them, who must by all means be
washed in holy water, that they may receive an immortal
soul, and one that can be saved. Nay, they have not been
ashamed to feign that certain women of them have been
joined in lawful marriage with men, and continued for a
long time with them, happily at first, but, for the most part,
with an ill or tragical conclusion.

" Their cattle, if not very numerous, are at least very pro-
fitable   They are invisible as their owners are, unless when

it pleases them to appear, which usually takes place when the
weather is serene and the sun shining very bright; for as
they do not see the sun within their dwellings, they frequently
walk out in the sunshine that they may be cheered by his
radiance.* Hence, even the coffins of dead kings and nobles,
such as are the oblong stones which are to be seen here and
there, in wildernesses and rough places, always lie in the open
air and exposed to the sun.

"They change their abodes and habitations occasionally
like mankind; this they do on new-year's night; whence
certain dreamers and mountebanks used on that night to
watch in the roads, that, by the means of various forms of
conjurations appointed for that purpose, they might extort
from them as they passed along the knowledge of future
events.† But people in general, who were not acquainted
with such things, especially the heads of families, used on
this evening strictly to charge their children and servants
to be sure to be serious and modest in their actions and
language, lest their invisible guests, and mayhap future
neighbours, should be aggrieved or any way offended.
Hence, when going to bed they did not shut the outer doors
of their houses, nor even the door of the sitting-room, but
having kindled a light, and laid out a table, they desired the
invisible personages who had arrived, or were to arrive, to
partake, if it was their pleasure, of the food that was laid out
for them; and hoped that if it pleased them to dwell within
the limits of their lands, they would live safe and sound,
and be propitious to them. As this superstitious belief
is extremely ancient, so it long continued in full vigour,
and was held by some even within the memory of our
fathers."‡

* The Icelandic dwarfs, it would appear, wore red clothes. In Nial's Saga
(p. 70), a person gaily dressed (*i litklœdum*) is jocularly called Red-elf
(*raud-álfr*).

† There was a book of prophecies called the *Kruckspá*, or Prophecy of
Kruck, a man who was said to have lived in the 15th century. It treated of
the change of religion and other matters said to have been revealed to him by
the Dwarfs. Johannæus says it was forged by Brynjalf Svenonius in or about
the year 1660.

‡ Finni Johannæi Historia Ecclesiastica Islandiæ, tom. ii. p. 368. Havniæ,
1774. We believe we might safely add, is held at the present day, for the
superstition is no more extinct in Iceland than elsewhere.

The Icelandic Neck, Kelpie, or Water-Spirit, is called Nickur, Ninnir, and Hnikur, one of the Eddaic names of Odin. He appears always in the form of a fine *apple-grey* horse on the sea-shore; but he may be distinguished from ordinary horses by the circumstance of his hoofs being reversed. If any one is so foolish as to mount him, he gallops off, and plunges into the sea with his burden. He can, however, be caught in a particular manner, tamed, and made to work.*

The Icelanders have the same notions respecting the seals which we shall find in the Feroes and Shetland. It is a common opinion with them that King Pharaoh and his army were changed into these animals.

FEROES.

◆

Sjûrur touk teâ besta svör
Sum Dvörgurin heji smuja.
QVÖRFINS THAATTUR.

Sigurd took the very best sword
That the Dwarfs had ever smithed.

THE people of the Feroes believe in the same classes of beings as the inhabitants of the countries whence their ancestors came.

They call the Trolls Underground-people, Hollow-men, Foddenskkmænd, and Huldefolk. These Trolls used frequently to carry people into their hills, and detain them there. Among several other instances, Debes† gives the following one of this practice:

" Whilst Mr. Taale was priest in Osteröe, it happened

---

* Svenska Visor, iii. 128. Grimm, Deut. Mythol., p. 458. At Bahus, in Sweden, a clever man contrived to throw on him an ingeniously made bridle so that he could not get away, and he ploughed all his land with him. One time the bridle fell off and the Neck, like a flash of fire, sprang into the lake and dragged the harrow down with him. Grimm, *ut sup.*, see p. 148.

† Færoæ et Færoa reserata. Lond. 1676.

that one of his hearers was carried away and returned again.
At last the said young man being to be married, and every
thing prepared, and the priest being arrived the Saturday
before at the parish, the bridegroom was carried away;
wherefore they sent folks to look after him, but he could
not be found. The priest desired his friends to have good
courage, and that he would come again; which he did at
last, and related that the spirit that led him away was in the
shape of a most beautiful woman, and very richly dressed,
who desired him to forsake her whom he was now to marry,
and consider how ugly his mistress was in comparison of her,
and what fine apparel she had. He said also that he saw the
men that sought after him, and that they went close by him
but could not see him, and that he heard their calling, and
yet could not answer them; but that when he would not be
persuaded he was again left at liberty."

The people of the Feroes call the Nisses or Brownies
Niägruisar, and describe them as little creatures with red
caps on their heads, that bring luck to any place where they
take up their abode.

It is the belief of the people of these islands that every
ninth-night the seals put off their skins and assume the
human form, and dance and sport about on the land. After
some time, they resume their skins and return to the water.
The following adventure, it is said, once occurred: *

" A man happening to pass by where a female seal was
disporting herself in the form of a woman, found her skin,
and took and hid it. When she could not find her skin to
creep into, she was forced to remain in the human form; and
as she was fair to look upon, that same man took her to wife,
had children by her, and lived right happily with her. After
a long time, the wife found the skin that had been stolen,
and could not resist the temptation to creep into it, and so
she became a seal again, and returned to the sea."

The Neck called Nikar is also an object of popular faith in
the Feroes. He inhabits the streams and lakes, and takes a
delight in drowning people.

---

* Thiele, iii. 51, from the MS. Travels of Svaboe in the Feroes.

SHETLAND.

Well, since we are welcome to Yule,
Up wi't Lightfoot, link it awa', boys!
Send for a fiddler, play up Foula reel,
The Shaalds will pay for a', boys.

SHETLAND SONG.

DR. HIBBERT's valuable work on the Shetland Islands *
fortunately enables us to give a tolerably complete account
of the fairy system of these islands.

The Shetlanders, he informs us, believe in two kinds of
Trows, as they call the Scandinavian Trolls, those of the land
and those of the sea.

The former, whom, like the Scots, they also term the *guid
folk* and *guid neighbours*, they conceive to inhabit the interior
of green hills. Persons who have been brought into their
habitations have been dazzled with the splendour of what
they saw there. All the interior walls are adorned with gold
and silver, and the domestic utensils resemble the strange
things that are found sometimes lying on the hills. These
persons have always entered the hill on one side and gone out
at the other.

They marry and have children, like their northern kindred.
A woman of the island of Yell, who died not long since, at
the advanced age of more than a hundred years, said, that
she once met some fairy children, accompanied by a little
dog, playing like other boys and girls, on the top of a hill.
Another time she happened one night to raise herself up in
the bed, when she saw a little boy with a white nightcap on
his head, sitting at the fire. She asked him who he was.
" I am Trippa's son," said he. When she heard this, she
instantly *sained*, i. e. blessed herself, and Trippa's son
vanished.

* Description of the Shetland Islands. Edinburgh, 1822.

Saining is the grand protection against them; a Shetlander always sains himself when passing by their hills.

The Trows are of a diminutive stature, and they are usually dressed in gay green garments. When travelling from one place to another they may be seen mounted on bulrushes, and riding through the air. If a person should happen to meet them when on these journeys, he should, if he has not a bible in his pocket, draw a circle round him on the ground, and in God's name forbid their approach. They then generally disappear.*

They are fond of music and dancing, and it is their dancing that forms the fairy rings. A Shetlander lying awake in bed before day one morning, heard the noise of a party of Trows passing by his door. They were preceded by a piper, who was playing away lustily. The man happened to have a good ear for music, so he picked up the tune he heard played, and used often after to repeat it for his friends under the name of the Fairy-tune.

The Trows are not free from disease, but they are possessed of infallible remedies, which they sometimes bestow on their favourites. A man in the island of Unst had an earthen pot that contained an ointment of marvellous power. This he said he got from the hills, and, like the widow's cruise, its contents never failed.

They have all the picking and stealing propensities of the Scandinavian Trolls. The dairy-maid sometimes detects a Trow-woman secretly milking the cows in the byre. She sains herself, and the thief takes to flight so precipitately as to leave behind her a copper pan of a form never seen before

When they want beef or mutton on any festal occasion, they betake themselves to the Shetlanders' *scatholds* or town-mails, and with elf-arrows bring down their game. On these occasions they delude the eyes of the owner with the appearance of something exactly resembling the animal whom they have carried off, and by its apparent violent death by some accident. It is on this account that the flesh of such animals as have met a sudden or violent death is regarded as improper food.

A Shetlander, who is probably still alive, affirmed that he

---

* Edmonston's View, &c., of Zetland Islands. Edin. 1809.

was once taken into a hill by the Trows. Here one of the
first objects that met his view was one of his own cows, that
was brought in to furnish materials for a banquet.   He
regarded himself as being in rather a ticklish situation if it
were not for the protection of the Trow-women, by whose
favour he had been admitted within the hill.   On returning
home, he learned, to his great surprise, that at the very
moment he saw the cow brought into the hill, others had
seen her falling over the rocks.

Lying-in-women and "unchristened bairns" they regard
as lawful prize. The former they employ as wet-nurses, the
latter they of course rear up as their own. Nothing will
induce parents to show any attention to a child that they
suspect of being a changeling. But there are persons who
undertake to enter the hills and regain the lost child.

A tailor, not long since, related the following story. He
was employed to work at a farm-house where there was a
child that was an idiot, and who was supposed to have been
left there by the Trows instead of some proper child, whom
they had taken into the hills.   One night, after he had
retired to his bed, leaving the idiot asleep by the fire, he was
suddenly waked out of his sleep by the sound of music, and
on looking about him he saw the whole room full of fairies,
who were dancing away their rounds most joyously.   Suddenly the idiot jumped up and joined in the dance, and
showed such a degree of acquaintance with the various steps
and movements as plainly testified that it must have been a
long time since he first went under the hands of the dancing-
master.   The tailor looked on for some time with admiration,
but at last he grew alarmed and *sained* himself.   On hearing
this, the Trows all fled in the utmost disorder, but one of
them, a woman, was so incensed at this interruption of their
revels, that as she went out she touched the big toe of the
tailor, and he lost the power of ever after moving it.*

In these cases of paralysis they believe that the Trows
have taken away the sound member and left a log behind.
They even sometimes sear the part, and from the want of
sensation in it boast of the correctness of this opinion.†

* We need hardly to remind the reader that in what precedes Dr. Hibbert
is to be regarded as the narrator in 1822.

† Edmonston, *ut supra*.

With respect to the Sea-Trows, it is the belief of the Shet-landers that they inhabit a region of their own at the bottom of the sea.* They here respire a peculiar atmosphere, and live in habitations constructed of the choicest submarine productions. When they visit the upper world on occasions of business or curiosity, they are obliged to enter the skin of some animal capable of respiring in the water. One of the shapes they assume is that of what is commonly called a merman or mermaid, human from the waist upwards, termi-nating below in the tail of a fish. But their most favourite vehicle is the skin of the larger seal or Haaf fish, for as this animal is amphibious they can land on some rock, and there cast off their sea-dress and assume their own shape, and amuse themselves as they will in the upper world. They must, however, take especial care of their skins, as each has but one, and if that should be lost, the owner can never re-descend, but must become an inhabitant of the supramarine world.

The following Shetland tales will illustrate this :—

Gioga's Son.

——◆——

A BOAT'S-CREW landed one time upon one of the stacks † with the intention of attacking the seals. They had consi-derable success; stunned several of them, and while they lay stupefied, stripped them of their skins, with the fat attached to them. They left the naked carcases lying on the rocks, and were about to get into their boat with their spoils and return to Papa Stour, whence they had come. But just as they were embarking, there rose such a tremendous swell that they saw there was not a moment to be lost, and every one flew as quickly as he could to get on board the boat. They were all successful but one man, who had imprudently loitered behind. His companions were very unwilling to leave him on the skerries, perhaps to perish, but the surge

* Dr. Hibbert says he could get but little satisfaction from the Shetlanders respecting this submarine country.
        † *Stacks* or *skerries* are bare rocks out in the sea.

increased so fast, that after many unsuccessful attempts to bring the boat in close to the stacks, they were obliged to depart, and leave the unfortunate man to his fate.

A dark stormy night came on, the sea dashed most furiously against the rocks, and the poor deserted Shetlander saw no prospect before him but that of dying of the cold and hunger, or of being washed into the sea by the breakers, which now threatened every moment to run over the stack.

At length he perceived several of the seals, who had escaped from the boatmen, approaching the skerry. When they landed they stripped off their seal-skin dresses and appeared in their proper forms of Sea-Trows. Their first object was to endeavour to recover their friends, who lay stunned and skinless. When they had succeeded in bringing them to themselves, they also resumed their proper form, and appeared in the shape of the sub-marine people. But in mournful tones, wildly accompanied by the raging storm, they lamented the loss of their sea-vestures, the want of which would for ever prevent them from returning to their native abodes beneath the deep waters of the Atlantic. Most of all did they lament for Ollavitinus, the son of Gioga, who, stripped of his seal-skin, must abide for ever in the upper world.

Their song was at length broken off by their perceiving the unfortunate boatman, who, with shivering limbs and despairing looks, was gazing on the furious waves that now dashed over the stack. Gioga, when she saw him, instantly conceived the design of rendering the perilous situation of the man of advantage to her son. She went up to him, and mildly addressed him, proposing to carry him on her back through the sea to Papa Stour, on condition of his getting ner the seal-skin of her son.

The bargain was soon made, and Gioga equipped herself in her phocine garb; but when the Shetlander gazed on the stormy sea he was to ride through, his courage nearly failed him, and he begged of the old lady to have the kindness to allow him to cut a few holes in her shoulders and flanks, that he might obtain a better fastening for his hands between the skin and the flesh.

This, too, her maternal tenderness induced Gioga to consent to. The man, having prepared everything, now

mounted, and she plunged into the waves with him, gallantly
ploughed the deep, and landed him safe and sound at Acres
Gio, in Papa Stour. He thence set out for Skeo, at Hamna
Voe, where the skin was, and honourably fulfilled his agreement by restoring to Gioga the means of bringing back her
son to his dear native land.

The Mermaid Wife.

ON a fine summer's evening, an inhabitant of Unst happened
to be walking along the sandy margin of a voe.* The moon
was risen, and by her light he discerned at some distance
before him a number of the sea-people, who were dancing
with great vigour on the smooth sand. Near them he saw
lying on the ground several seal-skins.

As the man approached the dancers, all gave over their
merriment, and flew like lightning to secure their garments;
then clothing themselves, plunged in the form of seals into the
sea. But the Shetlander, on coming up to the spot where
they had been, and casting his eyes down on the ground,
saw that they had left one skin behind them, which was
lying just at his feet. He snatched it up, carried it swiftly
away, and placed it in security.

On returning to the shore, he met the fairest maiden that
eye ever gazed upon: she was walking backwards and forwards, lamenting in most piteous tones the loss of her seal-
skin robe, without which she never could hope to rejoin her
family and friends below the waters, but must remain an
unwilling inhabitant of the region enlightened by the sun.

The man approached and endeavoured to console her, but
she would not be comforted. She implored him in the most
moving accents to restore her dress; but the view of her
lovely face, more beautiful in tears, had steeled his heart.
He represented to her the impossibility of her return, and

---

* A *voe* is a small bay.

that her friends would soon give her up; and finally, made an offer to her of his heart, hand, and fortune.

The sea-maiden, finding she had no alternative, at length consented to become his wife.   They were married, and lived together for many years, during which time they had several children, who retained no vestiges of their marine origin, saving a thin web between their fingers, and a bend of their hands, resembling that of the fore paws of a seal; distinctions which characterise the descendants of the family to the present day.

The Shetlander's love for his beautiful wife was unbounded, but she made but a cold return to his affection.   Often would she steal out alone and hasten down to the lonely strand, and there at a given signal, a seal of large size would make his appearance, and they would converse for hours together in an unknown language; and she would return home from this meeting pensive and melancholy.

Thus glided away years, and her hopes of leaving the upper world had nearly vanished, when it chanced one day, that one of the children, playing behind a stack of corn, found a seal-skin.   Delighted with his prize, he ran with breathless eagerness to display it before his mother.   Her eyes glistened with delight at the view of it; for in it she saw her own dress, the loss of which had cost her so many tears.   She now regarded herself as completely emancipated from thraldom; and in idea she was already with her friends beneath the waves.   One thing alone was a drawback on her raptures.   She loved her children, and she was now about to leave them for ever.   Yet they weighed not against the pleasures she had in prospect: so after kissing and embracing them several times, she took up the skin, went out, and proceeded down to the beach.

In a few minutes after the husband came in, and the children told him what had occurred.   The truth instantly flashed across his mind, and he hurried down to the shore with all the speed that love and anxiety could give.   But he only arrived in time to see his wife take the form of a seal, and from the ledge of a rock plunge into the sea.

The large seal, with whom she used to hold her conversations, immediately joined her, and congratulated her on her escape, and they quitted the shore together.   But ere she went she turned round to her husband, who stood in mute despair on the, rock, and whose misery excited feelings of compassion in her breast. "Farewell," said she to him, "and may all good fortune attend you. I loved you well while I was with you, but I always loved my first husband better."*

The water-spirit is in Shetland called Shoopiltee; he appears in the form of a pretty little horse, and endeavours to entice persons to ride on him, and then gallops with them into the sea.

ORKNEYS.

————◆————

Harold was born where restless seas
Howl round the storm-swept Orcades.

Scott.

OF the Orcadian Fairies we have very little information. Brand† merely tells us, they were, in his time, frequently seen in several of the isles dancing and making merry; so that we may fairly conclude they differed little from their Scottish and Shetland neighbours. One thing he adds, which is of some importance, that they were frequently seen in armour.

Brownie seems to have been the principal Orkney Fairy, where he possessed a degree of importance rather beyond what was allotted to him in the neighbouring realm of Scotland.

"Not above forty or fifty years ago," says Brand, "almost every family had a Brownie, or evil spirit, so called, which served them, to whom they gave a sacrifice for its service; as, when they churned their milk, they took a part thereof and sprinkled every corner of the house with it for Brownie's

---

* See below, *Germany.*
† Description of Orkney, Zetland, &c. Edin. 1703.

use; likewise, when they brewed, they had a stone which they called Brownie's stone, wherein there was a little hole, into which they poured some wort for a sacrifice to Brownie. My informer, a minister of the country, told me that he had conversed with an old man, who, when young, used to brew and sometimes read upon his bible; to whom an old woman in the house said that Brownie was displeased with that book he read upon, which, if he continued to do, they would get no more service of Brownie. But he being better instructed from that book which was Brownie's eyesore, and the object of his wrath, when he brewed, he would not suffer any sacrifice to be given to Brownie; whereupon, the first and second brewings were spilt and for no use, though the wort wrought well, yet in a little time it left off working and grew cold; but of the third browst or brewing, he had ale very good, though he would not give any sacrifice to Brownie, with whom afterwards they were no more troubled. I had also from the same informer, that a lady in Unst, now deceased, told him that when she first took up house, she refused to give a sacrifice to Brownie, upon which, the first and second brewings misgave, but the third was good; and Brownie, not being regarded and rewarded as formerly he had been, abandoned his wonted service: which cleareth the Scripture, 'Resist the devil and he will flee from you.' They also had stacks of corn which they called Brownie's stacks, which, though they were not bound with straw ropes, or any way fenced as other stacks use to be, yet the greatest storm of wind was not able to blow anything off them."

A very important personage once, we are told, inhabited the Orkneys in the character of Brownie.

"Luridan," says Reginald Scot, "a familiar of this kind, did for many years inhabit the island of Pomonia, the largest of the Orkades in Scotland, supplying the place of man-servant and maid-servant with wonderful diligence to those families whom he did haunt, sweeping their rooms and washing their dishes, and making their fires before any were up in the morning. This Luridan affirmed, that he was the *genius Astral* of that island; that his place or residence in the days of Solomon and David was at Jerusalem; that then he was called by the Jews Belelah; after that, he remained long in the dominion of Wales, instructing their bards in

British poesy and prophecies, being called Wrthin, Wadd, Elgin; 'and now,' said he, 'I have removed hither, and, alas! my continuance is but short, for in seventy years I must resign my place to Balkin, lord of the Northern Mountains.'

"Many wonderful and incredible things did he also relate of this Balkin, affirming that he was shaped like a satyr, and fed upon the air, having wife and children to the number of twelve thousand, which were the brood of the Norther_ Fairies, inhabiting Southerland and Catenes, with the adjacent islands. And that these were the companies of spirits that hold continual wars with the fiery spirits in the mountain Heckla, that vomits fire in Islandia. That their speech was ancient Irish, and their dwelling the caverns of the rocks and mountains, which relation is recorded in the antiquities of Pomonia."*

Concerning Luridan, we are farther informed from the Book of Vanagastus, the Norwegian, that it is his nature to be always at enmity with fire; that he wages war with the fiery spirits of Hecla; and that in this contest they do often anticipate and destroy one another, killing and crushing when they meet in mighty and violent troops in the air upon the sea. And at such times, many of the fiery spirits are destroyed when the enemy hath brought them off the mountains to fight upon the water. On the contrary, when the battle is upon the mountain itself, the spirits of the air are often worsted, and then great moanings and doleful noises are heard in Iceland, and Russia, and Norway, for many days after.†

The Water-spirit called Tangie, from Tang, the sea-weed with which he is covered, appears sometimes as a little horse, other times as a man.

---

* Reg. Scot. Discoverie of Witchcraft, b. 2. c. 4. Lond. 1665.
† Quarterly Review, vol. xxii. p. 367

ISLE OF RÜGEN.

Des Tagscheins Blendung drückt,
Nur Finsterniss beglückt;
Drum hausen wir so gern
Tief in des Erdballs Kern.

MATTHISSON.

Day's dazzling light annoys
Us, darkness only joys;
We therefore love to dwell
Deep underneath earth's shell.

WE now return to the Baltic, to the Isle of Rügen, once a chief seat of the Vendish religion; but its priests were massacred by the Scandinavians, and all traces of their system effaced. Its fairy mythology now agrees with that of its Gothic neighbours, and Mr. Arndt,* a native of the island, has enabled us to give the following tolerably full account of it:—

The inhabitants of Rügen believe in three kinds of Dwarfs, or underground people, the White, the Brown, and the Black; so named from the colour of their several habiliments.†

The White are the most delicate and beautiful of all, and are of an innocent and gentle disposition. During the winter, when the face of nature is cold, raw, and cheerless, they remain still and quiet in their hills, solely engaged in the fashioning of the finest works in silver and gold, of too delicate a texture for mortal eyes to discern. Thus they pass the winter; but no sooner does the spring return than they abandon their recesses, and live through all the

---

* Arndt, Märchen und Jugenderinnerungen. Berlin, 1818.
† See above p. 96.

summer above ground, in sunshine and starlight, in uninterrupted revelry and enjoyment. The moment the trees and flowers begin to sprout and bud in the early days of spring, they emerge from their hills, and get among the stalks and branches, and thence to the blossoms and flowers, where they sit and gaze around them. In the night, when mortals sleep, the White Dwarfs come forth, and dance their joyous roundels in the green grass, about the hills, and brooks, and springs, making the sweetest and most delicate music, bewildering travellers, who hear and wonder at the strains of the invisible musicians. They may, if they will, go out by day, but never in company; these daylight rambles being allowed them only when alone and under some assumed form. They therefore frequently fly about in the shape of party-coloured little birds, or butterflies, or snow-white doves, showing kindness and benevolence to the good who merit their favour.

The Brown Dwarfs, the next in order, are less than eighteen inches high. They wear little brown coats and jackets, and a brown cap on their head, with a little silver bell in it. Some of them wear black shoes with red strings in them; in general, however, they wear fine glass ones; at their dances none of them wear any other. They are very handsome in their persons, with clear light-coloured eyes, and small and most beautiful hands and feet. They are on the whole of a cheerful, good-natured disposition, mingled with some roguish traits. Like the White Dwarfs, they are great artists in gold and silver, working so curiously as to astonish those who happen to see their performances. At night they come out of their hills and dance by the light of the moon and stars. They also glide invisibly into people's houses, their caps rendering them imperceptible by all who have not similar caps. They are said to play all kinds of tricks, to change the children in the cradles, and take them away. This charge is perhaps unfounded, but certainly, children who fall into their hands must serve them for fifty years. They possess an unlimited power of transformation, and can pass through the smallest keyholes. Frequently they bring with them presents for children, or lay gold rings and ducats, and the like, in their way, and often are invisibly present, and save them from the perils of

fire and water. They plague and annoy lazy men-servants
and untidy maids with frightful dreams ; oppress them as
the nightmare ; bite them as fleas ; and scratch and tear
them like cats and dogs ; and often in the night frighten,
in the shape of owls, thieves and lovers, or, like Will-'o-the-
wisps, lead them astray into bogs and marshes, and perhaps
up to those who are in pursuit of them.

The Black Dwarfs wear black jackets and caps, are not
handsome like the others, but on the contrary are horridly
ugly, with weeping eyes, like blacksmiths and colliers. They
are most expert workmen, especially in steel, to which they
can give a degree at once of hardness and flexibility which
no human smith can imitate ; for the swords they make will
bend like rushes, and are as hard as diamonds. In old times
arms and armour made by them were in great request : shirts
of mail manufactured by them were as fine as cobwebs, and
yet no bullet would penetrate them, and no helm or corslet
could resist the swords they fashioned ; but all these things
are now gone out of use.

These Dwarfs are of a malicious, ill disposition, and
delight in doing mischief to mankind ; they are unsocial, and
there are seldom more than two or three of them seen together ; they keep mostly in their hills, and seldom come out
in the daytime, nor do they ever go far from home.
People say that in the summer they are fond of sitting under
the elder trees, the smell of which is very grateful to them,
and that any one that wants anything of them must go there
and call them. Some say they have no music and dancing,
only howling and whimpering ; and that when a screaming
is heard in the woods and marshes, like that of crying children, and a mewing and screeching like that of a multitude
of cats or owls, the sounds proceed from their midnight
assemblies, and are made by the vociferous Dwarfs.

The principal residence of the two first classes of the
underground-people in Rügen is what are called the Nine-
hills, near Rambin.   These hills lie on the west point of the
island, about a quarter of a mile from the village of Rambin
in the open country.   They are small mounds, or Giants'
graves (*Hünengräber*), as such are called, and are the subject of many a tale and legend among the people.   The
account of their origin is as follows :—

"A long, long time ago there lived in Rügen a mighty Giant named Balderich. He was vexed that the country was an island, and that he had always to wade through the sea when he wanted to go to Pomerania and the main land. He accordingly got an immense apron made, and he tied it round his waist and filled it with earth, for he wanted to make a dam of earth for himself from the island to the main-land. As he was going with his load over Rodenkirchen, a hole tore in the apron, and the clay that fell out formed the Nine-hills. He stopped the hole and went on; but when he had gotten to Gustau, another hole tore in the apron, and thirteen little hills fell out. He proceeded to the sea with what he had now remaining, and pouring the earth into the waters, formed the hook of Prosnitz, and the pretty little peninsula of Drigge. But there still remained a small space between Rügen and Pomerania, which so incensed the Giant that he fell down in a fit and died, from which unfortunate accident his dam was never finished." *

A Giant-maiden commenced a similar operation on the Pomeranian side "in order," said she, "that I may be able to go over the bit of water without wetting my little slip-pers." So she filled her apron with sand and hurried down to the sea-side. But there was a hole in the apron and just behind Sagard a part of the sand ran out and formed a little hill named Dubbleworth. "Ah!" said she, "now my mother will scold me." She stopped the hole with her hand and ran on as fast as she could. But her mother looked over the wood and cried, "You nasty child, what are you about? Come here and you shall get a good whip-ping." The daughter in a fright let go the apron, and all the sand ran out and formed the barren hills near Litzow.†

The Dwarfs took up their abode in the Nine-hills. The

---

* A Danish legend (Thiele, i. 79) tells the same of the sand-hills of Nestved in Zealand. A Troll who dwelt near it wished to destroy it, and for that purpose he went down to the sea-shore and filled his wallet with sand and threw it on his back. Fortunately there was a hole in the wallet, and so many sand-hills fell out of it, that when he came to Nestved there only remained enough to form one hill more. Another Troll, to punish a farmer, filled one of his gloves with sand, which sufficed to cover his victim's house completely. With what remained in the fingers he formed a row of hillocks near it. † Grimm, Deut. Myth., p. 502.

White ones own two of them, and the Brown ones seven,
for there are no Black ones there. These dwell chiefly on
the coast-hills, along the shore between the Ahlbeck and
Mönchgut, where they hold their assemblies, and plunder
the ships that are wrecked on the coast.

The Neck is called in Rügen Nickel. Some fishers once
launched their boat on a lonely lake. Next day when they
came they saw it in a high beech-tree. "Who the devil has
put the boat in the tree?" cried one. A voice replied, but
they saw no one, "'Twas no devil at all, but I and my
brother Nickel." *

The following stories Mr. Arndt, who, as we have
observed, is a native of Rügen, says he heard in his boyhood
from Hinrich Vieck, the Statthalter or Bailiff of Grabitz,
who abounded in these legends; "so that it is, properly
speaking," says he, "Hinrich Vieck, and not I, that relates."
We therefore see no reason to doubt of their genuineness,
though they may be a little embellished.†

Adventures of John Dietrich.

THERE once lived in Rambin an honest, industrious man,
named James Dietrich. He had several children, all of a
good disposition, especially the youngest, whose name was
John. John Dietrich was a handsome, smart boy, diligent
at school, and obedient at home. His great passion was for
hearing stories, and whenever he met any one who was well
stored, he never let them go till he had heard them all.

When John was about eight years old he was sent to
spend a summer with his uncle, a farmer in Rodenkirchen.

---

* Grimm, Deutsche Sagen, i. p. 70.
† Grimm also appears to regard them as genuine.

Here John had to keep cows with other boys, and they used to drive them to graze about the Nine-hills. There was an old cowherd, one Klas (*i. e.* Nick) Starkwolt, who used frequently to join the boys, and then they would sit down together and tell stories. Klas abounded in these, and he became John Dietrich's dearest friend. In particular, he knew a number of stories of the Nine-hills and the undergroundpeople in the old times, when the Giants disappeared from the country, and the little ones came into the hills. These tales John swallowed so eagerly that he thought of nothing else, and was for ever talking of golden cups, and crowns, and glass shoes, and pockets full of ducats, and gold rings, and diamond coronets, and snow-white brides, and such like. Old Klas used often to shake his head at him and say, "John! John! what are you about? The spade and sithe will be your sceptre and crown, and your bride will wear a garland of rosemary and a gown of striped drill." Still John almost longed to get into the Nine-hills; for Klas had told him that any one who by luck or cunning should get the cap of one of the little ones might go down with safety, and, instead of their making a servant of him, he would be their master. The person whose cap he got would be his servant, and obey all his commands.*

St. John's day, when the days are longest and the nights shortest, was now come. Old and young kept the holiday, had all sorts of piays, and told all kinds of stories. John could now no longer contain himself, but the day after the festival he slipt away to the Nine-hills, and when it grew dark laid himself down on the top of the highest of them, where Klas had told him the undergroundpeople had their principal dance-place. John lay quite still from ten till twelve at night. At last it struck twelve. Immediately there was a ringing and a singing in the hills, and then a whispering and a lisping and a whiz and a buzz all about him; for the little people were now some whirling round and round in the dance, and others sporting and tumbling about

---

* The population of Lusatia (*Lausatz*) is like that of Pomerania and Rügen, Vendish. Hence, perhaps, it is that in the Lusatian tale of the Fairy-sabbath, we meet with caps with bells, and a descent into the interior of a mountain in a kind of boat as in this tale: Wilcomm, Sagen und Märchen aus der Oberlausitz. Hanov. 1843. Blackwood's Magazine for June, 1844.

in the moonshine, and playing a thousand merry pranks and tricks. He felt a secret dread come over him at this whispering and buzzing, for he could see nothing of them, as the caps they wore made them invisible; but he lay quite still, with his face in the grass and his eyes fast shut, snoring a little, just as if he was asleep. Yet now and then he ventured to open his eyes a little and peep out, but not the slightest trace of them could he see, though it was bright moonlight.

It was not long before three of the underground-people came jumping up to where he was lying; but they took no heed of him, and flung their brown caps up into the air, and caught them from one another. At length one snatched the cap out of the hand of another and flung it away. It flew direct, and fell upon John's head. The moment he felt it he caught hold of it, and, standing up, bid farewell to sleep. He swung his cap about for joy, and made the little silver bell of it tingle, and then set it upon his head, and—O wonderful!—that instant he saw the countless and merry swarm of the little people.

The three little men came slily up to him, and thought by their nimbleness to get back the cap; but he held his prize fast, and they saw clearly that nothing was to be done in this way with him; for in size and strength John was a giant in comparison of these little fellows, who hardly came up to his knee. The owner of the cap now came up very humbly to the finder, and begged, in as supplicating a tone as if his life depended upon it, that he would give him back his cap. But "No," said John, "you sly little rogue, you'll get the cap no more. That's not the sort of thing that one gives away for buttered cake : I should be in a nice way with you if I had not something of yours ; but now you have no power over me, but must do what I please. And I will go down with you, and see how you live below, and you shall be my servant.—Nay, no grumbling, you know you must. I know that just as well as you do, for Klas Starkwolt told it to me often and often."

The little man looked as if he had not heard or understood one word of all this; he began all his crying and whining over again, and wept, and screamed, and howled most piteously for his little cap. But John cut the matter short by saying to him, "Have done; you are my servant, and I intend to take a trip with you." So he gave up, especially as the others told him that there was no remedy.

John now flung away his old hat, and put on the cap, and set it firm on his head, lest it should slip off or fly away, for all his power lay in the cap. He lost no time in trying its virtues, and commanded his new servant to fetch him food and drink. And the servant ran away like the wind, and in a second was there again with bottles of wine, and bread, and rich fruits. So John ate and drank, and looked on at the sports and the dancing of the little ones, and it pleased him right well, and he behaved himself stoutly and wisely, as if he was a born master.

When the cock had now crowed for the third time, and the little larks had made their first twirl in the sky, and the infant light appeared in solitary white streaks in the east, then it went hush, hush, hush, through the bushes, and flowers, and stalks; and the hills rang again, and opened up, and the little men went down. John gave close attention to everything, and found that it was exactly as he had been told. And behold! on the top of the hill, where they had just been dancing, and where all was full of grass and flowers, as people see it by day, there rose of a sudden, when the retreat was sounded, a bright glass point. Whoever wanted to go in stepped upon this; it opened, and he glided gently in, the glass closing again after him; and when they had all entered it vanished, and there was no farther trace of it to be seen. Those who descended through the glass point sank quite gently into a wide silver tun, which held them all, and could have easily harboured a thousand such little people. John and his man went down into such a one along with several others, all of whom screamed out and prayed him not to tread on them, for if his weight came on them they were dead men. He was, however, careful, and acted in a very friendly way toward them. Several tuns of this kind went up and down after each other, until all were in. They hung by long silver chains, which were drawn and held below.

In his descent John was amazed at the wonderful brilliancy of the walls between which the tun glided down. They were all, as it were, beset with pearls and diamonds, glittering and sparkling brightly, and below him he heard the most beautiful music tinkling at a distance, so that he did not know what was become of him, and from excess of pleasure he fell fast asleep.

He slept a long time, and when he awoke he found himself in the most beautiful bed that could be, such as he had never seen the like of in his father's house, and it was in the prettiest little chamber in the world, and his servant was beside him with a fan to keep away the flies and gnats. He had hardly opened his eyes when his little servant brought him a basin and towel, and held him the nicest new clothes of brown silk to put on, most beautifully made ; with these was a pair of new black shoes with red ribbons, such as John had never beheld in Rambin or in Rodenkirchen either. There were also there several pairs of beautiful shining glass shoes, such as are only used on great occasions. John was, we may well suppose, delighted to have such clothes to wear, and he put them upon him joyfully. His servant then flew like lightning and returned with a fine breakfast of wine and milk, and beautiful white bread and fruits, and such other things as little boys are fond of. He now perceived, every moment, more and more, that Klas Starkwolt, the old cowherd, knew what he was talking about, for the splendour and magnificence he saw here surpassed anything he had ever dreamt of. His servant, too, was the most obedient one possible : a nod or a sign was enough for him, for he was as wise as a bee, as all these little people are by nature.

John's bed-chamber was all covered with emeralds and other precious stones, and in the ceiling was a diamond as big as a nine-pin bowl, that gave light to the whole chamber. In this place they have neither sun, nor moon, nor stars to give them light ; neither do they use lamps or candles of any kind ; but they live in the midst of precious stones, and have the purest of gold and silver in abundance, and the skill to make it light both by day and by night, though, indeed, properly speaking, as there is no sun here, there is no distinction of day and night, and they reckon only by weeks. They set the brightest and clearest precious stones in their dwellings, and in the ways and passages leading under the ground, and in the places where they have their large halls, and their dances and feasts, where they sparkle so as to make it eternal day.

When John had finished his breakfast, his servant opened
a little door in the wall, where was a closet with the most
beautiful silver and gold cups and dishes and other vessels,
and baskets filled with ducats, and boxes of jewels and precious stones. There were also charming pictures, and the
most delightful story-books he had seen in the whole course
of his life.

John spent the morning looking at these things; and,
when it was mid-day, a bell rang, and his servant said, " Will
you dine alone, sir, or with the large company? "—" With
the large company, to be sure," replied John. So his servant
led him out. John, however, saw nothing but solitary halls,
lighted up with precious stones, and here and there little men
and women, who appeared to him to glide out of the clefts
and fissures of the rocks. Wondering what it was the bells
rang for, he said to his servant, " But where is the company?"
And scarcely had he spoken when the hall they were in
opened out to a great extent, and a canopy set with diamonds
and precious stones was drawn over it. At the same moment
he saw an immense throng of nicely-dressed little men and
women pouring in through several open doors: the floor
opened in several places, and tables, covered with the most
beautiful ware, and the most luscious meats, and fruits, and
wines, placed themselves beside each other, and the chairs
arranged themselves along the tables, and then the men and
women took their seats.

The principal persons now came forward, bowed to John,
and led him to their table, where they placed him among
their most beautiful maidens,—a distinction which pleased
John well. The party, too, was very merry, for the underground people are extremely lively and cheerful, and can
never stay long quiet. Then the most charming music
sounded over their heads; and beautiful birds, flying about,
sung most sweetly; and these were not real birds but artificial ones, which the little men make so ingeniously that they
can fly about and sing like natural ones.

The servants, of both sexes, who waited at table, and
handed about the gold cups, and the silver and crystal baskets
with fruit, were children belonging to this world, whom some
casualty or other had thrown among the undergroundpeople,
and who, having come down without securing any pledge,

were fallen into the power of the little ones. These were differently clad from them. The boys and girls were dressed in snow-white coats and jackets, and wore glass shoes, so fine that their steps could never be heard, with blue caps on their heads, and silver belts round their waists.

John at first pitied them, seeing how they were forced to run about and wait on the little people; but as they looked cheerful and happy, and were handsomely dressed, and had such rosy cheeks, he said to himself, " After all, they are not so badly off, and I was myself much worse when I had to be running after the cows and bullocks. To be sure, I am now a master here, and they are servants; but there is no help for it: why were they so foolish as to let themselves be taken and not get some pledge beforehand? At any rate, the time must come when they shall be set at liberty, and they will certainly not be longer than fifty years here." With these thoughts he consoled himself, and sported and played away with his little play-fellows, and ate, and drank, and made his servant and the others tell him stories, for he would know every thing exactly.

They sat at table about two hours; the principal person then rang a little bell, and the tables and chairs all vanished in a whiff, leaving the company all on their feet. The birds now struck up a most lively air, and the little people danced their rounds most merrily. When they were done, the joyous sets jumped, and leaped, and whirled themselves round and round, as if the world was grown dizzy. And the pretty little girls that sat next John caught hold of him and whirled him about; and, without making any resistance, he danced round and round with them for two good hours. Every afternoon while he remained there, he used to dance thus merrily with them; and, to the last hour of his life, he used to speak of it with the greatest glee. His language was—that the joys of heaven, and the songs and music of the angels, which the righteous hoped to enjoy there, might be excessively beautiful, but that he could conceive nothing to equal the music and the dancing under the earth, the beautiful and lively little men, the wonderful birds in the branches, and the tinkling silver bells on their caps. " No one," said he, " who has not seen and heard it, can form any idea whatever of it."

When the music and dancing were over, it might be about four o'clock. The little people then disappeared, and went each about their work or their pleasure. After supper they sported and danced in the same way; and at midnight, especially on starlight nights, they slipped out of their hills to dance in the open air. John used then, like a good boy, to say his prayers and go to sleep, a duty he never neglected either in the evening or in the morning.

For the first week that John was in the glass-hill, he only went from his chamber to the great hall and back again. After the first week, however, he began to walk about, making his servant show and explain everything to him. He found that there were in that place the most beautiful walks, in which he might ramble along for miles, in all directions, without ever finding an end of them, so immensely large was the hill that the little people lived in, and yet outwardly it seemed but a little hill, with a few bushes and trees growing on it.

It was extraordinary that, between the meads and fields, which were thick sown with hills, and lakes, and islands, and ornamented with trees and flowers in the greatest variety, there ran, as it were, small lanes, through which, as through crystal rocks, one was obliged to pass to come to any new place; and the single meads and fields were often a mile long, and the flowers were so brilliant and so fragrant, and the song of the numerous birds so sweet, that John had never seen anything on earth at all like it. There was a breeze, and yet one did not feel the wind; it was quite clear and bright, and yet there was no heat; the waves were dashing, still there was no danger; and the most beautiful little barks and canoes came, like white swans, when one wanted to cross the water, and went backwards and forwards of themselves. Whence all this came no one knew, nor could his servant tell anything about it; but one thing John saw plainly, which was, that the large carbuncles and diamonds that were set in the roof and walls gave light instead of the sun, moon, and stars.

These lovely meads and plains were, for the most part, quite lonesome. Few of the undergroundpeople were to be seen upon them, and those that were, just glided across them, as if in the greatest hurry. It very rarely happened that any of them danced out here in the open air; sometimes about three of them did so ; at the most half a dozen : John never saw a greater number together.   The meads were never cheerful, except when the corps of servants, of whom there might be some hundreds, were let out to walk.   This, however, happened but twice a-week, for they were mostly kept employed in the great hall and adjoining apartments, or at school.

For John soon found they had schools there also ; he had been there about ten months, when one day he saw something snow-white gliding into a rock, and disappearing. "What!" said he to his servant, "are there some of you too that wear white, like the servants?" He was informed that there were; but they were few in number, and never appeared at the large tables or the dances, except once a year, on the birthday of the great Hill-king, who dwelt many thousand miles below in the great deep.   These were the oldest men among them, some of them many thousand years old, who knew all things, and could tell of the beginning of the world, and were called the Wise.   They lived all alone, and only left their chambers to instruct the underground children and the attendants of both sexes, for whom there was a great school.

John was greatly pleased with this intelligence, and he determined to take advantage of it: so next morning he made his servant conduct him to the school, and was so well pleased with it that he never missed a day going there. They were taught there reading, writing, and accounts, to compose and relate histories and stories, and many elegant kinds of work ; so that many came out of the hills, both men and women, very prudent and knowing people, in consequence of what they were taught there.   The biggest, and those of best capacity, received instruction in natural science and astronomy, and in poetry and riddle-making, arts highly esteemed by the little people.   John was very diligent, and soon became extremely clever at painting and drawing ; he wrought, too, most ingeniously in gold, and silver, and stones, and in verse and riddle-making he had no fellow.

John had spent many a happy year here without ever thinking of the upper world, or of those he had left behind, so pleasantly passed the time—so many an agreeable playfellow he had among the children.

Of all his playfellows there was none of whom he was so fond as of a little fair-haired girl, named Elizabeth Krabbin. She was from his own village, and was the daughter of Frederick Krabbe, the minister of Rambin. She was but four years old when she was taken away, and John had often heard tell of her. She was not, however, stolen by the little people, but came into their power in this manner. One day in summer, she, with other children, ran out into the fields: in their rambles they went to the Nine-hills, where little Elizabeth fell asleep, and was forgotten by the rest. At night, when she awoke, she found herself under the ground among the little people. It was not merely because she was from his own village that John was so fond of Elizabeth, but she was a most beautiful child, with clear blue eyes and ringlets of fair hair, and a most angelic smile.

Time flew away unperceived: John was now eighteen, and Elizabeth sixteen. Their childish fondness had become love, and the little people were pleased to see it, thinking that by means of her they might get John to renounce his power, and become their servant; for they were fond of him, and would willingly have had him to wait upon them; for the love of dominion is their vice. But they were mistaken. John had learned too much from his servant to be caught in that way.

John's chief delight was in walking about alone with Elizabeth; for he now knew every place so well that he could dispense with the attendance of his servant. In these rambles he was always gay and lively, but his companion was frequently sad and melancholy, thinking on the land above, where men lived, and where the sun, moon, and stars, shine. Now it happened in one of their walks, that as they talked of their love, and it was after midnight, they passed under the place where the tops of the glass-hills used to open and let the undergroundpeople in and out. As they went along they heard of a sudden the crowing of several cocks above. At this sound, which she had not heard for twelve years, little Elizabeth felt her heart so affected that she could contain herself no longer, but throwing her arms about John's neck, she bathed his cheeks with her tears. At length she spake—

"Dearest John," said she, "everything down here is very

beautiful, and the little people are kind, and do nothing to
injure me, but still I have always been uneasy, nor ever
felt any pleasure till I began to love you; and yet that is
not pure pleasure, for this is not a right way of living, such
as it should be for human beings. Every night I dream of
my dear father and mother, and of our church-yard, where
the people stand so piously at the church-door waiting for
my father, and I could weep tears of blood that I cannot go
into the church with them, and worship God as a human
being should; for this is no Christian life we lead down
here, but a delusive half heathen one. And only think, dear
John, that we can never marry, as there is no priest to join
us. Do, then, plan some way for us to leave this place; for
I cannot tell you how I long to get once more to my father,
and among pious Christians."

John, too, had not been unaffected by the crowing of the
cocks, and he felt what he had never felt here before,
a longing after the land where the sun shines, and he
replied,

"Dear Elizabeth, all you say is true, and I now feel that
it is a sin for Christians to stay here; and it seems to me
as if our Lord said to us in that cry of the cocks, ' Come up,
ye Christian children, out of those abodes of illusion and
magic; come to the light of the stars, and act as children
of light.' I now feel that it was a great sin for me to come
down here, but I trust I shall be forgiven on account of my
youth; for I was a child and knew not what I did. But
now I will not stay a day longer. They cannot keep *me*
here."

At these last words, Elizabeth turned pale, for she recollected that she was a servant, and must serve her fifty years.
"And what will it avail me," cried she, "that I shall continue young and be but as of twenty years when I go out,
for my father and mother will be dead, and all my companions will be old and gray; and you, dearest John, will be
old and gray also," cried she, throwing herself on his bosom.

John was thunderstruck at this, for it had never before
occurred to him; he, however, comforted her as well as he
could, and declared he would never leave the place without
her. He spent the whole night in forming various plans;
at last he fixed on one, and in the morning he despatched

nis servant to summon to his apartment six of the principal of the little people. When they came, John thus mildly addressed them:

"My friends, you know how I came here, not as a prisoner or servant, but as a lord and master over one of you, and consequently, over all. You have now for the ten years I have been with you treated me with respect and attention, and for that I am your debtor. But you are still more my debtors, for I might have given you every sort of annoyance and vexation, and you must have submitted to it. I have, however, not done so, but have behaved as your equal, and have sported and played with you rather than ruled over you. I now have one request to make. There is a girl among your servants whom I love, Elizabeth Krabbin, of Rambin, where I was born. Give her to me, and let us depart. For I will return to where the sun shines and the plough goes through the land. I ask to take nothing with me but her, and the ornaments and furniture of my chamber."

He spoke in a determined tone, and they hesitated and cast their eyes to the ground; at last the oldest of them replied:

"Sir, you ask what we cannot grant. It is a fixed law, that no servant shall leave this place before the appointed time. Were we to break through this law, our whole subterranean empire would fall. Anything else you desire, for we love and respect you, but we cannot give up Elizabeth."

"You can and you shall give her up," cried John in a rage; "go think of it till to-morrow. Return here at this hour. I will show you whether or not I can triumph over your hypocritical and cunning stratagems."

The six retired. Next morning, on their return, John addressed them in the kindest manner, but to no purpose; they persisted in their refusal. He gave them till the next day, threatening them severely in case of their still proving refractory.

Next day, when the six little people appeared before him, John looked at them sternly, and made no return to their salutations, but said to them shortly, "Yes, or No?" And they answered with one voice, "No." He then ordered his servant to summon twenty-four more of the principal persons with their wives and children. When they came, they were in all five hundred, men, women, and children. John ordered them forthwith to go and fetch pickaxes, spades, and bars, which they did in a second.

He now led them out to a rock in one of the fields, and ordered them to fall to work at blasting, hewing, and dragging stones. They toiled patiently, and made as if it were only sport to them. From morning till night their task-master made them labour without ceasing, standing over them constantly, to prevent their resting. Still their obstinacy was inflexible; and at the end of some weeks his pity for them was so great, that he was obliged to give over.

He now thought of a new species of punishment for them. He ordered them to appear before him next morning, each provided with a new whip. They obeyed, and John commanded them to strip and lash one another till the blood should run down on the ground, and he stood looking on as grim and cruel as an eastern tyrant. Still the little people cut and slashed themselves, and mocked at John, and refused to comply with his wishes. This he did for three or four days.

Several other courses did he try, but all in vain; his temper was too gentle to struggle with their obstinacy, and he began now to despair of ever accomplishing his dearest wish. He began even to hate the little people whom he was before so fond of; he kept away from their banquets and dances, and associated alone with Elizabeth, and ate and drank quite solitary in his chamber. In short, he became almost a perfect hermit, and sank into moodiness and melancholy.

While in this temper, as he was taking a solitary walk in the evening, and, to divert his melancholy, was flinging the stones that lay in his path against each other, he happened to break a tolerably large one, and out of it jumped a toad. The moment John saw the ugly animal, he caught him up in ecstasy, and put him into his pocket and ran home, crying, " Now I have her! I have my Elizabeth! Now you shall get it, you little mischievous rascals! " And on getting home he put the toad into a costly silver casket, as if it was the greatest treasure.

To account for John's joy you must know that Klas Starkwolt had often told him that the underground people could not endure any ill smell, and that the sight or even the smell of a toad made them faint and suffer the most dreadful tortures, and that by means of stench and these odious ugly animals, one could compel them to anything. Hence there are no bad smells to be found in the whole glass empire, and a toad is a thing unheard of there; this toad must therefore have been inclosed in the stone from the creation, as it were for the sake of John and Elizabeth.

Resolved to try the effect of his toad, John took the casket under his arm and went out, and on the way he met two of the little people in a lonesome place. The moment he approached them they fell to the ground, and whimpered and howled most lamentably, as long as he was near them.

Satisfied now of his power, he next morning summoned the fifty principal persons, with their wives and children, to his apartment. When they came, he addressed them, reminding them once again of his kindness and gentleness toward them, and of the good terms on which they had hitherto lived. He reproached them with their ingratitude in refusing him the only favour he had ever asked of them, but firmly declared he would not give way to their obstinacy. "Wherefore," said he, "for the last time, think for a minute, and if you then say No, you shall feel that pain which is to you and your children the most terrible of all pains."

They did not take long to deliberate, but unanimously replied "No;" and they thought to themselves what new scheme has the youth hit on, with which he thinks to frighten wise ones like us, and they smiled as they said No. Their smiling enraged John above all, and he ran back a few hundred paces, to where he had laid the casket with the toad, under a bush.

He was hardly come within a hundred paces of them when they all fell to the ground as if struck with a thunderbolt, and began to howl and whimper, and to writhe, as if suffering the most excruciating pain. They stretched out their hands, and cried, "Have mercy! have mercy! we feel you have a toad, and there is no escape for us. Take the odious beast away, and we will do all you require." He let

them kick a few seconds longer, and then took the toad
away. They then stood up and felt no more pain. John
let all depart but the six chief persons, to whom he said:—

"This night between twelve and one Elizabeth and I will
depart. Load then for me three waggons, with gold, and
silver, and precious stones. I might, you know, take all that
is in the hill, and you deserve it, but I will be merciful.
Farther, you must put all the furniture of my chamber in
two waggons, and get ready for me the handsomest travèl-
ling-carriage that is in the hill, with six black horses.
Moreover, you must set at liberty all the servants who have
been so long here that on earth they would be twenty years
old and upwards, and you must give them as much silver
and gold as will make them rich for life, and make a law
that no one shall be detained here longer than his twentieth
year."

The six took the oath, and went away quite melancholy,
and John buried his toad deep in the ground. The little
people laboured hard and prepared everything. At midnight
everything was out of the hill, and John and Elizabeth got
into the silver tun, and were drawn up.

It was then one o'clock, and it was midsummer, the very
time that twelve years before John had gone down into the
hill. Music sounded around them, and they saw the glass
hill open, and the rays of the light of heaven shine on them
after so many years; and when they got out they saw the
first streaks of dawn already in the east. Crowds of the
undergroundpeople were around them busied about the
waggons. John bid them a last farewell, waved his brown
cap three times in the air, and then flung it among them.
And at the same moment he ceased to see them; he beheld
nothing but a green hill, and the well-known bushes and
fields, and heard the church clock of Rambin strike two.
When all was still, save a few larks, who were tuning their
morning songs, they all fell on their knees and worshiped
God, resolving henceforth to lead a pious and a Christian
life.

When the sun rose, John arranged the procession, and
they set out for Rambin. Every well-known object that
they saw awaked pleasing recollections in the bosom of John
and his bride; and as they passed by Rodenkirchen, John

recognised, among the people that gazed at and followed them, his old friend Klas Starkwolt, the cowherd, and his dog Speed. It was about four in the morning when they entered Rambin, and they halted in the middle of the village, about twenty paces from the house where John was born. The whole village poured out to gaze on these Asiatic princes, for such the old sexton, who had in his youth been at Moscow and Constantinople, said they were. There John saw his father and mother, and his brother Andrew, and his sister Trine. The old minister, Krabbe, stood there too, in his black slippers and white night cap, gaping and staring with the rest.

John discovered himself to his parents, and Elizabeth to hers, and the wedding-day was soon fixed, and such a wedding was never seen before or since in the island of Rügen; for John sent to Stralsund and Greifswald for whole boatloads of wine, and sugar, and coffee, and whole herds of oxen, sheep, and pigs were driven to the wedding. The quantity of harts, and roes, and hares that were shot on the occasion, it were vain to attempt to tell, or to count the fish that was caught. There was not a musician in Rügen and Pomerania that was not engaged, for John was immensely rich, and he wished to display his wealth.

John did not neglect his old friend Klas Starkwolt, the cowherd. He gave him enough to make him comfortable the rest of his days, and insisted on his coming and staying with him as often and as long as he wished.

After his marriage, John made a progress through the country with his beautiful Elizabeth, and they purchased towns, and villages, and lands, until he became master of nearly half Rügen, and a very considerable count in the country. His father, old James Dietrich, was made a nobleman, and his brothers and sisters gentlemen and ladies—for what cannot money do?

John and his wife spent their days in doing acts of piety and charity. They built several churches, and they had the blessing of every one that knew them, and died universally lamented. It was Count John Dietrich that built and richly endowed the present church of Rambin. He built it on the site of his father's house, and presented to it several of the cups and plates made by the underground people, and his own and Elizabeth's glass shoes, in memory of what had befallen them in their youth. But they were all taken away in the time of the great Charles the Twelfth of Sweden, when the Russians came on the island, and the Cossacks plundered even the churches, and took away everything.

The Little Glass Shoe.

A PEASANT, named John Wüde, who lived in Rodenkirchen, found one time a glass shoe on one of the hills where the little people used to dance. He clapped it instantly into his pocket and ran away with it, keeping his hand as close on his pocket as if he had a dove in it; for he knew that he had found a treasure which the underground people must redeem at any price.

Others say that John Wilde lay in ambush one night for the underground people, and gained an opportunity of pulling off one of their shoes, by stretching himself there with a brandy-bottle beside him, and acting like one that was dead drunk; for he was a very cunning man, not over scrupulous in his morals, and had taken in many a one by his craftiness, and, on this account, his name was in no good repute among his neighbours, who, to say the truth, were willing to have as little to do with him as possible. Many hold, too, that he was acquainted with forbidden arts, and used to carry on an intercourse with the fiends and old women that raised storms, and such like.

However, be this as it may, when John had gotten the shoe, he lost no time in letting the folk that dwell under the ground know that he had it. So at midnight he went to the Nine-hills, and cried with all his might, "John Wilde, of Rodenkirchen, has got a beautiful glass shoe. Who will buy it? Who will buy it?" For he knew that the little one who had lost the shoe must go barefoot till he got it again, and that is no trifle, for the little people have generally to walk upon very hard and stony ground.

John's advertisement was speedily attended to. The little fellow who had lost the shoe made no delay in setting about redeeming it. The first free day he got, that he might come out into the daylight, he came as a respectable merchant, and knocked at John Wilde's door, and asked if John had not a glass shoe to sell? "For," says he, "they are an article now in great demand, and are sought for in every market." John replied that it was true he had a very little little, nice, pretty little glass shoe, but it was so small that even a Dwarf's foot would be squeezed in it; and that God Almighty must make people on purpose for it before it could be of any use; but that, for all that, it was an extraordinary shoe, and a valuable shoe, and a dear shoe, and it was not every merchant that could afford to pay for it.

The merchant asked to see it, and when he had examined it, "Glass shoes," said he, "are not by any means such rare articles, my good friend, as you think here in Rodenkirchen, because you do not happen to go much into the world. However," said he, after hemming a little, "I will give you a good price for it, because I happen to have the very fellow of it." And he bid the countryman a thousand dollars for it.

"A thousand dollars are money, my father used to say when he drove fat oxen to market," replied John Wilde, in a mocking tone; "but it will not leave my hands for that shabby price; and, for my own part, it may ornament the foot of my daughter's doll. Harkye, friend: I have heard a sort of little song sung about the glass shoe, and it is not for a parcel of dirt that it will go out of my hands. Tell me now, my good fellow, should you happen to know the knack of it, that in every furrow I make when I am ploughing I should find a ducat? If not, the shoe is still mine, and you may inquire for glass shoes at those other markets."

The merchant made still a great many attempts, and twisted and turned in every direction to get the shoe; but when he found the farmer inflexible, he agreed to what John desired, and swore to the performance of it. Cunning John believed him, and gave him up the glass shoe, for he knew right well with whom he had to do. So the business being ended, away went the merchant with his glass shoe.

Without a moment's delay, John repaired to his stable,

got ready his horses and his plough, and drove out to the field. He selected a piece of ground where he would have the shortest turns possible, and began to plough. Hardly had the plough turned up the first sod, when up sprang a ducat out of the ground, and it was the same with every fresh furrow he made. There was now no end of his ploughing, and John Wilde soon bought eight new horses, and put them into the stable to the eight he already had —and their mangers were never without plenty of oats in them—that he might be able every two hours to yoke two fresh horses, and so be enabled to drive them the faster.

John was now insatiable in ploughing; every morning he was out before sunrise, and many a time he ploughed on till after midnight. Summer and winter it was plough, plough with him evermore, except when the ground was frozen as hard as a stone. But he always ploughed by himself, and never suffered any one to go out with him, or to come to him when he was at work, for John understood too well the nature of his crop to let people see what it was he ploughed so constantly for.

But it fared far worse with himself than with his horses, who ate good oats and were regularly changed and relieved, while he grew pale and meagre by reason of his continual working and toiling. His wife and children had no longer any comfort of him ; he never went to the alehouse or the club ; he withdrew himself from every one, and scarcely ever spoke a single word, but went about silent and wrapped up in his own thoughts. All the day long he toiled for his ducats, and at night he had to count them and to plan and meditate how he might find out a still swifter kind of plough.

His wife and the neighbours lamented over his strange conduct, his dullness and melancholy, and began to think that he was grown foolish. Everybody pitied his wife and children, for they imagined that the numerous horses that he kept in his stable, and the preposterous mode of agriculture that he pursued, with his unnecessary and superfluous ploughing, must soon leave him without house or land.

But their anticipations were not fulfilled. True it is, the poor man never enjoyed a happy or contented hour since he began to plough the ducats up out of the ground. The old saying held good in his case, that he who gives himself up to the pursuit of gold is half way in the claws of the evil one. Flesh and blood cannot bear perpetual labour, and John Wilde did not long hold out against this running through the furrows day and night. He got through the first spring, but one day in the second, he dropped down at the tail of the plough like an exhausted November fly. Out of the pure thirst after gold he was wasted away and dried up to nothing; whereas he had been a very strong and hearty man the day the shoe of the little underground man fell into his hands.

His wife, however, found after him a considerable treasure, two great nailed up chests full of good new ducats, and his sons purchased large estates for themselves, and became lords and noblemen. But what good did all that do poor John Wilde?

The Wonderful Plough.

THERE was once a farmer who was master of one of the little black ones, that are the blacksmiths and armourers; and he got him in a very curious way. On the road leading to this farmer's ground there stood a stone cross, and every morning as he went to his work he used to stop and kneel down before this cross, and pray for some minutes.

On one of these occasions he noticed on the cross a pretty bright insect, of such a brilliant hue that he could not recollect having ever before seen the like with an insect. He wondered greatly at this, yet still he did not disturb it; but the insect did not remain long quiet, but ran without ceasing backwards and forwards on the cross, as if it was in pain, and wanted to get away. Next morning the farmer again saw the very same insect, and again it was running to and fro, in the same state of uneasiness. The farmer began now to have some suspicions about it, and thought to himself, "Would this now be one of the little black enchanters? For certain, all is not right with that insect; it runs about just like one that had an evil conscience, as one that would,

yet cannot, go away:" and a variety of thoughts and conjectures passed through his mind; and he called to mind
what he had often heard from his father, and other old
people, that when the under groundpeople chance to touch
anything holy, they are held fast and cannot quit the spot,
and are therefore extremely careful to avoid all such things.
But he also thought it may as well be something else; and
you would perhaps be committing a sin in disturbing and
taking away the little animal; so he let it stay as it was.

But when he had found it twice more in the same place,
and still running about with the same marks of uneasiness,
he said, "No, it is not all right with it. So now, in the
name of God!" and he made a grasp at the insect, that
resisted and clung fast to the stone; but he held it tight,
and tore it away by main force, and lo! then he found he
had, by the top of the head, a little ugly black chap, about
six inches long, screeching and kicking at a most furious rate.

The farmer was greatly astounded at this sudden transformation; still he held his prize fast and kept calling to
him, while he administered to him a few smart slaps on the
buttocks: "Be quiet, be quiet, my little man! if crying was
to do the business, we might look for heroes in swaddling
clothes. We'll just take you with us a bit, and see what
you are good for."

The little fellow trembled and shook in every limb, and
then began to whimper most piteously, and to beg hard of
the farmer to let him go. But "No, my lad," replied the
farmer, "I will not let you go till you tell me who you are,
and how you came here, and what trade you know, that
enables you to earn your bread in the world." At this the
little man grinned and shook his head, but said not a word
in reply, only begged and prayed the more to get loose; and
the farmer found that he must now begin to entreat him if
he would coax any information out of him. But it was all
to no purpose. He then adopted the contrary method, and
whipped and slashed him till the blood run down, but just
to as little purpose; the little black thing remained as dumb
as the grave, for this species is the most malicious and obsti-
nate of all the underground race.

The farmer now got angry, and he said, "Do but be quiet,
my child; I should be a fool to put myself into a passion

with such a little brat. Never fear, I shall soon make you tame enough."

So saying, he ran home with him, and clapped him into a black, sooty, iron pot, and put the iron lid upon it, and laid on the top of the lid a great heavy stone, and set the pot in a dark cold room, and as he was going out he said to him, "Stay there, now, and freeze till you are black! I'll engage that at last you will answer me civilly."

Twice a-week the farmer went regularly into the room and asked his little black captive if he would answer him now; but the little one still obstinately persisted in his silence. The farmer had now, without success, pursued this course for six weeks, at the end of which time his prisoner at last gave up. One day as the farmer was opening the room door, he, of his own accord, called out to him to come and take him out of his dirty stinking dungeon, promising that he would now cheerfully do all that was wanted of him.

The farmer first ordered him to give him his history. The black one replied, "My dear friend you know it just as well as I, or else you never had had me here. You see I happened by chance to come too near the cross, a thing we little people may not do, and there I was held fast and obliged instantly to let my body become visible; so, then, that people might not recognise me, I turned myself into an insect. But you found me out. For when we get fastened to holy or consecrated things, we never can get away from them unless a man takes us off. That, however, does not happen without plague and annoyance to us, though, indeed, to say the truth, the staying fastened there is not over pleasant. And so I struggled against you, too, for we have a natural aversion to let ourselves be taken into a man's hand." "Ho, ho! is that the tune with you?" cried the farmer: "you have a natural aversion, have you? Believe me, my sooty friend, I have just the same for you; and so you shall be away without a moment's delay, and we will lose no time in making our bargain with each other. But you must first make me some present." "What you will, you have only to ask," said the little one: "silver and gold, and precious stones, and costly furniture—all shall be thine in less than an instant."—"Silver and gold, and precious stones, and all such glittering fine things will I none," said the farmer; "they have turned the heart and broken the neck of many a one before now, and few are they whose lives they make happy. I know that you are handy smiths, and have many a strange thing with you that other smiths know nothing about. So come, now, swear to me that you will make me an iron plough, such that the smallest foal may be able to draw it without being tired, and then run off with you as fast as your legs can carry you." So the black swore, and the farmer then cried out, "Now, in the name of God; there, you are at liberty," and the little one vanished like lightning.

Next morning, before the sun was up, there stood in the farmer's yard a new iron plough, and he yoked his dog Water to it, and though it was of the size of an ordinary plough, Water drew it with ease through the heaviest clay-land, and it tore up prodigious furrows. The farmer used this plough for many years, and the smallest foal or the leanest little horse could draw it through the ground, to the amazement of every one who beheld it, without turning a single hair. And this plough made a rich man of the farmer, for it cost him no horse-flesh, and he led a cheerful and contented life by means of it. Hereby we may see that moderation holds out the longest, and that it is not good to covet too much.

The Lost Bell.

A SHEPHERD'S boy belonging to Patzig, about half a mile from Bergen, where there are great numbers of the underground people in the hills, found one morning a little silver bell on the green heath, among the Giants'-graves, and fastened it on him. It happened to be the bell belonging to the cap of one of the little Brown ones, who had lost it while he was dancing, and did not immediately miss it, or observe that it was no longer tinkling in his cap. He had gone down into the hill without his bell, and having discovered his loss, was filled with melancholy. For the worst thing that can befall the underground people is to lose their cap, then their shoes; but even to lose the bell from their caps, or the buckle from their belts, is no trifle to them. Whoever loses his bell must pass some sleepless nights, for not a wink of sleep can he get till he has recovered it.

The little fellow was in the greatest trouble, and searched and looked about everywhere; but how could he learn who had the bell? For only on a very few days in the year may they come up to the daylight; nor can they then appear in their true form. He had turned himself into every form of birds, beasts, and men; and he had sung and rung, and groaned and moaned, and lamented and inquired about his bell, but not the slightest tidings, or trace of tidings, had he been able to get. For what was worst of all, the shepherd's boy had left Patzig the very day he found the little bell, and was now keeping sheep at Unruh, near Gingst: so it was not till many a day after, and then by mere chance, that the little underground fellow recovered his bell, and with it his peace of mind.

He had thought it not unlikely that a raven, or a crow, or a jackdaw, or a magpie, had found his bell, and from his thievish disposition, which is caught with anything bright and shining, had carried it into his nest; with this thought he had turned himself into a beautiful little bird, and searched all the nests in the island, and had sung before all kinds of birds, to see if they had found what he had lost, and could restore him his sleep; but nothing had he been able to learn from the birds. As he now, one evening, was flying over the waters of Ralov and the fields of Unruh, the shepherd's boy, whose name was Fritz Schlagenteufel (*Smite-devil*), happened to be keeping his sheep there at the very time. Several of the sheep had bells about their necks, and they tinkled merrily, when the boy's dog set them trotting. The little bird, who was flying over them thought of his bell, and sung, in a melancholy tone,

> Little bell, little bell,
> Little ram as well,
>   You, too, little sheep,
> If you've my Tingletoo,
> No sheep's so rich as you,
>   My rest you keep.

The boy looked up and listened to this strange song

which came out of the sky, and saw the pretty bird, which
seemed to him still more strange:—"Odds bodikins!" said
he to himself, "if one but had that bird that's singing up
there, so plain that one of us would hardly match him!
What can he mean by that wonderful song? The whole
of it is, it must be a feathered witch. My rams have only
pinchbeck bells, he calls them rich cattle; but I have a
silver bell, and he sings nothing about me." And with
these words he began to fumble in his pocket, took out his
bell, and rang it.

The bird in the air instantly saw what it was, and was
rejoiced beyond measure. He vanished in a second—flew
behind the nearest bush—alighted and drew off his speckled
feather-dress, and turned himself into an old woman dressed
in tattered clothes. The old dame, well supplied with sighs
and groans, tottered across the field to the shepherd's boy,
who was still ringing his bell, and wondering what was
become of the beautiful bird. She cleared her throat, and
coughing up from the bottom of her chest, bid him a kind
good evening, and asked him which was the way to Bergen.
Pretending then that she had just seen the little bell, she
exclaimed, "Good Lord! what a charming pretty little bell!
Well! in all my life I never beheld anything more beautiful! Harkye, my son, will you sell me that bell? And
what may be the price of it? I have a little grandson at
home, and such a nice plaything as it would make for him!"
"No," replied the boy, quite short, "the bell is not for
sale. It is a bell, that there is not such another bell in the
whole world. I have only to give it a little tinkle, and my
sheep run of themselves wherever I would have them go.
And what a delightful sound it has! Only listen, mother!"
said he, ringing it: "is there any weariness in the world
that can hold out against this bell? I can ring with
it away the longest time, so that it will be gone in a
second."

The old woman thought to herself, "We will see if he
can hold out against bright shining money." And she took
out no less than three silver dollars, and offered them to him:
but he still replied, "No, I will not sell my bell." She then
offered him five dollars. "The bell is still mine," said he.
She stretched out her hand full of ducats: he replied, this

third time, "Gold is dirt and does not ring." The old dame then shifted her ground, and turned the discourse another way. She grew mysterious, and began to entice him by talking of secret arts, and of charms by which his cattle might be made to thrive prodigiously, relating to him all kinds of wonders of them. It was then the young shepherd began to long, and he now lent a willing ear to her tales.

The end of the matter was, that she said to him, "Harkye, my child! give me the bell and see! here is a white stick for you," said she, taking out a little white stick which had Adam and Eve very ingeniously cut on it, as they were feeding the herds of Paradise, with the fattest sheep and lambs dancing before them; and there was the shepherd David too, as he stood with his sling against the giant Goliath. "I will give you," said the old woman, "this stick for the bell, and as long as you drive the cattle with it they will be sure to thrive. With this you will become a rich shepherd: your wethers will always be fat a month sooner than the wethers of other shepherds, and every one of your sheep will have two pounds of wool more than others, and yet no one will be ever able to see it on them."

The old woman handed him the stick. So mysterious was her gesture, and so strange and bewitching her smile, that the lad was at once in her power. He grasped eagerly at the stick, gave her his hand, and cried, "Done! Strike hands! The bell for the stick!" And cheerfully the old woman struck hands, and took the bell, and went like a light breeze over the field and the heath. He saw her vanish, and she seemed to float away before his eyes like a mist, and to go off with a slight whiz and whistle that made the shepherd's hair stand on end.

The underground one, however, who, in the shape of an old woman, had wheedled him out of his bell, had not deceived him. For the under groundpeople dare not lie, but must ever keep their word; a breach of it being followed by their sudden change into the shape of toads, snakes, dunghill-beetles, wolves and apes; forms in which they wander about, objects of fear and aversion for a long course of years before they are freed. They, therefore, have naturally a great dread of lying. Fritz Schlagenteufel gave close attention and made trial of his new shepherd's-staff, and he soon found that the old woman had told him the truth, for his flocks, and his work, and all the labour of his hands prospered with him and had wonderful luck, so that there was not a sheep-owner or head shepherd but was desirous of having Fritz Schlagenteufel in his employment.

It was not long, however, that he remained an underling. Before he was eighteen years of age, he had gotten his own flocks, and in the course of a few years was the richest sheep-master in the whole island of Rügen; until at last, he was able to purchase a knight's estate for himself, and that estate was Grabitz, close by Rambin, which now belongs to the lords of Sunde. My father* knew him there, and how from a shepherd's boy he was become a nobleman, and he always conducted himself like a prudent, honest and pious man, who had a good word from every one. He brought up his sons like gentlemen, and his daughters like ladies, some of whom are still alive and accounted people of great consequence. And well may people who hear such stories wish that they had met with such an adventure, and had found a little silver bell which the underground people had lost.

The Black Dwarfs of Granitz.

Not far from the Ahlbeck lies a little mansion called Granitz, just under the great wood on the sea-coast called the wood of Granitz. In this little seat lived, not many years ago, a nobleman named Von Scheele. Toward the close of his life he sank into a state of melancholy, though hitherto a very cheerful and social man, and a great sportsman. People said that the old man took to his lonesome way of living from the loss of his three beautiful daughters, who were called the three fair-haired maidens, and who grew up here in the solitude of the woods, among the herds and the birds, and who had all three gone off in the same night and never returned. The old man took this greatly

* Hinrich Vick's of course, for he is the narrator.

to heart, and withdrew himself from the world, and all cheerful society. He had great intercourse with the little black people, and he was many a night out of the house, and no one knew where he had been; but when he came home in the gray of the morning, he would whisper his housekeeper, and say to her, "Ha, ha! I was at a grand table last night."

This old gentleman used to relate to his friends, and confirm it with many a stout trooper's and sportsman's oath, that the underground people swarmed among the fir-trees of Granitz, about the Ahlbeck, and along the whole shore. He used often, also, to show to those whom he took to walk there, a great number of little foot-prints, like those of very small children, in the sand, and he has suddenly called out to his companions, "Hush! Listen how they are, buzzing and whispering!"

Going once with some friends along the sea-shore, he all of a sudden stood still, as if in amazement, pointed to the sea, and cried out, "My soul! there they are again at full work, and there are several thousands of them employed about a few sunken casks of wine that they are rolling to the shore; oh! what a jovial carouse there will be to-night!" He then told his companions that he could see them both by day and by night, and that they did nothing to him; nay, they were his most particular friends, and one of them had once saved his house from being burnt by waking him in the night out of a profound sleep, when a firebrand, that had fallen out on the floor, was just on the point of setting fire to some wood and straw that lay there. He said that almost every day some of them were to be seen on the sea-shore, but that during high storms, when the sea was uncommonly rough, almost all of them were there looking after amber and shipwrecks, and for certain no ship ever went to pieces but they got the best part of the cargo, and hid it safe under the ground. And how grand a thing, he added, it is to live under the sand-hills with them, and how beautiful their crystal palaces are, no one can have any conception who has not been there.

GERMANY.

Von wilden getwergen han ich gehöret sagen
Si sin in holren bergen; unt daz si ze scherme tragen
Einez heizet tarnkappen, von wunderlicher art—
Swerz hat an sime libe, der sol vil wohl sin bewart
Vor slegen unt vor stichen. NIBELUNGEN, LIED st. 342.

Of wild dwarfs I oft have heard men declare
They dwell in hollow mountains; and for defence they wear
A thing called a Tarn-cloke, of wonderful nature—
Who has it on his body will ever be secure
'Gainst cutting and 'gainst thrusting.

THE religion of the ancient Germans, probably the same with that of the Scandinavians, contained, like it, Alfs, Dwarfs, and Giants. The Alfs have fallen from the popular creed,* but the Dwarfs still retain their former dominion. Unlike those of the North, they have put off their heathen character, and, with their human neighbours, have embraced a purer faith. With the creed they seem to have adopted the spirit of their new religion also. In most of the traditions respecting them we recognise benevolence as one of the principal traits of their character.

The oldest monuments of German popular belief are the poems of the Heldenbuch (*Hero-book*) and the spirit-stirring Nibelungen Lied.† In these poems the Dwarfs are actors of importance.

In this last-named celebrated poem the Dwarf Albrich appears as the guardian of the celebrated Hoard which Sifrit (Siegfried) won from the Nibelungen. The Dwarf is

---

* The only remnant is *Alp*, the nightmare; the *elfen* of modern writers is merely an adoption of the English *elves*.

† The edition of this poem which we have used, is that by Schönhuth, Leipzig, 1841.

Illustration by Arthur Rackham from
"King of the Golden Mountain," by Grimm

Scene from the melodrama: *The Faery of Rheinfall*

twice vanquished by the hero who gains his Tarn-kappe, or Mantle of Invisibility.*

In the Heldenbuch we meet with the Dwarf-king Laurin, whose garden Dietrich of Bern and his warriors broke into and laid waste. To repel the invader the Dwarf appears in magnificent array: twenty-three stanzas are occupied with the description of his banner, helmet, shield, and other accoutrements. A furious combat ensues, in which the Dwarf has long the advantage, as his magic ring and girdle endow him with the strength of twenty-four men, and his Hel Keplein † (Tarnkappe) renders him invisible at pleasure. At length, by the advice of Hildebrand, Dietrich strikes off the Dwarf's finger, breaks his girdle, and pulls off his Hel Keplein, and thus succeeds in vanquishing his enemy. Laurin is afterwards reconciled to the heroes, and prevails on them to enter the mountain in which he dwelt, and partake of a banquet. Having them now in his power, he treacherously makes them all his prisoners. His queen, however, Ditlaub's sister, whom he had stolen away from under a linden, releases them: their liberation is followed by a terrific engagement between them and Laurin, backed by a numerous host of Dwarfs. Laurin is again overcome; he loses his queen; his hill is plundered of its treasures, and himself led to Bern, and there reduced to the extremity of earning his bread by becoming a buffoon.

In the poem named Hürnen Sifrit ‡ the Dwarf Eugel §

---

* Tarn from *taren*, to dare, says Dobenek, because it gave courage along with invisibility. It comes more probably we think from the old German *ternen*, to hide. Kappe is properly a cloak, though the Tarnkappe or Nebel-kappe is generally represented as a cap, or hat.

† From *hehlen*, to conceal.

‡ *Horny Siegfred*; for when he slew the dragon, he bathed himself in his blood, and became horny and invulnerable everywhere except in one spot between his shoulders, where a linden leaf stuck. In the Nibelungen Lied, (*st.* 100), Hagene says,

Yet still more know I of him—this to me is certaín,
A terrible Lind-dragon the hero's hand hath slain;
He in the blood him bathed, and horny grew his skin;
Hence woundeth him no weapon, full oft it hath been seen.

§ MM. Grimm thought at one time that this name was properly Engel, and that it was connected with the changes of Alp, Alf, to Engel (see above, p. 67). They query at what time the dim. *Engelein* first came into use, and when the angels were first represented under the form of children—a

renders the hero good service in his combat with the enchanted Dragon who had carried off the fair Chrimhild from Worms, and enclosed her in the Drachenstein. When Sifrit is treacherously attacked by the Giant Kuperan, the ally of the Dragon, the Dwarf flings his Nebelkappe over him to protect him.

But the most celebrated of Dwarfs is Elberich,* who aided the emperor Otnit or Ortnit to gain the daughter of the Paynim Soldan of Syria.

Otnit ruled over Lombardy, and had subdued all the neighbouring nations. His subjects wishing him to marry, he held a council to consider the affair. No maiden mentioned was deemed noble enough to share his bed. At last his uncle Elias, king of the "wild Russians," says :—

> "I know of a maiden, noble and high-born,
> Her no man yet hath wooed, his life who hath not lorn.

> "She shineth like the roses, and the gold ruddý,
> She fair is in her person, thou must credit me ;
> She shines o'er other women, as bright roses do,
> So fair a child was never; they say she good is too."

The monarch's imagination is inflamed, and, regardless of the remonstrances of his council, he determines to brave all dangers, to sail with a powerful army to Syria, where the maiden dwelt, and to win her or to die. He regulates his kingdom, and says to his uncle :—

> As soon as May appeareth, with her days so clear,
> Then pray thou of thy friends all, their warriors to cheer,
> To hold themselves all ready ; go things as they may,
> We will, with the birds' singing, sail o'er the sea away.

practice evidently derived from the idea of the Elves. In Otfried and other writers of the ninth and tenth centuries, they say, the angels are depicted as young men ; but in the latter half of the thirteenth, a popular preacher named Berthold, says : *Ir sehet wol daz si allesamt sint juncliche gemälet ; als ein kint daz dá vünf jár alt ist swá man sie málet.*

* Elberich, (the Albrich of the Nibelungen Lied,) as we have said (above p. 40), is Oberon. From the usual change of *l* into *u* (as *al, au, col, cou*, etc.), in the French language, Elberich or Albrich (derived from Alp, Alf) becomes Auberich ; and *ich* not being a French termination, the diminutive *on* was substituted, and so it became Auberon, or Oberon ; a much more likely origin than the usual one from *L'aube du jour*. For this derivation of Oberon we are indebted to Dr. Grimm.

The queen now endeavours to dissuade her son, but finding her efforts vain, resolves to aid him as far as she can. She gives him a ring, and desires him to ride toward Rome till he comes to where a linden stands before a hill, from which runs a brook, and there he will meet with an adventure. She farther tells him to keep the ring uncovered, and the stone of it will direct him.

Obeying his directions, Otnit rides alone from his palace at Garda, continually looking at his ring:

Unto a heath he came then, close by the Garda lake,
Where everywhere the flowers and clover out did break;
The birds were gaily singing, their notes did loudly ring,
He all the night had waked, he was weary with riding.

The sun over the mountains and through the welkin shone,
Then looked he full oft on the gold and on the stone;
Then saw he o'er the meadow, down trodden the green grass,
And a pathway narrow, where small feet used to pass.

Then followed he downwards, the rocky wall boldly,
Till he had found the fountain, and the green linden-tree,
And saw the heath wide spreading, and the linden branching high.
It had upon its boughs full many a guest worthy.

The birds were loudly singing, each other rivalling,
"I have the right way ridden," spake Otnit the king;
Then much his heart rejoiced, when he saw the linden spread;
He sprang down from his courser, he held him by the head.

And when the Lombarder had looked on the lindén
He began to laugh loud; now list what he said then:
"There never yet from tree came so sweet breathing a wind."
Then saw he how an infant was laid beneath the lind,

Who had himself full firmly rolled in the grass;
Then little the Lombarder knew who he was:
He bore upon his body so rich and noble a dress,
No king's child upon earth e'er did the like possess.

His dress was rich adorned with gold and precious stone;
When he beneath the linden the child found all alone:
"Where now is thy mother?" king Otnit he cries;
"Thy body unprotected beneath this tree here lies."

This child was Elberich, whom the ring rendered visible. After a hard struggle, Otnit overcomes him. As a ransom, Elberich promises him a magnificent suit of armour—

"I'll give thee for my ransom the very best harness
That either young or old in the world doth possess.

"Full eighty thousand marks the harness is worth well,
A sword too I will give thee, with the shirt of mail,
That every corselet cuts through as if steel it were not;
There ne'er was helm so strong yet could injure it a jot.

"I ween in the whole world no better sword there be,
I brought it from a mountain is called Almari;
It is with gold adorned, and clearer is than glass;
I wrought it in a mountain is called Göickelsass.

"The sword I will name to thee, it is bright of hue,
Whate'er thou with it strikest no gap will ensue,
It is Rossè called, I tell to thee its name;
Wherever swords are drawing it never will thee shame.

"With all the other harness I give thee leg armour,
In which there no ring is, my own hand wrought it sure;
And when thou hast the harness thou must it precious hold,
There's nothing false within it, it all is of pure gold.

"With all the armour rich I give thee a helmét,
Upon an emperor's head none a better e'er saw yet;
Full happy is the man who doth this helmet bear,
His head is recognised, a mile off though he were.

"And with the helmet bright I will give to thee a shield,
So strong and so good too, if to me thanks thou'lt yield;
It never yet was cut through by any sword so keen,
No sort of weapon ever may that buckler win."

Elberich persuades the king to lend him his ring; when
he gets it he becomes invisible, and amuses himself by telling him of the whipping he will get from his mother for
having lost it. At last when Otnit is on the point of going
away, Elberich returns the ring, and, to his no small surprise, informs him that he is his father, promising him, at
the same time, if he is kind to his mother, to stand his friend,
and assist him to gain the heathen maid.

When May arrives Otnit sails from Messina with his
troops. As they approach Sunders,* they are a little in
dread of the quantity of shipping they see in the port, and
the king regrets and bewails having proceeded without his
dwarf-sire. But Elberich has, unseen, been sitting on the

* Probably Saida, i.e. Sidon.

mast. He appears, and gives his advice, accompanied by a
stone, which, by being put into the mouth, endows its possessor with the gift of all languages. On the heathens
coming alongside the vessel, Otnit assumes the character of
a merchant, and is admitted to enter the port. He forthwith proposes to murder the inhabitants in the night, an act
of treachery which is prevented by the strong and indignant
rebukes of the Dwarf.

Elberich sets off to Muntabur,* the royal residence, to
demand the princess. The Soldan, enraged at the insolence
of the invisible envoy, in vain orders his men to put him to
death ; the "little man" returns unscathed to Otnit, and
bids him prepare for war. By the aid of Elberich, Otnit
wins, after great slaughter on both sides, the city of Sunders.
He then, under the Dwarf's advice, follows up his conquest
by marching for Muntabur, the capital. Elberich, still
invisible, except to the possessor of the ring, offers to act
as guide.

> "Give me now the horse here they lead by the hand,
> And I will guide thine army unto the heathens' land ;
> If any one should ask thee, who on the horse doth ride ?
> Thou shalt say nothing else, but—an angel is thy guide."

The army, on seeing the horse and banner advancing as it
were of themselves, blessed themselves, and asked Otnit why
he did not likewise.

> "It is God's messenger ! " Otnit then cried :
> "Who unto Muntabur will be our trusty guide ;
> Him ye should believe in, who like Christians debate,
> Who in the fight them spare not, he leads to heaven straight."

Thus encouraged, the troops cheerfully follow the invisible
standard-bearer, and soon appear before Muntabur, where
Elberich delivers the banner to king Elias, and directs them
to encamp. He meanwhile enters the city, flings down the
artillery from the walls, and when the Soldan again refuses
to give his daughter, plucks out some of his majesty's beard†
and hair, in the midst of his courtiers and guards, who in

---

* *i. e.* Mount Tabor.

† This may have suggested the well-known circumstance in Huon de
Bordeaux.

vain cut and thrust at the viewless tormentor. A furious
battle ensues. The queen and princess resort to prayers to
their gods Apollo and Mahomet for the safety of the Soldan.
The princess is thus described:

Her mouth flamed like a rose, and like the ruby stone,
And equal to the full moon her lovely eyes they shone.

With roses she bedecked had well her head,
And with pearls precious,—no one comforted the maid:
She was of exact stature, slender in the waist,
And turned like a taper was her body chaste.

Her hands and her arms, you nought in them could blame,
Her nails they so clear were, people saw themselves in them;
And her hair ribbons were of silk costly,
Which she left down hanging, the maiden fair and free.

She set upon her head high a crown of gold red,—
Elberich the little, he grieved for the maid;—
In front of the crown lay a carbuncle stone,
That in the royal palace like a taper shone.

Elberich endeavours to persuade her to become a Christian,
and espouse Otnit; and to convince her of the incapacity of
her gods, he tumbles their images into the fosse. Overcome
by his representations and her father's danger, the princess,
with her mother's consent, agrees to wed the monarch whom
Elberich points out to her in the battle, and she gives her
ring to be conveyed to him. The Dwarf, unperceived, leads
her out of the city, and delivers her to her future husband,
strictly forbidding all intercourse between them, previous to
the maiden's baptism.* When the old heathen misses his
daughter he orders out his troops to recover her. Elberich
hastens to king Elias, and brings up the Christians. A
battle ensues: the latter are victorious, and the princess is
brought to Sunders;—ere they embark Elberich and Elias
baptise her, and ere they reached Messina " the noble maiden
was a wife."

As yet not intimately acquainted with Christianity, the
young empress asks Otnit about his god, giving him to
understand that she knew his deity, who had come to her
father's to demand her for him. Otnit corrects her mistake,

* So Oberon in Huon de Bordeaux.

telling her that the envoy was Elberich, whom she then desires to see. At the request of Otnit the Dwarf reveals himself to the queen and court.

> Long time he refused,—he showed him then a stone,
> That like unto the sun, with the gold shone ;
> Ruby and carbuncle was the crown so rich,
> Which upon his head bare the little Elberich.
>
> The Dwarf let the people all see him then,
> They began to look upon him, both women and men ;
> Many a fair woman with rosy mouth then said,
> " I ween a fairer person no eye hath e'er survey'd."
>
>   *   *   *   *   *
>
> Then Elberich the little a harp laid hold upon ;
> Full rapidly he touched the strings every one
> In so sweet a measure that the hall did resound ;
> All that him beheld then, they felt a joy profound.

After giving Otnit abundance of riches, and counselling him to remunerate those who had lost their relatives in his expedition, Elberich takes leave of the king. He then vanishes, and appears no more.

Otnit is the most pleasing poem in the Heldenbuch. Nothing can be more amiable than the character of the Dwarf, who is evidently the model of Oberon. We say this, because the probability is much greater that a French writer should have taken a Dwarf from a German poet, than that the reverse should have occurred. The connexion between the two works appears indubitable.

An attempt has already been made to trace the origin of Dwarfs, and the historical theory respecting those of the North rejected. A similar theory has been given of those of Germany, as being a people subdued between the fifth and tenth centuries by a nation of greater power and size. The vanquished fled to the mountains, and concealed themselves in caverns, only occasionally venturing to appear ; and hence, according to this theory, the origin of Dwarf stories. As we regard them as an integrant part of Gotho-German religion, we must reject this hypothesis in the case of Germany also.

Beside the Dwarfs, we meet in the Nibelungen Lied with beings answering to the Nixes or Water-spirits. When* the Burgundians on their fatal journey to the court of Ezel (Attila) reached the banks of the Danube, they found that it could not be crossed without the aid of boats. Hagene then proceeded along the bank in search of a ferry. Suddenly he heard a plashing in the water, and on looking more closely he saw some females who were bathing. He tried to steal on them, but they escaped him and went hovering over the river. He succeeded, however, in securing their clothes, and in exchange for them the females, who were Watermaids (*Merewiper*) promised to tell him the result of the visit to the court of the Hunnish monarch. One of them then named Hadeburch assured him of a prosperous issue, on which he restored the garments. But then another, named Sigelint told him that Hadeburch had lied for the sake of the clothes; for that in reality the event of the visit would be most disastrous, as only one of the party would return alive. She also informed him where the ferry was, and told him how they might outwit the ferryman and get over.

We cannot refrain from suspecting that in the original legend these were Valkyrias and not Water-nymphs, for these last would hardly strip to go into the water, their native element. In the prose introduction to the Eddaic poem of Völundr we are told that he and his two elder brothers went to Wolfdale and built themselves a house by the water named Wolfsea or lake, and one morning early they found on the shore of the lake three women who were spinning flax: beside them were lying their *swan-dresses*. They were "Valkyrias, and king's daughters." The three brothers took them home and made them their wives, but after seven years they flew away and returned no more. It is remarkable, that in the poem there is not the slightest allusion to the swan-dresses, though it relates the coming and the departure of the maidens. We are then to suppose either that there were other poems on the subject, or that these dresses were so well known a vehicle that it was deemed needless to mention them. We are to suppose also that it was by securing these dresses that the brothers pre-

---

* Str. 1564, *seq.*

vented the departure of the maidens, and that it was by recovering them that they were enabled to effect their escape. In effect in the German legend of Wielant (Völundr), the hero sees three *doves* flying to a spring, and as soon as they touch the ground they become maidens. He then secures their clothes, and will not return them till one of them consents to become his wife.[*]

This legend resembles the tale of the Stolen Veil in Musæus, and those of the Peri-wife and the Mermaid-wife related above.[†] In the Breton tale of Bisclavaret, or the Warwolf, we learn that no one who became a wolf could resume his human form, unless he could recover the clothes which he had put off previous to undergoing the transformation.[‡]

Our readers may like to see how the preface to the old editions of the Heldenbuch accounts for the origin of the Dwarfs.

" God," says it, " gave the Dwarfs being, because the land and the mountains were altogether waste and uncultivated, and there was much store of silver and gold, and precious stones and pearls still in the mountains. Wherefore God made the Dwarfs very artful and wise, that they might know good and evil right well, and for what everything was good. They knew also for what stones were good. Some stones give great strength ; some make those who carry them about them invisible, that is called a mist-cloke (*nebelkap*) ; and therefore did God give the Dwarfs skill and wisdom. Therefore they built handsome hollow hills, and God gave them riches, etc.

" God created the Giants, that they might kill the wild beasts, and the great dragons (*würm*), that the Dwarfs might thereby be more secure. But in a few years the Giants would too much oppress the Dwarfs, and the Giants became altogether wicked and faithless.

" God then created the Heroes ; 'and be it known that the Heroes were for many years right true and worthy, and

---

[*] Grimm, Deut. Mythol., p. 398, *seq.*

[†] See above, pp. 19, 169 ; below, *Ireland ;* and Grimm, *ut sup.* p. 1216. The swan-dresses also occur in the Arabian tales of Jahânshâh and Hassan of Bassora in Trebutien's Arabian Nights.

[‡] Poésies de Marie de France, i. 177, *seq.*

they then came to the aid of the Dwarfs against the faithless Giants;'—God made them strong, and their thoughts
were of manhood, according to honour, and of combats and
war."

We will divide the objects of German popular belief at
the present day, into four classes:—1. Dwarfs; 2. Wild-
women; 3. Kobolds; 4. Nixes.

DWARFS.

Fort, fort! Mich schau' die Sonne nicht,
  Ich darf nicht langer harren;
Mich Elfenkind vor ihren Licht
  Sähst du zum Fels erstarren.
LA MOTTE FOUQUÉ.

Away! let not the sun view me,
  I dare no longer stay;
An Elfin-child thou wouldst me see,
  To stone turn at his ray.

THESE beings are called Zwerge (*Dwarfs*), Berg- and Erd-
mänlein (*Hill* and *Ground-mannikins*), the Stille Volk (*Still-
people*), and the Kleine Volk (*Little-people*).* The following account of the Still-people at Plesse will give the popular
idea respecting them.†

At Plesse, a castle in the mountains in Hesse, are various
springs, wells, clefts and holes in the rocks, in which, according to popular tradition, the Dwarfs, called the Still-people,
dwell. They are silent and beneficent, and willingly serve
those who have the good fortune to please them. If injured

---

* Another term is Wicht and its dim. Wichtlein, answering to the Scandinavian Vættr and the Anglo-Saxon *wiht*, English *wight*, all of which signify
a being, a person, and also a thing in general. Thus our words *aught* and
naught were *anwiht* and *nawiht*.

† See Grimm's Deutsche Sagen, vol. i. p. 38. As this work is our chief
authority for the Fairy Mythology of Germany, our materials are to be considered as taken from it, unless when otherwise expressed.

they vent their anger, not on mankind, but on the cattle, which they plague and torment. This subterranean race has no proper communication with mankind, but pass their lives within the earth, where their apartments and chambers are filled with gold and precious stones. Should occasion require their visit to the surface of the earth, they accomplish the business in the night, and not by day. This Hill-people are of flesh and bone, like mankind, they bear children and die, but in addition to the ordinary faculties of humanity, they have the power of making themselves invisible, and of passing through rocks and walls, with the same facility as through the air. They sometimes appear to men, lead them with them into clifts, and if the strangers prove agreeable to them, present them with valuable gifts.*

The Hill-Man at the Dance.

OLD people have positively asserted that some years ago, at the celebration of a wedding in the village of Glass, a couple of miles from the Wunderberg, and the same distance from the city of Saltzburg, there came toward evening a little Hill-man out of the Wunderberg. He desired all the guests to be merry and cheerful, and begged to be permitted to join in their dance, which request was not refused. He accordingly danced three dances with some of the maidens of good repute, and with a gracefulness that inspired all present with admiration and delight. After the dance he returned them his thanks, accompanied by a present to each of the bridal party of three pieces of money of an unknown coin, each of which they estimated to be worth four creutzers. Moreover, he recommended them to dwell in peace and concord, to live like Christians, and, by a pious education, to bring up their children in goodness. He told them to lay up these

* In Lusatia (Lausatz) if not in the rest of Germany, the same idea of the Dwarfs being fallen angels, prevails as in other countries : see the tale of the Fairies'-sabbath in the work quoted above, p. 179.

coins with their money, and constantly to think of him, and so they would rarely come to distress; but warned them against becoming proud, and advised them, on the contrary, to relieve their neighbours with their superfluities.

The Hill-man remained with them till night, and took some meat and drink from each as they offered it to him, but only very little. He then renewed his thanks, and concluded by begging of one of the company to put him over the river Satzach, opposite the mountain. There was at the wedding a boatman, named John Ständl, who got ready to comply with the dwarf's request, and they went together to the water's-edge. As they were crossing, the man asked for his payment, and the Hill-man humbly presented him three-pence. The boatman utterly rejected this paltry payment; but the little man gave him for answer, that he should not let that annoy him, but keep the threepence safe, and he would never suffer want, provided he put a restraint on arrogance. He gave him at the same time, a little stone with these words : " Hang this on your neck, and you will never be drowned in the water." And of this he had a proof that very year. Finally, the Hill-man exhorted him to lead a pious and humble life, and being landed on the opposite bank, departed speedily from the place.*

The Dwarf's Feast.

THERE appeared in the night to one of the Counts von Hoya, an extremely small little man. The count was utterly amazed at him, but he bid him not to be frightened; said he had a request to make of him, and entreated that he might not be refused. The count gave a willing assent, qualified with the provision, that the thing requested should be a matter which lay in his power, and would not be injurious to him or his. The little man then said, " There

* This tale is given by MM. Grimm, from the Brixener Volksbuch. 1782.

will come tomorrow night some people to thy house, and make a feast, if thou will lend them thy kitchen, and hall for as long as they want them, and order thy servants to go to sleep, and no one to look at what they are doing or are about; and also let no one know of it but thyself; only do this and we shall be grateful to thee for thy courtesy: thou and thy family will be the better of it; nor will it be in any way hurtful to thee or thine." The count readily gave his consent, and on the following night there came, as if they were a travelling party, over the bridge into the house a great crowd of little people, exactly such as the Hill-mannikins are described to be. They cooked, cut up wood, and laid out the dishes in the kitchen, and had every appearance of being about preparing a great entertainment.

When it drew near the morning, and they were about to take their departure, the little man came again up to the count, and with many thanks, presented him a sword, a salamander-cloth, and a golden ring, in which there was inserted a red-lion, with directions for himself and his descendants to keep these three articles safe; and so long as they kept them together all would be at unity and well in the county, but as soon as they were separated from each other it would be a token that there was evil coming on the county: the red lion too would always become pale when one of the family was to die.

They were long preserved in the family; but in the time when count Jobst and his brothers were in their minority, and Francis von Halle was governor of the land, two of the articles, the sword and the salamander-cloth, were taken away, but the ring remained with the family until they became extinct. What has become of it since is unknown.*

* Related by Hammelmann in the Oldenburg Chronicle, by Prætorius, Bräuner, and others.

The Friendly Dwarfs.

CLOSE to the little town of Dardesheim, between Halber-
stadt and Brunswick, is a spring of the finest water called
the Smansborn, and which flows out of a hill in which in
old times the dwarfs dwelt.   When the former inhabitants
of the country were in want of a holiday-dress, or, at a
family festival, of any rare utensils, they went and stood
before this Dwarf-hill, knocked three times, and pronounced
their petition in a distinct and audible tone, adding,

> Before the sun is up to-morrow.
> At the hill shall be the things we borrow.*

The Dwarfs thought themselves sufficiently compensated if
there was only some of the festive victuals set down before
the hill.

Wedding-Feast of the Little People.

THE little people of the Eilenburg in Saxony had occasion
to celebrate a wedding, and with that intent passed one
night through the key-hole and the window-slits into the
castle-hall, and jumped down on the smooth level floor like
peas on a barn floor.   The noise awoke the old count, who
was sleeping in the hall in his high four-post bed, and on
opening his eyes, he wondered not a little at the sight of
such a number of the little fellows.

One of them appareled as a herald came up to him, and
addressing him with the utmost courtesy and in very polite
terms invited him to share in their festivity. " We, however,"
added he, " have one request to make, which is, that you
alone should be present, and that none of your people

Frühmorgens eh die Sonn aufgeht
Schon alles vor dem Berge steht.

should presume to look on with you, or to cast so much as one glance." The old count answered in a friendly tone, "Since you have disturbed my sleep, I will join your company." A little small woman was now introduced to him; little torch-bearers took their places; and cricket-music struck up. The count found great difficulty to keep from losing the little woman in the dance, she jumped away fro n him so lightly, and at last whirled him about at such a rate that he could with difficulty recover his breath.

But in the very middle of their spritely dance, suddenly all became still, the music ceased, and the whole company hurried to the slits of the doors, mouse-holes, and everywhere else where there was a corner to slip into. The bride-pair, the heralds, and dancers, looked upwards to a hole that was in the ceiling of the hall, and there discovered the face of the old countess, who overflowing with curiosity, was looking down on the joyous assembly. They then bowed themselves before the count, and the person who had invited him stept forward again and thanked him for the hospitality he had shown them: "But," said he, "since our wedding and our festivity has been thus disturbed by another eye gazing on it, your race shall henceforward never count more than seven Eilenburgs." They then pressed out after one another with great speed, and soon all was silent, and the old count alone in the dark hall. The curse has lasted till the present time, and one of six living knights of Eilenburg has always died before the seventh was born.*

Smith Riechert.

On the east side of the Dwarf-hill of Dardesheim there is a piece of arable land. A smith named Riechert had sown this field with peas; but he observed that when they were just in perfection they were pulled in great quantities. Riechert built himself a little hut on his ground, there to

* This tale was orally related to MM. Grimm in Saxony. They do no mention the narrator's rank in life.

lie in wait for the thief; and there he watched day and night. In the daytime he could see no alteration, but every morning he found that, notwithstanding all his watchfulness, the field had been plundered during the night. Vexed to the heart at seeing that all his labour was in vain, he determined to thresh out on the ground what remained of the peas. So with the daybreak Smith Riechert commenced his work. Hardly was one half of his peas threshed when he heard a piteous wailing, and on going to look for the cause, he found on the ground under the peas one of the dwarfs whose skull he had rapped with his flail, and who was now visible, having lost his mist-cap with the blow. The Dwarf ran back into the hill as fast as his legs could carry him.

However, little tiffs like this disturbed but for a very short time the good understanding of the Dwarf-people and the inhabitants. But the Dwarfs emigrated at last, because the tricks and scoffs of several of the inhabitants were become no longer bearable, as well as their ingratitude for several services they had rendered them. Since that time no one has ever heard or seen anything of the Dwarfs in the neighbourhood.

Dwarfs Stealing Corn.

'Tis not very long since there were Dwarfs at Jüne near Göttingen, who used to go into the fields and steal the sheaves of corn. This they were able to do the more easily by means of a cap they wore, which made them invisible. They did much injury to one man in particular who had a great deal of corn. At length he hit on a plan to catch them. At noon one day he put a rope round the field, and when the Dwarfs went to creep under it, it knocked off their caps. Being now visible, they were caught. They gave him many fair words, promising if he would take away the rope to give him a peck (*mette*) of money if he came to that same place *before sunrise*. He agreed, but a friend whom he consulted told him to go not at sunrise but a little before twelve at night, as it was at that hour that the day really began. He did as directed, and there he found the Dwarfs, who did not expect him, with the peck of money. The name of the family that got it is Mettens.

A farmer in another part of the country being annoyed in a similar manner, was told to get willow-rods and beat the air with them, and he thus would knock of some of their caps and discover them. He and his people did so, and they captured one of the Dwarfs, who told the farmer that if he would let him go, he would give him a waggon-load of money, but he must come for it before sunrise. At the same time he informed him where his abode was. The farmer having enquired when the sun really rose, and being told at twelve o'clock, yoked his waggon and drove off, but when he came to the Dwarfs' hole, he heard them shouting and singing within:

> It is good that the bumpkin doth not know
> That up at twelve the sun doth go.*

When he asked for something, they showed him a dead horse, and bade him take it with him, as they could give him nothing else. He was very angry at this, but as he wanted food for his dogs, he cut off a large piece and laid it on his waggon. But when he came home, lo! it was all pure gold. Others then went to the place, but both hole and horse had vanished.†

Journey of Dwarfs over the Mountain.

On the north side of the Hartz there dwelt several thousand Dwarfs in the clefts of the rocks, and in the Dwarf-caves that still remain. It was, however, but rarely that they appeared to the inhabitants in a visible form; they generally

---

> * *Dat is gaut dat de büerkem dat nich weit*
> *Dat de sunne üm twölwe up geit.*

† Grimm, Deut. Mythol., p. 434. Both legends are in the **Low-Saxon** dialect.

went about among them protected by their mist-caps, unseen and unnoticed.

Many of these Dwarfs were good-natured, and, on particular occasions, very obliging to the inhabitants, who used, for instance, in case of a wedding or a christening, to borrow various articles for the table out of the caves of the Dwarfs, It was, however, highly imprudent to provoke their resentment ; as when injured or offended, they were malicious and wicked, and did every possible injury to the offender.

A baker, who lived in the valley between Blenkenburg and Quedlinburg, used to remark that a part of the loaves he baked was always missing, though he never could find out the thief. This continual secret theft was gradually reducing him to poverty. At last he began to suspect the Dwarfs of being the cause of his misfortune. He accordingly got a bunch of little twigs, and beating the air with them in all directions, at length struck the mist-caps off some Dwarfs, who could now conceal themselves no longer. There was a great noise made about it; several other Dwarfs were caught in the act of committing theft, and at last the whole of the Dwarf-people were forced to quit the country. In order, in some degree, to indemnify the inhabitants for what had been stolen, and at the same time to be able to estimate the number of those that departed, a large cask was set up on what is now called Kirchberg, near the village of Thele, into which each Dwarf was to cast a piece of money. This cask was found, after the departure of the Dwarfs, to be quite filled with ancient coins, so great was their number.

The Dwarf-people went by Warnstadt, a village not far from Quedlinburg, still going toward the east. Since that time the Dwarfs have disappeared out of this country ; and it is only now and then that a solitary one may be seen.

The Dwarfs on the south side of the Hartz were, in a similar manner, detected plundering the corn-fields. They also agreed to quit the country, and it was settled that they should pass over a small bridge near Neuhof, and that each, by way of transit-duty, should cast a certain portion of his property into a cask to be set there. The peasants, on their part, covenanted not to appear or look at them.

Some, however, had the curiosity to conceal themselves under the bridge, that they might at least hear them departing. They succeeded in their design, and heard during several hours, the trampling of the little men, sounding exactly as if a large flock of sheep was going over the bridge.

Other accounts of the departure of the Dwarfs relate as follows:—

The Dosenberg is a mountain in Hesse on the Schwalm, in which, not far from the bank of the stream, are two holes by which the Dwarfs* used to go in and out. One of them came frequently in a friendly way to the grandfather of Tobi in Singlis, when he was out in his fields. As he was one day cutting his corn he asked him if he would the next night, for a good sum of money, take a freight over the river. The farmer agreed, and in the evening the Dwarf brought him a sack of wheat as an earnest. Four horses were then put to the waggon, and the farmer drove to the Dosenberg, out of the holes of which the Dwarf brought heavy, but invisible loads to the waggon, which the farmer then drove through the water over to the other side. He thus kept going backwards and forwards from ten at night till four in the morning, by which time the horses were quite tired. Then said the Dwarf, "It is enough, now you shall see what you have been carrying!" He bade him look over his right shoulder, and then he saw the country far and near filled with the Dwarfs. "These thousand years," then said the Dwarf, "have we dwelt in the Dosenberg; our time is now up, and we must go to another land. But the hill is still so full of money that it would suffice for the whole country." He then loaded Tobi's waggon with money and departed. The farmer had difficulty in bringing home so heavy a load, but he became a rich man. His posterity are still wealthy people, but the Dwarfs have disappeared out of the country for ever.

At Offensen on the Aller in Lower Saxony, lived a great

* The terms used in the original are *Wichtelmänner Wichtelmännerchen,* and *Wichtel.*

farmer, whose name was Hövermann. He had a boat on
the river; and one day two little people came to him and
asked him to put them over the water. They went twice
over the Aller to a great tract of land that is called the
Allerô,* which is an uncultivated plain extending so wide
and far that one can hardly see over it. When the farmer
had crossed the second time one of the Dwarfs said to him,
"Will you have now a sum of money or so much a head?"
"I'd rather have a sum of money," said the farmer. One
of them took off his hat and put it on the farmer's head,
and said, "You'd have done better to have taken so much
a head." The farmer, who had as yet seen nothing and
whose boat had gone as if there was nothing in it, now
beheld the whole Allerô swarming (*krimmeln un wimmeln*)
with little men. These were the Dwarfs that he had brought
over. From that time forward the Hövermanns had the
greatest plenty of money, but they are all now dead and
gone, and the place is sold. But when was this? Oh! in
the old time when the Dwarfs were in the world, but now
there's no more of them, thirty or forty years ago.†

The Dwarfs Borrowing Bread.

—◆—

ALBERT STEFFEL, aged seventy years, who died in the year
1680, and Hans Kohmann, aged thirty-six, who died in
1679, two honest, veracious men, frequently declared that
as one time Kohmann's grandfather was working in his
ground which lay in the neighbourhood of the place called
the Dwarfs' hole, and his wife had brought out to the field
to him for his breakfast some fresh baked bread, and had
laid it, tied up in a napkin, at the end of the field, there
came up soon after a little Dwarf-woman, who spoke to him

---

* The Saxon *ô* seems to answer to the Anglo-Saxon I꜀, Irish *Inis*: see
below, *Ireland*.

† Grimm, Deut. Mythol., p. 428. The latter story is in the Low-Saxon
dialect.

about his bread, saying, that her own was in the oven, and that her children were hungry and could not wait for it, but that if he would give her his, she would be certain to replace it by noon. The man consented, and at noon she returned, spread out a very white little cloth, and laid on it a smoking hot loaf, and with many thanks and entreaties told him he might eat the bread without any apprehension, and that she would return for the cloth. He did as she desired, and when she returned she told him that there had been so many forges erected that she was quite annoyed, and would be obliged to depart and abandon her favourite dwelling. She also said that the shocking cursing and swearing of the people drove her away, as also the profanation of Sunday, as the country people, instead of going to church, used to go look at their fields, which was altogether sinful.*

The Changeling.

IT was the belief, in some parts of Germany, that if a child that was not thriving were taken to a place named Cyriac's Mead, near Neuhausen, and left lying there and given to drink out of Cyriac's Well, at the end of nine days it would either die or recover.

* In Scandinavia the Dwarfs used to borrow beer, even a barrel at a time, which one of them would carry off on his shoulders, Thiele i. 121. In the Highlands of Scotland, a firlot of meal. In all cases they paid honestly. On one occasion, a dwarf came to a lady named Fru (*Mrs.*) Mettè of Overgaard, in Jutland, and asked her to lend her silk gown to Fru Mettè of Undergaard, for her wedding. She gave it, but as it was not returned as soon as she expected, she went to the hill and demanded it aloud. The hill-man brought it out to her all spotted with wax, and told her that if she had not been so impatient, every spot on it would have been a diamond. Thiele iii. 48.

The Vends of Lüneburg, we are told, called the underground folk Görzoni (from *gora*, hill), and the hills are still shown in which they dwelt. They used to borrow bread from people; they intimated their desire invisibly, and people used to lay it for them outside of the door. In the evening they returned it, knocking at the window, and leaving an additional cake to express their thankfulness. Grimm, Deut. Mythol., p. 423.

The butler and cook of one of the spiritual lords of Germany, without being married, had a child, which kept crying day and night, and evermore craving for food and yet it never grew nor throve. It was finally resolved to try on it the effect of Cyriac's Mead, and the mother set out for that place with the child on her back, whose weight was so great that she hardly could endure it. As she was toiling along under her burden, she met a travelling student, who said to her, "My good woman, what sort of a wild creature is that you are carrying? I should not wonder if it were to crush in your neck." She replied that it was her dear child which would not grow nor thrive, and that she was taking it to Neuhausen to be rocked. "But," said he, "that is not your child; it is the devil. Fling it into the stream." But she refused, and maintained that it *was* her child, and kissed it. Then said he, "Your child is at home in the inner bedroom in a new cradle behind the ark. Throw, I tell you, this monster into the stream." With many tears and groans the poor woman at length did as he required and immediately there was heard under the bridge on which they were standing a howling and a growling as if wolves and bears were in the place. When the woman reached home she found her own child healthy and lively and laughing in its new cradle.

A Hessian legend tells that as a woman was reaping corn at the Dosenberg,* with her little child lying near her on the ground, a Dwarf-woman (*wichtelweib*) came and took it and left her own lying in its stead. When the mother came to look after her dear babe a great ugly jolterhead was there gaping at her. She cried out and roared Murder! so lustily that the thief came back with the child. But she did not restore it till the mother had put the changeling to her breast and given it some ennobling human milk.†

There was, it is said, in Prussian Samland, an inn-keeper whom the underground folk had done many good turns. It grieved him to see what bad clothes they had, and he desired his wife to leave new little coats for them. They took the

---

new clothes, but cried out, "Paid off! Paid off!" and went all away.

Another time they gave great help to a poor smith, and every night they made bran-new pots, pans, kettles and plates for him. His wife used to leave some milk for them, on which they fell like wolves, and drained the vessel to the bottom, and then cleaned it and went to their work. When the smith had grown rich by means of them, his wife made for each of them a pretty little red coat and cap, and left them in their way. "Paid off! Paid off!" cried they, slipped on the new clothes, and went away without working the iron that was left for them, and never returned.

There was a being named a Scrat or Schrat, Schretel, Schretlein.† This name is used in old German to translate *pilosus* in the narratives of those who wrote in Latin, and it seems sometimes to denote a House- sometimes a Wood-spirit. Terms similar to it are to be found in the cognate languages, and it is perhaps the origin of Old Scratch, a popular English name of the devil.

There is, chiefly in Southern Germany, a species of beings that greatly resemble the Dwarfs. They are called Wicht-lein (*Little Wights*), and are about three quarters of an ell high. Their appearance is that of old men with long beards. They haunt the mines, and are dressed like miners, with a white hood to their shirts and leather aprons, and are provided with lanterns, mallets, and hammers. They amuse themselves with pelting the workmen with small stones, but do them no injury, except when they are abused and cursed by them.

They show themselves most especially in places where there is an abundance of ore, and the miners are always glad to see them; they flit about in the pits and shafts, and appear to work very hard, though they in reality do nothing. Sometimes they seem as if working a vein, at other times putting the ore into buckets, at other times working at the windlass, but all is mere show. They frequently call, and when one comes there is no one to be seen.

* Grimm, Deut. Mythol., p. 453.
† See Grimm, *ut sup.*, p. 447 *seq.*

At Kuttenburg, in Bohemia, the Wichtlein have been seen in great numbers. They announce the death of a miner by knocking three times, and when any misfortune is about to happen they are heard digging, pounding, and imitating all other kinds of work. At times they make a noise, as if they were smiths labouring very hard at the anvil, hence the Bohemians call them Haus-Schmiedlein (*Little House-smiths*).

In Istria the miners set, every day, in a particular place, a little pot with food in it for them. They also at certain times in each year buy a little red coat, the size of a small boy's, and make the Wichtlein a present of it. If they neglect this, the little people grow very angry.[*]

In Southern Germany they believe in a species of beings somewhat like the Dwarfs, called Wild, Wood, Timber, and Moss-people. These generally live together in society, but they sometimes appear singly. They are small in stature, yet somewhat larger than the Elf, being the size of children of three years, grey and old-looking, hairy and clad in moss. The women are of a more amiable temper than the men, which last live further back in the woods; they wear green clothes faced with red, and cocked-hats. The women come to the wood-cutters and ask them for something to eat; they also take it away of themselves out of the pots; but they always make a return in some way or other, often by giving good advice. Sometimes they help people in their cooking or washing and haymaking, and they feed the cattle. They are fond of coming where people are baking, and beg of them to bake for them also a piece of dough the size of half a mill-stone, and to leave it in a certain place. They sometimes, in return, bring some of their own baking to the ploughman, which they lay in the furrow or on the plough, and they are greatly offended if it is rejected. The wood-woman sometimes comes with a broken wheel-barrow, and begs to have the wheel repaired, and she pays by the chips which turn into gold, or she gives to knitters a ball of thread which is never ended. A woman who good-naturedly gave her breast to a crying Wood-child, was rewarded by its

---

[*] Deutsche Sagen, from Prætorius., Agricola, and others.

mother by a gift of the bark on which it was lying. She broke a splinter off it and threw it into her faggot, and on reaching home she found it was pure gold. Their lives are attached, like those of the Hamadryads, to the trees, and if any one causes by friction the inner bark to loosen a Wood-woman dies.

Their great enemy is the Wild-Huntsman, who driving invisibly through the air pursues and kills them. A peasant one time hearing the usual baying and cheering in a wood, would join in the cry. Next morning he found hanging at his stable-door a quarter of a green Moss-woman as his share of the game. When the woodmen are felling timber they cut three crosses in a spot of the tree that is to be hewn, and the Moss-women sit in the middle of these and so are safe from the Wild-Huntsman.*

The following account of the popular belief in the parts of Germany adjacent to Jutland has been given by a late writer.†

In Friesland the Dwarfs are named Oennereeske, in some of the islands Oennerbänske, and in Holstein Unnerorske.‡ The same stories are told of them as of the Dwarfs and Fairies elsewhere. They take away, and keep for long periods, girls with whom they have fallen in love; they steal children and leave changelings in their stead, the remedy against which is to lay a bible under the child's pillow; they lend and borrow pots, plates, and such like, sometimes lending money with or even without interest; they aid to build houses and churches; help the peasant when his cart has stuck in the mire, and will bring him water and pancakes to refresh him when at work in the fields.

---

* Grimm, Deut. Mythol., pp. 451, 881.

† Kohl, Die Marschen und Inseln der Herzogthümer Schleswig und Holstein.

‡ These terms all signify *Underground folk.*

The Dwarf Husband.

A POOR girl went out one day and as she was passing by
a hill she heard a Dwarf hammering away inside of it, for
they are handy smiths, and singing at his work. She was
so pleased with the song, that she could not refrain from
wishing aloud that she could sing like him, and live like him
under the ground. Scarcely had she expressed the wish
when the singing ceased, and a voice came out of the hill,
saying, "Should you like to live with us?" "To be sure I
should," replied the girl, who probably had no very happy
life of it above ground. Instantly the Dwarf came out of
the hill and made a declaration of love, and a proffer of his
hand and a share in his subterranean wealth. She accepted
the offer and lived very comfortably with him, as he proved
an excellent little husband.

Inge of Rantum.

THE Friesland girls are, however, rather shy of these matches,
and if they have unwarily been drawn into an engagement they try to get out of it if they possibly can.

A girl named Inge of Rantum had some way or other
got into an engagement with one of the Underground
people. The wedding-day was actually fixed, and she could
only be released from her bond on one condition—that of
being able, before it came, to tell the real name of her lover.
All her efforts to that effect were in vain, the dreaded day
was fast approaching and she fell into deep melancholy. On
the morning of her wedding-day she went out and strolled
in sorrowful mood through the fields, saying to herself, as
she plucked some flowers, "Far happier are these flowers

than I." As she was stooping to gather them, she thought she heard a noise under the ground. She listened and recognised it as the voice of her lover, who, in the excess of his joy at the arrival of his wedding-day, was frolicking and singing, "To-day I must bake and boil and roast and broil and wash and brew; for this is my wedding-day. My bride is the fair Inge of Rantum, and my name is Ekke Nekkepem. Hurrah! Nobody knows *that* but myself!" "Aye, but *I* know it too!" said Inge softly to herself, and she placed her nosegay in her bosom and went home. Toward evening came the Dwarf to claim his bride. "Many thanks, dear Ekke Nekkepem," said she, "but if you please I would rather stay where I am." The smiling face of the bridegroom grew dark as thunder, but he recollected how he had divulged his secret, and saw that the affair was past remedy.*

The Nis of Jutland is called Puk† in Friesland. Like him he wears a pointed red cap, with a long grey or green jacket, and slippers on his feet. His usual abode is under the roof, and he goes in and out either through a broken window, which is never mended, or through some other aperture left on purpose for him. A bowl of groute must be left on the floor for him every evening, and he is very angry if there should be no butter in it. When well treated he makes himself very useful by cleaning up the house, and tending the cattle. He sometimes amuses himself by playing tricks on the servants, tickling, for example, their noses when they are asleep, or pulling off the bedclothes. Stories are told of the Puk, similar to some above related of the Juttish Nis.

---

* See above, p. 116.

† The Puk is also called Niss-Puk, Huis-Puk, Niske, Niske-Puk, Nise-Bok, Niss-Kuk—all compounds or corruptions of Nisse and Puk. He is also named from his racketing and noise Pulter-Claas, *i. e.* Nick Knocker, (the German Poltergeist,) Claas being the abbreviation of Nicolaus, Niclas ; see above, p. 139, for this same origin of Nisse.

THE WILD-WOMEN.

———✦———

Ein Mägdlein kam im Abendglanz,
Wie ich's noch nie gefunden.
                        SCHREIBER.

A maiden came in Evening's glow,
Such as I ne'er have met.

THE Wilde Frauen or Wild-women of Germany bear a very
strong resemblance to the Elle-maids of Scandinavia. Like
them they are beautiful, have fine flowing hair, live within
hills, and only appear singly or in the society of each other.
They partake of the piety of character we find among the
German Dwarfs.

The celebrated Wunderberg, or Underberg, on the great
moor near Salzburg, is the chief haunt of the Wild-women.
The Wunderberg is said to be quite hollow, and supplied
with stately palaces, churches, monasteries, gardens, and
springs of gold and silver. Its inhabitants, beside the Wild-
women, are little men, who have charge of the treasures it
contains, and who at midnight repair to Salzburg to perform
their devotions in the cathedral ; giants, who used to come
to the church of Grödich and exhort the people to lead a
godly and pious life; and the great emperor Charles V.,
with golden crown and sceptre, attended by knights and
lords. His grey beard has twice encompassed the table at
which he sits, and when it has the third time grown round
it, the end of the world and the appearance of the Anti-
christ will take place.*

---

* All relating to the Wild-women and the Wunderberg is given by MM.
Grimm from the Brixener Volksbuch, 1782. For an account of the various
Bergentrückte Helden, see the Deutsche Mythologie, ch. xxxii.

The following is the only account we have of the Wild-women.

The inhabitants of the village of Grödich and the peasantry of the neighbourhood assert that frequently, about the year 1753, the Wild-women used to come out of the Wunderberg to the boys and girls that were keeping the cattle near the hole within Glanegg, and give them bread to eat.

The Wild-women used frequently to come to where the people were reaping. They came down early in the morning, and in the evening, when the people left off work, they went back into the Wunderberg without partaking of the supper.

It happened once near this hill, that a little boy was sitting on a horse which his father had tethered on the headland of the field. Then came the Wild-women out of the hill and wanted to take away the boy by force. But the father, who was well acquainted with the secrets of this hill, and what used to occur there, without any dread hasted up to the women and took the boy from them, with these words: "What makes you presume to come so often out of the hill, and now to take away my child with you? What do you want to do with him?" The Wild-women answered: "He will be better with us, and have better care taken of him than at home. We shall be very fond of the boy, and he will meet with no injury." But the father would not let the boy out of his hands, and the Wild-women went away weeping bitterly.

One time the Wild-women came out of the Wunderberg, near the place called the Kugelmill, which is prettily situated on the side of this hill, and took away a boy who was keeping cattle. This boy, whom every one knew, was seen about a year after by some wood-cutters, in a green dress, and sitting on a block of this hill. Next day they took his parents with them, intending to search the hill for him, but they all went about it to no purpose, for the boy never appeared any more.

It frequently has happened that a Wild-woman out of the Wunderberg has gone toward the village of Anif, which is better than a mile from the hill. She used to make holes and beds for herself in the ground. She had uncommonly long and beautiful hair, which reached nearly to the soles of her feet. A peasant belonging to the village often saw this woman going and coming, and he fell deeply in love with her, especially on account of her beautiful hair. He could not refrain from going up to her, and he gazed on her with delight; and at last, in his simplicity, he laid himself, without any repugnance, down by her side. The second night the Wild-woman asked him if he had not a wife already? The peasant however denied his wife, and said he had not.

His wife meanwhile was greatly puzzled to think where it was that her husband went every evening, and slept every night. She therefore watched him and found him in the field sleeping near the Wild-woman:—"Oh, God preserve thy beautiful hair!" said she to the Wild-woman; "what are you doing there?" * With these words the peasant's wife retired and left them, and her husband was greatly frightened at it. But the Wild-woman upbraided him with his false denial, and said to him, "Had your wife manifested hatred and spite against me, you would now be unfortunate, and would never leave this place; but since your wife was not malicious, love her from henceforth, and dwell with her faithfully, and never venture more to come here, for it is written, 'Let every one live faithfully with his wedded wife;' though the force of this commandment will greatly decrease, and with it all the temporal prosperity of married people. Take this shoefull of money from me: go home, and look no more about you."

As the fair maiden who originally possessed the famed Oldenburg Horn was probably a Wild-woman, we will place the story of it here.

---

* In a similar tradition (Strack, Beschr. von Eilsen, p. 120) the wife cuts off one of her fair long tresses, and is afterwards most earnestly conjured by her to restore it.

The Oldenburg Horn.

IN the time of count Otto of Oldenburg, who succeeded his
father Ulrich in the year 967, a wonderful transaction
occurred. For as he, being a good sportsman, and one who
took great delight in the chase, had set out early one day
with his nobles and attendants, and had hunted in the
wood of Bernefeuer, and the count himself had put up a
roe, and followed him alone from the wood of Bernefeuer to
the Osenberg, and with his white horse stood on the top of
the hill, and endeavoured to trace the game, he said to himself, for it was an excessively hot day, "Oh God! if one had
now but a cool drink!"

No sooner had the count spoken the word than the Osenberg opened, and out of the cleft there came a beautiful
maiden, fairly adorned and handsomely dressed, and with her
beautiful hair divided on her shoulders, and a garland on
her head. And she had a rich silver vessel, that was gilded
and shaped like a hunter's horn, well and ingeniously made,
granulated, and fairly ornamented. It was adorned with
various kinds of arms that are now but little known, and
with strange unknown inscriptions and ingenious figures,
and it was soldered together and adorned in the same
manner as the old antiques, and it was beautifully and
ingeniously wrought. This horn the maiden held in her
hand, and it was full, and she gave it into the hand of the
count, and prayed that the count would drink out of it to
refresh himself therewith.

When the count had received and taken this gilded silver
horn from the maiden, and had opened it and looked into it,
the drink, or whatever it was that was in it, when he shook
it, did not please him, and he therefore refused to drink for
the maiden. Whereupon the maiden said, "My dear lord,
drink of it upon my faith, for it will do you no harm, but
will be of advantage;" adding farther, that if the count

would drink out of it, it would go well with him, count Otto, and his, and also with the whole house of Oldenburg after him, and that the whole country would improve and flourish. But if the count would place no faith in her, and would not drink of it, then for the future, in the succeeding family of Oldenburg, there would remain no unity. But when the count gave no heed to what she said, but, as was not without reason, considered with himself a long time whether he should drink or not, he held the silver gilded horn in his hand and swung it behind him, and poured it out, and some of its contents sprinkled the white horse, and where it fell and wetted him the hair all came off.

When the maiden saw this, she desired to have her horn back again, but the count made speed down the hill with the horn, which he held in his hand, and when he looked round he observed that the maiden was gone into the hill again. And when terror seized on the count on account of this, he laid spurs to his horse, and at full speed hasted to join his attendants, and informed them of what had befallen him. He moreover showed them the silver gilded horn, and took it with him to Oldenburg, and the same horn, as it was obtained in so wonderful a manner, was preserved as a costly jewel by him, and by all the succeeding reigning princes of the house of Oldenburg.*

---

* Given by Büsching (Volks-sagen Märchen und Legenden. Leipzig, 1820), from Hammelmann's Oldenburg Chronicle, 1599. Mme. Naubert has, in the second volume of her Volksmärchen, wrought it up into a tale of 130 pages.

The Oldenburg horn, or what is called such, is now in the King of Denmark's collection.

KOBOLDS.*

———◆———

Von Kobolt sang die Amme mir
Von Kobolt sing' ich wieder.
VON HALEM.

Of Kobold sang my nurse to me;
Of Kobold I too sing.

THE Kobold is exactly the same being as the Danish Nis,
and Scottish Brownie, and English Hobgoblin.† He performs the very same services for the family to whom he
attaches himself.

When the Kobold is about coming into any place, he first
makes trial of the disposition of the family in this way. He
brings chips and saw-dust into the house, and throws dirt
into the milk vessels. If the master of the house takes care
that the chips are not scattered about, and that the dirt is
left in the vessels, and the milk drunk out of them, the
Kobold comes and stays in the house as long as there is one
of the family alive.

The change of servants does not affect the Kobold, who
still remains. The maid who is going away must recommend
her successor to take care of him, and treat him well. If
she does not so, things go ill with her till she is also obliged
to leave the place.

The history of the celebrated Hinzelmann will give most

---

* This word is usually derived from the Greek κόβαλος, a knave, which
is found in Aristophanes. According to Grimm (p. 468) the German
Kobold is not mentioned by any writer anterior to the thirteenth century;
we find the French Gobelin in the eleventh; see *France*.

† In Hanover the Will-o'the-wisp is called the Tückebold, *i. e.* Tücke-
Kobold, and is, as his name denotes, a malicious being. Voss. Lyr. Ged.,
ii. p. 315.

full and satisfactory information respecting the nature and properties of Kobolds; for such he was, though he used constantly to deny it. His history was written at considerable length by a pious minister, named Feldmann. MM. Grimm gives us the following abridgement of it.*

Hinzelmann.†

A WONDERFUL house-spirit haunted for a long time the old castle of Hudemühlen, situated in the country of Lüneburg, not far from the Aller, and of which there is nothing remaining but the walls. It was in the year 1584 that he first notified his presence, by knocking and making various noises. Soon after he began to converse with the servants in the daylight. They were at first terrified at hearing a voice and seeing nothing, but by degrees they became accustomed to it and thought no more of it. At last he became quite courageous, and began to speak to the master of the house himself, and used, in the middle of the day and in the evening, to carry on conversations of various kinds; and at meal-times he discoursed with those who were present, whether strangers or belonging to the family. When all fear of him was gone he became quite friendly and intimate: he sang, laughed, and went on with every kind of sport, so long as no one vexed him: and his voice was on these occasions soft and tender like that of a boy or maiden. When he was asked whence he came, and what he had to do in that place, he said he was come from the Bohemian mountains, and that his companions were in the Bohemian forest —that they would not tolerate him, and that he was in consequence obliged to retire and take refuge with good people

* Deutsche Sagen, i. p. 103. Feldmann's work is a 12mo vol. of 379 pages.
† Heinze is the abbreviation of Heinrich (Henry). In the North of Germany the Kobold is also named Chimmeken and Wolterken, from Joachim and Walther.

till his affairs should be in a better condition. He added that his name was Hinzelmann, but that he was also called Lüring; and that he had a wife whose name was Hille Bingels. When the time for it was come he would let himself be seen in his real shape, but that at present it was not convenient for him to do so. In all other respects he was, he said, as good and honest a fellow as need be.

The master of the house, when he saw that the spirit attached himself more and more to him, began to get frightened, and knew not how he should get rid of him. By the advice of his friends he determined at last to leave his castle for some time, and set out for Hanover. On the road they observed a white feather that flew beside the carriage, but no one knew what it signified. When he arrived at Hanover he missed a valuable gold chain that he wore about his neck, and his suspicions fell upon the servants of the house. But the innkeeper took the part of his servants, and demanded satisfaction for the discreditable charge. The nobleman, who could prove nothing against them, sat in his chamber in bad spirits, thinking how he should manage to get himself out of this unpleasant affair, when all of a sudden he heard Hinzelmann's voice beside him, saying, " Why are you so sad ? If there is anything gone wrong with you tell it to me, and I shall perhaps know how to assist you. If I were to make a guess, I should say that you are fretting on account of a chain you have lost." " What are you doing here ?" replied the terrified nobleman; " why have you followed me ? Do you know anything about the chain ?" " Yes, indeed," said Hinzelmann, " I have followed you, and I kept you company on the road, and was always present : did you not see me ? why, I was the white feather that flew beside the carriage. And now I 'll tell you where the chain is :—Search under the pillow of your bed, and there you 'll find it." The chain was found where he said ; but the mind of the nobleman became still more uneasy, and he asked him in an angry tone why he had brought him into a quarrel with the landlord on account of the chain, since he was the cause of his leaving his own house. Hinzelmann replied, " Why do you retire from me ? I can easily follow you anywhere, and be where you are. It is much better for you to return to your own estate, and not be quitting it on my account.

You see well that if I wished it I could take away all you have, but I am not inclined to do so." The nobleman thought some time of it, and at last came to the resolution of returning home, and trusting in God not to retreat a step from the spirit.

At home in Hudemühlen, Hinzelmann now showed himself extremely obliging, and active and industrious at every kind of work. He used to toil every night in the kitchen; and if the cook, in the evening after supper, left the plates and dishes lying in a heap without being washed, next morning they were all nice and clean, shining like looking-glasses, and put up in proper order. She therefore might depend upon him, and go to bed in the evening after supper without giving herself any concern about them. In like manner nothing was ever lost in the kitchen; and if anything was astray Hinzelmann knew immediately where to find it, in whatever corner it was hid, and gave it into the hands of the owner. If strangers were expected, the spirit let himself be heard in a particular manner, and his labours were continued the whole night long: he scoured the pots and kettles, washed the dishes, cleaned the pails and tubs. The cook was grateful to him for all this, and not only did what he desired, but cheerfully got ready his sweet milk for his breakfast. He took also the charge of superintending the other men and maids. He noticed how they got through their business; and when they were at work he encouraged them with good words to be industrious. But if any one was inattentive to what he said, he caught up a stick and communicated his instructions by laying on heartily with it. He frequently warned the maids of their mistress's displeasure, and reminded them of some piece of work which they should set about doing. He was equally busy in the stable: he attended to the horses, and curried them carefully, so that they were as smooth in their coats as an eel; they also throve and improved so much, in next to no time, that everybody wondered at it.

His chamber was in the upper story on the right hand side, and his furniture consisted of only three articles. Imprimis, of a settle or arm-chair, which he plaited very neatly for himself of straw of different colours, full of handsome figures and crosses, which no one looked upon without admiration. Secondly, of a little round table, which was on his repeated entreaties made and put there. Thirdly, of a bed and bedstead, which he had also expressed a wish for. There never was any trace found as if a man had lain in it; there could only be perceived a very small depression, as if a cat had been there. The servants, especially the cook, were obliged every day to prepare a dish full of sweet milk, with crums of wheaten bread, and place it upon his little table; and it was soon after eaten up clean. He sometimes used to come to the table of the master of the house, and they were obliged to put a chair and a plate for him at a particular place. Whoever was helping, put his food on his plate, and if that was forgotten he fell into a great passion. What was put on his plate vanished, and a glass full of wine was taken away for some time, and was then set again in its place empty. But the food was afterwards found lying under the benches, or in a corner of the room.

In the society of young people Hinzelmann was extremely cheerful. He sang and made verses: one of his most usual ones was,

> If thou here wilt let me stay,
> Good luck shalt thou have alway;
> But if hence thou wilt me chase,
> Luck will ne'er come near the place.

He used also to repeat the songs and sayings of other people by way of amusement or to attract their attention. The minister Feldmann was once invited to Hudemühlen, and when he came to the door he heard some one above in the hall singing, shouting, and making every sort of noise, which made him think that some strangers had come the evening before, and were lodged above, and making themselves merry. He therefore said to the steward, who was standing in the court after having cut up some wood, "John, what guests have you above there?" The steward answered, "We have no strangers; it is only our Hinzelmann who is amusing himself; there is not a living soul else in the hall." When the minister went up into the hall, Hinzelmann sang out to him

> My thumb, my thumb,
> And my elbow are two.

The minister wondered at this unusual kind of song, and he

said to Hinzelmann, "What sort of music is that you come to meet me with?" "Why," replied Hinzelmann, "it was from yourself I learned the song, for you have often sung it, and it is only a few days since I heard it from you, when you were in a certain place at a christening."

Hinzelmann was fond of playing tricks, but he never hurt any one by them. He used to set servants and workmen by the ears as they sat drinking in the evening, and took great delight then in looking at the sport. When any one of them was well warmed with liquor, and let anything fall under the table and stooped to take it up, Hinzelmann would give him a good box on the ear from behind, and at the same time pinch his neighbour's leg. Then the two attacked each other, first with words and then with blows; the rest joined in the scuffle, and they dealt about their blows, and were repaid in kind; and next morning black eyes and swelled faces bore testimony of the fray. But Hinzelmann's very heart was delighted at it, and he used afterwards to tell how it was he that began it, on purpose to set them fighting. He however always took care so to order matters that no one should run any risk of his life.

There came one time to Hudemühlen a nobleman who undertook to banish Hinzelmann. Accordingly, when he remarked that he was in a certain room, of which all the doors and windows were shut fast, he had this chamber and the whole house also beset with armed men, and went himself with his drawn sword into the room, accompanied by some others. They however saw nothing, so they began to cut and thrust left and right in all directions, thinking that if Hinzelmann had a body some blow or other must certainly reach him and kill him; still they could not perceive that their hangers met anything but mere air. When they thought they must have accomplished their task, and were going out of the room tired with their long fencing, just as they opened the door, they saw a figure like that of a black marten, and heard these words, "Ha, ha! how well you caught me!" But Hinzelmann afterwards expressed himself very bitterly for this insult, and declared, that he would have easily had an opportunity of revenging himself, were it not that he wished to spare the two ladies of the house any uneasiness. When this same nobleman not long after went into an empty room in the house, he saw a large snake lying coiled up on an unoccupied bed. It instantly vanished, and he heard the words of the spirit—"You were near catching me."

Another nobleman had heard a great deal about Hinzelmann, and he was curious to get some personal knowledge of him. He came accordingly to Hudemühlen, and his wish was not long ungratified, for the spirit let himself be heard from a corner of the room where there was a large cupboard, in which were standing some empty wine-jugs with long necks. As the voice was soft and delicate, and somewhat hoarse, as if it came out of a hollow vessel, the nobleman thought it likely that he was sitting in one of these jugs, so he got up and ran and caught them up, and went to stop them, thinking in this way to catch the spirit. While he was thus engaged, Hinzelmann began to laugh aloud, and cried out, "If I had not heard long ago from other people that you were a fool, I might now have known it of myself, since you thought I was sitting in an empty jug, and went to cover it up with your hand, as if you had me caught. I don't think you worth the trouble, or I would have given you, long since, such a lesson, that you should remember me long enough. But before long you will get a slight ducking." He then became silent, and did not let himself be heard any more so long as the nobleman stayed. Whether he fell into the water, as Hinzelmann threatened him, is not said, but it is probable he did.

There came, too, an exorcist to banish him. When he began his conjuration with his magic words, Hinzelmann was at first quite quiet, and did not let himself be heard at all, but when he was going to read the most powerful sentences against him, he snatched the book out of his hand, tore it to pieces, so that the leaves flew about the room, caught hold of the exorcist himself, and squeezed and scratched him till he ran away frightened out of his wits. He complained greatly of this treatment, and said, "I am a Christian, like any other man, and I hope to be saved." When he was asked if he knew the Kobolds and Knocking-spirits (*Polter Geister*), he answered, "What have these to do with me? They are the Devil's spectres, and I do not belong to them. No one has any evil, but rather good, to expect from me. Let me alone and you will have luck in everything; the cattle will thrive, your substance will increase, and everything will go on well."

Profligacy and vice were quite displeasing to him; he used frequently to scold severely one of the family for his stinginess, and told the rest that he could not endure him on account of it. Another he upbraided with his pride, which he said he hated from his heart. When some one once said to him that if he would be a good Christian, he should call upon God, and say Christian prayers, he began the Lord's Prayer, and went through it till he came to the last petition, when he murmured "Deliver us from the Evil one" quite low. He also repeated the Creed, but in a broken and stammering manner, for when he came to the words, "I believe in the forgiveness of sins, the resurrection of the body, and life everlasting," he pronounced them in so hoarse and indistinct a voice that no one could rightly hear and understand him. The minister of Eicheloke, Mr. Feldmann, said that his father was invited to dinner to Hudemühlen at Whitsuntide, where he heard Hinzelmann go through the whole of the beautiful hymn, "*Nun bitten wir den heiligen Geist,*" in a very high but not unpleasant voice, like that of a girl or a young boy. Nay, he sang not merely this, but several other spiritual songs also when requested, especially by those whom he regarded as his friends, and with whom he was on terms of intimacy.

On the other hand, he was extremely angry when he was not treated with respect and as a Christian. A nobleman of the family of Mandelsloh once came to Hudemühlen. This nobleman was highly respected for his learning; he was a canon of the cathedral of Verden, and had been ambassador to the Elector of Brandenburg and the King of Denmark. When he heard of the house-spirit, and that he expected to be treated as a Christian, he said he could not believe that all was right with him: he was far more inclined to regard him as the Enemy and the Devil, for that God had never made men of that kind and form, that angels praised God their Lord, and guarded and protected men, with which the knocking and pounding and strange proceedings of the House-spirit did not accord. Hinzelmann, who had not let himself be heard since his arrival, now made a noise and cried out, "What say you Barthold? (that was the noble-man's name) am I the Enemy? I advise you not to say too much, or I will show you another trick, and teach you to deliver a better judgment of me another time." The nobleman was frightened when he heard a voice without seeing any one, broke off the discourse, and would hear nothing more of him, but left him in possession of his dignity.

Another time a nobleman came there, who, when he saw a chair and plate laid for Hinzelmann at dinner, refused to pledge him. At this the spirit was offended, and he said, "I am as honest and good a fellow as he is; why then does he not drink to me?" To this the nobleman replied, " Depart hence, and go drink with thy infernal companions ; thou hast nothing to do here." When Hinzelmann heard that, he became so highly exasperated, that he seized him by the strap with which, according to the custom of those days, his cloak was fastened under his chin, dragged him to the ground, and choked and pressed him in such a manner that all that were present were in pain lest he should kill him; and the gentleman did not come to himself for some hours after the spirit had left him.

Another time an esteemed friend of the master of Hude-mühlen was travelling that way, but he hesitated to come in on account of the House-spirit, of whose mischievous turn he had heard a great deal, and sent his servant to inform the family that he could not call upon them. The master of the house sent out and pressed him very much to come in and dine there, but the stranger politely excused himself, by saying that it was not in his power to stop; he, however, added, that he was too much terrified at the idea of sitting at the same table eating and drinking with a devil. Hinzel-mann, it appears, was present at this conversation out in the road; for when the stranger had thus refused they heard these words, "Wait, my good fellow, you shall be well paid for this talk." Accordingly, when the traveller went on and came to the bridge over the Meisse, the horses took fright, entangled themselves in the harness, and horses, carriage and all, were within an ace of tumbling down into the water. When everything had been set to rights, and the carriage had got on about a gun-shot, it was turned over in the sand on the level ground, without, however, those who were in it receiving any farther injury.

Hinzelmann was fond of society, but the society he chiefly delighted in was that of females, and he was to them very friendly and affable. There were two young ladies at Hude-mühlen, named Anne and Catherine, to whom he was par-·ticularly attached; he used to make his complaint to them whenever he was angry at anything, and held, besides, conversations of every kind with them. Whenever they travelled he would not quit them, but accompanied them everywhere in the shape of a white feather. When they went to sleep at night, he lay beneath, at their feet, outside the clothes, and in the morning there was a little hole to be seen, as if a little dog had lain there.

Neither of these ladies ever married; for Hinzelmann frightened away their wooers. Matters had frequently gone so far as the engagement, but the spirit always contrived to have it broken off. One lover he would make all bewildered and confused when he was about to address the lady, so that he did not know what he should say. In another he would excite such fear as to make him quiver and tremble. But his usual way was to make a writing appear before their eyes on the opposite white wall, with these words in golden letters: "Take maid Anne, and leave me maid Catherine." But if any one came to court lady Anne, the golden writing changed all at once, and became "Take maid Catherine, and leave me maid Anne." If any one did not change his course for this, but persisted in his purpose, and happened to spend the night in the house, he terrified and tormented him so in the dark with knocking and flinging and pounding, that he laid aside all wedding-thoughts, and was right glad to get away with a whole skin. Some, when they were on their way back, he tumbled, themselves and their horses, over and over, that they thought their necks and legs would be broken, and yet knew not how it had happened to them. In consequence of this, the two ladies remained unmarried; they arrived to a great age, and died within a week of each other.

One of these ladies once sent a servant from Hudemühlen to Rethem to buy different articles; while he was away Hinzelmann began suddenly to clapper in the ladies' chamber like a stork, and then said, "Maid Anne, you must go look for your things to-day in the mill-stream." She did not know what this meant; but the servant soon came in, and related, that as he was on his way home, he had seen a stork sitting at no great distance from him, which he shot at, and it seemed to him as if he had hit it, but that the stork had remained sitting, and at last began to clap its wings aloud and then flew away. It was now plain that Hinzelmann knew this, and his prophecy also soon came to pass. For the servant, who was a little intoxicated, wanted to wash his horse, who was covered with sweat and dirt, and he rode him into the mill-stream in front of the castle; but owing to his drunkenness he missed the right place, and got into a deep hole, where, not being able to keep his seat on the horse, he fell off and was drowned. He had not delivered the things he had brought with him ; so they and the body together were fished up out of the stream.

Hinzelmann also informed and warned others of the future. There came to Hudemühlen a colonel, who was greatly esteemed by Christian III. King of Denmark, and who had done good service in the wars with the town of Lübeck. He was a good shot and passionately fond of the chase, and used to spend many hours in the neighbouring woods after the harts and the wild sows. As he was getting ready one day to go to the chase as usual, Hinzelmann came and said, "Thomas (that was his name), I warn you to be cautious how you shoot, or you will before long meet with a mishap." The colonel took no notice of this, and thought it meant nothing. But a few days after, as he was firing at a roe, his gun burst, and took the thumb off his left hand. When this occurred, Hinzelmann was instantly by his side, and said, "See, now, you have got what I warned you of! If you had refrained from shooting this time, this mischance would not have befallen you."

Another time a certain lord Falkenberg, who was a soldier, was on a visit at Hudemühlen. He was a lively, jolly man, and he began to play tricks on Hinzelmann, and to mock and jeer him. Hinzelmann would not long put up with this, and he began to exhibit signs of great dissatisfaction. At last he said,—" Falkenberg, you are making very merry now at my expense, but wait till you come to Magdeburg, and there your cap will be burst in such a way that you will forget your jibes and your jeers." The nobleman was awed : he was persuaded that these words contained a hidden sense : he broke off the conversation with Hinzelmann, and shortly after departed.   Not long after the siege of Magdeburg, under the Elector Maurice, commenced, at which this lord Falkenberg was present, under a German prince of high rank.   The besieged made a gallant resistance, and night and day kept up a firing of double-harquebuses, and other kinds of artillery ; and it happened that one day Falkenberg's chin was shot away by a ball from a falconet, and three days after he died of the wound, in great agony.

Any one whom the spirit could not endure he used to plague or punish for his vices.   He accused the secretary at Hudemühlen of too much pride, took a great dislike to him on account of it, and night and day gave him every kind of annoyance.   He once related with great glee how he had given the haughty secretary a sound box on the ear.   When the secretary was asked about it, and whether the Spirit had been with him, he replied, " Ay, indeed, he has been with me but too often ; this very night he tormented me in such a manner that I could not stand before him."   He had a love affair with the chamber-maid ; and one night as he was in high and confidential discourse with her, and they were sitting together in great joy, thinking that no one could see them but the four walls, the crafty spirit came and drove them asunder, and roughly tumbled the poor secretary out at the door, and then took up a broomstick and laid on him with it, that he made over head and neck for his chamber, and forgot his love altogether.   Hinzelmann is said to have made some verses on the unfortunate lover, and to have often sung them for his amusement, and repeated them to travellers, laughing heartily at them.

One time some one at Hudemühlen was suddenly taken in the evening with a violent fit of the cholic, and a maid was despatched to the cellar to fetch some wine, in which the patient was to take his medicine.   As the maid was sitting before the cask, and was just going to draw the wine, Hinzelmann was by her side, and said, " You will be pleased to recollect that, a few days ago, you scolded me and abused me; by way of punishment for it, you shall spend this night sitting in the cellar. As to the sick person, he is in no danger whatever; his pain will be all gone in half an hour, and the wine would rather injure him. So just stay sitting here till the cellar door is opened." The patient waited a long time, but no wine came; another maid was sent down, and she found the cellar door well secured on the outside with a good padlock, and the maid sitting within, who told her that Hinzelmann had fastened her up in that way. They wanted to open the cellar and let the maid out, but they could not find a key for the lock, though they searched with the greatest industry. Next morning the cellar was open, and the lock and key lying before the door. Just as the spirit said, all his pain left the sick man in the course of half an hour.

Hinzelmann had never shown himself to the master of the house at Hudemühlen, and whenever he begged of him that if he was shaped like a man, he would let himself be seen by him, he answered, " that the time was not yet come; that he should wait till it was agreeable to him." One night, as the master was lying awake in bed, he heard a rushing noise on one side of the chamber, and he conjectured that the spirit must be there. So he said "Hinzelmann, if you are there, answer me." " It is I," replied he; "what do you want?" As the room was quite light with the moonshine, it seemed to the master as if there was the shadow of a form like that of a child, perceptible in the place from which the sound proceeded. As he observed that the spirit was in a very friendly humour, he entered into conversation with him, and said, " Let me, for this once, see and feel you." But Hinzelmann would not: "Will you reach me your hand, at least, that I may know whether you are flesh and bone like a man?" " No," said Hinzelmann; " I won't trust you; you are a knave; you might catch hold of me, and not let me go any more." After a long demur, however, and after he had promised, on his faith and honour, not to hold him, but to let him go again immediately, he said, "See, there is my hand." And as the master caught at it, it seemed to him as if he felt the fingers of the hand of a little child; but the spirit drew it back quickly. The master further desired that he would let him feel his face, to which he at last consented; and when he touched it, it seemed to him as if he had touched teeth, or a fleshless skeleton, and the face drew back instantaneously, so that he could not ascertain its exact shape; he only noticed that it, like the hand, was cold, and devoid of vital heat.

The cook, who was on terms of great intimacy with him, thought that she might venture to make a request of him, though another might not, and as she felt a strong desire to see Hinzelmann bodily, whom she heard talking every day, and whom she supplied with meat and drink, she prayed him earnestly to grant her that favour; but he would not, and said that this was not the right time, but that after some time, he would let himself be seen by any person. This refusal only stimulated her desire, and she pressed him more and more not to deny her request. He said she would repent of her curiosity if she would not give up her desire; and when all his representations were to no purpose, and she would not give over, he at last said to her, "Come to-morrow morning before sun-rise into the cellar, and carry in each hand a pail full of water, and your request shall be complied with." The maid inquired what the water was for: "That you will learn," answered he; "without it, the sight of me might be injurious to you."

Next morning the cook was ready at peep of dawn, took in each hand a pail of water, and went down to the cellar. She looked about her without seeing anything; but as she cast her eyes on the ground she perceived a tray, on which was lying a naked child apparently three years old, and two knives sticking crosswise in his heart, and his whole body streaming with blood. The maid was terrified at this sight to such a degree, that she lost her senses, and fell in a swoon on the ground. The spirit immediately took the water that she had brought with her, and poured it all over her head, by which means she came to herself again. She looked about for the tray, but all had vanished, and she only heard the voice of Hinzelmann, who said, "You see now how needful the water was; if it had not been at hand you had died here in the cellar. I hope your burning desire to see me is now pretty well cooled." He often afterwards illuded the cook with this trick, and told it to strangers with great glee and laughter.

He frequently showed himself to innocent children when at play. The minister Feldmann recollected well, that when he was about fourteen or fifteen years old, and was not thinking particularly about him, he saw the Spirit in the form of a little boy going up the stairs very swiftly. When children were collected about Hudemühlen house, and were playing with one another, he used to get among them and play with them in the shape of a pretty little child, so that all the other children saw him plainly, and when they went home told their parents how, while they were engaged in play, a strange child came to them and amused himself with them. This was confirmed by a maid, who went one time into a room in which four or six children were playing together, and among them she saw a strange little boy of a beautiful countenance, with curled yellow hair hanging down his shoulders, and dressed in a red silk coat; and while she wanted to observe him more closely, he got out of the party, and disappeared. Hinzelmann let himself be seen also by a fool, named Claus, who was kept there, and used to pursue every sort of diversion with him. When the fool could not anywhere be found, and they asked him afterwards where he had been so long, he used to reply, "I was with the little wee man, and I was playing with him." If he was farther asked how big the little man was, he held his hand at a height about that of a child of four years.*

When the time came that the house-spirit was about to depart, he went to the master of the house and said to him, "See, I will make you a present; take care of it, and let it remind you of me." He then handed him a little *cross*—it is doubtful from the author's words whether of silk (*seide*) or strings (*saiten*)—very prettily plaited. It was the length of a finger, was hollow within, and jingled when it was shaken. Secondly, a *straw hat*, which he had made himself, and in which might be seen forms and figures very ingeniously made in the variously-coloured straw. Thirdly, a

---

* This is a usual measure of size for the Dwarfs, and even the angels, in the old German poetry; see above, p. 208. In Otnit it is said of Elberich : *nu bist in Kindes máze des vierden jâres alt ;* and of Antilois in Ulrich's Alexander : *er war kleine und niht gróz in der máze als diu kint, wenn si in vier jâren sint,* Grimm, Deut. Mythol., p. 418. We meet with it even in Italian poetry :

E sovra il dorso un nano si piccino
Che sembri di quattr' anni un fanciullino.

B. Tasso, Amadigi, C. c. st. 78.

leathern *glove* set with pearls, which formed wonderful figures. He then subjoined this prophecy: "So long as these things remain unseparated in good preservation in your family, so long will your entire race flourish, and their good fortune continually increase; but if these presents are divided, lost, or wasted, your race will decrease and sink." And when he perceived that the master appeared to set no particular value on the present, he continued: "I fear that you do not much esteem these things, and will let them go out of your hands; I therefore counsel you to give them in charge to your sisters Anne and Catherine, who will take better care of them."

He accordingly gave the gifts to his sisters, who took them and kept them carefully, and never showed them to any but most particular friends. After their death they reverted to their brother, who took them to himself, and with him they remained so long as he lived. He showed them to the minister Feldmann, at his earnest request, during a confidential conversation. When he died, they came to his only daughter Adelaide, who was married to L. von H., along with the rest of the inheritance, and they remained for some time in her possession. The son of the minister Feldmann made several inquiries about what had afterwards become of the House-spirit's presents, and he learned that the straw-hat was given to the emperor Ferdinand II., who regarded it as something wonderful. The leathern glove was still in his time in the possession of a nobleman. It was short, and just exactly reached above the hand, and there was a snail worked with pearls on the part that came above the hand. What became of the little cross was never known.

The spirit departed of his own accord, after he had staid four years, from 1584 to 1588, at Hudemühlen. He said, before he went away, that he would return once more when the family would be declined, and that it would then flourish anew and increase in consequence.*

* The feats of House-spirits, it is plain, may in general be ascribed to ventriloquism and to contrivances of servants and others.

Hödeken.

—◆—

ANOTHER Kobold or House-spirit took up his abode in the palace of the bishop of Hildesheim. He was named Hödeken or Hütchen, that is Hatekin or Little Hat, from his always wearing a little felt hat very much down upon his face. He was of a kind and obliging disposition, often told the bishop and others of what was to happen, and he took good care that the watchmen should not go to sleep on their post.

It was, however, dangerous to affront him. One of the scullions in the bishop's kitchen used to fling dirt on him and splash him with foul water. Hödeken complained to the head cook, who only laughed at him, and said, " Are you a spirit and afraid of a little boy ?" "Since you won't punish the boy," replied Hödeken, "I will, in a few days, let you see how much afraid of him I am," and he went off in high dudgeon. But very soon after he got the boy asleep at the fire-side, and he strangled him, cut him up, and put him into the pot on the fire. When the cook abused him for what he had done, he squeezed toads all over the meat that was at the fire, and he soon after tumbled the cook from the bridge into the deep moat. At last people grew so much afraid of his setting fire to the town and palace, that the bishop had him exorcised and banished.

The following was one of Hödeken's principal exploits. There was a man in Hildesheim who had a light sort of wife, and one time when he was going on a journey he spoke to Hödeken and said, " My good fellow, just keep an eye on my wife while I am away, and see that all goes on right." Hödeken agreed to do so; and when the wife, after the departure of her husband, made her gallants come to her, and was going to make merry with them, Hödeken always threw himself in the middle and drove them away by assuming terrific forms; or, when any one had gone to bed, he invisibly flung him so roughly out on the floor as to crack his ribs. Thus they fared, one after another, as the light-o'-love dame introduced them into her chamber, so that no one ventured to come near her. At length, when the husband had returned home, the honest guardian of his honour presented himself before him full of joy, and said, "Your return is most grateful to me, that I may escape the trouble and disquiet that you had imposed upon me." "Who are you, pray?" said the man. "I am Hödeken," replied he, "to whom, at your departure, you gave your wife in charge. To gratify you I have guarded her this time, and kept her from adultery, though with great and incessant toil. But I beg of you never more to commit her to my keeping; for I would sooner take charge of, and be accountable for, all the swine in Saxony than for one such woman, so many were the artifices and plots she devised to blink me."

King Goldemar.

ANOTHER celebrated House-spirit was King Goldemar, who lived in great intimacy with Neveling von Hardenberg, on the Hardenstein at the Ruhr, and often slept in the same bed with him. He played most beautifully on the harp, and he was in the habit of staking great sums of money at dice. He used to call Neveling brother-in-law, and often gave him warning of various things. He talked with all kinds of people, and used to make the clergy blush by discovering their secret transgressions. His hands were thin like those of a frog, cold and soft to the feel; he let himself be felt, but no one could see him. After remaining there for three years, he went away without offending any one. Some call him King Vollmar, and the chamber in which he lived is still said to be called Vollmar's Chamber. He insisted on having a place at the table for himself, and a stall in the stable for his horse; the food, the hay, and the oats were consumed, but of man or horse nothing more than the shadow ever was seen. When one time a curious person had strewed ashes and tares in his way to make him fall, that his foot-prints might be seen, he came behind him as he was lighting the fire and hewed him to pieces, which he put on the spit and roasted, and he began to boil the head and legs. As soon as the meat was ready it was brought to Vollmar's chamber, and people heard great cries of joy as it was consumed. After this there was no trace of King Vollmar; but over the door of his chamber was found written, that in future the house would be as unfortunate as it had hitherto been fortunate; the scattered property would not be brought together again till the time when three Hardenbergs of Hardenstein should be living at the same time. The spit and the roast meat were preserved for a long time; but they disappeared in the Lorrain war in 1651. The pot still remains built into the wall of the kitchen.*

The Heinzelmänchen.

It is not over fifty years since the Heinzelmänchen, as they are called, used to live and perform their exploits in Cologne. They were little naked mannikins, who used to do all sorts of work; bake bread, wash, and such like house-work. So it is said, but no one ever saw them.

In the time that the Heinzelmänchen were still there, there was in Cologne many a baker, who kept no man, for the little people used always to make over-night, as much black and white bread as the baker wanted for his shop. In many houses they used to wash and do all their work for the maids.

Now, about this time, there was an expert tailor to whom they appeared to have taken a great fancy, for when he married he found in his house, on the wedding-day, the finest victuals and the most beautiful vessels and utensils, which the little folk had stolen elsewhere and brought to their favourite. When, with time, his family increased, the little ones used to give the tailor's wife considerable aid in her household affairs; they washed for her, and on holidays

* Von Steinen, Westfäl. Gesch. *ap.* Grimm, Deut. Mythol., p. 477

and festival times they scoured the copper and tin, and the house from the garret to the cellar. If at any time the tailor had a press of work, he was sure to find it all ready done for him in the morning by the Heinzelmänchen. But curiosity began now to torment the tailor's wife, and she was dying to get one sight of the Heinzelmänchen, but do what she would she could never compass it. She one time strewed peas all down the stairs that they might fall and hurt themselves, and that so she might see them next morning. But this project missed, and since that time the Heinzelmänchen have totally disappeared, as has been everywhere the case, owing to the curiosity of people, which has at all times been the destruction of so much of what was beautiful in the world. The Heinzelmänchen, in consequence of this, went off all in a body out of the town with music playing, but people could only hear the music, for no one could see the mannikins themselves, who forthwith got into a boat and went away, whither no one knows. The good times, however, are said to have disappeared from Cologne along with the Heinzelmänchen.*

NIXES.

Kennt ihr der Nixen, munt're Schaar?
Von Auge schwarz und grün von Haar
        Sie lauscht am Schilfgestade.
                        MATTHISSON.

Know you the Nixes, gay and fair?
Their eyes are black, and green their hair—
        They lurk in sedgy shores.

THE Nixes, or Water-people, inhabit lakes and rivers. The man is like any other man, only he has green teeth. He also wears a green hat. The female Nixes appear like beautiful maidens. On fine sunny days they may be seen sitting on the banks, or on the branches of the trees, combing their

* *Oral.* Cölns Vorzeit. Cöln. 1826.

Kobolds

Nixes

long golden locks. When any person is shortly to be drowned,
the Nixes may be previously seen dancing on the surface of
the water. They inhabit a magnificent region below the
water, whither they sometimes convey mortals. A girl from
a village near Leipzig was one time at service in the house
of a Nix. She said that everything there was very good; all
she had to complain of was that she was obliged to eat her
food without salt. The female Nixes frequently go to the
market to buy meat : they are always dressed with extreme
neatness, only a corner of their apron or some other part of
their clothes is wet. The man has also occasionally gone to
market. They are fond of carrying off women whom they
make wives of, and often fetch an earthly midwife to assist
at their labour. Among the many tales of the Nixes we
select the following :—

The Peasant and the Waterman.

—•—

A WATER-MAN once lived on good terms with a peasant who
dwelt not far from his lake. He often visited him, and at
last begged that the peasant would visit him in his house
under the water. The peasant consented, and went down
with him. There was everything down under the water as
in a stately palace on the land,—halls, chambers, and cabi-
nets, with costly furniture of every description. The Water-
man led his guest over the whole, and showed him everything
that was in it. They came at length to a little chamber,
where were standing several new pots turned upside down.
The peasant asked what was in them. " They contain," was
the reply, " the souls of drowned people, which I put under
the pots and keep them close, so that they cannot get away."
The peasant made no remark, and he came up again on the
land. But for a long time the affair of the souls continued
to give him great trouble, and he watched to find when the
Water-man should be from home. When this occurred, as
he had marked the right way down, he descended into the
water-house, and, having made out the little chamber, he
turned up all the pots one after another, and immediately

the souls of the drowned people ascended out of the water, and recovered their liberty.*

The Water-Smith.

THERE is a little lake in Westphalia called the Darmssen, from which the peasants in the adjacent village of Epe used to hear all through the night a sound as if of hammering upon an anvil. People who were awake used also to see something in the middle of the lake. They got one time into a boat and went to it, and there they found that it was a smith, who, with his body raised over the water, and a hammer in his hand, pointed to an anvil, and bid the people bring him something to forge. From that time forth they brought iron to him, and no people had such good plough-irons as those of Epe.

One time as a man from this village was getting reeds at the Darmssen, he found among them a little child that was rough all over his body. The smith cried out, " Don't take away my son!" but the man put the child on his back, and ran home with it. Since that time the smith has never more been seen or heard. The man reared the Roughy, and he became the cleverest and best lad in the place. But when he was twenty years old he said to the farmer, " Farmer, I must leave you. My father has called me!" " I am sorry for that," said the farmer. " Is there no way that you could stay with me?" " I will see about it," said the water-child. " Do you go to Braumske and fetch me a little sword; but you must give the seller whatever he asks for it, and not haggle about it." The farmer went to Braumske and bought the sword; but he haggled, and got something off the price. They now went together to the Darmssen, and the Roughy said, " Now mind. When I strike the water, if there comes

---

* This legend seems to be connected with the ancient idea of the water-deities taking the souls of drowned persons to themselves. In the Edda, this is done by the sea-goddess Ran.

up blood, I must go away; but if there comes milk, then I may stay with you." He struck the water, and there came neither milk nor blood. The Roughy was annoyed, and said, " You *have* been bargaining and haggling, and so there comes neither blood nor milk. Go off to Braumske and buy another sword." The farmer went and returned; but it was not till the third time that he bought a sword without haggling. When the Roughy struck the water with this it became as red as blood, and he threw himself into the lake, and never was seen more.*

The Working Waterman.

AT Seewenweiher, in the Black-Forest, a little Water-man (*Seemänlein*) used to come and join the people, work the whole day long with them, and in the evening go back into the lakes. They used to set his breakfast and dinner apart for him. When, in apportioning the work, the rule of "Not too much and not too little " was infringed, he got angry, and knocked all the things about. Though his clothes were old and worn, he steadily refused to let the people get him new ones. But when at last they would do so, and one evening the lake-man was presented with a new coat, he said, "When one is paid off, one must go away. After this day I 'll come no more to you." And, unmoved by the excuses of the people, he never let himself be seen again.†

The Nix-Labour.

A MIDWIFE related that her mother was one night called up, and desired to make haste and come to the aid of a woman in labour. It was dark, but notwithstanding she got up and

* Grimm, *ut sup.* p. 463.   † Grimm, *ut sup.* p. 453.

dressed herself, and went down, where she found a man waiting. She begged of him to stay till she should get a lantern, and she would go with him; but he was urgent, said he would show her the way without a lantern, and that there was no fear of her going astray.

He then bandaged her eyes, at which she was terrified, and was going to cry out; but he told her she was in no danger, and might go with him without any apprehension. They accordingly went away together, and the woman remarked that he struck the water with a rod, and that they went down deeper and deeper till they came to a room, in which there was no one but the lying-in woman.

Her guide now took the bandage off her eyes, led her up to the bed, and recommending her to his wife, went away. She then helped to bring the babe into the world, put the woman to bed, washed the babe, and did everything that was requisite.

The woman, grateful to the midwife, then secretly said to her: "I am a Christian woman as well as you; and I was carried off by a Water-man, who changed me. Whenever I bring a child into the world he always eats it on the third day. Come on the third day to your pond, and you will see the water turned to blood. When my husband comes in now and offers you money, take no more from him than you usually get, or else he will twist your neck. Take good care!"

Just then the husband came in. He was in a great passion, and he looked all about; and when he saw that all had gone on properly he bestowed great praise on the midwife. He then threw a great heap of money on the table, and said, "Take as much as you will!" She, however, prudently answered, "I desire no more from you than from others, and that is a small sum. If you give me that I am content; if you think it too much, I ask nothing from you but to take me home again." "It is God," says he, "has directed you to say that." He paid her then the sum she mentioned, and conducted her home honestly. She was, however, afraid to go to the pond at the appointed day.

There are many other tales in Germany of midwives, and even ladies of rank, who have been called in to assist at Nix or Dwarf labours. The Ahnfrau von Ranzau, for example, and the Frau von Alvensleben—the Ladies Bountiful of Germany—were waked up in the night to attend the little women in their confinement.* There is the same danger in touching anything in the Dwarf as in the Nix abodes, but the Dwarfs usually bestow rings and other articles, which will cause the family to flourish. We have seen tales of the same kind in Scandinavia, and shall meet with them in many other countries.

* A tale of this kind is to be seen in Luther's Table-talk, told by *die frau doctorin*, his wife. The scene of it was the river Mulda.

SWITZERLAND.

Denn da hielten auch im lande
Noch die guten Zwerglein Haus;
Kleingestalt, doch hochbegabet,
Und so hülfreich überaus!

MÜLLER.

For then also in the country
The good Dwarflings still kept house;
Small in form, but highly gifted,
And so kind and generous!

WE now arrive at Switzerland, a country with which are usually associated ideas of sublime and romantic scenery, simple manners, and honest hearts. The character of the Swiss Dwarfs will be found to correspond with these ideas. For, like the face of Nature, these personifications of natural powers seem to become more gentle and mild as they approach the sun and the south.

The Dwarfs, or little Hill- or Earth-men* of Switzerland, are described as of a lively, joyous disposition, fond of strolling through the valleys, and viewing and partaking in the labours of agriculture. Kind and generous, they are represented as driving home stray lambs, and leaving brushwood and berries in the way of poor children. Their principal occupation is keeping cattle—not goats, sheep, or cows, but the chamois, from whose milk they make excellent and well-flavoured cheese. This cheese, when given by the Dwarfs to any one, has the property of growing again when it has been cut or bitten. But should the hungry owner be improvident enough to eat up the whole of it and leave nothing from it to sprout from, he of course has seen the end of his cheese.

* In Swiss *Härdmandle*, pl. *Härdmändlene.*

The Kobolds are also to be met with in Switzerland. In the Vaudois, they call them Servants,[*] and believe that they live in remote dwellings and lonely shiels.[†] The most celebrated of them in those parts is Jean de la Boljéta, or, as he is called in German, Napf-Hans, *i. e.* Jack-of-the-Bowl, because it was the custom to lay for him every evening on the roof of the cow-house a bowl of fresh sweet cream, of which he was sure to give a good account. He used to lead the cows to feed in the most dangerous places, and yet none of them ever sustained the slightest injury. He always went along the same steep path on which no one ever saw even a single stone lying, though the whole side of the mountain was strewn as thickly as possible with boulders. It is still called Boliéta's Path.[‡]

Rationalising theory has been at work with the Swiss Dwarfs also. It is supposed, that the early inhabitants of the Swiss mountains, when driven back by later tribes of immigrants, retired to the high lands and took refuge in the clefts and caverns of the mountains, whence they gradually showed themselves to the new settlers—approached them, assisted them, and were finally, as a species of Genii, raised to the region of the wonderful.

For our knowledge of the Dwarf Mythology of Switzerland, we are chiefly indebted to professor Wyss, of Bern, who has put some of the legends in a poetical dress, and given others in the notes to his Idylls as he styles them.[§] These legends were related by the peasants to Mr. Wyss or his friends, on their excursions through the mountains; and he declares that he has very rarely permitted himself to add to, or subtract from, the peasants' narrative. He adds, that the belief in these beings is strong in the minds of the people, not merely in the mountain districts, but also at the foot of Belp mountain, Belp, Gelterfingen, and other places about Bern.[||]

[*] Wyss, Reise in das Berner Oberland, ii. 412. *Servants* is the term in the original.

[†] This Scottish word, signifying the summer cabin of the herdsmen on the mountains, exactly expresses the Sennhütten of the Swiss.

[‡] Alpenrosen for 1824, *ap.* Grimm, Introd. to Irish Fairy Legends.

[§] Idyllen, Volkssagen, Legenden, und Erzählungen aus der Schweiz. Von J. Rud Wyss, Prof. Bern, 1813.

[||] In Bilder und Sagen aus der Schweiz, von Dr. Rudolf. Müller. Glarus,

As a specimen of Mr. Wyss's manner of narrating these legends, we give here a faithful translation of his first Idyll.*

Gertrude and Rosy.

—◆—

GERTRUDE.

QUICK, daughter, quick! spin off what's on your rock.
'Tis Saturday night, and with the week you know
Our work must end; we shall the more enjoy
To-morrow's rest when all's done out of hand.*
Quick, daughter, quick! spin off what's on your rock.

ROSY.

True, mother, but every minute sleep
Falls on my eyes as heavy as lead, and I
Must yawn do what I will; and then God knows
I can't help nodding though 'twere for my life;
Or. . . . oh! it might be of some use if you
Would once more, dearest mother, tell about
The wonderful, good-natured little Dwarfs,
What they here round the country used to do,
And how they showed their kindness to the hinds.

GERTRUDE.

See now! what industry!—your work itself
Should keep you waking. I have told you o'er
A thousand times the stories, and we lose,
If you grow wearied of them, store of joy
Reserved for winter-nights; besides, methinks,
The evening's now too short for chat like this.

1842, may be found some legends of the Erdmännlein, but they are nearly all the same as those collected by Mr. Wyss. We give below those in which there is anything peculiar.
      * The original is in German hexameters.
    † It is a notion in some parts of Germany, that if a girl leaves any flax or tow on her distaff unspun on Saturday night, none of what remains will make good thread. Grimm, Deut. Mythol. Anhang, p. lxxii.

ROSY.

There's only one thing I desire to hear
Again, and sure, dear mother, never yet
Have you explained how 'twas the little men
Lived in the hills, and how, all through the year,
They sported round the country here, and gave
Marks of their kindness.   For you'll ne'er persuade
Me to believe that barely, one by one,
They wandered in the valleys, and appeared
Unto the people, and bestowed their gifts :
So, come now, tell at once, how 'twas the Dwarfs
Lived all together in society.

GERTRUDE.

'Tis plain, however, of itself, and well
Wise folks can see, that such an active race
Would never with their hands before them sit.
Ah! a right merry lively thing, and full
Of roguish tricks, the little Hill-man is,
And quickly too he gets into a rage,
If you behave not toward him mannerly,
And be not frank and delicate in your acts.
But, above all things, they delight to dwell,
Quiet and peaceful, in the secret clefts
Of hills and mountains, evermore concealed.
All through the winter, when with icy rind
The frost doth cover o'er the earth, the wise
And prudent little people keep them warm
By their fine fires, many a fathom down
Within the inmost rocks.   Pure native gold,
And the rock-crystals shaped like towers, clear,
Transparent, gleam with colours thousandfold
Through the fair palace, and the Little-folk,
So happy and so gay, amuse themselves
Sometimes with singing—Oh, so sweet! 'twould charm
The heart of any one who heard it sound.
Sometimes with dancing, when they jump and spring
Like the young skipping kids in the Alp-grass.
  Then when the spring is come, and in the fields

The flowers are blooming, with sweet May's approach,
They bolts and bars take from their doors and gates,
That early ere the hind or hunter stirs,
In the cool morning, they may sport and play;
Or ramble in the evening, when the moon
Lights up the plains.   Seldom hath mortal man
Beheld them with his eyes; but should one chance
To see them, it betokens suffering
And a bad year, if bent in woe they glide
Through woods and thickets; but the sight proclaims
Joy and good luck, when social, in a ring,
On the green meads and fields, their hair adorned
With flowers, they shout and whirl their merry rounds.
Abundance then they joyously announce
For barn, for cellar, and for granary,
And a blest year to men, to herds, and game.
Thus they do constantly foreshow what will
Befall to-morrow and hereafter; now
Sighing, and still, by their lamenting tones,
A furious tempest; and again, with sweet
And smiling lips, and shouting, clear bright skies.*
   Chief to the poor and good, they love to show
Kindness and favour, often bringing home
At night the straying lambs, and oftener still
In springtime nicely spreading, in the wood,
Brushwood, in noble bundles, in the way
Of needy children gone to fetch home fuel.
Many a good little girl, who well obeyed
Her mother,—or, mayhap, a little boy,—
Has, with surprise, found lying on the hills
Bright dazzling bowls of milk, and baskets too,
Nice little baskets, full of berries, left
By the kind hands of the wood-roaming Dwarfs.
   Now be attentive while I tell you one
Out of a hundred and a hundred stories;
'Tis one, however, that concerns us more
Than all the rest, because it was my own
Great-great-grandfather that the thing befell,
In the old time, in years long since agone.

* *Glanz* is the term employed in Switzerland.

Where from the lofty rocks the boundary runs
Down to the vale, Barthel, of herdsmen first
In all the country round, was ploughing up
A spacious field, where he designed to try
The seed of corn ; but with anxiety
His heart was filled, lest by any chance
His venture should miscarry, for his sheep
In the contagion he had lost, now poor
And without skill, he ventures on the plough.
  Deliberate and still, at the plough-tail,
In furrows he cuts up the grassy soil,
While with the goad his little boy drives on
The panting ox.   When, lo! along the tall
Rocky hill-side, a smoke ascends in clouds
Like snow-flakes, soaring from the summit up
Into the sky.   At this the hungry boy
Began to think of food, for the poor child
Had tasted nothing all the live-long day
For lunch, and, looking up, he thus began :
" Ah ! there the little Dwarf-folk are so gay
At their grand cooking, roasting, boiling now,
For a fine banquet, while with hunger I
Am dying.   Had we here one little dish
Of the nice savoury food, were it but as
A sign that there's a blessing on our work!"
  'Twas thus the boy spake, and his father ploughed
Silently on, bent forwards o'er his work.
They turn the plough ; when huzza! lo! behold
A miracle! there gleamed right from the midst
Of the dark furrow, toward them, a bright
Lustre, and there so charming! lay a plate
Heaped up with roast meat ; by the plate, a loaf
Of bread upon the outspread table-cloth,
At the disposal of the honest pair.
Hurra! long live the friendly, generous Dwarfs!
  Barthel had now enough—so had the boy—
And laughing gratefully and loud, they praise
And thank the givers ; then, with strength restored,
They quick return unto their idle plough.
  But when again their day's task they resume,
To break more of the field, encouraged now

To hope for a good crop, since the kind Dwarfs
Had given them the sign of luck they asked—
Hush! bread and plate, and crums, and knife and fork,
Were vanished clean; only—just for a sign
For ever of the truth—lay on the ridge
The white, nice-woven, pretty table-cloth.

ROSY.

O mother! mother! what? the glittering plate
And real? and the cloth with their own hands
Spun by the generous Dwarfs?   No, I can ne'er
Believe it!—Was the thread then, real drawn
And twisted thread, set in it evenly?
And was there too a flower, a pretty figure,
Nicely wrought in with warp and crossing woof?
Did there a handsome border go all round,
Enclosing all the figures?—Sure your great-
Great-grandfather, if really he was
The owner of the curious little cloth,
He would have left it carefully unto
His son and grandson for a legacy,
That, for a lasting witness of the meal
Given by the Dwarfs, it might to distant years,
The praise and wonder of our vale remain.

GERTRUDE.

Odds me! how wise the child is! what a loss
And pity 'tis that in old times the folk
Were not so thoughtful and so over-knowing!
Ah! our poor simple fathers should rise up
Out of their graves, and come to get advice
And comfort from the brooders that are now,—
As if they knew not what was right and fit!
    Have but a little patience, girl, and spin
What's on your rock; to-morrow when 'tis day
I 'll let you see the Dwarfs' flowered table-cloth,
Which, in the chest laid safe, inherited
From mother down to daughter, I have long
Kept treasured under lock and key, for fear
Some little girl, like some one that you know,
Might out of curiosity, and not
Acquainted with its worth, set it astray.

ROSY.

Ah, that is kind, dear mother; and see now
How broad awake I am, and how so smart
I'm finishing my work since you relate
These pretty tales; but I will call you up
Out of your bed to-morrow in the morning
So early! Oh, I wish now it were day
Already, for I'm sure I shall not get
One wink of sleep for thinking of the cloth.*

The Chamois-Hunter.

A CHAMOIS-HUNTER set out early one morning, and ascended
the mountains. He had arrived at a great height, and was
in view of some chamois, when, just as he was laying his
bolt on his crossbow, and was about to shoot, a terrible cry
from a cleft of the rock interrupted his purpose. Turning
round he saw a hideous Dwarf, with a battle-axe in his hand
raised to slay him. "Why," cried he, in a rage, "hast thou
so long been destroying my chamois, and leavest not with
me my flock? But now thou shalt pay for it with thy
blood." The poor hunter turned pale at the stranger's
words. In his terror he was near falling from the cliff.

---

* This legend was picked up by a friend of Mr. Wyss when on a topogra-
phical ramble in the neighbourhood of Bern. It was told to him by a peasant
of Belp; "but," says Mr. Wyss, "if I recollect right, this man said it was a
nice smoking-hot cake that was on the plate, and it was a servant, not the
man's son, who was driving the plough. The circumstance of the table-cloth
being handed down from mother to daughter," he adds, "is a fair addition
which I have allowed myself."

The writer recollects to have heard this story, when a boy, from an old
woman in Ireland; and he could probably point out the very field in the
county of Kildare where it occurred. A man and a boy were ploughing: the
boy, as they were about in the middle of their furrow, smelled roast beef, and
wished for some. As they returned, it was lying on the grass before them.
When they had eaten, the boy said "God bless me, and God bless the fairies!"
The man did not give thanks, and he met with misfortunes very shortly after.
—The same legend is also in Scotland. See below.

At length, however, he recovered himself, and begged forgiveness of the Dwarf, pleaded his ignorance that the chamois belonged to him, declaring at the same time that he had no other means of support than what he derived from hunting. The Dwarf was pacified, laid down his axe, and said to him, "'Tis well; never be seen here again, and I promise thee that every seventh day thou shalt find, early in the morning, a dead chamois hanging before thy cottage ; but beware and keep from the others." The Dwarf then vanished, and the hunter returned thoughtfully home, little pleased with the prospect of the inactive live he was now to lead.

On the seventh morning he found, according to the Dwarf's promise, a fat chamois hanging in the branches of a tree before his cottage, of which he ate with great satisfaction. The next week it was the same, and so it continued for some months. But at last he grew weary of this idle life, and preferred, come what might, returning to the chase, and catching chamois for himself, to having his food provided for him without the remembrance of his toils to sweeten the repast. His determination made, he once more ascended the mountains. Almost the first object that met his view was a fine buck. The hunter levelled his bow and took aim at the prey ; and as the Dwarf did not appear, he was just pulling the trigger, when the Dwarf stole behind him, took him by the ankle, and tumbled him down the precipice.

Others say the Dwarf gave the hunter a small cheese of chamois-milk, which would last him his whole life, but that he one day thoughtlessly ate the whole of it, or, as some will have it, a guest who was ignorant of the quality of it ate up the remainder. Poverty then drove him to return to the chamois-hunting, and he was thrown into a chasm by the Dwarf.*

* The former account was obtained by a friend in Glarnerland. The latter was given to Mr. Wyss himself by a man of Zweylütschinen, very rich, says Mr. Wyss, in Dwarf lore, and who accompanied him to Lauterbrunnen. Schiller has founded his poem Der Alpenjäger on this legend.

The Dwarfs on the Tree.

In the summer-time the troop of the Dwarfs came in great numbers down from the hills into the valley, and joined the men that were at work, either assisting them or merely looking on. They especially liked to be with the mowers in the hay-making season, seating themselves, greatly to their satisfaction, on the long thick branch of a maple-tree, among the dense foliage. But one time some mischief-loving people came by night and sawed the branch nearly through. The unsuspecting Dwarfs, as usual, sat down on it in the morning; the branch snapt in two, and the Dwarfs were thrown to the ground. When the people laughed at them they became greatly incensed, and cried out,

O how is heaven so high
And perfidy so great !
Here to-day and never more !

and they never let themselves again be seen.*

It is also related that it was the custom of the Dwarfs to seat themselves on a large piece of rock, and thence to look on the haymakers when at work. But some mischievous people lighted a fire on the rock and made it quite hot, and then swept off all the coals. In the morning the little people, coming to take their usual station, burned themselves in a lamentable manner. Full of anger, they cried out, "O wicked world! O wicked world!" called aloud for vengeance, and disappeared for ever.

Curiosity Punished.

In old times men lived in the valley, and around them, in the clefts and holes of the rocks, dwelt the Dwarfs. They

---

* Mr. Wyss heard this and the following tale in Haslithal and Gadmen.

were kind and friendly to the people, often performing hard and heavy work for them in the night; and when the country-people came early in the morning with their carts and tools, they saw, to their astonishment, that the work was already done, while the Dwarfs hid themselves in the bushes, and laughed aloud at the astonished rustics. Often, too, were the peasants incensed to find their corn, which was scarcely yet ripe, lying cut on the ground; but shortly after there was sure to come on such a hail-storm, that it became obvious that hardly a single stalk could have escaped destruction had it not been cut, and then, from the bottom of their hearts, they thanked the provident Dwarf-people. But at last mankind, through their own folly, deprived themselves of the favour and kindness of the Dwarfs; they fled the country, and since that time no mortal eye has seen them. The cause of their departure was this:

A shepherd had a fine cherry-tree* that stood on the mountain. When in the summer the fruit had ripened, it happened that, three times running, the tree was stript, and all the fruit spread out on the benches and hurdles, where the shepherd himself used to spread it out to dry for the winter. The people of the village all said, " It could be none but the good-natured Dwarfs, who come by night tripping along with their feet covered with long mantles, as light as birds, and industriously perform for mankind their daily work. People have often watched them," continued the narrators, " but no one disturbs them; they are left to come and go as they please." This talk only excited the curiosity of the shepherd, and he longed to know why it was that the Dwarfs so carefully concealed their feet, and whether they were differently formed from those of men. Accordingly, next year, when the summer came, and the time when the Dwarfs secretly pulled the cherries, and brought them to the barn, the shepherd took a sack full of ashes, and strewed them about under the cherry-tree. Next morning, at break of day, he hastened to the place: the tree was plucked completely empty, and he saw the marks of several goose-feet impressed on the ashes. The shepherd

---

* In several of the high valleys of Switzerland it is only a single cherry-tree which happens to be favourably situated that bears fruit. It bears abundantly, and the fruit ripens about the month of August. *Wyss.*

then laughed and jested at having discovered the Dwarfs'
secret. But soon after the Dwarfs broke and laid waste
their houses, and fled down deeper in the mountain to their
splendid secret palace, that had long lain empty to receive
them. Vexed with mankind, they never more granted them
their aid; and the imprudent shepherd who had betrayed
them became sickly, and continued so to the end of his life.*

The Rejected Gift.

A DWARF came down one night from the chestnut woods on
the side of the mountain over the village of Walchwyl, and
enquired for the house of a midwife, whom he earnestly
pressed to come out and go with him. She consented, and
the Dwarf, bearing a light, led the way in silence to the
woods. He stopped at last before a cleft in a rock, at which
they entered, and the woman suddenly found herself in a
magnificent hall. She was thence led through several rich
apartments to the chamber of state, where the queen of the
Dwarfs, for whom her services were required, was lying. She
performed her office, and brought a fair young prince to the
light. She was thanked and dismissed, and her former conductor appeared to lead her home. As he was taking leave
of her, he filled her apron with something, bidding her on no

* Compare the narrative in the Swiss dialect given by Grimm, Deut.
Mythol. p. 419. The same peasant of Belp who related the first legend was
Mr. Wyss's authority for this one. " The vanishing of the Bergmänlein," says
Mr. Wyss, " appears to be a matter of importance to the popular faith. It
is almost always ascribed to the fault of mankind—sometimes to their
wickedness."

We may in these tales recognise the box of Pandora under a different form,
but the ground is the same. Curiosity and wickedness are still the cause of
superior beings withdrawing their favour from man.

" I have never any where else," says Mr. Wyss, " heard of the goose-feet;
but that all is not right with their feet is evident from the popular tradition
giving long trailing mantles as the dress of the little people. Some will have
it that their feet are regularly formed, but set on their legs the wrong way, so
that the toes are behind and the heels before."

Heywood, in his Hierarchie of the Blessed Angels, p. 554, relates a story
which would seem to refer to a similar belief.

account to look at it till she was in her own house. But the woman could not control her curiosity, and the moment the Dwarf disappeared, she partly opened the apron, and lo! there was nothing in it but some black coals. In a rage, she shook them out on the ground, but she kept two of them in her hands, as a proof of the shabby treatment she had met with from the Dwarfs. On reaching home, she threw them also down on the ground. Her husband cried out with joy and surprise, for they shone like carbuncles. She asserted that the Dwarf had put nothing but coals into her apron; but she ran out to call a neighbour, who knew more of such things than they did, and he on examining them pronounced them to be precious stones of great value. The woman immediately ran back to where she had shaken out the supposed coals, but they were all gone.*

The Wonderful Little Pouch.

At noon one day a young peasant sat by the side of a wood, and, sighing, prayed to God to give him a morsel of food. A Dwarf suddenly emerged from the wood, and told him that his prayer should be fulfilled. He then gave him the pouch that he had on his side, with the assurance that he would always find in it wherewithal to satisfy his thirst and hunger, charging him at the same time not to consume it all and to share with any one who asked him for food. The Dwarf vanished, and the peasant put his hand into the pouch to make trial of it, and there he found a cake of new bread, a cheese, and a bottle of wine, on which he made a hearty meal. He

---

* Müller, Bilder und Sagen, p. 119; see above, p. 81. Coals are the usual form under which the Dwarfs conceal the precious metals. We also find this trait in Scandinavia. A smith who lived near Aarhuus in Jutland, as he was going to church, saw a Troll on the roadside very busy about two straws that had got across each other on a heap of coals, and which, do what he would, he could not remove from their position. He asked the smith to do it for him; but he who knew better things took up the coals with the cross straws on them, and carried them home in spite of the screams of the Troll, and when he reached his own house he found it was a large treasure he had got, over which the Troll had lost all power. Thiele, i. 122.

then saw that the pouch swelled up as before, and looking in
he found that it was again full of bread, cheese, and wine.
He now felt sure of his food, and he lived on in an idle
luxurious way, without doing any work. One day, as he was
gorging himself, there came up to him a feeble old man, who
prayed him to give him a morsel to eat. He refused in a
brutal, churlish tone, when instantly the bread and cheese
broke, and scattered out of his hands, and pouch and all
vanished.*

Aid and Punishment.

On the side of Mount Pilatus is a place named the Kastler-
Alpe, now covered with stones and rubbish, but which once
was verdant and fertile. The cause of the change was as
follows.

The land there was formerly occupied by a farmer, a
churlish, unfeeling man, who, though wealthy, let his only
sister struggle with the greatest poverty in the valley
beneath. The poor woman at length having fallen sick, and
seeing no other resource, resolved to apply to her hard-
hearted brother for the means of employing a doctor. She
sent her daughter to him; but all the prayers and tears of
the poor girl failed to move him, and he told her he would,
sooner than give her anything, see the Alpe covered with
stones and rubbish. She departed, and as she went along a
Dwarf suddenly appeared to her. She would have fled, but
he gently detained her, and telling her he had heard all that
had passed, gave her a parcel of herbs, which he assured her
would cure her mother, and a little cheese, which he said
would last them a long time.

On trial, the herbs quickly produced the promised effect;
and when they went to cut the cheese they found the knife
would not penetrate it, and no wonder, for it was pure gold.
There also came a sudden storm on the mountain, and the
Kastler-Alpe was reduced to its present condition.†

* Müller, *ut sup.* p. 123.   † Müller, *ut sup.* p. 126.

The Dwarf in Search of Lodging.

ONE night, during a tremendous storm of wind and rain, a
Dwarf came travelling through a little village, and went from
cottage to cottage, dripping with rain, knocking at the doors
for admission.   None, however, took pity on him, or would
open the door to receive him : on the contrary, the inhabitants even mocked at his distress.

At the very end of the village there dwelt two honest poor
people, a man and his wife.   Tired and faint, the Dwarf crept
on his staff up to their house, and tapped modestly three
times at the little window.   Immediately the old shepherd
opened the door for him, and cheerfully offered him the little
that the house afforded.   The old woman produced some
bread, milk, and cheese : the Dwarf sipped a few drops of the
milk, and ate some crums of the bread and cheese.   " I am
not used," said he, laughing, " to eat such coarse food : but
I thank you from my heart, and God reward you for it : now
that I am rested, I will proceed on farther."   " God forbid ! "
cried the good woman ; " you surely don't think of going out
in the night and in the storm !   It were better for you to
take a bed here, and set out in the daylight."   But the Dwarf
shook his head, and with a smile replied, " You little know
what business I have to do this night on the top of the mountain.   I have to provide for you too ; and to-morrow you
shall see that I am not ungrateful for the kindness you have
shown to me."   So saying, the Dwarf departed, and the
worthy old couple went to rest.

But at break of day they were awaked by storm and
tempest ; the lightnings flashed along the red sky, and tor-
rents of water poured down the hills and through the valley.
A huge rock now tumbled from the top of the mountain,
and rolled down toward the village, carrying along with it,
in its course, trees, stones, and earth.   Men and cattle, every
thing in the village that had breath in it, were buried beneath

it. The waves had now reached the cottage of the two old people, and in terror and dismay they stood out before their door. They then beheld approaching in the middle of the stream a large piece of rock, and on it, jumping merrily, the Dwarf, as if he was riding and steering it with a great trunk of a pine till he brought it before the house, where it stemmed the water and kept it from the cottage, so that both it and the good owners escaped. The Dwarf then swelled and grew higher and higher till he became a monstrous Giant, and vanished in the air, while the old people were praying to God and thanking him for their deliverance.*

* This story is told of two places in the Highlands of Berning, of Ralligen, a little village on the lake of Thun, where there once stood a town called Roll; and again, of Schillingsdorf, a place in the valley of Grinderwald, formerly destroyed by a mountain slip.

The reader need scarcely be reminded of the stories of Lot and of Baucis and Philemon : see also Grimm's Kinder und Hausmärchen, iii. 153, for other parallels.

GREAT BRITAIN.

In old wives daies that in old time did live,
To whose odde tales much credit men did give,
Great store of goblins, fairies, bugs, nightmares,
Urchins and elves to many a house repaires.

OLD POEM.

WE use the term Great Britain in a very limited sense, as merely inclusive of those parts of the island whose inhabitants are of Gotho-German origin—England and the Lowlands of Scotland.

We have already seen* that the Anglo-Saxon conquerors of Britain had in their language the terms from which are derived Elf and Dwarf, and the inference is natural that their ideas respecting these beings corresponded with those of the Scandinavians and Germans. The same may be said of the Picts, who, akin to the Scandinavians, early seized on the Scottish Lowlands. We therefore close our survey of the Fairy Mythology of the Gotho-German race with Great Britain.

ENGLAND.

Merry elves, their morrice pacing,
To aërial minstrelsy,
Emerald rings on brown heath tracing,
Trip it deft and merrily.

SCOTT.

THE Fairy Mythology of England divides itself into two branches, that of the people and that of the poets. Under the former head will be comprised the few scattered tradi-

* See above pp. 66, 75.

The Snow Drop

A fairy messenger

Flying away

THE FAIRY SCHOOL.

The Fairy School

tions which we have been able to collect respecting a system, the belief in which is usually thought to be nearly extinct; the latter will contain a selection of passages, treating of fairies and their exploits, from our principal poets.

The Fairies of England are evidently the Dwarfs of Germany and the North, though they do not appear to have been ever so denominated.* Their appellation was Elves, subsequently Fairies; but there would seem to have been formerly other terms expressive of them, of which hardly a vestige is now remaining in the English language.

They were, like their northern kindred, divided into two classes—the rural Elves, inhabiting the woods, fields, mountains, and caverns; and the domestic or house-spirits, usually called Hobgoblins and Robin Goodfellows. But the Thames, the Avon, and the other English streams, never seem to have been the abode of a Neck or Kelpie.

The following curious instances of English superstition, occur in the twelfth century.

The Green Children.

"ANOTHER wonderful thing," says Ralph of Coggeshall,† "happened in Suffolk, at St. Mary's of the Wolf-pits. A boy and his sister were found by the inhabitants of that place near the mouth of a pit which is there, who had the form of all their limbs like to those of other men, but they differed in the colour of their skin from all the people of our habitable world; for the whole surface of their skin was tinged of a green colour. No one could understand their speech. When they were brought as curiosities to the house of a certain knight, Sir Richard de Calne, at Wikes, they wept

---

* The Anglo-Saxon Dweorg, Dworh, and the English Dwarf, do not seem ever to have had any other sense than that of the Latin *nanus*.

† As quoted by Picart in his Notes on William of Newbridge. We could not find it in the Collection of Histories, etc., by Martène and Durand,—the only place where, to our knowledge, this chronicler's works are printed.

bitterly. Bread and other victuals were set before them, but they would touch none of them, though they were tormented by great hunger, as the girl afterwards acknowledged. At length, when some beans just cut, with their stalks, were brought into the house, they made signs, with great avidity, that they should be given to them. When they were brought, they opened the stalks instead of the pods, thinking the beans were in the hollow of them; but not finding them there, they began to weep anew. When those who were present saw this, they opened the pods, and showed them the naked beans. They fed on these with great delight, and for a long time tasted no other food. The boy, however, was always languid and depressed, and he died within a short time. The girl enjoyed continual good health; and becoming accustomed to various kinds of food, lost completely that green colour, and gradually recovered the sanguine habit of her entire body. She was afterwards regenerated by the laver of holy baptism, and lived for many years in the service of that knight (as I have frequently heard from him and his family), and was rather loose and wanton in her conduct. Being frequently asked about the people of her country, she asserted that the inhabitants, and all they had in that country, were of a green colour; and that they saw no sun, but enjoyed a degree of light like what is after sunset. Being asked how she came into this country with the aforesaid boy, she replied, that as they were following their flocks, they came to a certain cavern, on entering which they heard a delightful sound of bells; ravished by whose sweetness, they went for a long time wandering on through the cavern, until they came to its mouth. When they came out of it, they were struck senseless by the excessive light of the sun, and the unusual temperature of the air; and they thus lay for a long time. Being terrified by the noise of those who came on them, they wished to fly, but they could not find the entrance of the cavern before they were caught."

This story is also told by William of Newbridge,* who places it in the reign of King Stephen. He says he long

* *Guilielmi Neubrigensis Historia, sive Chronica Rerum Anglicarum.* Oxon. 1719, lib. i. c. 27.

hesitated to believe it, but he was at length overcome by the weight of evidence. According to him, the place where the children appeared was about four or five miles from Bury St. Edmund's: they came in harvest-time out of the Wolf-pits; they both lost their green hue, and were baptised, and learned English. The boy, who was the younger, died; but the girl married a man at Lenna, and lived many years. They said their country was called St. Martin's Land, as that saint was chiefly worshiped there; that the people were Christians, and had churches; that the sun did not rise there, but that there was a bright country which could be seen from theirs, being divided from it by a very broad river.

The Fairy Banquet.

In the next chapter of his history, William of Newbridge relates as follows:—

"In the province of the Deiri (Yorkshire), not far from my birth-place, a wonderful thing occurred, which I have known from my boyhood. There is a town a few miles distant from the Eastern Sea, near which are those celebrated waters commonly called Gipse. . . . A peasant of this town went once to see a friend who lived in the next town, and it was late at night when he was coming back, not very sober; when lo! from the adjoining barrow, which I have often seen, and which is not much over a quarter of a mile from the town, he heard the voices of people singing, and, as it were, joyfully feasting. He wondered who they could be that were breaking in that place, by their merriment, the silence of the dead night, and he wished to examine into the matter more closely. Seeing a door open in the side of the barrow, he went up to it, and looked in; and there he beheld a large and luminous house, full of people, women as well as men, who were reclining as at a solemn banquet. One of the attendants, seeing him standing at the door, offered him a cup. He took it, but would not drink; and pouring out the contents, kept the vessel. A great tumult arose at the banquet

on account of his taking away the cup, and all the guests
pursued him; but he escaped by the fleetness of the beast
he rode, and got into the town with his booty. Finally, this
vessel of unknown material, of unusual colour, and of extraordinary form, was presented to Henry the Elder, king of
the English, as a valuable gift, and was then given to the
queen's brother David, king of the Scots, and was kept for
several years in the treasury of Scotland; and a few years
ago (as I have heard from good authority), it was given by
William, king of the Scots, to Henry the Second, who wished
to see it."

The scene of this legend, we may observe, is the very
country in which the Danes settled; and it is exactly the
same as some of the legends current at the present day
among the Danish peasantry.* It is really extraordinary to
observe the manner in which popular traditions and superstitions will thus exist for centuries.

Gervase of Tilbury, the Imperial Chancellor, gives the
following particulars respecting the Fairy Mythology of
England in the thirteenth century.

The Fairy Horn.

"THERE is," says he,† "in the county of Gloucester, a forest
abounding in boars, stags, and every species of game that
England produces. In a grovy lawn of this forest there is a
little mount, rising in a point to the height of a man, on which
knights and other hunters are used to ascend when fatigued
with heat and thirst, to seek some relief for their wants. The
nature of the place, and of the business, is, however, such,
that whoever ascends the mount must leave his companions,
and go quite alone.

"When alone, he was to say, as if speaking to some other
person, 'I thirst,' and immediately there would appear a
cupbearer in an elegant dress, with a cheerful countenance,
bearing in his stretched-out hand a large horn, adorned with

---

* See above, p. 109.

† Otia Imperialia *apud Leibnitz Scriptores rerum Brunsvicarum*, vol. i.
p. 981.

gold and gems, as was the custom among the most ancient English. In the cup * nectar of an unknown but most delicious flavour was presented, and when it was drunk, all heat and weariness fled from the glowing body, so that one would be thought ready to undertake toil instead of having toiled. Moreover, when the nectar was taken, the servant presented a towel to the drinker, to wipe his mouth with, and then having performed his office, he waited neither for a recompense for his services, nor for questions and enquiry.

" This frequent and daily action had for a very long period of old times taken place among the ancient people, till one day a knight of that city, when out hunting, went thither, and having called for a drink and gotten the horn, did not, as was the custom, and as in good manners he should have done, return it to the cup-bearer, but kept it for his own use. But the illustrious Earl of Gloucester, when he learned the truth of the matter, condemned the robber to death, and presented the horn to the most excellent King Henry the Elder, lest he should be thought to have approved of such wickedness, if he had added the rapine of another to the store of his private property."

The Portunes.

In another part of this work the Chancellor says,†—

" They have in England certain demons, though I know not whether I should call them demons or figures of a secret and unknown generation, which the French call Neptunes, the English Portunes.‡ It is their nature to embrace the simple life of comfortable farmers, and when, on account of their domestic work, they are sitting up at night, when the

---

* Vice calicis.

† Otia Imperialia *apud Leibnitz Scriptores rerum Brunsvicarum,* vol. i. p. 980.

‡ There is, as far as we are aware, no vestige of these names remaining in either the French or English language, and we cannot conceive how the Latin names of sea-gods came to be applied to the Gotho-German Kobolds, etc.

doors are shut, they warm themselves at the fire, and take little frogs out of their bosom, roast them on the coals, and eat them. They have the countenance of old men, with wrinkled cheeks, and they are of a very small stature, not being quite half-an-inch high.* They wear little patched coats, and if anything is to be carried into the house, or any laborious work to be done, they lend a hand, and finish it sooner than any man could. It is their nature to have the power to serve, but not to injure. They have, however, one little mode of annoying. When in the uncertain shades of night the English are riding any where alone, the Portune sometimes invisibly joins the horseman; and when he has accompanied him a good while, he at last takes the reins, and leads the horse into a neighbouring slough; and when he is fixed and floundering in it, the Portune goes off with a loud laugh, and by sport of this sort he mocks the simplicity of mankind.

The Grant.

" THERE is," says he, again† "in England a certain kind of demon whom in their language they call Grant,‡ like a yearling foal, erect on its hind legs, with sparkling eyes. This kind of demon often appears in the streets in the heat of the day, or about sunset. If there is any danger impending on the following day or night, it runs about the streets provoking the dogs to bark, and, by feigning flight, draws the dogs after it, in the vain hope of catching it. This illusion warns the inhabitants to beware of fire, and the friendly demon, while he terrifies those who see him, puts by his coming the ignorant on their guard."

Thus far the Chancellor of the Holy Roman Empire, and,

---

* Dimidium *pollicis.* Should we not read *pedis?*

† Otia Imperialia *apud Leibnitz Scriptores rerum Brunsvicarum,* vol. i. p. 980.

‡ Can this name be connected with that of Grendel, the malignant spirit in Beówulf?

except in the poets, we have met with no further account of, or allusion to, fairies, until the reign of Elizabeth, when a little work appeared, named, The mad Pranks and merry Jests of Robin Goodfellow,* from which Shakespeare seems in a good measure to have derived his Puck.

This work consists of two parts. In the first we are informed that Robin was the offspring of a "proper young wench by a hee-fayrie, a king or something of that kind among them." By the time he was six years old he was so mischievous and unlucky that his mother found it necessary to promise him a whipping. He ran away and engaged with a tailor, from whom also he soon eloped. When tired he sat down and fell asleep, and in his sleep he had a vision of fairies; and when he awoke he found lying beside him a scroll, evidently left by his father, which, in verses written in letters of gold, informed him that he should have any thing he wished for, and have also the power of turning himself "To horse, to hog, to dog, to ape," etc., but he was to harm none but knaves and queans, and was to "love those that honest be, and help them in necessity." He made trials of his power and found that he really possessed it. His first exploit was to turn himself into a horse, to punish a churlish clown, whom he induced to mount him, and gave him a fall that went well nigh to break his neck. The fellow then went to ride him through a great plash of water, "and in the middle of it he found himself with nothing but a pack-saddle between his legs, while Robin went off laughing, *Ho, ho, hoh!* He next exerted himself in the cause of two young lovers, and secured their happiness.

In the Second Part we find him more in the character of the Nis or Brownie. Coming to a farmer's house, he takes a liking to a "good handsome maid," that was there, and in the night does her work for her, at breaking hemp and flax, bolting meal, etc. Having watched one night and seen him at work, and observed that he was rather bare of clothes, she

---

* Edited for the Percy Society by J. P. Collyer, Esq., 1841. Mr. Collyer says there is little doubt but that this work was printed before 1588, or even 1584. We think this is true only of the First Part; for the Second, which is of a different texture, must have been added some time after tobacco had come into common use in England: see the verses in p. 34.

provided him with a waistcoat against the next night.　But when he saw it he started and said :—

> Because thou layest me himpen hampen
> I will neither bolt nor stampen :
> 'Tis not your garments, new or old,
> That Robin loves : I feel no cold.
> Had you left me milk or cream,
> You should have had a pleasing dream :
> Because you left no drop or crum,
> Robin never more will come.

He went off laughing *Ho, ho, hoh !* and the maid in future had to do all the work herself.

A company of young fellows who had been making merry with their sweethearts were coming home over a heath. Robin met them, and to make himself merry took the form of *a walking fire*, and led them up and down till daylight, and then went off saying :—

> Get you home, you merry lads :
> Tell your mammies and your dads,
> And all those that news desire,
> How you saw a walking fire.
> Wenches that do smile and lispe,
> Use to call me Willy Wispe.
> If that you but weary be,
> It is sport alone for me.
> Away : unto your houses go,
> And I 'll go laughing, *Ho, ho, hoh !*

A fellow was attempting to offer violence to a young maiden. Robin came to her aid, ran between his legs in the shape of a hare, then turning himself into a horse, carried him off on his back, and flung him into a thick hedge.

Robin fell in love with a weaver's pretty wife, and for her sake took service with her husband.　The man caught them one day kissing, and next night he went and took Robin as he was sleeping, up out of his bed, and went to the river and threw him in.　But instantly he heard behind him—

> For this your service, master, I you thank.
> Go swim yourself ; I 'll stay upon the bank ;

and was pushed in by Robin, who had put a bag of yarn in his bed, and now went off with, *Ho, ho, hoh !*

Robin went as a fiddler to a wedding. When the candles came he blew them out, and giving the men boxes in the ears he set them a-fighting. He kissed the prettiest girls, and pinched the others, till he made them scratch one another like cats. When the posset was brought forth, he turned himself into a bear, and frightening them away, had it all to himself.

At length his father who we now find was king Obreon (i. e. Oberon),* called him up out of his bed one night, and took him to where the fairies were dancing to the music of Tom Thumb's bagpipe, and thence to Fairy-land, where he " did show him many secrets which he never did open to the world."

In the same work Sib says of the woman-fairies :

" To walk nightly as do the men-fairies we use not; but now and then we go together, and at good housewives' fires we warm our fairy children.† If we find clean water and clean towels we leave them money, either in their basins, or in their shoes; but if we find no clean water in their houses, we wash our children in their pottage, milk, or beer, or whatever we find: for the sluts that have not such things fitting, we wash their faces and hands with a gilded child's clout, or else carry them to some river and duck them over head and ears. We often use to dwell in some great hill, and from thence we do lend money to any poor man or woman that hath need; but if they bring it not again at the day appointed, we do not only punish them with pinching, but also in their goods, so that they never thrive till they have paid us."

The learned and strong-minded Reginald Scot, thus notices the superstitions of his own and the preceding age.‡

" Indeed your grandams' maids were wont to set a bowl of milk before him (Incubus) and his cousin Robin Good-fellow, for grinding of malt or mustard, and sweeping the house at midnight; and you have also heard that he would chafe exceedingly if the maid or good-wife of the house, having compassion of his nakedness, laid any clothes for him

---

* Mr. Collyer does not seem to have recollected that Huon de Bordeaux had been translated by Lord Berners; see above, p. 56.

† It is, according to this authority the man-fairy Gunn that steals children and leaves changelings.

‡ Discoverie of Witchcrafte, iv. ch. 10.

besides his mess of white bread and milk, which was his
standing fee; for in that case he saith,

> What have we here?   Hemten, hamten,
> Here will I never more tread nor stampen.

Again : *
" The Faeries do principally inhabit the mountains and
caverns of the earth, whose nature is to make strange apparitions on the earth, in meadows or on mountains, being like
men and women, soldiers, kings, and ladies, children and
horsemen, clothed in green, to which purpose they do in the
night steal hempen stalks from the fields where they grow, to
convert them into horses, as the story goes.

" Such jocund and facetious spirits," he continues, " are
said to sport themselves in the night by tumbling and fool-
ing with servants and shepherds in country houses, pinching
them black and blue, and leaving bread, butter, and cheese,
sometimes with them, which, if they refuse to eat, some mischief shall undoubtedly befal them by the means of these
Faeries ; and many such have been taken away by the said
spirits for a fortnight or a month together, being carried
with them in chariots through the air, over hills and dales,
rocks and precipices, till at last they have been found lying
in some meadow or mountain, bereaved of their senses, and
commonly one of their members to boot."

Elsewhere ‡ he gives the following goodly catalogue of
these objects of popular terror :—" Our mother's maids have
so frayed us with Bull-beggars, Spirits, Witches, Urchins,
Elves, Hags, Faeries, Satyrs, Pans, Faunes, Sylens, Kit-wi-
the-Canstick, Tritons, Centaurs, Dwarfs, Gyants, Impes,
Calcars, Conjurors, Nymphs, Changelings, Incubus, Robin
Goodfellow, the Spoorn, the Mare, the Man-in-the-Oak, the
Hell-wain, the Firedrake, the Puckle, Tom-thombe, Hob-
goblin, Tom-tumbler, Boneless, and such other Bugs, that
we are afraid of our shadow." †

---

* R. Scot, Discoverie of Witchcrafte, ii. ch. 4.   † *Ib.* vii. 15.

‡ This appears to us to be rather a display of the author's learning than an
actual enumeration of the objects of popular terror; for the maids hardly
talked of Satyrs, Pans, etc. For Bull-beggar, see p. 316; for Urchin, p. 319.
Hag is the Anglo-Saxon hæƷerre, German *hexe*, " witche," and hence the
Nightmare (see p. 332) which was ascribed to witches ; we still say *Hag-ridden.*

Burton, after noticing from Paracelsus those which in Germany "do usually walk in little coats, some two foot long," says,* "A bigger kind there is of them called with us Hobgoblins and Robin Goodfellows, that would, in those superstitious times, grind corn for a mess of milk, cut wood, or do any manner of drudgery work." And again: "Some put our Fairies into this rank (that of terrestrial devils), which have been in former times adored with much superstition, with sweeping their houses, and setting of a pail of clean water, good victuals, and the like, and then they should not be pinched, but find money in their shoes, and be fortunate in their enterprises." In another place (p. 30,) he says, "And so those which Miyaldus calls *Ambulones*, that walk about midnight, on heaths and desert places, which (saith Lavater) draw men out of the way and lead them all night a by-way, or quite barre them of their way; these have several names, in several places; we commonly call them *Pucks*."

Harsenet thus speaks of them in his Declaration : †—

"And if that the *bowl* of curds and *cream* were not *duly set* out for Robin Goodfellow, the *friar*, and Sisse the dairymaid, why then, either the pottage was burned the next day in the pot, or the cheeses would not curdle, or the butter would not come, or the ale in the fat never would have good head. But if a Peter-penny or a Housle-egge‡ were behind, or a patch of tythe unpaid—then 'ware of bull-beggars, spirits, &c."

Nash thus describes them : §—

"Then ground they malt, and had hempen shirts for their

Calcar and Sporn (spurs?) may be the same, from the idea of riding: the French call the Nightmare, *Cauchemare*, from *Caucher, calcare.* Kit-wi-the-Canstick is Jack-with-the-Lanthorn. The Man in the Oak is probably Puck, "Turn your cloakes, quoth hee, for Pucke is busy in these oakes."—Iter Boreale. The Hell-wain is perhaps the Death-coach, connected with Northern and German superstitions, and the Fire-drake an Ignis Fatuus. Boneless may have been some impalpable spectre; the other terms seem to be mere appellations of Puck.

   * Anat. of Mel. p. 47.   † Chap. xx. p. 134. Lond. 1604.

   ‡ This is, we apprehend, an egg at Easter or on Good Friday. *Housle* is the Anglo-Saxon huŗel; Goth. *hunsl*, sacrifice or offering, and thence the Eucharist.

§ Terrors of the Night, 1594.

labours; daunced in rounds in green meadows; pincht maids
in their sleep that swept not their houses clean, and led poor
travellers out of their way."

As the celebrated Luck of Eden Hall is supposed to have
been a chalice, due respect for the piety of our forefathers
will not allow of our placing the desecration of it any higher
than the reign of Elizabeth, or that of her father at farthest.
We will therefore introduce its history in this place.

The Luck of Eden Hall.

IN this house (Eden Hall, a seat of the Musgraves,) are some
good old-fashioned apartments.   An old painted drinking-
glass, called the *Luck of Eden Hall*, is preserved with great
care.   In the garden near to the house is a well of excellent
spring water, called St. Cuthbert's Well.   (The church is
dedicated to that saint.)   This glass is supposed to have
been a sacred chalice; but the legendary tale is, that the
butler, going to draw water, surprised a company of Fairies,
who were amusing themselves upon the green near the well;
he seized the glass which was standing upon its margin.
They tried to recover it; but, after an ineffectual struggle,
flew away, saying,—

> If that glass either break or fall,
> Farewell the luck of Eden Hall.*

"In the year 1633-4 (says Aubrey†) soon after I had
entered into my grammar, at the Latin schoole of Yatton-
Keynel, [near Chippenham, Wilts,] our curate, Mr. Hart,
was annoyed one night by these elves or fayeries.   Comming
over the downes, it being neere darke, and approaching one
of the faiery dances, as the common people call them in

------

* Hutchinson, History of Cumberland, vol. i. p. 269.
† As quoted by Thoms in his Essay on Popular Songs, in the Athenæum
for 1847.

these parts, viz. the greene circles made by those sprites on the grasse, he all at once saw an innumerable quantitie of pigmies, or very small people, dancing rounde and rounde, and singing and making all maner of small odd noyses. He, being very greatly amazed, and yet not being able, as he says, to run away from them, being, as he supposes, kept there in a kinde of enchantment, they no sooner perceave him but they surround him on all sides, and what betwixte feare and amazement he fell down, scarcely knowing what he did; and thereupon these little creatures pinched him all over, and made a quick humming noyse all the tyme; but at length they left him, and when the sun rose he found himself exactly in the midst of one of these faiery dances. This relation I had from him myselfe a few days after he was so tormented; but when I and my bed-fellow, Stump, wente soon afterwards, at night time, to the dances on the downes, we sawe none of the elves or faieries. But, indeed, it is saide they seldom appeare to any persons who go to seeke for them."

The next account, in order of time, that occurs, is what Sir Walter Scott calls the Cock Lane narrative of Anne Jefferies, who was born in 1626, in the parish of St. Teath, in Cornwall, and whose wonderful adventures with the Fairies were, in 1696, communicated by Mr. Moses Pitt, her master's son, to Dr. Fowler, bishop of Gloucester.[*]

According to this account, Anne described the Fairies, who she said came to her, as "six small people, all in green clothes." They taught her to perform numerous surprising cures; they fed her from harvest-time till Christmas; they always appeared in even numbers. When seen dancing in the orchard among the trees, she said she was dancing with the fairies. These fairies scorned the imputation of being evil spirits, and referred those who termed them such to Scripture.

The following "relation of the apparition of Fairies, their seeming to keep a fair, and what happened to a certain man that endeavoured to put himself in amongst them," is given by Bovet.[†]

[*] Morgan, Phœnix Britannicus, Lond. 1732.
[†] Pandemonium, p. 207. Lond. 1684.

The Fairy-Fair.

"Reading once the eighteenth of Mr. Glanvil's relations, p. 203, concerning an Irishman that had like to have been carried away by spirits, and of the banquet they had spread before them in the fields, etc., it called to mind a passage I had often heard, of Fairies or spirits, so called by the country people, which showed themselves in great companies at divers times. At some times they would seem to dance, at other times to keep a great fair or market. I made it my business to inquire amongst the neighbours what credit might be given to that which was reported of them, and by many of the neighbouring inhabitants I had this account confirmed.

"The place near which they most ordinarily showed themselves was on the side of a hill, named Black-down, between the parishes of Pittminster and Chestonford, not many miles from Tanton. Those that have had occasion to travel that way have frequently seen them there, appearing like men and women, of a stature generally near the smaller size of men. Their habits used to be of red, blue, or green, according to the old way of country garb, with high crowned hats. One time, about fifty years since, a person living at Comb St. Nicholas, a parish lying on one side of that hill, near Chard, was riding towards his home that way, and saw, just before him, on the side of the hill, a great company of people, that seemed to him like country folks assembled as at a fair. There were all sorts of commodities, to his appearance, as at our ordinary fairs; pewterers, shoemakers, pedlars, with all kind of trinkets, fruit, and drinking-booths. He could not remember anything which he had usually seen at fairs but what he saw there. It was once in his thoughts that it might be some fair for Chestonford, there being a considerable one at some time of the year; but then again he considered that it was not the season for it. He was under very great surprise, and admired what the meaning of what he saw should be. At length it came into his mind what he had heard concerning the Fairies on the side of that hill, and it being near the road he was to take, he resolved to ride in amongst them, and see what they were. Accordingly he put on his horse that way, and, though he saw them perfectly all along as he came, yet when he was upon the place where all this had appeared to him, he could discern nothing at all, only seemed to be crowded and thrust, as when one passes through a throng of people. All the rest became invisible to him until he came to a little distance, and then it appeared to him again as at first. He found himself in pain, and so hastened home; where, being arrived, lameness seized him all on one side, which continued on him as long as he lived, which was many years; for he was living in Comb, and gave an account to any that inquired of this accident for more than twenty years afterwards; and this relation I had from a person of known honour, who had it from the man himself.

"There were some whose names I have now forgot, but they then lived at a gentleman's house, named Comb Farm, near the place before specified: both the man, his wife, and divers of the neighbours, assured me they had, at many times, seen this *fair-keeping* in the summer-time, as they came from Tanton-market, but that they durst not adventure in amongst them; for that every one that had done so had received great damage by it."

The Fairies' Caldron.

"In the vestry of Frensham church, in Surrey, on the north side of the chancel, is an extraordinary great kettle or caldron, which the inhabitants say, by tradition, was brought hither by the fairies, time out of mind, from Borough-hill, about a mile hence. To this place, if anyone went to borrow a yoke of oxen, money, etc., he might have it for a year or longer, so he kept his word to return it. There is a cave where some have fancied to hear music. In this Borough hill is a great stone, lying along of the length of about six feet. They went to this stone and knocked at it, and declared what they would borrow, and when they would repay, and a voice would answer when they should come, and that they should find what they desired to borrow at that stone. This caldron, with the trivet, was borrowed here after the manner aforesaid, and not returned according to promise; and though the caldron was afterwards carried to the stone, it could not be received, and ever since that time no borrowing there."*

The Cauld Lad of Hilton.

"HILTON HALL, in the vale of the Wear, was in former times the resort of a Brownie or House-spirit called The Cauld Lad. Every night the servants who slept in the great hall heard him at work in the kitchen, knocking the things about if they had been set in order, arranging them if otherwise, which was more frequently the case. They were resolved to banish him if they could, and the spirit, who seemed to have an inkling of their design, was often heard singing in a melancholy tone:

> Wae's me! wae's me!
> The acorn is not yet
> Fallen from the tree,
> That's to grow the wood,
> That's to make the cradle,
> That's to rock the bairn,
> That's to grow to a man,
> That's to lay me.

The servants, however, resorted to the usual mode of banishing a Brownie: they left a green cloke and hood for him by the kitchen fire, and remained on the watch. They saw him come in, gaze at the new clothes, try them on,

* Aubrey, Natural History of Surrey, iii. 366, *ap.* Ritson, Fairy Tales, p. 166.

and, apparently in great delight, go jumping and frisking about the kitchen. But at the first crow of the cock he vanished, crying—

> Here 's a cloak, and here 's a hood !
> The Cauld Lad of Hilton will do no more good;

and he never again returned to the kitchen; yet it was said that he might still be heard at midnight singing those lines in a tone of melancholy.

There was a room in the castle long called the Cauld Lad's Room, which was never occupied unless the castle was full of company, and within the last century many persons of credit had heard of the midnight wailing of the Cauld Lad, who some maintained was the spirit of a servant whom one of the barons of Hilton had killed unintentionally in a fit of passion."*

In the beginning of the last century Bourne thus gives the popular belief on this subject:

"Another part of this (winter's evening) conversation generally turns upon Fairies. These, they tell you, have frequently been seen and heard; nay, that there are some still living who were stolen away by them, and confined seven years. According to the description they give of them, who pretend to have seen them, they are in the shape of men exceeding little: they are always clad in green, and frequent the woods and fields. When they make cakes (which is a work they have been often heard at), they are very noisy; and when they have done, they are full of mirth and pastime. But generally they dance in moonlight, when mortals are asleep, and not capable of seeing them; as may be observed on the following morning, their dancing places being very distinguishable: for as they dance hand in hand, and so make a circle in their dance, so next day there will be seen rings and circles on the grass."†

The author of "Round about our Coalfire" says : ‡

* The Local Historian's Table-Book, by M. A. Richardson, iii. 239. Newcastle-upon-Tyne, 1846.

† Bourne, Antiquitates Vulgares, 1725.

‡ Quoted by Brand in his Popular Antiquities, an enlarged edition of Bourne's work.

" My grandmother has often told me of Fairies dancing upon our green, and they were *little little creatures, clothed in green.*

" The moment any one saw them, and took notice of them, they were struck blind of an eye. They lived under ground, and generally came out of a mole-hill.

" They had fine music always among themselves, and danced in a moonshiny night around, or in a ring, as one may see at this day upon every common in England, where mushrooms grow.

" When the master and mistress were laid on their pillows, the men and maids, if they had a game at romp, and blundered upstairs, or jumbled a chair, the next morning every one would swear it was the fairies, and that they heard them stamping up and down stairs all night, crying ' Water 's locked! Water 's locked!' when there was not water in every pail in the kitchen."

To come to the present times. There is no stronger proof of the neglect of what Mr Thoms has very happily designated " Folk-lore " in this country, than the fact of there having been no account given anywhere of the Pixies or Pisgies * of Devonshire and Cornwall, till within these last few years. In the year 1836, Mrs. Bray, a lady well known as the author of several novels, and wife of a clergyman at Tavistock, published, in a series of letters to Robert Southey, interesting descriptions of the part of Devonshire bordering on the Tamar and the Tavy. In this work there is given an account of the Pixies, from which we derive the following information :

According to the Devon peasant, the Pixies are the souls of infants who died before they were baptised. They are of

---

* This word Pixy, is evidently Pucksy, the endearing diminutive *sy* being added to Puck, like Betsy, Nancy, Dixie. So Mrs. Trimmer in her Fabulous Histories—which we read with wonderful pleasure in our childhood, and would recommend to our young readers—calls her hen-robins Pecksy and Flapsy. Pisgy is only Pixy transposed. Mrs. Bray derives Pixy from Pygmy. At Truro, in Cornwall, as Mr. Thoms informs us, the *moths,* which some regard as departed souls, others as fairies, are called *Pisgies.* He observes the curious, but surely casual, resemblance between this and the Greek ψυχὴ, which is both soul and moth. Grimm (p. 430) tells us from an old glossary, that the caterpillar was named in Germany, *Alba,* i. e. *Elbe,* and that the Alp often takes the form of a butterfly.

small dimensions, generally handsome in their form. Their attire is always green. Dancing is their chief amusement, which they perform to the music of the cricket, the grass-hopper, and the frog,—always at night; and thus they form the fairy-rings. The Pixy-house is usually in a rock. By moon-light, on the moor, or under the dark shade of rocks, the Pixy-monarch, Mrs. Bray says, holds his court, where, like Titania, he gives his subjects their several charges. Some are sent to the mines, where they will kindly lead the miner to the richest lode, or maliciously, by noises imitating the stroke of the hammer, and by false fires, draw him on to where the worst ore in the mine lies, and then laugh at his disappointment. Others are sent

> To make the maids their sluttery rue,
> By pinching them both black and blue.

On this account, says Mrs. Bray, " the good dames in this part of the world are very particular in sweeping their houses before they go to bed; and they will frequently place a basin of water beside the chimney-nook, to accommo-date the Pixies, who are great lovers of water; and some-times they requite the good deed by dropping a piece of money into the basin. A young woman of our town, who declared she had received the reward of sixpence for a like service, told the circumstance to her gossips; but no six-pence ever came again, and it was generally believed that the Pixies had taken offence by her chattering, as they do not like to have their deeds, good or evil, talked over by mortal tongues."

The office of some is to steal children; of others, to lead travellers astray, as Will-o'-the-wisps, or to *Pixy-lead* them, as it is termed. Some will make confusion in a house by blowing out the candle, or kissing the maids " with a smack, as they 'shriek Who's this?' as the old poet writes, till their grandams come in and lecture them for allowing unseemly freedoms with their bachelors." Others will make noises in walls, to frighten people. In short, everything that is done elsewhere by fairies, boggarts, or other like beings, is done in Devon by the Pixies.

It is said that they will sometimes aid their favourites in spinning their flax. "I have heard a story about an old

woman in this town," says Mrs. Bray, "who suspected she
received assistance of the above nature; and one evening,
coming suddenly into the room, she spied a ragged little
creature, who jumped out of the door. She thought she
would try still further to win the services of her elfin friend,
and so bought some smart new clothes, as big as those made
for a doll. These pretty things she placed by the side of
her wheel. The Pixy returned, and put them on; when,
clapping her tiny hands, she was heard to exclaim—

> Pixy fine, Pixy gay,
> Pixy now will run away;

and off she went. But the ungrateful little creature never
spun for the poor old woman after."

Mrs. Bray has been assured that mothers used frequently
to pin their children to their sides, to prevent their being
stolen by the Pixies; and she heard of a woman in Tavistock
who avowed that her mother had a child which was stolen
by them, as she was engaged hanging out clothes to dry in
her garden. She almost broke her heart when she discovered
it; but she took great care of the changeling, which so
pleased the Pixy, that she soon after gave the woman back
her child, who proved eminently lucky in after life.

The being *Pixy-led* is a thing very apt to befall worthy
yeomen returning at night from fair or market, especially
if they sat long at the market-table; and then, says our
authority, "he will declare, and offer to take his Bible-oath
upon it, that, as sure as ever he 's alive to tell it, whilst his
head was running round like a mill-wheel, he heard with
his own ears they bits of Pisgies a-laughing and a-*tacking*
their hands, all to see he led-astray, and never able to find
the right road, though he had travelled it scores of times
long agone, by night or by day, as a body might tell."
Mr. Thoms, too, was told by a Devon girl, who had often
heard of the Pixies, though she had never seen any, that
"she once knew a man who, one night, could not find his
way out of his own fields, all he could do, until he recollected
to *turn his coat;* and the moment he did so, he heard the
Pixies all fly away, up into the trees, and there they sat
and laughed. Oh! how they did laugh! But the man then
soon found his way out of the field."

This turning of the coat, or some other article of dress, is found to be the surest remedy against Pixy-illusion. Mrs. Bray says that the old folk in Tavistock have recourse to it as a preventive against being *Pixy-led*, if they have occasion to go out after sun-down. It appears to have been formerly in use in other parts of England also; for Bishop Corbet thus notices it in his "Iter Boreale:"

> William found
> A mean for our deliverance, *Turne your cloakes*
> Quoth hee, for Pucke is busy in these oakes;
> If ever wee at Bosworth will be found
> Then *turne your cloakes*, for this is fairy ground.

In Scandinavia, also, we learn the remedy against being led astray by the Lygtemand, Lyktgubhe, or Will-o'-the-Wisp, is to turn one's cap inside out.

Mrs. Bray gives, in addition, the following legends, which we have taken the liberty of abridging a little.

The Pixy-Labour.

ONE night, about twelve o'clock in the morning, as the good folks say, who tell this good tale, Dame —— the *sage femme* of Tavistock, had just got comfortably into bed, when rap, rap, rap, came on her cottage door, with such bold and continued noise, that there was a sound of authority in every individual knock. Startled and alarmed by the call, she arose from her bed, and soon learnt that the summons was a hasty one to bid her attend on a patient who needed her help. She opened her door, when the summoner appeared to be a strange, squint-eyed, little, ugly old fellow, who had a look, as she said, very like a certain dark personage, who ought not at all times to be called by his proper name. Not at all prepossessed in favour of the errand by the visage of the messenger, she nevertheless could not, or dared not, resist the command to follow him straight, and attend on " his wife."

"Thy wife!" thought the good dame; "Heaven forgive me, but as sure as I live I be going to the birth of a little divil." A large coal-black horse, with eyes like balls of fire, stood at the door. The ill-looking old fellow, without more ado, whisked her up on a high pillion in a minute, seated himself before her, and away went horse and riders as if sailing through the air rather than trotting on the ground. How she got to the place of her destination she could not tell; but it was a great relief to her fears when she found herself set down at the door of a neat cottage, saw a couple of tidy children, and remarked her patient to be a decent looking woman, having all things about her fitting the time and occasion. A fine bouncing babe soon made its appearance, who seemed very bold on its entry into life, for it gave the good dame a box on the ear, as, with the coaxing and cajolery of all good old nurses, she declared the "sweet little thing to be very like its father." The mother said nothing to this, but gave nurse a certain ointment, with directions that she should *strike* (i. e. *rub*) the child's eyes with it. The nurse performed her task, considering what it could be for. She thought that, as no doubt it was a good thing, she might just as well try it upon her own eyes as well as those of the baby; so she made free to *strike* one of them by way of trial, when, O ye powers of fairy land! what a change was there!

The neat, but homely cottage, and all who were in it, seemed all on a sudden to undergo a mighty transformation; some for the better, some for the worse. The new-made mother appeared as a beautiful lady attired in white; the babe was seen wrapped in swaddling clothes of a silvery gauze. It looked much prettier than before, but still maintained the elfish cast of the eye, like his father, whilst two or three children more had undergone a strange metamorphosis. For there sat on either side the bed's head, a couple of little flat-nosed imps, who with "mops and mows," and with many a grimace and grin, were busied to no end in scratching their own polls, or in pulling the fairy lady's ears with their long and hairy paws. The dame who beheld all this, fearing she knew not what, in the house of enchantment, got away as fast as she could, without saying one word about *striking* her own eye with the magic ointment and what she had seen. The sour-looking old fellow once more handed her up on the coal-black-horse, and sent her home in a *whip sissa* * much faster than she came.

On the next market-day, when she sallied forth to sell her eggs, she saw the same old fellow busy pilfering sundry articles from stall to stall, and going up to him she enquired about his wife and child. "What!" exclaimed he, "do you see me to-day?" "See you! to be sure I do, as plain as I see the sun in the sky; and I see you are busy, too." "Do you?" says he, "and pray with which eye do you see all this?" "With the right eye to be sure."

"The ointment! the ointment!" cried he. "Take that, for meddling with what did not belong to you; you shall see me no more."

He struck her eye as he spoke, and from that hour till the day of her death she was blind of that eye.

Pixy-Vengeance.

Two serving-girls in Tavistock said that the Pixies were very kind to them, and used to drop silver for them into a bucket of fair water which they took care to place for them in the chimney-nook every night. Once it was forgotten, and the Pixies forthwith came up to the girls' room, and loudly complained of the neglect. One of them, who happened to be awake, jogged the other, and proposed going down to rectify the omission, but she said, "for her part she would not stir out of bed to please all the pixies in Devonshire." The other went down and filled the bucket, in which, by the way, she found next morning a handfull of silver pennies. As she was returning, she heard the Pixies debating about what they would do to punish the other. Various modes were proposed and rejected; at last it was agreed to give her a lame leg for a term of seven years, then to be cured by an herb growing on Dartmoor, whose name of seven

---

* *Whip says he,* as Mrs. Bray conjectures.

syllables was pronounced in a clear and audible tone. This the girl tried by every known means to fix in her memory. But when she awoke in the morning, it was gone, and she could only tell that Molly was to be lame for seven years, and then be cured by an herb with a strange name. As for Molly, she arose dead lame, and so she continued till the end of the period, when one day, as she was picking up a mushroom, a strange-looking boy started up and insisted on *striking* her leg with a plant which he held in his hand. He did so, and she was cured and became the best dancer in the town.

Pixy-Gratitude.

An old woman who lived near Tavistock had in her garden a splendid bed of tulips. To these the Pixies of the neighbourhood loved to resort, and often at midnight might they be heard singing their babes to rest among them. By their magic power they made the tulips more beautiful and more permanent than any other tulips, and they caused them to emit a fragrance equal to that of the rose. The old woman was so fond of her tulips that she would never let one of them be plucked, and thus the Pixies were never deprived of their floral bowers.

But at length the old woman died; the tulips were taken up, and the place converted into a parsley-bed. Again, however, the power of the Pixies was shown; the parsley withered, and nothing would grow even in the other beds of the garden. On the other hand, they tended diligently the grave of the old woman, around which they were heard lamenting and singing dirges. They suffered not a weed to grow on it; they kept it always green, and evermore in spring-time spangled with wild flowers.

Thus far for the Pixies of Devon; as for the adjoining Somerset, all we have to say is, that a good woman from that county, with whom we were acquainted, used, when making

a cake, always to draw a cross upon it. This, she said, was
in order to prevent the Vairies from dancing on it. She
described these Vairies as being very small people, who,
with the vanity natural to little personages, wear high-
heeled shoes, and if a new-made cake be not duly crossed,
they imprint on it in their capers the marks of their heels.
Of the actual existence of the Vairies, she did not seem to
entertain the shadow of a doubt.

In Dorset also, the Pixy-lore still lingers. The being is
called *Pexy* and *Colepexy*; the fossil belemnites are named
Colepexies'-fingers; and the fossil echini, Colepexies'-heads.
The children, when naughty, are also threatened with the
Pexy, who is supposed to haunt woods and coppices.*

"In Hampshire," says Captain Grose, "they give the
name of Colt-Pixy to a supposed spirit or fairy, which in the
shape of a horse *wickers*, i. e. neighs, and misleads horses
into bogs, etc."

The following is a Hampshire legend: †

The Fairy-Thieves.

A FARMER in Hampshire was sorely distressed by the
unsettling of his barn. However straightly over-night he
laid his sheaves on the threshing-floor for the application of
the morning's flail, when morning came, all was topsy-turvy,
higgledy-piggledy, though the door remained locked, and
there was no sign whatever of irregular entry. Resolved to
find out who played him these mischievous pranks, Hodge
couched himself one night deeply among the sheaves, and
watched for the enemy. At length midnight arrived, the
barn was illuminated as if by moonbeams of wonderful
brightness, and through the key-hole came thousands of
elves, the most diminutive that could be imagined. They
immediately began their gambols among the straw, which

---

* Brand, Popular Antiquities, ii. 513. Bohn's edit.
† Given in the Literary Gazette for 1825. No. 430.

was soon in a most admired disorder. Hodge wondered, but interfered not; but at last the supernatural thieves began to busy themselves in a way still less to his taste, for each elf set about conveying the crop away, a straw at a time, with astonishing activity and perseverance. The key-hole was still their port of egress and regress, and it resembled the aperture of a bee-hive, on a sunny day in June. The farmer was rather annoyed at seeing his grain vanish in this fashion, when one of the fairies said to another in the tiniest voice that ever was heard—"*I weat, you weat?* Hodge could contain himself no longer. He leaped out crying, "The devil sweat ye. Let me get among ye!" when they all flew away so frightened that they never disturbed the barn any more.

In Suffolk the fairies are called *farisees*. Not many years ago, a butcher near Woodbridge went to a farmer's to buy a calf, and finding, as he expressed it, that "the cratur was all o' a muck," he desired the farmer to hang a flint by a string in the crib, so as to be just clear of the calf's head. "Becaze," said he, "the calf is rid every night by the *farisees*, and the stone will brush them off." *

We once questioned a girl from Norfolk on the subject of Fairy-lore. She said she had often heard of and even seen the *Frairies*. They were dressed in white, and lived under the ground, where they constructed houses, bridges, and other edifices. It is not safe, she added, to go near them when they appear above ground.

We now proceed to Yorkshire, where the Boggart and the Barguest used to appear in by-gone days. The former, whose name we will presently explain, is the same as the Brownie or Kobold; the latter, whose proper name perhaps is Barn-ghaist, or Barn-spirit, keeps without, and usually takes the form of some domestic animal.

* Brand, Popular Antiquities, ii. 503. Bohn's edit.

𝕮𝖍𝖊 𝕭𝖔𝖌𝖌𝖆𝖗𝖙.

IN the house of an honest farmer in Yorkshire, named George Gilbertson, a Boggart had taken up his abode. He here caused a good deal of annoyance, especially by torment-ing the children in various ways. Sometimes their bread and butter would be snatched away, or their porringers of bread and milk be capsized by an invisible hand; for the Boggart never let himself be seen; at other times, the cur-tains of their beds would be shaken backwards and forwards, or a heavy weight would press on and nearly suffocate them. The parents had often, on hearing their cries, to fly to their aid. There was a kind of closet, formed by a wooden parti-tion on the kitchen-stairs, and a large knot having been driven out of one of the deal-boards of which it was made, there remained a hole.* Into this one day the farmer's youngest boy stuck the shoe-horn with which he was amusing himself, when immediately it was thrown out again, and struck the boy on the head. The agent was of course the Boggart, and it soon became their sport (which they called *laking* † *with Boggart*) to put the shoe-horn into the hole and have it shot back at them.

The Boggart at length proved such a torment that the farmer and his wife resolved to quit the house and let him have it all to himself. This was put into execution, and the farmer and his family were following the last loads of furni-ture, when a neighbour named John Marshall came up— "Well, Georgey," said he, "and soa you're leaving t'ould hoose at last?"—"Heigh, Johnny, my lad, I'm forced tull it; for that damned Boggart torments us soa, we can

---

* The *Elfbore* of Scotland, where it is likewise ascribed to the fairies, Jamieson, *s. v.* The same opinion prevails in Denmark, where it is said that any one who looks through it will see things he would not otherwise have known : see Thiele, ii. 18.

† The Anglo-Saxon *léan, laécan,* to play.

neither rest neet nor day for't. It seems loike to have such a malice again t'poor bairns, it ommost kills my poor dame here at thoughts on't, and soa, ye see, we're forced to flitt loike." He scarce had uttered the words when a voice from a deep upright churn cried out, "Aye, aye, Georgey, we're flitting ye see."—"Od damn thee," cried the poor farmer, "if I'd known thou'd been there, I wadn't ha' stirred a peg. Nay, nay, it's no use, Mally," turning to his wife, "we may as weel turn back again to t'ould hoose as be tormented in another that's not so convenient." *

Addlers and Menters.

An old lady in Yorkshire related as follows:—My eldest daughter Betsey was about four years old; I remember it was on a fine summer's afternoon, or rather evening, I was seated in this chair which I now occupy. The child had been in the garden, she came into that entry or passage from the kitchen (on the right side of the entry was the old parlour-door, on the left the door of the common sitting-room; the mother of the child was in a line with both the doors); the child, instead of turning towards the sitting-room made a pause at the parlour-door, which was open. She stood several minutes quite still; at last I saw her draw her hand quickly towards her body; she set up a loud shriek and ran, or rather flew, to me crying out "Oh! Mammy, green man will hab me! green man will hab me!" It was a long time before I could pacify her; I then asked her why she was so frightened. "O Mammy," she said, "all t'parlour is full of *addlers* and *menters*." Elves and fairies (spectres?) I suppose she meant. She said they

---

* We have abridged this legend from a well-written letter in the Literary Gazette, No. 430 (1825), the writer of which says, he knew the house in which it was said to have occurred. He also says he remembered an old tailor, who said the horn was often pitched at the head of himself and his apprentice, when in the North-country fashion they went to work at the farm-house. Its identity with other legends will be at once perceived.

were dancing, and a little man in a green coat with a gold-laced cocked hat on his head, offered to take her hand as if he would have her as his partner in the dance. The mother, upon hearing this, went and looked into the old parlour, but the fairy vision had melted into thin air. " Such," adds the narrator, " is the account I heard of this vision of fairies. The person is still alive who witnessed or supposed she saw it, and though a well-informed person, still positively asserts the relation to be strictly true.*

Ritson, who was a native of the bishoprick of Durham, tells us † that the fairies frequented many parts of it; that they were described as being of the smallest size, and uniformly habited in green. They could, however, change their size and appearance. "A woman," he says, "who had been in their society challenged one of the guests whom she espied in the market selling fairy-butter.‡ This freedom was deeply resented, and cost her the eye she first saw him with. Some one informed him that an acquaintance of his in Westmoreland, wishing to see a fairy, was told that on such a day on the side of such a hill, he should be gratified. He went, and there, to use his own words, " the hobgoblin stood before him in the likeness of a green-coat lad," but vanished instantly. This, he said, the man told him. A female relation of his own told Mr. Ritson of Robin Good-fellow's, it would seem, thrashing the corn, churning the butter, drinking the milk, etc., and when all was done, lying before the fire " *like a great rough hurgin* (hugging ?) *bear.* " §

* And true no doubt it is, *i. e.* the impression made on her imagination was as strong as if the objects had been actually before her. The narrator is the same person who told the preceding Boggart story.

† Fairy Tales, pp. 24, 56.

‡ In Northumberland the common people call a certain fungous excrescence, sometimes found about the roots of old trees, Fairy-butter. After great rains and in a certain degree of putrefaction, it is reduced to a consistency, which, together with its colour, makes it not unlike butter, and hence the name. Brand, Popular Antiquities, ii. 492, Bohn's edit.

The Menyn Tylna Têg or Fairy-butter of Wales, we are told in the same place, is a substance found at a great depth in cavities of limestone-rocks when sinking for lead-cre.

§ Comp. Milton, L'Allegro, 105 *seq.*

The Barguest used also to appear in the shape of a mastiff-dog and other animals, and terrify people with his *skrikes* (shrieks). There was a Barguest named the Picktree Brag, whose usual form was that of a little galloway, "in which shape a farmer, still or lately living thereabouts, reported that it had come to him one night as he was going home; that he got upon it and rode very quietly till it came to a great pond, to which it ran and threw him in, and *went laughing away.*"

In Northumberland the belief in the fairies is not yet extinct. The writer from whom we derive the following legends tells us * that he knew an old man whose dog had *pointed* a troop of fairies,† and though he could not see them he plainly heard their music sounding like a fiddle and a *very small* pair of pipes. He also tells us, that many years ago a girl who lived near Nether Witton, as she was returning from milking with her pail on her head, saw the fairies playing in the fields, and though she pointed them out to her companions they could not see them. The reason it seemed was her *weise* or pad for bearing the pail on her head was composed of four-leaved clover, which gives the power of seeing fairies. Spots are pointed out in sequestered places as the favourite haunts of the elves. A few miles from Alnwick is a fairy-ring, round which if people run more than nine times, some evil will befall them. The children constantly run this number, but nothing will induce them to venture a tenth run.

The Fary Nurseling.

A COTTAGER and his wife residing at Nether Witton were one day visited by a *fary* and his spouse with their young

---

* Richardson, Table-Book, iii. 45 ; see above, p. 297.

† This word, as we may see, is spelt *faries* in the following legends; so we may suppose that *fairy* is pronounced *farry* in the North, which has a curious coincidence with *Peri :* see above, p. 15.

child, which they wished to leave in their charge. The cottager agreed to take care of the child for a certain period when it had to be taken thence. The fary gave the man a box of ointment with which to anoint the child's eyes; but he had not on any account to touch himself with it, or some misfortune would befal him. For a long time he and his wife were very careful to avoid the dangerous unction; but one day when his wife was out curiosity overcame his prudence, and he anointed his eyes without any noticeable effect; but after a while, when walking through Long Horsley Fair, he met the male fary and accosted him. He started back in amazement at the recognition; but instantly guessing the truth, blew on the eyes of the cottager, and instantly blinded him. The child was never more seen.

The Fary Labour.

ANOTHER tale relates that a messenger having visited a country midwife or *howdie* requested her professional assistance in a case where so much secrecy was required that she must be conducted to and from the destined place blindfolded; she at first hesitated, but her scruples were overcome by a handsome present, the promise of a future reward, and assurance of perfect personal safety. She then submitted to the required condition, mounted behind the messenger on a fleet charger, and was carried forward in an unaccountable manner. The journey was not of long continuance, the steed halted, she dismounted, and was conducted into a cottage where the bandage was removed from her eyes; everything appeared neat and comfortable. She was shown the woman "in the straw," and performed her office; but when ready to dress the babe, an old woman, (who, according to the narration, appears to have been the nurse,) put a box of ointment into her hand, requiring her to anoint the child all over with it, but to be careful that it did not touch her own person; she prudently complied, though wondering at the motive. Whilst this operation was going on, she felt an itching in one of her eyes, and in an unguarded moment rubbed it with a finger which had touched the mysterious ointment. And now a new scene forced itself upon her astonished vision, and she saw everything in a different light; instead of the neat cottage, she perceived the large overhanging branches of an ancient oak, whose hollow and moss-grown trunk she had before mistaken for the fire place, glowworms supplied the place of lamps, and, in short, she found herself in the abode of a family of faries, with faries was she surrounded, and one of their number reposed on her lap. She however retained her self-possession, finished her task, and was conducted homeward in the same manner as she was brought. So far all went well, and the *howdie* might have carried the secret to her grave, but in after time, on a market-day (in what town the legend saith not,) forgetful of her former caution, she saw the old nurse among the countrywomen, gliding about from one basket to another, passing a little wooden scraper along the rolls of butter, and carefully collecting the particles thus purloined into a vessel hung by her side. After a mutual but silent recognition, the nurse addressed her thus, "Which eye do you see me with?" "With this," innocently answered the other. No sooner had she spoken than a puff from the withering breath of her unearthly companion extinguished the ill-fated orb for ever, and the hag instantly vanished.

Another version says the Doctor is presented with a box of eye-salve by his conductor; on using it he sees a splendid portico in the side of a steep hill, through this he is shown into the faries' hall in the interior of the mountain: he performs his office, and on coming out receives a second box; he rubs one eye, and with it sees the hill in its natural shape; then thinking to cheat the devil, feigns to rub the other, and gallops off. Afterwards he sees the fary's husband stealing corn in the market, when similar consequences befal him as those which occurred unto the woman.

Ainsel.

A WIDOW and her son, a little boy, lived together in a cottage in or near the village of Rothley, Northumberland. One winter's evening the child refused to go to bed with his mother, as he wished to sit up for a while longer, "for," said he, "I am not sleepy." The mother finding remonstrance in vain, at last told him that if he sat up by himself the faries would most certainly come and take him away. The boy laughed as his mother went to bed, leaving him sitting by the fire; he had not been there long, watching the fire and enjoying its cheerful warmth, till a beautiful little figure, about the size of a child's doll, descended the chimney and alighted on the hearth! The little fellow was somewhat startled at first, but its prepossessing smile as it paced to and fro before him soon overcame his fears, and he inquired familiarly, " What do they ca' thou ?" " Ainsel," answered the little thing haughtily, at the same time retorting the question, " And what do they ca' *thou ?*" " *My* ainsel'," answered the boy; and they commenced playing together like two children newiy acquainted. Their gambols continued quite innocently until the fire began to grow dim; the boy then took up the poker to stir it, when a hot cinder accidently fell upon the foot of his playmate; her tiny voice was instantly raised to a most terrific roar, and the boy had scarcely time to crouch into the bed behind his mother, before the voice of the old fary-mother was heard shouting, " Who's done it ? Who's done it ? " " Oh! it was my ainsel!" answered the daughter. " Why, then," said the mother, as she kicked her up the chimney, " what's all this noise for : there's nyon (*i.e.* no one) to blame."

Such is the sum of what we have been able to collect respecting the popular fairy-lore of England, the largest and most complete collection that, to our knowledge, has ever been made.   We might venture to add that little more is ever likely to be collected, for the sounds of the cotton-mill, the steam-engine, and, more than all, the whistle of the railway train, more powerful than any exorcists, have banished, or soon will banish, the fairy tribes from all their accustomed haunts, and their name and their exploits will in future be found in works like the present rather than in village tradition.

As the merry spirit, Puck, is so prominent an actor in the scenes forming our next division, this may be deemed no unfitting place for the consideration of his various appellations; such as Puck, Robin Good-fellow, Robin Hood, Hobgoblin.

Puck is evidently the same with the old word *Pouke*,* the original meaning of which would seem to be devil, demon, or evil spirit.   We first meet with it in the Vision of Piers Ploughman, where it undoubtedly signifies 'the grand adversary of God and man.'

When, in this poem,† the Seer beholds Abraham, the personification of Faith, with his "wide clothes," within which lay a Lazar,

> Amonges patriarkes and prophetes,
> Pleying togideres,

and asks him what was there,

> Loo ! quod he, and leet me see.
> Lord mercy ! I seide ;
> This is a present of muche pris,
> What prynce shal it have?
> It is a precious present, quod he,
> Ac the *pouke* it hath attached,
> And me theremyde, 'quod that man,
> May no wed us quyte,
>
> Ne no buyrn be oure borgh,
> Ne bringe us from his daunger ;
> Out of the *poukes pondfold*
> No maynprise may us fecche,
> Til he come that I carpe of,
> Crist is his name,
> That shall delivere us som day
> Out of the *develes* power.

Golding also must have understood Pooke in the sense of devil, when in the ninth book of his translation of Ovid,

---

* Probably pronounced *Poke*, as still in Worcestershire.   Our ancestors frequently used *ou* or *oo* for the long *o* while they expressed the sound of *oc* by *o* followed by *e*, as *rote* root, *coke* cook, *more* moor, *pole* pool.

† Passus xvii. *v.* 11,323 *seq.* ed. 1842.   Comp. *vv.* 8363, 9300, 10,902.

unauthorised however by the original, he applies it to the Chimæra,

> The country where Chymæra, that same *pooke*
> Hath goatish body, lion's head and brist, and dragon's tayle.

Spenser employs the word, and he clearly distinguishes it from hob-goblin :

> Ne let housefires nor lightnings helpless harms,
> Ne let the *pouke** nor other evil sprites,
> Ne let mischievous witches with their charms,
> Ne let *hob-goblins,* names whose sense we see not,
> Fray us with things that be not.—*Epithalamion,* v. 340.

These terms are also distinguished in the poem named The Scourge of Venus :

> And that they may perceive the heavens frown,
> The *poukes* and *goblins* pull the coverings down.

In Ben Jonson's play of The Devil is an Ass, the unlucky fiend who gives origin to its name is called Pug, and in the same author's Sad Shepherd the personage named Puck-hairy is, as Gifford justly observes, "not the Fairy or Oriental Puck, though often confounded with him." † In truth, it is first in Shakespeare that we find Puck confounded with the House-spirit, and having those traits of character which are now regarded as his very essence, and have caused his name Pug to be given to the agile mischievous monkey, and to a kind of little dog.

We will now discuss the origin of this far-famed appellation and its derivation.

In the Slavonic tongues, which are akin to the Teutonic, *Bôg* is God, and there are sleights of etymology which would identify the two terms ; the Icelandic Puki is an evil spirit, and such we have seen was the English Pouke, which easily became Puck, Pug, and Bug ; finally, in Friesland the

---

* Mr. Todd is right, in reading *pouke* for *ponke,* an evident typographic error : wrong in saying, " He is the Fairy, Robin Good-fellow, known by the name of Puck." Robin is the " hob-goblin " mentioned two lines after.

† We know nothing of the Oriental origin of Puck, and cannot give our ful. assent to the character of our ancestry, as expressed in the remaining part of Mr. Gifford's note : " but a fiend engendered in the moody minds, and rude a.id gloomy fancies of the barbarous invaders of the North." It is full time to have done with describing the old Gothic race as savages.

Kobold is called Puk, and in old German we meet with Putz or Butz as the name of a being not unlike the original English Puck.* The Devonshire fairies are called Pixies, and the Irish have their Pooka, and the Welsh their Pwcca, both derived from Pouke or Puck. From Bug comes the Scottish Bogle, (which Gawin Douglas expressly distinguishes from the Brownie) and the Yorkshire Boggart.† The Swedish language has the terms *spöka, spöke;* the Danish *spöge, spögelse,* the German, *spuken, spuk,* all used of spirits or ghosts, and their apparitions. Perhaps the Scottish *pawkey,* sly, knowing, may belong to the same family of words. Akin to Bogle was the old English term Puckle, noticed above, which is still retained in the sense of mischievous, as in Peregrine Pickle and Little Pickle. It has been conjectured‡ that *Pickleharing,* the German term for zany or merry-andrew, may have been properly *Picklehärin, i.e.* the hairy sprite, answering to Jonson's Puck-hairy, and that he may have worn a vesture of hair or leaves to be rough like the Brownie and kindred beings.

From Bug also come Bugbear, and Bugleboo, or Bugaboo. They owe their origin probably to the Ho! Ho! Ho! given to Puck or Robin Goodfellow, as it was to the Devil (*i.e.,* Pouke) in the Mysteries. Bull-beggar may be only a corruption of Bugbear.§

The following passage from a writer of the present day proves that in some places the idea of Puck as a spirit haunting the woods and fields is still retained. " The pea-

* *Der Putz würde uns über berg und thäler tragen.* To frighten children they say *Der Butz kommt!* see Grimm, Deut. Mythol. p. 474.

† The former made by adding the Anglo-Saxon and English *el, le;* the latter by adding the English *art* : see p. 318.

‡ By Sir F. Palgrave, from whose article in the Quarterly Review, we have derived many of the terms named above. He adds that the Anglo-Saxon *pæcan* is to deceive, seduce; the Low-Saxon *picken* to gambol; *pickeln* to play the fool; *pukra* in Icelandic to make a murmuring noise, to steal secretly; and *pukke* in Danish to scold. He further adds the Swedish *poika* boy, the Anglo-Saxon and Swedish *piga* and Danish *pige* girl. If, however, Pouke is connected with the Sclavonic Bog, these at the most can be only derivations from it. By the way *boy* itself seems to be one of these terms; the Anglo-Saxon *piga* was probably pronounced *piya,* and *a* is a masculine termination in that language.

§ See above, p. 291. In Low German, however, the Kobold is called Bull-mann, Bullermann, Bullerkater, from *bullen, bullern,* to knock : see Grimm, *ut sup.* p. 473.

Puck and the Fairies

Shakespeare's *A Midsummer Night's Dream*

santry," says Mr. Allies,* "of Alfrick and those parts of Worcestershire, say that they are sometimes what they call *Poake-ledden*, that is, that they are occasionally waylaid in the night by a mischievous sprite whom they call Poake, who leads them into ditches, bogs, pools, and other such scrapes, and then sets up a loud laugh and leaves them quite bewildered in the lurch." This is what in Devon is called being *Pixy-led*. We may observe the likeness here to the Puck of Shakspeare and Drayton, who were both natives of the adjoining county.

A further proof perhaps of Puck's rural and extern character is the following rather trifling circumstance. An old name of the fungus named *puff ball* is *puck fist*, which is plainly Puck's-fist, and not *puff-fist* as Nares conjectured; for its Irish name is *Cos-a-Phooka*, or Pooka's-foot, *i.e.*, Puck's-foot. We will add by the way, that the Anglo-Saxon Ɍ ulꞃeꞃ-ꞃiꞃꞇ, Wolf's-fist, is rendered in the dictionaries toadstool, mushroom, and we cannot help suspecting that as wolf and elf were sometimes confounded, and wolf and fist are, in fact, incompatible terms, this was originally Ælꞃeꞃ-ꞃiꞃꞇ Elf's-fist, and that the mushrooms meant were not the thick ugly toadstools, the "grislie todestooles," of Spenser, but those delicate fungi called in Ireland *fairy-mushrooms*, and which perhaps in England also were ascribed to the fairies.†

So much then for Puck; we will now consider some other terms.

Robin Goodfellow, of whom we have given above a full account, is evidently a domestic spirit, answering in name and character to the Nisse God-dreng of Scandinavia, the Knecht Ruprecht, *i.e.*, Robin of Germany. He seems to unite in his person the Boggart and Barguest of Yorkshire.

Hob-goblin is, as we have seen, another name of the same spirit. Goblin is the French *gobelin*, German Kobold; Hob is Rob, Robin, Bob; just as Hodge is Roger. We still have the proper names Hobbs, Hobson, like Dix, Dixon, Wills, Wilson; by the way, Hick, *i. e.* Dick, from Richard, still remains in Hicks, Hickson.

---

* Essay on the Ignis Fatuus, quoted by Thoms.
†   And you whose pastime
 Is to make midnight mushrooms.—*Tempest*, v. 1.

Robin Hood, though we can produce no instance of it, must, we think, also have been an appellation of this spirit, and been given to the famed outlaw of merry Sherwood, from his sportive character and his abiding in the recesses of the greenwood. The hood is a usual appendage of the domestic spirit.

Roguery and sportiveness are, we may see, the characteristics of this spirit. Hence it may have been that the diminutives of proper names were given to him, and even to the Ignis Fatuus, which in a country like England, that was in general dry and free from sloughs and bog-holes, was mischievous rather than dangerous.* But this seems to have been a custom of our forefathers, for we find the devil himself called Old Nick, and Old Davy is the sailor's familiar name for Death.

In the Midsummer Night's Dream the fairy says to Puck "Thou Lob of spirits;" Milton has the *lubber-fiend*, and Fletcher says,† "There is a pretty tale of a witch that had a giant to be her son that was called Lob Lie-by-the-fire." This might lead us to suppose that *Lob*, whence *loby* (looby), *lubbard*, *lubber*,‡ and adding the diminutive *kin*, Lubberkin, a name of one of the clowns in Gay's Pastorals, was an original name of some kind of spirit. We shall presently see that the Irish name of the Leprechaun is actually Lubberkin. As to the origin of the name we have little to say, but it may have had a sense the very opposite of the present one of *lubber*, and have been connected with the verb *to leap*.§ Grimm‖ tells of a spirit named the Good

---

* Jack-o'-the-lanthorn, Will-o'-the-wisp. In Worcestershire they call it Hob-and-his-lanthorn, and Hobany's- or Hobredy's-lanthorn. Allies, *ut sup.*

† Knight of the Burning Pestle : see above, p. 309.

‡ *Ard* is the German *hart*, and is, like it, depreciatory. It is not an Anglo-Saxon termination, but from the Anglo-Saxon *boll*, *dull*, we have *dullard*. May not *haggard* be *hawk-ard*, and the French *hagard* be derived from it, and not the reverse?

§ For in Anglo-Saxon *áttorcoppe* (*Poison-head*?) is spider, and from *áttor-coppe-web*, by the usual aphœresis of the two first syllables we put *coppe-web*, cobweb. May not the same have been the case with *lob*? and may not the nasty *bug* be in a similar manner connected with Puck ? As *dvergsnat* is in Swedish a cobweb, one might be tempted to suppose that this last, for which no good etymon has been offered, was *lob-web;* but the true etymon is *cop-web*, from its usual site.

Upon the *cop* right of his nose he hedde
A wert.—Chaucer, *Cant. Tales, v.* 556.

‖ Deut. Mythol. p. 492.

Lubber, to whom the bones of animals used to be offered at Mansfield in Germany; but we see no resemblance between him and our Lob of spirits; we might rather trace a connexion with the French Lutin, Lubin.* The phrase of *being in* or *getting into Lob's Pound* (like the "Pouke's pondfold,") is easy of explanation, if we suppose Lob to be a sportive spirit. It is equivalent to being *Poake-ledden* or *Pixy-led.*

Wight, answering to the German *Wicht*, seems to have been used in the time of Chaucer for elf or fairy, most probably for such as haunted houses, or it may have had the signification of *witch*, which is evidently another form of it. In the Miller's Tale the carpenter says,

> I crouchè thee from elvès and from *wights.*

And

> Jesu Crist, and Seint Benedight,
> Blisse this house from every wicked *wight!*†

Urchin is a term which, like *elf* and such like, we still apply to children, but which seems formerly to have been one of the appellations of the fairies. Reginald Scott, as we have seen, places it in his list, and we find it in the following places of the poets:—

> *Urchins*
> Shall for the vast of night that they may work
> All exercise on thee.—*Tempest*, i. 2.

---

* See *France*. *In* is a mere termination, perhaps. like *on*, a diminutive, as in *Catin* Kate, *Robin* Bob. *Lutin* was also spelt *Luyton* : see p. 42.

† The two lines which follow

> Fro the nightes mare the witè Paternoster !
> Where wonest thou Seint Peter's suster?

are rather perplexing. We would explain them thus. Bergerac, as quoted by Brand (Pop. Antiq. i. 312. Bohn's edit.) makes a magician say " I teach the shepherds the wolf's paternoster," *i. e.* one that keeps off the wolf. *Wite* may then be *i. q. wight*, and *wight paternoster* be a safeguard against the wights, and we would read the verse thus : " Fro the nightes mare the wite paternoster" *sc. blisse it* or *us*. St. Peter's *suster, i. e.* wife (see 1 Cor. ix. 5) may have been canonised in the popular creed, and held to be potent against evil beings. The term *suster* was used probably to obviate the scandal of supposing the first Pope to have been a married man. This charm is given at greater length and with some variations by Cartwright in his Ordinary, Act iii. sc. 1.

His spirits hear me,
And yet I needs must curse; but they'll not pinch.
Fright me with *urchin-shows*, pitch me i' the mire,
Nor lead me like a fire-brand in the dark
Out of my way, unless he bid 'em.—*Ib.* ii. 2.

Like *urchins*, ouphs, and fairies.
　　　　　　　Merry Wives of Windsor, iv. 4.

Elves, *urchins*, goblins all, and little fairyes.
　　　　　　　Mad Pranks, etc., p. 38.

Great store of goblins, fairies, bugs, nightmares,
Urchins, and elves, to many a house repairs.
　　　　　　　Old Poem, in Brand, ii. 514.

Trip it, litttle *urchins* all.
　　　　　　　Maid's Metamorphosis.

Helping all *urchin-blasts* and ill-luck signs,
That the shrewd meddling elfe delights to make.
　　　　　　　Comus, 845.

Urchin is a hedgehog, as Stevens has justly observed,[*] and in these lines of Titus Andronicus (ii. 3.)

A thousand fiends, a thousand hissing snakes,
Ten thousand swelling toads, as many *urchins*,

it probably has this sense. We still call the *echinus marinus* the Sea-urchin. Still as we have no analogy, but rather the contrary, for transferring the name of an animal to the elves, we feel inclined to look for a different origin of the term as applied to these beings. The best or rather only hypothesis we have met with[†] is that which finds it in the hitherto unexplained word *Orcneas* in Beówulf, which may have been *Orcenas*, and if, as we have supposed,[‡] the Anglo-Saxons sometimes pronounced *c* before *e* and *i* in the Italian manner, we should have, if needed, the exact word. We would also notice the old German *urkinde*, which Grimm renders *nanus*.[§]

We now come to the poets.

In Beówulf, an Anglo-Saxon poem, supposed not to be

---

[*] He derives it from the French *oursin*, but the Ang.-Sax. name of the hedgehog is eɲꞇcen.

[†] Athenæum, Oct. 9, 1847.

[‡] Hist. of England, i. 478, 8vo edit.　　　[§] Deut. Mythol. p. 419

later than the seventh century, we meet with the following verse,

> " Eotenas, and Ylfe,
> And Orcneas."

The first of these words is evidently the same as the Iötunn or Giants of the northern mythology; the second is as plainly its Alfar, and we surely may be excused for supposing that the last may be the same as its Duergar.

Layamon, in the twelfth century, in his poetic paraphrase of Wace's Brut,* thus expands that poet's brief notice of the birth of Arthur :—

> " Ertur son nom ; de sa bunte
> Ad grant parole puis este."

Soné swa he com on eorthe,	So soon he came on earth,
Alven hine ivengen.	Elves received him.
Heo bigolen that child	They enchanted that child
Mid galdere swith stronge.	With magic most strong.
Heo zeven him mihte	They gave him might
To beon best alre cnihton.	To be the best of all knights.
Heo zeven him an other thing	They gave him another thing
That he scolde beon riche king.	That he should be a rich king.
Heo zeven him that thridde	They gave him the third
That he scolde longe libben.	That he should long live.
Heo zeven that kin-bern	They gave to that kingly child
Custen swithe gode.	Virtues most good.
That he was mete-custi	That he was most generous
Of alle quike monnen.	Of all men alive.
This the Alven him zef.	This the Elves him gave.

vv. 19254 : *seq.*

If we have made any discovery of importance in the department of romantic literature, it is our identification of Ogier le Danois with the Eddaic Helgi.† We have shown among other points of resemblance, that as the Norns were at the birth of the one, so the Fées were at that of the other. With this circumstance Layamon was apparently acquainted, and when he wished to transfer it to Arthur as

---

* Layamon's Brut, etc., by Sir Frederick Madden.

† Tales and Popular Fictions, ch. viii. We do not wonder that this should have eluded previous observation, but it is really surprising that we should have been the first to observe the resemblance between Ariosto's tale of Giocondo and the introductory tale of the Thousand and One Nights. It is also strange that no one should have noticed the similarity between Ossian's Carthon and the tale of Soohráb in the Shâh-nâmeh.

the Norns were no longer known and the Fées had not yet risen into importance, there only remained for him to employ the Elves, which had not yet acquired tiny dimensions. Hence then we see that the progress was Norns, Elves, Fées, and these last held their place in the subsequent Fairy tales of France and Italy.

These potent Elves are still superior to the popular Fairies which we first met with in Chaucer.

Yet nothing in the passages in which he speaks of them leads to the inference of his conceiving them to be of a diminutive stature. His notions, indeed, on the subject seem very vague and unsettled; and there is something like a confusion of the Elves and Fairies of Romance, as the following passages will show: —

The Wife of Bathes Tale is evidently a Fairy tale. It thus commences:

> In oldè dayès of the king Artoúr,
> Of which that Bretons speken gret honoúr,
> All was this lond fulfilled of faërie;*
> The Elf-quene with her joly compagnie,
> Danced ful oft in many a grenè mede.
> This was the old opinion as I rede;
> I speke of many hundred yeres ago.
> But now can no man see non elvès mo,
> For now the gretè charitee and prayéres
> Of limitoures, and other holy freres,
> That serchen every land and every streme,
> As thikke as motès in the sonnè-beme,
> Blissing halles, chambres, kichenès, and boures,
> Citees and burghès, castles highe, and toures,
> Thropès† and bernès, shepenes and dairiés,
> This maketh that there ben no faëries;
> For there as wont to walken was an elf,
> There walketh now the limitour himself,
> In undermelès, ‡ and in morweninges,
> And sayth his matines and his holy thinges,
> As he goth in his limitatioun.
> Women may now go safely up and down;
> In every bush and under every tree
> There is none other incubus but he,
> And he ne will don hem no dishonoúr.

* Both here and lower down we would take *faërie* in its first sense.

† *Thrope, thorpe,* or *dorp,* is a village, the German *dorf ;* Dutch *dorp ;* we may still find it in the names of places, as Althorpe. *Dorp* occurs frequently in Drayton's Polyolbion; it is also used by Dryden, Hind and Panther, *v.* 1905.

‡ *Undermeles,* i. e. *undertide* (p. 51), aftermeal, afternoon.

The Fairies therefore form a part of the tale, and they are thus introduced :

> The day was come that homward must he turne;
> And in his way it happed him to ride,
> In all his care, under a forest side,
> Wheras he saw upon a dancè go
> Of ladies foure and twenty, and yet mo :
> Toward this ilke dance he drow ful yerne,
> In hope that he som wisdom shuldè lerne ;
> But certainly, er he came fully there,
> Yvanished was this dance, he n'iste not wher ;
> No creäture saw he that barè lif,
> Save on the grene he saw sitting a wif,
> A fouler wight ther may no man devise.

These ladies bear a great resemblance to the Elle-maids of Scandinavia. We need hardly inform our readers that this "foul wight" becomes the knight's deliverer from the imminent danger he is in, and that, when he has been forced to marry her, she is changed into a beautiful young maiden. But who or what she was the poet sayeth not.

In the Marchantes Tale we meet the Faerie attendant on Pluto and Proserpina, their king and queen, a sort of blending of classic and Gothic mythology :

> for to tell
> The beautee of the gardin, and the well
> That stood under a laurer alway grene ;
> Ful often time he Pluto, and his quene
> Proserpina, and alle hir faërie *
> Disporten hem, and maken melodie
> About that well, and daunced, as men told.

Again, in the same Tale :

> And so befel in that bright morwe tide,
> That, in the gardin, on the ferther side,
> Pluto, that is the king of Faërie,
> And many a ladye in his compagnie,
> Folwing his wif, the quene Proserpina,
> Which that he ravisshed out of Ethná,
> While that she gadred floures in the mede,
> (In Claudian ye may the story rede,
> How that hire in his grisely carte he fette);
> This king of Faërie adoun him sette
> Upon a benche of turvès, fresh and grene.

---

* This is the third sense of *Faërie.* In the next passage it is doubtful whether it be the second or third sense ; we think the latter.

In the conversation which ensues between these august personages, great knowledge of Scripture is displayed; and the queen, speaking. of the "sapient prince," passionately exclaims—

> I setè nat of all the vilanie
> That he of women wrote a boterflie;
> I am a woman nedès moste I speke,
> Or swell unto that time min hertè breke.

Some might suspect a mystery in the queen's thus emphatically styling herself a woman, but we lay no stress upon it, as Faire Damoselle Pertelote, the hen, who was certainly less entitled to it, does the same.

In the Man of Lawes Tale the word Elfe is employed, but whether as equivalent to witch or fairy is doubtful.

> This lettre spake, the quene delivered was
> Of so horríble a fendliche creätúre,
> That in the castle, non so hardy was,
> That any whilè dorste therein endure.
> The mother was an *elfe* by áventure,
> Y come, by charmès or by sorcerie,
> And everich man hateth hire compagnie.*

The Rime of Sir Thopas has been already considered as belonging to romance.

It thus appears that the works of manners-painting Chaucer give very little information respecting the popular belief in Fairies of his day. Were it not for the sly satire of the passage, we might be apt to suspect that, like one who lived away from the common people, he was willing to represent the superstition as extinct—" But now can no man see non elves mo." The only trait that he gives really characteristic of the popular elves is their love of dancing.

In the poets that intervene between Chaucer and the Maiden Reign, we do not recollect to have noticed anything of importance respecting Fairies, except the employment, already adverted to, of that term, and that of Elves, by

---

> * This wife which is of *faërie*,
> Of such a childe delivered is,
> Fro kindè which stante all amis.
>   GOWER, *Legende of Constance.*

translators in rendering the Latin *Nymphæ.* Of the size of these beings, the passages in question give no information.

But in Elizabeth's days, "Fairies," as Johnson observes, "were much in fashion; common tradition had made them familiar, and Spenser's poem had made them great." A just remark, no doubt, though Johnson fell into the common error of identifying Spenser's Fairies with the popular ones.

The three first books of the Faerie Queene were published in 1590, and, as Warton remarks, Fairies became a familiar and fashionable machinery with the poets and poetasters. Shakspeare, well acquainted, from the rural habits of his early life, with the notions of the peasantry respecting these beings, and highly gifted with the prescient power of genius, saw clearly how capable they were of being applied to the production of a species of the wonderful, as pleasing, or perhaps even more so, than the classic gods; and in the Midsummer-Night's Dream he presented them in combination with the heroes and heroines of the mythic age of Greece. But what cannot the magic wand of genius effect? We view with undisturbed delight the Elves of Gothic mythology sporting in the groves of Attica, the legitimate haunts of Nymphs and Satyrs.

Shakspeare, having the Faerie Queene before his eyes, seems to have attempted a blending of the Elves of the village with the Fays of romance. His Fairies agree with the former in their diminutive stature,—diminished, indeed, to dimensions inappreciable by village gossips,—in their fondness for dancing, their love of cleanliness, and their child-abstracting propensities. Like the Fays, they form a community, ruled over by the princely Oberon and the fair Titania.* There is a court and chivalry: Oberon would have the queen's sweet changeling to be a " Knight of his

---

* The derivation of Oberon has been already given (p. 208). The Shakspearean commentators have not thought fit to inform us why the poet designates the Fairy-queen, Titania. It, however, presents no difficulty. It was the belief of those days that the Fairies were the same as the classic Nymphs, the attendants of Diana: "That fourth kind of spritis," says King James, " quhilk be the gentilis was called Diana, and her wandering court, and amongst us called the *Phairie.*" The Fairy-queen was therefore the same as Diana, whom Ovid (Met. iii. 173) styles Titania; Chaucer, as we have seen, calls her Proserpina.

train to trace the forest wild." Like earthly monarchs, he has his jester, " the shrewd and knavish sprite, called Robin Good-fellow."

The luxuriant imagination of the poet seemed to exult in pouring forth its wealth in the production of these new actors on the mimic scene, and a profusion of poetic imagery always appears in their train. Such lovely and truly British poetry cannot be too often brought to view; we will therefore insert in this part of our work several of these gems of our Parnassus, distinguishing by a different character such acts and attributes as appear properly to belong to the Fairy of popular belief.

MIDSUMMER-NIGHT'S DREAM.

ACT II.—SCENE I.

Puck and a Fairy.

Puck. How now, spirit! whither wander you?
Fai. Over hill, over dale,
  Thorough bush, thorough briar,
 Over park, over pale,
  Thorough flood, thorough fire.
 I do wander every where,
 Swifter than the moonès sphere,
 And I serve the Fairy-queen,
 To dew her orbs upon the green.
 The cowslips tall her pensioners be ;
 In their gold coats spots you see.
 Those be rubies, fairy favours,
 In those freckles live their savours.
I must go seek some dew-drops here,
And hang a pearl in every cowslip's ear.*
Farewell, thou lob of spirits ! I 'll be gone ;
Our queen and all her elves come here anon.
 Puck. The king doth keep his revels here to-night.
Take heed the queen come not within his sight ;
For Oberon is passing fell and wroth,
Because that she, as her attendant, hath
A lovely boy stolen from an Indian king,—
She never had so sweet a changeling ;

---

 * 'Twas I that led you through the painted meads,
  Where the light Fairies danced upon the flowers,
  Hanging on every leaf an orient pearl.
      Wisdom of Dr. Dodypoll, 1600. *Steevens.*
Men of fashion, in that age, wore earrings.

And jealous Oberon would have the child
Knight of his train, to trace the forests wild ;
But she, perforce, withholds the loved boy,
Crowns him with flowers, and makes him all her joy ;
And now they never meet in grove or green,
By fountain clear, or spangled star-light sheen,
But they do square ; that all their elves, for fear,
Creep into acorn cups, and hide them there.

 Fai. Either I mistake your shape and making **quite,**
Or else you are that shrewd and knavish sprite
Call'd Robin Good-fellow. Are you not he
That frights the maidens of the villagery,
Skims milk, and sometimes labours in the quern,
And bootless makes the breathless housewife churn ;
And sometimes makes the drink to bear no barm ;
Misleads night-wanderers, laughing at their harm ?
Those that Hob-goblin call you, and sweet Puck,
You do their work, and they shall have good luck,
Are not you he ?

 Puck.   Thou speakest aright,
I am that merry wanderer of the night.
I jest to Oberon, and make him smile,
When I a fat and bean-fed horse beguile,
Neighing in likeness of a filly-foal ;
And sometimes lurk I in a gossip's bowl,
In very likeness of a roasted crab ,
And when she drinks, against her lips I bob,
And on her withered dewlap pour the ale.
The wisest aunt, telling the saddest tale,
Sometimes for three-foot stool mistaketh me :
Then slip I from her bum,—down topples she,
And *tailor* cries, and falls into a cough ;
And then the whole quire hold their hips and loffe,
And waxen in their mirth, and neeze, and swear
A merrier hour was never wasted there.

The haunts of the Fairies on earth are the most rural and
romantic that can be selected. They meet

    On hill, in dale, forest or mead,
  By paved fountain, or by rushy brook,
  Or on the beached margent of the sea,
  To dance their ringlets to the whistling wind.

And the place of Titania's repose is

    A bank whereon the wild thyme blows,
  Where oxlips and the nodding violet grows,
  Quite over-canopied with lush woodbine,
  With sweet musk-roses, and with eglantine.

> There sleeps Titania, some time of the night
> Lull'd in these flowers with dances and delight;
> And there the snake throws her enamell'd skin,
> Weed wide enough to wrap a fairy in.

The powers of the poet are exerted to the utmost, to convey an idea of their minute dimensions; and time, with them, moves on lazy pinions. " Come," cries the queen,

> Come now, a roundel and a fairy song,
> Then for the third part of a minute hence :
> Some to kill cankers in the musk-rose buds;
> Some war with rear-mice for their leathern wings,
> To make my small elves coats.

And when enamoured of Bottom, she directs her Elves that they should

> Hop in his walks and gambol in his eyes ;
> Feed him with apricocks and dewberries,
> With purple grapes, green figs, and mulberries.
> The honey-bags steal from the humble-bees,
> And for night-tapers crop their waxen thighs,
> And light them at the fiery glow-worm's eyes ;
> To have my love to bed, and to arise
> And pluck the wings from painted butterflies,
> To fan the moon-beams from his sleeping eyes.

Puck goes " swifter than arrow from the Tartar's bow;" he says, " he 'll put a girdle round about the earth in forty minutes;" and " We," says Oberon—

> We the globe can compass soon,
> Swifter than the wandering moon.

They are either not mortal, or their date of life is indeterminately long; they are of a nature superior to man, and speak with contempt of human follies.   By night they revel beneath the light of the moon and stars, retiring at the approach of " Aurora's harbinger," * but not compulsively like ghosts and " damned spirits."

---

* And the yellow-skirted Fayes
  Fly after the night-steeds, leaving their moon-loved maze.
              MILTON, *Ode on the Nativity*, 235.

> But we (says Oberon) are spirits of another sort;
> I with the morning's love have oft made sport,
> And like a forester the groves may tread,
> Even till the eastern gate, all fiery red,
> Opening on Neptune with fair blessed beams,
> Turns into yellow gold his salt-green streams.

In the Merry Wives of Windsor, we are introduced to mock-fairies, modelled, of course, after the real ones, but with such additions as the poet's fancy deemed itself authorised to adopt.

Act IV., Scene IV., Mrs. Page, after communicating to Mrs. Ford her plan of making the fat knight disguise himself as the ghost of Herne the hunter, adds—

> Nan Page, my daughter, and my little son,
> And three or four more of their growth, we'll dress
> Like urchins, ouphes,* and fairies, green and white,
> With rounds of waxen tapers on their heads,
> And rattles in their hands.
>
> *   *   *   *   *
>
> Then let them all encircle him about,
> And, *fairy-like, to-pinch*† the unclean knight,
> And ask him why that hour of fairy revel
> In their so sacred paths he dares to tread
> In shape profane.

And

> My Nan shall be the queen of all the fairies,
> Finely attired in a robe of white.

In Act V., Scene V., the plot being all arranged, the Fairy

---

* *Ouph*, Steevens complacently tells us, in the Teutonic language, is a fairy; if by Teutonic he means the German, and we know of no other, he merely showed his ignorance. Ouph is the same as *oaf* (formerly spelt *aulf*), and is probably to be pronounced in the same manner. It is formed from *elf* by the usual change of *l* into *u*.

† *i. e.* Pinch severely. The Ang.-Sax. ⱦo joined to a verb or part. answers to the German *zu* or *zer*. ⱦo-bꞃecan is to break to pieces, ⱦo-ꝺꞃiꝼan to drive asunder, scatter. Verbs of this kind occur in the Vision of Piers Ploughman, in Chaucer and elsewhere. The part. is often preceded by *all*, in the sense of the German *ganz*, quite, with which some ignorantly join the *to* as *all-to ruffled* in Comus, 380, instead of *all to-ruffled*. In Golding's Ovid (p. 15) we meet "With rugged head as white as down, and garments *all to-torn;*" in Judges ix. 53, "and *all to-brake* his skull." See also Faerie Queene, iv. 7, 8; v. 8, 4, 43, 44; 9, 10.

rout appears, headed by Sir Hugh, as a Satyr, by ancient
Pistol as Hobgoblin, and by Dame Quickly.

> *Quick.* Fairies black, grey, green, and white,
> You moonshine revellers and shades of night,
> You orphan heirs of fixed destiny,*
> Attend your office and your quality.
> Crier Hob-goblin, make the fairy O-yes.
> *Pist.* Elves, list your names! silence, you airy toys!
> *Cricket*, to Windsor chimneys shalt thou leap;
> *Where fires thou findest unraked, and hearths unswept,*
> *There pinch the maids as blue as bilberry:*
> *Our radiant queen hates sluts and sluttery.*
> *Fals.* They are fairies; *he that speaks to them shall die.*
> I 'll wink and couch; no man their works must eye.
> *Pist.* Where's Bead?—Go you, and where you find a maid
> That, ere she sleep, has thrice her prayers said,
> Raise up the organs of her fantasy,
> Sleep she as sound as careless infancy;
> But those as sleep and think not on their sins,
> Pinch them, arms, legs, backs, shoulders, sides, and shins.
> *Quick.* About, about,
> Search Windsor castle, elves, within and out;
> *Strew good luck, ouphes, on every sacred room,*
> That it may stand till the perpetual doom,
> In state as wholesome as in state 'tis fit;
> Worthy the owner, and the owner it.
> The several chairs of order look you scour
> With juice of balm and every precious flower;
> Each fair instalment, coat, and several crest,
> With loyal blazon evermore be blest;
> *And nightly, meadow-fairies, look, you sing,*
> Like to the Garter's compass, *in a ring:*
> *The expressure that it bears green let it be,*
> *More fertile-fresh than all the field to see;*
> And "Hony soit qui mal y pense" write,
> In emerald tufts, flowers, purple, blue, and white;
> Like sapphire, pearl, and rich embroidery,
> Buckled below fair knighthood's bending knee:
> Fairies use flowers for their charactery.
> Away—disperse!—but, till 'tis one o'clock,
> Our dance of custom, round about the oak
> Of Herne the hunter, let us not forget.
> *Eva.* Pray you, lock hand in hand, yourselves in order set,
> And twenty glow-worms shall our lanterns be,

---

* After all the commentators have written, this line is still nearly unin-
telligible to us. It may relate to the supposed origin of the fairies. For
orphan, Warburton conjectured *ouphen*, from *ouph.*

To guide our measure round about the tree ;
But stay, I smell a man of middle earth.*
   Fal.   Heaven defend me from that Welsh fairy, lest
He transform me to a piece of cheese.
   Pist.   Vile worm ! thou wast o'erlook'd even in thy birth.
   Quick. With trial fire touch we his finger-end :
If he be chaste the flame will back descend,
And turn him to no pain ; but if he start,
It is the flesh of a corrupted heart.
   Pist.   A trial, come.
   Eva.   Come, will this wood take fire ?
   Fal.   Oh, oh, oh !
   Quick. Corrupt, corrupt, and tainted in desire :
About him, fairies, sing a scornful rime ;
And, as you trip, still pinch him to your time.

In Romeo and Juliet the lively and gallant Mercutio
mentions a fairy personage, who has since attained to great
celebrity, and completely dethroned Titania, we mean Queen
Mab,* a dame of credit and renown in Faëry.

" I dreamed a dream to-night," says Romeo.

" O then," says Mercutio :—

O then, I see Queen Mab hath been with you.
She is the fairies' midwife ; and she comes,
In shape no bigger than an agate-stone
On the forefinger of an alderman,
Drawn with a team of little atomies,
Over men's noses as they lie asleep :
Her waggon-spokes made of long spinners' legs ;
The cover, of the wings of grasshoppers ;
The traces, of the smallest spider's web ;
The collars of the moonshine's watery beams :
Her whip of cricket's bone ; the lash of film :
Her waggoner, a small gray-coated gnat,
Not half so big as a round little worm

---

* The Anglo-Saxon ᛗiᛞan eaþᛞ or ᵹeaþᛞ ; and is it not also plainly the
Midgard of the Edda ?

† The origin of Mab is very uncertain ; it may be a contraction of Habundia,
see below *France.* " Mab," says Voss, one of the German translators of
Shakspeare, " is not the Fairy-queen, the same with Titania, as some, misled
by the word *queen,* have thought. That word in old English, as in Danish,
designates the female sex." He might have added the Ang.-Sax. cþen
woman, whence both *queen* and *quean.* Voss is perhaps right and *elf-queen*
may have been used in the same manner as the Danish *Elle-quinde,*
Elle-kone for the female Elf. We find Phaer (see above, p. 11) using *Fairy-*
queen, as a translation for *Nympha.*

Prick'd from the lazy finger of a maid:
Her chariot is an empty hazel-nut,
Made by the joiner squirrel or old grub,
Time out of mind the fairies' coachmakers.

    *   *   *   *   *

         This is that very Mab
That plats the manes of horses in the night ;
And bakes the elf-locks in foul sluttish hairs,
Which once untangled, much misfortune bode.
This is the hag,* when maids lie on their backs,
That presses them.

In an exquisite and well-known passage of the Tempest,
higher and more awful powers are ascribed to the Elves:
Prospero declares that by their aid he has "bedimmed the
noon-tide sun;" called forth the winds and thunder; set
roaring war "'twixt the green sea and the azured vault;"
shaken promontories, and plucked up pines and cedars.
He thus invokes them:—

Ye elves of hills, brooks, standing lakes, and groves; †
And ye, that on the sands with printless foot
Do chase the ebbing Neptune, and do fly him,
When he comes back; you demi-puppets that
By moonshine do the green-sour ringlets make,
Whereof the ewe not bites ; and you whose pastime
Is to make midnight-mushrooms, that rejoice
To hear the solemn curfew.

The other dramas of Shakspeare present a few more
characteristic traits of the Fairies, which should not be
omitted.

Some say that ever 'gainst that season comes
Wherein our Saviour's birth is celebrated,

---

* *i. e,* Night-mare. "Many times," says Gull the fairy, "I get on men and
women, and so lie on their stomachs, that I cause them great pain ; for which
they call me by the name of Hagge or Night-mare." *Merry Pranks,* etc. p. 42.

   † Auræque et venti, montesque, amnesque, lacusque,
Díque omnes nemorum, díque omnes noctis, adeste.
                      Ovid, Met. 1. vii. 198.

Ye ayres and winds, ye *elves* of hills, of brooks, of woods, alone,
Of standing lakes, and of the night—approach ye everich one.
                              GOLDING.

Golding seems to have regarded, by chance or with knowledge, the Elves as
a higher species than the Fairies. Misled by the word *elves,* Shakspeare makes
sad confusion of classic and Gothic mythology.

This bird of dawning singeth all night long;
And then they say no spirit dares stir abroad;
The nights are wholesome; then no planet strikes,
No fairy takes,* no witch hath power to charm,
So hallow'd and so gracious is that time.

Hamlet, Act. i. sc. 1.

King Henry IV. wishes it could be proved,

That some night-tripping fairy had exchanged
In cradle-clothes our children where they lay,
And called mine—Percy, his—Plantagenet!

The old shepherd in the Winter's Tale, when he finds Perdita, exclaims,

It was told me, I should be rich, by the fairies: this is some changeling.

And when his son tells him it is gold that is within the "bearing-cloth," he says,

This is fairy-gold, boy, and 'twill prove so. We are lucky, boy, and *to be so still requires nothing but secresy.*†

In Cymbeline, the innocent Imogen commits herself to sleep with these words:—

To your protection I commit me, gods!
From fairies and the tempters of the night,
Guard me, beseech ye!

And when the two brothers see her in their cave, one cries—

But that it eats our victuals, I should think
Here were a fairy.

---

* *Take* signifies here, to strike, to injure.

And there he blasts the tree and *takes* the cattle.

Merry Wives of Windsor, iv. 4

Thou farest as fruit that with the frost is taken.

SURREY, *Poems,* p. 13, Ald. edit.

In our old poetry *take* also signifies, to give.

† But not a word of it,—'tis fairies' treasure,
Which but revealed brings on the blabber's ruin.

MASSINGER, *Fatal Dowry,* Act iv. sc. 1.

A prince's secrets are like fairy favours,
Wholesome if kept, but poison if discovered.

Honest Man's Fortune.

And thinking her to be dead, Guiderius declares—

> If he be gone, he'll make his grave a bed;
> With female fairies will his tomb be haunted,
> And worms will not come to thee.

The Maydes Metamorphosis of Lylie was acted in 1600, the year the oldest edition we possess of the Midsummer Night's Dream was printed. In Act II. of this piece, Mopso, Joculo, and Frisio are on the stage, and "Enter the Fairies singing and dancing."

> By the moon we sport and play,
> With the night begins our day;
> As we dance the dew doth fall—
> Trip it, little urchins all,
> Lightly as the little bee,
> Two by two, and three by three;
> And about go we, and about go we.

> *Jo.* What mawmets are these?
> *Fris.* O they be the faieries that haunt these woods.
> *Mop.* O we shall be pinched most cruelly!
> *1st Fai.* Will you have any music, sir?
> *2d Fai.* Will you have any fine music?
> *3d Fai.* Most dainty music?
> *Mop.* We must set a face on it now; there is no flying.
> No, sir, we very much thank you.
> *1st Fai.* O but you shall, sir.
> *Fris.* No, I pray you, save your labour.
> *2d Fai.* O, sir! it shall not cost you a penny.
> *Jo.* Where be your fiddles?
> *3d Fai.* You shall have most dainty instruments, sir?
> *Mop.* I pray you, what might I call you?
> *1st Fai.* My name is Penny.
> *Mop.* I am sorry I cannot purse you.
> *Fris.* I pray you, sir, what might I call you?
> *2d Fai.* My name is Cricket.
> *Fris.* I would I were a chimney for your sake.
> *Jo.* I pray you, you pretty little fellow, what's your name?
> *3d Fai.* My name is little little Prick.
> *Jo.* Little little Prick? O you are a dangerous faierie!
> I care not whose hand I were in, so I were out of yours.
> *1st Fai.* I do come about the coppes.
> > Leaping upon flowers' toppes;
> > Then I get upon a fly,
> > She carries me about the sky,
> > And trip and go.

2d *Fai.* When a dew-drop falleth down,
And doth light upon my crown.
Then I shake my head and skip,
And about I trip.
3d *Fai.* When I feel a girl asleep,
Underneath her frock I peep,
There to sport, and there I play,
Then I bite her like a flea,
And about I skip.
Jo. I thought where I should have you.
1st *Fai.* Will 't please you dance, sir?
Jo. Indeed, sir, I cannot handle my legs.
2d *Fai.* O you must needs dance and sing,
Which if you refuse to do,
We will pinch you black and blue;
And about we go.

They all dance in a ring, and sing as followeth :—

Round about, round about, in a fine ring a,
Thus we dance, thus we dance, and thus we sing a;
Trip and go, to and fro, over this green a,
All about, in and out, for our brave queen a.

Round about, round about, in a fine ring a,
Thus we dance, thus we dance, and thus we sing a;
Trip and go, to and fro, over this green a,
All about, in and out, for our brave queen a.

We have danced round about, in a fine ring a,
We have danced lustily, and thus we sing a;
All about, in and out, over this green a,
To and fro, trip and go, to our brave queen a.

The next poet, in point of time, who employs the Fairies, is worthy, long-slandered, and maligned Ben Jonson. His beautiful entertainment of the Satyr was presented in 1603, to Anne, queen of James I. and prince Henry, at Althorpe, the seat of Lord Spenser, on their way from Edinburgh to London. As the queen and prince entered the park, a Satyr came forth from a "little spinet" or copse, and having gazed the "Queen and the Prince in the face" with admiration, again retired into the thicket; then "there came tripping up the lawn a bevy of Fairies attending on Mab, their queen, who, falling into an artificial ring, began to dance a round while their mistress spake as followeth :"

Mab.　　Hail and welcome, worthiest queen !
　　　　Joy had never perfect been,
　　　　To the nymphs that haunt this green,
　　　　Had they not this evening seen.
　　　　Now they print it on the ground
　　　　With their feet, in figures round ;
　　　　Marks that will be ever found
　　　　To remember this glad stound.

Satyr (peeping out of the bush).
　　　　Trust her not, you bonnibell,
　　　　She will forty leasings tell ;
　　　　I do know her pranks right well.

Mab.　　Satyr, we must have a spell,
　　　　For your tongue it runs too fleet.

Sat.　　Not so nimbly as your feet,
　　　　When about the cream-bowls sweet
　　　　You and all your elves do meet.

*(Here he came hopping forth, and mixing himself with the Fairies,
skipped in, out, and about their circle, while they made many offers
to catch him.)*

　　　　This is Mab, the mistress Fairy,
　　　　That doth nightly rob the dairy ;
　　　　And can hurt or help the churning
　　　　As she please, without discerning.

1st Fai.　Pug, you will anon take warning.

Sat.　　*She that pinches country wenches,*
　　　　If they rub not clean their benches,
　　　　And, with sharper nail, remembers
　　　　When they rake not up their embers ;
　　　　But if so they chance to feast her,
　　　　In a shoe she drops a tester.

2d Fai.　Shall we strip the skipping jester?

Sat.　　*This is she that empties cradles,*
　　　　Takes out children, puts in ladles ;
　　　　Trains forth midwives in their slumber,
　　　　With a sieve the holes to number,
　　　　And then leads them from her burrows,
　　　　Home through ponds and water-furrows.*

1st Fai.　Shall not all this mocking stir us?

Sat.　　She can start our Franklin's daughters
　　　　In her sleep with shouts and laughters ;
　　　　And on sweet St. Anna's † night
　　　　Feed them with a promised sight,

---

* We do not recollect having met with any account of this prank ; but
Jonson is usually so correct, that we may be certain it was a part of the
popular belief.

† Whalley was certainly right in proposing to read Agnes.　This ceremony
is, we believe, still practised in the north of England on St. Agnes' night.
See Brand, i. 34.

> Some of husbands, some of lovers,
> Which an empty dream discovers.
> *1st Fai.* Satyr, vengeance near you hovers.

At length Mab is provoked, and she cries out,

> Fairies, pinch him black and blue.
> Now you have him make him rue.
> *Sat.* O hold, mistress Mab, I sue!

Mab, when about to retire, bestows a jewel on the Queen, and concludes with,

> *Utter not, we you implore,*
> *Who did give it, nor wherefore.*
> And whenever you restore
> Yourself to us you shall have more.
> Highest, happiest queen, farewell,
> But, beware you do not tell.

The splendid Masque of Oberon, presented in 1610, introduces the Fays in union with the Satyrs, Sylvans, and the rural deities of classic antiquity; but the Fay is here, as one of them says, not

> The coarse and country fairy,
> That doth haunt the hearth and dairy;

it is Oberon, the prince of Fairy-land, who, at the crowing of the cock, advances in a magnificent chariot drawn by white bears, attended by Knights and Fays. As the car advances, the Satyrs begin to leap and jump, and a Sylvan thus speaks:—

> Give place, and silence; you were rude too late—
> This is a night of greatness and of state;
> Not to be mixed with light and skipping sport—
> A night of homage to the British court,
> And ceremony due to Arthur's chair,
> From our bright master, Oberon the Fair,
> Who with these knights, attendants here preserved
> In Fairy-land, for good they have deserved
> Of yond' high throne, are come of right to pay
> Their annual vows, and all their glories lay
> At 's feet.

Another Sylvan says,

> Stand forth, bright faies and elves, and tune your lay
> Unto his name ; then let your nimble feet
> Tread subtile circles, that may always meet
> In point to him.

In the Sad Shepherd, Alken says,

> There in the stocks of trees white fays* do dwell,
> And span-long elves that dance about a pool,
> With each a little changeling in their arms !

The Masque of Love Restored presents us " Robin Good-fellow, he that sweeps the hearth and the house clean, riddles for the country maids, and does all their other drudgery, while they are at hot-cockles," and he appears therefore with his *broom* and his *canles*.

In Fletcher's Faithful Shepherdess we read of

> A virtuous well, about whose flowery banks
> The nimble-footed fairies dance their rounds,
> By the pale moonshine ; dipping oftentimes
> Their stolen children, so to make them free
> From dying flesh and dull mortality.

And in the Little French Lawyer (iii. 1), one says, " You walk like Robin Goodfellow all the house over, and every man afraid of you."

In Randolph's Pastoral of Amyntas, or the Impossible Dowry, a " knavish boy," called Dorylas, makes a fool of a " fantastique sheapherd," Jocastus, by pretending to be Oberon, king of Fairy. In Act i., Scene 3, Jocastus' brother, Mopsus, " a foolish augur," thus addresses him :—

> *Mop.* Jocastus, I love Thestylis abominably,
> The mouth of my affection waters at her.
> *Jo.* Be wary, Mopsus, learn of me to scorn
> The mortals ; choose a better match : go love
> Some fairy lady ! Princely Oberon
> Shall stand thy friend, and beauteous Mab, his queen,
> Give thee a maid of honour.

---

* Shakespeare gives different colours to the Fairies ; and in some places they are still thought to be white. See p. 306.

Mop.   How, Jocastus?
Marry a puppet? Wed a mote i' the sun?
Go look a wife in nutshells? Woo a gnat,
That's nothing but a voice? No, no, Jocastus,
I must have flesh and blood, and will have Thestylis:
A fig for fairies!

Thestylis enters, and while she and Mopsus converse, Jocastus muses. At length he exclaims,

Jo. It cannot choose but strangely please his highness.
The. What are you studying of Jocastus, ha?
Jo. A rare device; a masque to entertain
His Grace of Fairy with.
The.   A masque! What is 't?
Jo. An anti-masque of fleas, which I have taught
To dance corrantos on a spider's thread.
    *   *   *   *   *
                    And then a jig of pismires
Is excellent.

Enter DORYLAS. *He salutes* MOPSUS, *and then*

Dor. Like health unto the president of the jigs.
I hope King Oberon and his joyall Mab
Are well.
Jo.   They are. I never saw their Graces
Eat such a meal before.
Dor.   E'en much good do 't them!
Jo. They're rid a hunting.
Dor.   Hare or deer, my lord?
Jo. Neither. A brace of snails of the first head.

ACT I.—SCENE 6.

Jo. Is it not a brave sight, Dorylas? Can the mortals
Caper so nimbly?
Dor.   Verily they cannot.
Jo. Does not King Oberon bear a stately presence?
Mab is a beauteous empress.
Dor.   Yet you kissed her
With admirable courtship.
Jo.   I do think
There will be of Jocastus' brood in Fairy.
    *   *   *   *   *
    The. But what estate shall he assure upon me?

Jo.   A royal jointure, all in Fairy land.

    *   *   *   *   *

    Dorylas knows it.
A curious park—
    Dor. Paled round about with pickteeth.
    Jo.   Besides a house made all of mother-of-pearl,
An ivory tennis-court.
    Dor. A nutmeg parlour.
    Jo.   A sapphire dairy-room.
    Dor. A ginger hall.
    Jo.   Chambers of agate.
    Dor. Kitchens all of crystal.
    Am.   O admirable ! This it is for certain.
    Jo.   The jacks are gold.
    Dor. The spits are Spanish needles.
    Jo.   Then there be walks—
    Dor. Of amber.
    Jo.   Curious orchards—
    Dor. That bear as well in winter as in summer.
    Jo.   'Bove all, the fish-ponds, every pond is full—
    Dor. Of nectar.   Will this please you !   Every grove
Stored with delightful birds.

ACT III.—SCENE 2.

Dorylas says,

Have at Jocastus' orchard !   Dainty apples,
How lovely they look !   Why these are Dorylas' sweetmeats.
Now must I be the princely Oberon,
And in a royal humour with the rest
Of royal fairies attendant, go in state
To rob an orchard.   I have hid my robes
On purpose in a hollow tree.

ACT III.—SCENE 4.

Dorylas with a bevy of Fairies.

    Dor. How like you now, my Grace ?   Is not my countenance
Royal and full of majesty ?   Walk not I
Like the young prince of pygmies ?   Ha, my knaves,
We'll fill our pockets.   Look, look yonder, elves ;
Would not yon apples tempt a better conscience
Than any we have, to rob an orchard ?   Ha !
Fairies, like nymphs with child, must have the things
They long for.   You sing here a fairy catch
In that strange tongue I taught you, while ourself
Do climb the trees.   Thus princely Oberon
Ascends his throne of state.

Elves. Nos beata Fauni proles,
Quibus non est magna moles,
Quamvis Lunam incolamus.
Hortos sæpe frequentamus.

Furto cuncta magis bella,
Furto dulcior puella,
Furto omnia decora,
Furto poma dulciora.

Cum mortales lecto jacent,
Nobis poma noctu placent;
Illa tamen sunt ingrata
Nisi furto sint parata.

Jocastus and his man Bromius come upon the Elves while plundering the orchard: the latter is for employing his cudgel on the occasion, but Jocastus is overwhelmed by the condescension of the princely Oberon in coming to his orchard, when

His Grace had orchards of his own more precious
Than mortals can have any.

The Elves, by his master's permission, pinch Bromius, singing,

Quoniam per te violamur,
Ungues hic experiamur;
Statim dices tibi datam
Cutem valde variatam.

Finally, when the coast is clear, Oberon cries,

So we are got clean off; come, noble peers
Of Fairy, come, attend our royal Grace.
Let's go and share our fruit with our queen Mab
And the other dairy-maids; where of this theme
We will discourse amidst our cakes and cream.

Cum tot poma habeamus,
Triumphos læti jam canamus;
Faunos ego credam ortos,
Tantum ut frequentent hortos.

I domum, Oberon, ad illas,
Quæ nos manent nunc, ancillas,
Quarum osculemur sinum,
Inter poma lac et vinum.

In the old play of Fuimus Troes are the following lines:[*]

> Fairies small,
> Two foot tall,
> With caps red
> On their head,
> Danse around
> On the ground.

The pastoral poets also employed the Fairy Mythology. Had they used it exclusively, giving up the Nymphs, Satyrs, and all the rural rout of antiquity, and joined with it faithful pictures of the scenery England then presented, with just delineations of the manners and character of the peasantry, the pastoral poetry of that age would have been as unrivalled as its drama.   But a blind admiration of classic models, and a fondness for allegory, were the besetting sins of the poets.   They have, however, left a few gems in this way.

Britannia's Pastorals furnish the following passages:[†]

> Near to this wood there lay a pleasant mead,
> Where fairies often did their measures tread,
> Which in the meadows made such circles green,
> As if with garlands it had crowned been;
> Or like the circle where the signs we track,
> And learned shepherds call 't the Zodiac;
> Within one of these rounds was to be seen
> A hillock rise, where oft the fairy-queen
> At twilight sate, and did command her elves
> To pinch those maids that had not swept their shelves;
> And, further, if, by maiden's oversight,
> Within doors water was not brought at night,
> Or if they spread no table, set no bread,
> They should have nips from toe unto the head;
> And for the maid who had perform'd each thing,
> She in the water-pail bade leave a ring.
>   Song 2.
>
> Or of the faiery troops which nimbly play,
> And by the springs dance out the summer's day,
> Teaching the little birds to build their nests,
> And in their singing how to keepen rests.
>   Song 4.

---

[*] Act i. sc. 5.   Dodsley's Old Plays, vii. p. 394.   We quote this as the first notice we have met of the red caps of the fairies.

[†] Brown, their author, was a native of Devon, the Pixy region; hence their accordance with the Pixy legends given above.

As men by fairies led fallen in a dream.

Ibid.

In his Shepherd's Pipe, also, Brown thus speaks of the Fairies:—

> Many times he hath been seen
> With the fairies on the green,
> And to them his pipe did sound
> While they danced in a round.
> Mickle solace they would make him,
> And at midnight often wake him
> And convey him from his room
> To a field of yellow-broom;
> Or into the meadows where
> Mints perfume the gentle air,
> And where Flora spreads her treasure;
> There they would begin their measure.
> If it chanced night's sable shrouds
> Muffled Cynthia up in clouds,
> Safely home they then would see him,
> And from brakes and quagmires free him.

But Drayton is the poet after Shakespeare for whom the Fairies had the greatest attractions. Even in the Polyolbion he does not neglect them. In Song xxi., Ringdale, in Cambridgeshire, says,

> For in my very midst there is a swelling ground
> About which Ceres' nymphs dance many a wanton round;
> The frisking fairy there, as on the light air borne,
> Oft run at barley-break upon the ears of corn;
> And catching drops of dew in their lascivious chases,
> Do cast the liquid pearl in one another's faces.

And in Song iv., he had spoken of

> The feasts that underground the faëry did him (Arthur) make,
> And there how he enjoyed the Lady of the Lake.

Nymphidia is a delicious piece of airy and fanciful invention. The description of Oberon's palace in the air, Mab's amours with the gentle Pigwiggin, the mad freaks of the jealous Oberon, the pygmy Orlando, the mutual artifices of Puck and the Fairy maids of honour, Hop, Mop, Pip, Trip, and Co., and the furious combat of Oberon and the doughty

Pigwiggin, mounted on their earwig chargers—present altogether an unequalled fancy-piece, set in the very best and most appropriate frame of metre.

It contains, moreover, several traits of traditional Fairy lore, such as in these lines :—

> Hence shadows, seeming idle shapes
> Of little frisking elves and apes,
> To earth do make their wanton skapes
> 　As hope of pastime hastes them ;
> Which maids think on the hearth they see,
> When fires well near consumed be,
> There dancing hays by two and three,
> 　Just as their fancy casts them.*
>
> These make our girls their sluttery rue,
> By pinching them both black and blue,
> And put a penny in their shoe,
> 　The house for cleanly sweeping ;
> And in their courses make that round,
> In meadows and in marshes found,
> Of them so call'd the fairy ground,
> 　Of which they have the keeping.
>
> These, when a child haps to be got,
> That after proves an idiot,
> When folk perceive it thriveth not,
> 　The fault therein to smother,
> Some silly, doating, brainless calf,
> That understands things by the half,
> Says that the fairy left this aulf,
> 　And took away the other.

And in these :—

> Scarce set on shore but therewithal
> He meeteth Puck, whom most men call
> Hobgoblin, and on him doth fall
> 　With words from frenzy spoken ;
> "Ho ! ho !" quoth Puck, "God save your Grace !
> Who drest you in this piteous case?
> He thus that spoiled my sovereign's face,
> 　I would his neck were broken.

---

* This is perhaps the dancing on the hearth of the fairy-ladies to which Milton alludes : see above, p. 42. "Doth not the warm zeal of an Englishman's devotion make them maintain and defend the social hearth as the sanctuary and chief place of residence of the tutelary lares and household gods, and the only court where the *lady-fairies convene to dance and revel ?*"— Paradoxical Assertions, etc. 1664, quoted by Brand, ii. p. 504.

This Puck seems but a dreaming dolt,
Still walking like a ragged colt,
And oft out of a bush doth bolt,
    Of purpose to deceive us;
And leading us, makes us to stray
Long winter nights out of the way;
And when we stick in mire and clay,
    He doth with laughter leave us.

In his Poet's Elysium there is some beautiful Fairy poetry, which we do not recollect to have seen noticed any where. This work is divided into ten Nymphals, or pastoral dialogues. The Poet's Elysium is, we are told, a paradise upon earth, inhabited by Poets, Nymphs, and the Muses.

The poet's paradise this is,
To which but few can come,
The Muses' only bower of bliss,
Their dear Elysium.

In the eighth Nymphal,

A nymph is married to a fay,
Great preparations for the day,
All rites of nuptials they recite you
To the bridal, and invite you.

The dialogue commences between the nymphs Mertilla and Claia:—

M. But will our Tita wed this fay?
C. Yes, and to-morrow is the day.
M. But why should she bestow herself
    Upon this dwarfish fairy elf?
C. Why, by her smallness, you may find
    That she is of the fairy kind;
    And therefore apt to choose her make
    Whence she did her beginning take;
    Besides he's deft and wondrous airy,
    And of the noblest of the fairy,*

* The reader will observe that the third sense of Fairy is the most usual one in Drayton. It occurs in its second sense two lines further on, twice in Nymphidia, and in the following passage of his third Eclogue,
    For learned Colin (Spenser) lays his pipes to gage,
    And is to *Fayrie* gone a pilgrimage,
        The more our moan.

> Chief of the Crickets,* of much fame,
> In Fairy a most ancient name.

The nymphs now proceed to describe the bridal array of Tita: her jewels are to be dew-drops; her head-dress the "yellows in the full-blown rose;" her gown

> Of pansy, pink, and primrose leaves,
> Most curiously laid on in threaves;

her train the "cast slough of a snake;" her canopy composed of "moons from the peacock's tail," and "feathers from the pheasant's head;"

> Mix'd with the plume (of so high price),
> The precious bird of paradise;

and it shall be

> Borne o'er our head (by our inquiry)
> By elfs, the fittest of the fairy.

Her buskins of the "dainty shell" of the lady-cow. The musicians are to be the nightingale, lark, thrush, and other songsters of the grove.

> But for still music, we will keep
> The wren and titmouse, which to sleep
> Shall sing the bride when she's alone,
> The rest into their chambers gone;
> And like those upon ropes that walk
> On gossamer from stalk to stalk,
> The tripping fairy tricks shall play
> The evening of the wedding day.

Finally, the bride-bed is to be of roses; the curtains, tester, and all, of the "flower imperial;" the fringe hung with harebells; the pillows of lilies, "with down stuft of the butterfly;"

> For our Tita is to-day,
> To be married to a fay.

---

* Mr. Chalmers does not seem to have known that the Crickets were a family of note in Fairy. Shakspeare (*Merry Wives of Windsor*) mentions a Fairy named Cricket; and no hint of Shakspeare's was lost upon Drayton.

In Nymphal iii.,

> The fairies are hopping,
> The small flowers cropping,
> And with dew dropping,
>   Skip thorow the greaves.
>
> At barley-break they play
> Merrily all the day:
> At night themselves they lay
>   Upon the soft leaves.

And in Nymphal vi. the forester says,

> The dryads, hamadryads, the satyrs, and the fawns,
> Oft play at hide-and-seek before me on the lawns;
> The frisking fairy oft, when horned Cynthia shines,
> Before me as I walk dance wanton matachines.

Herrick is generally regarded as the Fairy-poet, *par excellence;* but, in our opinion, without sufficient reason, for Drayton's Fairy pieces are much superior to his. Indeed Herrick's Fairy-poetry is by no means his best; and we doubt if he has anything to exceed in that way, or perhaps equal, the light and fanciful King Oberon's Apparel of Smith.*

Milton disdained not to sing

> How faëry Mab the junkets eat.
> She was pinch'd and pull'd, she said;
> And he, by *friar's* lantern led,†
> Tells how the drudging Goblin sweat
> To earn his *cream bowl duly set,*
> When in one night, ere glimpse of morn,
> His shadowy flail hath thresh'd the corn

---

* In the Musarum Deliciæ.

† This is a palpable mistake of the poet's. The Friar (see above, p. 291) is the celebrated Friar Rush, who haunted houses, not fields, and was never the same with Jack-o'-the-Lanthorn. It was probably the name Rush, which suggested *rushlight,* that caused Milton's error. He is the Brüder Rausch of Germany, the Broder Ruus of Denmark. His name is either as Grimm thinks, *noise,* or as Wolf (Von Bruodor Rauschen, p. xxviii.) deems *drunkenness,* our old word, *rouse.* Sir Walter Scott in a note on Marmion, says also " Friar Rush, *alias* Will-i-o'-the-Wisp. He was also a sort of Robin Goodfellow and Jack-o'-Lanthorn," which is making precious confusion. Reginald Scot more correctly describes him as being " for all the world such another fellow as this Hudgin," *i. e.* Hödeken: see above, p. 255.

That ten day-labourers could not end ;
Then lies him down, the lubber fiend,
And stretch'd out all the chimney's length,
Basks at the fire his hairy strength,
And, crop-full, out of doors he flings,
Ere the first cock his matin rings.

Regardless of Mr. Gifford's sneer at "those who may
undertake the unprofitable drudgery of tracing out the property of every word, and phrase, and idea in Milton," * we
will venture to trace a little here, and beg the reader to
compare this passage with one quoted above from Harsenet,
and to say if the resemblance be accidental. The truth is,
Milton, reared in London, probably knew the popular
superstitions chiefly or altogether from books ; and almost
every idea in this passage may be found in books that he
must have read.

In the hands of Dryden the Elves of Chaucer lose their
indefiniteness. In the opening of the Wife of Bath her
Tale,

The king of elves and *little* fairy queen
Gamboled on heaths and danced on every green.

And

In vain the dairy now with mint is dressed,
The dairy-maid expects no fairy guest
To skim the bowls, and after pay the feast.
She sighs, and shakes her empty shoes in vain,
No silver penny to reward her pain.

In the Flower and the Leaf, unauthorised by the old
bard, he makes the knights and dames, the servants of the
Daisy and of the Agnus Castus, Fairies, subject, like the
Italian Fate, to "cruel Demogorgon."

Pope took equal liberties with his original, as may be
seen by a comparison of the following verses with those
quoted above :—

About this spring, if ancient fame say true,
The dapper elves their moonlight sports pursue :

* Ben Jonson's Works, vol. ii. p. 499. We shall never cease to regret
that the state to which literature has come in this country almost precludes
even a hope of our ever being able to publish our meditated edition of Milton's
poems for which we have been collecting materials these five and twenty
years. It would have been very different from Todd's. [Published in 1859.]

Their pigmy king and little fairy queen
In circling dances gamboled on the green,
While tuneful sprites a merry concert made,
And airy music warbled through the shade.

January and May, 459.

It so befel, in that fair morning tide,
The fairies sported on the garden's side,
And in the midst their monarch and his bride.
So featly tripp'd the light-foot ladies round,
The knight so nimbly o'er the greensward bound,
That scarce they bent the flowers or touch'd the ground.
The dances ended, all the fairy train
For pinks and daisies search'd the flowery plain.*

Ibid., 617.

With the Kensington Garden† of Tickell, Pope's contemporary, our Fairy-poetry may be said to have terminated.‡ Collins, Beattie, and a few other poets of the last century make occasional allusions to it, and some attempts to revive it have been made in the present century. But vain are such efforts, the belief is gone, and divested of it such poetry can produce no effect. The Fairies have shared the fate of the gods of ancient Hellas.

---

* Evidently drawn from Dryden's Flower and Leaf.

† We meet here for the last time with Fairy in its collective sense, or rather, perhaps, as the country:

All Fairy shouted with a general voice.

‡ In Mr. Halliwell's Illustrations of Fairy Mythology, will be found a good deal of Fairy poetry, for which we have not had space in this work.

SCOTTISH LOWLANDS.

———•———

When from their hilly dens, at midnight hour,
Forth rush the airy elves in mimic state,
And o'er the moonlight heath with swiftness scour,
In glittering arms the little horsemen shine.
ERSKINE.

THE Scottish Fairies scarcely differ in any essential point from those of England. Like them they are divided into the rural and the domestic. Their attire is green, their residence the interior of the hills. They appear more attached than their neighbours to the monarchical form of government, for the Fairy king and queen, who seem in England to have been known only by the poets, were recognised by law in Caledonia, and have at all times held a place in the popular creed. They would appear also to be more mischievously inclined than the Southrons, and less addicted to the practice of dancing. They have, however, had the advantage of not being treated with contempt and neglect by their human countrymen, and may well be proud of the attention shown them by the brightest genius of which their country can boast. There has also been long due from them an acknowledgment of the distinction conferred on them by the editor of the Nithsdale and Galloway Song,* for the very fanciful manner in which he has described their attributes and acts.

The Scottish Fairies have never been taken by the poets for their heroes or machinery, a circumstance probably to be attributed to the sterner character of Scottish religion. We cannot, therefore, as in England, make a distinction between popular and poetic fairies.

* Mr. Cromek. There was, we believe, some false dealing on the part of Allan Cunningham toward this gentleman, such as palming on him his own verses as traditionary ones. But the legends are genuine.

The earliest notice we have met with of the Fairies is in Montgomery's Flyting against Polwart, where he says,

In the hinder end of harvest, at All-hallowe'en,
  When our *good neighbours* * dois ride, if I read right,
Some buckled on a beenwand, and some on a been,
  Ay trottand in troops from the twilight;
Some saidled on a she-ape all graithed in green,
  Some hobland on a hempstalk hovand to the sight;
The king of Phairie and his court, with the elf-queen,
  With many elfish incubus, was ridand that night.

Elf-land was the name of the realm ruled by the king of Phairie. King James† speaks of him and his queen, and " of sic a jolie court and traine as they had ; how they had a teinde and a dewtie, as it were, of all guidis ; how they naturally raid and yeid, eat and drank, and did all other actions lyke natural men and women. I think," concludes the monarch, "it is lyker Virgilis *Campi Elysii* nor anything that ought to be believed by Christianis." And one of the interlocutors in his dialogue asks how it was that witches have gone to death confessing that they had been " transported with the Phairie to such and such a hill, which, opening, they went in, and there saw a faire queene, who, being now lighter, gave them a stone which had sundry virtues."

According to Mr. Cromek, who, however, rather sedulously keeps their darker attributes out of view, and paints everything relating to them *couleur de rose*, the Lowland Fairies are of small stature, but finely proportioned; of a fair complexion, with long yellow hair hanging over their shoulders, and gathered above their heads with combs of gold. They wear a mantle of green cloth, inlaid with wild flowers ; green pantaloons, buttoned with bobs of silk ; and silver shoon. They carry quivers of " adder-slough," and bows made of the ribs of a man buried where *three lairds'*

---

* This answers to the *Deenè Máh*, Good People, of the Highlands and Ireland. An old Scottish name, we may add, for a fairy seems to have been Bogle, akin to the English Pouke, Puck, Puckle; but differing from the Boggart. Thus Gawain Douglas says,

Of *Brownyis* and of *Boggles* full is this Beuk.

† Daemonologie, B. III. c. 5.

lands meet ; their arrows are made of bog-reed, tipped with white flints, and dipped in the dew of hemlock ; they ride on steeds whose hoofs "would not dash the dew from the cup of a harebell." With their arrows they shoot the cattle of those who offend them ; the wound is imperceptible to common eyes, but there are gifted personages who can discern and cure it.*

In their intercourse with mankind they are frequently kind and generous. A young man of Nithsdale, when out on a love affair, heard most delicious music, far surpassing the utterance of 'any mortal mixture of earth's mould.' Courageously advancing to the spot whence the sound appeared to proceed, he suddenly found himself the spectator of a Fairy-banquet. A green table with feet of gold, was laid across a small rivulet, and supplied with the finest of bread and the richest of wines. The music proceeded from instruments formed of reeds and stalks of corn. He was invited to partake in the dance, and presented with a cup of wine. He was allowed to depart in safety, and ever after possessed the gift of second sight. He said he saw there several of his former acquaintances, who were become members of the Fairy society.

We give the following legend on account of its great similarity to a Swiss tradition already quoted :—

Two lads were ploughing in a field, in the middle of which was an old thorn-tree, a trysting place of the Fairy-folk. One of them described a circle round the thorn, within which the plough should not go. They were surprised, on ending the furrow, to behold a green table placed there, heaped up with excellent bread and cheese, and even wine. The lad who had drawn the circle sat down without hesitation, ate and drank heartily, saying, "Fair fa' the hands whilk gie." His companion whipped on the horses, refusing to partake of the Fairy-food. The other, said Mr.

---

* These elf-arrows are triangular pieces of flint, supposed to have been the heads of the arrows used by the aborigines. Though more plentiful in Scotland they are also found in England and Ireland, and were there also attached to the fairies, and the wounds were also only to be discerned by gifted eyes. In an Anglo-Saxon poem, there occur the words æʏa ʒeʏcoꞇ and ýlꝼa ʒeʏcoꞇ, *i. e.* arrow of the Gods, and arrow of the Elves. Grimm, Deut. Mythol., p. 22.

Cromek's informant, "thrave like a breckan," and was a proverb for wisdom, and an oracle for country knowledge ever after.*

The Fairies lend and borrow, and it is counted *uncanny* to refuse them. A young woman was one day sifting meal warm from the mill, when a nicely dressed beautiful little woman came to her with a bowl of antique form, and requested the loan of as much meal as would fill it. Her request was complied with, and in a week she returned to make repayment. She set down the bowl and breathed over it, saying, "Be never toom." The woman lived to a great age, but never saw the bottom of the bowl.

Another woman was returning late one night from a gossiping. A pretty little boy came up to her and said, " Coupe yere dish-water farther frae yere door-step, it pits out our fire." She complied with this reasonable request, and prospered ever after.

The Fairies' Nurse.

THE Fairies have a great fondness for getting their babes suckled by comely, healthy young women. A fine young woman of Nithsdale was one day spinning and rocking her first-born child. A pretty little lady in a green mantle, and bearing a beautiful babe, came into the cottage and said, " Gie my bonny thing a suck." The young woman did so, and the lady left her babe and disappeared, saying, "Nurse kin' and ne'er want." The young woman nursed the two children, and was astonished to find every morning, when she awoke, rich clothes for the children, and food of a most

---

* "It was till lately believed by the ploughmen of Clydesdale, that if they repeated the rhyme

    Fairy, fairy, bake me a bannock and roast me a collop,
    And I'll gie ye a spurtle off my gadend !

three several times on turning their cattle at the terminations of ridges, they would find the said fare prepared for them on reaching the end of the fourth furrow."—Chambers' Popular Rhymes of Scotland, p. 33.

delicious flavour.   Tradition says this food tasted like wheaten-bread, mixed with wine and honey.

When summer came, the Fairy lady came to see her child. She was delighted to see how it had thriven, and, taking it in her arms, desired the nurse to follow her.   They passed through some scroggy woods skirting the side of a beautiful green hill, which they ascended half way.   A door opened on the sunny side—they went in, and the sod closed after them. The Fairy then dropped three drops of a precious liquid on her companion's left eyelid, and she beheld a most delicious country, whose fields were yellow with ripening corn, watered by *looping burnies,* and bordered by trees laden with fruit.   She was presented with webs of the finest cloth, and with boxes of precious ointments.   The Fairy then moistened her right eye with a green fluid, and bid her look.   She looked, and saw several of her friends and acquaintances at work, reaping the corn and gathering the fruit.   "This," said the Fairy, "is the punishment of evil deeds!"   She then passed her hand over the woman's eye, and restored it to its natural power.   Leading her to the porch at which she had entered, she dismissed her ; but the woman had secured the wonderful salve.   From this time she possessed the faculty of discerning the Fairy people as they went about invisibly ; till one day, happening to meet the Fairy-lady, she attempted to shake hands with her.   "What ee d'ye see me wi'?" whispered she.   "Wi' them baith," said the woman.   The Fairy breathed on her eyes, and the salve lost its efficacy, and could never more endow her eyes with their preternatural power.*

The Fairy Rade.

THE *Fairy Rade,* or procession, was a matter of great importance.   It took place on the coming in of summer, and the peasantry, by using the precaution of placing a branch

---

* See above, pp. 302, 311.   Graham also relates this legend in his Picturesque Sketches of Perthshire.

of rowan over their door, might safely gaze on the cavalcade, as with music sounding, bridles ringing, and voices mingling, it pursued its way from place to place. An old woman of Nithsdale gave the following description of one of these processions :

"In the night afore Roodmass I had trysted with a neebor lass a Scots mile frae hame to talk anent buying braws i' the fair. We had nae sutten lang aneath the haw-buss till we heard the loud laugh of fowk riding, wi' the jingling o' bridles, and the clanking o' hoofs. We banged up, thinking they wad ride owre us. We kent nae but it was drunken fowk ridin' to the fair i' the forenight. We glowred roun' and roun', and sune saw it was the *Fairie-fowks Rade.* We cowred down till they passed by. A beam o' light was dancing owre them mair bonnie than moonshine : they were a' wee wee fowk wi' green scarfs on, but ane that rade foremost, and that ane was a good deal larger than the lave wi' bonnie lang hair, bun' about wi' a strap whilk glinted like stars. They rade on braw wee white naigs, wi' unco lang swooping tails, an' manes hung wi' whustles that the win' played on. This an' their tongue when they sang was like the soun' o' a far awa psalm. Marion an' me was in a brade lea fiel', where they came by us; a high hedge o' haw-trees keepit them frae gaun through Johnnie Corrie's corn, but they lap a' owre it like sparrows, and gallopt into a green know beyont it. We gaed i' the morning to look at the treddit corn ; but the fient a hoof mark was there, nor a blade broken."

The Changeling.

BUT the Fairies of Scotland were not, even according to Mr. Cromek, uniformly benevolent. Woman and child abstraction was by no means uncommon with them, and the substitutes they provided were, in general, but little attractive.

A fine child at Caerlaveroc, in Nithsdale, was observed on

the second day after its birth, and before it was baptised, to have become quite ill-favoured and deformed. Its yelling every night deprived the whole family of rest; it bit and tore its mother's breasts, and would lie still neither in the cradle nor the arms. The mother being one day obliged to go from home, left it in charge of the servant girl. The poor lass was sitting bemoaning herself—" Were it nae for thy girning face, I would knock the big, winnow the corn, and grun the meal."—" Lowse the cradle-band," said the child, "and tent the neighbours, and I 'll work yere work." Up he started—the wind arose—the corn was chopped—the outlyers were foddered—the hand-mill moved around, as by instinct—and the knocking-mill did its work with amazing rapidity. The lass and child then rested and diverted themselves, till, on the approach of the mistress, it was restored to the cradle, and renewed its cries. The girl took the first opportunity of telling the adventure to her mistress. "What 'll we do with the wee diel? " said she. " I 'll work it a pirn," replied the lass. At midnight the chimney-top was covered up, and every chink and cranny stopped. The fire was blown till it was glowing hot, and the maid speedily undressed the child, and tossed him on the burning coals. He shrieked and yelled in the most dreadful manner, and in an instant the Fairies were heard moaning on every side, and rattling at the windows, door, and chimney. " In the name of God bring back the bairn," cried the lass. The window flew up, the real child was laid on the mother's lap, and the *wee diel* flew up the chimney laughing.

Departure of the Fairies.

On a Sabbath morning, all the inmates of a little hamlet had gone to church, except a herd-boy, and a little girl, his sister, who were lounging beside one of the cottages, when just as the shadow of the garden-dial had fallen on the line of noon, they saw a long cavalcade ascending out of the ravine, through the wooded hollow. It winded among the knolls and bushes, and turning round the northern gable of the cottage, beside which the sole spectators of the scene were stationed, began to ascend the eminence towards the south. The horses were shaggy diminutive things, speckled dun and grey; the riders stunted, misgrown, ugly creatures, attired in antique jerkins of plaid, long grey clokes, and little red caps, from under which their wild uncombed locks shot out over their cheeks and foreheads. The boy and his sister stood gazing in utter dismay and astonishment, as rider after rider, each more uncouth and dwarfish than the other which had preceded it, passed the cottage and disappeared among the brushwood, which at that period covered the hill, until at length the entire rout, except the last rider, who lingered a few yards behind the others, had gone by. " What are you, little manie? and where are ye going? " inquired the boy, his curiosity getting the better of his fears and his prudence. " Not of the race of Adam," said the creature, turning for a moment in its saddle, " the people of peace shall never more be seen in Scotland." *

The Brownie.

THE Nis, Kobold, or Goblin, appears in Scotland under the name of Brownie.† Brownie is a personage of small stature, wrinkled visage, covered with short curly brown hair, and wearing a brown mantle and hood. His residence is the

---

* Hugh Miller, The Old Red Sandstone, p. 251. We are happy to have an opportunity of expressing the high feelings of respect and esteem which we entertain for this extraordinary man. Born in the lowest rank of society, and commencing life as a workman in a stone-quarry, he has, by the mere force of natural genius, become not only a most able geologist but an elegant writer, and a sound and discerning critic. Scotland seems to stand alone in producing such men.

† He is named as we have seen (p. 351) by Gawain Douglas. King James says of him " The spirit called Brownie appeared like a rough man, and haunted divers houses without doing any evill, but doing, as it were, necessarie turns up and down the house; yet some are so blinded as to believe that their house was all the sonsier, as they called it, that such spirits resorted there."

hollow of an old tree, a ruined castle, or the abode of man. He is attached to particular families, with whom he has been known to reside, even for centuries, threshing the corn, cleaning the house, and doing everything done by his northern and English brethren. He is, to a certain degree, disinterested; like many great personages, he is shocked at anything approaching to the name of a bribe or *douceur*, yet, like them, allows his scruples to be overcome if the thing be done in a genteel, delicate, and secret way. Thus, offer Brownie a piece of bread, a cup of drink, or a new coat and hood, and he flouted at it, and perhaps, in his huff, quitted the place for ever; but leave a nice bowl of cream, and some fresh honeycomb, in a snug private corner, and they soon disappeared, though Brownie, it was to be supposed, never knew anything of them.

A good woman had just made a web of linsey-woolsey, and, prompted by her good nature, had manufactured from it a snug mantle and hood for her little Brownie. Not content with laying the gift in one of his favourite spots, she indiscreetly called to tell him it was there. This was too direct, and Brownie quitted the place, crying,

> A new mantle and a new hood;
> Poor Brownie! ye 'll ne'er do mair gude !

Another version of this legend says, that the gudeman of a farm-house in the parish of Glendevon having left out some clothes one night for Brownie, he was heard to depart, saying,

> Gie Brownie coat, gie Brownie sark,
> Ye 'se get nae mair o' Brownie's wark !*

At Leithin-hall, in Dumfrieshire, a Brownie had dwelt, as he himself declared, for three hundred years. He used to show himself but once to each master; to other persons he rarely discovered more than his hand. One master was greatly beloved by Brownie, who on his death bemoaned him exceedingly, even abstaining from food for many successive days. The heir returning from foreign parts to take possession of the estate, Brownie appeared to do him homage, but the Laird, offended at his mean, starved appearance, ordered him

---

* Popular Rhymes of Scotland, p. 33.

meat and drink, and new livery. Brownie departed, loudly crying,

Ca', cuttee, ca' !
A' the luck of Leithin Ha'
Gangs wi' me to Bodsbeck Ha'.

In a few years Leithin Ha' was in ruins, and "bonnie Bodsbeck" flourishing beneath the care of Brownie.

Others say that it was the gudeman of Bodsbeck that offended the Brownie by leaving out for him a mess of bread and milk, and that he went away, saying,

Ca, Brownie, ca',
A' the luck of Bodsbeck awa to Leithenha'.

Brownie was not without some roguery in his composition. Two lasses having made a fine bowlful of buttered brose, had taken it into the byre to sup in the dark. In their haste they brought but one spoon, so, placing the bowl between them, they supped by turns. "I hae got but three sups," cried the one, "and it's a' dune."—"It's a' dune, indeed," cried the other.—"Ha, ha, ha!" cried a third voice, "Brownie has got the maist o' it."—And Brownie it was who had placed himself between them, and gotten two sups for their one.

The following story will remind the reader of Hinzelmann. A Brownie once lived with Maxwell, Laird of Dalswinton, and was particularly attached to the Laird's daughter, the comeliest lass in all the holms of Nithsdale. In all her love affairs Brownie was her confidant and assistant; when she was married, it was Brownie who undressed her for the bridal bed; and when a mother's pains first seized her, and a servant, who was ordered to go fetch the *cannie wife*, who lived on the other side of the Nith, was slow in getting himself ready, Brownie, though it was one of dark December's stormy nights, and the wind was howling through the trees, wrapped his lady's fur cloak about him, mounted the servant's horse, and dashed through the waves of the foaming Nith. He went to the cannie wife, got her up behind him, and, to her terror and dismay, plunged again into the torrent. "Ride nae by the auld pool," said she, "lest we suld meet wi' Brownie." "Fear nae, dame," replied he, "ye've met a' the Brownies ye will meet." He set her down at the hall

steps, and went to the stable.   There finding the lad, whose
embassy he had discharged, but drawing on his boots, he
took off the bridle, and by its vigorous application instilled
into the memory of the loitering loon the importance of
dispatch.   This was just at the time of the Reformation, and
a zealous minister advised the Laird to have him baptised.
The Laird consented, and the worthy minister hid himself in
the barn.   When Brownie was beginning his night's work,
the man of God flung the holy water in his face, repeating
at the same time the form of baptism.   The terrified Brownie
gave a yell of dismay, and disappeared for ever.

Another name by which the domestic spirit was known in
some parts of Scotland was Shellycoat, of which the origin is
uncertain.*

Scotland has also its water-spirit, called Kelpie, who in
some respects corresponds with the Neck of the northern
nations.   "Every lake," says Graham,† "has its *Kelpie*, or
Water-horse, often seen by the shepherd, as he sat in a
summer's evening upon the brow of a rock, dashing along
the surface of the deep, or browsing on the pasture-ground
upon its verge.   Often did this malignant genius of the
waters allure women and children to his subaqueous haunts,
there to be immediately devoured.   Often did he also swell
the torrent or lake beyond its usual limits, to overwhelm the
hapless traveller in the flood."‡

We have now gone through nearly the whole of the Gotho-
German race, and everywhere have found their fairy system
the same—a proof, we conceive, of the truth of the position
of its being deeply founded in the religious system originally
common to the whole race.   We now proceed to another,
and, perhaps, an older European family, the Celts.

---

* Grimm (Deut. Mythol., p. 479) says it is the German Schellenrock, *i. e.*
Bell-coat, from his coat being hung with bells like those of the fools.   A *Pück*
he says, once served in a convent in Mecklenburg, for thirty years, in kitchen,
and stable, and the only reward he asked was " tunicam de diversis coloribus
et *tintinnabulis*-plenam."
                    † Sketches of Perthshire, p. 245.
‡ In what precedes, we have chiefly followed Mr. Cromek.   Those anxious
for further information will meet it in the Minstrelsy of the Scottish Border,
and other works.

Brownies—A relatively modern representation of an ancient myth

Kelpie—the treacherous water demon

CELTS AND CYMRY.

There every herd by sad experience knows,
How winged with fate their elf-shot arrows fly;
When the sick ewe her summer-food foregoes,
Or, stretched on earth, the heart-smit heifers lie.

COLLINS.

UNDER the former of these appellations we include the inhabitants of Ireland, the Highlands of Scotland, and the Isle
of Man; under the latter, the people of Wales and Brittany.
It is, not, however, by any means meant to be asserted that
there is in any of these places to be found a purely Celtic or
Cymric population. The more powerful Gotho-German
race has, every where that they have encountered them,
beaten the Celts and Cymry, and intermingled with them,
influencing their manners, language, and religion.

Our knowledge of the original religion of this race is very
limited, chiefly confined to what the Roman writers have
transmitted to us, and the remaining poems of the Welsh
bards. Its character appears to have been massive, simple,
and sublime, and less given to personification than those of
the more eastern nations. The wild and the plastic powers
of nature never seem in it to have assumed the semblance of
huge giants and ingenious dwarfs.

Yet in the popular creed of all these tribes, we meet at
the present day beings exactly corresponding to the Dwarfs
and Fairies of the Gotho-German nations. Of these beings
there is no mention in any works—such as the Welsh
Poems, and Mabinogion, the Poems of Ossian, or the different Irish poems and romances—which can by any possi-
bility lay claim to an antiquity anterior to the conquests of

the Northmen.   Is it not then a reasonable supposition that
the Picts, Saxons, and other sons of the North, brought with
them their Dwarfs and Kobolds, and communicated the
knowledge of, and belief in, them to their Celtic and Cymric
subjects and neighbours ?   Proceeding on this theory, we
have placed the Celts and Cymry next to and after the
Gotho-German nations, though they are perhaps their pre-
cursors in Europe.

IRELAND.

Like him, the Sprite,
Whom maids by night
Oft meet in glen that's haunted.
MOORE.

WE commence our survey of the lands of Celts and Cymry
with Ireland, as being the first in point of importance, but
still more as being the land of our birth.   It is pleasing to
us, now in the autumn of our life, to return in imagination
to where we passed its spring—its most happy spring.   As
we read and meditate, its mountains and its vales, its verdant fields and lucid streams, objects on which we probably
never again shall gaze, rise up in their primal freshness and
beauty before us, and we are once more present, buoyant
with youth, in the scenes where we first heard the fairy-
legends of which we are now to treat.   Even the forms of
the individual peasants who are associated with them in our
memory, rise as it were from their humble resting-places and
appear before us, again awaking our sympathies ; for, we
will boldly assert it, the Irish peasantry, with all their faults,
gain a faster hold on the affections than the peasantry of
any other country.   We speak, however, particularly of
them as they were in our county and in our younger days ;
for we fear that they are somewhat changed, and not for the
better.   But our present business is with the Irish fairies
rather than with the Irish people.

The fairies of Ireland can hardly be said to differ in any respect from those of England and Scotland. Like them they are of diminutive size, rarely exceeding two feet in height; they live also in society, their ordinary abode being the interior of the mounds, called in Irish, Raths (*Ráhs*), in English, Moats, the construction of which is, by the peasantry, ascribed to the Danes from whom, it might thence perhaps be inferred, the Irish got their fairies direct and not *viâ* England. From these abodes they are at times seen to issue mounted on diminutive steeds, in order to take at night the diversion of the chase. Their usual attire is green with red caps.* They are fond of music, but we do not in general hear much of their dancing, perhaps because on account of the infrequency of thunder, the fairy-rings are less numerous in Ireland than elsewhere. Though the fairies steal children and strike people with paralysis and other ailments (which is called being *fairy-struck*), and shoot their elf-arrows at the cattle, they are in general kind to those for whom they have contracted a liking, and often render them essential service in time of need. They can make themselves visible and invisible, and assume any forms they please. The pretty tiny conical mushrooms which grow so abundantly in Ireland are called Fairy-mushrooms; a kind of nice regularly-formed grass is named Fairy-flax, and the bells of the foxglove called in some places Fairy-bells, are also said to have some connexion with the Little People.

The popular belief in Ireland also is, that the Fairies are a portion of the fallen angels, who, being less guilty than the rest, were not driven to hell, but were suffered to dwell on earth. They are supposed to be very uneasy respecting their condition after the final judgement.

The only names by which they are known in those parts of Ireland in which the English language is spoken are, Fairies, the Good People,† and the Gentry, these last terms being placatory, like the Greek Eumenides. When, for example, the peasant sees a cloud of dust sweeping along the road, he raises his hat and says, "God speed you, gentlemen!" for it is the popular belief that it is in these cloudy vehicles

---

* Mr. Croker says, that according to the Munster peasantry the ordinary attire of the Fairy is a black hat, green coat, white stockings, and red shoes.

† In Irish as in Erse, ᚁᚐᚔᚅᚉ ᚋᚐᚔᚈ (*deenè máh*).

that the Good People journey from one place to another.[*]
The Irish language has several names for the fairies; all
however are forms or derivations of the word *Shia,*[†] the
proper meaning of which seems to be Spirit. The most
usual name employed by the Munster peasantry is *Shifra;*
we are not acquainted with the fairy-belief and terminology
of the inhabitants of Connemara and the other wilds of
Connaught.[‡]

Most of the traits and legends of the Irish fairies are contained in the Fairy Legends and Traditions of the South of
Ireland, compiled by Mr. Crofton Croker. As we ourselves
aided in that work we must inform the reader that our contributions, both in text and notes, contain only Leinster
ideas and traditions, for that was the only province with
which we were acquainted. We must make the further confession, that some of the more poetic traits which MM. Grimm,
in the Introduction to their translation of this work, give
as characteristic of the Irish fairies, owe their origin to
the fancy of the writers, who were, in many cases, more
anxious to produce amusing tales than to transmit legends
faithfully.

The Legend of Knockshegowna (*Hill of the Fairy-calf*) the
first given in that work, relates how the fairies used to
torment the cattle and herdsmen for intruding on one of
their favourite places of resort which was on this hill. The
fairy-queen, it says, having failed in her attempts to daunt
a drunken piper who had undertaken the charge of the
cattle, at last turned herself into a calf, and, with the piper
on her back, jumped over the Shannon, ten miles off, and
back again. Pleased with his courage, she agreed to abandon
the hill for the future.

The Legend of Knock-Grafton tells how a little hunchback, while sitting to rest at nightfall at the side of a Rath
or Moat, heard the fairies within singing over and over again,
Da Luan, Da Mart! (*i.e.,*Monday,Tuesday!) and added,weary

---

* See above, p. 26.

† They are ꞃɪᴀ (*shia*), ꞃᴀбꞃᴀ (*shifra*), ꞃɪᴀcᴀɪꞁe (*shicárè*), ꞃɪ̄ʒ (*shee*),
ꞃɪ̄ʒe (*sheeè*), ꞃɪ̄ʒɪᴅ (*sheeidh*) all denoting, spirit, fairy. The term ꞃɪ̄ʒ also
signifies a hag, and a hillock, and as an adjective, spiritual.

‡ We never heard a fairy-legend from any of the Connaught-men with
whom we conversed in our boyhood. Their tales were all of Finn-mac-Cool
and his heroes.

with the monotony, *Agus da Cadin!* (*i.e.*, and Wednesday!)
The fairies were so delighted with this addition to their
song that they brought him into the Moat, entertained him,
and finally freed him from the incumbrance of his hump.
Another hunchback hearing the story went to the Moat to
try if he could meet with the same good fortune. He heard
the fairies singing the amended version of the song, and,
anxious to contribute, without waiting for a pause or attending to the rhythm or melody, he added *Agus da Hena!* (*i.e.*,
and Friday.)* His reward was, being carried into the Moat,
and having his predecessor's hump placed on his back in
addition to his own.†

In the story named the Priest's Supper, a fisherman, at
the request of the fairies, asks a priest who had stopt at his
house, whether they would be saved or not at the last day.
The priest desired him to tell them to come themselves and
put the question to him, but this they declined doing, and
the question remained undecided.

The next three stories are of changelings. The Young
Piper, one of our own contributions, will be found in the
Appendix. The Changeling has nothing peculiar in it; but
the Brewery of Eggshells is one which we find in many
places, even in Brittany and Auvergne. In the present
version, the mother puts down eggshells to boil, and to the
enquiry of the changeling she tells him that she is brewing
them, and clapping his hands he says, " Well! I'm fifteen
hundred years in the world, and I never saw a brewery of
eggshells before!"

In the Capture of Bridget Purcel, a girl is struck with a
little switch between the shoulders, by something in the form
of a little child that came suddenly behind her, and she
pined away and died.

The Legend of Bottle Hill gives the origin of that name,
which was as follows. A poor man was driving his only cow

---

* In Irish, ᴅıᴀ ᴀoıꞃe (*dhia eenè*). We are inclined to think that he
must have added, ᴅıᴀ ᴅᴀꞃᴅᴀoıꞃ, ᴅıᴀ ᴀoıꞃe (*dhia dhardheen, dhia eenè*), *i. e.*
Thursday, Friday; for we can see no reason for omitting Thursday.

† See below, *Brittany* and *Spain*, in both of which the legend is more
perfect; but it is impossible to say which is the original. Parnell's pleasing
Fairy Tale is probably formed on this Irish version, yet it agrees more with
the Breton legend.

to Cork to sell her. As he was going over that hill he was suddenly joined by a strange-looking little old man with a pale withered face and red eyes, to whom he was eventually induced to give his cow in exchange for a bottle, and both cow and purchaser then disappeared. When the poor man came home he followed the directions of the stranger, and spreading a cloth on the table, and placing the bottle on the ground, he said, "Bottle, do your duty!" and immediately two little beings rose out of it, and having covered the table with food in gold and silver dishes, went down again into the bottle and vanished. By selling these he got a good deal of money and became rich for one in his station. The secret of his bottle however transpired, and his landlord induced him to sell it to him. But his prosperity vanished with it, and he was again reduced to one cow, and obliged to drive her to Cork for sale. As he journeyed over the same hill he met the same old man, and sold him the cow for another bottle. Having made the usual preparations, he laid it on the ground and said, "Bottle, do your duty!" but instead of the tiny little lads with their gold and silver dishes, there jumped up out of it two huge fellows with cudgels, who fell to belabouring the whole family. When they had done and were gone back into the bottle, the owner of it, without saying a word, put it under his coat and went to his landlord, who happened to have a great deal of company with him, and sent in word that he was come with another bottle to sell. He was at once admitted, the bottle did its duty, and the men with cudgels laid about them on all present, and never ceased till the original wealth-giving bottle was restored. He now grew richer than ever, and his son married his landlord's daughter, but when the old man and his wife died, the servants, it is recorded, fighting at their wake, broke the two bottles.*

The Confessions of Tom Bourke, as it contains a faithful transcript of the words and ideas of that personage, is perhaps the most valuable portion of the work. From this we learn that in Munster the fairies are, like the people themselves, divided into *factions*. Thus we are told that, on the

---

* This story may remind one of the Wonderful Lamp, and others. There is something of the same kind in the Pentamerone.

occasion of the death of Bourke's mother, the two parties fought for three continuous nights, to decide whether she should be buried with her own or her husband's *people* (*i. e.* family). Bourke also had sat for hours looking at two parties of the Good People playing at the popular game of hurling, in a meadow at the opposite side of the river, with their coats and waistcoats off, and white handkerchiefs on the heads of one, and red on these of the other party.

A man whom Tom knew was returning one evening from a fair, a little elevated of course, when he met a *berrin* (*i. e.* funeral), which he joined, as is the custom; but, to his surprise, there was no one there that he knew except one man, and *he* had been dead for some years. When the *berrin* was over, they gathered round a piper, and began to dance in the churchyard. Davy longed to be among them, and the man that he knew came up to him, and bid him take out a partner, but on no account to give her the usual kiss. He accordingly took out the *purtiest girl in the ring*, and danced a jig with her, to the admiration of the whole company; but at the end he forgot the warning, and complied with the custom of kissing one's partner. All at once everything vanished; and when Davy awoke next morning, he found himself lying among the tombstones.

Another man, also a little in liquor, was returning one night from a *berrin*. The moon was shining bright, and from the other side of the river came the sounds of merriment, and the notes of a bagpipe. Taking off his shoes and stockings, he waded across the river, and there he found a great crowd of people dancing on the Inch* on the other side. He mingled with them without being observed, and he longed to join in the dance; for he had no mean opinion of his own skill. He did so, but found that it was not to be compared to theirs, they were so light and agile. He was going away quite in despair, when a little old man, who was looking on with marks of displeasure in his face, came up to him, and telling him he was his friend, and his father's

---

* *Inis*, pronounced sometimes *Inch*, (like the Hebrew *Ee* (ʻא) and the Indian *Dsib*) is either island or coast, bank of sea or river. The Ang.-Sax. ᛁᚷ (*ee*) seems to have had the same extent of signification, hence Chelsea, Battersea, etc., which never could have been islands. Perhaps þeoɲ'ðɪᵹ (*worthy, worth*) was similar, as *werd, werth,* in German is an island.

friend, bade him go into the ring and call for a lilt. He
complied, and all were amazed at his dancing; he then got
a table and danced on it, and finally he span round and
round on a trencher. When he had done, they wanted him
to dance again; but he refused with a great oath, and
instantly he found himself lying on the Inch with only a
white cow grazing beside him. On going home, he got a
shivering and a fever. He was for many days out of his
mind, and recovered slowly; but ever after he had great
skill in fairy matters. The dancers, it turned out, had
belonged to a different faction, and the old man who gave
him his skill to that to which he himself was attached.

In these genuine confessions it is very remarkable that
the Good People are never represented as of a diminutive
size; while in every story that we ever heard of them in
Leinster, they were of pygmy stature. The following account
of their mode of entering houses in Ulster gives them
dimensions approaching to those of Titania's 'small elves.'

A Fairy, the most agile, we may suppose, of the party, is
selected, who contrives to get up to the keyhole of the door,
carrying with him a piece of thread or twine. With this he
descends on the inside, where he fastens it firmly to the
floor, or some part of the furniture. Those without then
'haul taut and belay,' and when it is fast they prepare
to march along this their perilous Es-Sirat, leading to the
paradise of pantry or parlour, in this order. First steps up
the Fairy-piper, and in measured pace pursues his adventurous route, playing might and main an invigorating elfin-
march, or other spirit-stirring air; then one by one the
rest of the train mount the cord and follow his steps. Like
the old Romans, in their triumphal processions, they pass
beneath the lofty arch of the keyhole, and move down along
the other side. Lightly, one by one, they then jump down
on the floor, to hold their revels or accomplish their thefts.

We have never heard of any being, in the parts of Ireland
with which we are acquainted, answering to the Boggart,
Brownie, or Nis. A farmer's family still, we believe, living
in the county of Wicklow, used to assert that in their grandfather's time they never had any trouble about washing up
plates and dishes; for they had only to leave them collected

in a certain part of the house for the Good People, who would come in and wash and clean them, and in the morning everything would be clean and in its proper place.

Yet in the county of Cork it would seem that the Cluricaun, of which we shall presently speak, used to enact the part of Nis or Boggart. Mr. Croker tells a story of a little being, which he calls a Cluricaun, that haunted the cellar of a Mr. Macarthy, and in a note on this tale he gives the contents of a letter informing him of another ycleped Little Wildbean, that haunted the house of a Quaker gentleman named Harris, and which is precisely the Nis or Boggart. This Wildbean, who kept to the cellar, would, if one of the servants through negligence left the beer-barrel running, wedge himself into the cock and stop it, till some one came to turn it. His dinner used to be left for him in the cellar, and the cook having, one Friday, left him nothing but part of a herring and some cold potatoes, she was at midnight dragged out of her bed, and down the cellar-stairs, and so much bruised that she kept her bed for three weeks. In order at last to get rid of him, Mr. Harris resolved to remove, being told that if he went beyond a running stream the Cluricaun could not follow him. The last cart, filled with empty barrels and such like, was just moving off, when from the bung-hole of one of them Wildbean cried out, "Here, master! here we go all together!" "What!" said Mr. Harris, "dost thou go also?" "Yes, to be sure, master. Here we go, all together!" "In that case, friend," replied Mr. Harris, "let the carts be unloaded; we are just as well where we are." It is added, that "Mr. Harris died soon after, but it is said the Cluricaun still haunts the Harris family."

In another of these Fairy Legends, Teigue of the Lee, who haunted the house of a Mr. Pratt, in the county of Cork, bears a strong resemblance to the Hinzelmann of Germany. To the story, which is exceedingly well told by a member of the society of Friends, now no more, also the narrator of the Legend of Bottle-hill, Mr. Croker has in his notes added some curious particulars.

A being named the Fear Dearg (*i. e.* Red Man) is also known in Munster. A tale named The Lucky Guest, which Mr. Croker gives as taken down *verbatim* from the mouth of

the narrator by Mr. M'Clise, the artist, gives the fullest
account of this being. A girl related that, when she was
quite a child, one night, during a storm of wind and rain, a
knocking was heard at the door of her father's cabin, and a
voice like that of a feeble old man craving admission.   On
the door's being opened, there came in a little old man,
about two feet and a half high, with a red sugar-loaf hat and
a long scarlet coat, reaching down nearly to the ground, his
hair was long and grey, and his face yellow and wrinkled.
He went over to the fire (which the family had quitted in
their fear), sat down and dried his clothes, and began smoking
a pipe which he found there.   The family went to bed, and
in the morning he was gone.   In about a month after he
began to come regularly every night about eleven o'clock.
The signal which he gave was thrusting a hairy arm through
a hole in the door, which was then opened, and the family
retired to bed, leaving him the room to himself.   If they did
not open the door, some accident was sure to happen next
day to themselves or their cattle.   On the whole, however,
his visits brought good luck, and the family prospered, till
the landlord put them out of their farm, and they never saw
the Fear Dearg more.

As far as our knowledge extends, there is no being in the
Irish rivers answering to the Nix or Kelpie; but on the
sea coast the people believe in beings of the same kind as
the Mermen and Mermaids.   The Irish name is Merrow,* and
legends are told of them similar to those of other countries.
Thus the Lady of Gollerus resembles the Mermaid-wife and
others which we have already related.   Instead, however, of
an entire dress, it is a kind of cap, named *Cohuleen Driuth*,
without which she cannot return to her subaqueous abode.
Other legends tell of matrimonial unions formed by mortals
with these sea-ladies, from which some families in the south
claim a descent.   The Lord of Dunkerron, so beautifully
told in verse by Mr. Croker, relates the unfortunate termination of a marine amour of one of the O'Sullivan family.
The Soul-cages alone contains the adventures of a Mermau.

---

* Mr. Croker says this is *moruach*, sea-maid ; the only word we find in
O'Reilly is ᵐᵘᵢᵣᵢᵐᵹᵉᵃċ (*múrivgach*).   We have met no term answering
to *merman*.

The Irish Pooka* (ꝑuc⸪) is plainly the English Pouke, Puck, and would seem, like it, to denote an evil spirit. The notions respecting it are very vague. A boy in the mountains near Killarney told Mr. Croker that " old people used to say that the Pookas were very numerous in the times long ago. They were wicked-minded, black-looking, bad things, that would come in the *form of wild colts*, with chains hanging about them. They did great hurt to benighted travellers." Here we plainly have the English Puck; but it is remarkable that the boy should speak of Pookas in the plural number. In Leinster, it was always *the*, not *a* Pooka, that we heard named. When the blackberries begin to decay, and the seeds to appear, the children are told not to eat them any longer, as *the* Pooka has dirtied on them.

The celebrated fall of the Liffey, near Ballymore Eustace, is named Pool-a-Phooka, or The Pooka's Hole. Near Macroom, in the county of Cork, are the ruins of a castle built on a rock, named Carrig-a-Phooka, or The Pooka's Rock. There is an old castle not far from Dublin, called Puck's Castle, and a townland in the county of Kildare is named Puckstown. The common expression *play the Puck* is the same as *play the deuce, play the Devil*.

The most remarkable of the Fairy-tribe in Ireland, and one which is peculiar to the country, is the Leprechaun.† This is a being in the form of an old man, dressed as he is described in one of the following tales. He is by profession a maker of brogues; he resorts in general only to secret and retired places, where he is discovered by the sounds which he makes hammering his brogues. He is rich, like curmudgeons of his sort, and it is only by the most violent threats

---

* It is a rule of the Irish language, that the initial consonant of an oblique case, or of a word *in regimine*, becomes aspirated; thus *Pooka* (nom.), *na Phooka* (gen.), *mac* son, *a mhic* (*vic*) my son.

† In Irish lobⱥⱦncⱦn (*lubárkin*); the Ulster name is Logheryman, in Irish loċⱥⱦmⱥn (*lucharman*). For the Cork term Cluricaun, the Kerry Luricaun and the Tipperary Lurigadaun, we have found no equivalents in the Irish dictionaries. The short *o* in Irish, we may observe, is pronounced as in French and Spanish, *i. e.* as *u* in *but, cut; ai* nearly as *a* in *fall*. It may be added, on account of the following tales, that in Kildare and the adjoining counties the short English *u*, in *but, cut*, etc., is invariably pronounced as in *pull, full*, while this *u* is pronounced as that in *but, cut*.

of doing him some bodily harm, that he can be made to show the place where his treasure lies; but if the person who has caught him can be induced (a thing that always happens, by the way) to take his eyes off him, he vanishes, and with him the prospect of wealth. The only instance of more than one Leprechaun being seen at a time is that which occurs in one of the following tales, which was related by an old woman, to the writer's sister and early companion, now no more.

Yet the Leprechaun, though, as we said, peculiar to Ireland, seems indebted to England, at least, for his name. In Irish, as we have seen, he is called *Lobaircin*, and it would not be easy to write the English Lubberkin more accurately with Irish letters and Irish sounds. Leprechaun is evidently a corruption of that word.* In the time of Elizabeth and James, the word Lubrican was used in England to indicate some kind of spirit. Thus Drayton gives as a part of Nymphidia's invocation of Proserpina:

> By the mandrake's dreadful groans;
> By the Lubrican's sad moans;
> By the noise of dead men's bones
> In charnel-house rattling.

That this was the Leprechaun is, we think, clear; for in the Honest Whore of Decker and Middleton, the following words are used of an Irish footman:

> As for your Irish Lubrican, that spirit
> Whom by preposterous charms thy lust has raised.
> Part II. i. 1.†

We thus have the Leprechaun as a well-known Irish fairy, though his character was not understood, in the sixteenth century.

The two following tales we ourselves heard from the peasantry of Kildare in our boyhood: ‡

---

* The Ulster *Lucharman* also has such an English look, that we should be tempted to derive it from the Ang.-Sax. *lácan*, *lǽcan*, to play. Loki *Löjemand*, or Loki Playman, is a name of the Eddaic deity Loki in the Danish ballads.

† In the place of the Witch of Edmonton usually quoted with this, *Lubrick* is plainly the Latin *lubricus*.

‡ It will be observed that these, as well as the Young Piper in the Appen-

Clever Tom and the Leprechaun.

OLIVER Tom Fwich-(i.e. Fitz)pathrick, as people used to call him, was the eldest son o' a comfortable farmer, who lived nigh hand to Morristown-Lattin, not far from the Liffey. Tom was jist turned o' nine-an'-twinty, whin he met wid the follyin' advinthur, an' he was as cliver, clane, tight, good-lukin' a boy as any in the whole county Kildare. One fine day in harvist (it was a holiday) Tom was takin' a ramble by himsilf thro' the land, an' wint saintherin' along the sunny side uv a hidge, an' thinkin' in himsilf, whare id be the grate harm if people, instid uv idlin' an' goin' about doin' nothin' at all, war to shake out the hay, an' bind and stook th' oats that was lyin' an the ledge, 'specially as the weather was raither brokin uv late, whin all uv a suddint he h'ard a clackin' sort o' n'ise jist a little way fornint him, in the hidge. "Dear me," said Tom, "but isn't it now raaly surprisin' to hear the stonechatters singin' so late in the saison." So Tom stole an, goin' on the tips o' his toes to thry iv he cud git a sight o' what was makin' the n'ise, to see iv he was right in his guess. The n'ise stopt; but as Tom luked sharp thro' the bushes, what did he see in a neuk o' the hidge but a brown pitcher that might hould about a gallon an' a haff o' liquor; an' bye and bye he seen a little wee deeny dawny bit iv an ould man, wid a little motty iv a cocked hat stuck an the top iv his head, an' a deeshy daushy leather apron hangin' down afore him, an' he pulled out a little wooden stool, an' stud up upon it, and dipped a little piggen into the pitcher, an' tuk out the full av it, an' put it beside the stool, an' thin sot down undher the pitcher, an' begun to work at puttin' a heelpiece an a bit iv a brogue jist fittin' fur himsilf.

dix, are related in the character of a peasant. This was in accordance with a frame that was proposed for the Fairy Legends, but which proved too difficult of execution to be adopted.

"Well, by the powers!" said Tom to himsilf, "I aften hard tell o' the Leprechauns, an', to tell God's thruth, I nivir rightly believed in thim, but here's won o' thim in right airnest; if I go knowin'ly to work, I'm a med man. They say a body must nivir take their eyes aff o' thim, or they'll escape."

Tom now stole an a little farther, wid his eye fixed an the little man jist as a cat does wid a mouse, or, as we read in books, the rattlesnake does wid the birds he wants to inchant. So, whin he got up quite close to him, "God bless your work, honest man," sez Tom. The little man raised up his head, an' "Thank you kindly," sez he. "I wundher you'd be workin' an the holiday," sez Tom. "That's my own business, an' none of your's," was the reply, short enough. "Well, may be, thin, you'd be civil enough to tell us, what you've got in the pitcher there," sez Tom. "Aye, will I, wid pleasure," sez he: "it's good beer." "Beer!" sez Tom: "Blud an' turf, man, whare did ye git it?" "Whare did I git it, is it? why I med it to be shure; an' what do ye think I med it av?" "Divil a one o' me knows," sez Tom, "but av malt, I 'spose; what ilse?" "'Tis there you're out; I med it av haith." "Av haith!" sez Tom, burstin' out laughin'. "Shure you don't take me to be sich an omedhaun as to b'lieve that?" "Do as ye plase," sez he, "but what I tell ye is the raal thruth. Did ye nivir hear tell o' the Danes?" "To be shure I did," sez Tom, "warn't thim the chaps we gev such a lickin' whin they thought to take Derry frum huz?" "Hem," sez the little man dhryly, "is that all ye know about the matther?" "Well, but about thim Danes," sez Tom. "Why all th' about thim is," said he, "is that whin they war here they taught huz to make beer out o' the haith, an' the saicret's in my family ivir sense." "Will ye giv a body a taste o' yer beer to thry?" sez Tom. "I'll tell ye what it is, young man, it id be fitther fur ye to be lukin' afther yer father's propirty thi'n to be botherin' dacint, quite people wid yer foolish questions. There, now, while you're idlin' away yer time here, there's the cows hav' bruk into th' oats, an' are knockin' the corn all about."

Tom was taken so by surprise wid this, that he was jist an the very point o' turnin' round, whin he recollicted himsilf

So, afeard that the like might happin agin, he med a grab at the Leprechaun, an' cotch him up in his hand, but in his hurry he ovirset the pitcher, and spilt all the beer, so that he couldn't git a taste uv it to tell what sort it was. He thin swore what he wouldn't do to him iv he didn't show him whare his money was. Tom luked so wicked, an' so bloody-minded, that the little man was quite frightened. "So," sez he, "come along wid me a couple o' fields aff, an' I'll show ye a crock o' gould." So they wint, an' Tom held the Leprechaun fast in his hand, an' nivir tuk his eyes frum aff uv him, though they had to crass hidges an' ditches, an' a cruked bit uv a bog (fur the Leprechaun seemed, out o' pure mischief, to pick out the hardest and most conthrairy way), till at last they come to a grate field all full o' *bolyawn buies,** an' the Leprechaun pointed to a big bolyawn, an' sez he, "Dig undher that bolyawn, an' you'll git a crock chuck full o' goulden guineas."

Tom, in his hurry, had nivir minded the bringin' a fack †
wid him, so he thought to run home and fetch one, an' that he might know the place agin, he tuk aff one o' his red garthers, and tied it round the bolyawn. "I s'pose," sez the Leprechaun, very civilly, "ye've no further occashin fur me?" "No," sez Tom, "ye may go away now, if ye like, and God speed ye, an' may good luck attind ye whareivir ye go." "Well, good bye to ye, Tom Fwichpathrick," sed the Leprechaun, "an' much good may do ye wid what ye'll git."

So Tom run fur the bare life, till he come home, an' got a fack, an' thin away wid him as hard as he could pilt back to the field o' bolyawns; but whin he got there, lo an' behould, not a bolyawn in the field, but had a red garther, the very idintical model o' his own, tied about it; an' as to diggin' up the whole field, that was all nonsinse, fur there was more nor twinty good Irish acres in it. So Tom come home agin wid his fack an his shouldher, a little cooler nor he wint; and many's the hearty curse he gev the Leprechaun ivry time he thought o' the nate turn he sarved him.‡

* Lit. Yellow-stick, the ragwort or ragweed, which grows to a great size in Ireland.

† A kind of spade with but one step, used in Leinster.

‡ All that is said in this legend about the beer is a pure fiction, for we

The Leprechaun in the Garden.

THERE'S a sort o' people that every body must have met wid sumtime or another. I mane thim people that purtinds not to b'lieve in things that in their hearts they *do* b'lieve in, an' are mortially afeard o' too. Now Failey[*] Mooney was one o' these. Failey (iv any o' yez knew him) was a rollockin', rattlin', divil-may-care sort ov a chap like— but that 's neither here nor there ; he was always talkin' one nonsinse or another ; an' among the rest o' his fooleries, he purtinded not to b'lieve in the fairies, the Leprechauns, an' the Poocas, an' he evin sumtimes had the impedince to purtind to doubt o' ghosts, that every body b'lieves in, at any rate. Yit sum people used to wink an' luk knowin' whin Failey was gostherin', fur it was obsarved that he was mighty shy o' crassin' the foord o' Ahnamoe afther nightfall ; an' that whin onst he was ridin' past the ould church o' Tipper in the dark, tho' he 'd got enough o' pottheen into him to make any man stout, he med the horse trot so that there was no keepin' up wid him, an' iv'ry now an' thin he 'd throw a sharp luk-out ovir his lift shouldher.

Well, one night there was a parcel o' the neighbours sittin' dhrinkin' an' talkin' at Larry Reilly's public-house, an' Failey was one o' the party. He was, as usual, gittin' an wid his nonsinse an' baldherdash about the fairies, an' swearin' that he didn't b'lieve there was any live things, barrin' min

never heard of a Leprechaun drinking or smoking. It is, however, a tradition of the peasantry, that the Danes used to make beer of the heath. It was a Protestant farmer in the county of Cavan, that showed such knowledge of the siege of Derry ; the Catholic gardener who told us this story, knew far better. It is also the popular belief that the Danes keep up their claim on Ireland, and that a Danish father, when marrying his daughter, gives her a portion in Ireland.

[*] *i. e.* Felix. On account of the Romish custom of naming after Saints, Felix, Thaddæus, Terence, Augustine, etc., are common names among the peasantry.

an' bastes, an' birds and fishes, an' sich like things as a body
cud see, an' he wint on talkin' in so profane a way o' the
good people, that som o' the company grew timid an' begun
to crass thimsilves, not knowin' what might happin', whin
an ould woman called Mary Hogan wid a long blue cloak
about her, that was sittin' in the chimbly corner smokin'
her pipe widout takin' the laste share in the conversation,
tuk the pipe out o' her mouth, an' threw the ashes out o' it,
an' spit in the fire, an' turnin' round, luked Failey straight
in the face. "An' so you don't b'lieve there's sich things
as Leprechauns, don't ye?" sed she.

Well, Failey luked rayther daunted, but howsumdivir
he sed nothin'. "Why, thin, upon my throth, an' it well
becomes the likes o' ye, an' that's nothin' but a bit uv a
gossoon, to take upon yer to purtind not to b'lieve what yer
father, an' yer father's father, an' his father afore him,
nivir med the laste doubt uv. But to make the matther
short, seein''s b'lievin' they say, an' I, that might be yer
gran'mother, tell ye there is sich things as Leprechauns, an'
what's more, that I mysilf seen one o' thim,—there's fur ye,
now!"

All the people in the room luked quite surprised at this,
an' crowded up to the fireplace to listen to her. Failey
thried to laugh, but it wouldn't do, nobody minded him.

"I remimber," sed she, "some time afther I married the
honest man, that's now dead and gone, it was by the same
token jist a little afore I lay in o' my first child (an' that's
many a long day ago), I was sittin', as I sed, out in our little
bit o' a gardin, wid my knittin' in my hand, watchin' sum
bees we had that war goin' to swarm. It was a fine sun-
shiny day about the middle o' June, an' the bees war hum-
min' and flyin' backwards an' forwards frum the hives, an'
the birds war chirpin' an' hoppin' an the bushes, an' the
buttherflies war flyin' about an' sittin' an the flowers, an'
ev'ry thing smelt so fresh an' so sweet, an' I felt so happy,
that I hardly knew whare I was. Well, all uv a suddint, I
heard among sum rows of banes we had in a corner o' the
gardin, a n'ise that wint tick tack, tick tack, jist fur all the
world as iv a brogue-maker was puttin' an the heel uv a
pump. 'The Lord presarve us,' sed I to mysilf, 'what in
the world can that be?' So I laid down my knittin', an'

got up, an' stole ovir to the banes, an' nivir believe me iv I
didn't see, sittin' right forenint me, in the very middle of
thim, a bit of an ould man, not a quarther so big as a new-
born child, wid a little cocked hat an his head, an' a dudeen
in his mouth, smokin' away; an' a plain, ould-fashioned,
dhrab-coloured coat, wid big brass buttons upon it, an his
back, an' a pair o' massy silver buckles in his shoes, that
a'most covered his feet they war so big, an' he workin' away
as hard as ivir he could, heelin' a little pair o' pumps. The
instant minnit I clapt my two eyes upon him I knew him to
be a Leprechaun, an' as I was stout an' foolhardy, sez I to
him ' God save ye honist man! that 's hard work ye 're at
this hot day.' He luked up in my face quite vexed like; so
wid that I med a run at him an' cotch hould o' him in
my hand, an' axed him whare was his purse o' money!
' Money? ' sed he, ' money *annagh!* an' whare on airth id a
poor little ould crathur like mysilf git money?' 'Come, come,'
sed I, ' none o' yer thricks upon thravellers; doesn't every
body know that Leprechauns, like ye, are all as rich as the
divil himsilf.' So I pulled out a knife I'd in my pocket,
an' put on as wicked a face as ivir I could (an' in throth,
that was no aisy matther fur me thin, fur I was as comely
an' good-humoured a lukin' girl as you 'd see frum this to
Ballitore)—an' swore by this and by that, if he didn't
instantly gi' me his purse, or show me a pot o' goold, I'd
cut the nose aff his face. Well, to be shure, the little man
did luk so frightened at hearin' these words, that I a'most
found it in my heart to pity the poor little crathur. ' Thin,'
sed he, ' come wid me jist a couple o' fields aff, an' I 'll show
ye whare I keep my money.' So I wint, still houldin' him
fast in my hand, an' keepin' my eyes fixed upon him, whin
all o' a suddint I h'ard a whiz-z behind me. ' There! there!'
cries he, ' there's yer bees all swarmin' an' goin' aff wid
thimsilves like blazes.' I, like a fool as I was, turned my
head round, an' whin I seen nothin' at all, an' luked back at
the Leprechaun, an' found nothin' at all at all in my hand—
fur whin I had the ill luck to take my eyes aff him, ye see,
he slipped out o' my fingers jist as iv he was med o' fog or
smoke, an' the sarra the fut he iver come nigh my garden
agin."

The Three Leprechauns.

———◆———

MRS. L. having heard that Molly Toole, an old woman who held a few acres of land from Mr. L., had seen Leprechauns, resolved to visit her, and learn the truth from her own lips. Accordingly, one Sunday, after church, she made her appearance at Molly's residence, which was—no very common thing—extremely neat and comfortable. As she entered, every thing looked gay and cheerful. The sun shone bright in through the door on the earthen floor. Molly was seated at the far side of the fire in her arm-chair; her daughter Mary, the prettiest girl on the lands, was looking to the dinner that was boiling; and her son Mickey, a young man of about two-and-twenty, was standing lolling with his back against the dresser.

The arrival of the mistress disturbed the stillness that had hitherto prevailed. Mary, who was a great favourite, hastened to the door to meet her, and shake hands with her. Molly herself had nearly got to the middle of the floor when the mistress met her, and Mickey modestly staid where he was till he should catch her attention. "O then, musha! but isn't it a glad sight for my ould eyes to see your own silf undher my roof? Mary, what ails you, girl? and why don't you go into the room and fetch out a good chair for the misthress to sit down upon and rest herself?" "'Deed faith, mother, I'm so glad I don't know what I'm doin'. Sure you know I didn't see the misthress since she cum down afore."

Mickey now caught Mrs. L.'s eye, and she asked him how he did. "By Gorra, bravely, ma'am, thank you," said he, giving himself a wriggle, while his two hands and the small of his back rested on the edge of the dresser.

"Now, Mary, stir yourself, alanna," said the old woman, "and get out the bread and butther. Sure you know the misthress can't but be hungry afther her walk."—"O, never mind it, Molly; it's too much trouble."—"Throuble, indeed!

it's as nice butther, ma'am, as iver you put a tooth in; and it was Mary herself that med it."—"O, then I must taste it."

A nice half griddle of whole-meal bread and a print of fresh butter were now produced, and Molly helped the mistress with her own hands. As she was eating, Mary kept looking in her face, and at last said, "Ah then, mother, doesn't the misthress luk mighty well? Upon my faikins, ma'am, I never seen you luking half so handsome."—"Well! and why wouldn't she luk well? And niver will she luk betther nor be betther nor I wish her."—"Well, Molly, I think I may return the compliment, for Mary is prettier than ever; and as for yourself, I really believe it's young again you're growing."—"Why, God be thanked, ma'am, I'm stout and hearty; and though I say it mysilf, there's not an ould woman in the county can stir about betther nor me, and I'm up ivery mornin' at the peep of day, and rout them all up out of their beds. Don't I?" said she, looking at Mary.—"Faith, and sure you do, mother," replied Mickey; "and before the peep of day, too; for you have no marcy in you at all at all."—"Ah, in my young days," continued the old woman, "people woren't slugabeds; out airly, home late—that was the way wid thim."—"And usedn't people to see Leprechauns in thim days, mother?" said Mickey, laughing.—"Hould your tongue, you saucy cub, you," cried Molly; "what do you know about thim?"—"Leprechauns?" said Mrs. L., gladly catching at the opportunity; "did people really, Molly, see Leprechauns in your young days?"—"Yes, indeed, ma'am; some people say they did," replied Molly, very composedly.—"O com' now, mother," cried Mickey, "don't think to be goin' it upon us that away; you know you seen thim one time yoursilf, and you hadn't the gumption in you to cotch thim, and git their crocks of gould from thim."—"Now, Molly, is that really true that you saw the Leprechauns?"—"'Deed, and did I, ma'am; but this boy's always laughin' at me about thim, and that makes me rather shy in talkin' o' thim."—"Well, Molly, I won't laugh at you; so, come, tell me how you saw them."

"Well, ma'am, you see it was whin I was jist about the age of Mary, there. I was comin' home late one Monday

evenin' from the market; for my aunt Kitty, God be mar-
ciful to her! would keep me to take a cup of tay. It was in
the summer time, you see, ma'am, much about the middle of
June, an' it was through the fields I come. Well, ma'am, as
I was sayin', it was late in the evenin', that is, the sun was
near goin' down, an' the light was straight in my eyes, an' I
come along through the bog-meadow; for it was shortly
afther I was married to him that 's gone, an' we wor livin' in
this very house you 're in now; an' thin whin I come to the
castle-field — the pathway you know, ma'am, goes right
through the middle uv it—an' it was thin as fine a field of
whate, jist shot out, as you 'd wish to luk at; an' it was a
purty sight to see it wavin' so beautifully wid every air of
wind that was goin' over it, dancin' like to the music of a
thrush, that was singin' down below in the hidge.* Well,
ma'am, I crasst over the style that 's there yit, and wint
along fair and aisy, till I was near about the middle o' the
field, whin somethin' med me cast my eyes to the ground, a
little before me; an' thin I saw, as sure as I 'm sittin' here,
no less nor three o' the Leprechauns, all bundled together
like so miny tailyors, in the middle o' the path before me.
They worn't hammerin' their pumps, nor makin' any kind of
n'ise whatever; but there they wor, the three little fellows,
wid their cocked hats upon thim, an' their legs gothered up
undher thim, workin' away at their thrade as hard as may be.
If you wor only to see, ma'am, how fast their little ilbows
wint as they pulled out their inds! Well, every one o' thim
had his eye cocked upon me, an' their eyes wor as bright as
the eye of a frog, an' I cudn't stir one step from the spot

---

* In our Tales and Popular Fictions, p. 16, we noticed the coincidence
between this and a passage in an Arabic author. We did not then recollect
the following verses of Milton,

> The willows and the hazle copses green
> Shall now no more be seen
> Fanning their joyous leaves to thy soft lays.
> *Lycidas,* 42.

The simile of the moon among the stars in the same place, we have since
found in the Nibelungen Lied (st. 285), and in some of our old poets, and
Hammer says (Schirin i. note 7), that it occurs even to satiety in Oriental
poetry. In like manner Camoens' simile of the mirror, mentioned in the same
place, occurs in Poliziano's Stanze i. 64.

for the life o' me.. So I turned my head round, and prayed
to the Lord in his marcy to deliver me from thim, and when
I wint to luk at thim agin, ma'am, not a sight o' thim was
to be seen: they wor gone like a dhrame."—"But, Molly,
why did you not catch them?"—"I was afeard, ma'am,
that's the thruth uv it; but maybe I was as well widout
thim. I niver h'ard tell of a Leprechaun yit that wasn't too
many for any one that cotch him."—"Well, and Molly, do
you think there are any Leprechauns now?"—"It's my
belief, ma'am, they're all gone out of the country, cliver and
clane, along wid the Fairies; for I niver hear tell o' thim
now at all."

Mrs. L. having now attained her object, after a little more
talk with the good old woman, took her leave, attended by
Mary, who would see her a piece of the way home. And
Mary being asked what she thought of the Leprechauns,
confessed her inability to give a decided opinion: her mother,
she knew, was incapable of telling a lie, and yet she had her
doubts if there ever were such things as Leprechauns.

The following tale of a Cluricaun, related by the writer of
the Legend of Bottle Hill, is of a peculiar character. We
have never heard anything similar of a Leprechaun.

The Little Shoe.

"Now tell me, Molly," said Mr. Coote to Molly Cogan, as
he met her on the road one day, close to one of the old gate-
ways of Kilmallock, "did you ever hear of the Cluricaun?"
—"Is it the Cluricaun? Why, thin, to be shure; aften an'
aften. Many's the time I h'ard my father, rest his sowl!
tell about 'em over and over agin."—"But did you ever
see one, Molly—did you ever see one yourself?"—"Och!
no, I niver seen one in my life; but my gran'father, that's
my father's father, you know, he seen one, one time, an'
cotch him too."—"Caught him! Oh! Molly, tell me how
was that."

"Why, thin, I'll tell ye. My gran'father, you see, was out there above in the bog, dhrawin' home turf, an' the poor ould mare was tir't afther her day's work, an' the ould man wint out to the stable to look afther her, an' to see if she was aitin' her hay; an' whin he come to the stable door there, my dear, he h'ard sumthin' hammerin', hammerin', hammerin', jist for all the wurld like a shoemaker makin' a shoe, and whis'lin' all the time the purtiest chune he iver h'ard in his whole life afore. Well, my gran'father he thought it was the Cluricaun, an' he sed to himsilf, sez he, 'I'll ketch you, if I can, an' thin I'll have money enough always.' So he opened the door very quitely, an' didn't make a taste o' n'ise in the wurld, an' luked all about, but the niver a bit o' the little man cud he see anywhare, but he h'ard his hammerin' and whis'lin', an' so he luked and luked, till at last he seen the little fellow; an' whare was he, do ye think, but in the girth undher the mare; an' there he was, wid his little bit ov an apron an him, an' his hammer in his hand, an' a little red night-cap an his head, an' he makin' a shoe; an' he was so busy wid his work, an' was hammerin' an' whis'lin' so loud, that he niver minded my gran'father, till he cotch him fast in his hand. 'Faix, I have ye now,' says he, 'an' I'll niver let ye go till I git yer purse—that's what I won't; so give it here at onst to me, now.' 'Stop, stop,' says the Cluricaun; 'stop, stop,' says he, 'till I get it for ye.' So my gran'father, like a fool, ye see, opened his hand a little, an' the little weeny chap jumped away laughin', an' he niver seen him any more, an' the divil a bit o' the purse did he git; only the Cluricaun left his little shoe that he was makin'. An' my gran'father was mad enough wid himself for lettin' him go; but he had the shoe all his life, an' my own mother tould me she aftin seen it, an' had it in her hand; an' 'twas the purtiest little shoe she ivir seen."—"An' did you see it yourself, Molly?"—"Oh! no, my dear, 'twas lost long afore I was born; but my mother tould me aftin an' aftin enough."

SCOTTISH HIGHLANDS.

Huar Prownie coad agus curochd,
Agus cha dían Prownie opar tullidh.

Brownie has got a cowl and coat,
And never more will work a jot.
STEWART.

COLONIES of Gothic Fairies, it would appear, early established themselves in the Highlands, and almost every Lowland, German, and Scandinavian Fairy or Dwarf-tale will there find its fellow. The Gaelic Fairies are very handsome in their persons; their usual attire is green. They dance and sing, lend and borrow, and they make cloth and shoes in an amazingly short space of time. They make their *raids* upon the low country, and carry off women and children; they fetch midwives to assist at the birth of their children, and mortals have spent a night at the fairy revels, and next morning found that the night had extended a hundred years. Highland fairies also take the diversion of the chase. "One Highlander," says Mc.Culloch,* "in passing a mountain, hears the tramp of horses, the music of the horn, and the cheering of the huntsmen; when suddenly a gallant crew of thirteen fairy hunters, dressed in green, sweep by him, the silver bosses of their bridles jingling in the night breeze."

The Gael call the Fairies Daoine Shi',† (*Dheenè Shee*) and their habitations Shians, or Tomhans. These are a sort of turrets, resembling masses of rock or hillocks. By day they are indistinguishable, but at night they are frequently lit up with great splendour.

Brownie, too, 'shows his honest face' in the Highlands;

---

* Account of the Highlands, etc. iv. 358.
† *Men of Peace*, perhaps the *Stille-folk*, Still-people, or rather, merely Fairy- or Spirit-people. See above p. 364.

ar.d the mischievous water-Kelpie also appears in his equine form, and seeks to decoy unwary persons to mount him, that he may plunge with his rider into the neighbouring loch or river.

The Highlanders have nearly the same ideas as their Shetland neighbours, respecting the seals.

The following legends will illustrate what we have stated.*

The Fairy's Inquiry.

A CLERGYMAN was returning home one night after visiting a sick member of his congregation. His way led by a lake, and as he proceeded he was surprised to hear most melodious strains of music. He sat down to listen. The music seemed to approach coming over the lake accompanied by a light. At length he discerned a man walking on the water, attended by a number of little beings, some bearing lights, others musical instruments. At the beach the man dismissed his attendants, and then walking up to the minister saluted him courteously. He was a little grey-headed old man, dressed in rather an unusual garb. The minister having returned his salute begged of him to come and sit beside him. He complied with the request, and on being asked who he was, replied that he was one of the Daoine Shi. He added that he and they had originally been angels, but having been seduced into revolt by Satan, they had been cast down to earth where they were to dwell till the day of doom. His object now was, to ascertain from the minister what would be their condition after that awful day. The minister then questioned him on the articles of faith; but as his answers did not prove satisfactory, and as in repeating the Lord's Prayer, he persisted in saying *wert* instead of *art*

---

* See Stewart, The Popular Superstitions of the Highlanders. Edinburgh, 1823. As Mr. Stewart's mode of narrating is not the very best, we have taken the liberty of re-writing and abridging the legends.

in heaven, he did not feel himself justified in holding out any hopes to him. The fairy then gave a cry of despair and flung himself into the loch, and the minister resumed his journey.

The Young Man in the Shian.

A FARMER named Macgillivray, one time removed from the neighbourhood of Cairngorm in Strathspey to the forest of Glenavon, in which the fairies are said to reside. Late one night, as two of his sons, Donald and Rory, were in search of some of his sheep that had strayed, they saw lights streaming from the crevices of a fairy turret which in the day time had only the appearance of a rock. They drew nigh to it, and there they heard jigs and reels played inside in the most exquisite manner. Rory was so fascinated that he proposed that they should enter and take part in the dance. Donald did all he could to dissuade him, but in vain. He jumped into the Shian, and plunged at once into the whirling movements of its inhabitants. Donald was in great perplexity, for he feared to enter the Shian. All he could do therefore was to put his mouth to one of the crevices, and calling, as the custom was, three times on his brother, entreating him in the most moving terms, to come away and return home. But his entreaties were unheeded and he was obliged to return alone.

Every means now was resorted to for the recovery of Rory, but to no purpose. His family gave him up for lost, when a *Duin Glichd* or Wise man, told Donald to go to the place where he had lost his brother, a year and a day from the time, and placing in his garments a rowan-cross, to enter the Shian boldly, and claim him in the divine name, and if he would not come voluntarily, to seize him and drag him out; for the fairies would have no power to prevent him. After some hesitation Donald assented. At the appointed time he approached the Shian at midnight. It was full of revelry, and the merry dance was going on as before. Donald had his terrors no doubt, but they gave way to his fraternal affection. He entered and found Rory in the midst of a Highland Fling, and running up to him, seized him by the collar, repeating the words dictated by the Wise man. Rory agreed to go provided he would let him finish his dance; for he had not been, he assured him, more than half an hour in the place, but Donald was inexorable, and took him home to his parents. Rory would never have believed that his half-hour had been a twelvemonth, "did not the calves grown now into stots, and the new-born babes now toddling about the house, at length convince him that in his single reel he had danced for a twelvemonth and a day."

The Two Fiddlers.

NEARLY three hundred years ago, there dwelt in Strathspey two fiddlers, greatly renowned in their art. One Christmas they resolved to go try their fortune in Inverness. On arriving in that town they took lodgings, and as was the custom at that time, hired the bellman to go round announcing their arrival, their qualifications, their fame, and their terms. Soon after they were visited by a venerable-looking grey-haired old man, who not only found no fault with, but actually offered to double their terms if they would go with him. They agreed, and he led them out of the town, and brought them to a very strange-looking dwelling which seemed to them to be very like a Shian. The money, however, and the entreaties of their guide induced them to enter it, and their musical talents were instantly put into requisition, and the dancing was such as in their lives they had never witnessed.

When morning came they took their leave highly gratified with the liberal treatment they had received. It surprised them greatly to find that it was out of a hill and not a house that they issued, and when they came to the town, they could not recognise any place or person, every thing seemed so altered. While they and the townspeople were in mutual amazement, there came up a very old man, who on hearing their story, said: "You are then the two men who lodged with my great-grandfather, and whom Thomas Rimer, it was supposed, decoyed to Tomnafurach. Your friends were greatly grieved on your account, but it is a hundred years ago, and your names are now no longer known." It was the Sabbath day and the bells were tolling; the fiddlers, deeply penetrated with awe at what had occurred, entered the church to join in the offices of religion. They sat in silent meditation while the bell continued ringing, but the moment that the minister commenced the service they crumbled away into dust.

The Fairy-Labour.

MANY years ago there dwelt in Strathspey a midwife of great repute. One night just as she was going to bed, she heard a loud knocking at the door, and on opening it she saw there a man and a grey horse, *both out of breath*. The rider requested her to jump up behind him and come away to assist a lady who was in great danger. He would not even consent to her stopping to change her dress, as it would cause delay. She mounted and away they went at full speed. On the way she tried to learn from the rider whither she was going, but all she could get from him was, that she would be well paid. At length he let out that it was to a fairy-lady he was taking her. Nothing daunted, however, she went on, and on reaching the Shian, she found that her services were really very much needed. She succeeded in bringing a fine boy to the light, which caused so much joy, that the fairies desired her to ask what she would, and if it was in their power, it should be granted. Her desire was that success might attend herself and her posterity in all similar operations. The gift was conferred and it continued, it was said, with her great-grandson, at the time the collector of these legends wrote.

The Fairy borrowing Oatmeal.

A FAIRY came one day from one of the turrets of Craig-ail-naic to the wife of one of the tenants in Delnabo, and asked her to lend her a firlot of oatmeal for food for her family, promising to repay it soon, as she was every moment expecting an ample supply. The woman complied with this request, and after, as was the custom of the country, having regaled her with bread, cheese, and whiskey, she went, as was usual, to see her a part of the way home. When they had reached the summit of an eminence near the town, the *Béanshi* told her she might take her meal home again as she was now abundantly supplied. The woman did as desired, and as she went along she beheld the corn-kiln of an adjacent farm all in a blaze.

The Fairy-Gift.

A FARMER in Strathspey was one day engaged in sowing one of his fields and singing at his work. A fairy damsel of great beauty came up to him and requested him to sing for her a favourite old Gaelic song named *Nighan Donne na Bual*. He complied, and she then asked him to give her some of his corn. At this he demurred a little and wished to know what she would give him in return. She replied with a significant look that his seed would never fail him. He then gave to her liberally and she departed. He went on sowing, and when he had finished a large field, he found that his bag was as full and as heavy as when he began. He then sowed another field of the same size, with the same result, and satisfied with his day's work, he threw the bag on his shoulder and went home. Just as he was entering

the barn-door he was met by his wife, a foolish talkative body
with a tongue as long, and a head as empty as the church
bell, who, struck with the appearance of the bag after a day's
sowing, began to ask him about it.   Instantly it became
quite empty.   "I'll be the death of you, you foolish woman,"
roared out the farmer; "if it were not for your idle talk,
that bag was worth its weight in gold."

The Stolen Ox.

THE tacksman (*i. e.* tenant) of the farm of Auchriachan in
Strathavon, while searching one day for his goats on a hill
in Glenlivat, found himself suddenly enveloped in a dense
fog.   It continued till night came on when he began to give
himself up to despair.   Suddenly he beheld a light at no
great distance.   He hastened toward it, and found that it
proceeded from a strange-looking edifice.   The door was
open, and he entered, but great was his surprise to meet
there a woman whose funeral he had lately attended.   From
her he learned that this was an abode of the fairies for whom
she kept house, and his only chance of safety, she said, was
in being concealed from them; for which purpose she hid him
in a corner of the apartment.   Presently in came a troop of
fairies, and began calling out for food.   An old dry-looking
fellow then reminded them of the miserly, as he styled him,
tacksman of Auchriachan, and how he cheated them out of
their lawful share of his property, by using some charms
taught him by his old grandmother.   "He is now from
home," said he, "in search of our allies,* his goats, and his
family have neglected to use the charm, so come let us have
his favourite ox for supper."   The speaker was Thomas
Rimer, and the plan was adopted with acclamation.   "But
what are we to do for bread?" cried one.   "We'll have

---

* "The goats are supposed to be upon a very good understanding with the
fairies, and possessed of more cunning and knowledge than their appearance
bespeaks."—*Stewart: see Wales.*

Auchriachan's new baked bread," replied Thomas; "his wife forgot to cross the first bannock."* So said, so done. The ox was brought in and slaughtered before the eyes of his master, whom, while the fairies were employed about their cooking, his friend gave an opportunity of making his escape.

The mist had now cleared away and the moon was shining. Auchriachan therefore soon reached his home. His wife instantly produced a basket of new-baked bannocks with milk and urged him to eat. But his mind was running on his ox, and his first question was, who had served the cattle that night. He then asked the son who had done it if he had used the charm, and he owned he had forgotten it. "Alas! alas!" cried he, "my favourite ox is no more." "How can that be?" said one of the sons, "I saw him alive and well not two hours ago." "It was nothing but a fairy stock," cried the father. "Bring him out here." The poor ox was led forth, and the farmer, after abusing it and those that sent it, felled it to the ground. The carcase was flung down the brae at the back of the house, and the bread was sent after it, and there they both lay untouched, for it was observed that neither cat nor dog would put a tooth in either of them.

The Stolen Lady.

JOHN ROY, who lived in Glenbroun, in the parish of Abernethy, being out one night on the hills in search of his cattle, met a troop of fairies, who seemed to have got a prize of some sort or other. Recollecting that the fairies are obliged to exchange whatever they may have with any one who offers them anything, however low in value, for it, he flung his bonnet to them, crying *Shuis slo slumus sheen* (*i. e.*, mine is yours and yours is mine). The fairies dropped their booty, which proved to be a Sassenach (English) lady whom the dwellers of the Shian of Coir-laggac had carried away

* See above, p. 305.

from her own country, leaving a stock in her place which, of course, died and was buried. John brought her home, and she lived for many years in his house. "It happened, however, in the course of time," said the Gaelic narrator, "that the *new king* found it necessary to make the great roads through these countries by means of soldiers, for the purpose of letting coaches and carriages pass to the northern cities; and those soldiers had officers and commanders in the same way as our fighting army have now. Those soldiers were never great favourites in these countries, particularly during the time that our kings were alive; and consequently it was no easy matter for them, either officers or men, to procure for themselves comfortable quarters." But John Roy would not keep up the national animosity to the *cottan dearg* (red-coats), and he offered a residence in his house to a *Saxon* captain and his son. When there they could not take their eyes off the English lady, and the son remarked to his father what a strong likeness she bore to his deceased mother. The father replied that he too had been struck with the resemblance, and said he could almost fancy she *was* his wife. He then mentioned her name and those of some persons connected with them. The lady by these words at once recognised her husband and son, and honest John Roy had the satisfaction of reuniting the long-separated husband and wife, and receiving their most grateful acknowledgments.*

---

* There is a similar legend in Scandinavia. As a smith was at work in his forge late one evening, he heard great wailing out on the road, and by the light of the red-hot iron that he was hammering, he saw a woman whom a Troll was driving along, bawling at her " A little more! a little more!" He ran out, put the red-hot iron between them, and thus delivered her from the power of the Troll (see p. 108). He led her into his house and that night she was delivered of twins. In the morning he waited on her husband, who he supposed must be in great affliction at the loss of his wife. But to his surprise he saw there, in bed, a woman the very image of her he had saved from the Troll. Knowing at once what she must be, he raised an axe he had in his hand, and cleft her skull. The matter was soon explained to the satisfaction of the husband, who gladly received his real wife and her twins.— Thiele, i. 88. *Oral.*

The Changeling.

A COUPLE of Strathspey lads who dealt in whiskey that never paid duty, which they used to purchase in Glenlivat, and sell at Badenoch and Fort William, were one night laying in stock at Glenlivat when they heard the child in the cradle give a piercing cry, just as if it had been shot. The mother, of course, blessed it, and the Strathspey lads took no further notice, and soon after set out with their goods. They had not gone far when they found a fine healthy child lying all alone on the road-side, which they soon recognised as that of their friend. They saw at once how the thing was. The fairies had taken away the real child and left a stock, but, owing to the pious ejaculation of the mother, they had been forced to drop it. As the urgency of their business did not permit them to return, they took the child with them, and kept it till the next time they had occasion to visit Glenlivat. On their arrival they said nothing about the child, which they kept concealed. In the course of conversation, the mother took occasion to remark that the disease which had attacked the child the last time they were there had never left it, and she had now little hopes of its recovery. As if to confirm her statement, it continued uttering most piteous cries. To end the matter at once, the lads produced the real child healthy and hearty, and told how they had found it. An exchange was at once effected, and they forthwith proceeded to dispose of their new charge. For this purpose they got an old *creel* to put him in and some straw to light under it. Seeing the serious turn matters were likely to take, he resolved not to await the trial, but flew up the *smoke-hole*, and when at the top he cried out that things would have gone very differently with them had it not been for the arrival of their guests.

The Wounded Seal.

THERE once dwelt on the northern coast, not far from Taigu
Jan Crot Callow (*John o' Groat's House*), a man who gained
his living by fishing.   He was particularly devoted to the
killing of the seals, in which he had great success.   One
evening just as he had returned home from his usual occupation, he was called upon by a man on horseback who was an
utter stranger to him, but who said that he was come on the
part of a person who wished to make a large purchase of seal-
skins from him, and wanted to see him for that purpose that
very evening.   He therefore desired him to get up behind
him and come away without any delay.   Urged by the hope
of profit he consented, and away they went with such speed
that the wind which was in their backs seemed to be in their
faces.   At length they reached the verge of a stupendous
precipice overhanging the sea, where his guide bade him
alight, as they were now at the end of their journey.   "But
where," says he, "is the person you spoke of?"   "You'll
see him presently," said the guide, and, catching hold of him,
he plunged with him into the sea.   They went down and
down, till at last they came to a door which led into a range
of apartments inhabited by seals, and the man to his amazement now saw that he himself was become one of these
animals.   They seemed all in low spirits, but they spoke
kindly to him, and assured him of his safety.   His guide
now produced a huge *gully* or *joctaleg*, at sight of which,
thinking his life was to be taken away, he began to cry for
mercy.   "Did you ever see this knife before?" said the
guide. He looked at it and saw it was his own, which he had
that very day stuck into a seal who had made his escape
with it sticking in him.   He did not, therefore, attempt to
deny that it had been his property.   "Well," said the guide,
"that seal was my father.   He now lies dangerously ill, and
as it is only you that can cure him, I have brought you
hither."   He then led him into an inner room, where the old

seal lay suffering grievously from a cut in his hind quarters. He was then desired to lay his hand on the wound, at which it instantly healed, and the patient arose hale and sound. All now was joy and festivity in the abode of the seals, and the guide, turning to the seal-hunter, said, " I will now take you back to your family, but you must first take a solemn oath never again to kill a seal as long as you live." Hard as the condition was, he cheerfully accepted it. His guide then laid hold on him, and they rose up, up, till they reached the surface of the sea, and landed at the cliff. He breathed on him and they resumed the human form. They then mounted the horse and sped away like lightning till they reached the fisherman's house. At parting his companion left with him such a present as made him think light of giving over his seal-hunting.

The Brownies.

Two Brownies, man and woman, were attached to the ancient family of Tullochgorm, in Strathspey. The former was named Brownie-Clod, from a habit he had of flinging clods at passers-by ; the latter was called Maug Vuluchd (*i.e.*, Hairy Mag), on account of her great quantity of hair. She was a capital housekeeper, and used invisibly to lay out the table in the neatest and handiest manner. Whatever was called for came as if floating through the air. She kept a very strict hand over the maids, with whom she was no great favourite, as she reported their neglect of duty to their mistress. Brownie-Clod was not so pawky, and he was constantly overreached by the servants, with whom he used to make contracts. He, however, was too able for them on one occasion. He had agreed with two of them to do their whole winter's threshing for them, on condition of get- ting in return an old coat and a Kilmarnock hood to which he had taken a fancy. He wrought away manfully, and they had nothing to do but lie at their ease on the straw and look on. But before the term was expired they laid the coat and hood for him in the barn. The moment Brownie laid his eyes upon them he struck work, using the words prefixed to this section of our volume.

Martyn describes the Brownie of the Western Isles as a *tall man*, and he tells a story of his invisibly directing a person, at Sir Norman M'Leod's, who was playing at draughts, where to place his men.

The Urisk.

THERE is also in the Highlands a rough hairy spirit, called the Urisk. The following legend will display his nature and character:

To the very great annoyance of a Highland miller, and to the injury of the machinery, his mill, he found, used to be set to work at night when there was nothing in it to grind. One of his men offered to sit up, and try to discover who it was that did it; and, having kindled a good turf-fire, sat by it to watch. Sleep, however, overcame him, and when he awoke about midnight, he saw sitting opposite him a rough shaggy being. Nothing daunted, he demanded his name, and was told that it was Urisk. The stranger, in return, asked the man his name, who replied that it was Myself. The conversation here ended, and Urisk soon fell fast asleep. The man then tossed a panful of hot ashes into his shaggy lap, which set his hair all on fire. In an agony, and screaming with the pain, he ran to the door, and in a loud yelling tone several of his brethren were heard to cry out, " What's the matter with you? " " Oh! he set me on fire!" "Who?" " Myself!" "Then put it out yourself," was the reply.*

---

* Told, without naming his authority, by the late W. S. Rose, in the Quarterly Review for 1825.

ISLE OF MAN.

Mona once hid from those that search the main,
Where thousand elfin shapes abide.

COLLINS.

THE Isle of Man, peopled by Celts, and early and frequently
visited and colonised by the Northmen, has also its Fairies,
which differ little from those of the greater islands between
which it lies. An English gentleman, named Waldron, who
resided in the island in the early part of the last century,
was curious about its Fairy-lore, and he has recorded a
number of the legends which he heard.* His book, indeed,
has been the chief source whence Ritson, Sir Walter Scott,†
and others, have drawn their illustrations of English Fairy-
lore in general, and the subsequent inquiries of Mr. Train
have enabled him to add but very little to it. We will here
relate some of these legends :

The great peculiarity of the Manks Fairies, according to
Mr. Waldron, is their fondness for riding, and this not on
little steeds of their own, or on the small breed of the
country, but on the large English and Irish horses, which
are brought over and kept by the gentry. Nothing, it was
said, was more common than to find in the morning horses
covered with foam and sweat, and tired to death, which had
been shut up at night in the stable. One gentleman assured
Mr. Waldron that three or four of his best horses had been
killed with these nocturnal exercises.

They called them the Good People, and said that their
reason for dwelling in the hills and woods was, their dislike
of the vices of towns. Hence the houses which they deigned
to visit were thought to be blest. In these houses, a tub or

---

* Description of the Isle of Man. London, 1731.
† In his Essay on Fairies in the Minstrelsy of the Scottish Border, and in
the notes on Peveril of the Peak.

pail of clean water was always left for them to bathe in. Good, however, as they were, they used to change children. Mr. Waldron saw one of these changelings; it was nearly six years old, but was unable to walk or even stand, or move its limbs. Its complexion was delicate, and it had the finest hair in the world. It never cried or spoke, and it ate scarcely anything; it rarely smiled, but if any one called it *Fairy-elf*, it would frown and almost look them through. Its mother, who was poor, was often obliged to go out for whole days a-charing, and leave it by itself, and when the neighbours would look in on it through the window, they always saw it laughing and in great delight, whence they judged that it had agreeable company with it, more especially as let it be left ever so dirty, the mother on her return found it with a clean face, and its hair nicely combed out.

The Fairy-Chapman.

A MAN being desirous of disposing of a horse he had at that time no great occasion for, and riding him to market for that purpose, was accosted in passing over the mountains by a little man in a plain dress, who asked him if he would sell his horse. " 'Tis the design I am going on," replied he : on which the other desired to know the price. " Eight pounds," said he. " No," returned the purchaser, " I will give no more than seven, which if you will take, here is your money." The owner thinking he had bid pretty fair, agreed with him, and the money being told out, the one dismounted and the other got on the back of the horse, which he had no sooner done than both beast and rider sunk into the earth immediately, leaving the person who had made the bargain in the utmost terror and consternation. As soon as he had a little recovered himself, he went directly to the parson of the parish, and related what had passed, desiring he would give his opinion whether he ought to make use of the money he had received or not. To which

he replied, that as he had made a fair bargain, and no way
circumvented nor endeavoured to circumvent the buyer, he
saw no reason to believe, in case it was an evil spirit, it
could have any power over him. On this assurance, he went
home well satisfied, and nothing afterwards happened to give
him any disquiet concerning this affair. This was told to
Waldron by the person to whom it happened.

The Fairy-Banquet.

A MAN one time was led by invisible musicians for several
miles together, and not being able to resist the harmony,
followed till it conducted him to a large common, where
were a great number of little people sitting round a table,
and eating and drinking in a very jovial manner. Among
them were some faces whom he thought he had formerly
seen, but forbore taking any notice, or they of him, till the
little people offering him drink, one of them, whose features
seemed not unknown to him, plucked him by the coat, and
forbade him whatever he did to taste anything he saw before
him, "For if you do," added he, "you will be as I am, and
return no more to your family." The poor man was much
affrighted, but resolved to obey the injunction. Accordingly,
a large silver cup, filled with some sort of liquor, being put
into his hand, he found an opportunity to throw what it
contained on the ground. Soon after, the music ceasing, all
the company disappeared, leaving the cup in his hand, and
he returned home, though much wearied and fatigued. He
went the next day, and communicated to the minister of the
parish all that had happened, and asked his advice, how he
should dispose of the cup, to which the parson replied, he
could not do better than to devote it to the service of the
church, and this very cup, they say, is that which is now
used for the consecrated wine in Kirk Merlugh.

The Fairies' Christening.

A WOMAN related that being great with child, and expecting every moment the good hour, as she lay awake one night in her bed, she saw seven or eight little women come into her chamber, one of whom had an infant in her arms. They were followed by a man of the same size with themselves, but in the habit of a minister. One of them went to the pail, and finding no water in it, cried out to the others, what must they do to christen the child? On which they replied it should be done in beer. With that the seeming parson took the child in his arms, and performed the ceremony of baptism, dipping his head into a great tub of strong beer, which the woman had brewed the day before to be ready for her lying-in. She said they baptised the infant by the name of Joan, which made her know she was pregnant of a girl, as it proved a few days after when she was delivered. She added, that it was common for the fairies to make a mock christening when any person was near her time, and that, according to what child, male or female, they brought, such should the woman bring into the world.

The Fairy-Whipping.

A WOMAN who lived about two miles distant from Balla-salli, and used to serve Mr. Waldron's family with butter, made him once very merry with a story she told him of her daughter, a girl of about ten years old, who being sent over the fields to the town for a pennyworth of tobacco for her father, was on the top of a mountain surrounded by a great number of little men, who would not suffer her to pass any farther. Some of them said she should go with them, and accordingly laid hold of her; but one, seeming more pitiful, desired they would let her alone, which they refusing, there ensued a quarrel, and the person who took her part fought bravely in her defence. This so incensed the others, that to be revenged on her for being the cause, two or three of them seized her, and pulling up her clothes, whipped her heartily; after which, it seems, they had no farther power over her, and she ran home directly telling what had befallen her, and showing her buttocks, on which were the prints of several small hands. Several of the town's-people went with her to the mountain; and she conducting them to the spot, the little antagonists were gone, but had left behind them proofs, as the good woman said, that what the girl had informed them was true, for there was a great deal of blood to be seen on the stones. This did she aver with all the solemnity possible.

The Fairy-Hunt.

A YOUNG sailor coming off a long voyage, though it was late at night, chose to land rather than lie another night in the vessel. Being permitted to do so, he was set on shore at Douglas. It happened to be a fine moonlight night, and very dry, being a small frost; he therefore forbore going into any house to refresh himself, but made the best of his way to the house of a sister he had at Kirk-Merlugh. As he was going over a pretty high mountain, he heard the noise of horses, the halloo of a huntsman, and the finest horn in the world. He was a little surprised that any one pursued those kinds of sports in the night; but he had not time for much reflection before they all passed by him so near, that he was able to count what number there was of them, which he said was thirteen, and that they were all dressed in green, and gallantly mounted. He was so well pleased with the sight, that he would gladly have followed could he have kept pace with them. He crossed the footway, however, that he might see

them again, which he did more than once, and lost not the
sound of the horn for some miles. At length being arrived
at his sister's, he tells her the story, who presently clapped
her hands for joy that he was come home safe; "for," said
she, "those you saw were *fairies,* and 'tis well they did not
take you away with them."

The Fiddler and the Fairy.

A FIDDLER having agreed with a person, who was a stranger,
for so much money, to play to some company he should bring
him to, all the twelve days of Christmas, and received earnest
for it, saw his new master vanish into the earth the moment
he had made the bargain. Nothing could be more terrified
than was the poor fiddler. He found he had entered himself
into the Devil's service, and looked on himself as already
damned; but having recourse to a clergyman, he received
some hope. He ordered him, however, as he had taken
earnest, to go when he should be called, but that whatever
tunes should be called for, to play none but psalms. On the
day appointed the same person appeared, with whom he
went, but with what inward reluctance it is easy to guess;
and punctually obeying the minister's directions, the company to whom he played were so angry, that they all vanished
at once, leaving him at the top of a high hill, and so bruised
and hurt, though he was not sensible when or from what
hand he received the blows, that he got not home without
the utmost difficulty.

The Phynnodderee.

THE Phynnodderee, or Hairy-one, is a Manks spirit of the
same kind with the Brownie or the Kobold. He is said to
have been a fairy who was expelled from the fairy society.

The cause was, he courted a pretty Manks maid who lived
in a bower beneath *the blue tree* of Glen Aldyn, and therefore was absent from the Fairy court during the *Re-hollys
vooar yn ouyr*, or harvest-moon, being engaged dancing in
the merry glen of Rushen.   He is condemned to remain in
the Isle of Man till doomsday, in a wild form, covered with
long shaggy hair, whence his name.

He is very kind and obliging to the people, sometimes
driving home the sheep, or cutting and gathering the hay, if
he sees a storm coming on.   On one of these occasions, a
farmer having expressed his displeasure with him for not
having cut the grass close enough to the ground, he let him
cut it himself the next year; but he went after him stubbing
up the roots so fast, that it was with difficulty that the
farmer could escape having his legs cut off.   For several
years no one would venture to mow that meadow; at length
a soldier undertook it, and by beginning in the centre of the
field, and cutting round, as if on the edge of a circle, keeping
one eye on the scythe, and looking out for the Phynnodderee
with the other, he succeeded in cutting the grass in safety.

A gentleman having resolved to build a large house on his
property, at a place called Sholt-e-will, near the foot of Sna-
field mountain, caused the stones to be quarried on the
beach.   There was one large block of white stone which he
was very anxious to have, but all the men in the parish could
not move it.   To their surprise, the Phynnodderee in the
course of one night conveyed all the stones that had been
quarried, the great white one included, up to the proposed
site, and the white stone is there still to be seen.   The
gentleman, to reward the Phynnodderee, caused some clothes
to be left for him in one of his usual haunts.   When he saw
them, he lifted them up one by one, saying in Manks:

Bayrm da'n choine, dy doogh da'n choine,
Cooat da'n dreeym, dy doogh da'n dreeym,
Breechyn da'n toyn, dy doogh da'n toyn,
Agh my she lhiat ooiley, shoh cha nee lhiat Glen reagh Rushen.

Cap for the head, alas, poor head !
Coat for the back, alas, poor back !
Breeches for the breech, alas, poor breech !
If these be all thine, thine cannot be the merry glen of Rushen.

And he departed with a melancholy wail, and has never been seen since. The old people say, "There has not been a merry world since he lost his ground."[*]

WALES.

It was the Druid's presage, who had long
In Geirionydd's[†] airy temple marked
The songs that from the Gwyllion[‡] rose, of eve
The children, in the bosom of the lakes.
                                        TALIESIN.

THE oldest account we have met with of Welsh Fairies is in the Itinerary of Giraldus Cambrensis, who, in the year 1188, accompanied Archbishop Baldwin in his tour through Wales, undertaken for the purpose of exciting the zeal of the people to take part in the crusade then in contemplation.

Giraldus, who was an attentive observer of nature and of mankind, has in this work given many beautiful descriptions of scenery, and valuable traits of manners. He is liberal of legends of saints, but such was the taste of his age. Among his narratives, however, he gives the two following, which show that there was a belief in South Wales in beings similar to the Fairies and Hobgoblins of England.

Tale of Elidurus.

A SHORT time before our days, a circumstance worthy of note occurred in these parts, which Elidurus, a priest, most strenuously affirmed had befallen himself. When he was a

---

[*] Train, Account of the Isle of Man, ii. p. 148.
[†] A lake, on whose banks Taliesin resided.
[‡] These Mr. Davies thinks correspond to the Gallicenæ of Mela: see *Brittany*.

The leprechaun, a shoe maker, is as a rule, a solitary
and rather morose creature

Welsh fairies

youth of twelve years,—since, as Solomon says, " The root of learning is bitter, although the fruit is sweet,"—and was following his literary pursuits, in order to avoid the discipline and frequent stripes inflicted on him by his preceptor, he ran away, and concealed himself under the hollow bank of a river; and, after fasting in that situation for two days, two little men of pygmy stature appeared to him, saying, " If you will come with us, we will lead you into a country full of delights and sports." Assenting, and rising up, he followed his guides through a path, at first subterraneous and dark, into a most beautiful country, adorned with rivers and meadows, woods and plains, but obscure, and not illuminated with the full light of the sun. All the days were cloudy, and the nights extremely dark, on account of the absence of the moon and stars. The boy was brought before the king, and introduced to him in the presence of the court; when, having examined him for a long time, he delivered him to his son, who was then a boy. These men were of the smallest stature, but very well proportioned for their size. They were all fair-haired, with luxuriant hair falling over their shoulders, like that of women. They had horses proportioned to themselves, of the size of greyhounds. They neither ate flesh nor fish, but lived on milk diet, made up into messes with saffron. They never took an oath, for they detested nothing so much as lies. As often as they returned from our upper hemisphere, they reprobated our ambition, infidelities, and inconstancies. They had no religious worship, being only, as it seems, strict lovers and reverers of truth.

The boy frequently returned to our hemisphere, sometimes by the way he had first gone, sometimes by another; at first in company with others, and afterwards alone, and confided his secret only to his mother, declaring to her the manners, nature, and state of that people. Being desired by her to bring a present of gold, with which that region abounded, he stole, while at play with the king's son, the golden ball with which he used to divert himself, and brought it to his mother in great haste; and when he reached the door of his father's house, but not unpursued, and was entering it in a great hurry, his foot stumbled on the threshold, and, falling down into the room where his mother was sitting, the two Pygmies seized the ball, which had dropped from his hand, and departed, spitting at and deriding the boy. On recovering from his fall, confounded with shame, and execrating the evil counsel of his mother, he returned by the usual track to the subterraneous road, but found no appearance of any passage, though he searched for it on the banks of the river for nearly the space of a year. Having been brought back by his friends and mother, and restored to his right way of thinking and his literary pursuits, he attained in process of time the rank of priesthood. Whenever David the Second, bishop of St. David's, talked to him in his advanced state of life concerning this event, he could never relate the particulars without shedding tears.

He had also a knowledge of the language of that nation, and used to recite words of it he had readily acquired in his younger days. These words, which the bishop often repeated to me, were very conformable to the Greek idiom. When they asked for water, they said, *Udor udorum*, which signifies "Bring water;" for Udor, in their language, as well as in the Greek, signifies water; and Dwr also, in the British language, signifies water. When they want salt, they say, *Halgein udorum*, "Bring salt." Salt is called ἁλς in Greek, and Halen in British; for that language, from the length of time which the Britons (then called Trojans, and afterwards Britons from Brito, their leader) remained in Greece after the destruction of Troy, became, in many instances, similar to the Greek.*

"If," says the learned archdeacon, "a scrupulous inquirer should ask my opinion of the relation here inserted, I answer, with Augustine, 'admiranda fore divina miracula non disputatione discutienda;' nor do I, by denial, place bounds to the Divine power; nor, by affirming insolently, extend that power which cannot be extended. But on such occasions I always call to mind that saying of Hieronymus: "Multa," says he, 'incredibilia reperies et non verisimilia, quæ nihilominus tamen vera sunt.' These, and any such that might occur, I should place, according to Augustine's opinion, among those things which are neither to be strongly affirmed nor denied."

---

* Giraldus Cambrensis, Itinerarium Cambriæ, l. i. c. 8, translated by Sir R. C. Hoare.

David Powel, who edited this work in 1585, thinks that this legend is written in imitation of the relation of Eros the Armenian, in Plato, or taken from Polo's account of the garden of the Old Man of the Mountain.*

Again Giraldus writes,—" In these parts of Penbroch it has happed, in our times, that unclean spirits have conversed with mankind, not indeed visibly, but sensibly; for they manifested their presence at first in the house of one Stephen Wiriet, and some time after of William Not, by throwing dirt and such things as rather indicate an intention of mockery and injury. In the house of William, the spirit used to make rents and holes in both linen and woollen garments, to the frequent loss of both host and guest, from which injury no care and no bolts could protect them. In the house of Stephen, which was still more extraordinary, the spirit used to converse with people; and when they taunted him, which they frequently did out of sport, he used to charge them openly with those actions of theirs, from their birth, which they least wished to be heard or known by others. If you ask the cause and reason of this matter, I do not take on me to assign it; only this, that it, as is said, used to be the sign of a sudden change, either from poverty to riches, or rather from riches to desolation and poverty, as it was found to be a little after with both of these. But this I think worthy of remark, that places cannot be freed from illusions of this kind by the sprinkling of holy water, not merely of the ordinary, but even of the great kind; nor by the aid of any ecclesiastical sacrament. Nay, the priests themselves, when coming in with devotion, and fortified as well with the cross as with holy water, were forthwith among the first defiled by the dirt thrown at them. From which it would appear that both sacramentals and sacraments defend from hurtful, not harmless things, and from injury, not from illusion." †

---

* Very likely indeed that Elidurus, or Giraldus either, should know any thing of Plato or of Marco Polo, especially as the latter was not yet born !
† Book i. chap. 12.

The Tylwyth Teg.

In the mountains near Brecknock, says Davies,* there is a
small lake, to which tradition assigns some of the properties
of the fabled Avernus. I recollect a Mabinogi, or mythologic tale, respecting this piece of water, which runs thus :—

In ancient times a door in a rock near this lake was
found open upon a certain day every year. I think it was
May-day. Those who had the curiosity and resolution to
enter were conducted by a secret passage, which terminated
in a small island in the centre of the lake. Here the
visitors were surprised with the prospect of a most enchant-
ing garden stored with the choicest fruits and flowers, and
inhabited by the Tylwyth Têg, or Fair Family, a kind of
Fairies, whose beauty could be equalled only by the courtesy
and affability which they exhibited to those who pleased
them. They gathered fruit and flowers for each of their
guests, entertained them with the most exquisite music, dis-
closed to them many secrets of futurity, and invited them to
stay as long as they should find their situation agreeable.
But the island was secret, and nothing of its produce must
be carried away. The whole of this scene was invisible to
those who stood without the margin of the lake. Only an
indistinct mass was seen in the middle ; and it was observed
that no bird would fly over the water, and that a soft strain
of music at times breathed with rapturous sweetness in the
breeze of the morning.

It happened upon one of these annual visits that a sacrilegious wretch, when he was about to leave the garden, put
a flower, with which he had been presented, in his pocket ;
but the theft boded him no good. As soon as he had touched
unhallowed ground the flower vanished and he lost his
senses. Of this injury the Fair Family took no notice at
the time. They dismissed their guests with their accustomed courtesy, and the door was closed as usual. But their

* Mythology and Rites of the British Druids.

resentment ran high. For though, as the tale goes, the Tylwyth Têg and their garden undoubtedly occupy the spot to this day, though the birds still keep at a respectful distance from the lake, and some broken strains of music are still heard at times, yet the door which led to the island has never re-opened, and from the date of this sacrilegious act the Cymry have been unfortunate.

Some time after this, an adventurous person attempted to draw off the water, in order to discover its contents, when a terrific form arose from the midst of the lake, commanding him to desist, or otherwise he would drown the country.

These Tylwyth Têg are, as we see, regarded as Fairies, but we think improperly; for diminutive size is an attribute of the Fairies in all parts of the British Isles, and Mr. Owen (in his Welsh Dictionary, *s. v.*) expressly says that such is not the case with these beings.

The Spirit of the Van.

AMONG the mountains of Carmarthen, lies a beautiful and romantic piece of water, named The Van Pools. Tradition relates, that after midnight, on New Year's Eve, there appears on this lake a being named The Spirit of the Van. She is dressed in a white robe, bound by a golden girdle; her hair is long and golden, her face is pale and melancholy; she sits in a golden boat, and manages a golden oar.

Many years ago there lived in the vicinity of this lake a young farmer, who having heard much of the beauty of this spirit, conceived a most ardent desire to behold her, and be satisfied of the truth. On the last night of the year, he therefore went to the edge of the lake, which lay calm and bright beneath the rays of the full moon, and waited anxiously for the first hour of the New Year. It came, and then he beheld the object of his wishes gracefully guiding her golden gondola to and fro over the lake. The moon at length sank

behind the mountains, the stars grew dim at the approach
of dawn, and the fair spirit was on the point of vanishing,
when, unable to restrain himself, he called aloud to her to
stay and be his wife; but with a faint cry she faded from his
view.   Night after night he now might be seen pacing the
shores of the lake, but all in vain.   His farm was neglected,
his person wasted away, and gloom and melancholy were
impressed on his features.   At length he confided his secret
to one of the mountain-sages, whose counsel was—a Welsh
one, by the way—to assail the fair spirit with gifts of cheese
and bread!   The counsel was followed; and on Midsummer
Eve the enamoured swain went down to the lake, and let fall
into it a large cheese and a loaf of bread.   But all was vain;
no spirit rose.   Still he fancied that the spot where he had
last seen her shone with more than wonted brightness, and
that a musical sound vibrated among the rocks.   Encouraged
by these signs, he night after night threw in loaves and
cheeses, but still no spirit came.   At length New Year's
Eve returned.   He dressed himself in his best, took his
largest cheese and seven of his whitest loaves, and repaired
to the lake.   At the turn of midnight, he dropped them
slowly one by one into the water, and then remained in
silent expectation.   The moon was hid behind a cloud, but
by the faint light she gave, he saw the magic skiff appear,
and direct its course for where he stood.   Its owner stepped
ashore, and hearkened to the young man's vows, and consented to become his wife.   She brought with her as her
dower flocks and herds, and other rural wealth.   One charge
she gave him, never to strike her, for the third time he
should do so she would vanish.

They married, and were happy.   After three or four years
they were invited to a christening, and to the surprise of all
present, in the midst of the ceremony, the spirit burst into
tears.   Her husband gave an angry glance, and asked her
why she thus made a fool of herself?   She replied, "The
poor babe is entering in a world of sin and sorrow, and
misery lies before it; why should I rejoice?"   He gave her
a push.   She warned him that he had struck her once.
Again they were, after some time, invited to attend the
funeral of that very child.   The spirit now laughed, and
danced, and sang.   Her husband's wrath was excited, and he

asked her why she thus made a fool of herself? "The babe," she said, "has left a world of sin and sorrow, and escaped the misery that was before it, and is gone to be good and happy for ever and ever. Why, then, should I weep?" He gave her a push from him, and again she warned him. Still they lived happily as before. At length they were invited to a wedding, where the bride was young and fair, the husband a withered old miser. In the midst of the festivity, the spirit burst into a copious flood of tears, and to her husband's angry demand of why she thus made a fool of herself, she replied in the hearing of all, "Because summer and winter cannot agree. Youth is wedded to age for paltry gold. I see misery here, and tenfold misery hereafter, to be the lot of both. It is the devil's compact." Forgetful of her warnings, the husband now thrust her from him with real anger. She looked at him tenderly and reproachfully, and said, "You have struck me for the third and last time. Farewell!"

So saying, she left the place. He rushed out after her, and just reached his home in time to see her speeding to the lake, followed by all her flocks and herds. He pursued her, but in vain; his eyes never more beheld her.*

As far as we have been able to learn, the belief in Fairies is confined in Wales to the southern counties of Glamorgan,

---

* Abridged from " A Day at the Van Pools ;" MS. of Miss Beale, the author of " Poems" and of " The Vale of the Towey," a most delightful volume. We have since received from our gifted friend the following additional information. " Since writing this letter, I have heard a new version of the last part of the Spirit of the Van. The third offence is said to be, that she and her husband were *ploughing*; he guiding the plough, and she driving the horses. The horses went wrong, and the husband took up something and threw it at them, which struck her. She seized the plough and went off, followed by the flocks and herds she had brought with her to Van Pool, where they all vanished, and the *mark of the ploughshare* is shown on the mountain at this present day. She left her children behind her, who became famous as doctors. Jones was their name, and they lived at a place called Muddfi. In them was said to have originated the tradition of the seventh son, or Septimus, being born for the healing art ; as for many generations, seven sons were regularly born in each family, the seventh of whom became the doctor, and wonderful in his profession. It is said even now, that the Jones of Muddfi are, or were, until very recently, clever doctors."—A. B. A somewhat different version of this legend is given by Mr. Croker, iii. 256.

Carmarthen, and Pembroke, the parts into which the Saxons had penetrated farthest, and where they of course had exercised most influence. In these counties the popular belief in these beings is by no means yet extinct, and their attributes in the creed of the Welsh peasant are similar to those of their British and Irish kindred.

The usual name given to the fairies in these parts of Wales, is Y Dynon Bach Têg, i. e. *The Little Fair People.* Ellyll, in the plural Ellyllon, also signifies an Elf, from which word, indeed, it may have been derived. The bells of the Digitalis or fox-glove are called Menyg·Ellyllon, or the Elves'-gloves; in Ireland, also, they are connected with the fairies. The toadstools or poisonous mushrooms are named Bwyd Ellyllon, or Elves'-food. Perhaps, however, it is not the large ugly toadstools that are so named, but those pretty small delicate fungi, with their conical heads, which are named Fairy-mushrooms in Ireland, where they grow so plentifully. Finally, there was formerly in the park of Sir Robert Vaughan a celebrated old oak-tree, named Crwben-yr-Ellyll, or The Elf's Hollow-tree. The popular belief respecting these Ellyllon is, that they are the souls of the ancient Druids, who, being too good for relegation to Hell, and too evil for re-admittance to Heaven, are permitted to wander among men upon earth till the last day, when they also will enter on a higher state of being.*

The legends of which we will now proceed to give a specimen, were collected and published in the latter half of the eighteenth century, by a Welsh clergyman, who seems to have entertained no doubt whatever of the truth of the adventures contained in them.†

The two daughters of a respectable farmer in the parish of Bedwellty were one day out hay-making with their man

---

* For the chief part of our knowledge respecting the fairy lore of Wales we are indebted to the third or supplemental volume of the Fairy Legends, in which Mr. Croker, with the aid of Dr. Owen Pugh and other Welsh scholars, has given a fuller account of the superstitions of the people of the Principality, than is, we believe, to be found any where else.

† A Relation of Apparitions of Spirits in the County of Monmouth and the Principality of Wales, by the Rev. Edward Jones of the Tiarch.—For our extracts from this work we are indebted to Mr. Croker.

and maid servant and a couple of their neighbours, when on a hill, about quarter of a mile distant, they saw a large flock of sheep. Soon after, they saw them going up to a place half a mile off, and then going out of their sight as if they vanished in the air. About half-an-hour before sunset, they saw them again, but not all alike; for some saw them like sheep, some like greyhounds, some like swine, and some like naked infants. They appeared in the shade of the mountain between them and the sun, and the first sight was as if they rose out of the earth. "This was a notable appearance of the fairies, seen by credible witnesses. The sons of infidelity are very unreasonable not to believe the testimonies of so many witnesses of the being of spirits."

E. T. going home by night over Bedwellty Mountains, saw the fairies on each side of him. Some of them were dancing. He also heard the sound of a bugle-horn, as if people were hunting. He began to grow afraid, but recollecting to have heard that if, on seeing the fairies, you draw out your knife, they will vanish, he did so, and saw them no more. "This the old gentleman sincerely related to me. He was a sober man, and of the strictest veracity."

A young man having gone early one morning to a barn to feed oxen, when he had done, lay down on the hay to rest. As he lay he heard the sound of music approaching the barn, and presently came in a large company, wearing striped clothes (some more gay than others), and commenced dancing to their music. He lay quite still, thinking to escape their notice; but a woman, better dressed than the others, came up to him with a striped cushion, with a tassel at each corner, and put it under his head. Some time after, a cock was heard to crow, which seemed either to surprise or displease them, and they hastily drew the cushion from under his head, and went away.

P. W., "an honest virtuous woman," related that one time, when she was a little girl on her way to school, she saw the fairies dancing under a crab-tree. As they appeared to be children of her own size, and had small pleasant music, she went and joined in their exercise, and then took them to dance in an empty barn. This she continued to do for three or four years. As she never could hear the sound of their feet, she always took off her shoes, supposing noise to be displeasing to them. They were of small stature, looked rather old, and wore blue and green aprons. Her grandfather, who kept school in the parish-church, used, when going home from it late in the evening, to see the fairies dancing under an oak, within two or three fields of the church.

The learned writer gives finally a letter to himself, from a "pious young gentleman" of Denbighshire, dated March 24, 1772, in which he informs him, that about fifteen years before, as himself, his sister, and two other little girls were playing at noon of a summer's day in a field, they saw a company of dancers, about seventy yards from them. Owing to the rapidity of their whirling motions, they could not count them, but guessed them at fifteen or sixteen. They were in red, like soldiers, with red handkerchiefs spotted with yellow, on their heads. As they were gazing and wondering at them, one of the dancers came running towards them. The children, in a fright, made for an adjacent stile. The girls got over, but the boy was near being caught, and on looking back when over, he saw the red man stretching his arms after him over the stile, which it would seem he had not the power to cross. When they came to the house, which was close at hand, they gave the alarm, and people went out to search the fields, but could see nothing. The little man was very grim-looking, with a copper-coloured face. His running-pace was rather slow, but he took great strides for one of his size.

The following legends were collected in 1827, in the Vale of Neath, in Glamorganshire, by a lady with whom we became acquainted when travelling through North Wales, in the preceding autumn.*

An old woman assured our fair friend, that she one time, many years before, saw the fairies to the number of some hundreds. They were very small, were mounted on little white horses, not bigger than dogs, and rode four a-breast. It was almost dusk at the time, and they were not a quarter

---

* The lady's name was Williams. The legends were originally intended for the present work, but circumstances caused them to appear in the supplemental volume of the Irish Fairy Legends. We have abridged them.

of a mile from her. Another old woman said that her
father had often seen the fairies riding in the air on little
white horses, but he never saw them come down on the
ground. He also used to hear their music in the air. She
had heard, too, of a man who had been five-and-twenty years
with the fairies, and thought he had been away only five
minutes.

Rhys at the Fairy-Dance.

RHYS and Llewellyn, two farmer's servants, who had been
all day carrying lime for their master, were driving in the
twilight their mountain ponies before them, returning home
from their work. On reaching a little plain, Rhys called to
his companion to stop and listen to the music, saying it was
a tune to which he had danced a hundred times, and must go
and have a dance now. He bade him go on with the horses,
and he would soon overtake him. Llewellyn could hear
nothing, and began to remonstrate ; but away sprang Rhys,
and he called after him in vain. He went home, put up the
ponies, ate his supper, and went to bed, thinking that Rhys
had only made a pretext for going to the ale-house. But
when morning came, and still no sign of Rhys, he told his
master what had occurred. Search was then made everywhere, but no Rhys could be found. Suspicion now fell
upon Llewellyn of having murdered him, and he was thrown
into prison, though there was no evidence against him. A
farmer, however, skilled in fairy-matters, having an idea of
how things might have been, proposed that himself and some
others should accompany Llewellyn to the place where he
parted with Rhys. On coming to it, they found it green as
the mountain ash. "Hush!" cried Llewellyn, "I hear
music, I hear sweet harps." We all listened, says the
narrator, for I was one of them, but could hear nothing.
"Put your foot on mine, David," said he to me (his own
foot was at the time on the outward edge of the fairy-ring).
I did so, and so did we all, one after another, and then we
heard the sound of many harps, and saw within a circle,

about twenty feet across, great numbers of little people, of
the size of children of three or four years old, dancing
round and round. Among them we saw Rhys, and Llewellyn
catching him by the smock-frock, as he came by him, pulled
him out of the circle. "Where are the horses? where are
the horses?" cried he. "Horses, indeed!" said Llewellyn.
Rhys urged him to go home, and let him finish his dance, in
which he averred he had not been engaged more than five
minutes. It was by main force they took him from the
place. He still asserted he had been only five minutes away,
and could give no account of the people he had been with.
He became melancholy, took to his bed, and soon after died.
"The morning after," says the narrator, "we went to look
at the place, and we found the edge of the ring quite red, as
if trodden down, and I could see the marks of little heels,
about the size of my thumb-nail."

Gitto Bach.

GITTO BACH,* who was a fine boy, used often to ramble to
the top of the mountain to look after his father's sheep. On
his return, he would show his brothers and sisters pieces
of remarkably white paper, like crown-pieces, with letters
stamped upon them, which he said were given him by the
little children with whom he used to play on the mountain.
One day he did not return, and during two whole years no
account could be got of him, and the other children were
beginning to go up the mountain, and bring back some of
those white crown-pieces. At length, one morning, as their
mother opened the door, she saw Gitto sitting on the
threshold, with a bundle under his arm. He was dressed,
and looked exactly as when she last had seen him. To her
inquiry of where he had been for so long a time, he replied
that it was only the day before he had left her; and he bade
her look at the pretty clothes the little children on the
mountain had given him for dancing with them to the music

* Gitto is the dim. of Griffith : *bach* (*beg* Ir.) is little.

of their harps. The dress in the bundle was of very white paper, without seam or sewing. The prudent mother committed it to the flames.

"This," said the narrator, "made me more anxious than ever to see the fairies," and his wish was gratified by a gipsy, who directed him to find a four-leaved clover, and put it with nine grains of wheat on the leaf of a book which she gave him. She then desired him to meet her next night by moonlight on the top of Craig y Dinis. She there washed his eyes with the contents of a phial which she had, and he instantly saw thousands of fairies, all in white, dancing to the sounds of numerous harps. They then placed themselves on the edge of the hill, and sitting down and putting their hands round their knees, they tumbled down one after another, rolling head-over-heels till they disappeared in the valley.

Another old man, who was present at the preceding narration, averred that he had often seen the fairies at waterfalls; particularly at that of Sewyd yr Rhyd in Cwm Pergwm, Vale of Neath, where a road runs between the fall and the rock. As he stood behind the fall, they appeared in all the colours of the rainbow, and their music mingled with the noise of the water. They then retired into a cavern, which they had made in the rock, and, after enjoying themselves there, ascended the rock, and went off through the mountains, the sounds of their harps dying away as they receded.

The Fairies Banished.

ONE of those old farm-houses, where the kitchen and cow-house are on the same floor, with only a low partition between them, was haunted by the fairies. If the family were at their meals in the kitchen, *they* were racketing in the cow-house, and if the people were engaged about the cows, the fairies were making a riot in the kitchen. One day, when a parcel of reapers were at their harvest-dinner in the kitchen, the elves, who were laughing and dancing above, threw down such a quantity of dust and dirt as quite spoiled the dinner. While the mistress of the house was in perplexity about it, there came in an old woman, who, on hearing the case, said she could provide a remedy. She then told her in a whisper to ask six of the reapers to dinner next day in the hearing of the fairies, and only to make as much pudding as could be boiled in an egg-shell. She did as directed, and when the fairies saw that a dinner for six men was put down to boil in an egg-shell, there was great stir and noise in the cow-house, and at length one angry voice was heard to say, "We have lived long in this world; we were born just after the earth was made, and before the acorn was planted, and yet we never saw a harvest-dinner dressed in an egg-shell! There must be something wrong in this house, and we will stop here no longer." They went away and never returned.

The fairies are said to take away children, and leave changelings.* They also give pieces of money, one of which is found every day in the same place as long as the finder keeps his good fortune a secret. One peculiarity of the Cambrian fairies is, that every Friday night they comb the goats' beards "to make them decent for Sunday."

We hear not of Brownies or Kobolds in the Welsh houses now, but Puck used to haunt Wales as well as Ireland. His Welsh name, Pwcca, is the same as his Irish one. In Brecon there is Cwm Pwcca, or Puck's Glen, and though an iron-foundry has in a great measure scared him from it, yet he occasionally makes his appearance. As a man was returning one night from his work, he saw a light before him, and thought he discerned some one that carried it. Supposing it to be one of his fellow-workmen with a lanthorn, he quickened his pace to come up with him, wondering all the while how so short a man as he appeared to be could get over the ground so fast. He also fancied he was not going the right way, but still thought that he who had the light must know best. At last, he came up

* See *Brittany*.

with him, and found himself on the very edge of one of the precipices of Cwm Pwcca, down which another step would have carried him. The Pwcca, for it was he, sprang over the glen, turned round, held the light above his head, and then with a loud laugh put it out and vanished.

BRITTANY.

Mut unt este noble Barun
Cil de Bretaine li Bretun.
                    MARIE DE FRANCE.

Thise oldè gentil Bretons in hir dayes
Of diverse áventurès maden layes.
                    CHAUCER.

BRITTANY, the ancient Armorica, retains perhaps as un-mixed a population as any part of Western Europe. Its language has been, however, like the Welsh and the Celtic dialects, greatly affected by the Latin and Teutonic. The ancient intercourse kept up with Wales and Cornwall by the Bretons, who were in a great measure colonists from these parts of Britain, caused the traditions and poetry of the latter to be current and familiar in Little Britain, as that country was then called. To poetry and music, indeed, the whole Celto-Cymric race seem to have been strongly addicted; and, independently of the materials which Brit-tany may have supplied for the history of Geoffrey of Monmouth, many other true or romantic adventures were narrated by the Breton poets in their Lais. Several of these Lais were translated into French verse in the thirteenth century by a poetess named Marie de France, resident at the court of the English monarchs of the house of Plantagenet, to one of whom, probably Henry the Third, her Lais are dedicated.* This circumstance may account

---

* Poésies de Marie de France, par De Roquefort. Paris, 1820. If any one should suspect that these are not genuine translations from the Breton, his doubts will be dispelled by reading the original of the Lai du Laustic in the Barzan-Breiz (i. 24) presently to be noticed.

for the Lais being better known in England than in France. The only manuscript containing any number of them is in the Harleian Library; for those of France contain but five Lais. The Lai du Fresne was translated into English; and from the Lai de Lanval and Lai de Graelent—which last by the way is not in the Harleian Collection—Chestre made his Launfal Miles, or Sir Launfal. Chaucer perhaps took tne concluding circumstance of his Dream from the Lai de Eliduc.

In some of these Lais we meet with what may be regarded as Fairy machinery. The word Fée, indeed, occurs only once;* but in the Lais de Gugemer, de Lanval, d'Ywenec, and de Graelent, personages are to be met with differing in nothing from the Fays of Romance, and who, like them, appear to be human beings endowed with superior powers.

The origin of the Breton Korrigan, as they are called, has been sought, and not improbably, in the Gallicenæ† oɪ ancient Gaul, of whom Pomponius Mela thus writes:— "Sena,‡ in the British sea, opposite the Ofismician coast, is remarkable for an oracle of the Gallic God. Its priestesses, holy in perpetual virginity, are said to be *nine* in number. They are called Gallicenæ, and are thought to be endowed with singular powers, so as to raise by their charms the winds and seas, *to turn themselves into what animals they will*, to cure wounds and diseases incurable by others, to know and predict the future; but this they do only to navigators who go thither purposely to consult them."§

We have here certainly all the attributes of the Damoiselles of the Lais of Marie de France. The doe whom Gugemer wounds speaks with a human voice. The lady who loved Lanval took him away into an island, and Graelent and his mistress crossed a deep and broad river to arrive at her country, which perhaps was also an island in the original Breton Lai. The part most difficult of explanation is the secret manner in which these dames used to visit their

---

* See above, p. 21.

† The Bas-Breton *Korrigan* or *Korrigwen* differs, as we may see, but little from *Gallican*. Strabo (i. p .304) says that Demeter and *Kora* were worshipped in an island in these parts.

‡ Sena is supposed to be L'Isle des Saints, nearly opposite Brest.

§ Pomp. Mela, iii. 6.

Korrigans

A Swedish elf

.overs; but perhaps the key is to be found in the Lai d'Ywenec, of which, chiefly on that account, we give an analysis. The hero of that Lai differs not in point of power from these ladies, and as he is a real man, with the power of assuming at will the shape of a bird, so it is likely they were real women, and that it was in the bird-shape they entered the chambers of their lovers. Graelent's mistress says to him,*

> I shall love you trewely;
> But one thing I forbid straitlý,
> You must not utter a word apérte
> Which might our love make discovérte.
> I will give unto you richlý,
> Gold and silver, clothes, and fee.
> Much love shall be between us two—
> Night and day I'll go to you:
> You'll see me come to you alwáy—
> With me laugh and talk you may.
> You shall no comrade have to see,
> Or who shall know my privacy,
> *   *   *
> Take care now that you do not boast
> Of things by which I may be lost.

The lady says to Lanval,

> When you would speak to me of ought—
> You must in no place form the thought
> Where no one could meet his amie
> Without reproach and villainie—
> I will be presently with you,
> All your commands ready to do ;
> No one but you will me see,
> Or hear the words that come from me.

She also had previously imposed on the knight the obligation of secresy.

As a further proof of the identity of the Korrigan and the Gallicenæ, it may be remarked, that in the evidently very ancient Breton poem, Ar-Rannou, or The Series, we

---

* It might seem hardly necessary to inform the reader that these verses and those that follow, are our own translations, from Marie de France. Yet some have taken them for old English verses.

meet the following passage:—"There are *nine* Korrigen, who dance, with flowers in their hair, and robes of white wool, around the fountain, by the light of the full moon." *

Lai D'ywenec.

I HAVE in thought and purpose too,
Of Ywenec to tellen you—
Of whom he born was, his sire's fame,
How first he to his mother came.
He who did beget Ywenec
Y-cleped was Eudemarec.

There formerly lived in Britain a man who was rich and old. He was Avoez or governor of Caerwent on the Doglas, and lord of the surrounding country. Desirous of having an heir to his estates, he espoused a maiden " courteous and sage, and passing fair." She was given to him because he was rich, and loved by him for her beauty. Why should I say more, but that her match was not to be found between Lincoln and Ireland ? " Great sin did they who gave her him," adds the poet.

On account of her rare beauty, the jealous husband now turned all his thoughts to keeping her safe. To this end he shut her up in his tower, in a large room, to which no one had access but himself and his sister, an old widow, without whose permission the young wife was forbidden to speak to any even of her female attendants. In this tower the suspicious husband immured his lovely bride for seven years, during which time they had no children, nor did she ever leave her confinement on any account. She had neither chamberlain nor huissier to light the tapers in her chamber when she would retire, and the poor lady passed her time

---

* E korole nao c'horrigan,
Bleunvek ho bleo, gwisket gloan,
Kelc'h ar feunteun, d'al loar-gann.

VILLEMARQUÉ, *Barzan-Breiz*, i. 8.

The *c'h* expresses the guttural.

weeping, sighing, and lamenting; and from grief and neglect
of herself losing all her beauty.

> The month of April was entering,
> When every bird begins to sing;
> Her lord arose at early day,
> And to the wood he takes his way.

Before he set out he called up the old dame to fasten the
door after him. This done, she took her psalter and retired
to another room to chant it. The imprisoned lady awoke in
tears, seeing the brightness of the sun, and thus began
her moan:

> Alas! said she, why born was I?
> Right grievous is my destiny:
> In this towére imprisoned,
> I ne'er shall leave it till I'm dead.

She marvels at the unreasonable jealousy of her old husband,
curses her parents, and all concerned in giving her to a man
not only so unamiable, but who was of so tough a constitution that the chance of his dying seemed infinitely remote.

> When baptised he was to be,
> In hell's rivere deep dipt was he;
> Hard are his sinews, hard each vein,
> And lively blood they all contain.
>   Oft have I heard the people tell,
> That in this country there befell
> Adventures in the days of yore,
> That did to joy grieved hearts restore;
> Knights met with damsels, fair and gent,
> In all things unto their talént;
> And dames met lovers courteoús,
> Handsome, and brave, and generous;
> So that they never blamed were,
> For save themselves none saw them e'er.*
> If this may be, or ever was,
> Or any it befallen has,
> May God, who hath all might and power,
> My wish perform for me this hour.

Scarcely had she uttered this pious wish, when she per-

---

* This manifestly alludes to Lanval or Graelent, or similar stories.

ceived the shadow of a large bird at a narrow window. The bird now flew into the room. He had jesses on his legs, and appeared to be a goss-hawk.* He placed himself before the lady, and in a few minutes after became a handsome gentle knight. The lady was terrified at the sight, and covered her head; but the knight was courteous, and addressed her,

> Lady, said he, be not thus stirred;
> A goss-hawk is a gentle bird.
> If my secréte should be obscure,
> Attend, and I will you assure;
> Maketh now of me your lovére,
> For that it is I am come here.
> Long have I loved you and admired,
> And in my heart have much desired;
> I ne'er have loved save you alone,
> And save you never shall love none;
> But I could never come to you,
> Nor from own countrie issúe,
> If you had not required me:
> Your lover now I may well be.

The lady was now re-assured: she uncovered her head, and told the knight she would accept him as her *Dru*, if she were satisfied that he believed in God. On this head, he assures her,

> I in the Créator believe,
> Who did from misery us relieve,
> In which us Adam our sire put,
> By eating of that bitter fruit:
> He is, and was, and ever he
> To sinners life and light will be.

And to put the matter out of all doubt, he directs her to feign sickness, and send for the chaplain, when he undertakes to assume her form, and receive the holy Sacrament. The dame does accordingly; and the old woman, after many objections, at length sends for the chaplain.

---

* It follows, in M. de Roquefort's edition,

> "Deci ne muez fu ou désis."

Of which we can make no sense, and the French translation gives no aid. In the Harleian MS. it is

> "De cinc muez fu ou de sis,"

which is more intelligible.

And he with all due speed did hie,
And brought the Corpus Domini.
The knight received the holy sign,
And from the chalice drank the wine :*
The chaplain then his way is gone—
The old dame shut the doors anon.

The scruples of the lady being now entirely removed, she grants *le don d'amoureuse merci*, and the bliss of the lovers is complete. At length the knight takes his leave, and in reply to the lady's question, of when she should see him again, he tells her that she has only to wish for him, and the wish will be fulfilled by his appearance ;† but he warns her to beware of the old woman, who will closely watch her, assuring her at the same time that a discovery will be his certain death.

The lady now bids adieu to all sadness and melancholy, and gradually regains all her former beauty. She desires no longer to leave her tower ; for, night or day, she has only to express a wish, and her knight is with her. The old lord marvels greatly at this sudden change, and begins to distrust the fidelity of his sister. On revealing his suspicions, her replies fully satisfy him on that head, and they concert between them how to watch the young wife, and to discover her secret. After an interval of three days, the old lord tells his wife that the king has sent for him, and that he must attend him, but will soon return. He sets out, and the old woman having closed the door as usual after him,

---

* This tends to prove that this is a translation from the Breton ; for Innocent III., in whose pontificate the cup was first refused to the laity, died in 1216, when Henry III., to whom Marie is supposed to have dedicated her Lais, was a child.

† The same was the case with the Wünschelweib (*Wish-woman*) of German romance.

> Swenne du einêst wünschest nâch mir,
> Sô bin ich endelîchen bî dír,

says the lady to the Staufenberger. She adds,

> Wâr ich wil dâ bin ich,
> Den Wunsch hât mir Got gegeben.

He finds it to be true,

> Er wûnschte nach der frouwen sîn,
> Bî îm sô war diu schöne sîn.

GRIMM, *Deut. Mythol.*, p. 391.

gets behind a curtain to watch. The lady now wishes for her lover, and instantly he is with her, and they continue together till it is time to rise. He then departs, leaving the spy, who had seen how he came and went, terrified at the strange metamorphosis.

When the husband, who was at no great distance, came home, his spy informed him of the strange affair. Greatly grieved and incensed at this, he began to meditate the destruction of his rival. He accordingly got four pikes made, with steel-heads so sharp that

> No razor under heaven's sheen
> Was ever yet so sharp and keen.

These he set at the window through which the knight was used to enter. Next day he feigns to go to the chase, the old woman returns to her bed to sleep, and the lady anxiously expects " him whom she loveth loyally,"

> And says that he may come safelý,
> And with her at all leisure be.

So said, so done: the bird was at the window; but alas! too eager for caution, he overlooked the pikes, and, flying against them, was mortally wounded. Still he entered the chamber and threw himself on the bed, which his blood soon filled, and thus addressed his distracted mistress :

> He said unto her—" My sweet friend,
> For you my life comes to an end ;
> I often told you 't would be so,
> That your fair cheer would work us woe."
> When she heard this she swooned away,
> And long time there for dead she lay ;
> Her gently to herself he brought,
> And said, that grief availeth nought ;
> That she by him a son would bear,
> Valiant and wise, and debonair ;
> He would dispel her sorrows all.
> Ywenec she should him call.
> He wouldè vengeance for their sake
> Upon their trait'rous enemy take.*

* In the Shâh-nâmeh, Siyawush, when he foresees his own death by the

Exhausted with loss of blood, he can stay no longer. He departs; and the lady, uttering loud cries of woe, leaps after him, unapparelled as she is, out of the window, which was twenty feet from the ground, and pursues him by the traces of his blood.

> Along his path strayed the dame,
> Until unto a hill she came.*
> Into this hill one entrance led;
> It with the blood was all sprinkléd.
> Before her she can nothing see;
> Whereat she thinketh full surelý
> Her lover thither is gone in.
> She entereth with mickle teen;
> Within it light ne found she none;
> Thorow it still she goeth on,
> Until she from the hill issúed
> In a fair meadow, rich and good.
> With blood she stained found the grass,
> At which she much dismayed was;
> The trace lay of it on the ground.
> Quite near she there a city found;
> With walls it was enclosed all.—
> There was not house, nor tower, nor hall,
> That did not seem of silver fair:
> The Mandevent† right wealthy are.
> Before the town lay marshes rude,
> The forest, and wild solitude.
> On the other side, toward the donjón,
> The water all around did run;
> And here the shippès did entér,
> More thannè three hundréd they were.
> The lower gate wide open lay;
> Therein the lady took her way,

treachery of Afrasiâb, tells his wife Ferengis, the daughter of that monarch, that she will bear a son whom she is to name Ky Khosroo, and who will avenge the death of his father : see Görres, Heldenbuch von Iran, ii. 32.

> * Desi k'a une hoge vint :
> En cele hoge ot une entree.

M. de Roquefort, in his Glossaire de la Langue Romaine, correctly renders *hoge* by *colline.* In his translation of this Lai he renders it by *cabane*, not, perhaps, understanding how a hill could be pervious. The story, however, of Prince Ahmed, and the romance of Orfeo and Heurodis (see above, p. 52), are good authority on this point : see also above, pp. 405, 408.

† In the Harleian MS. Mandement. M. de Roquefort confesses his total ignorance of this people ; we follow his example. May it not, however, be connected with *manant*, and merely signify people, inhabitants?

> Stil following the blood, that fell
> The townè thorow to the castél.
> Unto her spaké there no one,
> Ne man nor woman found she none.
> She to the palace came; with blood
> The steps she found were all embrued;
> She entered then a low chambére;
> A knight she found fast sleeping there;
> She knew him not—she passed on—
> To a larger chamber came anon;
> A bed, and nothing more, there found,
> A knight was on it sleeping sound.
> Still farther passed on the dame;
> Unto the third chambére she came,
> Where she gan find her lover's bed.
> The posts were gold enamelled;
> I could not price the clothes aright:
> The chandeliers and tapers bright,
> Which night and day burned constantly,
> Were worth the gold of a citee.

She finds her lover at the point of death.

At seeing his wretched state the unhappy lady swoons again. The expiring knight endeavours to console her; and, foretelling his own death on that day, directs her to depart, lest his people in their grief should ill treat her as the cause of his death. She, however, protests that she will stay and die with him, as, if she returns, her husband will put her to death. The knight repeats his consolations, and gives her a ring, which, while she wears, her husband will retain no remembrance of what relates to her. At the same time he gives her his sword, which she is to keep safely and to give to her son when grown up and become a valiant knight. He says, she then

> Unto a festival will go;
> Her lord will thither wend also;
> Unto an abbey they will come,
> Where they will see a stately tomb,
> Will learn the story of the dead,
> And how he was there buried.
> There thou the sword shalt to him reach,
> And all the ádventure then teach,
> How he was born, who was his sire;
> His deeds enough will then admire.

He then gave her a dress of fine silk, and insisted on her

departure. She is with difficulty induced to leave him, and is hardly half a league from the place when she hears the bells tolling, and the cries of grief of the people for the death of their lord. She faints four times, but at length recovering retraces her steps, and returns to her tower. Her husband makes no inquiry, and gives her no farther uneasiness. She bare a son, as Eudemarec had foretold, and named him Ywenec. As he grew up, there was not his peer in the kingdom for beauty, valour, and generosity.

After Ywenec had been dubbed a knight, his supposed father was summoned to attend the feast of St. Aaron at Carlion. He went, accompanied by his wife and Ywenec. On their way, they stopped at a rich abbey, where they were received with the utmost hospitality. Next day, when they asked to depart, the abbot entreated them to stay a little longer till he should show them the rest of the abbey. They consented, and after dinner,

> On entering the chapter-room,
> They found a large and stately tomb,
> Covered with rich tapestry,
> Bordered with gold embroidery.
> At head and feet and sides there were
> Twenty tapers burning clear;
> Of fine gold were the chandeliers;
> Of amethyst were the censéres,
> With which they incensed alwáy,
> For great honoúr, this tomb each day.

The curiosity of the visitors was excited by the sight of this magnificent tomb, and they learned, on inquiry, that therein lay one of the noblest and most valiant knights that had ever lived. He had been king of that country, and had been slain at Caerwent for the love of a lady, leaving a vacancy in the throne which had never been since filled, it being reserved, according to his last commands, for his son by that lady.

When the Dame heard this, she called aloud to her son,

> "Fair son, you now have heard," she said,
> "That God hath us to this place led.
> It is your father here doth lie,
> Whom this old man slew wrongfully."

She then gave him the sword she had kept so long, relating

the whole story to him. At the conclusion she fainted on
the tomb, and expired. Filled with rage and grief, Ywenec
at one blow struck off the head of the old man, and avenged
both his father and mother. The lady was buried in the
coffin with him whom she had loved, and the people joyfully
acknowledged Ywenec as king of the country.

> Long time after maden they,
> Who heard this ádventure, a Lay
> Of the grief and the doloúr
> That for love these did endure.

There are still to be seen in Brittany the rock, the cavern,
the fountain, the hole, the valley, etc., of the Fées.

The forest of Brezeliande, near Quintin, was, in the twelfth
and thirteenth centuries, regarded as the chief seat of Breton
wonders. It contained the tomb of Merlin. Robert de
Wace, hearing of the wonders of this forest, visited it; but,
by his own account, to little purpose.

> La allai je merveilles querre (*chercher*),
> Vis la forêt et vis la terre;
> Merveilles quis (*cherchai*) mais ne trovai,
> Fol m'en revins, fol y allai;
> Fol y allai, fol m'en revins,
> Folie quis, por fol me tins.*

There were also the Fountain of Berenton and the Perron
(*block*, or *steps*) Merveilleux.

> En Bretagne ce treuve-on
> Une Fontaine et un Perron;
> Quant on gette l'iaue (*eau*) dessus
> Si vente et tonne et repluit jus (*à bas*).

Huon de Méry was more fortunate than Wace. He
sprinkled the Perron from the golden basin which hung
from the oak that shaded it, and beheld all the marvels.†

Such is the result of our inquiries respecting the Fairy

---

* Roman de Roux, *v.* ii. 234.

† See Roquefort, Supplément au Glossaire de la Langue Romaine, *s. v.*
Perron.

system of the "oldè gentil Bretons." Owing to the praise-
worthy labours of a Breton gentleman of the present day,*
we are enabled to give the following account of it as it
actually prevails in Brittany.

Our author divides the Breton fairies into two classes,—
the Fays (*Fées*) and the Dwarfs (*Nains*); of which the
Breton name seems to be Korrig or Korrigan, and Korr or
Korred.† The former he identifies, as we have seen, very
plausibly, with the Gallicenæ of Mela; for he says that the
ancient Welsh bards declare that they reverenced a being of
the female sex named Korid-gwen, *i. e.* Korid-woman, to
whom they assigned *nine* virgins as attendants. To this
being Taliesin gives a magic vase, the edges of which are
adorned with pearl, and it contains the wondrous water of
bardic genius and of universal knowledge.

The Korrigan, our authority further states, can predict the
future, assume any form they please, move from place to
place with the rapidity of thought, cure maladies by the aid
of charms which they communicate to their favourites. Their
size is said not to exceed two feet, but their proportions are
most exact; and they have long flowing hair, which they
comb out with great care. Their only dress is a long white
veil, which they wind round their body. Seen at night, or
in the dusk of the evening, their beauty is great; but in the
daylight their eyes appear red, their hair white, and their
faces wrinkled; hence they rarely let themselves be seen by
day. They are fond of music, and have fine voices, but are
not much given to dancing. Their favourite haunts are the
springs, by which they sit and comb their hair. They are

---

* Barzan-Breiz, Chants Populaires de la Bretagne, recueilles et publiés par
Th. Hersart de la Villemarqué. Paris, 1846. This is a most valuable work
and deserving to take its place with the Ballads of Scotland, Scandinavia, and
Servia, to none of which is it inferior. To the credit of France the edition
which we use is the fourth. How different would the fate of such a work be
in this country!

† We make this distinction, because in the ballads in which the personage
is a Fay, the word used is Korrigan or Korrig, while in that in which the
Dwarfs are actors, the words are Korr and Korred. But the truth is, they are
all but different forms of Korr. They are all the same, singular and plural.
The Breton changes its first consonant like the Irish: see p. 371. We also
meet with Crion, Goric, Couril, as names of these beings, but they are only
forms of those given above.

said to celebrate there every returning spring a great nocturnal festival. On the sod at its brink is spread a table-cloth
white as the driven snow, covered with the most delicious
viands. In the centre is a crystal cup, which emits such
light that there is no need of lamps. At the end of the
banquet a cup goes round filled with a liquor, one drop of
which would make one as wise as God himself. At the
approach of a mortal the whole vanishes.

Like fairies in general the Korrigan steal children, against
which the remedy usually employed is, to place the child
under the protection of the Virgin, by putting a rosary or
a scapulary about its neck. They are also fond of uniting
themselves with handsome young men to regenerate, as the
peasants say, their accursed race. The general belief respecting them is, that they were great princesses who,
having refused to embrace Christianity when it was preached
in Armorica by the Apostles, were struck by the curse of
God. Hence it is that they are said to be animated by a
violent hatred of religion and the clergy. The sight of a
soutane, or the sound of a bell, puts them to flight; but
the object of greatest abhorrence to them is the Holy
Virgin. The last trait to be noticed of these beings is,
that, like similar beings in other countries, their breath is
deadly.

The reader must have observed the strong resemblance
which the Korrigan bear to the Elle-maids of Scandinavia.
In like manner the Korred are very similar to the Trolls.*
These are usually represented as short and stumpy with
shaggy hair, dark wrinkled faces, little deep-set eyes, but
bright as carbuncles. Their voice is cracked and hollow:
their hands have claws like a cat's; their feet are horny like
those of a goat. They are expert smiths and coiners; they
are said to have great treasures in the *dolmen*† in which
they dwell, and of which they are regarded as the builders.
They dance around them by night, and wo to the belated
peasant who, passing by, is forced to join in their roundel;

---

* Hence we may infer that they came originally from Scandinavia, communicated most probably by the Normans.

† Stone-tables. They are called by the same name in Devon and Cornwall;
in Irish their appellation is Cromleach.

he usually dies of exhaustion. Wednesday is their holiday; the first Wednesday in May their annual festival, which they celebrate with dancing, singing, and music. They have the same aversion to holy things as the Korrigan; like them, too, they can fortell events to come. The Korrid is always furnished with a large leathern purse, which is said to be full of gold; but if any one succeeds in getting it from him, he finds nothing in it but hair and a pair of scissors.

The Bretons also believe in Mermaids; they name them Morgan (*sea-women*) and Morverc'h (*sea-daughters*), and say that they draw down to their palaces of gold and crystal at the bottom of the sea or of ponds, those who venture imprudently too near the edge of the water. Like the mermaids they sing and comb their golden hair. In one of the ballads we read, "Fisher, hast thou seen the mermaid combing her hair, yellow as gold, by the noontide sun, at the edge of the water?" "I have seen the fair mermaid. I have also heard her singing; her songs were plaintive as the waves."*

In M. Villemarqué's collection there are three ballads relating to the Korrigan and Korred. The following is a faithful translation of the first of them in the exact measure of the original. All the Breton poetry is rimed, very frequently in triads or tercets.

Lord Nann and the Korrigan.

THE Lord Nann and his bride so fair
In early youth united were,
In early youth divided were.

The lady lay-in yesternight
Of twins, their skin as snow was white,
A boy and girl, that glad his sight.

"What doth thy heart desire, loved one,
For giving me so fair a son?
Say, and at once it shall be done.

---

* Barzan-Breiz., t. xlix. 69.

" A woodcock from the pool of the glyn,
Or roebuck from the forest green ? "

" The roebuck's flesh is savoury,
But for it thou to the wood should'st hie."

Lord Nann when he these words did hear,
He forthwith grasped his oaken spear,

And vaulting on his coal-black steed
Unto the green-wood hied with speed.

When he unto the wood drew nigh,
A fair white doe he there did spy,

And after her such chase he made,
The ground it shook beneath their tread.

And after her such chase made he,
From his brows the water copiously

And from his horse's sides ran down.
The evening had now come on,

And he came where a streamlet flowed
Fast by a Korrigan's abode ;

And grassy turf spread all around.
To quench his thirst he sprang to ground.

The Korrig at her fount sat there
A-combing of her long fair hair.

She combed it with a comb of gold—
These ladies ne'er are poor, we 're told.

" Rash man," cried she, " how dost thou **dare**
To come disturb my waters fair !

" Thou shalt unto me plight thy fay,
Or seven years thou shalt waste away,
Or thou shalt die ere the third day."

" To thee my faith plight will I ne'er,
For I am married now a year.

"I shall not surely waste away,
Nor shall I die ere the third day;

"I shall not die within three days,
But when it unto God shall please."—

"Good mother, mine, if you love me,
See that my bed made ready be,
For I have ta'en a malady.

"Let not one word to my wife be told;
In three days I shall lie in the mould,
A Korrigan has thus foretold."

And when three days were past and gone,
The young wife asked this question,—

"My mother-in-law, now tell me why
The bells all ring thus constantly?

"And why the priests a low mass sing,
All clad in white, as the bells ring?"

"Last night a poor man died whom we
A lodging gave through charity."

"My mother-in-law, tell me, I pray,
My Lord Nann whither is he gone away?"

"My daughter, to the town he's gone,
To see thee he will come anon."

"Good mother-in-law, to church to fare,
Shall I my red or blue gown wear?"

"The custom now is, daughter dear,
At church always in black to appear."

As they crossed o'er the churchyard-wall,
On her husband's grave her eye did fall.

"Who is now dead of our family,
That thus fresh dug our ground I see?"

" Alas ! my child, the truth can I
Not hide : thy husband there doth lie."

On her two knees herself she cast
And rose no more, she breathed her last.

It was a marvel to see, men say,
The night that followed the day,
The lady in earth by her lord lay,

To see two oak-trees themselves rear
From the new-made grave into the air ;

And on their branches two doves white,
Who there were hopping gay and light ;

Which sang when rose the morning-ray
And then toward heaven sped away.

This ballad is very remarkable.   Its similarity to that of
Sir Olof, so celebrated in Scandinavia, and of which we have
already given two variations out of fifteen, must strike
every one ; in its concluding stanzas also it resembles other
Scandinavian and English ballads.   On the other,hand, the
White Doe and the Korrigan at the fount remind us of the
Lais of Marie de France.   Our opinion on the whole is,
that the ballad belongs to Scandinavia, whence it was
brought at an early period—by the Normans, we might say
only for its Christian air in both countries—and naturalised
in the usual manner.   It is rather strange that there is
neither an English nor a Scottish version of it.

The next lay, which is entirely composed in tercets, is the
story of a changeling.   In order to recover her own child
the mother is advised by the Virgin, to whom she has
prayed, to prepare a meal for ten farm-servants in an egg-
shell, which will make the Korrid speak, and she is then to
whip him well till he cries, and when he does so he will be
taken away.   The woman does as directed : the Korr asks
what she is about : she tells him : " For ten, dear mother, in
an eggshell !   I have seen the egg before I saw the white
hen : I have seen the acorn before I saw the tree : I have

seen the acorn and I have seen the shoot: I have seen the oak in the wood of Brézal, but never saw I such a thing as this." "Thou hast seen too many things, my son," replied she, and began to whip him, when one came crying, "Don't beat him, give him back to me; I have not done yours any injury. He is king in our country." When the woman went home she found her own child sleeping sweetly in the cradle. He opened his eyes and said, "Ah! mother, I have been a long time asleep!"

Among the Welsh legends above related, that of the Fairies Banished has some resemblance to this; but M. Villemarqué says that he was told a changeling-story by the Glamorgan peasantry, precisely the same as the Breton legend. In it the changeling is heard muttering to himself in a cracked voice, "I have seen the acorn before I saw the oak: I have seen the egg before I saw the white hen: I have never seen the like of this." It is remarkable that these words form a rimed triad or tercet nearly the same with that in the Breton ballad,* whence M. Villemarqué is led to suspect that the legend is anterior to the seventh century, the epoch of the separation of the Britons of Wales and Armorica. But as changelings seem to have come from the North, we cannot consent to receive this theory. He also quotes from Geoffrey of Monmouth's Life of Merlin, "There is in this forest," said Merlin the Wild, "an oak laden with years: I saw it when it was beginning to grow... I saw the acorn whence it rose, germinate and become a twig... I have then lived a long time." This would, in our opinion, tend to show that this was an ordinary formula in the British language.

The third and last of those ballads tells, and not without humour, how Paskou-Hir, *i. e.*, Long-Paskou, the tailor, one Friday evening, entered the abode of the Korred, and there dug up and carried home a concealed treasure. They

---

* WELSH.

Gweliz mez ken gwelet derven,
Gweliz vi ken gwelet iar wenn,
Eriocz ne wiliz evelhenn.

BRETON.

Gweliz vi ken guelet iar wenn,
Gweliz mez ken gwelet gwezen.
Gweliz mez ha gweliz gwial,
Gweliz derven e Koat Brezal,
Biskoaz na weliz kemend all.

pursued him, and came into the court-yard dancing with might and main, and singing,—

> Dilun, dimeurs, dimerc'her
> Ha diriaou, ha digwener.
>
> Monday, Tuesday, Wednesday,
> And Thursday, and Friday.

Finding the door secured* they mount the roof and break a hole through which they get in, and resume their dance on the floor, still singing, Monday, Tuesday, etc., and calling on the tailor to come and join them and they would teach him a dance that would crack his back-bone, and they end by telling him that the money of the Korr is good for nothing.

Another version says, that it was a baker who stole the treasure, and, more cunning than the tailor, he strewed the floor of his house with hot ashes and cinders on which the Korred burned their feet. This made them scamper off, but before they went they smashed all his crockery and earthen-ware. Their words were, "In Iannik-ann-Trevou's house we burnt our horny feet and made a fine mess of his crockery."

The following legend will explain the song of the Korred.

The Dance and Song of the Korred.

THE valley of Goel was a celebrated haunt of the Korred.† It was thought dangerous to pass through it at night lest one should be forced to join in their dances, and thus perhaps lose his life. One evening, however, a peasant and

---

* The tailor cries "Shut the door! Here are the little *Duz* of the night" (*Setu ann Duzigou nouz*), and St. Augustine (De Civ. Dei, c. xxiii.) speaks of "Daemones quos *Duscios* Galli nuncupant." It may remind us of our own word *Deuce.*

     † In the original the word is Korrigan, but see above, p. 431.

his wife thoughtlessly did so, and they soon found themselves enveloped by the dancing sprites, who kept singing—

> Lez y, Lez hon,
> Bas an arer zo gant hon;
> Lez on, Lez y,
> Bas an arer zo gant y.

> Let him go, let him go,
> For he has the wand of the plough;
> Let her go, let her go,
> For she has the wand of the plough.

It seems the man had in his hand the *fourche*, or short stick, which is used as a plough-paddle in Brittany, and this was a protection, for the dancers made way for them to go out of the ring.

When this became known, many persons having fortified themselves with a *fourche*, gratified their curiosity by witnessing the dance of the Korred. Among the rest were two tailors, Peric and Jean, who, being merry fellows, dared each other to join in the dance. They drew lots, and the lot fell upon Peric, a humpbacked red-haired, but bold stout little fellow. He went up to the Korred and asked permission to take share in their dance. They granted it, and all went whirling round and round, singing

> Dilun, Dimeurs, Dimerc'her.

> Monday, Tuesday, Wednesday.

Peric, weary of the monotony, when there was a slight pause at the last word, added

> Ha Diriaou, ha Digwener.

> And Thursday and Friday.

Mat! mat! (good! good!) cried they, and gathering round him, they offered him his choice of beauty, rank, or riches. He laughed, and only asked them to remove his hump and change the colour of his hair. They forthwith took hold of him and tossed him up into the air, throwing him from hand to hand till at last he lighted on his feet with a flat back and fine long black hair.

When Jean saw and heard of the change he resolved to
try what *he* could get from the potent Korred, so a few
evenings after he went and was admitted to the dance, which
now went to the words as enlarged by Peric. To make his
addition he shouted out,

> Ha Disadarn, ha Disul.
>
> And Saturday and Sunday.

" What more ? what more ? " cried the Korred, but he only
went on repeating the words. They then asked him what
he would have, and he replied riches. They tossed him up,
and kept bandying him about till he cried for mercy, and on
coming to the ground, he found he had got Peric's hump and
red hair.

It seems that the Korred were condemned to this continual dancing, which was never to cease till a mortal should
join in their dance, and after naming all the days of the
week, should add, *Ha cetu chu er sizun,* "And now the week
is ended." They punished Jean for coming so near the end
and then disappointing them.*

We add the following circumstances from other authorities:
At Carnac, near Quiberon, says M. de Cambry, in the
department of Morbihan, on the sea-shore, is the Temple of
Carnac, called in Breton "Ti Goriquet" (*House of the Gorics*),
one of the most remarkable Celtic monuments extant. It is
composed of more than four thousand large stones, standing
erect in an arid plain, where neither tree nor shrub is to be
seen, and not even a pebble is to be found in the soil on
which they stand. If the inhabitants are asked concerning
this wonderful monument, they say it is an old camp of
Cæsar's, an army turned into stone, or that it is the work of
the Crions or Gorics. These they describe as little men
between two and three feet high, who carried these enormous
masses on their hands; for, though little, they are stronger
than giants. Every night they dance around the stones;

---

* From an article signed H—Y in a cheap publication called Tracts for
the People. The writer says he heard it in the neighbourhood of the Vale of
Goel, and it has every appearance of being genuine. Villemarqué (i. 61) mentions the last circumstance as to the end of the penance of the Korred.

and woe betide the traveller who approaches within their reach! he is forced to join in the dance, where he is whirled about till, breathless and exhausted, he falls down, amidst the peals of laughter of the Crions. All vanish with the break of day.*

In the ruins of Tresmaïouen dwell the Courils.† They are of a malignant disposition, but great lovers of dancing. At night they sport around the Druidical monuments. The unfortunate shepherd that approaches them must dance their rounds with them till cock-crow; and the instances are not few of persons thus ensnared who have been found next morning dead with exhaustion and fatigue. Woe also to the ill-fated maiden who draws near the Couril dance! nine months after, the family counts one member more. Yet so great is the power and cunning of these Dwarfs, that the young stranger bears no resemblance to them, but they impart to it the features of some lad of the village.

A number of little men, not more than a foot high, dwell under the castle of Morlaix. They live in holes in the ground, whither they may often be seen going, and beating on basins. They possess great treasures, which they sometimes bring out; and if any one pass by at the time, allow him to take one handful, but no more. Should any one attempt to fill his pockets, the money vanishes, and he is instantly assailed by a shower of boxes in the ear from invisible hands.

The Bretons also say that there are spirits who silently skim the milk-pans in the dairies. They likewise speak of Sand Yan y Tad (*St. John and Father*), who carry five lights at their finger-ends, which they make spin round and round like a wheel.‡

There is a species of malignant beings, called Night-

---

* Monumens Celtiques, p. 2. An old sailor told M. de Cambry, that one of these stones covers an immense treasure, and that these thousands of them have been set up the better to conceal it. He added that a calculation, the key to which was to be found in the Tower of London, would alone indicate the spot where the treasure lies.

† For what follows we are indebted to the MS. communication of Dr. W. Grimm. He quotes as his authority the *Zeitung der Gesellschafter* for 1826.

‡ The former seems to be a house spirit, the *Goblin*, *Follet*, or *Lutin* of the north of France; the latter is apparently the *Ignis Fatuus*.

washers (*Eur cunnerez noz*), who appear on the banks of streams, and call on the passers-by to aid them to wash the linen of the dead. If any one refuses, they drag him into the water and break his arms.

About Morlaix the people are afraid of evil beings they call Teurst. One of these, called Teursapouliet, appears in the likeness of some domestic animal.* In the district of Vannes is a colossal spirit called Teus,† or Bugelnoz, who appears clothed in white between midnight and two in the morning. His office is to rescue victims from the Devil. He spreads his mantle over them, and they are secure. The Devil comes over the ocean; but, unable to endure the look of the good spirit, he sinks down again, and, the object of the spirit accomplished, he vanishes.

* So the Yorkshire Bar-guest.
† See above, p. 438.

SOUTHERN EUROPE.

O faretrate Ninfe, o agresti Pani,
O Satiri e Silvani, o Fauni e Driadi,
Najadi ed Amadriadi, e Semidee,
Oreadi, e Napee, or siete sole.

SANAZZARO.

UNDER the title of Southern Europe, we comprise Greece
and those nations whose languages are derived from the
Latin; Italy, Spain, and France. Of the Fairy-system, if
there ever was one, of Portugal we have met with nothing,
at least in the works of Camoens, Bernardes, and Lobo.

The reader will, in this part of our work, find little corresponding to the Gothic Dwarfs who have hitherto been our
companions. The only one of our former acquaintances
that will attend us is honest Hob-goblin, Brownie, Kobold,
Nis, or however else he may style himself. And it is very
remarkable that we shall meet with him only in those places
where the Northmen, the Visigoths or other Scandinavian
tribes settled. Whence perhaps it might be concluded that
they brought him with them to the South of Europe.

GREECE.

'Ως τέρεινα Νύμφα
δροσερῶν ἐσωθεν ἄντρων.   EURIPIDES.

Like a tender Nymph
Within the dewy caves.

THE Grecian mythology, like its kindred systems, abounded
in personifications.* Modified by scenery so beautiful, rich,

---

* See our Mythology of Ancient Greece and Italy, where (p. 237) most of
what follows will be found, with notes.

and various as Hellas presented, it in general assigned the supposed intelligences who presided over the various parts of external nature more pleasing attributes than they elsewhere enjoyed. They were mostly conceived to be of the female sex, and were denominated Nymphs, a word originally signifying a new-married woman.

Whether it be owing to soil, climate, or to an original disposition of mind and its organ, the Greeks have above all other people possessed a perception of beauty of form, and a fondness for representing it. The Nymphs of various kinds were therefore always presented to the imagination, in the perfection of female youth and beauty. Under the various appellations of Oreades, Dryades, Naïdes, Limniades, Nereides, they dwelt in mountains, trees, springs, lakes, the sea, where, in caverns and grottos, they passed a life whose occupations resembled those of females of human race. The Wood-nymphs were the companions and attendants of the huntress goddess Artemis; the Sea-nymphs averted shipwreck from pious navigators; and the Spring- and River-nymphs poured forth fruitfulness on the earth. All of them were honoured with prayer and sacrifice; and all of them occasionally 'mingled in love' with favoured mortals.

In the Homeric poems, the most ancient portion of Grecian literature, we meet the various classes of Nymphs. In the Odyssey, they are the attendants of Calypso, herself a goddess and a nymph. Of the female attendants of Circe, the potent daughter of Helios, also designated as a goddess and a nymph, it is said,

> They spring from fountains and from sacred groves,
> And holy streams that flow into the sea.

Yet these nymphs are of divine nature, and when Zeus, the father of the gods, calls together his council,

> None of the streams, save Ocean, stayed away,
> Nor of the Nymphs, who dwell in beauteous groves,
> And springs of streams, and verdant grassy slades.

The good Eumæus prays to the Nymphs to speed the return of his master, reminding them of the numerous sacrifices

Ulysses had offered to them.   In another part of the poem,
their sacred cave is thus described :—

> But at the harbour's head a long-leafed olive
> Grows, and near to it lies a lovely cave,
> Dusky and sacred to the Nymphs, whom men
> Call Naïdes.   In it large craters lie,
> And two-eared pitchers, all of stone, and there
> Bees build their combs.   In it, too, are long looms
> Of stone, and there the Nymphs do weave their robes,
> Sea-purple, wondrous to behold.   Aye-flowing
> Waters are there ; two entrances it hath ;
> That to the north is pervious unto men ;
> That to the south more sacred is, and there
> Men enter not, but 'tis the Immortals' path.

Yet though thus exalted in rank, the Homeric Nymphs frequently 'blessed the bed' of heroes; and many a warrior
who fought before Troy could boast descent from a Naïs or
a Nereis.

The sweet, gentle, pious, Ocean-nymphs, who in the Prometheus of Æschylus appear as the consolers and advisers
of its dignified hero, seem to hold a nearly similar relation
with man to the supernal gods.   Beholding the misery
inflicted on Prometheus by the power of Zeus, they
cry,—

> May never the all-ruling
> Zeus set his rival power
>   Against my thoughts ;
> Nor may I ever fail
> The gods, with holy feasts
> Of sacrifices, drawing near,
> Beside the ceaseless stream
>   Of father Ocëan :
> Nor may I err in words ;
> But this abide with me
>   And never fade away.

One of the most interesting species of Nymphs is the
Dryads, or Hamadryads, those personifications of the vegetable life of plants.   In the Homeric hymn to Aphroditè,
we find the following full and accurate description of them.
Aphroditè, when she informs Anchises of her pregnancy,

and her shame to have it known among the gods, says of the child :—

> But him, when first he sees the sun's clear light,
> The Nymphs shall rear, the mountain-haunting Nymphs,
> Deep-bosomed, who on this mountain great
> And holy dwell, who neither goddesses
> Nor women are.   Their life is long ; they eat
> Ambrosial food, and with the deathless frame
> The beauteous dance.   With them, in the recess
> Of lovely caves, well-spying Argos-slayer
> And the Sileni mix in love.   Straight pines
> Or oaks high-headed spring with them upon
> The earth man-feeding, soon as they are born ;
> Trees fair and flourishing ; on the high hills
> Lofty they stand ; the Deathless' sacred grove
> Men call them, and with iron never cut.
> But when the fate of death is drawing near,
> First wither on the earth the beauteous trees,
> The bark around them wastes, the branches fall,
> And the Nymph's soul at the same moment leaves
> The sun's fair light.

They possessed power to reward and punish those who prolonged or abridged the existence of their associate-tree. In the Argonautics of Apollonius Rhodius, Phineus thus explains to the heroes the cause of the poverty of Peræbius :—

> But he was paying the penalty laid on
> His father's crime ; for one time, cutting trees
> Alone among the hills, he spurned the prayer
> Of the Hamadryas Nymph, who, weeping sore,
> With earnest words besought him not to cut
> The trunk of an oak tree, which, with herself
> Coeval, had endured for many a year.
> But, in the pride of youth, he foolishly
> Cut it ; and to him and to his race the Nymph
> Gave ever after a lot profitless.

The Scholiast gives on this passage the following tale from Charon of Lampsacus :

A man, named Rhœcus, happening to see an oak just ready to fall to the ground, ordered his slaves to prop it. The Nymph, who had been on the point of perishing with the tree, came to him and expressed her gratitude to him for having saved her life, and at the same time desired him to ask what reward he would. Rhœcus then requested her to permit him to be her lover, and the Nymph acceded to his wishes. She at the same time charged him strictly to avoid the society of every other woman, and told him that a bee should be her messenger. One time the bee happened to come to Rhœcus as he was playing at draughts, and he made a rough reply. This so incensed the Nymph that she deprived him of sight.

Similar was the fate of the Sicilian Daphnis.* A Naïs loved him and forbade him to hold intercourse with any other woman under pain of loss of sight. Long he abstained, though tempted by the fairest maids of Sicily. At length a princess contrived to intoxicate him: he broke his vow, and the threatened penalty was inflicted.

ITALY.

Faune Nympharum fugientum amator,
Per meos fines et aprica rura
Lenis incedas, abeasque parvis
Æquus alumnis.

HORATIUS.

UNFORTUNATELY for our knowledge of the ancient Italian mythology, the ballad-poetry of Rome is irrecoverably lost. A similar fate has befallen the literature of Etruria, Umbria, and other parts of the peninsula. The powerful influence exercised by Grecian genius over the conquerors of the Grecian states utterly annihilated all that was national and domestic in literature. Not but that Latin poetry abounds in mythologic matter; but it is the mythology of Greece, not of Italy; and the reader of Virgil and Ovid will observe with surprise how little of what he meets in their works is Italian.

So much however of the population of ancient Italy,

* Parthenius Erotica, chap. xxix.

particularly of Latium, was Pelasgian, that it is natural to suppose a great similarity between the religious systems of Latium and Hellas. The Latins do not, however, appear to have believed in choirs of Nymphs. Those we read of, such as Egeria, Anna Perenna, Juturna, are all solitary, all dwellers of fountains, streams, and lakes. The Italian Diana did not, like the Grecian Artemis, speed over the mountains attended by a train of buskined nymphs. No Dryads sought to avert the fate of their kindred trees—no Nereides sported on the waves.

Dwarfish deities they had none. We are indeed told of the Lars, particularly the rural Lars, as answering to the Gothic Dwarfs; but no proofs are offered except the diminutive size of their statues. This we hold to amount to nothing. Are we to suppose the following lines of Plautus to have been delivered by an "eyas?"

> Lest any marvel who I am, I shall
> Briefly declare it. I am the family Lar
> Of this house whence you see me coming out.
> 'Tis many years now that I keep and guard
> This family; both father and grandsire
> Of him that has it now, I aye protected.
> Now his grandsire intrusted me a treasure
> Of gold, that I, unknown to all, should keep it.
>   *   *   *   *   *
> He has one daughter, who, each day with wine
> Or incense, or with something, worships me.
> She gives me crowns, and I in recompense
> Have now made Euclio find the treasure out,
> That if he will, he may more readily
> Get her a match.*

The Lars were a portion of the Etrurian religion. The Etruscan word Lar signifies Lord, with which it has a curious but casual resemblance.† The Lars were regarded, like the Grecian heroes, as being the souls of men who, after death, still hovered about their former abodes, averting dangers from, and bestowing blessings on, the inhabitants. They differed from the Penates, who were, properly speak-

---

* Aulularia, Prologue.

† See our Mythology of Greece and Italy, p. 543; and our Ovid's Fasti, Excursus IV.

ing, Gods, beings of a higher nature, personifications of natural powers, the givers of abundance and wealth.

The old Italians, it appears, believed in a being, we know not of what size, called an Incubo, that watched over treasure. " But what they say I know not," says Petronius,* but I have heard how he snatched the cap of an Incubo and found a treasure."

Respecting the Fairy mythology of the modern Italians, what we have been able to collect is very little.

The people of Naples, we are told,† believe in a being very much resembling the Incubo, whom they call the Monaciello, or Little Monk. They describe him as a short, thick kind of little man, dressed in the long garments of a monk, with a broad-brimmed hat. He appears to people in the dead of the night, and beckons to them to follow him. If they have courage to do so, he leads them to some place where treasure is concealed. Several are said to have made sudden fortunes through him. In the Neapolitan story-book, named the Pentamerone, of which we shall presently give an account, we meet with a Monaciello of a very different character from this guardian of hidden treasure.

In the second tale of the first day of that work, when the prince in the night heard the noise made by the Fairy in his room, " he thought it was some chamber-boy coming to lighten his purse for him, or some Monaciello to pull the clothes off him." And in the seventh tale of the third day of the same collection, when Corvetto had hidden himself under the Ogre's ‡ bed to steal his quilt, " he began to pull

---

* Satyricon, ch. 38. *Sunt qui eundem* (Hercules) *Incubonem esse velint.* Schol. Hor. Sat. ii. 6, 13.

† Viessieux, Italy and the Italians, vol. i. pp. 161, 162.

‡ *L'huorco,* the Orco of Bojardo and Ariosto, probably derived from the Latin Orcus : see Mythol. of Greece and Italy, p. 527. In this derivation we find that we had been anticipated by Minucci in his notes on the Malmantile Racquistato, c. ii. st. 50.

In a work, from which we have derived some information (Lettres sur les Contes des Fées, Paris, 1826), considerable pains are taken, we think to little purpose, to deduce the French Ogre from the Oïgours, a Tartar tribe, who with the other tribes of that people invaded Europe in the twelfth century. In the Glossaire de la Langue Romaine, Ogre is explained by Hongrois. Any one, however, that reads the Pentamerone will see that the ugly, cruel, man-eating

quite gently, when the Ogre awoke, and bid his wife not to pull the clothes that way, or she 'd strip him, and he would get his death of cold." "Why, it 's you that are stripping me," replied the Ogress, "and you have not left a stitch on me." "Where the devil is the quilt?" says the Ogre; and putting his hand to the gronnd, he happened to touch the face of Corvetto, and immediately began to shout out, "The Monaciello, the Monaciello, hola! candles! run, run!" Corvetto, meanwhile, got off with his prize through the window.*

It is quite clear that the Monaciello is the same kind of being as the House-spirit of the Gotho-German nations. He seems to belong peculiarly to Naples, for we have not heard of him in any other part of Italy. Now we are to recollect that this was the very place in which the Normans settled, and so he may be their Nis or Kobold;† or, as he is so very like the Spanish Duende, he may be that being introduced by the Aragonese, who seem to have exercised so much influence over the language and manners of the people of Naples.

The belief in Mermaids also prevailed in modern Italy. In the reign of Roger, king of Sicily, a young man happening to be bathing in the sea late in the evening, perceived that something was following him. Supposing it to be one of his companions, he caught it by the hair, and dragged it on shore. But finding it to be a maiden of great beauty and of most perfect form, he threw his cloak about her, and took her home, where she continued with him till they had a son. There was one thing however which greatly grieved him, which was the reflection that so beautiful a form should be dumb, for he had never heard her speak. One day he was reproached by one of his companions, who said that it

---

Huorco is plainly an Ogre; and those expert at the *tours de passe passe* of etymology will be at no loss to deduce Ogre from Orco. See Tales and Popular Fictions, p. 223.

* In another of these tales, it is said of a young man, who, on breaking open a cask, found a beautiful maiden in it, that he stood for a while *comme o chillo che ha visto lo Monaciello.*

† See Tales and Popular Fictions, chap. ix. p. 269; see also *Spain* and *France.*

was a spectre, and not a real woman, that he had at home:
being both angry and terrified, he laid his hand on the hilt
of his sword, and urged her with vehemence to tell him who
or what she was, threatening if she did not do so, to kill the
child before her eyes. The spirit only saying, that he had
lost a good wife by forcing her to speak, instantly vanished,
leaving her son behind. A few years after, as the boy was
playing on the sea-shore with his companions, the spirit his
mother dragged him into the sea, where he was drowned.*

We now come to the Fate of romance and tale.

The earliest notice that we can recollect to have seen of
these potent ladies is in the Orlando Innamorato, where we
meet the celebrated Fata Morgana, who would at first appear
to be, as a personification of Fortune, a being of a higher
order.

> Ivi è una fata nomata Morgana,
> Che a le genti diverse dona l'oro ;
> Quanto e per tutto il mondo or se ne spande
> Convien che ad essa prima si dimande.
>
> L. I. c. xxv. st. 5. ed. 1831.

But we afterwards find her in her proper station, subject,
with the Fate and Witches, to the redoubtable Demogorgon.†
When Orlando, on delivering Zilante from her, makes her
swear by that awful power, the poet says :

> Sopra ogni fata è quel Demogorgone
> (Non so se mai l'odiste raccontare)
> E giudica tra loro e fa ragione,
> E quel che piace a lui può di lor fare.
> La notte si cavalca ad un montone,
> Travarca le montagne e passa il mare,
> E *strigie,* e *fate,* e fantasime vane
> Batte con serpi vive ogni dimane.
>
> Se le ritrova la dimane al mondo,
> Perchè non ponno al giorno comparire,
> Tanto le batte al colpo furibondo
> Che volentier vorrien poter morire.

---

* Vincentius apud Kornmann, *de Miraculis Vivorum.*

† This being, unknown to classic mythology, is first mentioned by Lactantius. It was probably from Boccaccio's Genealogia Deorum that Bojardo got his knowledge of him.

Or le incatena giù nel mar profondo,
Or sopra il vento scalze le fa gire,
Or per il fuoco dietro a sè le mena;
A cui dà questa, a cui quell' altra pena.

L. II. c. xiii. st. 27, 28.

According to Ariosto,* Demogorgon has a splendid temple
palace in the Himalaya mountains, whither every fifth
year the Fate are all summoned to appear before him,
and give an account of their actions. They travel through
the air in various strange conveyances, and it is no easy
matter to distinguish between their convention and a Sabbath
of the Witches.

We meet with another Fata in Bojardo,† the beautiful
Silvanella, who raised a tomb over Narcissus, and then dis-
solved away into a fountain.

When Brandamarte opens the magnificent tomb and kisses
the hideous serpent that thrusts out its head, it gradually
becomes a beautiful maiden.

Questa era Febosilla quella fata,
Che edificato avea l'alto palaccio
E 'l bel giardino e quella sepoltura,
Ove un gran tempo è stata in pena dura.

Perchè una fata non può morir mai,
Sin che non giunge il giorno del giudizio,
Ma ben ne la sua forma dura assai,
Mill' anni o più, sì come io aggio indizio.
Poi (siccome di questa io vi contai
Qual fabbricato avea il bell' edifizio)
In serpe si tramuta e stavvi tanto
Che di baciarla alcun si doni il vanto.

L. II. c. xxvi. st. 14, 15.

The other Fate who appear in this poem are Le Fate
Nera and Bianca, the protectresses of Guidone and Aquilante;
the Fata della Fonte, from whom Mandricardo obtains the
arms of Hector, and finally Alcina, the sister of Morgana,
who carries off Astolfo. Dragontina and Falerina, the
owners of such splendid gardens, may also have been Fate,
though they are not called so by the poet.

* I Cinque Canti, c. i. st. 1. *seq.*   † Lib. II. xvii. 56, *seq.*

Alcina re-appears in great splendour in the Orlando Furioso, where she is given a sister named Logistilla, and both, like Morgana in the preceding poem, are in a great measure allegorical. We also obtain there a glimpse of the White and Black Fate. The Maga Manto of Dante becomes here a Fata, and we meet her in the form of a serpent; to account for which she says,

> Nascemmo ad un punto che d' ogni altro male
> Siamo capaci fuor che della morte.
> Ma giunta è con questo essere immortale
> Condizion non men del morir forte ;
> Ch' ogni settimo giorno ognuna è certa
> Che la sua forma in biscia si converta.
>
> C. xliii. st. 98.

Elsewhere (x. 52) the poet tells us that

> Morir non puote alcuna fata mai
> Fin che il Sol gira, o il ciel non muta stilo.

In the Amadigi of Bernardo Tasso the Fate appear for the last time in Italian poetry;* but in greater number, and, we may say, greater splendour than elsewhere. There are two classes of them, the beneficent and protective, and the seductive and injurious. The terms Maga and Incantatrice, as well as Fata, are applied to them all indifferently. The good Fairy-ladies are Urganda, termed *La savia* and *La sconosciuta*,† the guardian of Amadigi, and the fair Oriana; Silvana or Silvanella who stands in a similar relation to Alidoro; Lucina, also named La Donna del Lago, another protectress of Alidoro and of his lady-love, the fair warrior Mirinda, sister of Amadigi; Eufrosina, the sister of Lucina; Argea, called La Reina della Fate, the protectress of Floridante, to whom, after making him undergo various trials, she gives her daughter Filidora in marriage; finally, Argea's sister Filidea. The Fate whose character resembles that of Alcina are Morganetta, Nivetta, and Carvilia, the

---

* There is, however, a Maga or Fata named Falsirena in the Adone of Marini.

† La Sabia and La Desconocida of the original romance, which Tasso follows very closely in everything relating to Amadis and Oriana.

three daughters of Morgana. Beside these then are two Fate of neutral character, Dragontina, who formed a palace, temple and gardens, in which, at the desire of her father, she enchanted a young prince and his wife ; and Montana, who, to avenge the fate of her lover, slain by Alidoro, enchanted that warrior in a temple which she had raised to the memory of the fallen.*

> Ma veggiam ch' io non stessi troppo a bada
> Con queste Alcine e Morgane.

The earliest collections of European Fairy-tales in prose belong to Italy. In 1550, Straparola, a native of Caravaggio, in the Milanese, published at Venice his Notti Piacevoli, a collection of tales, jokes, and riddles, of which several, and those the best, are Fairy-tales. These were translated into French in 1560-76, and seem to have been the origin of the so well known Contes des Feés. Perrault's Puss in Boots (*Le Chat Botté,*) and the Princess Fairstar (*Belle Etoile,*) and many others of Madame D'Aulnoy's, who borrowed largely from the Notti Piacevoli, are to be found in Straparola. In 1637, eighty-seven years after the Notti Piacevoli appeared at Naples, and in the Neapolitan dialect, the Pentamerone, the best collection of Fairy-tales ever written.† The author, Giambattista Basile,‡ had spent his youth in Candia, and then passed several years rambling through Italy. He seems to have carefully treasured up all the tales

---

* Few of our readers, we presume, are acquainted with this poem, and they will perhaps be surprised to learn that it is, after the Furioso, the most beautiful romantic poem in the Italian language, graceful and sweet almost to excess. It is strange that it should be neglected in Italy also. One cause may be its length (One Hundred Cantos), another the constant and inartificial breaking off of the stories, and perhaps the chief one, its serious moral tone so different from that of Ariosto. It might be styled The Legend of Constancy, for the love of its heroes and heroines is proof against all temptations. Mr. Panizzi's charge of abounding in scandalous stories, is not correct, for it is in reality more delicate than even the Faerie Queene. Ginguené, who admired it, appreciates it far more justly.

† See Tales and Popular Fictions, p. 183. The Pentamerone we may observe, was not a title given to it by the author; in like manner the only title Fielding gave his great work was The History of a Foundling.

‡ He was brother to Adriana and uncle to Leonora Baroni, the ladies whose musical talents Milton celebrates.

he heard, and he wrote and published them, under the feigned name of Gian Alesio Abbatutis, in his native dialect, not long before his death.

In the Tales and Popular Fictions we gave some translations from the Notti Piacevoli, the only ones in English, and they will probably remain such, as the work is not one likely ever to be translated. In the same work we gave two from the Pentamerone, and three (the Dragon, Gagliuso, and the Goatface) in the former edition of the present work. Most certainly we were the first to render any of these curious tales into English, and we look back with a mixture of pleasure and surprise at our success in the unaided struggle with an idiom so different from the classic Italian.* We fancied that we had been the first to make translations from it into any language, but we afterwards learned that of the two tales in our other work, the one, Peruonto, had been translated into French (probably by the Abbé Galiani) for the Cabinet des Fées, the other, the Serpent into German, by M. Grimm.† Of late, this most original work has been brought within the reach of ordinary readers by two translations, the one in German by Felix Liebrecht, who has given the work complete with few omissions; the other in English by Mr. J. E. Taylor, who has made a selection of thirty tales, and these most carefully expurgated, in order that agreeably to its second title, it might form a book of amusement even for children—a most difficult task, and in which his success has been far greater than might have been anticipated. All our own translations have been incorporated in it, and we can safely refer to it those who wish to know the real character and nature of the Pentamerone.

Whatever name Basile might give his book it is quite plain that he never could have meant it merely for children. The language alone is proof enough on that head. It is, besides, full of learned allusions and of keen satire, so that it

---

* Ex. gr. Fiume is *shiume ;* Fiore, *shiure ;* Piaggia, *chiaja ;* Piombo, *chiummo ;* Biondo, *ghiunno.* There are likewise numerous Hispanicisms. Thus *gaiola* in Gagliuso which we all rendered *coffin,* is the Spanish *jaula,* cage, and the meaning apparently is that he would have the cat stuffed and put in a glass-case; in like manner calling the eyes suns (as in *na bellezza a doje sole*) occurs in the plays of Calderon.

† In the Taschenbuch für altdeutscher Zeit und Kunst, 1816.

could only be understood and relished by grown persons, for whose amusement it was apparently designed; and its tales are surely not much more extravagant than some of those in Ariosto and the other romantic poets. It in fact never was a child's book like the Contes de ma Mère l' Oie. It has now become very scarce; we could not at Naples meet with a copy of it, or even with any one who had read it.

SPAIN.

Duendecillo, duendecillo,
Quien quiera que seas ó fueras,
El dinero que tú das
En lo que mandares vuelve.

CALDERON, *La Dama Duende.*

WHEN we inquired after the fairy-system of Spain, we were told that there was no such thing, for that the Inquisition had long since eradicated all such ideas. Most certainly we would not willingly be regarded as partisans of the Holy Office, yet still we must express our doubt of the truth of this charge. In Señor Llorente's work, as far as we can recollect, there is no account of prosecutions for Duende-heresy; and even to the Holy Office we should give its due. Still, with all our diligence, our collection of Iberian fairy-lore is extremely scanty.

Our earliest authority for Spain, as for other countries, is the celebrated marshall of Champagne, Gervase of Tilbury, who thus relates:—

The Daughter of Peter De Cabinam.

IN the bishoprick of Gerunda (*i. e.* Gerona), and the province of Catalonia, stands a mountain which the natives call Convagum. It is very steep, and on its summit is a lake of dark water, so deep that it cannot be fathomed. The abode of the Demons is in this lake; and if a stone, or anything else, be thrown into it, there rises from it an awful tempest.

Not far from this mountain, in a village named Junchera, lived a man named Peter de Cabinam, who being one day annoyed by the crying of his little girl, wished in his anger that the Demons might fetch her away. The child instantly vanished—snatched away by invisible hands—and was seen no more. Time passed on; and it was seven years after this event, when a man belonging to the village, as he was one day rambling about the foot of the mountain, met a man weeping bitterly, and bewailing his hard fate. On inquiry, he said that he had now been seven years in the mountain under the power of the Demons, who employed him as a beast of burden. He added, that there was also a girl in the mountain, the daughter of Peter de Cabinam of Junchera, a servant like himself; but that they were tired of her, and would restore her to her father if he came to claim her. When this information came to Peter de Cabinam, he forthwith ascended the mountain, and going to the edge of the lake, he besought the Demons to give him back his child. Like a sudden gust of wind she came, tall in stature, but wasted and dirty, her eyes rolling wildly, and her speech inarticulate. The father, not knowing what to do with her, applied to the Bishop of Gerunda, who took this opportunity of edifying his people by exhibiting the girl to them, and warning them against the danger of wishing that the Demons had their children. Some time after the man also was released, and from him the people learned that at the bottom of the lake there was a large palace, with a wide gate, to which palace the Demons repaired from all parts of the world, and which no one could enter but themselves, and those they brought thither.*

* Otia Imperialia, p. 982. The Demons must have been some kind of fairies : see above, p. 4.

Origin of the House of Haro.

As Don Diego Lopez, lord of Biscay, was one day lying
in wait for the wild boar, he heard the voice of a woman
who was singing.　On looking around, he beheld on the
summit of a rock a damsel, exceedingly beautiful, and richly
attired.　Smitten with her charms, he proffered her his
hand.　In reply, she assured him that she was of high
descent, but frankly accepted his proffered hand; making,
however, one condition—he was never to pronounce a holy
name.　Tradition says that the fair bride had only one
defect, which was, that one of her feet was like that of a
goat.　Diego Lopez, however, loved her well, and she bore
him two children, a daughter, and a son named Iniguez
Guerra.

Now it happened one day, as they were sitting at dinner,
that the lord of Biscay threw a bone to the dogs, and a
mastiff and a spaniel quarrelled about it, and the spaniel
griped the mastiff by the throat, and throttled him.　"Holy
Mary!" exclaimed Don Diego, "who ever saw the like?"
Instantly the lady caught hold of the hands of her children;
Diego seized and held the boy, but the mother glided through
the air with the daughter, and sought again the mountains
whence she had come.　Diego remained alone with his son;
and some years after, when he invaded the lands of the
Moors, he was made captive by them, and led to Toledo.
Iniguez Guerra, who was now grown up, was greatly grieved
at the captivity of his father, and the men of the land told
him that his only hope was to find his mother, and obtain
her aid.　Iniguez made no delay; he rode alone to the well-
known mountains, and when he reached them, behold! his
fairy-mother stood there before him on the summit of a rock.
"Come unto me," said she, "for well do I know thy errand."
And she called to her Pardalo, the horse that ran without a
rider in the mountains, and she put a bridle into his mouth,
and bade Iniguez mount him, and told him that he must not

give him either food or water, or unsaddle or unbridle him,
or put shoes upon his feet, and that in one day the demon-
steed would carry him to Toledo.   And Iniguez obeyed the
injunctions of his mother, and succeeded in liberating his
father; but his mother never returned.*

In the large collection of Spanish ballads named El
Romancero Castellano, the only one that treats of fairy-lore
is the following, which tells of the enchantment of the King
of Castille's daughter by seven fairies,† for a period of seven
years. It is of the same character as the fairy-tales of France
and Italy.

La Infantine.

—•—

Á CAZAR va el caballero,
Á cazar como solia.—
Los perros lleva cansados,
El falcon perdido avia.

Arrimarase á un roble,
Alto es á maravilla,
En un ramo mas alto
Viera estar una Infantina.

Cabellos de su cabeza
Todo aquel roble cobrian;
" No te espantes, caballero.
Ni tengas tamaña grima.

" Hija soy del buen rey
Y de la reina de Castilla;
Siete fadas me fadaron,‡
En brazos de una ama mia,

----

* Related by Sir Francis Palgrave, but without giving any authority, in
the Quarterly Review, vol. xxii.   See *France.*

† In Don Quixote (part i. chap. 50) we read of "los siete castillos de las
siete Fadas " beneath the lake of boiling pitch, and of the fair princess who
was enchanted in one of them.

‡ *Fada* is certainly the elided part. of this verb, for the Latin mode of

" Que andase los siete años
Sola en esta montina.*
Hoy se cumplan los años
O mañana, en aquel dia.

" Por Dios te ruego, caballero,
Llevesme en tu compañia,
Si quisieres por muger,
Si no sea por amiga."

" Espereis me vos, señora,
Esta mañana, aquel dia;
Iré yo tomar consejo
De una madre que tenia."

La niña le respondiera,
Y estas palabras, decia:
" O mal haya el caballero
Que sola deja la niña!"

El se va á tomar consejo,
Y ella queda en la montina.
Aconsejóle su madre
Que la tomase por amiga.

Quando volvió el caballero
No la hallara en la montina.
Vió la que la llevaban,
Com muy grande caballeria.

El caballero, que lo ha visto,
En el suelo se caia.
Desque en si hubo tornado
Estas palabras decia:

---

elision (see above p. 7.) was retained in Spanish as well as Italian. Thus *quedo,
junto, harto, marchito, vacio, enjuto, violento*, &c., come from *quedar, juntar,
hartar*, &c. As the Spanish, following the Latin, also frequently uses the
past as a present participle, as *un hombre atrevido*, "a daring man;" and the
same appears to take place in Italian, as *un huomo accorto, saputo, avveduto,
dispietato*; and even in French, as *un homme réfléchi, désespéré;* may we
not say that *fada, fata, fée*, is enchant*ing* rather than enchant*ed* ?
　　 * *Montina* is a small wood.

" Caballero que tal pierde
Muy grandes penas merecia.
Yo mismo seré el alcalde,
Yo me seré la justicia,
Que me cortan pies y manos,
Y me arrastran por la villa."*

Pepito el Corcobado.

PEPITO EL CORCOVADO,† a gay lively little hunchback, used
to gain his living by his voice and his guitar; for he was a
general favourite, and was in constant request at weddings
and other festivities. He was going home one night from
one of these festive occasions, being under engagement for
another in the morning, and, as it was in the celebrated
Sierra Morena, he contrived to lose his way. After trying
in vain to find it, he wrapped his cloak about him, and lay
down for the night at the foot of a cork-tree. He had
hardly, however, gone to sleep, when he was awakened by
the sound of a number of little voices singing to an old air
with which he was well acquainted,

Lunes y Martes y Miercoles tres

over and over again. Deeming this to be imperfect, he
struck in, adding,

Jueves y Viernes y Sabado seis.

The little folk were quite delighted, and for hours the
mountain rang with

Lunes y Martes y Miercoles tres,
Jueves y Viernes y Sabado seis.

Monday and Tuesday and Wednesday three,
Thursday and Friday and Saturday, six.

---

* Romancero Castellano por Depping, ii. p. 198, 2nd edit. A translation of
this romance will be found in Thoms's Lays and Legends of Spain.
† *i.e.* Joey the Hunchback. Pepito is the dim. of Pepe, *i.e.* José, Joseph.

They finally crowded round Pepito, and bade him ask what he would for having completed their song so beautifully. After a little consideration, he begged to have his hump removed. So said so done, he was in an instant one of the straightest men in all Spain. On his return home, every one was amazed at the transformation. The story soon got wind, and another hunchback, named Cirillo, but unlike Pepito, as crooked in temper as in person, having learned from him where the scene of his adventure lay, resolved to proceed thither and try his luck. He accordingly reached the spot, sat under the cork-tree, and saw and heard all that Pepito had heard and seen. He resolved also to add to the song, and he struck in with "Y Domingo siete" (*and Sunday seven*); but whether it was the breach of rhythm, or the mention of the Lord's Day that gave offence, he was instantly assailed with a shower of blows or pinches, and to make his calamity the greater, Pepito's hump was added to his own.[*]

We thus may see that there are beings in Spain also answering to the various classes of Fairies. But none of these have obtained the same degree of reputation as the House-spirit, whose Spanish name is Duende or Trasgo. In Torquemada's Spanish Mandeville, as the old English version of it is named, there is a section devoted to the Duende, in which some of his feats, such as pelting people with stones, clay, and such like, are noticed, and in the last century the learned Father Feijoo wrote an essay on Duendes,[†] *i.e.* on House-spirits; for he says little of the proper Spanish Duende, and his examples are Hödiken and the Kobolds, of

---

[*] See Thoms's Lays and Legends of Spain, p. 83. It was related, he says, to a friend of his by the late Sir John Malcolm, who had heard it in Spain. It is also briefly related (probably on the same authority) in the Quarterly Review, vol. xxii. (see above pp. 364, 438). Redi, in his Letters, gives another form of it, in which the scene is at Benevento, the agents are witches, and the hump is taken off, *senza verun suo dolor*, with a saw of butter. *Y Domingo siete* is, we are told, a common phrase when any thing is said or done *mal à propos*.

[†] Teatro Critico, tom. ii. His object is to disprove their existence, and he very justly says that the Duende was usually a knavish servant who had his own reasons for making a noise and disturbing the family. This theory will also explain the Duende-tales of Torquemada.

which he had read in Agricola and other writers. On the whole, perhaps, the best account of the Duende will be found in Calderon's spritely comedy, named La Dama Duende.

In this piece, when Cosme, who pretends that he had seen the Duende when he put out his candle, is asked by his master what he was like, he replies:

> Era un fraile
> Tamañito, y tenia puesto
> Un cucurucho tamaño;
> Que por estas señas creo
> Que era duende capuchino.

This *cucurucho* was a long conical hat without a brim worn by the clergy in general, and not by the Capuchins alone. A little before, Cosme, when seeking to avert the appearance of the Duende, recites the following lines, which have the appearance of being formed from some popular charm against the House-spirit:

> Señora dama duende,
> Duelase de mi;
> Que soy niño y solo,
> Y nunca en tal me ví.

In De Solis' very amusing comedy of Un Bobo hace Ciento, Doña Ana makes the following extremely pretty application of the popular idea of the Duende:

> Yo soy, don Luis, una dama
> Que no conozco este duende
> Del amor, si no es por fama.

In another of his plays (*El Amor al Uso*), a lady says:

> Amor es duende importuno
> Que al mundo asombrando trae;
> Todos dicen que le ay,
> Y no le ha visto ninguno.

The lines from Calderon prefixed to this section of our work, show that money given by the Duende was as unsubstantial as fairy-money in general. This is confirmed by Don Quixote, who tells his rather covetous squire, that "los

tesoros de los caballeros andantes son, como los de los
Duendes, aparentes y falsos."

The Spaniards seem also to agree with the people of other
countries in regarding the Fairies as being fallen angels.
One of their most celebrated poets thus expresses himself:

> Disputase por hombres entendidos
> Si fué de *los caidos* este duende.

Some Spanish etymologists say that Duende is a contraction of *Dueño de casa;* others, that it comes from the Arabic
Dúar, (dwelling) the term used for the Arab camps on the
north-coast of Africa.   To us it appears more probable that
the Visigoths brought their ancient popular creed with them
to Spain * also, and that as Duerg became Drac in Provence, it was converted into Duende in Spain.†   It is further
not quite impossible that Duerg may be also the original of
Trasgo, a word for which we believe no etymon has been
proposed.

---

* See Tales and Popular Fictions, p. 269.

† The change of *r* and *n* is not without examples.   Thus we have
ἄργυρον and *argentum ; water,* English ; *vand,* Danish; *vatn,* Swedish.
Cristofero is *Cristofano* in Tuscan ; *homine, nomine, sanguine,* are *hombre,*
nombre, sangre, Spanish.   In *Duerg* when *r* became *n,* euphony changed *g*
to *d,* or *vice versâ.*   The changes words undergo when the derivation is
certain, are often curious.   *Alguacil,* Spanish, is *Él-wezeer* Arab, as *Azucena*
Spanish, *Cecem* Portuguese (white-lily) is *Súsan* Arab; *Guancia* (cheek) Italian,
is *Wange* German ; Ναύπακτος has become *Lépanto.*   It might not be safe
to assert that the Persian *gurk* and our *wolf* are the same, and yet the letters
in them taken in order are all commutable.   Our *God be with you* has shrunk
to *Goodbye,* and the Spanish *Vuestra merced* to *Usted,* pr. *Usté.*   There must,
by the way, some time or other, have been an intimate connexion between
Spain and England, so many of our familiar words seem to have a Spanish
origin.   Thus *ninny* is from *niño ; booby* from *bobo ; pucker* from *puchero ;*
launch (a boat) from *lancha ;* and perhaps *monkey* (if not from *mannikin*)
from *mono, monico.*   We pronounce our *colonel* like the Spanish *coronel.*

French firefly fairies

Breton fairies from a tale of fairies turning into mortals

FRANCE.

Pourquoi faut-il s'émerveiller
Que la raison la mieux sensée,
Lasse souvent de veiller,
Par des contes d'ogre et de fée
Ingenieusement bercée,
Prenne plaisir à sommeiller?
PERRAULT.

THE Fairy mythology of France may be divided, as respects its locality, into two parts, that of Northern and that of Southern France, the Langue d'Oil and the Langue d'Oc. We will commence with the latter, as adjacent to Spain. Of its mythology, Gervase of Tilbury, who resided in the kingdom of Arles, has left us some interesting particulars, and other authorities enable us to trace it down to the present day. Speaking of the inhabitants of Arles, Gervase thus expresses himself:

"They also commonly assert, that the Dracs assume the human form, and come early into the public market-place without any one being thereby disturbed. These, they say, have their abode in the caverns of rivers, and occasionally, floating along the stream in the form of gold rings or cups, entice women or boys who are bathing on the banks of the river; for, while they endeavour to grasp what they see, they are suddenly seized and dragged down to the bottom: and this, they say, happens to none more than to suckling women, who are taken by the Dracs to rear their unlucky offspring; and sometimes, after they have spent seven years there, they return to our hemisphere. These women say that they lived with the Dracs and their wives in ample palaces, in the caverns and banks of rivers. We have ourselves seen one of these women, who was taken away while washing clothes on the banks of the Rhone. A wooden bowl floated along by her, and, in endeavouring to catch it, having got out into the deep water, she was carried down by a Drac, and made nurse to his son below the water. She returned uninjured, and was hardly recognised by her husband and friends after seven years' absence.

"After her return she related very wonderful things, such as that the Dracs lived on people they had carried off, and turned themselves into human forms; and she said that one day, when the Drac gave her an eel-pasty to eat, she happened to put her fingers, that were greasy with the fat, to one of her eyes and one side of her face, and she immediately became endowed with most clear and distinct vision under the water. When the third year of her time was expired, and she had returned to her family, she very early one morning met the Drac in the market-place of Beaucaire. She knew him at once, and saluting him, inquired about the health of her mistress and the child. To this the Drac replied, 'Harkye,' said he, 'with which eye do you see me?' She pointed to the eye she had touched with the fat: the Drac immediately thrust his finger into it, and he was no longer visible to any one."*

Respecting the Dracs, Gervase farther adds:

"There is also on the banks of the Rhone, under a guardhouse, at the North-gate of the city of Arles, a great pool of the river. . . . In these deep places, they say that the Dracs are often seen of bright nights, in the shape of men. A few years ago there was, for three successive days, openly heard the following words in the place outside the gate of the city, which I have mentioned, while the figure as it were of a man ran along the bank: 'The hour is passed, and the man does not come.' On the third day, about the ninth hour, while that figure of a man raised his voice higher than usual, a young man ran simply to the bank, plunged in, and was swallowed up; and the voice was heard no more."

The word Drac is apparently derived from Draco; but we are inclined to see its origin in the Northern *Duerg*. We must recollect that the Visigoths long occupied Provence and Languedoc. It is, we apprehend, still in use. *Fa le Drac*, in Provençal, signifies *Faire le diable*.† Goudelin, a

* *Otia Imperialia*, p. 987: see above p. 302 *et alib.*
† Like the Irish *Play the Puck*, above, p. 371.

Provençal poet of the seventeenth century, begins his Castel
en l'Ayre with these lines :

> Belomen qu' yeu *faré le Drac*
> Se jamay trobi dins un sac
> Cinc ô siés milante pistolos
> Espessos como de redolos.

The following curious narrative also occurs in Gervase's
work, and might seem to belong to Provence :—

"Seamen tell that one time as a ship was sailing in the
Mediterranean sea, which sea we call ours, she was surrounded by an immense number of porpoises (*delphinos*), and
that when an active young man, one of the crew, had wounded
one of them with a weapon, and all the rest of them had
rapidly sought the bottom, a sudden and awful tempest
enveloped the ship. While the sailors were in doubt of their
lives, lo! one in the form of a knight came borne on a steed
on the sea, and demanded that, for the salvation of all the
rest, the person who had wounded the porpoise should be
delivered up to him. The sailors were in an agony between
their own danger and their aversion to expose their comrade
to death, which seemed to them to be most cruel, and they
thought it infamous to consult their own safety at the
expense of the life of another. At last the man himself,
deeming it better that all should be saved at the cost of one,
as they were guiltless, than that such a number of people
should run the risk of destruction on account of his folly,
and lest by defending him they should become guilty, devoted
himself to the death he merited, and voluntarily mounted
the horse behind the rider, who went over the firm water,
taking his road along it as if it had been the solid land. In
a short time he reached a distant region, where he found
lying in a magnificent bed the knight whom he had wounded
the day before as a porpoise. He was directed by his guide
to pull out the weapon which was sticking in the wound, and
when he had done so, *the guilty right hand gave aid to the wound.*
This being done, the sailor was speedily brought back to the
ship, and restored to his companions. Hence it is, that from
that time forth sailors have ceased to hunt the porpoises."*

* *Otia Imper.* p. 981 : see above, p. 394. It does not appear that the
abode of these porpoise-knights was beneath the water.

Gervase also describes the Kobold, or House-spirit, the
Esprit Follet, or Goblin of the North of France.

"There are," says he, "other demons, commonly called
Follets, who inhabit the houses of simple country people,
and can be kept away neither by water nor exorcisms; and
as they are not seen, they pelt people as they are going in
at the door with stones, sticks, and domestic utensils. Their
words are heard like those of men, but their form does not
appear. I remember to have met several wonderful stories
of them in the Vita Abbreviata, et Miraculis beatissimi
Antonii."*

Elsewhere† he speaks of the beings which he says are
called Lamiæ, who, he relates, are used to enter houses suddenly, ransack the jars and tubs, pots and pitchers, take the
children out of the cradles, light lamps or candles, and
sometimes oppress those who are sleeping.

Either Gervase mistook, or the Fadas of the south of
France were regarded as beings different from mankind. The
former is, perhaps, the more likely supposition. He thus
speaks of them: "This, indeed, we know to be proved every
day by men who are beyond all exception; that we have heard
of some who were lovers of phantoms of this kind,‡ which
they call Fadas; and when they married other women, they
died before consummating the marriage. We have seen most
of them live in great temporal felicity, who when they withdrew themselves from the embraces of these Fadas, or discovered the secret, lost not only their temporal prosperity,
but even the comfort of wretched life."§

"In the legend of St. Armentaire, composed about 1300,
by Raymond, a gentleman of Provence, we read of the Fée
Esterelle, and of the sacrifices to her, who used to give
barren women beverages to drink, to make them fruitful;
and of a stone called *La Lauza de la Fada;* that is the Fairy-
stone on which they used to sacrifice to her." ∥

---

* *Otia Imper.* p. 897. See above p. 407. Orthone, the House-spirit, who,
according to Froissart, attended the Lord of Corasse, in Gascony, resembled
Hinzelmann in many points.   † Ibid.

‡ *Hujusmodi larvarum.* He classes the Fadas with Sylvans and Pans.

§ P. 989. Speaking of the wonderful horse of Giraldus de Cabreriæ ;
Gervase says, *Si Fadus erat, i. e.* says Leibnitz, incantatus, ut *Fadæ, Fatæ,*
Fées.

∥ Cambry, Monumens Celtiques, p. 342. The author says, that Esterelle,

Even at the present day the belief in the Fadas seems to linger in Provence and the adjoining districts.

"On the night of the 31st of December," says Du Mege,[*] the "Fées (*Hadas*)` enter the dwellings of their worshipers. They bear good-luck in their right, ill-luck in their left-hand. Care has been taken to prepare for them in a clean retired room, such a repast as is suited to them. The doors and windows are left open; a white cloth is laid on a table with a loaf, a knife, a vessel full of water or wine, and a cup. A lighted candle or wax taper is set in the centre of the table. It is the general belief that those who present them with the best food may expect all kinds of prosperity for their property and their family; while those who acquit themselves grudgingly of their duty toward the Fées, or who neglect to make preparations worthy of these divinities, may expect the greatest misfortunes."

From the following passage of the Roman de Guillaume au Court-Nez it would appear that three was the number of the Hadas.

> Coustume avoient les gens, par véritez,
> Et *en Provence* et en autres regnez.
> Tables métoient et siéges ordenez,
> Et sur la table iij blans pains bulétez,
> Iij poz de vins et iij hénez de lès
> Et par encoste iert li enfès posez.[†]

---

es well as all the Fairies, was the moon. This we very much doubt. He derives her name from the Breton *Escler,* Brightness, Lauza, from *Lac'h* (Irish *Cloch*), a flat stone.

[*] Monuments religieux des Volces Tectosages, *ap.* Mlle. Bosquet, Normandie, etc., p. 92 : see above, pp. 161, 342.

[†] See Leroux de Lincy, *ap.* Mlle. Bosquet, p. 93, who adds " In Lower Normandy, in the arrondissement of Bayeux, they never neglect laying a table for the protecting genius of the babe about to be born ;" see our note on Virg. Buc. iv. 63. In a collection of decrees of Councils made by Burchard of Worms, who died in 1024, we read as follows : " Fecisti, ut quaedam mulieres in quibusdam temporibus anni facere solent, ut in domo tua *mensam praepares* et tuos cibos et potum cum *tribus cultellis* supra mensam poneres, ut si venissent *tres illae sorores* quas antiqua posteritas et antiqua stultitia Parcas nominavit, ibi reficirentur ... ut credens illas quas tu dicis esse sorores tibi posse aut hic aut in futuro prodesse?" GRIMM. *Deut. Mythol. Anhang*, p. xxxviii., where we are also told that these Parcæ could give a man at his birth the power of becoming a Werwolf. All this, however, does not prove that they were the origin of the *Fées* : see above, p. 6.

Some years ago a lady, named Marie Aycard, published a volume named "Ballades et Chants populaires de la Provence," two of which seem to be founded on popular legends. She names the one La Fée aux Cheveux Verts, and in it relates the story of a young mariner of Marseilles who was in the habit of rowing out to sea by himself in the evening. On one of these occasions he felt himself drawn down by an invisible power, and on reaching the bottom found himself at the gate of a splendid palace, where he was received by a most beautiful fairy, only her hair was green. She at once told him her love, to which he responded as she wished, and after detaining him some time she dismissed him, giving him two fishes, that he might account for his absence by saying that he had been fishing. The same invisible power brought him back to his boat, and he reached home at sunrise. The size and form of his fishes, such as had never been seen, excited general wonder; but he feared the fairy too much to reveal his secret. An invincible attraction still drew him to the submarine palace, but at last he saw a maiden whose charms, in his eyes, eclipsed those of the fairy. He now fled the sea-shore, but every time he approached his mistress he received an invisible blow, and he continually was haunted by threatening voices. At length he felt an irresistible desire to go out again to sea. When there he was drawn down as before to the palace, but the fairy now was changed, and saying, "You have betrayed me—you shall die," she caused him to be devoured by the sea-monsters. But other accounts say that she kept him with her till age had furrowed his brow with wrinkles, and then sent him back to poverty on earth.

The other legend named Le Lutin tells how seven little boys, regardless of the warnings of their old grandmother, would go out at night on various affairs. As they went along a pretty little black horse came up to them, and they all were induced to mount on his back. When they met any of their playmates they invited them also to mount, and the back of the little horse, stretched so that at last he had on him not less than thirty little boys. He then made with all speed for the sea, and plunging into it with them they were all drowned.*

* This may remind us of the Neck or Kelpie above, p. 162. It seems confirmatory of our theory respecting the Visigoths, p. 466.

Passing to Auvergne we find Gregory of Tours in the sixth century thus relating an event which happened in his youth. A man was going one morning to the forest, and he took the precaution to have his breakfast, which he was taking with him, blessed before he set out. Coming to the river, before it was yet day, he drove his bullock-cart into the ferry-boat (*in ponte qui super navem est*), and when he was about half-way over he heard a voice saying, "Down with him! down with him! be quick!" (*Merge, merge, ne moreris!*) to which another replied, "I should have done it without your telling me if something holy did not prevent me; for I would have you to know that he is fortified with the priest's blessing, so that I cannot hurt him."[*]

Miss Costello [†] heard in Auvergne a story of a changeling, which the mother, by the direction of the Curé, took to the market-place, where she whipped it well, till its mother, La Fée du Grand Cascade, brought her back her own child. She also relates at great length a legend which she styles La Blonde de la Roche, in which a young lady, instructed by her nurse, learns to change her form, and thus become a companion of the Fées, who are beings of tiny dimensions. Afterwards, when she is married, they take away her children, but she manages to recover them.

" La Tioul de las Fadas is within five and a half leagues of St. Flour, at Pirols, a village of Haute Auvergne. It is composed of six large rude stones, covered by a seventh, larger and more massive than the rest; it is twelve feet long, and eight and a half wide. The tradition relates that a Fée who was fond of keeping her sheep on the spot occupied by this monument, resolved to shelter herself from the wind and rain. For this purpose she went far, very far, (*bien loin, bien loin*) in search of such masses of granite, as six yoke of oxen could not move, and she gave them the form of a little house. She carried, it is said, the largest and heaviest of them on the top of her spindle, and so little was she incommoded by the weight of it, that she continued to spin all the way." [‡]

[*] Greg. Tur. De Glor. Confess. ch. xxxi., *ap.* Grimm. p. 466.

[†] Pilgrimage to Auvergne, ii. p. 294, *seq.*

[‡] Cambry, Monuments Celtiques, p. 232.

The following legend is traditional in Périgord :—

Embosomed in the forest of the canton of La Double, near the road leading from Périgueux to Ribérac, is a monument named Roque Brun. It consists of four enormous rocks placed two and two, so as to form an alley ten feet long and six wide. A fifth rock, higher and thicker than the others, closes this space on the west. The whole is covered by a huge mass of rock, at least twelve feet by seven, and from three to four feet thick. There can be no doubt of its being the work of man, and it is remarkable that the stone composing it is different from that of the soil on which it stands.* The tradition of the canton, however, is, that many thousand years ago there was a Fée who was the sovereign of the whole country, and having lost her husband in a battle fought in this very place she resolved to bury him on the spot. She therefore called six of her pages, and ordered them to fetch, each one of these stones, and to place them in the order which they still maintain. They instantly obeyed, and they carried and arranged the huge masses as easily as if they had been only rose-leaves. When the tomb was completed, the Fairy ascended it, and turning to the east, she thrice cursed, in a voice of thunder, whoever should henceforth dare even to touch this monument of her royal spouse. Many an instance is still recorded by the peasantry of those who dared and were punished.†

The Fairy-lore of the North of France, at least of Normandy, is, as was to be expected, similar to that of the other portions of the Gotho-German race. We meet it in the *fées* or fairies, and the *lutins* or *gobelins*, which answer to the Kobolds, Nisses, and such like of those nations.‡

The Fées are small and handsome in person; they are

---

* It is evidently a *cromleach*. What is said of the nature of the stones is also true of Stonehenge.

† Lettres de Madame S. à sa Fille. Périgueux, 1830 : by M. Jouannet of Bordeaux.

‡ See Mlle. Bosquet, La Normandie Romanesque et Merveilleuse, and the works there quoted by this learned and ingenious lady. What follows is so extremely like what we have seen above of the Korrigan of the adjacent Brittany, that we hope she has been careful not to transfer any of their traits to her Fées.

fond of dancing in the night-time, and in their dances which are circular they form the *Cercles des Fées*, or fairy-rings. If any one approaches their dance, he is irresistibly impelled to take part in it. He is admitted with the greatest courtesy; but as the whirling movement increases, and goes faster and faster, his head becomes giddy, and he falls to the ground utterly exhausted. Sometimes the *fées* amuse themselves by flinging him up to a great height in the air, and, if not killed by the fall, he is found next morning full of bruises. These little beings, it is also said, haunt solitary springs, where they wash their linen, which they then dry by way of preference on the Druidic stones, if at hand, and lay up in the hollows of rocks or barrows, thence named *Chambres* or *Grottes des Fées*. But, further, it is said of them, like the *Lutins*, they select particular farms to which they resort at night, and there making use of horses, harness and utensils of all kinds, they employ themselves at various kinds of work, of which, however, no traces remain in the morning. They are fond of mounting and galloping the horses; their seat is on the neck, and they tie together locks of the mane to form stirrups. Their presence, however, always brings luck, the cattle thrive where they are, the utensils of which they have made use, if broken are mended and made as good as new. They are altogether most kind and obliging, and have been known to give cakes to those to whom they have taken a fancy.

The Fées of Normandy are, like others, guilty of child-changing. A countrywoman as she was one day carrying her child on her arm met a Fée similarly engaged, who proposed an exchange. But she would not consent, even though, she said, the Fée's babe were *nine times finer than her own*. A few days after, having left her child in the house when she went to work in the fields, it appeared to her on her return that it had been changed. She immediately consulted a neighbour, who to put the matter to the proof, broke a dozen eggs and ranged the shells before the child, who instantly began to cry out, *Oh! what a number of cream-pots! Oh! what a number of cream-pots!* The matter was now beyond doubt, and the neighbour next advised to make it cry lustily in order to bring its real mother to it. This also succeeded; the Fée came

imploring them to spare her child, and the real one should
be restored.

There is another kind of Fées known in Normandy by the
name of *Dames Blanches*, or White Ladies, who are of a less
benevolent character. These lurk in narrow places, such as
ravines, fords and bridges, where passengers cannot well
avoid them, and there seek to attract their attention. The
Dame Blanche sometimes requires him whom she thus meets
to join her in a dance, or to hand her over a plank. If he
does so she makes him many courtesies, and then vanishes.
One of these ladies named La Dame d' Aprigny, used to
appear in a winding narrow ravine which occupied the place
of the present Rue Saint Quentin at Bayeux, where, by her
involved dances, she prevented any one from passing. She
meantime held out her hand, inviting him to join her, and if
he did so she dismissed him after a round or two; but if he
drew back, she seized him and flung him into one of the
ditches which were full of briars and thorns. Another Dame
Blanche took her station on a narrow wooden bridge over the
Dive, in the district of Falaise, named the Pont d' Angot. She
sat on it and would not allow any one to pass unless he went
on his knees to her; if he refused, the Fée gave him over to
the *lutins*, the cats, owls, and other beings which, under her
sway, haunt the place, by whom he was cruelly tormented.

Near the village of Puys, half a league to the north-east of
Dieppe, there is a high plateau, surrounded on all sides by
large entrenchments, except that over the sea, where the
cliffs render it inaccessible. It is named *La Cité de Limes*
or *La Camp de César* or simply *Le Catel* or *Castel*. Tradition
tells that the Fées used to hold a fair there, at which all
sorts of magic articles from their secret stores were offered
for sale, and the most courteous entreaties and blandishments
were employed to induce those who frequented it to become
purchasers. But the moment any one did so, and stretched
forth his hand to take the article he had selected, the
perfidious Fées seized him and hurled him down the cliffs.

Such are the accounts of the Fées still current in Normandy. To these we may add that of Dame Abonde or
Habonde, current in the middle ages. William of Auvergne,
bishop of Paris, who died in the year 1248, thus writes :—

" Sunt et aliæ ludificationes malignorum spiritorum quas

faciunt interdum in nemoribus et locis amœnis, et frondosis arboribus, ubi apparent in similitudine *puellarum* aut *matronarum* ornatu muliebri et *candido;* interdum etiam *in stabulis, cum luminaribus cereis, ex quibus apparent distillationes in comis et collis equorum et comæ ipsorum diligenter tricatæ;* et audies eos, qui talia se vidisse fatentur, dicentes veram ceram esse quæ de luminaribus hujusmodi stillaverat. De illis vero substantiis quæ apparent in domibus quas *dominas nocturnas* et *principem* earum vocant *Dominam Abundiam* pro eo quod domibus, quas frequentant, abundantiam bonorum temporalium præstare putantur non aliter tibi sentiendum est neque aliter quam quemadmodum de illis audivisti. Quapropter eo usque invaluit stultitia hominum et insania vetularum ut vasa vini et receptacula ciborum discooperta relinquant, et omnino nec obstruent neque claudant eis noctibus quibus ad domos suos eas credunt adventuras ; ea de causa videlicet ut cibos et potus quasi paratos inveniant, et eos absque difficultate apparitionis pro beneplacito sumant."*

Dame Abonde is also mentioned in the same century in the celebrated Roman de la Rose as follows :—

> Qui les cinc sens ainsinc deçoit
> Par les fantosmes qu'il reçoit,
> Dont maintes gens par lor folie
> Cuident estre par nuit estries (*allés*)
> *Errans* avecques *Dame Habonde.*
> Et dient que par tout le monde
> Si tiers enfant de nacion (*naissance*)
> Sunt de ceste condicion,
> Qu'ils vont trois fois en la semaine,
> Li cum destinée les maine (*mène*),
> Et par tous ces ostex (*hôtels*) se boutent,
> Ne cles ne barres ne redoutent.
> Ains sen entrent par les fendaces (*fentes*)
> Par chatieres et par crevaces.
> Et se partent des cors les ames
> Et vont avec les *bonnes dames*
> Par leur forains et par maisons.
> Et le prouvent par tiex (*ces*) raisons :
> Que les diversités veues
> Ne sont pas en lor liz (*lits*) venues,

---

* Opera i. 1036; Paris, 1674, *ap.* Grimm, Deut. Mythol. p. 263.

Ains (*anzi* It.) sunt lor ames que laborent
Et par le monde ainsinc sen corent.*

In these places we find that Abundia is a queen or ruler
over a band of what we may call fairies, who enter houses at
night, feast there, twist the horses' manes, etc.   This may
remind us at once of Shakespeare's Queen Mab, whom, though
only acquainted with Habundia through a passage in Heywood,† we conjectured to have derived her name from that
of this French dame.‡   Chaucer, by the way, always spells
habundance with an *h*, which may have become *m* as it does
n in Numps from Humphrey ; so Edward makes Ned, Oliver
Noll, etc.

The Lutin or Gobelin§ of Normandy hardly differs in any
respect from the domestic spirit of Scandinavia and Germany.
He is fond of children and horses ; and if the proverb

> Ou il y a belle fille et bon vin
> Là aussi hante le lutin

lie not, of young maidens also.   He caresses the children,
and gives them nice things to eat, but he also whips and
pinches them if naughty.‖   He takes great care of the
horses, gallops them at times, and *lutines* their manes, *i.e.*, *elfs*

---

* *Ap.* Grimm, *ut sup.* Douce (Ill. of Shak. i. 382) was, we believe, the
firs⸍ who directed attention to Abundia.   He quotes from an old *fabliau :*
> Ceste richesse nus abonde,
> Nos l'avons de par Dame Abonde.

† One kind of these the Italians Fatæ name ;
Fée the French ; we Sybils ; and the same
Others White Nymphs ; and those that have them seen,
Night Ladies some, of which Habundia queen.
Hierarchie, viii. p. 507.

‡ Mr. Thoms prefers a derivation from the Cymric, *Mab*, boy, child.

§ There is no satisfactory derivation of *Lutin*, for we cannot regard as such
Grimm's *à luctu*.   *Gobelin, Goblin,* or *Goubelin*, is evidently the same as
Kobold.   *Follet* (from *fol, fou*) and *Farfadet*, are other names.   Both
Gobelin and *Lutin* were in use in the 11th century.   Orderic Vitalis, speaking
of the demon whom St. Taurin drove out of the temple of Diana, says, *Hunc
vulgus Gobelinum appellat*, and Wace (Roman de Rou, *v.* 9715) says of the
familiar of bishop Mauger who excommunicated the Conqueror
> *Ne sei s'esteit lutin ou non.*

‖ Mothers also threaten their children with him.   *Le gobelin vous mangera,
le gobelin vous emportera.*   Père L'Abbé, *Etymologie*, i. p. 262.

or plaits and twists them in an inexplicable manner. So fond, indeed, is he of this amusement, that it is related that when one time two young girls fell asleep in a stable, he *lutined* their hair in such a way that they had to cut it all off. Sometimes the Lutin takes the form of a young villager, and struts about with great complacency. On such occasions it is necessary to call him Bon Garçon, a thing the Norman peasant never neglects to do. At other times he appears under the form of a horse ready bridled and saddled. If any peasant, weary after his day's work, is induced to mount him in order to ride home, he begins to kick and fling and rear and bound, and ends by jerking him into a marsh or a ditch full of water. When he takes this form he is called Le Cheval Bayard, probably after the famous steed of the Paladin Rinaldo.

The following tradition of "*Le Lutin, ou le Fé amoureux,*" is related in the neighbourhood of Argentan :—

A Fé was fond of a pretty young *paysanne*, and used to come every evening when she was spinning at her fireside, and take his seat on a stool opposite to her, and keep gazing on her fair face. The ungrateful object of this respectful attention, however, told her husband the whole story, and in his jealous mood he resolved to have his revenge of the amorous Lutin. Accordingly, he heated the girdel (*galetière*) red-hot, and placed it on the seat which he used to occupy, and then dressing himself in his wife's clothes, he sat in her place, and began to spin as well as he could. The Fé came as usual, and instantly perceived the change. "Where," said he, "is La-belle belle of yesterday evening, who draws, draws, and keeps always twirling, while you, you turn, turn, and never twirl?" He, however, went and took his usual seat, but immediately jumped up, screaming with pain. His companions, who were at hand, inquired the cause. "I am burnt," cried he. "Who burned you?" cried they. "Myself," replied he; for this the woman had told him was her husband's name. At this they mocked at him and went away.*

The best way, it is said, to banish a Lutin who haunts a

---

* In another French tale a man to deceive a Fée, put on his wife's clothes and was minding the child, but she said as she came in, " Non, tu ne point la belle d'hier au soir, tu ne files, ni ne vogues, ni ton fuseau ne t'enveloppes," and to punish him she turned some apples that were roasting on the hearth into peas. SCHREIBER *ap.* GRIMM, p. 385.

house, is to scatter flax-seed in the room that he most frequents. His love of neatness and regularity will not allow him to let it lie there, and he soon gets tired of picking it up, and so he goes away.

A Lutin, named the Nain Rouge, haunts the coast of Normandy. He is kind in his way to the fishermen, and often gives them valuable aid; but he punishes those who do not treat him with proper respect. Two fishermen who lived near Dieppe, were going one day to Pollet. On their way they found a little boy sitting on the road-side; they asked him what he was doing there. "I am resting myself," said he, "for I am going to Berneville" (a village within a league of Pollet.) They invited him to join company; he agreed, and amused them greatly with his tricks as they went along. At last, when they came to a pond near Berneville, the malicious urchin caught up one of them, and flung him, like a shuttlecock, up into the air over it; but, to his great disappointment, he saw him land safe and sound at the other side. "Thank your patron-Saint," cried he, with his cracked voice, "for putting it into your mind to take some holy water when you were getting up this morning. But for that you'd have got a nice dip." *

A parcel of children were playing on the strand at Pollet, when Le Petit Homme Rouge came by. They began to make game of him, and he instantly commenced pelting them with stones at such a rate that they found it necessary to seek refuge in a fishing-boat, where, for the space of an hour, as they crouched under the hatches, they heard the shower of stones falling so that they were sure the boat must be buried under them. At length the noise ceased, and when they ventured to peep out, not a stone was to be seen.

There is also in Normandy a kind of spirits called Lubins, which take the form of wolves, and enter the churchyards under the guidance of a chief, who is quite black. They are very timorous, and at the least noise they fly, crying " *Robert est mort! Robert est mort!* " People say of a timorous man, " *Il a peur de Lubins!* " †

---

* See above, p. 471.

† Lubin may be only another form of Lutin, and connected with the English Lob. Its likeness to *loup* may have given occasion to the fiction of their taking the lupine form.

Illustration for ''Hop o' my Thumb'' by Gustave Doré

The Fay Mélusine

A belief in Fées, similar to those which we nave denominated Fairies of Romance, seems to have prevailed all over France during the middle ages.

The great Bertrand Duguesclin married a lady named Tiphaine, "extraite de noble lignée," says his old biographer; "laquelle avoit environ vingt-quatre ans, ne onques n'avoit été mariée et éstoit bonne et sage, et moult experte aux arts d'astronomie; aucuns disoient qu'elle éstoit *faée* mais non éstoit, mais éstoit ainsi inspirée et de la Grace de Dieu."

One of the chief articles of accusation against the heroic and unfortunate Maid of Orleans, was " Que souvent alloit à une belle fontaine au pais de Lorraine, laquelle elle nommoit *bonne fontaine aux Fées* nostre Seigneur, et en icelui lieu tous ceulx de pays quand ils avoient fiebvre ils alloient pour recouvrer garison, et la alloit souvent la dite Jehanne la Pucelle, sous un grand arbre qui la fontaine ombroit, et s'apparurent à elle St. Katerine et St. Marguerite." * She was also asked " Si elle sçait rien de *ceux qui vont avecq les Fées?* " †

Of these Fées the most celebrated is Melusina, who was married to the Count of Lusignan. Toward the end of the fourteenth century, Jean d'Arras collected the traditions relating to her, and composed what he called her " Chronicle." Stephen, a Dominican of the house of Lusignan, took up the history written by Jean D'Arras, gave it consistency, and cast such splendour about his heroine, that several noble houses were ambitious of showing a descent from her. Those of Luxembourg and Rohan even falsified their genealogies for that purpose; and the house of Sassenage, though it might claim its descent from a monarch, preferred Melusina, and to gratify them it was feigned that when she quitted Lusignan she retired to the grot of Sassenage, in Dauphiny.

The following is a slight sketch of the story of the fair Melusina.‡

> Ange par la figure, et serpent par le reste.
> DE LILLE.

---

* Chartier.   † See above, p. 475.
‡ Histoire de Mélusine, tirée des Chroniques de Poitou. Paris, 1698. Dobeneck, des Deutschen Mittelalter und Volksglauben.

Legend of Melusina.

Elinas, king of Albania, to divert his grief for the death of his wife, amused himself with hunting. One day, at the chase, he went to a fountain to quench his thirst: as he approached it he heard the voice of a woman singing, and on coming to it he found there the beautiful Fay Pressina.

After some time the Fay bestowed her hand upon him, on the condition that he should never visit her at the time of her lying-in. She had three daughters at a birth : Melusina, Melior, and Palatina. Nathas, the king's son by a former wife, hastened to convey the joyful tidings to his father, who, without reflection, flew to the chamber of the queen, and entered as she was bathing her daughters. Pressina, on seeing him, cried out that he had broken his word, and she must depart; and taking up her three daughters, she disappeared.

She retired to the Lost Island ;* so called because it was only by chance any, even those who had repeatedly visited it, could find it. Here she reared her children, taking them every morning to a high mountain, whence Albania might be seen, and telling them that but for their father's breach of promise they might have lived happily in the distant land which they beheld. When they were fifteen years of age, Melusina asked her mother particularly of what their father had been guilty. On being informed of it, she conceived the design of being revenged on him. Engaging her sisters to join in her plans, they set out for Albania : arrived there, they took the king and all his wealth, and, by a charm, inclosed him in a high mountain, called Brandelois. On telling their mother what they had done, she, to punish them for the unnatural action, condemned Melusina to become every Saturday a serpent, from the waist downwards, till she

* _i. e._ Cephalonia, see above, p. 41.

should meet a man who would marry her under the condition of never seeing her on a Saturday, and should keep his promise. She inflicted other judgements on her two sisters, less severe in proportion to their guilt. Melusina now went roaming through the world in search of the man who was to deliver her. She passed through the Black Forest, and that of Ardennes, and at last she arrived in the forest of Colombiers, in Poitou, where all the Fays of the neighbourhood came before her, telling her they had been waiting for her to reign in that place.

Raymond having accidentally killed the count, his uncle, by the glancing aside of his boar-spear, was wandering by night in the forest of Colombiers. He arrived at a fountain that rose at the foot of a high rock. This fountain was called by the people the Fountain of Thirst, or the Fountain of the Fays,* on account of the many marvellous things which had happened at it. At the time, when Raymond arrived at the fountain, three ladies were diverting themselves there by the light of the moon, the principal of whom was Melusina. Her beauty and her amiable manners quickly won his love : she soothed him, concealed the deed he had done, and married him, he promising on his oath never to desire to see her on a Saturday. She assured him that a breach of his oath would for ever deprive him of her whom he so much loved, and be followed by the unhappiness of both for life. Out of her great wealth, she built for him, in the neighbourhood of the Fountain of Thirst, where he first saw her, the castle of Lusignan. She also built La Rochelle, Cloitre Malliers, Mersent, and other places.

But destiny, that would have Melusina single, was incensed against her. The marriage was made unhappy by the deformity of the children born of one that was enchanted; but still Raymond's love for the beauty that ravished both heart and eyes remained unshaken. Destiny now renewed her attacks. Raymond's cousin had excited him to jealousy and to secret concealment, by malicious suggestions of the purport of the Saturday retirement of

* It is at this day (1698) corruptly called La Font de Séc; and every year in the month of May a fair is held in the neighbouring mead, where the pastry-cooks sell figures of women, *bien coiffées*, called Merlusines.—*French Author's Note*

the countess. He hid himself; and then saw how the lovely
form of Melusina ended below in a snake, gray and sky-
blue, mixed with white. But it was not horror that seized
him at the sight, it was infinite anguish at the reflection
that through his breach of faith he might lose his lovely wife
for ever. Yet this misfortune had not speedily come on him,
were it not that his son, Geoffroi with the tooth,* had burned
his brother Freimund, who would stay in the abbey of
Malliers, with the abbot and a hundred monks. At which
the afflicted father, count Raymond, when his wife Melusina
was entering his closet to comfort him, broke out into these
words against her, before all the courtiers who attended
her :—" Out of my sight, thou pernicious snake and odious
serpent! thou contaminator of my race! "

Melusina's former anxiety was now verified, and the evil
that had lain so long in ambush had now fearfully sprung on
him and her. At these reproaches she fainted away; and
when at length she revived, full of the profoundest grief, she
declared to him that she must now depart from him, and, in
obedience to a decree of destiny, fleet about the earth in pain
and suffering, as a spectre, until the day of doom; and that
only when one of her race was to die at Lusignan would she
become visible.

Her words at parting were these :

" But one thing will I say unto thee before I part, that
thou, and those who for more than a hundred years shall
succeed thee, shall know that whenever I am seen to hover
over the fair castle of Lusignan, then will it be certain that
in that very year the castle will get a new lord; and though
people may not perceive me in the air, yet they will see me
by the Fountain of Thirst; and thus shall it be so long as
the castle stands in honour and flourishing—especially on
the Friday before the lord of the castle shall die." Immediately, with wailing and loud lamentation, she left the castle
of Lusignan,† and has ever since existed as a spectre of the
night. Raymond died as a hermit on Monserrat.

---

* A boar's tusk projected from his mouth. According to Brantôme, a
figure of him, cut in stone, stood at the portal of the Mélusine tower, which
was destroyed in 1574.

† At her departure she left the mark of her foot on the stone of one of the
windows, where it remained till the castle was destroyed.

The president de Boissieu says,* that she chose for her retreat one of the mountains of Sassenage, near Grenoble, on account of certain vats that are there, and to which she communicated a virtue which makes them, at this day, one of the seven wonders of Dauphiné. They are two in number, of great beauty, and so admirably cut in the rock, that it is easy to see they are not the work of unaided nature. The virtue which Melusina communicated to them was, that of announcing, by the water they contain, the abundance or scantiness of the crops. When there is to be an abundant harvest, it rises over the edges, and overflows; in middling years, the vats are but half full; and when the crops are to fail, they are quite dry. One of these vats is consecrated to corn, the other to wine.

The popular belief was strong in France that she used to appear on what was called the tower of Melusina as often as any of the lords of the race of Lusignan was to die; and that when the family was extinct, and the castle had fallen to the crown, she was seen whenever a king of France was to depart this life. Mézeray informs us that he was assured of the truth of the appearance of Melusina on this tower previous to the death of a Lusignan, or a king of France, by people of reputation, and who were not by any means credulous. She appeared in a mourning dress, and continued for a long time to utter the most heart-piercing lamentation.

The following passage occurs in Brantôme's Eloge of the Duke of Montpensier, who in 1574 destroyed Lusignan, and several other retreats of the Huguenots:

"I heard, more than forty years ago, an old veteran say, that when the Emperor Charles V. came to France, they brought him by Lusignan for the sake of the recreation of hunting the deer, which were there in great abundance in fine old parks of France; that he was never tired admiring and praising the beauty, the size, and the chef d'œuvre of that house, built, which is more, by such a lady, of whom he made them tell him several fabulous tales, which are there quite common, even to the good old women who washed their linen at the fountain, whom Queen Catherine of Medicis, mother to the king, would also question and listen to. Some

---

* In his poem of Melusina, dedicated to Christina of Sweden.

told her that they used sometimes to see her come to the fountain to bathe in it, in the form of a most beautiful woman, and in the dress of a widow. Others said that they used to see her, but very rarely, and that on Saturday evening, (for in that state she did not let herself be seen,) bathing, half her body being that of a very beautiful lady, the other half ending in a snake: others, that she used to appear a-top of the great tower in a very beautiful form, and as a snake. Some said, that when any great disaster was to come on the kingdom, or a change of reign, or a death, or misfortune among her relatives, who were the greatest people of France, and were kings, that three days before she was heard to cry, with a cry most shrill and terrible, three times.

"This is held to be perfectly true. Several persons of that place, who have heard it, are positive of it, and hand it from father to son; and say that, even when the siege came on, many soldiers and men of honour who were there affirmed it. But it was when the order was given to throw down and destroy her castles that she uttered her loudest cries and wails. This is perfectly true, according to the saying of people of honour. Since then she has not been heard. Some old wives, however, say she has appeared to them, but very rarely."

Jean d'Arras declares that Serville, who defended the castle of Lusignan for the English against the Duke of Berri, swore to that prince, upon his faith and honour, "that, three days before the surrender of the fortress, there entered into his chamber, though the doors were shut, a large serpent, enamelled with white and blue, which came and struck its tail several times against the feet of the bed where he was lying with his wife, who was not at all frightened at it, though he was very much so; and that when he seized his sword, the serpent changed all at once into a woman, and said to him, *How, Serville, you who have been at so many sieges and battles, are you afraid! Know that I am the mistress of this castle, which I have built, and that you must surrender it very soon.* When she had ended these words she resumed her serpent-shape, and glided away so swiftly that he could not perceive her." The author adds, that the prince told him that other credible people had sworn to him that they too had seen her at the same time in other places in the neighbourhood, and in the same form.

The old castle of Pirou, on the coast of the Cotentin, in Lower Normandy, likewise owes its origin to the Fées.* These were the daughters of a great lord of the country, who was a celebrated magician. They built the castle long before the time of the invasions of the Northmen, and dwelt there in peace and unity. But when these pirates began to make their descents on the coast, the Fées, fearing their violence, changed themselves into wild geese, and thus set them at defiance. They did not, however, altogether abandon their castle; for the elders of the place assert that every year, on the first of March, a flock of wild geese returns to take possession of the nests they had hollowed out for themselves in its walls. It was also said that when a male child was born to the illustrious house of Pirou, the males of these geese, displaying their finest grey plumage, strutted about on the pavement in the courts of the castle; while, if it was a girl, the females, in plumage whiter than snow, took precedence then over the males. If the new-born maiden was to be a nun, it was remarked that one of them did not join with the rest, but kept alone in a corner, eating little, and deeply sighing.

The following traditions are attached to the castles of Argouges and Rânes, in Normandy :—†

One of the lords of Argouges, when out hunting one day, met a bevy of twenty ladies of rare beauty, all mounted on palfreys white as the driven snow. One of them appeared to be their queen, and the lord of Argouges became all at once so deeply enamoured of her, that he offered on the spot to marry her. This lady was *fée*; she had for a long time past secretly protected the Sire d'Argouges, and even caused him to come off victorious in a combat with a terrible giant. As she loved the object of her care, she willingly accepted his troth, but under the express condition that he should never pronounce in her presence the name of Death. So light a

---

* Mlle Bosquet, *ut sup.* p. 100.

† Mlle. Bosquet, *ut sup.* p. 98. The castle of Argouges is near Bayeux, that of Rânes is in the arrondissement of Argentan.

condition caused no difficulty ; the marriage took place under the happiest auspices, and lovely children crowned their union. The fatal word was never heard, and their happiness seemed without alloy. It came to pass, however, one day at length, that the wedded pair were preparing to give their presence at a tournament. The lady was long at her toilet, and her husband waited for her with impatience. At length she made her appearance. "Fair dame," said he, when he saw her, "you would be a good person to send to fetch Death ; for you take long enough to perform what you are about."* Hardly had he pronounced the fatal word when, uttering a piercing cry, as if actually struck by death, the Fée lady disappeared, leaving the mark of her hand on the gate. She comes every night clad in a white robe, and wanders round and round the castle, uttering deep and continuous groans, amid which may be heard, in funereal notes, *Death ! Death !*†

The same legend, as we have said, adheres to the castle of Rânes, where, however, it was on the top of a tower that the Fée vanished, leaving, like Melusina, the mark of her foot on the battlements, where it is still to be seen.

In explication of the former legend, M. Pluque observes, that at the siege of Bayeux by Henry I., in 1106, Robert d'Argouges vanquished in single combat a German of huge stature ; and that the crest of the house of Argouges is Faith, under the form of a woman naked to the waist, seated in a bark, with the motto, or war-cry, *A la Fé !* (i. e. *à la foi !*) which the people pronounce *A la Fée !*

So far the genuine French Fées. On the revival of learning they appear to have fallen into neglect, till the memory of them was awakened by the appearance of the translation of the Italian tales of Straparola, many of which seem to have become current among the people ; and in the end of the seventeenth century, the Contes des Fées of Perrault, Madame d'Aulnoy, and their imitators and successors, gave them vogue throughout Europe. These tales are too well known to our readers to require us to make any observations on them.

* This proverbial expression is to be met with in various languages : see Grimm, Deut. Mythol. p. 802. † See above, p. 458.

EASTERN EUROPE.

Up the hill I went, and gazed round,
  Hoping golden maids to see;
Trooping lovely maidens came, who
  Round the hill danced merrily.

All the sweetest ditties singing,
  Sweetest ditties that might be;
Bearing fragrant apple-blossoms,
  These fair maidens came to me.

                    LETTISH SONG.

EUROPE is inhabited on the east and north-east, from the
Frozen Ocean to the Adriatic, by two extensive races named
the Finns and the Slaves.   The former dwell round the
northern edge of Scandinavia by the Icy Ocean, and on the
east and south-east of the Baltic.   The Majjars, or the
dominant portion of the people of Hungary, are also of
Finnish origin.   The Slaves who are akin to the Gotho-
German race are also widely spread.   This stem numbers
among its branches the Russians, Poles, Bohemians, Servians, and the nations dwelling north-east of the Adriatic.
Our knowledge of the popular mythology of both races is
very limited.

FINNS.

Bee! thou little mundane bird!
Fly away to where I bid thee;
O'er the moon, beneath the sun,
Behind the lofty heaven's stars,
Close by the Wain's axle—fly
To the great Creator's court.

                    FINNISH RUNE.

OF the mythology of the Finnish race, the first possibly that
appeared in Europe, and one of the most widely spread in
the world, our knowledge, as we have just stated, is very

slight. It appears, however, either to have influenced that of the Gothic race, or to have been affected by it.

The Finlanders, Laplanders, and other nations of this race, who are neighbours of the Scandinavians and Germans, believe, like them, in Dwarfs and Kobolds. The former they describe as having a magnificent region under the ground, to which mortals are sometimes admitted and are there sumptuously entertained, getting plenty of tobacco and brandy, and other things esteemed by them delicious.

It is an article of faith with the Finns that there dwell under the altar in every church little misshapen beings which they call *Kirkonwaki, i. e.*, Church-folk. When the wives of these little people have a difficult labour they are relieved if a Christian woman visits them and lays her hand upon them. Such service is always rewarded by a gift of gold and silver.*

The Kobold of Finland is called Para (from the Swedish Bjära) ; he steals the milk from other people's cows, carries and coagulates it in his stomach, and then disgorges it into the churn of his mistress. There is a species of mushroom, which if it be fried with tar, salt and sulphur, and then beaten with a rod, the woman who owns the Kobold will quickly appear, and entreat to spare him.

The Alp, or nightmare, is called Painajainen, *i. e.*, Presser. It resembles a white maid, and its brightness illumines the whole room. It causes people to scream out wofully ; it also hurts young children, and makes them squint. The remedy against it is *steel* or a broom placed under the pillow. The House-spirit named Tonttu (the Swedish Tomtegubbe) is also common in Finland.† The Esthonians believe that the Neck has fish's teeth.

An Esthonian legend relates that one time a girl was stopt by a pretty boy that had on him a handsome peasant's belt and forced to scratch his head a little. She did so, and while she was so engaged she was, without her knowledge, fastened to him by his belt, but the rubbing of her hand set him to sleep. Meanwhile a woman passed by, who came up and asked the girl what she was doing there. She told her

---

* Mnemosyne, Abo 1821, *ap.* Grimm, Deut. Mythol. p. 426.
† Rühs, Finland und seine Bewohner.

the whole matter, and as she was speaking she freed herself from the belt. The boy, however, slept sounder than ever and his mouth was wide open. The woman who had come nearer cried at once, Ha! that's a *Näkki* (Neck,) see his *fish's teeth!* The Neck instantly vanished.[*]

The following Esthonian legend, though the Devil is the subject, strongly resembles some of those of France and Great Britain:—

A man who had charge of the granary of a farm-house was sitting one day moulding buttons in lead. The Devil came by, saluted him, and said, "What are you doing there?" "I am moulding eyes." "Eyes! could you make me new ones?" "To be sure I could; but I have none by me at present." "Will you then do it another time?" "That will I." "When shall I come again?" "Whenever you please." Next day the Devil came to get his new eyes. "Will you have them large or small?" said the man. "Very large." The man then put a large quantity of lead down to melt, and said, "I cannot make them for you, unless you first let me tie you fast." He then made him lie on his back on a bench and tied him down with good strong thick ropes. When the Devil was thus fast bound he asked the man what his name was. "My name is Myself (*Issi*)," replied he. "That's a good name, I know none better." The lead was now melted; the Devil opened his eyes as wide as he could, expecting to get the new ones. "Now, I'm going to pour it out," said the man, and he poured the melting lead into the eyes of the Devil, who jumped up with the bench on his back, and ran away. As he passed by some people who were ploughing, they asked him "Who did that to you?" "Myself did it (*Issi teggi*)," replied the Devil. The people laughed and said, "If you did it yourself, keep it yourself." The Devil died of his new eyes, and since then no one has seen the Devil any more.[†]

The Hungarians or Madyars (Magyars) as they call them-

---

[*] Grimm, Deut. Mythol. p. 459.

[†] Grimm, Deut. Mythol. p. 979. This is the fourth place where we have met this story. Could they have all come from the Odyssey, the hero of which tells the Cyclops, whom he blinds, that his name is Nobody?

selves, are, as we have seen, a portion of the Finnish race.
Two collections of their popular tales have been published of
late years. The editor of one of them which we have read,*
assures us that he took them from the lips of an old
Hungarian soldier, who knew no language but his own.
We therefore cannot but regard the tales as genuine,
though the mode and tone in which they are narrated by the
editor are not always the best. They contain no traits of
popular mythology,—a circumstance not a little remarkable,
rather resembling the French and Italian Fairy tales.
Several of them, however, are very pleasing. We regret
that we have not seen the other collection, which is apparently of greater value.†

SLAVES.

Whatsoe'er at eve had raised the workmen,
Did the Vila raze ere dawn of morning.
BOWRING, *Servian Popular Poetry.*

A DEMON, in the attire of a mourning widow, used, in the
Eastern Russia, to go through the fields at noon in harvest-
time, and break the legs and arms of the workmen, who
failed, when they saw her, to fall on their faces. There was
a remedy, however, against this. Trees, long venerated,
grew in the adjacent wood, the bark of which being laid on
the wound, removed the pain and healed it.‡

The Vends believe in a similar being; but a Vend knows
that when he converses with her for an hour together about
flax and the preparation of it, if he always contradicts her,
or says the paternoster backwards without stopping, he is
secure.§

The Russians also believe in a species of water and wood-

* Gaal, Märchen der Magyaren. Wien, 1822.
† Mailath, Magyarische Sagen Mährchen, etc., 2 vols, 8vo. Stutg. 1837.
‡ Delrio, Lib. ii. Sect. 2. Boxhorn Resp. Moscov. Pars I.
§ Grimm, Deut. Mythol. p. 447.

maids, called Rusalki. They are of a beautiful form, with
long green hair; they swing and balance themselves on the
branches of trees—bathe in lakes and rivers—play on the
surface of the water—and wring their locks on the green
meads at the water's-edge. It is chiefly at Whitsuntide
that they appear, and the people then singing and dancing,
weave garlands for them, which they cast into the stream.*

The following is the Polish form of a legend which we
have already met with in several places : †

There came to a nobleman an unknown man, who called
himself Iskrzycki (*spark* or *firestone*), and offered to engage
in his service. The contract was drawn up and signed, when
the master perceived that Iskrzycki had horse's hoofs, and
he accordingly wanted to break off the agreement; but the
servant stood on his right, and declared that he would enter
on his duties, even against his master's will. From this
time forwards he took up his abode invisibly in the stove,
and performed all the tasks set him. People gradually grew
accustomed to him, but at last the lady prevailed on her
lord to remove, and he hired another estate. His people
left the castle, and they had already gone the greater part of
the way, when on a bad part of the road the carriage was
near turning over, and the lady gave a loud cry of terror.
Immediately a voice answered from behind the carriage—
" Never fear! Iskrzycki is with you! " The lord and his
lady now saw that there was no way of getting rid of him,
so they went back to the old house, and lived there on good
terms with their servant till the term of the engagement had
arrived.

The Servian ballads, that have lately appeared,‡ have
made us acquainted with an interesting species of beings
called Vilas. These are represented as mountain-nymphs,
young and beautiful, clad in white, with long flying hair.
Their voice is said to resemble that of the woodpecker.
They shoot, according to popular belief, deadly arrows at

---

* Mone, vol. i. p. 144. Grimm, Deut. Mythol. p. 460.
† Grimm, *ut sup.* p. 480.
‡ Published by Wuk and translated by Talvi and others into German, by
Bowring into English.

men, ar d sometimes carry off children, whom their mothers
in their anger have consigned to them or the devil: yet the
general character of the Vilas is to injure none but those who
intrude upon their *kolos*, or roundels.

The Vilas sometimes appear gaily dancing their kolos
beneath the branches of the Vishnia or Vistula cherry; sometimes a Vila is introduced comforting the sorrows of an
enamoured deer; at other times collecting storms in the
heavens;* now foretelling to a hero his impending death;†
now ruthlessly casting down each night the walls of a rising
fortress, till a young and lovely female is immured within
them.‡ She usually rides a seven-year old hart, with a bridle
made of snakes.

The following are specimens of these Servian ballads:

Vilas.

—·—

CHERRY! dearest Cherry!
Higher lift thy branches,
Under which the Vilas
Dance their magic roundels.
Them before Radisha
Dew from flowers, lashes,
Leadeth on two Vilas,
To the third he sayeth—
"Be thou mine, O Vila!
Thou shalt, with my mother,
In the cool shade seat thee;
Soft silk deftly spinning
From the golden distaff." ‡

---

* Bowring, p. 175. *Sabejam oblake,* Cloud-gatherer, is an epithet of the
Vila, answering to the Νεφεληγερέτης of the Grecian Zeus.
† Death of Kralwich Marko. Bowring, p. 97.
‡ The building of Skadra. Ibid. p. 64.
§ We have made this translation from a German version in the Wiener
Jahrbücher, vol. xxx. which is evidently more faithful than Bowring's.

Deer and Vila.

A YOUNG deer track'd his way through the lone forest
One lonely day—another came in sadness—
And the third dawn'd, and brought him sighs and sorrow;
Then he address'd him to the forest Vila:
"Young deer," she said, "thou wild one of the forest!
Now tell me what great sorrow has oppress'd thee;
Why wanderest thou thus in the forest lonely:
Lonely one day—another day in sadness—
And the third day with sighs and anguish groaning?"
  And thus the young deer to the Vila answered:
"O thou sweet sister! Vila of the forest!
Me has indeed a heavy grief befallen;
For I once had a fawn, mine own beloved,
And one sad day she sought the running water;
She enter'd it, but came not back to bless me.
Then, tell me, has she lost her way and wander'd?
Was she pursued and captured by the huntsman?
Or has she left me?—has she wholly left me—
Loving some other deer—and I forgotten?
Oh, if she has but lost her way, and wanders,
Teach her to find it—bring her back to love me!
Oh, if she has been captured by the huntsman,
Then may a fate as sad as mine await him!
But if she has forsaken me—if, faithless,
She loves another deer, and I forgotten—
Then may the huntsman speedily o'ertake her." *

We have already observed how almost all nations compare
female beauty to that of the beings of their legendary creed.
With the Servians the object of comparison is the lovely

---

* Bowring, This version differs considerably from the German one of Talvi.
We feel quite convinced that the English translator has mistaken the sense.

Vila. "She is fairer than the mountain-Vila," is the highest praise of woman's beauty. In the ballad of The Sister of the Kapitan Leka, it is said of the heroine Rossandra, that in no country, either Turkey, or the land of the Kauran, or Jewrs, was her fellow to be found. No white Bula (Mohammedan), no Vlachin (Greek), no slender Latiness (Roman Catholic), could compare with her,

> And who on the hills hath seen the Vila—
> E'en the Vila, brother, must to her yield.

The swiftness of the Vila also affords a subject of comparison : a fleet horse is said to be " Vilaish," or " swift as a Vila."

The Morlacchi of Dalmatia, as Sir Gardner Wilkinson informs us,* believe also in the Vila. They describe her as a handsome female, who accompanies the man who is her favourite everywhere he goes, and causes all his undertakings to prosper. One thus favoured is termed Vilénik. Another of their objects of belief is the Maçieh, who appears in the form of a boy, with a cap on his head, and is always laughing. Any one to whom he appears gets the power of commanding him. If ordered to bring money, he usually steals it from one of the neighbours, and if taxed with his dishonesty, he goes to the sea and comes back dripping and with money.

* Dalmatia and Montenegro, etc.

AFRICANS, JEWS, Etc.

Loud from the hills the voice of riot comes,
Where Yumboes shout and beat their Jaloff drums.

T. K.

THIS division of our work is somewhat miscellaneous, not being restricted to any particular race, or to any determinate part of the earth's surface. It contains merely such matters as appeared to us to be worthy of note, but which we could not include in any of the preceding sections.

AFRICANS.

When evening's shades o'er Goree's isle extend,
The nimble Yumboes from the Paps descend,
Slily approach the natives' huts, and steal,
With secret hand, the pounded coos-coos meal.

T. K.

THE Jaloff inhabitants of the mainland of Africa, opposite the isle of Goree, believe in a species of beings who have a striking and surprising correspondence with the Gothic Fairies. They call them Yumboes, and describe them as being about two feet high, of a white colour, as every thing preternatural is in Africa. It is remarkable that, acting on the same principle as the Greeks, who called their Furies Eumenides, and the Scots and Irish, who style the Fairies Good Neighbours, or Good People, the Africans call the Yumboes, Bakhna Rakhna, or Good People. The dress of the Yumboes exactly corresponds with that of the natives, and they imitate their actions in every particular. They attach themselves to particular families; and whenever any of their members die, the Yumboes are heard to lament them, and to dance upon their graves. The Moors believe the Yumboes to be the souls of their deceased friends.

The chief abode of the Yumboes is a subterraneous dwelling on the Paps, the hills about three miles distant from the coast. Here they dwell in great magnificence, and many wonderful stories are told of those persons, particularly Europeans, who have been received and entertained in the subterraneous residence of the Yumboes: of how they were placed at richly furnished tables; how nothing but hands and feet were to be seen, which laid and removed the various dishes; of the numerous stories the underground abode consisted of; the modes of passing from one to the other without stairs, etc., etc.

In the evening the Yumboes come down to the habitation of man, wrapped close in their *pangs*,* with only their eyes and nose visible. They steal to the huts, where the women are pounding in mortars the coos-coos, or corn, watch till the pounders are gone for sieves to searce the meal, and then slily creep to the mortars, take out the meal, and carry it off in their pangs, looking every moment behind them, to see if they are observed or pursued; or they put it into calabashes, and arranging themselves in a row, like the monkeys, convey it from hand to hand, till it is placed in safety.

They are also seen at night in their canoes, out fishing in the bay. They bring their fish to land, and, going to the fires kindled by the natives to keep away the wild beasts, they steal each as much fire as will roast his fish. They bury palm-wine, and when it becomes sour they drink of it till it intoxicates them, and then make a great noise, beating Jaloff drums on the hills.†

---

* The Pang (Span. *paño*, cloth) is an oblong piece of cotton cloth, which the natives manufacture and wear wrapped round their bodies.

† For the preceding account of the Yumboes we are indebted to a young lady, who spent several years of her childhood at Goree. What she related to us she had heard from her maid, a Jaloff woman, who spoke no language but Jaloff.

JEWS..

———•———

ומזיקיא לא יקרבון במכניך

PSALM XCI. 5. *Chaldaicà.*

And the Mazikeen shall not come near thy tents.

IT has long been an established article of belief among the
Jews that there is a species of beings which they call
Shedeem,* Shehireem,† or Mazikeen.‡ These beings exactly
correspond to the Arabian Jinn;§ and the Jews hold that it
is by means of them that all acts of magic and enchantment
are performed.

 The Talmud says that the Shedeem were the offspring of
Adam. After he had eaten of the Tree of life, Adam was
excommunicated for one hundred and thirty years. " In all
those years," saith Rabbi Jeremiah Ben Eliezar, " during
which Adam was under excommunication, he begat spirits,
demons, and spectres of the night, as it is written, ' Adam
lived one hundred and thirty years, and begat children in his
likeness and in his image,' which teaches, that till that time
he had not begotten them in his own likeness." In
Berashith Rabba, R. Simon says, " During all the one
hundred and thirty years that Adam was separate from Eve,
male spirits lay with her, and she bare by them, and female
spirits lay with Adam, and bare by him."

 These Shedeem or Mazikeen are held to resemble the

---

 * שרים from שדד to lay waste, Deut. xxxii. 17.
 † שעירים from שער horreo, Isaiah, xiii. 22.
 ‡ מזיקין from נזק to hurt.
 § Moses Edrehi, our informant, says that the Mazikeen are called in the
Arabic language, *znoon* (زنون), *i. e.* Jinn.

angels in three things. They can see and not be seen; they have wings and can fly; they know the future. In three respects they resemble mankind: they eat and drink; they marry and have children; they are subject to death. It may be added, they have the power of assuming any form they please; and so the agreement between them and the Jinn of the Arabs is complete.

Moses Edrehi, a learned Jew of Morocco, has translated into Spanish for us several of the tales of the Mazikeen contained in the Talmud and Rabbinical writings. We select the following as specimens; and according to our usual custom, adhere strictly to our original.

The Broken Oaths.

THERE was a man who was very rich, and who had but one only son. He bestowed upon him every kind of instruction, so that he became very learned and of great talent.

Before his death the old man gave a great entertainment, and invited all the chief people of the city; and when the entertainment was over, he called his son, and made him swear, in the name of the great God of the whole universe, that he never would travel or go out of his own country. He then left him the whole of his riches on this condition, and made him sign a paper to that effect, with sufficient witnesses, in the presence of all that company, and he gave the paper into the custody of one of the principal persons.

Some years after the death of his father, there came a very large ship from India, laden with merchandise of great value. The captain when he arrived inquired after the father of this young man, and the people said unto him that he was dead, but that he had left a son, and they conducted the captain to the young man's dwelling. The captain then said unto him, " Sir, I have brought hither much property belonging to thy father, and as there is much property of thy father's still remaining, if thou wilt come with me, thou wilt be able to obtain much riches, for thou canst recover all that is owing unto thy father." He made answer unto the captain and said, that he could not travel, as he had taken an oath unto his father that he never would go out of the country. The captain, however, ceased not every day to persuade him, until at length he gave him his word that he would go with him. He then went unto the learned Rabbin that were at that time, to see if they would give him absolution respecting the oath he had sworn unto his father. But they counselled him not to leave the country. But his eagerness to acquire more riches was so great, that he would not hearken unto the counsel of any one. So he finally took his resolution, and went away with the captain.

Now, when they were in the midst of the sea, lo! the ship went to pieces, and all the merchandise that was on board was lost, and all the people were drowned, save only this young man, who got upon a plank. And the water carried him about from one place unto another, until it cast him upon the land. But here he was in danger of starving, and had nothing to eat but the herbs of the field, or to drink but the running water.

One day an exceeding large eagle drew near unto him, and seated himself on the ground before him. As he was now reduced to despair, and had little hopes of being able to preserve his life, and knew not where he was, he resolved to mount this eagle, and to sit upon his back. He accordingly mounted the bird, and the eagle flew with him until he brought him unto a country that was inhabited, where he left him.* When he saw that he was in a land where there were people, he was greatly rejoiced, and he immediately inquired where the great Rabbi of that country dwelt. But all the people that were there stood mocking at him, and cursing him, and saying that he should die, because he had broken the oath he had sworn unto his father. When he heard this he was greatly astonished at their knowing it, but he went to the house of the chief person among them who said unto him that he should abide in his house until

* Comp. Lane, Thousand and One Nights, iii. p. 91.

they did him justice, because in that country they were all Mazikeen, and they wanted to kill him because he deserved death on account of the oath to his father, which he had broken. "Therefore," said he, "when they will sentence thee, and will lead thee forth to punishment, cry aloud and say, I call for justice before God and the king! The king will then do his utmost to deliver thee out of their hands, and thou wilt remain alive."

Accordingly, when he was tried before the senate, and before their princes and great men, he was found guilty, and sentenced to death, according to the law of God. And when they led him forth to be slain, he put his fingers before God, and before his majesty the king.* When they heard this, they took him before the king, who examined him, and saw that, in justice, he was worthy of death. But the king asked him if he had studied or knew the law of Moses, or had studied the Talmud, and various authors; and he saw that he was very learned, and a great Rabbi, and it grieved him much that he should be put to death. The king, therefore, begged that they would defer his execution until the following day, for he wished to give his case a little further consideration. At this they all held their peace, and departed.

Next day all the senators, governors, chief men, and all the people of the city, came together to see and hear the sentence of the king, and also to behold the death of this man, as it would be for them a very curious sight. Now, while they were all standing there assembled, before the king came forth from his palace to give his judgement, he called for this man who was condemned to death, and asked him if he was willing to remain with him and teach his children what he knew, as, in such case, he would do his utmost to deliver him from death. He made answer that he was willing. The king then went forth from his palace, and seated himself upon his throne of judgement, and called all the chief men, and all the people, and spake unto them in this sort :—

"Sirs, it is a truth that you have adjudged this man to death, which he deserves : but there is no rule without an

* To signify that he appealed to them.

exception, and I believe that this man hath not yet come to his time that he should die. For if it was the will of God that he should die, he would have died along with the rest of the people who were on board the same ship with him when the ship went to pieces, and not have escaped as he hath done. Again, if it was the will of God that he should die, he would not have reached the land, and an eagle would not have come and brought him hither amongst us. In like manner, God hath delivered him from you, for he might have been slain by you. He hath thus been delivered out of these manifold and great perils, and it therefore seemeth unto me that he should live; as for the sin that he hath committed, in breaking his oath, it is between him and God, who shall reward him for it one day or other. He shall therefore be free from us; and I ordain that no one shall touch him, or do him any evil; and whosoever troubleth him shall be put to death."

When they heard these words of the king, they all expressed themselves well pleased at his decision; and the man remained in the house of the king, teaching his children. He continued in the palace for three years, highly respected by every one, and greatly esteemed by the king for his talents and his capacity.

Now it came to pass that the king was obliged to set forth with an army, to war against one of the provinces of his kingdom which had rebelled. As he was on the point to set out, he called for this man, and gave him all the keys of his palaces and his treasures, and said unto him, "Behold! thou mayest view every thing that is in the land and in the palaces; but thou hast here a golden key of one palace which thou must beware of opening, for on the day that thou openest it I will slay thee." Then, charging the people to respect and attend to him, the king took his leave of him and departed. When the king was gone, he began to open and examine all the palaces, and all the curiosities, which were such as he had never seen in his life, and all the treasures of the greatest riches that could be in the world; in short, he saw mountains upon mountains of diamonds of great weight, and other things of various kinds, most admirable to behold. But when he had seen all, he was not satisfied; he wanted to see more. And as his desire was very great, he would open the other palace; and he thought he should suffer no injury thereby, so that he resolved to open it. Five or six times he drew nigh to open it, and as often he drew back in fear: at length he took courage and opened it.

There were seven apartments, one within the other, and every apartment was full of different rich and curious things. In the seventh apartment was the princess, with other women, all richly dressed, and very beautiful. When the princess saw him, she gave a sigh, and said, "Man, it grieveth me for thee! how art thou come hither? Where is thy regard for the advice of my father, who entreated thee not to open this palace, when he gave thee the keys of his palaces and his treasures, and straitly charged thee not to come hither? Know now that my father is coming, and that he will surely slay thee. But if thou wilt follow my counsel, and wilt espouse me, I will save thee; but thou must give unto me thy oath, that thou wilt do it." He replied that he would, and he sware unto her, and gave it unto her in writing. She then said unto him, "When my father asketh thee why thou hast opened the palace, thou shalt make answer, and say that thou desirest to marry me, and then he will let thee escape, and not slay thee."

He had scarcely ended speaking with her, when the king entered, with his sword drawn in his hand, to slay him. Then he threw himself on the ground, and began to entreat him, and said that he was desirous to marry the princess. When the king heard this, he was rejoiced that he would remain there, and so teach his children all the knowledge he possessed; for he was of great capacity in everything. He therefore told him, that he would leave it to his daughter, whether she would have him or not. The king then asked his daughter, and she replied, "What your majesty doth for me is well done." The king then gave his consent for her marriage with him. The contract was made, and notice was given to all the chief persons of the city, and the wedding was appointed to be in two months.

When the appointed time was come, all the chief men of all the provinces of the kingdom were invited, and a great feast was made to celebrate the marriage of the princess; and they were married to their great joy and happiness.

On the first night of their marriage, when the husband and the wife were alone, she said unto him, "Behold! I am not like one of you, and thou seest that, thanks be unto God! there is no defect in my body; if, therefore, though we have been publicly married with the consent of my father, thou art not content to live with me as husband and wife, thou art at liberty, and no one shall know it; but if thou art content with all thy will, thou must swear unto me that thou wilt never leave me." He replied, that he was well content with everything; and he sware unto her, and wrote it down on paper, and signed it with his hand, and gave it unto her; and they lived happily as man and wife for many years, and they had children; and his first-born he named Solomon, after the name of king Solomon.

Immediately after the marriage, the king caused it to be proclaimed that his son-in-law should be the second person in the kingdom to give judgement, and to punish such as should be deserving of punishment. This the king did with the consent of all the great men of the country.

But, after some years, this man began to be very anxious and melancholy; and his wife asked him many times what it was that ailed him, but he would never tell her the cause: yet she persuaded him so much, that at length he told it unto her, and said, that when he looked upon his children he remembered the other children that he had, and his other wife, and that he yearned to behold them once more. His wife replied, "My dear husband, let not this give thee any uneasiness, for if thou wishest to see them, thou canst see them." He answered, "If thou wilt do me this favour and grace, I shall thank thee much." She asked him how long he wished to stay with his wife and children, and he answered, three months; but she said, "No; I will give thee the space of a year, on condition, that as soon as the year is expired thou return again unto me." He answered, "If thou show me this favour, I will do all that thou wilt command me." She said, "Take an oath that thou wilt keep thy word." He then sware, and wrote it down on paper, and gave it unto her.

She then called one of her servants, and ordered him to convey him to his own house with all the speed he could make; and in the space of a few minutes he found himself in his own house with his wife and children. The man then asked him if he had any commands for his lady? He replied, "I have nothing to do with thee or thy lady. I am now with my wife and children; I know no other, and therefore I have no message to give." The servant then returned to his mistress; and she asked him what his master had said, and if he had given him any message. He answered, "Madam, if I tell thee what he hath said, thou wilt not believe me." She then pressed him, and he told her all. She said, "It doth not signify."

He remained, then, very happy with his family; but at the end of the year his wife sent a messenger unto him to call him back unto her, as the year was expired. But he answered that he would not, and that he had nothing to do with them, as he was a man, and had nothing more to say with them. The messenger returned and told his mistress, and she sent other messengers of greater dignity, for she said this one is not sufficient for him. But he made the same reply that he had made unto the first. She then sent greater still, three or four times; and at last she was obliged to send her son Solomon. When he saw his son he embraced him, and asked him what he wanted. He told him that his mother had sent him, that he might come back with him, and that if he would not, she would come and avenge herself upon him. His father replied, that he had no mind to depart from his house; that he would stay with his wife and children, who were human beings like himself. So when his son saw that there was no remedy, and that he would not come with him, he returned unto his mother, and related the whole unto her.

His mother was then obliged to go herself with her great army. When they arrived at the city where the man dwelt, they said unto the princess that they would go up and slay the man that was her husband, and all the people of the city; but she answered, "No; they had not permission to kill any one, as all the Hebrews, when they lie down to sleep at night, make their prayers unto God to protect and guard them from all Mazikeen; so that we have no right or permission to touch them; and if we do them a mischief, we shall be chastised for it by the God of Israel, who governeth the whole world. Do you, therefore, bide here without the city, and in the morning I and my son Solomon will arise and go unto the school of the Rabbin and the Sanhedrim, and if they will do me justice with him, well; if not, I will avenge myself upon him and upon them." They all made answer and said, " It is well said."

In the morning she arose with her son Solomon, and went unto the great school, where the divine Law was taught. They were consulting, when they heard the voice of one crying aloud, and saying, " Sirs, justice before God, and before you, upon such a one, my husband;" and all the people were amazed, and were in astonishment when they heard the voice three times, and saw no one. They then sent for the man, who came unto them and related the whole story, and said that he had no mind to go with her. They again heard the voice, which said, " Sirs, here are his oaths, signed by himself, which he sware and signed each time;" and then three written papers fell before them. They read them, and asked him if that was his signature. He said it was. They said unto him, " It is ill done to break so many oaths," and that there was no remedy, but that he should go with her to where he had lived so many years with her, and where she had saved him from death, and he had had children by her. " As for us, we advise thee to go with her, and if thou dost not, it will not come to good; for she is not an ordinary person, but is a princess, and merits attention, more especially as she hath right on her side." He answered that he would give her Guet (a bill of divorce); but she made answer, that that would not be for her honour. In fine, he refused absolutely to go with her.

After a great deal of argument, and when she saw that there were no means to persuade him, she said, " Sirs, I am highly obliged and grateful to you; for I see that you do me the justice of God, and he will not accept it. You are free, and the sin will be upon his soul. Wherefore, sirs, since there is no remedy with him, I entreat that he will suffer me to take leave of him, and to embrace him." He replied that she might, and as soon as she embraced him she drew out his soul, and he died. She then said, " Sirs, here is his son Solomon, who is one of yourselves. I will give him sufficient riches, and he shall be heir along with the children of his other wife, and you will make him among you a great Rabbi; for he is of sufficient ability, as you may see if you will examine him. Farewell." So saying, she departed with her army.*

The Moohel.

THERE was once a man who was exceedingly rich, but out of all measure avaricious, and who never had done a good deed in his life, and never had given even the value of a farthing unto the poor.

It happened one winter's night, between the hours of twelve and one, that a man came and knocked loudly at the door of this miser. He opened the window, and saw a man at the door, and he asked him what it was he wanted. He said that he wanted him to go with him to a village twelve miles distant from the town, to circumcise a young child that would be eight days old in the morning.

Now you must know, that this man of whom we treat was a Jew and a Moohel, that is, one whose office it is to circumcise the young children; and with all his avarice in money matters, he was not avaricious in his office, for he believed in the end of the world, and therefore he did this good action.

He accordingly agreed to go with the man, and he kindled a fire, and put his clothes before it, and got ready the instruments he required for performing the ceremony. He then set out along with the strange man, whom he knew not, though it was winter, and dark and rainy; and they went along, journeying through the wilderness. This

* From a rabbinical book called Mahasee Yerusalemee, *i. e.* History of a Hebrew of Jerusalem.—" Very old," says Moses Edrehi, " and known by the Hebrews to be true." " Moreover," saith he of another tale, "it really happened, because every thing that is written in the Jewish books is true; for no one can print any new book without its being examined and approved of by the greatest and chiefest Rabbin and wise men of that time and city, and the proofs must be very strong and clear; so that all the wonderful stories in these books are true." The Jews are not singular in this mode of vouching for the truth of wonderful stories.

unfortunate Moohel, who did not know his way in the wilderness, and in the dark, every now and then fell over the stones on the way; but they still went on until they came to a great and lofty mountain in the midst of the wilderness, where people never passed, and where there are no people to be seen, but only dark, dark mountains, that fill with terror those who look upon them.

The man who came with the Moohel now laid his hand on a great stone of the mountain, so large that five hundred persons could not remove or raise it; yet he raised it with only one hand. The place then opened, and they both descended. There were many flights of steps, and it was very deep within the earth, and below there was an entire city. They entered then into a palace that was very large and handsome; it had fine gardens, and there was a great deal of light, and music, and much dancing of men and women. When they saw this Moohel approach, they began to laugh and to mock at him; but the poor Moohel was greatly astonished at all the things that he saw, and as he stood looking on, he began to consider and reflect upon them; and then he saw that they were not human beings like us, and great fear came upon him; but he had no means of getting out, or of saving himself, so he constrained himself, and remained quiet.

Now the man who had brought him thither was one of their commanders, and a great personage among them. He took him then to the apartment of the lying-in woman, that he might view the child. The man then went away, and left him with the lying-in woman. But the woman groaned in great affliction, and began to weep. The Moohel asked her what ailed her? Then said the woman unto the Moohel, "How didst thou come hither? Knowest thou in what place thou art, and amongst whom thou art?" The Moohel replied that he did not, as he had not ventured to speak. The woman then explained, "Thou art in the land of the Mazikeen, and all the people that are here are Mazikeen; but I am a being like unto thyself; for when I was yet young and little, I was once alone in a dark place, and these people took me and brought me hither; and I was married to this husband, who is one of their great men, and who is, moreover, a Jew, for there are different religions among them; and I also am a Jewess; and when this child was born, I spake unto my husband, and entreated of him, that he would get a Moohel to circumcise the babe; and so he brought thee hither. But thou art in great danger here, and art lost; for thou wilt never be able to go out from here, and wilt be like one of them. Yet, as I have compassion for thee, and particularly as thou hast, out of kindness, come hither to circumcise the babe, and out of humanity, I will give thee a counsel that may be of service unto thee; and that is, when they ask thee to eat or to drink, take good heed not to touch anything; for if thou taste anything of theirs thou wilt become like one of them, and wilt remain here for ever."

The husband now came in, and they went to the congregation to perform the morning prayer. After the prayer, they returned to the house to perform the ceremony of circumcision. The Moohel took a cup of wine, and gave it to taste to the lying-in woman, to the babe, and to all who were invited to the ceremony; for this is the manner and the custom. But the man who had fetched the Moohel said unto him, "Thou also shouldst taste." The Moohel replied, that he could not, for he had dreamed an evil dream, and that he must fast; and by this excuse he escaped. But he waited for him till night, and then they brought him meat and drink; but he replied that he could not eat until he had passed two or three days fasting. When the man who had brought him thither saw that he would neither eat nor drink for so long a time, he took compassion upon him, and said unto him, "What is the matter with thee, that thou wilt neither eat nor drink?"—"Sir," replied the Moohel, "I ask and desire no other thing but to go home unto my family; for this week we hold a feast, and I should be with my family. I therefore most humbly supplicate thee to take me unto my own house." He then began to beg and entreat him most earnestly, and the woman also entreated for him.

The man then said unto him, "Since thou desirest to go home unto thy house, come then with me; I will give thee a present for thy trouble. Come with me, where thou mayest see and take whatever will seem good unto thee." The Moohel answered, "I do not wish for anything. Thanks be to God! I am very rich—I want for nothing, but to return home unto my family."—"Nevertheless," said he, "come with me, till I show thee curious things that thou hast never seen in thy life." He was accordingly persuaded; he went with him, and he showed him divers apartments all full of silver, of gold, of diamonds, of all sorts of precious stones, and of other curious and magnificent things, such as he had never seen in his life.

He thus led him from one chamber to another, and continually asked him if he wished for anything; for if he did, he might take it. But he still refused, and would take nothing. At length they came to the last chamber, where there was nothing but bunches of keys hanging. The Moohel raised his eyes at seeing such a number of keys, and, lo! he beheld a bunch of keys that was his own. He began then to reflect deeply; and the man said unto him, "What dost thou stand gazing at? I have shown thee many precious and curious things, and yet thou didst not bestow so much attention upon them as upon these old keys, that are of little worth." "Be not offended, sir," answered the Moohel, "but these keys are so like mine, and I believe they are the same." He took the keys and began to examine them, and to point out each key separately to the man, who at length said unto him, "Thou art right, they are thy keys. Know that I am lord over the hearts of the people who never at any time do good; and as thou performest this good deed of circumcision, and riskest thy life in dangerous journeys, and goest with all sorts of people to do the commandment of the God of Israel, here, take the keys! From henceforward thy heart will be opened,* and will be good toward the poor, which will cause thee to live a long and a happy life with thy family. Come now with me; I will carry thee home to thy house and to thy family. Now shut thine eyes."

He shut his eyes, and instantly found himself in his own house amidst his family. He then began to distribute money to all the poor that were in the land, every week and every month. But the world is always curious to hear novelties and strange events, and the people, and even his own wife, as this was a very wonderful thing, pressed him and persuaded him, until at length he was obliged to relate the whole history of what had befallen him, from the beginning

---

* The moral here is apparent.

even unto the end; and it was a matter of great delight to all the world; and they did much good to the poor, and they all became rich, with great prosperity. And the Moohel lived very long, and spent a great and a happy life with his family, a pattern and an example unto the whole world.*

The Mazik-Ass.

It came to pass in the countries of Africa, in a particular month, during which it is the usage and the custom of the Jews to rise in the night to say their prayers, that a servant, whose business it was to knock at the doors, and to call up the people, found one night an ass (*jumento*) in the street; and he mounted upon him, and went riding along and calling up the people. And, as he rode, lo! the ass began to swell and to increase in size, until he became three hundred yards in height, and reached up even unto the top of the loftiest tower of the church, upon which he set the man, and then went away; and on the morrow the man was found sitting upon the tower. Now, thou must know that this ass was one of the Mazikeen.

The Jews have, as it were, brought us back to Asia. As we proceed eastwards from Persia, where we commenced, India first meets our view, but of the numerous beings of its copious and intricate mythology, no class seems to belong to earth unless it be the Yakshas who attend on Kuveras, the Hindoo Plutos, and have charge of his enchanted gardens on the summit of Himalaya, and who bear some resemblance to the Dwarfs. There are also the misshapen Pisachas, who love to dwell in gloom; the Vidhyadharas, *i. e.*, Masters of Magic, are said to resemble the Jinn of the Arabs; and the dancing and singing Gandharvas and Apsaresas may be compared with the Nymphs of Grecian mythology.

Eastwards still lies China. Here there is a species of

---

* From a very ancient rabbinical book called R. H. It is needless to point out its resemblance to German and other tales.

beings named Shinseën, who are said to haunt the woods and mountains, where, exempt from the passions and the cares of life, they dwell in a state of blissful ease; but still exercise an influence over human affairs. Sometimes they appear as old men with long beards; at other times as young maidens, sauntering amid rocks and woods by moonlight.*

We do not recollect to have met, in our reading, with any other beings bearing a resemblance to what we term Fairies.

CONCLUSION.

HERE, then, we conclude. The task which we imposed on ourselves was to collect, arrange, classify, and give under one point of view the various ideas and legends respecting Fairies and similar beings of the popular creed, which lay scattered in a variety of books and a variety of languages. We have marked resemblances, traced coincidences, and offered etymologies. Many legends, especially German ones, we know, exist, which are not to be found in this work; but, in general, they offer no new traits of popular lore, and most persons will, we apprehend, be content with what we have given.

The labours of MM. Grimm in this department of philosophy can never be too highly praised. They have been, in fact, the creators of it; and the German Mythology is a work of the most extensive learning, and written in the spirit of true philosophy. And this is no light praise; for of all subjects, Mythology appears to be the one on which imagination is most apt to run riot. Hence, it has been frequently almost brought into contempt by the wild vagaries of those who have presumed to write on it without judgement or common sense. Though all may not agree with the opinions or deductions in the preceding pages, we trust that they will find in them no traces of ill-regulated imagination.

As works of this kind have no bearing on material enjoyments, the number of those who will think lightly of them in these days will, of course, not be small. But in the view of sane reason and philosophy, the subject is by no means

* See Davis's translation of The Fortunate Union, i. 68.

unimportant, nay, it is even more important than many of higher pretensions. To trace the corruption and degradation of the pure religion of the Gospel, has always been held to be a task worthy of the highest intellect: we should not, therefore, despise the present one, which is the same in kind though different in degree. We have seen that all these legendary beings and their characters and acts are remnants of ancient religious systems, the mental offspring of deep-thinking sages. It is surely, then, not uninteresting to trace them to their present form and condition. Even in a historic point of view they are not undeserving of attention. Thus, should our theory on the subject be correct, it is of importance to observe how the tribes around the Baltic, when they made conquests in the Roman Empire, brought with them the religious ideas of their forefathers, and left traces of them, which are discernible even at the present day. Again, nothing more interests the botanist than to find the same plants, modified by local circumstances, growing in widely-distant regions. The interest is similar when we find the same legends, modified also by circumstances, springing up in distant countries, and amongst tribes and nations who could hardly have had any communication.*

This work is therefore to be regarded as a part of the philosophy of popular fiction. It is not by any means intended to be a work of mere amusement, and those who view or represent it in that light will do it manifest injustice. Many of the legends, no doubt, may possess attractions even for children; but the same is true of the narratives of Herodotus, and still more of those of the Old Testament, and therefore should not derogate from its real importance. At the same time, we have adopted a light and facile style, as that which we deemed best suited to the character of the subject and the taste of this country; but we trust that this will not lower either our subject or ourselves in the eyes of our readers.†

* Under the title Similar Legends in the Index, legends of this kind are arranged with references to the places where they occur.

† The legends from the German and other languages are, in general, faithfully translated, whence the style is at times rude and negligent; English legends are for the most part, also, merely transcribed.

APPENDIX.

———◆———

THE following tales are some of those which we contributed to the Irish Fairy Legends. Subjoined is a selection from the verses which we have written on various occasions, chiefly to oblige our lady-friends. They are inserted merely to show that the writer could compose well-rimed stanzas, while he lays no claim whatever to the title of poet.

The Harvest Dinner.

———◆———

IT was Monday, and a fine October morning. The sun had been some time above the mountains, and the hoar frost and the dew-drops on the gossamers * were glittering in the light, when Thady

---

* As we have above given an etymon of *cobweb*, we will here repeat our note on the word *gossamer* in the Fairy Legends.

" Gossamers, Johnson says, are the long white cobwebs which fly in the air in calm sunny weather, and he derives the word from the Low Latin *gossapium*. This is altogether unsatisfactory. The gossamers are the cobwebs which may be seen, particularly of a still autumnal morning, in such numbers on the furze-bushes, and which are raised by the wind and floated through the air, as thus exquisitely pictured by Browne in his Britannia's Pastorals (ii. 2),

> The milk-white gossamers not upwards snowed.

Every lover of nature must have observed and admired the beautiful appearance of the gossamers in the early morning, when covered with dew-drops, which, like prisms, separate the rays of light, and shoot the blue, red, yellow, and other colours of the *spectrum*, in brilliant confusion. Of King Oberon we are told—

> A riche mantle he did wear,
> Made of tinsel gossamer,
> Bestrew'd over with a few
> Diamond drops of morning dew.

A much more probable origin of *gossamer* than that proposed by Johnson is

Byrne, on coming in to get his breakfast, saw his neighbour Paddy Cavenagh, who lived on the other side of the road, at his own door tying his brogues.

"A good morrow to you, Paddy, honey," said Thady Byrne.

"Good morrow, kindly, Thady," said Paddy.

"Why, thin, Paddy, avick, it isn't your airly risin', anyhow, that 'ill do you any harm this mornin'."

"It's thrue enough for you, Thady Byrne," answered Paddy, casting a look up at the sky; "for I b'leeve it's purty late in the day. But I was up, you see, murdherin' late last night."

"To be shure, thin, Paddy, it was up at the great dinner, yisterday, above at the big house you wor."

"Ay was it; an' a rattlin' fine dinner we had uv it. too."

"Why, thin, Paddy, agrah, what's to ail you now, but you'd jist sit yourself down here on this piece o' green sod, an' tell us all about it from beginnin' to ind."

"Niver say the word twist, man; I'll give you the whole full an' thrue account uv it, an' welcome."

They sat down on the roadside, and Paddy thus began.

"Well, you see, Thady, we'd a powerful great harvist uv it, you know, this year, an' the min all worked like jewels, as they are; an' the masther was in great sperits, an' he promis'd he'd give us all a grand dinner whin the dhrawin'-in was over, an' the corn all safe in the haggard. So this last week, you see, crown'd the business; an' on Satherday night the last shafe was nately tied an' sint in to the misthress, an' everything was finisht, all to the tatchin' o' the ricks. Well, you see, jist as Larry Toole was come down from headin' the last rick, an' we war takin' away the laddher, out comes the misthress herself—long life to her—by the light o' the moon; an', 'Boys,' sez she, 'yez hav' finish'd the harvist bravely, an' I invite yez all to dinner here to-morrow; an' if yez come airly, yez 'ill git mass in the big hall, widout the throuble o' goin' up all the ways to the chapel for it.'"

"Why, thin, did she raally say so, Paddy?"

"That she did—the divil the word o' lie in it."

"Well, go on."

"Well, if we didn't set up a shout for her, it's no matther!"

"Ay, an' a good right yez had too, Paddy, avick."

"Well, you see, yistherday mornin'—which, God be praised, was as fine a day as iver come out of the sky—whin I tuk the beard off o' me, Tom Conner an' I set off together for the big

suggested by what has been now stated. *Gossamer* is, we think, a corruption of *gorse*, or *goss samyt*, i. e. the *samyt*, or finely-woven silken web that lies on the *gorse* or furze. Voss, in a note on his Luise (iii. 17), says that the popular belief in Germany is, that the gossamers are woven by the Dwarfs.

house. An' I don't know, Thady, whether it was the fineness o' the day, or the thoughts o' the good dinner we wor to have, or the kindness o' the misthress, that med my heart so light, but I filt, anyhow, as gay as any skylark. Well, whin we got up to the house, there was every one o' the people that's in the work, min, women and childher, all come together in the yard; an' a purty sight it was to luk upon, Thady: they wor all so nate an so clane, an' so happy."

"Thrue for you, Paddy, agrah; an' a fine thing it is, too, to work wid a raal gintleman like the masther. But till us, avick, how was it the misthress conthrived to get the mass for yez: shure Father Miley himself, or the codjuthor, didn't come over."

"No, in troth didn't they, but the misthress managed it betther nor all that. You see, Thady, there's a priest, an ould friend o' the family's, one Father Mulhall's on a visit, this fortnight past, up at the big house. He's as gay a little man as iver spoke, only he's a little too fond o' the dhrop,—the more's the pity,— an' it's whispered about among the sarvints that by manes uv it he lost a parish he had down the counthry; an' he was an his way up to Dublin, whin he stopt to spind a few days wid his ould frinds the masther an' misthress.

"Well, you see, the misthress on Satherday, widout sayin' a single word uv it to any livin' sowl, writes a letther wid her own hand, an' sinds Tom Freen off wid it to Father Miley, to ax him for a loan o' the vistmints. Father Miley, you know's a mighty ginteel man intirely, and one that likes to obleege the quolity in anything that doesn't go agin' his juty; an' glad he was to hav' it in his power to sarve the misthress; an' he sint off the vistmints wid all his heart an' sowl an' as civil a letther, Tommy Freen says, for he hard the misthress readin' it, as ivir was pinned."

"Well, there was an alther, you see, got up in the big hall, jist bechune the two doors—if ivir you wor in it—ladin' into the store-room, an' the room the childher sleep in; and whin iviry thing was ready we all come in, an' the priest gev' us as good mass iviry taste as if we wor up at the chapel for it. The mis-thress an' all the family attinded thimsilves, an' they stud jist widinside o' the parlour-door; and it was raaly surprisin', Thady, to see how dacently they behaved thimsilves. If they wor all their lives goin' to chapel they cudn't have behaved thimsilves betther nor they did."

"Ay, Paddy, mavourneen; I'll be bail they didn't skit and laugh the way some people would be doin'."

"Laugh! not thimsilves, indeed. They'd more manners, if nothin' else, nor to do that. Well, to go an wid my story: whin the mass was ovir we wint sthrollin' about the lawn an' place till three o'clock come, an' thin you see the big bell rung out for dinner, an' may be it wasn't we that wor glad to hear it. So away wid us to the long barn where the dinner was laid out ; an' 'pon my conscience, Thady Byrne, there's not one word o' lie in what I'm goin' to tell you ; but at the sight o' so much vittles iviry taste uv appetite in the world lift me, an' I thought I'd ha' fainted down an the ground that was undher me. There was, you see, two rows o' long tables laid the whole linth o' the barn, an' table cloths spred upon iviry inch o' them ; an' there was rounds o' beef, an' rumps o' beef, an' ribs o' beef, both biled an' roast, an' there was ligs o' mootton, and han's o' pork, and pieces o' fine bacon, an' there was cabbage an' pratees to no ind, an' a knife an' fork laid for iviry body ; an' barrils o' beer an' porther, with the cocks in iviry one o' them, an' moogs an' porringirs in hapes. In all my born days, Thady dear, I nivir laid eyes on sich a load o' vittles."

"By the powers o' dilph ! Paddy, ahaygar, an' it *was* a grand sight shure enough. Tare an' ayjirs ! what ill loock I had not to be in the work this year ! But go on, agra."

"Well, you see, the masther himself stud up at the ind uv one o' the tables, an' coot up a fine piece o' the beef for us ; and right forenint him at the other ind, sot ould Paddy Byrne, for, though you know he is a farmer himself, yet the misthress is so fond uv him—he is sich a mighty dacint man—that she would by all manner o' manes hav' him there. Then the priest was at the head o' th' other table, an' said grace for us, an' thin fill to slashin' up another piece o' the beef for us : and forenint him sot Jim Murray the stchewart ; an' shure enough, Thady, it was oursilves that played away in grand style at the beef an' the mootton, an' the cabbage, an' all th' other fine things. An' there was Tom Freen, and all th' other sarvints waitin' upon us an' handin' us dhrink, jist as if we wor so many grand gintle-min that wor dinin' wid the masther. Well, you see, whin we wor about half doon, in walks the misthress hursilf, an' the young masther, an' the young ladies, an' the ladies from Dublin that's down on a visit wid the misthress, jist, as she said, to see that we wor happy and merry ovir our dinner ; an' thin, Thady, you see, widout anybody sayin' a single word, we all stud up like one man, an' iviry man an' boy wid his full porringer o' porther in his hand dhrank long life an' success to the misthress and masther an' iviry one o' the family. I don't know for others, Thady, but for mysilf, I nivir said a prayer in all my life more from the heart ; and a good right I had, shure, and iviry one that was there, too ; for, to say nothin' o' the dinner, is there the likes uv her in the whole side o' the counthry for goodness to the poor,

whethir they're sick or they 're well. Wouldn't I mysilf, if it
worn't but for her, be a lone an' desolate man this blissed
day ? "

" It 's thrue for you, avick, for she brought Judy through it
betther nor any docther o' thim all."

" Well, to make a long story short, we et, an' we dhrank, an'
we laughed, an' we talked, till we wor tirt, an' as soon as it grew
dusk, we wor all called agin into the hall : an' there, you see, the
misthress had got ovir Tim Connel, the blind piper, an' had sint
for all the women that could come, an' the cook had tay for thim
down below in the kitchen ; an' they come up to the hall, an'
there was chairs set round it for us all to sit upon, an' the misthress
come out o' the parlour, an' ' Boys,' says she, ' I hope yez med a
good dinnir, an' I 've bin thinkin' uv yez, you see, an' I 've got
yez plinty o' partnirs, an' it 's your own faults if yez don't spind
a pleasint evinin'.' So wid that we set up another shout for the
misthress, an' Tim sthruck up, an' the masther tuk out Nilly
Mooney into the middle of the flure to dance a jig, and it was
they that futted it nately. Thin the masther called out Dinny
Moran, an' dhragged him up to one o' the Dublin young ladies,
an' bid Dinny be stout an' ax her out to dance wid him. So
Dinny, you see, though he was ashamed to make so free wid the
lady, still he was afeard not to do as the masther bid him ; so,
by my conscience, he bowled up to her manfully, an' hild out
the fist an' axed her out to dance wid him, an' she gev' him her
hand in a crack, an' Dinny whipt her out into the middle o' the
hall, forenint us all, an' pulled up his breeches an' called out to
Tim to blow up ' The Rocks of Cashel ' for thim. An' thin *my*
jewil if you wor but to see thim ! Dinny flingin' the ligs about
as if they 'd fly from off him, an' the lady now here, now there,
jist for all the world as if she was a sperit, for not a taste o'
n'ise did she make on the flure that ivir was hard ; and Dinny
callin' out to Tim to play it up fasther an' fasther, an' Tim almost
workin' his elbow through the bag, till at last the lady was fairly
tirt, an' Dinny thin clapt his hands an' up jumpt Piggy Reilly,
an' she attacked him bouldly, an' danced down Dinny an' thin
up got Johnny Regan an' put her down complately. An' sence
the world was a world, I b'leeve there nivir was such dancin'
seen."

" The sarra the doubt uv it, avick I 'm sartin' ; they 're all o'
thim sich rael fine dancers. An' only to think o' the lady dancin'
wid the likes o' Dinny ! "

" Well, you see, poor ould Paddy Byrne, whin he hears that
the womin wor all to be there, in he goes into the parlor to the
misthress, an' axes her if he might make so bould as to go home
and fetch *his* woman. So the misthress, you see, though you

know Katty Byrne's no great favourite wid hur, was glad tí
obleege Paddy, an' so Katty Byrne was there too. An' thin ould
Hugh Carr axt hur out to move a minnet wid him, an' there was
Hugh, as stiff as if he dined on one o' the spits, wid his black
wig an' his long brown coat, an' his blue stockin's, movin' about
wid his hat in his hand, an' ladin' Katty about, an' lukin' so soft
upon her ; an' Katty, in her stiff mob-cap, wid the ears pinned
down undher her chin, an' hur little black hat on the top uv her
head ; an' she at one corner curcheyin' to Hugh, an' Hugh at
another bowin' to her, an' iviry body wundherin' at thim, they
moved it so iligantly."

"Troth, Paddy, avourneen, that was well worth goin' a mile o'
ground to see."

"Well, you see ; whin the dancin' was ovir they tuk to the
singin', an' Bill Carey gev' the 'Wounded Hussar,' an' the ' Poor
but Honest So'dger,' in sich style that yi 'd have h'ard him on
the top o' Slee Roo ; an' Dinny Moran an' ould Tom Freen gev'
us the best songs they had, an' the priest sung the ' Cruiskeen
Laun' for us gaily, an' one o' the young ladies played an' sung
upon a thing widin in the parlor, like a table, that was purtier
nor any pipes to listen to."

"An' didn't Bill giv' yez 'As down by Banna's Banks I
sthrayed ?' Shure that 's one o' the best songs he has."

"An' that he did, till he med the very sates shake undher us ;
but a body can't remimber iviry thing, you know. Well, where
was I ? Oh, ay ! You see, my dear, the poor little priest was all
the night long goin' backwards an' forwards, iviry minit, bechune
the parlor an' the hall ; an' the sperits, you see, was lyin' opin on
the sideboord, an' the dear little man he cudn't, for the life
uv him, keep himself from it, so he kipt helpin' himself to a
dhrop now an' a dhrop thin, till at last he got all as one as tipsy.
So thin he comes out into the hall among us, an' goes about
whisperin' to us to go home, an' not to be keepin' the family out
o' their bids. But the misthress she saw what he was at, an'
she stud up, an' she spoke out an' she said, ' Good people,' sez she,
'nivir mind what the priest says to yez ; yez are my company,
an' not his, an' yez are heartily welcum to stay as long as yez
like.' So whin he found he cud get no good uv us at all, he
rowled off wid himself to his bid ; an' his head, you see, was so
bothered wid the liquor he 'd bin takin', that he nivir once
thought o' takin' off his boots, but tumbled into bed wid thim
upon him, Tommy Freen tould us, whin he wint into the room
to luk afther him ; and divil be in Tim, when he h'ard it but he
lilts up the ' Priest in his Boots ;' and, God forgive us, we all burst
out laughin', for shure who could hilp it, if it was the bishop
himsilf ?"

"Troth, it was a shame for yez, anyhow. But Paddy, agrah, did yez come away at all?"

"Why at last we did, afther another round o' the punch to the glory an' success o' the family. And now, Thady, comes the most surprisintest part o' the whole story. I was all alone, you see, for my woman, you know, cudn't lave the childher to come to the dance; so, as it was a fine moonshiny night, nothin' 'ud sarve me but I must go out into the paddock, to luk afther poor Rainbow the plough bullock, that's got a bad shouldher, and so by that manes, you see, I misst o' the cumpany, an' had to go home all alone by myself. Well, you see, it was out by the back gate I come, an' it was thin about twelve in the night, as well as I cud jidge by the Plough, an' the moon was shinin' as bright as a silver dish, and there wasn't a sound to be hard, barrin' the screechin' o' the ould owl down in the ivy-wall; an' I filt it all very pleasant, for I was sumhow rather hearty, you see, wid the dhrink I'd bin takin'; for you know, Thady Byrne, I'm a sober man."

"That's no lie for you, Paddy, avick. A little, as they say, goes a great way wid you."

"Well, you see, an I wint whistlin' to mysilf some o' the chunes they wor singin', and thinkin' uv any thing, shure, but the good people; whin jist as I come to the cornir o' the plantation, an' got a sight o' the big bush, I thought, faith, I seen sum things movin' backwards an' for'ards, an' dancin' like, up in the bush. I was quite sartin it was the fairies that, you know, resort to it, for I cud see, I thought, their little red caps an' green jackits quite plain. Well, I was thinkin', at first, o' goin' back an' gittin' home through the fields; but, says I to myself, says I, what sh'uld I be afeard uv? I'm an honest man that does nobody any harm; an' I h'ard mass this mornin'; an' it's neither Holly eve nor St. John's eve, nor any other o' their great days, an' they can do me no harm, I'm sartin. So I med the sign o' the crass, an' an I wint in God's name, till I come right undher the bush; and what do you think they wor, Thady, afther all?"

"Arrah, how can I till? But you wor a stout man anyhow, Paddy, agrah!"

"Why, thin, what was it but the green laves o' the ould bush, an' the rid bunches o' the haves that war wavin' and shakin' in the moonlight. Well on I goes till I come to the cornir o' the Crab road, whin I happined to cast my eyes ovir tow'st the little moat in the Moatfield, an' there, by my sowl! (God forgive me for swaerin',) I seen the fairies in rael airnist."

"You did, thin, did you?"

"Ay, by my faith, did I, an' a mighty purty sight it was to see, too, I can tell you, Thady. The side o' the moat, you see, that

luks into the field was opin, and out uv it there come the darlint-
est little calvacade o' the purtiest little fellows you ivir laid your
eyes upon. They wor all dhrest in green huntin' frocks, wid nice
little rid caps on their heads, an' they wor all mounted on purty
little, long-tailed, white ponies, not so big as young kids, an' they
rode two and two so nicely. Well, you see, they tuk right acrass
the field, jist abuv the san'pit, an' I was wundherin' in myself
what they 'd do whin they come to the big ditch, thinkin' they 'd
nivir git ovir it. But I 'll tell you what it is, Thady. Misther
Tom and the brown mare, though they 're both o' thim gay good
at either ditch or wall, they 're not to be talked uv in the same
day wid thim. They tuk the ditch, you see, big as it is, in full
sthroke ; not a man o' thim was shuk in his sate, nor lost his
rank ; it was pop, pop, pop, ovir wid thim ; and thin, hurra, away
wid thim like shot acrass the High Field, in the direction o' the
ould church. Well, my dear, while I was sthrainin' my eyes
lukin' afther thim, I hears a great rumblin' noise cumin' out o'
the moat, an' whin I turned about to luk at it, what did I see but
a great ould family coach-an'-six comin' out o' the moat, and
makin' direct for the gate where I was stannin'. Well, says I,
I 'm a lost man now, anyhow. There was no use at all, you see,
in thinkin' to run for it, for they wor dhrivin' at the rate uv a
hunt ; so down I got into the gripe o' the ditch, thinkin' to snake
off wid mysilf while they war op'nin' the gate. But, be the laws,
the gate flew opin widout a sowl layin' a finger to it, the very
instant minnet they come up to it, an' they wheeled down the
road jist close to the spot where I was hidin', an' I seen thim as
plain as I now see you ; an' a quare sight it was, too, to see ; for
not a morsel uv head that ivir was, was there upon one o' the
horses, nor on the coachman neither, and yit, for all that, Thady,
the Lord Lef'nint's coach cudn't ha' med a handier nor a shorter
turn nor they med out o' the gate; an' the blind thief uv a coachman, jist as they wor makin' the wheel, was near takin' the eye
out o' me wid the lash uv his long whip, as he was cuttin' up the
horses to show off his dhrivin'. I 've my doubts that the schamer
knew I was there well enough, and that he did it all a purpose.
Well, as it passed by me, I peept in at the quolity widinside, an'
not a head, no not as big as the head uv a pin, was there among
the whole kit o' thim, an' four fine futmin that war stannin'
behind the coach war jist like the rest o' thim."

" Well, to be shure, but it *was* a quare sight."

" Well, away they wint tattherin' along the road, makin' the
fire fly out o' the stones at no rate. So whin I seen they 'd no
eyes, I knew it was onpossible they could ivir see *me*, so up I got
out o' the ditch, and afther thim wid me along the road as fast as
ivir I culd lay fut to ground. But whin I got to the rise o' the

hill I seen they wor a great ways a-head o' me, an' they 'd takin to the fields, an' war makin' off for the ould church too. I thought they might have some business o' their own there, an' that it might not be safe for sthrangers to be goin' afther thim; so as I was by this time near my own house, I wint in and got quietly to bid, widout sayin' anything to the woman about it; an' long enough it was before I cud git to sleep for thinkin' o' thim, an' that's the raison, Thady, I was up so late this mornin'. But wasn't it a sthrange thing, Thady?"

"Faith, an' shure it was, Paddy ahayger, as sthrange a thing as ivir was. But are you quite sartin an' shure that you seen thim?"

"Am I sartin an' shure I seen thim? Am I sartin an' shure I see the nose there on your face? What was to ail me not to see thim? Wasn't the moon shinin' as bright as day? An' didn't they pass widin a yard o' me? And did ivir any one see me dhrunk, or hear me tell a lie?"

"It 's thrue for you, Paddy, no one ivir did, and myself doesn't rightly know what to say to it?"*

The Young Piper.

THERE was livin', it 's not very long ago, on the bordhers o' the county Wicklow, a dacint honest couple, whose names wor Mick Flanagan and Judy Muldoon. These poor people wor

---

* In the notes on this story Mr. Croker gives the following letter:—

"The accuracy of the following story I can vouch for, having heard it told several times by the person who saw the circumstances.

"About twenty years back, William Cody, churn-boy to a person near Cork, had, after finishing his day's work, to go through six or eight fields to his own house, about twelve o'clock at night. He was passing alongside of the ditch of a large field, and coming near a quarry, he heard a great cracking of whips on the other side. He went on to a gap in the same ditch, and out rode a little horseman, dressed in green, and mounted in the best manner, who put a whip to his breast, and made him stop until several hundred horsemen, all dressed alike, rode out of the gap at full speed, and swept round a glen. When the last horseman was clear off, the sentinel clapt spurs to his horse, gave three cracks ot his whip, and was out of sight in a second.

"The person would swear to the truth of the above, as he was quite sober and sensible at the time. The place had always before the name of being very airy [the Scottish eirie].

"Royal Cork Institution,   P. BATH.
June 3, 1825."

blist, as the saying is, wid four childher, all buys : three o' them
wor as fine, stout, healthy, goodlukin' childher as ivir the sun
shone upon ; an' it was enough to make any Irishman proud of
the breed of his counthrymen to see thim about one o'clock on a
find summer's day stannin' at their father's cabin-door, wid their
beautiful, fine flaxen hair hangin' in curls about their heads, an'
their cheeks like two rosy apples, an' a big, laughin' potato
smokin' in their hand. A proud man,·was Mick, o' these fine
childher, an' a proud woman, too, was Judy ; an' raison enough
they had to be so. But it was far otherwise wid the remainin'
one, which was the ouldest ; he was the most miserable, ugly,
ill-conditioned brat that ivir God put life into: he was so ill thriven,
that he was nivir able to stand alone or to lave his cradle ; he
had long, shaggy, matted, curly hair, as black as the sut ; his face
was uv a greenish yollow colour ; his eyes wor like two burnin'
coals, an' wor for ever movin' in his head, as if they had the
parpaitual motion. Before he was a twel'month ould he had a
mouth full o' great teeth ; his hands wor like kite's claws, and
his legs wor no thicker nor the handle of a whip, and about as
straight as a rapin' hook ; to make the matther worse, he had
the gut uv a cormorant, and the whinge, and the yelp, and the
screech, and the yowl, was never out of his mouth.

The neighbours all suspicted that he was somethin' not right,
more especialy as it was obsarved, that whin people, as they use
to do in the counthry, got about the fire, and begun to talk o'
religion and good things, the brat, as he lay in the cradle which
his mother ginerally put near the fireplace that he might be snug,
used to sit up, as they wor in the middle of their talk, and
begin to bellow as if the divil was in him in right airnest : this,
as I said, led the neighbours to think that all wasn't right wid
him, an' there was a gineral consultashion held one day, about
what id be best to do wid him. Some advised to put him out an
the shovel, but Judy's pride was up at that. A purty thing,
indeed, that a child of her's shud be put an a shovel, an' flung
out on the dunghill jist like a dead kitten or a pisoned rat ; no,
no, she wouldn't hear to that at all. One ould woman, who was
considhered mighty skilful an' knowin' intirely in fairy matthers
sthrongly recommended to put the tongs in the fire, an' to hate
thim rid hot, an' thin to take his nose in thim, an' that that id,
beyant all manner o' doubt, make him tell what he was, an'
whare he come from (for the gineral suspishion was, that he was
changed by the good people) ; but Judy was too saft-harted, an'
too fond o' the imp, so she wouldn't giv' into this plan neither,
though iverybody said she was wrong ; and may be so she was,
but it's a hard thing, you know, to blame a mother. Well some
advised one thing and some another, at last one spoke of sindin

fur the priest, who was a very holy an' a very larned man, to see it;
to this Judy uv coorse had no objection, but one thing or another
always purvinted her doing so, an' the upshot o' the business was
that the priest niver seen him at all. Well, things wint on in the
ould way for some time longer. The brat continued yelpin' an'
yowlin', an' aitin' more nor his three brothers put together, an'
playin' all sorts uv unlucky thricks, for he was mighty mis-
chievyously inclined, till it happened one day that Tim Carrol,
the blind piper, goin' his rounds, called in and sot down by the
fire to hav' a bit o' chat wid the woman o' the house. So afther
some time, Tim, who was no churl uv his music, yoked an the
pipes an' begun to bellows away in high style; whin the
instant minnit he begun, the young fellow, who was lyin' as still
as a mouse in his cradle, sot up, an' begun to grin an' to twist his
ugly phiz, an' to swing about his long tawny arms, an' to kick
out his crucked ligs, an' to show signs o' grate glee at the music.
At last nothin' id sarve him but he must git the pipes into his
own hands, an', to humour him, his mother axt Tim to lind thim
to the child for a minnit. Tim, who was kind to childher, readily
consinted ; and, as Tim hadn't his sight, Judy herself brought
thim to the cradle, an' wint to put thim an him, but she had no
need, for the youth seemed quite up to the business. He buckled
an the pipes, set the bellows undher one arm and the bag undher
th' other, an' worked 'thim both as knowingly as iv he was twinty
years at the thrade, an' lilted up " Sheela na Guira," in the finest
style that iver was hard.

Well, all was in amazemint ; the poor woman crast herself.
Tim, who, as I tould you afore, was dark an' didn't well know
who was playin,' was in grate delight ; an' whin he hard that it was
a little *prechaun*,[*] not aight years ould, that nivir seen a set of
pipes in all his days afore, he wished the mother joy iv her
son ; offered to take him aff her han's iv she 'd part wid him,
swore he was a born piper, a nath'ral jainus, an' declared that
in a little time more, wid the help uv a little good tachein' frum
himsilf, there wouldn't be his match in the whole counthry round.
The poor woman was grately delighted to hear all this, partick-
larly as what Tim sed about nath'ral jainises put an ind to some
misgivin's that war risin' in hur mind, laist what the naybours
sed about his not bein' right might be only too thrue ; an' it
gratified hur too to think that her dear child (for she raely loved
the whelp) wouldn't be forced to turn out an' big, but might
airn dacent, honest bread fur himsilf. So whin Mick come home
in the evenin' frum his work, she up an' she tould him all that
happined, an' all that Tim Carrol sed ; an Mick, as was nath'ral,

* An abridgment of *Leprechaun,* see p. 371.

was very glad to hear it, for the helpless condition o' the poor crather was a grate throuble to him ; so nixt fair-day he tuk the pig to the fair of Naas, and wid what it brought he whipt up, the nixt holiday that come, to Dublin, an' bespoke a bran new set o' pipes o' the proper size fur him, an' the nixt time Tom Doolan wint up wid the cars, in about a fortnight after, the pipes come home, an' the minnit the chap in the cradle laid eyes on thim, he squealed wid delight, an' threw up his purty legs, an' bumped himsilf in his cradle, an' wint an wid a grate many comical thricks ; till at last, to quite him, they gev him the pipes, an' immajetly he set to an' pulled away at "Jig Polthog," to th' admirashin uv all that hard him.

Well, the fame uv his skill an the pipes soon spread far an' near, for there wasn't a piper in the nixt three counties cud come near him at all, in Ould Maudha Roo, or the Hare in the Corn, or The Fox Hunther's Jig, or The Piper's Maggot, or any uv the fine ould Irish jigs, that make people dance whether they will or no : an' it was surprisin' to hear him rattle away The Fox Hunt ; you 'd raaly think you hard the hounds givin' tongue, an' the tarriers yelpin' always behind, an' the huntsman an' the whippers-in cheerin' or correctin' the dogs ; it was, in short, the very nixt thing to seein' the hunt itself. The best uv him was, he was no way stingy uv his music, an' many 's the merry dance the boys an' the girls o' the neighbourhood used to hav' in his father's cabin ; an' he 'd play up music fur thim that, they sed, used, as it wor, to put quicksilver in their feet ; an' they all declared they nivir moved so light an' so airy to any piper's playin' that ivir they danced to.

But besides all his fine Irish music, he had one quare chune uv his own, the oddest that iver was hard ; fur the minnit he begun to play it iverything in the house seemed disposed to dance ; the plates an' porringers used to jingle an the dhresser, the pots an' pot-hooks used to rattle in the chimbley, an' people used even to fancy they felt the stools movin' frum undher thim ; but, how-iver it might be wid the stools, it is sartin that no one cud keep long sittin' an them, fur both ould and young always fell to caperin' as hard as ivir they cud. The girls complained that whin he begun this chune it always threw thim out in their dancin', an' that they nivir cud handle their feet rightly, fur they felt the flure like ice undher thim, an' thimsilves ready ivery minnit to come sprawlin' an their backs or their faces ; the young bachelors that wanted to show aff their dancin' an' their new pumps, an' their bright red or green an' yellow garthers, swore that it con-fused thim so that they cud nivir go rightly through the heel-and-toe, or cover-the-buckle, or any uv their best steps, but felt thimsilves always bedizzied an' bewildhered, an' thin ould an' young id go jostlin' an' knockin' together in a frightful manner an' whin the anlooky brat had thim all in this way whirligiggin' about the flure, he'd grin an' he'd chuckle an' he'd chather, jist fur all the world like Jocko, the monkey, whin he's played off sum uv his roguery.*

The oulder he grew the worse he grew, an' by the time he was noine year ould there was no stannin' the house for him ; he was always makin' his brothers burn or scald thimsilves, or brake their shins ovir the pots an' stools. One time in harvist, he was left at home by himself, an' whin his mother come in she found the cat a horseback on the dog wid hur face to the tail, an' hur legs tied round him, an' the urchin playin' his quare chune to thim, so that the dog wint barking an jumpin' about, an' puss was miowin' fur the dear life, an' slappin' her tail backwards an' forwards, which whin it id hit agin the dog's chaps, he'd snap at it an' bite it, an' thin there was the philliloo. Another time the farmer Mick worked wid, a mighty dacint kind uv a man, happened to call in, an' Judy wiped a stool wid her apron an' axed him to sit down an rest himself afther his walk. He was sittin' wid his back to the cradle, an' behind him was a pan o' blood, fur Judy was makin' hog's puddin's ; the lad lay quite still in his nist, an' watched his opportunity till he got ready a hook at the ind uv a piece o' packthread an' he conthrived to fling it so handy that it cotcht in the bob o' the man's nice new wig, an' soused it in the pan o' blood. Another time his mother was comin' in from milkin' the cow, wid the pail an her head, an' the very minnit he saw her, he lilted up his infernal chune, an' the poor woman lettin' go the pail, clapped her hands aside an' begun to dance a jig, an' tumbled the milk all atop uv her husband, who was bringin' in some turf to bile the supper. In short there id be no ind to tellin' all his pranks, an' all the mischievyous tricks he played.

Soon afther, some mischances begun to happen to the farmer's cattle ; a horse tuk the staggers, a fine vale calf died o' the black-lig, an' some uv his sheep o' the rid wather ; the cows begun to grow vicious, an' to kick down the milkpails, an' the roof o' one ind o' the barn fell in ; an' the farmer tuk it into his head that Mick Flannagan's onlooky child was the cause uv all the mischief. So, one day, he called Mick aside, an' sed to him, " Mick," sez he, " you see things are not goin' on wid me as they ought to go ; an' to be plain an' honest wid you, Mick, I think that child o' yours is the cause uv it. I am raaly fallin' away to nothin', wid frettin', an' I can hardly sleep an my bed at night

* This wonderful tune is, we fear, a transference we made from Scandinavia. See above, p. 79.

for thinkin' o' what may happen afore the mornin'. So I'd be
glad af you'd luk out fur work somewhare else; you're as good
a man as any in the whole counthry, there's no denyin' it, an'
there's no fear but you'll have yer choice o' work." To this
Mick med answer, and sed, "that he was sorry indeed for his
losses, and still sorrier that he or his shud be thought to be the
cause o' thim; that, for his own part, he wasn't quite aisy in
his mind about that child, but he had him, an' so he must
keep him;" an' he promised to luk out fur another place
immajetly.

So nixt Sunday at chapil, Mick gev out that he was about
lavin' the work at John Riordan's, an' immajetly a farmer,
who lived a couple o' miles aff, an' who wanted a ploughman (the
last one havin' jist left him), come up to Mick, an' offered him a
house an' garden, an' work all the year round. Mick, who knew
him to be a good employer, immajetly closed wid him. So
it was agreed that the farmer shud sind his car to take his
little bit o' furniture, an' that he shud remove an the following
Thursday.

Whin Thursday come, the car come accordin' to promise, an'
Mick loaded it, an' put the cradle wid the child an' his pipes an
the top, an' Judy sat beside it to take care uv him, laste he
shud tumble out an' be kilt; they druv the cow afore thim,
the dog follied; but the cat, uv coorse, was lift behind: an' the
other three childer wint along the road, pickin' haves and blackberries; for it was a fine day towst the latther ind uv harvist.
They had to crass a river; but as it run through the bottom
between two high banks, you didn't see it till you wor close up
an it. The young fellow was lyin' purty quite in the bottom o'
the cradle, till they come to the head o' the bridge, whin hearin'
the roarin' o' the wather (for there was a grate flood in the river,
as there was heavy rain for the last two or three days), he sot up
in his cradle, an' luked about him; an' the minnit he got a sight
ov the wather, an' found they wor goin' to take him acrass it,
oh! how he did bellow, an' how he did squeal. "Whisht,
alanna," sed Judy, "there's no fear o' yer; shure it's only ovir
the stone bridge we're goin'." "Bad luck to yer, ye ould rip,"
sez he, "what a purty thrick yuv played me, to bring me here;"
an' he still wint an yellin', and the farther they got an the bridge,
the loudher he yelled; till at last Mick cud hould out no longer;
so givin' him a skelp o' the whip he had in his han', "Divil
choke you, you crukked brat," sez he; "will you nivir stop
bawlin'? a body can't hear their ears for you." Well, my dear,
the instant minnit he felt the thong o' the whip, he jumped up
in the cradle, clapped the pipes undher his arm, an' lept clane
ovir the battlemints o' the bridge down into the wather. "Oh,

my child ! my child !" shouted Judy ; "he's clane gone for ivir frum me." Mick an' the rest o' the childher run to the other side o' the bridge an' lukt down, an' they seen him comin' out from undher the arch o' the bridge, sittin' crass-liggs an the top uv a big white-headed wave, an' playin' away an the pipes, jist as if nothin' had happened at all. The river was runnin' very hard, so he was whirled away at a grate rate ; but he played away as fast, ay, and faster nor the river run. They set aff as hard as they cud along the bank ; but as the river med a suddint turn round the hill, about a hundred yards below the bridge, by the time they got there he was out o' sight, an' no one ivir led eyes an him sence ; but the gineral belief is, that he wint home wid the pipes to his own relations—the good people—to make music fur thim.

The Soul Cages.

JACK DOGHERTY lived on the coast of the county Clare. Jack was a fisherman, as his father and his grandfather before him had been. Like them, too, he lived all alone (but for the wife), and just in the same spot, too. People used to wonder why the Dogherty family were so fond of that wild situation, so far away from all human kind, and in the midst of huge scattered rocks, with nothing but the wide ocean to look upon. But they had their own good reasons for it.

The place was just, in short, the only spot on that part of the coast where anybody could well live ; there was a neat little creek, where a boat might lie as snug as a puffin in her nest, and out from this creek a ledge of sunken rocks ran into the sea. Now, when the Atlantic, according to custom, was raging with a storm, and a good westerly wind was blowing strong on the coast, many's the richly-laden ship that went to pieces on these rocks ; and then the fine bales of cotton and tobacco, and such like things ; and the pipes of wine, and the puncheons of rum, and the casks of brandy, and the kegs of Hollands that used to come ashore. Why, bless you ! Dunbeg Bay was just like a little estate to the Doghertys.

Not but that they were kind and humane to a distressed sailor, if ever one had the good luck to get to land ; and many a time, indeed, did Jack put out in his little *corragh*, that would breast the billows like any gannet, to lend a hand towards bringing off the crew from a wreck. But when the ship was gone to pieces, and the crew were all lost, who would blame Jack for *picking* up all he could find ? "And who's the worse of it ?" said he. "For as to the king, God bless him ! everybody knows he's rich enough already, without gettin' what's floatin' in the say."

Jack, though such a hermit, was a good-natured, jolly fellow. No other, sure, could ever have coaxed Biddy Mahony to quit her father's snug and warm house in the middle of the town of Ennis, and to go so many miles off to live among the rocks, with the seals and sea-gulls for her next door neighbours. But Biddy knew what's what, and she knew that Jack was the man for a woman who wished to be comfortable and happy ; for, to say nothing of the fish, Jack had the supplying of half the gentlemen's houses of the country with the Godsends that came into the bay. And she was right in her choice, for no woman ate, drank, or slept better, or made a prouder appearance at Chapel on Sundays than Mrs. Dogherty.

Many a strange sight, it may well be supposed, did Jack see, and many a strange sound did he hear, but nothing daunted him. So far was he from being afraid of Merrows, or such like beings, that the very first wish of his heart was fairly to meet with one. Jack had heard that they were mighty like Christians, and that luck had always come out of an acquaintance with them. Never, therefore, did he dimly discern the Merrows moving along the face of the waters in their robes of mist, but he made direct for them ; and many a scolding did Biddy, in her own quiet way, bestow upon Jack for spending his whole day out at sea, and bringing home no fish. Little did poor Biddy know the fish Jack was after.

It was rather annoying to Jack that, though living in a place where the Merrows were as plenty as lobsters, he never could get a right view of one. What vexed him more was, that both his father and grandfather had often and often seen them ; and he even remembered hearing, when a child, how his grandfather, who was the first of the family that had settled down at the Creek, had been so intimate with a Merrow, that, only for fear of vexing the priest, he would have had him stand for one of his children. This, however, Jack did not well know how to believe.

Fortune at length began to think that it was only right that Jack should know as much as his father and grandfather knew. Accordingly, one day, when he had strolled a little farther than usual along the coast to the northward, just as he was turning a point, he saw something, like to nothing he had ever seen before, perched upon a rock at a little distance out to sea: it looked green in the body, as well as he could discern at that distance, and he would have sworn, only the thing was impossible, that it had a cocked hat in his hand. Jack stood, for a good half hour, straining his eyes and wondering at it, and all the time the thing did not stir hand or foot. At last Jack's patience was quite worn out, and he gave a loud whistle and a hail, when the Merrow (for such it was) started up, put the cocked hat on its head, and dived down, head foremost, from the rock.

Jack's curiosity was now excited, and he constantly directed his steps toward the point; still he could never get a glimpse of the sea-gentleman with the cocked hat; and with thinking and thinking about the matter, he began at last to fancy he had been only dreaming. One very rough day, however, when the sea was running mountains high, Jack determined to give a look at the Merrow's rock, (for he had always chosen a fine day before,) and then he saw the strange thing cutting capers upon the top of the rock, and then diving down, and then coming up, and then diving down again. Jack had now only to choose his time, (that is, a good blowing day,) and he might see the man of the sea as often as he pleased. All this, however, did not satisfy him,—"much will have more;"—he wished now to get acquainted with the Merrow, and even in this he succeeded. One tremendous blustery day, before he got to the point whence he had a view of the Merrow's rock, the storm came on so furiously that Jack was obliged to take shelter in one of the caves which are so numerous along the coast, and there, to his astonishment, he saw, sitting before him, a thing with green hair, long green teeth, a red nose, and pig's eyes. It had a fish's tail, legs with scales on them, and short arms like fins. It wore no clothes, but had the cocked hat under its arm, and seemed engaged thinking very seriously about something. Jack, with all his courage, was a little daunted; but now or never, thought he; so up he went boldly to the cogitating fish-man, took off his hat, and made his best bow.

"Your sarvint, sir," said Jack.—"Your servant, kindly, Jack Dogherty," answered the Merrow.—"To be shure, thin, how well your honour knows my name," said Jack.—"Is it I not know your name, Jack Dogherty? Why, man, I knew your grandfather long before he was married to Judy Regan, your grandmother. Ah, Jack, Jack, I was fond of that grandfather of yours; he was a mighty worthy man in his time. I never met his match above or below, before or since, for sucking in a shellful of brandy," said the old fellow, "I hope, my boy," said the old fellow, "I hope you're his own grandson."—"Never fear me for that," said Jack; "if my mother only reared me on brandy, 'tis myself that 'ud be a suckin infant to this hour."—"Well, I like to hear you talk so manly; you and I must be better acquainted, if it were only for your grandfather's sake. But, Jack, that father of yours was not the thing; he had no head at all, not he."—" I 'm shure," said Jack, " sense your honour lives down undher the wather, you must be obleeged to dhrink a power to keep any hate in you, at all at all, in such a cruel, damp, cowld place. Well, I often hard of Christhens dhrinkin' like fishes ;—and might I be so bould as to ax where you get the sperits ?"—" Where do you get them yourself, Jack ?" said the Merrow, with a knowing look.— " Hubbubboo," cries Jack, " now I see how it is ; but I suppose, sir, your honour has got a fine dhry cellar below to keep them in."—" Let me alone for that," said the Merrow, with another knowing look.—" I 'm shure," continued Jack, " it must be mighty well worth the luking at."—" You may say that, Jack, with your own pretty mouth," said the Merrow ; " and if you meet me here next Monday, just at this time of the day, we will have a little more talk with one another about the matter."

Jack and the Merrow parted the best friends in the world ; and on Monday they met, and Jack was not a little surprised to see that the Merrow had two cocked hats with him, one under each arm. " Might I make so bould as to ask you, sir," said Jack, " why yer honour brought the two hats wid you to-day ? You wouldn't, shure, be goin' to giv' me one o' them, to keep for the curosity of the thing ?"—" No, no, Jack," said he, " I don't get my hats so easily, to part with them that way ; but I want you to come down and eat a bit of dinner with me, and I brought you the hat to dive with."—" The Lord bless and presarve us !" cried Jack, in amazement, " would you want me to go down to the bottom of the salt say ocean ? Shure I 'd be smoothered and choked up wid the wather, to say nothin' of bein' dhrownded ! And what would poor Biddy do for me, and what would she say ?" —" And what matter what she says, you pinkeen you ? Who cares for Biddy's squalling ? It 's long before your grandfather would have talked in that way. Many 's the time he stuck that same hat on his head, and dived down boldly after me, and many 's the snug bit of dinner, and good shellful of brandy, he and I had together, below under the water."—" Is it raally, sir, and no joke ?" said Jack ; " why, thin, sorra' be from me for ivir and a day afther, if I 'll be a bit a worse man nor my grandfather was ! So here goes ; but play me fair now. Here 's nick or nothin' ! " cried Jack.—" That 's your grandfather all over," said the old fellow. " So come along, my boy, and do as I do."

They both left the cave, walked into the sea, and then swam a piece until they got to the rock. The Merrow climbed to the top of it, and Jack followed him. On the far side it was as straight as the wall of a house, and the sea looked so deep that Jack was almost cowed.

" Now, do you see, Jack," said the Merrow, " just put this hat on your head, and mind to keep your eyes wide open. Take hold of my tail, and follow after me, and you 'll see what you 'll see." In he dashed, and in dashed Jack after him boldly. They went and they went, and Jack thought they 'd never stop going. Many a time did he wish himself sitting at home by the fireside with Biddy: yet, where was the use of wishing now, when he was so many miles as he thought below the waves of the Atlantic? Still he held hard by the Merrow's tail, slippery as it was. And, at last, to Jack's great surprise, they got out of the water, and he actually found himself on dry land at the bottom of the sea. They landed just in front of a nice little house that was slated very neatly with oyster-shells; and the Merrow, turning about to Jack, welcomed him down. Jack could hardly speak, what with wonder, and what with being out of breath with travelling so fast through the water. He looked about him, and could see no living things, barring crabs and lobsters, of which there were plenty walking leisurely about on the sand. Overhead was the sea like a sky, and the fishes like birds swimming about in it.

"Why don't you speak, man?" said the Merrow: "I dare say you had no notion that I had such a snug little concern as this? Are you smothered, or choked, or drowned, or are you fretting after Biddy, eh?" "Oh! not mysilf, indeed," said Jack, showing his teeth with a good-humoured grin, "but who in the world 'ud ivir ha' thought uv seein' sich a thing?" "Well, come along my lad, and let 's see what they 've got for us to eat?"

Jack was really hungry, and it gave him no small pleasure to perceive a fine column of smoke rising from the chimney, announcing what was going on within. Into the house he followed the Merrow, and there he saw a good kitchen, right well provided with everything. There was a noble dresser, and plenty of pots and pans, with two young Merrows cooking. His host then led him into the *room*, which was furnished shabbily enough. Not a table or a chair was there in it; nothing but planks and logs of wood to sit on, and eat off. There was, however, a good fire blazing on the hearth—a comfortable sight to Jack. "Come, now, and I 'll show you where I keep—you know what," said the Merrow, with a sly look; and opening a little door, he led Jack into a fine long cellar, well filled with pipes, and kegs, and hogsheads, and barrels. "What do you say to that, Jack Dogherty?—Eh!—May-be a body can't live snug down under the water!" "The divil the doubt of that," said Jack, "anyhow."

They went back to the room, and found dinner laid. There was no table-cloth, to be sure—but what matter? It was not always Jack had one at home. The dinner would have been no discredit to the first house in the county on a fast-day. The choicest of fish, and no wonder, was there. Turbots, and soles, and lobsters, and oysters, and twenty other kinds, were on the planks at once, and plenty of foreign spirits. The wines, the old fellow said, were too cold for his stomach. Jack ate and drank till he could eat no more : then, taking up a shell of brandy, "Here 's to your honour 's good health, sir," said he, "though beggin' your pardon, its mighty odd, that as long as we 're acquainted, I don't know your name yit." "That 's true, Jack," replied he ; "I never thought of it before, but better late than never. My name is Coomara." "Coomara! And a mighty dacint sort of a name it is, too," cried Jack, taking another shellful : "here 's, then, to your good health, Coomara, and may you live these fifty years." "Fifty years !" repeated Coomara ; "I 'm obliged to you, indeed; if you had said five hundred, it would have been something worth wishing." "By the laws, sir," said Jack, "yez live to a powerful great age here undher the wather ! Ye knew my grandfather, and he 's dead and gone betther nor sixty years. I 'm shure it must be a mighty healthy place to live in." "No doubt of it ; but come, Jack, keep the liquor stirring."

Shell after shell did they empty, and to Jack's exceeding surprise, he found the drink never got into his head, owing, I suppose, to the sea being over them, which kept their noddles cool. Old Coomara got exceedingly comfortable, and sang several songs ; but Jack, if his life had depended on it, never could remember any of them. At length said he to Jack, "Now, my dear boy, if you follow me, I 'll show you my curosities !" He opened a little door, and led Jack into a large room, where Jack saw a great many odds and ends that Coomara had picked up at one time or another. What chiefly took his attention, however, were things like lobster-pots, ranged on the ground along the wall.

"Well, Jack, how do you like my curosities ?" said old Coo. "Upon my sowkins, sir," said Jack, "they 're mighty well worth the lukin' at ; but might a body make so bould as to ax what thim things like lobster-pots are ?" "Oh, the soul-cages, is it ?" "The what, sir ?" "These things here that I keep the souls in." "Arrah ! what sowls, sir ?" said Jack in amazement : "shure the fish ha' got no sowls in them ?" "Oh, no," replied Coo, quite coolly, "that they haven't ; but these are the souls of drowned sailors." "The Lord presarve us from all harm !" muttered Jack, "how in the world did you conthrive to get thim ?" "Easily enough. I 've only when I see a good storm coming on, to set a couple of dozen of these, and then, when the sailors are drowned, and the souls get out of them under the water, the poor things are almost perished to death, not being used to the cold ; so they make into my pots for shelter, and then I have them snug, and fetch them home, and keep them here dry and warm ; and is it not well for them, poor souls, to get into such good quarters ? "

Jack was so thunderstruck he did not know what to say, so he said nothing. They went back into the dining-room, and had some more brandy, which was excellent, and then, as Jack knew that it must be getting late, and as Biddy might be uneasy, he stood up, and said he thought it was time for him to be on the road.

" Just as you like, Jack," said Coo, " but take a *doch an durrus* before you go ; you 've a cold journey before you." Jack knew better manners than to refuse the parting glass. " I wondher" said he, " will I ivir be able to make out my way home." " What should ail you," said Coo, " when I show you the way ? " Out they went before the house, and Coomara took one of the cocked hats, and put it on Jack's head the wrong way, and then lifted him up on his shoulder that he might launch him up into the water. " Now," says he, giving him a heave, " you 'll come up just in the same spot you came down in ; and, Jack, mind and throw me back the hat." He canted Jack off his shoulder, and up he shot like a bubble—whirr, whirr, whiz—away he went up through the water, till he came to the very rock he had jumped off, where he found a landing-place, and then in he threw the hat, which sunk like a stone.

The sun was just going down in the beautiful sky of a calm summer's evening. The evening star was seen brightly twinkling in the cloudless heaven, and the waves of the Atlantic flashed in a golden flood of light. So Jack, perceiving it was getting late, set off home ; but when he got there, not a word did he say to Biddy of where he had spent his day.

The state of the poor souls cooped up in the lobster-pots, gave Jack a great deal of trouble, and how to release them cost him a great deal of thought. He at first had a mind to speak to the priest about the matter ; but what could the priest do, and what did Coo care for the priest ? Besides, Coo was a good sort of an old fellow, and did not think he was doing any harm. Jack had a regard for him too, and it also might not be much to his own credit if it were known that he used to go dine with the Merrows under the sea. On the whole, he thought his best plan would be to ask Coo to dinner, and to make him drunk, if he was able, and then to take the hat and go down and turn up the pots. It was first of all necessary, however, to get Biddy out of the way ; for Jack was prudent enough, as she was a woman, to wish to keep the thing secret from her.

Accordingly, Jack grew mighty pious all of a sudden, and said to Biddy, that he thought it would be for the good of both their souls if she was to go and take her rounds at Saint John's Well,

near Ennis. Biddy thought so too, and accordingly off she set
one fine morning at day dawn, giving Jack a strict charge to
have an eye to the place. The coast being clear, away then went
Jack to the rock to give the appointed signal to Coomara, which
was, throwing a big stone into the water; Jack threw, and up
sprang Coo. "Good morrow, Jack," said he; "what do you
want with me?" "Jist nothin' at all to spake about, sir," replied
Jack; "only to come and take pot-luck wid me, now that Biddy's
out of the way; if I might make so free as to ax you, an' shure
it's myself that's afther doin' so." "It's quite agreeable, Jack,
I assure you; what's your hour?" "Any time that's most con-
vanient to yoursilf, sir : say one o'clock, that you may go home, if
you wish it, wid the daylight." "I'll be with you," said Coo,
"never fear me."

Jack went home and dressed a noble fish dinner, and got out
plenty of his best foreign spirits, enough for that matter to make
twenty men drunk. Just to the minute came Coo, with his
cocked hat under his arm. Dinner was ready; they sat down,
and ate and drank manfully. Jack thinking of the poor souls
below in the pots, plied old Coo well with brandy, and encouraged
him to sing, hoping to put him under the table, but poor Jack
forgot that he had not the sea over his own head now to keep it
cool. The brandy got into it and did his business for him, and
Coo reeled off home, leaving his entertainer as dumb as a haddock on a Good Friday.

Jack never woke till the next morning, and then he was in a
sad way. "'Tis no use at all for me thinkin' to make that ould
Rapperee dhrunk," said Jack; "an' how in this world can I
help the poor sowls out o' the lobster pots." After ruminating
nearly the whole day, a thought struck him. "I have it," said
he, slapping his thigh; "I'll be bail Coo nivir saw a dhrop o'
raal potyeen as ould as he is, an' that's the thing to settle him!
Och! thin isn't it well that Biddy won't be home these two days
yit; I can have another twist at him." Jack asked Coo again,
and Coo laughed at him for having no better head; telling him,
he'd never come up to his grandfather. "Well, but thry me
agin," said Jack, "and I'll be bail to dhrink you dhrunk and
sober, and dhrunk agin."—"Any thing in my power," said Coo,
"to oblige you."

All this dinner, Jack took care to have his own liquor watered,
and to give the strongest brandy he had to Coo. At last, says
he, "Pray, sir, did you ivir dhrink any potyeen? any raal moun-
tain-jew?"—"No," says Coo; what's that, and where does it
come from?"—"Oh! that's a sacret," said Jack, "but it's the
right stuff; nivir believe me agin if it isn't fifty times better
nor brandy or rum either. Biddy's brother jist sint me a prisent

of a little dhrop, in exchange for some brandy, and as you 're an ould frind o' the family, I kep it to thrate you wid."—"Well, let 's see what sort of thing it is," said Coo.

The potyeen was the right sort. It was first-rate, and had the real smack on it. Coo was delighted with it; he drank and he sang, and he laughed and he danced, till he fell on the floor fast asleep. Then Jack, who had taken good care to keep himse. sober, snapt up the cocked hat, ran off to the rock, leaped in, anu soon arrived at Coo's habitation.

All was as still as a churchyard at midnight—not a Merrow young or old, was there. In he went and turned up the pots but nothing did he see, only he heard, he thought, a sort of a little whistle or chirp as he raised each of them. At this he was surprised, till he recollected what the priest had often said. that nobody living could see the soul, no more than they could see the wind or the air. Having now done all he could do for them he set the pots as they were before, and sent a blessing after the poor souls to speed them on their journey wherever they were going. He now began to think of returning; he put on the hat (as was right,) the wrong way; but when he got out, he found the water so high over his head that he had no hopes of ever getting up into it now that he had not old Coomara to give him a lift. He walked about looking for a ladder, but not one could he find, and not a rock was there in sight. At last he saw a spot where the sea hung rather lower than anywhere else, so he resolved to try there. Just as he came to it, a big cod happened to put down his tail. Jack made a jump and caught hold of it, and the cod, all in amazement, gave a bounce and pulled Jack up. The minute the hat touched the water, pop away Jack was whisked; and up he shot like a cork, dragging the poor cod, that he forgot to let go, up with him tail foremost. He got to the rock in no time, and without a moment's delay hurried home rejoicing in the good deed he had done. But, meanwhile, there was fine work at home; for our friend Jack had hardly left the house on his soul-freeing expedition, when back came Biddy from her soul-saving one to the well. When she entered the house and saw the things lying *thrie-na heelah* on the table before her—"Here's a purty job," said she, "that blackguard of mine—what ill-luck I had ivir to marry him—he's picked up some vagabone or other, while I was prayin' for the good of his sowl; and they've bin dhrinkin' up all the potyeen that my own brother gev' him, and all the sperits, to be shure, that he was to have sould to his honour." Then hearing an outlandish kind of grunt, she looked down and saw Coomara lying under the table. "The blessed Vargin help an' save me," shouted she, "if he hasn't made a rael baste of himself. Well, well, well to be

shure, I often hard till of a man makin' a baste of himself
wid dhrink, but I niver saw it afore! Oh hone, oh hone,—
Jack, honey, what 'ill I do wid you, or what 'ill I do widout
you? How can any dacint woman ivir think of livin' wid a
baste?"

With such like lamentations, Biddy rushed out of the house,
and was going, she knew not where, when she heard the well
known voice of Jack, singing a merry tune. Glad enough was
Biddy to find him safe and sound, and not turned into a thing
that was like neither fish nor flesh. Jack was obliged to tell her
all; and Biddy, though she had half a mind to be angry with
him for not telling her before, owned that he had done a great
service to the poor souls. Back they both went most lovingly to
the house, and Jack wakened up Coomara; and perceiving the
old fellow to be rather dull, he bid him not be cast down, for 'twas
many a good man's case; said it all came of his not being used
to the potyeen, and recommended him, by way of cure, to swallow
a hair of the dog that bit him. Coo, however, seemed to think
he had had quite enough: he got up, quite out of sorts, and without having the good manners to say one word in the way of civi-
lity, he sneaked off to cool himself by a jaunt through the salt
water.

Coomara never missed the souls. He and Jack continued the
best friends in the world; and no one, perhaps, ever equalled
Jack at freeing souls from purgatory; for he contrived fifty
excuses for getting into the house below the sea, unknown to the
old fellow; and then turned up the pots, and let out the souls.
It vexed him, to be sure, that he could never see them; but as
he knew the thing to be impossible, he was obliged to be satisfied.
Their intercourse continued for several years. However, one
morning, on Jack's throwing in a stone, as usual, he got no
answer. He flung another, and another; still there was no reply.
He went away, and returned the next morning; but it was to no
purpose. As he was without the hat, he could not go down to
see what had become of old Coo; but his belief was, that the old
man, or the old fish, or whatever he was, had either died, or had
removed away from that part of the country.*

* We must here make an honest confession. This story had no foundation
but the German legend in p. 259. All that is not to be found there is our
own pure invention. Yet we afterwards found that it was well-known on the
coast of Cork and Wicklow. "But," said one of our informants, "It was
things like flower-pots he kept them in." So faithful is popular tradition in
these matters! In this and the following tale there are some traits by another
hand which we are now unable to discriminate.

Barry of Cairn Thierna.

FERMOY, though now so pretty and so clean a town, was once as poor and as dirty a village as any in Ireland. It had neither barracks, nor church, nor school, nor anything to admire. Two-storied houses were but few : its street (for it had but one) was chiefly formed of miserable mud cabins ; nor was the fine scenery around sufficient to induce the traveller to tarry in its paltry, dirty inn, beyond the limits actually required.

In those days it happened that a regiment of foot was proceeding from Dublin to Cork. One company, which left Caher in the morning, had, with 'toilsome march,' passed through Mitchelstown, tramped across the Kilworth mountains ; and, late of an October evening, tired and hungry, reached Fermoy, the last stage but one to their quarters. No barracks, as we have said, were then built there to relieve them ; and every voice was raised, calling to the gaping villagers for the name and residence of the billet-master.

" Why, thin, can't ye be aisy, now, and let a body tell you," said one. " Shure, thin, how can I answer you all at onst," said another. " Anan ! " cried a third, affecting not to understand the sergeant, who addressed him. " Is it Mr. Consadine you want ? " replied a fourth, answering, à l' Irlandaise, the question, by asking another. " Bad luck to the whole breed and seed of the sogers ! " muttered a fifth villager, between his teeth. " It 's come to ate poor people that work for their bread, out of house and home, yez are ? " " Whisht, Teigue, can't you, now ? " said his neighbour, jogging the last speaker ; " there 's the house, gintlemen. You see it there, yondher, forenint you, at the bottom of the sthreet, wid the light in the winddy ; or, stay, shure it 's mysilf id think little of runnin' down wid you, poor crathurs ! for 'tis tirt and wairy yez must be afther the road."—" That 's an honest fellow," said several of the dust-covered soldiers ; and away scampered Ned Flynn, with all the men of war following close at his heels.

Mr. Consadine, the billet-master, was, as may be supposed, a person of some, and on such occasions as the present, of no small consideration in such a place as Fermoy. He was of a portly build, and of a grave and slow movement, suited at once to his importance and to his size. Three inches of fair linen were at all times visible between his waistband and waistcoat. His

breeches-pockets were never buttoned ; and, scorning to conceal
the bull-like proportions of his chest and neck, his shirt-collar was
generally open, as he wore no cravat ; and a flaxen bob-wig commonly sat fairly on his head, and squarely on his forehead. Such,
then, was Mr. Consadine, billet-master-general and barony sub-
constable, who was now just getting to the end of his eighth
tumbler, in company with the proctor, who at that moment had
begun to talk of coming to something like a fair settlement
about his tithes, when Ned Flynn knocked.

"See who's at the door, Nilly," said the eldest Miss Consadine, raising her voice, and calling to the barefooted servant
girl. "'Tis the sogers, sir, is come !" cried Nelly, running back
into the room without opening the door. "I hear the jinketin'
of their swoords and bagnets on the pavin'-stones."—"Divil welcome them at this hour o' the night," said Mr. Consadine, taking
up the candle, and moving off to the room on the opposite side of
the hall, which served him for an office.

Mr. Consadine's own pen, and that of his son Tom were now in
full employment. The officers were sent to the inn ; the
sergeants, corporals, etc., were billeted on those who were on
indifferent terms with Mr. Consadine ; for, like a worthy man
as he was, he leaned as light as he could on his friends. The
soldiers had nearly all departed for their quarters, when one
poor fellow, who had fallen asleep, leaning on his musket against
the wall, was awakened by the silence, and starting up, he went
over to the table at which Mr. Consadine was seated, hoping his
worship would give him a good billet. "A good billet, my lad,"
said the billet-master-general, "that you shall have, and on the
biggest house in the whole place. Do you hear, Tom ! make
out a billet for this honest man upon Mr. Barry of Cairn Thierna."
"On Mr. Barry of Cairn Thierna !" said Tom, with a look of
amazement. "Yes, to be sure, on Mr. Barry of Cairn Thierna—
the great Barry !" replied his father, giving a nod. "Isn't he
said to keep the grandest house in this part of the counthry ?—or
stay, Tom, jist hand me over the paper, and I'll write the billet
myself."

The billet was made out accordingly ; the sand glittered on the
signature and broad flourishes of Mr. Consadine, and the weary
grenadier received it with becoming gratitude and thanks. Taking
up his knapsack and firelock, he left the office, and Mr. Consadine waddled back to the proctor to chuckle over the trick he had
played on the soldier, and to laugh at the idea of his search after
Barry of Cairn Thierna's house. Truly had he said no house
could vie in capacity with Mr. Barry's ; for like Allan A-Dale's,
its roof was

The blue vault of Heaven, with its crescent so pale.

Barry of Cairn Thierna was one of the chieftains who, of old, lorded it over the barony of Barrymore, and for some reason or other, he had become enchanted on the mountain of Cairn Thierna, where he was known to live in great state, and was often seen by the belated peasant.

Mr. Consadine had informed the soldier that Mr. Barry lived a little way out of the town, on the Cork road; so the poor fellow trudged along for some time with eyes right and eyes left, looking for the great house; but nothing could he see only the dark mountain of Cairn Thierna before him, and an odd cabin or two on the road-side. At last he met a man, of whom he asked the way to Mr. Barry's. "To Mr. Barry's?" said the man; "what Barry is it you want?" "I can't say exactly in the dark," returned the soldier. "Mr. What's-his-name, the billet-master, has given me the direction on my billet; but he said it was a large house, and I think he called him the great Mr. Barry." "Why, sure, it wouldn't be the great Barry of Cairn Thierna you're asking after?" "Aye," said the soldier, "Cairn Thierna—that's the place. Can you tell me where it is?" "Cairn Thierna!" repeated the man—"Barry of Cairn Thierna! I'll show you the way, and welcome; but it's the first time in all my born days that ever I h'ard of a soger bein' billeted on Barry of Cairn Thierna. 'Tis a quare thing, anyhow, for ould Dick Consadin to be sindin' you up there," continued he; "but you see that big mountain before you—that's Cairn Thierna. Any one will show you Mr. Barry's when you get to the top of it, up to the big hape of stones."

The weary soldier gave a sigh as he walked forwards toward the mountain; but he had not proceeded far when he heard the clatter of a horse coming along the road after him, and, turning his head round, he saw a dark figure rapidly approaching. A tall gentleman, richly dressed, and mounted on a noble gray horse, was soon at his side, when the rider pulled up, and the soldier repeated his inquiry after Mr. Barry of Cairn Thierna. "Why, I'm Barry of Cairn Thierna, myself," said the gentleman, "and pray what's your business with me, friend." "I have got a billet on your house, sir," replied the soldier, "from the billet-master of Fermoy." "Did you, indeed," said Mr. Barry; "well, then, it is not very far off; follow me and you shall be well taken care of, depend upon it."

He turned off the road, and led his horse up the steep side of the mountain, followed by the soldier, who was astonished at seeing the horse proceed with so little difficulty, where *he* was obliged to scramble up, and could hardly find or keep his footing. When they got to the top, there was a house, sure enough, far beyond any house in Fermoy. It was three stories high, with fine windows, and all lighted up within, as if it was full of grand company. There was a hall-door, too, with a flight of stone steps before it, at which Mr. Barry dismounted, and the door was opened to him by a servant-man, who took his horse round to the stable. Mr. Barry, as he stood at the door, desired the soldier to walk in, and, instead of sending him down to the kitchen, as any other gentleman would have done, brought him into the parlour, and desired to see his billet. "Ay," said Mr. Barry, looking at it and smiling, "I know Dick Consadine well—he's a merry fellow, no doubt, and, if I mistake not, has got some capital good cows down on the inch-field of Carrickabrick; a sirloin of beef would be no bad thing for supper, my man, eh?"

Mr. Barry then called out to some of his attendants, and desired them to lay the cloth, and make all ready, which was no sooner done than a smoking sirloin of beef was placed before them. "Sit down, now, my honest fellow," said Mr. Barry, "you must be hungry after your long day's march." The soldier with a profusion of thanks for such hospitality, and acknowledgments for such condescension, sat down and made, as might be expected, an excellent supper; Mr. Barry never letting his jaws rest for want of helping until he was fairly unable to eat more. Then the boiling water was brought in, and such a jug of whiskey punch as was made! Take my word for it,—it did not, like honest Robin Craig's, require to be hung out on the bush to let the water drain out of it.

They sat together a long time, talking over the punch, and the fire was so good, and Mr. Barry himself was so free a gentleman, and had such fine conversation about everything in the world, far or near, that the soldier never felt the night going over him. At last Mr. Barry stood up, saying it was a rule with him that every one in his house should be in bed by twelve o'clock, "And," said he, pointing to a bundle which lay in one corner of the room, "take that to bed with you, it's the hide of the cow I had killed for your supper; give it to the billet-master when you go back to Fermoy, in the morning, and tell him that Barry of Cairn Thierna sent it to him. He will soon understand what it means, I promise you; so, good night, my brave fellow; I wish you a comfortable sleep and every good fortune; but I must be off and away out of this long before you are stirring." The soldier gratefully returned his host's good wishes, and went off to the room which was shown him, without claiming, as every one knows he had a right to do, the second best bed in the house.

Next morning the sun awoke him. He was lying on the broad of his back, and the skylark was singing over him in the beautiful blue sky, and the bee was humming close to his ear among the heath. He rubbed his eyes ; nothing did he see but the clear sky, with two or three light morning clouds floating away. Mr. Barry's fine house and soft feather bed had melted into air, and he found himself stretched on the side of Cairn Thierna, buried in the heath, with the cowhide which had been given him, rolled up under his head for a pillow.*

"Well," said he, "this bates cockfighting, any how ! Didn't I spind the plisantest night I iver spint in my life with Mr. Barry last night ? And what in the world has becom' of the house, and the hall door with the steps, and the very bed that was undher me ? " He stood up. Not a vestige of a house or any thing like one, but the rude heap of stones on the top of the mountain, could he see ; and ever so far off lay the Blackwater, glittering with the morning sun, and the little quiet village of Fermoy on its banks, from whose chimneys white wreaths of smoke were beginning to rise upwards into the sky. Throwing the cowhide over his shoulder, he descended, not without some difficulty, the steep side of the mountain, up which Mr. Barry had led his horse the preceding night with so much ease ; and he proceeded along the road, pondering on what had befallen him.

When he reached Fermoy, he went straight to Mr. Consadine's, and asked to see him. "Well, my gay fellow," said the official Mr. Consadine, recognising, at a glance, the soldier; "what sort of an entertainment did you meet with from Barry of Cairn Thierna ? " "The best of good thratement, sir," replied the soldier ; "and well did he spake of you, and he disired me to give you this cowhide as a token to remimber him by." "Many thanks to Mr. Barry for his generosity," said the billet-master, making a low bow, in mock solemnity ; "many thanks indeed, and a right good skin it is, wherever he got it."

Mr. Consadine had scarcely finished the sentence, when he

---

* It is not very likely that the inventor of this legend knew anything about the Amadigi of B. Tasso, yet in that poem we meet this circumstance more than once. In c. ii., when night falls on the young knight Alidoro, in the open country, he finds a pavilion pitched beside a fountain, with lights in it, and hears a voice which invites him to enter it. He there sups and goes to sleep in a rich bed, and on awaking in the morning (iii. 38) finds himself lying in the open air. Another time (c. viii) he comes to a fair inn, in a wild region, where he is entertained and his wounds are dressed by a gentle damsel, and on awaking in the morning he finds himself lying under a tree. The tent and inn were the work of his protectress, the Fairy Silvana. Another Fairy, Argea, entertains (c. xxxiii.) a king, queen, knight and ladies, in a stately palace. At night they retire to magnificent chambers, and in the morning they find themselves lying in a mead, some under trees, others on the sides of a stream, with more of the beauties of the ladies displayed than they could have desired.

saw his cow-boy running up the street, shouting and crying aloud, that the best cow in the Inch-field was lost and gone, and nobody knew what had become of her, or could give the least tidings of her.

The soldier had spread out the skin on the ground for Mr. Consadine to see it ; and the cow-boy looking at it, exclaimed— "That is her hide, wherever she is ; I 'd take my Bible oath to the two small white spots, with the glossy black about thim; and there 's the very place where she rubbed the hair off her shouldher last Martinmas." Then clapping his hands together, he literally sang "the tune the old cow died of." This lamentation was stopped short by Mr. Consadine : "There is no manner of doubt about it," said he. "It was Barry that kilt my best cow, and all he has left me is the hide o' the poor baste to comfort myself with ; but it will be a warnin' to Dick Consadine, for the rest of his life, nivir again to play off his thricks upon thravellers."

Aileen a Roon,

(ELLEN MY LOVE.)

CARROL O'DALY is the Lochinvar of Ireland. He and Ellen Cavanagh were intimate from childhood. The result was love ; but Ellen's father insisted on her marrying a wealthier suitor. On the wedding-night Carrol came disguised as a harper, and played and sung this air, which he had composed for the occasion. Ellen's tenderness revived in full force ; she contrived to make her father, the bridegroom, and the guests drink to excess, and by morning she and Carrol were beyond pursuit.

The following lines were written one evening to gratify a lady who wished to have the writer's idea of what Carrol might have sung. The air is generally known under the name of Robin Adair :—

What are the joys wealth and honours bestow ?
Do they endure like true love's steady glow ?
　　Shadows of vanity,
　　Mists of the summer sky,
　　Soon they disperse and fly,
　　　Aileen a roon !

Time was when Aileen tripped light as the fawn,
Spying young Carrol approach in the dawn,
 Ere the sun's early beam
 Glittered on lake and stream,—
 Oh! that was bliss supreme,
  Aileen a roon!

Or when mild even's star beamed in the west,
Bringing to nature the season of rest—
 At that sweet hour to rove,
 Down by yon spreading grove,
 Breathing forth vows of love,
  Aileen a roon!

Aileen forgets, but her Carrol more true,
As these past scenes memory brings to his view.
 Heaves many a heavy sigh,
 Breaking his heart is nigh—
 And canst thou let him die?
  Aileen a roon!

Rousseau's Dream.

◆

THESE verses are adapted to the well-known air. They were
suggested by a passage from Rousseau's works, quoted by Alison
in his Essay on Taste. Though real names are mentioned, the
scenery and subject are purely ideal.

Calmly at eve shone the sun o'er Lake Leman,
Bright in his beam lay the watery expanse,
Softly the white sails reflected his gleaming,
Groves, banks, and trees their slow shadows advance.
Cool from the mountains the summer-gale breathed,
Laden with fragrance the lake it came o'er;
Leman, exulting, danced joyous beneath it,
Light crisped waves gently roll to the shore.

At that soft hour on the blue Leman rowing,
Slowly a sage urged his bark by a grove,
Silently musing, his lofty mind glowing,
Viewing earth's pomp and the glories above

As o'er the lake the long shadows extended,
Whispering the breeze, lulled each sense to repose ;
Calm he reclined, and as slumber descended,
Visions of bliss to his fancy arose.

Heaven to his view seemed arrayed in new glory,
Earth breathed forth fragrance and basked in the ray
Clad in loose raiment, more white than the hoary
Front of Mont Blanc, came a son of the day.
Lightly his wand o'er the slumberer extending,
While with new joy laughed the earth, sky, and lake ;
Love in his accents with soft pity blending,
Shedding content, thus the bright vision spake :—

" Hither I come, from my cloud-crowned station,
Touched with thy grief, to shed balm o'er thy mind '
I am the Spirit to whom, at creation,
Charge was by Heaven o'er this region assigned.
List to my accents, thou hunted by malice !
Let what I utter sink deep in thy breast :
Fly from mankind, to the lakes, hills, and valleys,
Thus, thus alone, shall thy spirit find rest.

" But if again to the world thou now fliest,
Thou should return, and again meet thy foes,
Think on this hour, when for comfort thou sighest,
And the bright scene will dispel all thy woes."
Gone was the vision : eve's star now was glancing,
Cold came the breeze o'er the blue curling stream ;
Waked from his slumber, his heart with joy dancing,
Homeward he turned, and still mused on his dream.

Alexander Selkirk's Dream.

COMPOSED ONE DAY WHEN CONFINED TO BED BY A COLD
AND UNABLE TO READ.

O'ER the isle of Juan Fernandez
    Cooling shades of evening spread,
While upon the peaks of Andes
    Still the tints of day were shed.

From the sea-beat shore returning
　Homeward hied the lonely man,
O'er his cheerless fortune mourning,
　As through past days memory ran.

Soon his brief repast was ended
　And he sought his lowly bed;
Balmy slumber there descended,
　Shedding influence o'er his head.

Then a vision full of gladness
　Came, sent forth by Him supreme,
Who his suffering servants' sadness
　Oft dispelleth in a dream.

In his view the lively dream sets
　Hills and vales in verdure bright;
Where the gaily-prattling streamlets
　Sparkle in the morning-light.

Hark! the holy bell is swinging,
　Calling to the house of prayer;
Loud resounds the solemn ringing
　Through the still and balmy air.

Youths and maids from glen and mountain
　Hasten at the hallowed sound,
Old men rest by shady fountain,
　Children lay them on the ground.

Now the pious throng is streaming
　Through the temple's portal low;
Rapture in each face is beaming
　Pure devotion's genuine glow.

Fervently the hoary pastor,
　Humbly bent before his God,
Supplicates their heavenly Master
　Them to lead on Sion's road;

Owns that all have widely erred
　From the true, the narrow way,
That with Him we have no merit,
　And no claim of right can lay.

Loud then rise in choral measure
    Hymns of gratitude and praise,
As, inspired with solemn pleasure,
    Unto Heaven their strains they raise.

Now the grave discourse beginneth,
    Which, ungraced by rhetoric's arts,
Quick the rapt attention winneth,
    While it glorious truths imparts;

While it tells how kind is Heaven
    To the race of him who fell;
How of old the Son was given
    To redeem from pains of hell;

How the Holy Spirit abideth
    In their hearts that hear his call;
How our God for all provideth,
    How His mercy 's over all;

How, beyond the grave extending,
    Regions lie of endless bliss;
How our thoughts on that world bending,
    We should careless be of this.

Once again the raised hymn pealeth
    Notes of joy and jubilee,
Praising Him who truth revealeth,
    Dweller of Eternity!

Night's dim shades were now retreating,
    Over Andes rose the day,
On the hills the kids' loud bleating
    Lingering slumber chased away.

Birds their merry notes were singing,
    Joyous at the approach of morn—
Morn that, light and fragrance flinging,
    Earth doth cherish and adorn.

Waked by Nature's general chorus
    Selkirk quits his lonely couch,
While o'er heaven run colours glorious,
    Heralding the sun's approach.

Still the vision hovers o'er him,
  Still the heavenly strains he hears,
Setting those bright realms before him
  Where are wiped away all tears.

All this vain and transitory
  State of mankind here on earth,
Weighed with that exceeding glory,
  Now he deems as nothing worth.

Low he bends in adoration,
  As the sun ascends the sky;
Doubt and fear and lamentation
  With the night's last shadows fly.

A Moonlight Scene,

CONCEIVED AND COMMENCED WHEN PASSING OVER PUTNEY BRIDGE ON
A FINE MOONLIGHT NIGHT IN SUMMER.

THE moonbeams on the lake are glancing,
The nimble bark is now advancing,
  That for this grove is bound.
Ye gentle clouds, ah! hear a lover,
And hasten not the moon to cover
  And darkness pour around.

Doth fancy sport, or do I hear her,
As nearer still she comes and nearer,
  Cutting the billows bright?—
How still! scarce even a light breeze flying!
Earth, water, air, at peace are lying
  Beneath the calm moonlight.

My heart beats high, my soul rejoices,
Methinks I hear their merry voices—
  She soon will reach the shore.—
Ah me! my hopes, my hopes are failing,
Yon sable cloud is onwards sailing—
  The moon it covers o'er.

Now o'er the lake they dubious wander,
And on some part remote may strand her,
   Unless they aid obtain.—
I 'll wave a signal from the summit
Of yon high bank, and haply from it
   Some guidance they may gain.

The cloud moves on, the moonlight beameth,
And o'er the lovely lady streameth,
   Upon her lofty stand.
With joyful shout the boatmen greet her,
Her anxious lover hastes to meet her,
   And eager springs to land.

Lines Written in a Lady's Album.

In those blest days, when free from care,
And happy as the birds in air,
   I roamed the hills and dales,
By purling rills oft passed the day,
Or on green banks recumbent lay,
   Listening the shepherds' tales,

My fancy, rising on the wing,
Would visions fair before me bring,
   Of castles high. and towers,
With knights in radiant panoply,
And ladies of the beaming eye,
   Within their fragrant bowers ;

Or lead me thence away to shades
Of woods, and show me, in the glades,
   The cottages serene,
Where Peace dwelt with Content, among
The happy, gay Arcadian throng
   That tenanted the scene.

But whether cot or tower arose
In vision, at the dawn or close
    Of summer-days, to me,
The lovely form of woman still
Shone bright by dale, by mead, by rill,
    Amid my extacy.

I saw her robed in every grace
With youth, with loveliness of face,
    And virtue's gentle eye ;
And from her tongue heard accents fall,
That would the rudest heart enthral,
    And raise emotions high.

But like the Eastern prince, who loved
The pictured form of one that moved
    In life full many a year
Ere he beheld the light, I deemed
The lovely form of which I dreamed
    Would ne'er to me appear.

And years came on, and years went by,
And yet I never found me nigh
    My youthful vision bright.
I said,—I might as well, I ween,
Expect to see the Fairy-queen
    Descend, to bless my sight.

But often, when we hope it least,
And when our search has well nigh ceased,
    Good fortune will befall :
So I one evening saw a maid,
Who every grace and charm displayed
    That decked my *Ideal*.

Her portrait here I need not show,
For, reader, thou must surely know
    That peerless, gentle maid :
To her these lines I consecrate ;
And if she smiles I 'll deem, elate,
    My toil far overpaid.

To Amanda.

—◆—

[These are the verses quoted in the Introduction to the " Tales and Popular
Fictions." The author was very young when he wrote them ; and Amanda
was, like Beatrice and Laura, a mere *donna di mente*, having no real
existence.]

As when a storm in vernal skies
    The face of day doth stain,
And o'er the smiling landscape flies,
    With mist and drizzling rain ;
If chance the sun look through the shower
    O'er flowery hill and dale,
Reviving Nature owns his power,
    And softly sighs the gale :

So when, by anxious thoughts oppressed,
    My soul sinks in despair,
When smiling hope deserts my breast,
    And all is darkness there ;
If chance Amanda's form appear,
    The gloom is chased away,
My soul once more her soft smiles cheer,
    And joy resumes his sway.

Then, dear Amanda, since thy smile
    Has power all gloom to charm,
Oh ! ever thus my cares beguile,
    And guard my soul from harm.
Let Hymen's bands our fates unite,
    What bliss may then be ours !—
Our days will glide, like streamlets bright,
    O'erhung with fragrant flowers.

Lines,

WRITTEN AT ROME IN THE SPRING OF 1842.

FAIR Tibur, once the Muses' home,
  Before us lay ; around
Was spread the plain which mighty Rome
  Oft saw with victory crowned.

The sun rode high, the sky was clear,
  The lark poured forth his strain,
And flowers, the firstlings of the year,
  Shed fragrance o'er the plain.

A gentle lady turned on me
  Her bright expressive eyes,
And bade the flame of poesy
  Within my bosom rise.

'Twas then I felt, I felt, alas !
  How Time has dealt with me,
And how the rays of fancy pass,
  And vanish utterly.

For time has been when such a view
  And mandate of the fair,
With images of brightest hue,
  Had fill'd the land and air :

While now I strive, and strive in vain,
  To twine poetic flowers,
Since from me Time away has ta'en
  Imagination's powers.

Then lady, be thou gentle still,
  Let pity sway thy breast ;
Accept for deeds the fervent will
  To honour thy behest.

A Farewell.

FAREWELL ! farewell ! the parting hour
　　Is come, and I must leave thee !
Oh ! ne'er may aught approach thy bower
　　That might of bliss bereave thee !

But ever a perennial rill
　　Of joy, so brightly flowing,
Keep each fair thought in fragrance still
　　Within thy pure mind blowing.

For life all charm had lost for me,
　　My thoughts were only sadness,
When fortune led me unto thee
　　To taste once more of gladness.—

I 've seen the sullen shades of night
　　Fair nature's face concealing,
And marked how scattered rays of light
　　Came morn's approach revealing.

The light increased, the orb of day
　　Clomb to the mountain's summit ;
And vale and plain, and stream and bay,
　　Drew life and lustre from it.

And as it towered in majesty,
　　Light all around it shedding,
It seemed a monarch, seated high,
　　Bliss through his realms wide spreading.

All nature joyed ; I felt my heart
　　Distend, and fill with pleasure ;
For heavenly light and warmth impart
　　A bliss we cannot measure.

This glorious sun to me art thou,
　　Whose light all gloom dispelleth,
Before whose majesty I bow
　　When he his power revealeth.

Thy golden locks, thine eyes so blue,
  Thy smile so sweetly playing,
Were those first shafts of light that flew,
  The gloom of night warraying.

But when, more intimately known,
  I found not only beauty,
But genius, taste, and truth, thine own,
  Combined with filial duty :

Then rose the sun, o'er all my soul
  In full effulgence beaming,
And tides of joy began to roll
  Beneath his radiance gleaming.—

Time still his noiseless course pursues
  With unremitting vigour,
And lovely Spring each year renews
  The waste of Winter's rigour.

Were mine the power, thus, like Time,
  To wake again life's flowers,
And days recall of youthful prime
  Passed in the Muses' bowers ;

Then, lovely maiden ! fancy-free,
  Rich in each mental treasure,
In me thou wouldst a votary see—
  Thy will would be my pleasure.

But while such bliss might not be mine,
  A friendship pure and holy
I offered at the hallowed shrine,
  To which my heart turned solely.—

When distant from thee many a mile,
  High waves between us swelling,
I'll think upon thy lovely smile,
  Of pure emotion telling.

The sky will show me thy blue eye ;
  The whispering breeze of even
Recall that voice, whose melody
  Oft lapped my soul in heaven !

The sinking sun thy ringlets' gold
  Will show ; but memory only
The treasures of thy mind unfold
  To me when musing lonely.

Oh ! may I hope that memory,
   That power for ever changing,
Will make thee sometimes think on me,
   O'er distant mountains ranging ?

Say me not nay ; let Fancy cheat
   My soul with bland illusion ;
And let not Doubt my vision sweet
   Dispel by rude intrusion.

Verses,

WRITTEN AT BATH IN 1840, FOR A LITTLE BOY WHO KEPT AN ALBUM, AND WAS
A GREAT ADMIRER OF ROBIN HOOD AND HIS MERRY MEN.

Had the kind Muse, young friend, on me
   Her pleasing gifts bestowed,
And taught to tread of poesy
   The smooth and flowery road ;

Then should the deeds of Robin Hood,
   And Little John, so bold,
And of the Friar, stout and good,
   In numbers high be told.

The merry greenwood should resound
   With feats of archery,
And antlered deer along should bound
   So light and gracefully !

But vain the hopes : 'gainst Fate's decrees
   To struggle I must cease ;
I only can write histories
   Of England, Rome, and Greece.

Father Cuddy's Song.

IN THE LEGEND OF CLOUGH NA CUDDY.

QUAM pulchra sunt ova,
　Cum alba et nova
In stabulo scite leguntur ;
　Et à Margery bella,
　Quæ festiva puella !
Pinguis lardi cum frustis coquuntur.

　Ut belles in prato
　Aprico et lato
Sub sole tam læte renident,
　Ova tosta, in mensa
　Mappa bene extensa,
Nitidissima lance consident.

TRANSLATION.

OH ! 'tis eggs are a treat,
　When so white and so sweet
From under the manger they 're taken,
　And by fair Margery,
　Och ! 'tis she 's full of glee,
They are fried with fat rashers of bacon.

　Just like daisies all spread
　O'er a broad sunny mead,
In the sunbeams so beauteously shining,
　Are fried eggs fair displayed
　On a dish, when we 've laid
The cloth and are thinking of dining.

The Praises of Mazenderân.

FROM THE SHÂH-NÂMEH OF FERDOUSEE.

◆

[The object of this version was to give a correct idea of the animated anapæstic measure in which the Shâh-Nâmeh is written. Our knowledge of Persian was extremely slight; but a friendly Orientalist gave us a faithful line-for-line translation, which we versified, and he and Ram Mohun Roy then compared our version with the original.]

His hand from the lute hath its melody drawn,
And thus rose the song of Mazenderân :—
　May Mazenderân, the land of my birth,
Its hills and its dales, be e'er famed o'er the earth :
For evermore blooms in its gardens the rose,
On its hills nods the tulip, the hyacinth blows ;
Its air ever fragrant, its earth flourishing,
Cold or heat is not felt,—'tis perpetual spring.
The nightingale's lays in the gardens resound ;
On the sides of the mountains the stately deer bound,
In search evermore of their pastime and food ;
With fragrance and colour each season 's bedewed ;
Its streams of rose-water unceasingly roll,
Whose perfume doth gladness diffuse o'er the soul.
In November, December, and January,
Full of tulips the ground thou mayest everywhere see ;
The springs, unexhausted, flow all through the year ;
The hawk at his chase everywhere doth appear.
The region of bliss is adorned all o'er
With dinars, with rich stuffs, and with all costly store ;
The idol-adorers with fine gold are crowned,
And girdles of gold gird the heroes renowned.
Whoe'er hath not dwelt in that region so bright,
His soul knows no pleasure, his heart no delight.

INDEX.

The words printed in *Italics* are those whose origin or meaning is explained. The word "Fairy" is inclusive of all similar beings.

THE END.